Richard Hudson, womaniser and successful used-car salesman, decides to pursue his life's dream – to make a movie. But forces beyond his control reject and destroy his cherished work. An epic bender finds him drinking his way through the underbelly of LA, wreaking revenge on those who have crossed him.

Cockfighter

Frank Mansfield is a cockfighter, obsessed with an illegal sport that is horribly cruel and bloody – and incredibly exciting. Pursuit of the champion's medal takes him into the hot, dusty small-town circuits of the seamy, rural South, where greed and corruption vie with lust and violence . . .

The Burnt Orange Heresy

Art critic James Figueras is psychotic: an amoral, unrepentant killer. Wanting to make a name for himself, he seeks out the greatest painter in the world, now a hermit in the Florida swamplands. But Figueras is after more than just the man. He wants the work . . . and something more horrible than can be imagined.

The Machine in Ward Eleven

'I had a hunch that madness was a predominant theme and normal condition for Americans living in the second half of this century.' At a time when we still had some faith in our leaders, Willeford laid bare the

American Dream in these six fresh, incisive tales. Fifty years later, his revelations are as chilling and relevant as ever.

Charles Willeford was a professional horse trainer, boxer, radio announcer and painter. He was also a highly decorated tank commander (Silver Star, Bronze Star, Purple Heart, Luxembourg Croix de Guerre) with the Third Army in the Second World War. Willeford is the author of twenty novels, and created the Miami detective series featuring Hoke Moseley.

By Charles Willeford

CHARLES WILLEFORD
OMNIBUS 2

The Woman Chaser

Cockfighter

The Burnt Orange Heresy

The Machine in Ward Eleven

An Orion paperback

The Woman Chaser first published in the USA in 1960 by
by Newsstand Library
Cockfighter first published in the USA in 1962
by Chicago Paperback House
The Burnt Orange Heresy first published in the USA in 1971
by Crown Publishers
The Machine in Ward Eleven first published in the USA in 1963
by Belmont Books
This omnibus edition published in 2015
by Orion Books,
an imprint of The Orion Publishing Group Ltd,
Carmelite House, 50 Victoria Embankment,
London EC4Y 0DZ

An Hachette UK company

1 3 5 7 9 10 8 6 4 2

A CIP catalogue record for this book
is available from the British Library.

ISBN 978-1-4091-6061-8

Printed and bound in Great Britain by
CPI Group (UK) Ltd Croydon, CR0 4YY
Typeset by Born Group within Book Cloud

The Orion Publishing Group's policy is to use papers that
are natural, renewable and recyclable products and
made from wood grown in sustainable forests. The logging
and manufacturing processes are expected to conform to
the environmental regulations of the country of origin.

www.orionbooks.co.uk

Contents

Contents

BOOK ONE

The Woman Chaser

START HERE

Using the thumb and forefinger of the right hand, get a little slack and pull the film through this little thingamajig. Clamp here. Leave a small loop so it won't flutter, and then go up over this, down under this, around this, and then tight around the big one. (It has to fit tight on the sound drum). Then under this, over this, under this again, around this, and down. Insert the feeder in the lower reel and you are almost ready. Turn on the sound and let it warm up. See the tiny red light? Now out with the house-lights and flip the toggle switch to ON. If the sound is loud enough the incidental slithering of the film won't bother you a bit . . .

Richard Hudson pressed the counter in his hand one more time before he took a look at it. 873. That was a lot of iron to pass one spot in fifteen minutes. And more passed the other way going toward Hollywood. 927. The Los Angeles Transit Company bus stopped at the corner every fourteen minutes discharging an average of six passengers, taking on five. Across the street on the other corner a streetcar stopped every seven minutes, and three men and one woman and one child got aboard, while two women and one child dismounted. That was the average for the location. Richard Hudson had been checking it for two days.

A beautiful average and a wonderful location. And yet, the used-car dealer across the street sat on his big fat keister smoking cigarettes and gurgling Coca-Colas all day long when he had thirty-five unsold automobiles glaring under the California sun.

With an impatient movement of his fingers Richard noosed his rep tie and slid across the hot leather seat of his 1940 Continental convertible (a very clean car) and climbed out on the sidewalk side. It had been very warm for May sitting in the direct rays of the sun and he blotted his face with an Irish linen handkerchief, jerked his jacket down in back. He was wearing a new black silk suit, and it was well wrinkled. One day's wear and the suit was ready for the cleaners, but it gave Richard an air of prosperity, and at the moment he was prosperous.

Richard Hudson was about to steal a used-car lot and every automobile on it.

At the corner he waited for the green light before crossing the busy street. In San Francisco he would have dashed across, dodging between cars, but in Los Angeles, to cross against a red light means a ticket for jaywalking and/or sudden death. This was Crenshaw Boulevard; 873 cars one way and 927 cars the other way every fifteen minutes.

Upon reaching the lot Richard walked slowly around a vintage Buick, eyeing it critically and kicking the tires. Such obvious shopping tactics should have roused the owner from his lethargy, but he didn't even look up from his comic book. A lazy mixed-up skid. Richard was forced to go to him.

'You selling used cars today?' Richard asked, smiling down at the heavy man in the chair.

'Yes, sir. See anything you like?'

'Yeah,' Richard mused, 'I like all thirty-five.'

'Can't make up your mind, huh?' The owner wiped his sweating neck with the back of his hand, leaned his chair back comfortably against the wall of the small stucco office building.

Richard broadened his thin smile. 'Yeah,' he said, 'I can make up my mind. Can you?'

'What do you mean?' The dealer was beginning to get suspicious of Richard's manner, and he got uneasily to his feet.

'I mean all thirty-five. You own them all. You have a lease on the lot with three more years to run and you aren't doing worth a damn. You should have hung onto the two apartment houses you owned in St Louis.'

'Now wait a minute, Mr—'

'Don't get excited, Mr Ehlers.' Richard handed the dealer his card. 'My name is Richard Hudson and my business is used cars. I'll take all of these heaps off your hands and buy your lease. You don't want to work anyway. Why not retire permanently and enjoy the sun at the beach instead of sitting on a Crenshaw used-car lot?'

'You've got a point there; Mr Hudson, wasn't it?' Mr Ehlers reached out a soft white hand for Richard to shake.

'Richard Hudson is right. Chief representative of Honest Hal Parker, San Francisco. And I'll give you seventeen thousand, five for the cars on the lot as they stand, including the lease. Final price. No dickering.'

Mr Ehlers looked blankly across the white gravel of the lot, at the flapping, fading bunting strung on wires above the shiny merchandise, and performed some slow mental arithmetic. Richard could have done it for him a lot quicker. At midnight the night before, Richard had gone through the lot with THE BOOK, and his offer was exactly $300 below list on every car, not counting two pre-WWII models Mr Ehlers would probably have thrown in for nothing anyway.

Ehlers lit a filter-tipped cigarette and Richard perceived the trembling of his fingers. The price was very right for a slipping business and Ehlers knew it. But when a person offers good money for something it is the nature of man to want more than was offered.

'What about my lease?' Ehlers asked timidly.

'I said I'd take that too.'

'You didn't mention what you'd pay me for my lease.'

'That's right.' Richard lit a cigarette, but his hands did not tremble. 'I'll give you nothing for the lease,' he said in a flat, even voice, 'but I'll take over your burden of the $250 a month payments. Now just what in the hell would you do with an empty parking lot?'

'It cost me a lot of dough—'

'I'm not you!' Richard reminded the dealer sharply. 'Is it a deal or isn't it?'

Mr Ehlers sat down wearily in his chair, pressed the fingers of his right hand against his forehead, cradled his right elbow in the palm of his left hand. A few moments later a notebook came out of his shirt pocket and he started figuring with a ballpoint pen. After five minutes of figuring with the pen and notebook a beautiful smile creased his round perspiring face.

'I figure it at about $150 off list on each car, and you've made me a fair price, Mr Hudson. I'll take it!'

Richard could hardly believe his ears. Ehlers was wrong, dead wrong, but so what? The deal was merely that much easier to wrap in a package.

'You've made a deal then, Mr Ehlers. How about meeting me at my lawyers at three this afternoon. O'Keeffe and Cullinan. The Redstone Building. And bring your papers.'

'That's pretty fast!' the fat dealer marveled.

'You bet it is!' Richard laughed. 'I don't want you to change your mind.'

'Don't worry. I'll be there.'

They shook hands. Richard returned to his car, drove to the Fig Hotel where he had been staying the past six weeks. He was in exceptionally good spirits, well pleased with himself. Honest Hal would be happy with the transaction and the low price, and Richard was glad the search was over. Now he could get back to selling used cars.

In his hotel room Richard raised a glass of Scotch and tap water to his reflection in the mirror above the chest of drawers.

'To me!' he said happily.

EXPOSITION

That was the beginning. It is also a flashback and narrative hook. This much about writing I have learned from the movies. Also, I don't want to fool anybody, including myself. Especially myself. I believe now, that I should have remained Richard Hudson, Used-Car Dealer, and I should never have become Richard Hudson, Writer-Director-Producer. At least I think I know this, but I do not really know. Thereby this story, or narrative, or notebook, or whatever it turns out to be. Somewhere along the way I may discover the exact point, or the turning point perhaps, or the error, if it was an error that I made, or someone else made, or just exactly what it was that happened to me.

I have the time. God knows I have the time. If it were possible I would put down every thought, every word of conversation, every minute of every day that followed this beginning. But I cannot. Not only is my memory too faulty for total recall, I would soon be bogged down in the insignificant. Instead, I intend to put on paper the sequence of events, some in order, some out of order. I shall include some of the people involved, and somewhere during this journey from backward to forward in time I may find myself. However, I doubt this very much. But in any case it will be an interesting journey. Long or short.

A movie is ninety minutes long, six short reels in time. This is something I learned in Hollywood. An insane rule, I know, but there it is; let no man tear it asunder.

This is not a story about used cars, and it isn't altogether about movies or the making of movies, although it has something of each. Mostly it is about people, and of and about me. Already I sense that I am breaking some cardinal rule of writing.

If I continue in this vein how will I be able to establish a strong reader-identification? The average reader has a tendency to identify himself with a lead character and to project himself into the story and actually live the story through the thoughts, emotions and actions of the lead character. Poor reader. I am the reader and I dread the thought of going through it all again, and at the same time I welcome and relish the opportunity. Perhaps I am a masochist?

This is what I learned about a story at Mammoth Studios: A likeable and sympathetic hero, one who affords a good measure of viewer-identification, and around whom the story revolves, is faced with the necessity of solving a serious and urgent problem which affects his vital interests. The hero makes an effort to solve his problem, but this only succeeds in making matters worse. (This is me all right.) The hero's efforts all lead to a series of increasingly harder complications. Each new complication is related to the original problem. (This isn't me, or is it?) Anyway, there is an integrated series of complications which build up in intensity until a definite point or crisis is reached. It is here that the reader cannot possibly understand how the hero can possibly succeed. But now the hero makes one last and heroic attempt to resolve his difficulties, and in every case it must be his own individual efforts that solve the dilemma(s). Under no circumstances can he accept any form of outside aid to make things easier for him.

As I think things over, maybe this is a conventional story after all. But not really, because it is too personal. It happened to me and therefore it is important to me, if not to anybody else. But everything a man does affects somebody else directly or indirectly. So my story should be important to everybody. Some of my story is too personal to write in the first person, and some of it is too personal to write in the third person. Most of it is too personal to write at all.

But the decision is mine. If nothing else, Richard Hudson has always made his own decisions. Right or wrong, they were his own. Maybe I am on the right track after all. Six months ago I would never have admitted, not even to myself, that I ever made a wrong decision.

FLASHBACK

The actual purchase of George Ehler's used-car lot by Richard Hudson went back several months; it was not a quick business deal, by any means. For ten years Richard Hudson had been the star used-car salesman for Honest Hal Parker in San Francisco. Honest Hal had gotten so big in San Francisco he wanted to expand his empire. He trusted Richard, and he had faith in the ability of Richard to the tune of a transfer of $40,000 to a Los Angeles bank, and his blessing in the establishment of an Honest Hal used-car lot in Los Angeles.

The distance between San Francisco and Los Angeles is approximately 447 miles, but the people who live and work in the two cities are as different as lox and cream cheese. This difference is well-known to the dealers in the necessity of life in California: the used automobile.

Example: The driver of a laundry truck in San Francisco makes $75 a week. His counterpart in Los Angeles considers himself fortunate if he makes $60 a week. A clerk in San Francisco with simple filing and typing duties can easily command a $65 weekly salary. Her sister in Los Angeles will only take home $40 a week. Why is this? Union now in San Francisco. In Los Angeles, the unions lag behind. Perhaps this explanation is an over-simplification. Maybe it costs more to live in San Francisco and the employers must pay more to get employees. Maybe it costs less to live in Los Angeles, but I doubt it. I only know that these are the facts insofar as salaries are concerned. A cursory comparison of the classified advertisements in the San Francisco *Chronicle* with those of the Los Angeles *Times* will graphically show the difference in salary for the same types of work in the two California cities.

This difference in salaries has always been the same, even during the years of the Great Depression. Those who *were* working during the thirties made more money per week in San Francisco than those who *were* working in Los Angeles. These are the facts; the why is a question of economics or something that is not important to this chronicle. Except for the business of used cars. In San Francisco it is nice to own a used car. In Los Angeles it is necessary to own an automobile of some kind whether you want one or not.

A man in San Francisco who walks onto a used-car lot may walk away from it. He must be sold an automobile. In Los Angeles, a man who walks onto a used car lot will drive away. He is already sold on buying some kind of transportation before he puts his tired feet on the gravel of the lot. It is only necessary for the salesman to determine his financial status and sell him an automobile slightly above his means.

As far as Richard Hudson was concerned there were no exceptions to these rules. Practically, there are bound to be some exceptions. But by not recognizing any exceptions, Richard Hudson was a used-car salesman in the $1,000 per month class. His salary varied but slightly. There were bad months when he made but $850, but on the other hand there were months when he made as much as $1,500. It is a question of values. It is the American way of life. Once the American way of life is reasoned out and thoroughly understood, the achievement of success in any given field becomes a matter of the *desire* of the man concerned.

I find that it is almost impossible to write in the third person, if that is what I have been doing. Damn it all, anyway! Everything concerning myself is personal, and that is the way I am taking it. What gives me the right to state categorically that *any* man can become successful? (Even though I know it is true.)

The trouble with the American people is their credulity. Or is it idealism? Take the Hungarians. Big Deal! THE BID FOR FREEDOM. ESCAPE. RED CROSS. FREEDOM FUNDS. Millions of Americans, with tears in their eyes, donated millions of dollars for the BRAVERY, the SACRIFICES, the NOBLENESS of the Hungarians in their bid for FREEDOM. The gates were opened, the safeguards ignored, the McCarran Act forgotten. Six months later the same American who donated five bucks from his $65 weekly paycheck is working for some Hungarian who readily grasped the American way of life.

We see things and we do not see things. We say one thing and we do another. General MacArthur said, 'There is no security, there is only opportunity.' He was right, of course. And yet the man who stated this basic truth clung to the security of the US Army until he was kicked out. But why should I go on?

As a used-car salesman I saw the world through a pair of dark glasses. They were necessary to protect my eyes from the rays of the hot California sun as I twisted arms on the used-car lots of Los Angeles and San Francisco. But the lenses were purple, not rose-colored. To the really successful used-car salesman there are only two types of people: Insiders and Feebs. Feebs are the feeble-minded, and Insiders are those who are wise to themselves and to things as the way they are. A simple uncomplicated distinction, but a true one nonetheless.

When a man knows the truth it is no longer necessary to search for it. As I see things now, in retrospection, the only thing the matter with me was my compassion for others. I felt sorry for the Feebs, and that was fatal. Down

11

inside myself, in some hidden pocket of a fold in my heart, compassion lay for the poor ignorant slob. It was too bad.

When I made the move from San Francisco to Los Angeles I was being kicked upstairs, as the saying goes. I was at the top as a used-car salesman. There are only so many hours in a day, and one salesman, no matter how good he is, can only sell so many cars in one day. My earning capacity as a salesman had been reached. It was necessary to either become a partner with Honest Hal Parker or leave him altogether and establish my own business. Honest Hal wanted it both ways so he took the road in the middle. Sensing my restlessness, Insider Hal handed me a golden deal on a platter.

For several months Honest Hal had wanted to expand. He too, was aware of the American way of life. An outlet and inlet was needed in Los Angeles to get rid of the cars that didn't move in San Francisco due to the discrimination that comes with the heavier paycheck of the San Franciscans – I've explained that – and to replace cars that were needed for his big lot. And a new big lot in Los Angeles would enhance Honest Hal's prestige.

By establishing a new lot in Los Angeles with a trustworthy hotshot in command, namely me, Richard Hudson, these birds could be stoned.

My commissions would roll in from *all* cars sold instead of only those I sold myself. Hal would make more money. I would make more money. And the clincher for me was that it was Hal's dough that was going into the expansion. Not mine. Not a penny of mine. If everything went wrong, if every nickel was lost due to my lack of acumen, business sense, stupidity, or if things just didn't work out as they were planned, I was still way ahead of the game. I could still sell used cars. And if things did work out, I would, in time, make enough money to buy a partnership with Honest Hal. Or if I *really* made money, I could cut Honest Hal's throat and take the entire pie. Is not this the American Way?

DISSOLVE

The search for a likely location for an Honest Hal used-car lot in Los Angeles was not as difficult as I had thought it would be. Los Angeles was my hometown; I had been born and reared there, and I knew my way around. A stranger who moves to Los Angeles as an adult will never learn the city like a native. Although many of the streets are numbered, many are named instead, and between the two systems, a stranger becomes confused and discouraged. Take 41st Street as an example. Next to 41st Street is 41st Drive and next to 41st Drive is 41st Place. If you were counting blocks from 9th Street to 60th Street your count would be wrong, and besides, 60th Street is actually Slauson Avenue to the native, although there is a 60th Street on the map.

San Francisco had been my home for ten years, and except for infrequent visits to Los Angeles to see Mother, the city had changed a great deal, even for me. About 200 families move into Los Angeles daily to stay permanently, and this migration has caused a fantastic outward growth. The resettlement, divided about equally between Negroes and Others, has caused the Negro section, as I used to know it, to become a mere suburb of the current Negro community. It was impossible for 500,000 Negroes to live in one small area, and they now have a city within a city extending from downtown all the way to Long Beach, and on either side of Central Avenue as far in each direction as they have been able to buy or rent.

Los Angeles is such a lousy city to live in it is a wonder

13

to me why anybody would want to live there. But on the other hand, I moved back to make money and I suppose that is the reason everybody makes the move. There couldn't possibly be any other reason.

Another peculiarity is that no matter where a man lives in Los Angeles, he is required to drive at least twenty miles to get to work. If you live in Montebello you work in Inglewood. If you live in Inglewood your job is in Burbank. If you live in Burbank you work in Watts. And so on. Why Angelenos select a residence at least twenty miles away from their employment has always been a mystery. However, it is a well-known fact. The great masses of people moving in from the Dust Bowl and other areas of the United States have to live somewhere. So the project house came into being following World War II. These projects are a blight on the face of Southern California. Orange groves were torn down, desert land beyond Van Nuys was cleared and row on row of houses appeared from nowhere like peas in a pod. The Feebs moving in from elsewhere can buy one of these excellent $6,000 houses for $15,000. Of coarse, by the time the Feeb pays mortgage interest, assessments, loan charges, closing costs, etc., and finally pays off the house twenty years later, it has cost him $30,000 for his $6,000 house, which is then worth $1,500 due to the rundown condition of the neighborhood.

But this influx of migrant Feebs, in addition to the people already there, makes good business for used-car dealers. The man who got along wonderfully in Ogden, Utah with a one-family car, now finds that he needs the car every day to drive twenty miles to work. His wife also needs a car to drive six miles to the shopping center, or fifteen miles to pay the light bill. The son has to have an automobile to drive to high school. His sister-in-law, who made the move to Los Angeles also, and shares the third bedroom with the youngest daughter, and who hopes to land a husband at the Hollywood Friendship Club for those who are over thirty-five years of age, needs a car to take an out-of-work plumber she met at this wonderful meeting place out to show him a good time at a drive-in movie.

Two-and-one/half automobiles per capita in Los Angeles. That is the official ratio. I checked it with the Chamber of Commerce. The single street of iron, Figueroa Avenue, which met the used-car requirements of Los Angeles for many years, is just another used-car center today. There are many others. Crenshaw Boulevard, an unpaved street twenty-five years ago, is one of the largest used-car selling areas in the world today. Crenshaw Boulevard makes Van Ness Avenue in San Francisco resemble a small neighborhood parking lot. In every section of Los Angeles there were small and large used-car centers and I investigated them all before concentrating my search to Crenshaw Boulevard. Figueroa Avenue no longer had the volume of traffic I wanted to move cars. The Los Angeles branch office of the Triple A Finance Company, which handles all of Honest Hal's credit business in San Francisco, opened their files to my investigations. More research unearthed Mr George Ehler's unhappy situation; personal investigation confirmed my findings; and when I made my indecent offer, he grabbed it.

That evening I called Honest Hal in San Francisco and told him we were in business.

'Already,' Hal asked sarcastically over the phone. 'After six weeks without a single call I was beginning to think you were on a vacation.'

'I suppose I should have called you,' I said, 'but I wanted to wait until I was set.'

'Do you need any help, Richard? I could send Don down for a couple of weeks—'

'Look, Hal,' I replied belligerently, 'we discussed all that. The deal was for me to run things in my own way, hire local people. When I need any help, I'll ask for it!'

'OK, Richard, it's your baby. Sounds like you've made a good start, but keep in touch with me for Christ's sake. Don't wait six weeks before you call me again even if it's just to say, "Hello."'

'OK, Hal. I'll drop you a line as soon as I find an apartment and get settled. I'm still staying at a hotel.'

'Which hotel?'

'The Fig, but I'll probably move out tomorrow. So long, Hal.'

That afternoon, after concluding the deal with Ehlers at my lawyers' office, I had promised to meet him for a drink at the 222 Club. Ehlers wanted to celebrate, and I sympathized with him, although he could have made a better deal than the one I gave him by merely lifting his telephone off the hook. The only trouble was that Ehlers was a Feeb and didn't know where to call. I didn't care about seeing him again. He was a bore. And besides, I wanted to see Mother.

Although I digress a lot I actually have a one-track mind once I have set myself a task, and I hadn't even called Mother during my six weeks' stay. Much harder work lay ahead of me in getting the new lot under full-scale operation and I didn't want to get sidetracked into anything else. But now that I was committed to Los Angeles residence for at least a few years I wanted to see Mother.

She was wonderful!

ALEXANDRA HOROTSOFF HUDSON BLAKE STEINBERG

I didn't know how old Mother was at this time, and I still don't know. It isn't important. In order for her to be my mother she was bound to be older than me, and I was then thirty. But Mother didn't look thirty; in a flattering light she could easily pass for twenty-five. Alexandra was

16

a retired ballerina and still worked four hours a day, seven days a week, at the *barre* in her basement rehearsal hall.

Her figure was the most remarkable I have ever seen for any woman of any age. Tall for a woman, with long slim legs, she was topped with the firm proud bust of a coloratura soprano. A narrow waist, flat, truly feminine hips, and a white, unblemished skin made her the most beautiful woman in the world. In a vague way, she wasn't quite bright, but in my opinion, her vagueness added to her beauty.

Certainly I am prejudiced. Why not? A man's mother is always the most beautiful woman in the world. But more often than not, she is beautiful for what she has done for him. Home cooking, the biased admiration of his small achievements, and generous portions of daily love, including lavish endearments, strengthen a man's belief in the beauty of his mother. But my mother never did a damned thing for me. I never expected her to do anything for me. She was beautiful because she was beautiful and she had scrapbooks full of newspaper clippings to prove it.

Her pale face was narrow, and perhaps her eyes were set a mite too close together, but her waist-length hair was usually knotted in an enormous bun on the nape of her long white neck, and male attention was usually diverted from her blue eyes. I can remember, with amusement, the startling effect she created at parties when for one reason or another all of the attention was not concentrated upon her beauty. She would rise grandly to her feet, grasp a hairpin in each hand, make a quick movement with her arms, and the enormous mass of coal-colored hair would cascade down her back completely hiding her narrow waist. This little feminine display centered the attention on Mother immediately and brought gasps of admiration from all of the men present. In the 1930s, other women at the same party, with their short bobbed hair, feather cuts, and short permanents, never fully appreciated this display of Mother's crowning glory.

Mother's nose was overly large, but then it was thin enough to minimize the size. Her lips were full, generous, sensuous, and never painted off-stage. She bit them into redness instead. Most of the time Mother wore a pair of slanted, blue-tinted prescription glasses, and they successfully diminished the slight defection of her close-set eyes. But most striking, the absence of makeup on a clown-white face gave Mother an appearance of clean phthisic beauty I have never seen any other woman equal.

I loved Alexandra as much as I could love anything or anybody, and I suppose she loved me, in her absent-minded way. Her way would have to be effortless, because except for her daily stint of dancing – which did everything for her figure and nothing for her mind – Mother did absolutely nothing.

Alexandra slept from 8 p.m. to 8 a.m., twelve restful hours every night. For breakfast she ate a head of lettuce which fortified her legs for dancing until noon in her basement studio. Lunch, for Mother, consisted of a cup of clear soup and a cup of hot tea. For dinner she ate a small steak with all of the fat trimmed away, a small boiled potato and a green salad with a dash of lemon juice. She was ravenous most of the time and it gave a kind of wild look to her eyes that showed behind the tinted glasses. Only when it was absolutely necessary did she ever leave the house; she filled her waking hours by painting insipid watercolors of food, by reading true love story magazines, and by listening to the radio.

I shall never understand how she managed to find and marry and divorce my father, an instructor of romance languages at the University of Chicago. And I do not know the circumstances surrounding her marriage to my first stepfather, Harry Blake. Harry Blake was a very good friend of mine when I was growing up and one of the world's worst songwriters. But he taught me how to play 'Chopsticks', and he played a damned fine piano and I missed him around the house when he committed suicide.

My new stepfather was Leo Steinberg, an ex-movie director, thirty-seven years of age, and if it ever embarrassed him when I called him Pop he never gave any indication that it did. But more about Pop later.

DISSOLVE TO:

The House of Lumpy Grits occupied a fall acre of expensive ground in an area containing mostly hotel-apartments and a large, sprawling shopping center. At one time a favorite residential neighborhood, when large houses were in style, and before the California stucco period, Mother's dilapidated three-story house was the only reminder of the spendthrift twenties when taxes did not have the meaning that they have today. The other homes that once poked their badly designed eaves at the sun were gone, sold to realtors, and this old section of Los Angeles, on the mythical boundary between Los Angeles and Hollywood, had taken on a new glittering life. But Mother doggedly hung on, refusing all offers for the house out of apathy, or reluctance to change, or perhaps sentimental reasons for dear old Harry Blake. There it squatted, its flaking, scaling exterior a mute reminder of the thousands of hot sunny days it had suffered. A small, square, cracking concrete swimming pool, half full of trash and debris, hadn't been filled in two decades. There was a four-car garage with empty servant's quarters above, and behind the house there was a huge greenhouse with all of the glass windows broken. This monster nestled, if nestled can be applied to such a monstrosity, in a full acre of dried, parched jungle, enclosed by an ivy-choked brick wall, ten feet high all of the way around.

I loved the place because of boyhood memories. A boy of twelve couldn't ask for a better yard to play Tarzan of the Apes, and a young teenager could find a dozen secret crannies to sneak a forbidden cigarette and drift quietly down the river with Huckleberry Finn.

Long ago Mother and I had laughingly christened the house as The House of Lumpy Grits, because its purchase had been made possible by the popularity of the only hit song ever written by Harry Blake. The lyrics of this unspeakably rotten song are engraved forever upon my mind, because it took Harry three months to write it, pounding on the grand piano in the music room and singing at the top of his nastily nasal voice. 'Lumpy Grits' was on the Grand Ole Opry radio program for twenty-four straight weeks, warbled by one over-alled singer or another in a plaintive, mournful manner, and evidently it sent the ruralist Feebs. In turn, juke box popularity brought it to The Ten Top Tunes radio show for one week only when it became Number Ten in the overall poll of hit songs for the week. A rendition by Lupe Runoz, a calypso singer employed by Ten Top Tunes, and the horrid arrangement of the Ten Top Tunes orchestra finished off 'Lumpy Grits', and it disappeared like any other popular song. But 'Lumpy Grits' fitfully lingers on, and Mother still gets a royalty check – every three months – for approximately $1.35. The melody, without the lyrics, isn't too bad. How could it be? Harry stole the tune from a dozen New Orleans blues numbers, a measure at a time, and blended them beautifully.

Because such a hodgepodge could become popular, and roll blithely off the lips of children and grown-ups alike, I include the lyrics here as Americana. Not a single tear to either one of my eyes does it bring. Harry Blake, old song-writer, you broke *many* a heart with this one, and wherever you are, you left your mark upon us!

LUMPY GRITS*

By

Harry Blake

(Indignantly)
Lumpy Grits!
Ain't nothin' to serve no hongry man!
Lumpy Grits!
Ain't nothin' to serve no hongry man!
And when I saw your grits,
I turned around and ran!
(Sadly, with feeling)
I love gravy,
With my grits and eggs.
I love gravy,
With my grits and eggs.
But when I ate your gravy,
I used my longest legs.

(Sotto voce)
I bought you a 'lectric stove
And a 'lectric fryin' pan.
Yet you went ahead and served me—!
Lumpy Grits to a hongry man!
Lumpy Grits! Lumpy Grits! Lumpy Grits!
Is somethin' no good man can stand!
(Bitterly, with much feeling)
Goin' to the Ho-tel
To get grits for my inner man!
Goin' to the Ho-tel

* 'Lumpy Grits' has been reprinted with the permission of the M. N. Norton
Music Pub. Corp.

To get grits for my inner man!
An' if the Ho-tel won't feed me,
I'll go where someone can . . .
(Gradually fading away to heartrending, sobbing whisper)
Lumpy Grits . . . Lumpy Grits . . .
Lumpy Grits . . . Lumpy Grits . . .

And that is the song that bought the house that Mother now lives in. I believe I have already mentioned it, but it won't hurt anything to put it down again: Harry Blake died by his own hand, probably because he could never again scale the heights reached by the epic 'Lumpy Grits'.

FADEOUT

A round-faced, sweet, chubby, adorable, cute, gay-voiced, bright-eyed teenager of not more than sixteen and not less than sixteen opened the door to The House of Lumpy Grits in answer to my ring. A single bead of perspiration lay in the delicious hollow above her short, full upper lip. Her white forehead was also perspiring, and her short-cropped jet hair curled damply about tiny pink ears.

This sweet little girl shook her head and smiled. 'I've been skipping rope!'

'Well,' I said, 'isn't that nice? Now who are you, and why do you skip here?'

'I live here,' she laughed happily. 'My name is Becky Steinberg.'

I remembered then. Leo Steinberg had a daughter, I knew that much, and this was she. I had never seen her before; she was supposed to be in an expensive private school in New Jersey.

'Do you know who I am?' I asked Becky. 'I'm your big brother, Richard.' I grinned disarmingly. She was bound to know about me, but she could hardly have thought of me as her brother. I was only seven years younger than her father, and to a girl of sixteen, thirty is near-senility. Becky's dark eyes widened and her face flushed prettily.

'Come in, come in,' she stammered. 'I don't think Daddy's expecting you—'

'I wasn't expecting you,' I cut in, 'but now that we're both here I expect a brotherly kiss.'

The color in Becky's round cheeks deepened to tomato. I grasped her elbows lightly, kissed her O of a mouth, and ran my tongue experimentally between her white, parted teeth. Becky spluttered, jerked away from me fiercely, and ran down the hall.

'Daddy! Daddy!' she called out loudly as she ran. I laughed and closed the door gently behind me.

LEO STEINBERG

One of the first things anyone noticed about Leo Steinberg was the tonsure encircling his pale bald head. It was a thin black-and-white fringe and every other hair was black, or if you prefer, every other hair was white. Any normal man, not even a vain man, would have done something about this hirsute horror. There was very little hair anyway, and a single bottle of Colorback would have lasted Leo for years.

Leo was an ex-wonder boy insofar as movies were concerned. In my opinion, and I do not stand alone, his contribution to the movies was enormous. An exceptional movie never sets the world on fire because a new movie starts this coming Friday with a larger cast, and now tells for the first time a story that could never be told before. But Leo's movies were exceptional, even the last one, which took him out of the business altogether and into enforced retirement. You can lose money, but not *too* much money on a movie . . .

I suppose this is as good a time as any to state that I am a movie fan. I *like* movies, all kinds of movies. The big ones, the little ones, the westerns, love stories, tragedies, spectacles, all of them. I like movies in CinemaScope, Todd-AO, 16 mm, 8mm, and in 3-D. I like the successes, the stinkers, and the in-betweens. Of course, I am unhappy when a movie is lousy, and I am glad when a movie is good. But I *like* movies.

When I entered the living room Leo was watching television and Becky was standing behind his chair. Leo turned the set off immediately and shook hands with me warmly, genuinely glad to see me.

'My son!' Leo said proudly, feigning strong emotion in the little game we played. 'You are home! Home at last!'

'Hi, Pop,' I said. 'How in hell are you?' I removed my hand from his and carefully counted the fingers. 'What's with my little sister, Becky? I thought she was going to school in New Jersey.'

'Private schools cost money, Richard.' Leo shrugged elaborately. 'And I'm broke. Here, she can ride the bus to Hollywood High for fifteen cents.'

'That's true enough. How do you like California, Becky?'

'All right. I guess.' She blushed prettily.

'Hollywood High is different from a convent anyway.' I turned to Leo. 'Where's Mother?'

'In bed. It's after eight o'clock.'

'Sure, sure,' I said, remembering. 'But just this once, I believe I'll wake her.'

I climbed the stairs to the second floor, pushed open the door to Mother's bedroom, and let the light from the hallway fall across her bed instead of flipping the bedroom wall switch. The opened door and sudden light didn't wake her. She lay quietly in the center of a large double bed, a black eye mask guarding her eyes, crescent-shaped pieces of adhesive plaster on each temple, and a large triangle of adhesive filling the space between her lower lip and her heart-shaped chin. The portions of her face not hidden by adhesive plaster were shiny with cold cream. A piece of gauze was looped tightly beneath her chin and the cords were tied in a lovely bow across the top of her head. Her hands were on top of the covers and deep inside a pair of rubber gloves. I knew that the inside of the gloves contained great globs of cold cream. So Mother took good care of herself— why not?

I sat down on the edge of the bed, leaned over and kissed Mother lightly on the lips. Out of a sound sleep Mother wrapped her arms hard about my head and kissed back fiercely. I jerked away, laughing, and Mother sat up quickly in bed exposing her large, unencumbered, firm jutting breasts. They had never known the touch of a brassiere. Leo was a fortunate man. Using the heels of her palms Mother raised her sleep mask and blinked at me in the dim light.

'It's sonny boy, Mother dear,' I said. 'Your own little darling boy.'

'I thought it was Leo,' Mother replied through her teeth. She loosened the bow on top of her head so that she could speak better. 'What brings you home in the middle of the night?'

'It's only eight thirty. I didn't want to wake you, but thought I'd better. It's been a long time, Sweetie.'

'Almost two years, you damned expatriate. How do I look, Richard?' Mother straightened her back and pulled her shoulders back. Her bare white breasts stood forth proudly, the dark nipples canting up toward the ceiling.

'Just wonderful, Mother dear. Wonderful! You really are taking care of yourself.' I said admiringly. It was what she wanted me to say.

'I'm trying anyway.' Mother smiled coyly and looked at me through lowered lashes. 'Did you know that your

25

mother was fifty-one last week?' She was lying, of course.

'No, I didn't. I thought my mother was fifty-three.'

'Let's change the subject.' Mother scooted under the covers, pulled the sheets up to her chin. 'What is my baby doing in Los Angeles? Why did they run you out of San Francisco? Where are you staying? Tell me.'

'I'm down here for good, starting a new agency for Honest Hal. Right now I'm staying at the Fig Hotel, but I'm going to get an apartment as soon as I can find one.'

'Why don't you stay with us, Angel Pants?'

'I don't know.'

I hadn't thought about the possibility, but why not? Certainly there was room enough. Of course, with an apartment of my own I could have a girl in to spend the night once in awhile. But I could do the same thing at home if I wanted to – Mother was in bed asleep by eight every night. Leo wouldn't give a damn, and I didn't care what Becky thought. Why not?

'I'm used to having my own place, Mother dear. And all of my furniture and my hi-fi is in storage in San Francisco . . .' I hesitated.

Mother pursed her lips thoughtfully. 'How about the old servant's quarters over the garage? We just have Leona now, and she doesn't sleep in. She married again and lives with her new husband down on 39th Street. The apartment is too small anyway for a couple, but it would be fine for you. A large living room, bedroom and kitchenette. There's a refrigerator in the kitchenette for your Schweppes and ice cubes.'

'I remember what it's like.' I thought it over. 'I could have the place redecorated, I suppose. OK, Mother dear, I'll send for my furniture.'

'Good! It's nice to have you home again. Now kiss me good night and close the door on your way out. It's late and I have to get my sleep.'

26

I pulled her sleep mask down, kissed her lightly, and closed the door quietly behind me. No man in the world ever had a mother as wonderful as mine. She is the greatest.

At the foot of the stairs Leo greeted me with an opened bottle of beer. He had sent Becky to bed and we went into his study to talk. The beer was cold, and I enjoyed talking to Leo more than I've ever enjoyed talking to anybody. Why? Maybe it is because Leo lets the other person do most of the talking? But he listens, he really knows how to listen. And when Leo talks, he doesn't need many words. A lift of the shoulder, a slight rise of eyebrow, an expressive gesture with the hand, a slow and meaningful nod, a carefully raised forefinger; this was the way Leo talked, and his gestures and body movements were always punctuated with carefully chosen words. It was a pleasure to talk to Leo. And it was easy to see why he was a great director.

Lubricating my discourse with two quarts of beer I told Leo about my adventures in the search for a used-car lot, and about closing the deal with Ehlers.

'Then you're in Los Angeles to stay?' Leo pursed his lips.

'If everything works out all right. And how can I fail?'

'Then stay here with us, Richard. It will help me out.'

'Mother already asked me, Leo. I should have mentioned it. She said I could have the garage apartment, and it will suit my needs very well. But I appreciate your second to the invitation.'

'It will make me very happy to have you,' Leo said simply.

'No time like the present then. If you don't mind, I'll telephone the moving company in San Francisco right now and have them ship my furniture down.' I reached for the phone on the desk.

Leo spread his fingers and examined them. 'The telephone is not connected, Richard. I couldn't afford it any longer,' he said quietly.

I could hardly believe it, but there was no tone – 'But you've got to have a telephone! The studio—'

'No!' Leo broke in sharply. 'They didn't call me for *months!* And they will never call me. Neither will any other studio call me. I'm broke, Richard. I'm down to my last Roualt, and I can go no further.' Leo lifted his chin and looked at the single painting on the wall; a painted clown done in opaque reds and yellows, with a white face, blocked in by thick gobs of black. The light above the painting, in combination with the desk lamp, gave the picture an effect of stained glass.

'This is an original Roualt, isn't it, Pop?'

'Of course.' Leo shrugged. 'And all I have left.'

'Well, you certainly aren't broke then. Isn't an original Roualt worth about a hundred thousand dollars?'

'Worth is relative.' Leo said as I got up to look at the painting. He sat down at his desk and smiled sadly. The light above the painting made his bald head shine. He spread his hands flat on the desk and closed his eyes. 'As a symbol, Richard, that clown represents my life. It is my life. When I say it is all I have left, I don't just mean that the other paintings are gone; I mean that this painted clown represents the sum of my artistic endeavors, my contribution to the motion picture, my final paycheck.

'My painting is like the framed one-dollar bill businessmen hang on their office wall – a symbolic treatment of the first dollar they ever made for themselves. You've seen framed one-dollar bills?'

'Of course,' I said.

'Except that—' Leo hesitated, shrugged his shoulders and held them in an elevated position, 'my clown symbolizes the last dollar I'll ever make at what I do best.'

We were both silent for a moment. This kind of talk I could understand, and it got under my skin. For the first time in many months I didn't know what to say and I had difficulty in swallowing.

'I suppose,' Leo dropped his shoulders, looked fondly at his painting, 'if I tried hard enough, let certain dealers know that it was for sale, I could get a hundred thousand. Maybe more. Eventually. The intrinsic value of any painting is whatever anyone is willing or able to pay. But actually, by a single phone call,' Leo smiled wryly, 'if I had a telephone, a man in Pasadena would drive over here immediately with a check for thirty thousand in his hand made out to cash.'

A man with a more practical mind than mine, I suppose, would have said, 'There's a hell of a lot of difference between a framed one-dollar bill and a framed thirty-thousand dollar bill!' But I knew exactly what Leo meant and I was all for him. This was real integrity, artistic integrity, the only kind that means anything.

I sat down in the deep leather chair next to the desk and lit a cigarette. 'Mother has money,' I said. 'Jesus! A damned telephone!'

Leo smiled wearily, repeated his elaborate shrug. 'You know Alexandra as well, if not better, than I do, Richard. She pays the taxes on the house because it is her house. But she figures, and rightly so, that the upkeep is my responsibility. I am now at the point where I must economize. The telephone has been disconnected, my car is gone, and I buy the groceries myself. Becky is here to stay, and Leona . . . I owe her two months back wages. I don't know why she doesn't quit.' It was agony for Leo to say these things and he turned his head and eyes away from me. 'That's why I wanted you to stay with us, Richard. I am selfish. I need you. A few dollars from you . . .' The top of Leo's head turned a delicate rose.

'You knew my address in San Francisco, Pop. Why didn't you let me know?'

Leo shook his head and raised his left hand with a gesture that explained everything – frustration, pride, embarrassment, shame.

I took out my checkbook and ballpoint pen. 'Look, Pop,' I said without hesitation. 'I paid two hundred a month for my apartment in San Francisco, and I'd have to pay the same here in LA. So I'll give you the same.' I made out a check payable to Leo. 'Here is a thousand bucks for the first five months in advance. Take it. It will help you get even for awhile. As your eldest son,' I grinned at him, patted his shoulder friendlily, 'I consider it a privilege to help you around the house. We're a family aren't we?'

Leo accepted the check with trembling fingers, folded it three times, and dropped it into his shirt pocket. We both got to our feet. Leo embraced me hard, kissed me on the cheek. His eyes were wet. I looked over Leo's shoulder at the white face of the clown. The clown was Leo all right, every wavering, tragic line, and as far as I was concerned, he would never have to sell his painting for a lousy thirty thousand bucks. I made a decision on that, right then and there.

What a sentimental slob I was!

MONTAGE

I was busy for the next few weeks and I put in some mighty long days. Liaison was established between the Triple A Finance Company in the person of Mr Raymond Moore, the assistant manager, and we set up some standard contracts based on the material I had brought down with me from San Francisco. I contacted jobbers and did some buying, ensuring an even flow of cars to the new Honest Hal lot. A large neon sign, which I designed myself, was constructed, and the glowing honest face of Honest Hal, in blue and red tubing, smiled down on Crenshaw Boulevard from a vantage point atop a fifty-foot pole.

To improve the looks of the lot I had two truckloads of white gravel dumped and spread on the lot, and new red-and-blue triangular flags of bunting strung from the wires above the cars. Then I dug into an advertising campaign, doing copy and layout work myself to ensure that it was correct, catchy and colorful. I wrote several radio spots, but I was especially proud of one singing commercial which I had aired over three radio stations at irregular intervals. This commercial really dragged in the Feebs:

First Girl: *Well, honestly . . . !*
Second Girl: *Did you ever . . . ?*
Third Girl: *Why I never . . . !*
All Girls: *Bargains! Honest Hal has Got 'em!*
All Girls: (singing)
For an honest steal.

For an honest Deal,

See Honest Hal . . .

See Honest Hal . . .

Announcer: The glittering new used-car emporium on Crenshaw Boulevard, ladies and gentlemen, under the exclusive management of Honest Hal Parker, California's top automobile dealer, offers you honest transportation at honest prices. Only volume sales can keep prices so low, and Honest Hal passes his profits on to you! Honest Hal will give you the best trade-in allowance in town, and his cars are the cleanest, in tip-top mechanical condition, and guaranteed! And remember, there is never a down payment required at Honest Hal's!

All Girls: (singing)

31

For an honest steal.

For an honest deal,

See Honest Hal . . .

See Honest Hal . . .

I sent a record of this commercial, and a dozen color photographs of the new lot to Honest Hal (including the new sign with Hal's smiling map) and received a glowing, ecstatic letter of praise from the old thief.

The advertising was all true, of course. No down payment was needed – if you owned your own furniture outright, or something else equally valuable. A second mortgage was arranged by the Triple-A Finance Company to cover the down payment with your furniture as security. And every car *was* guaranteed, for an entire *month*, or *1,000 miles*, whichever came first. And the cars were in tip-top mechanical condition; put into that condition by an on-the-premises Negro mechanic I hired called Graphite Sam. I had promised him a swift kick in the ass if any car was turned in before it had completed 1,000 miles. Yessiree, Bob, them cars at Honest Hal's glittering new used-car emporium were in *tip-top* condition!

I hired three salesmen, drifters and drunks, but the best I could get at the time. I needed somebody, and I planned to fire them later. For the one serious-minded hotshot car salesman in ten there are nine drifter types who prefer to receive their commission money at the end of each day instead of waiting until Saturday. Whiskey is an occupational hazard of the used-car industry.

But I sorely needed a completely trustworthy office-type. After a Feeb is sold on a car on the lot by a salesman wearing dark glasses, the real take begins in the office. The buyer is sized up, his credit rating is examined, and his gullibility is tested on the spot. If it is possible to add the line in the next higher column of the insurance table without the buyer being aware of it, this is done in front of his eyes. The extra dollar or so is added to the monthly payment and is kicked back, of course, to the dealer. If it is possible, and it is almost always possible, a small charge for handling and delivery of the car is added to the total. This modest charge of five dollars for handling and delivery pays for the services of the salesman who drives the buyer's choice from its place in the line all of the way to the door of the lot office where the keys to the car are ceremoniously deposited into the buyer's impatient hand.

Until I could find the right man, I handled these administrative details myself. But I don't like this kind of work. Attention to detail, sitting at a desk with pencil and paper and columns of figures bores me. I like the selling end, the excitement of fisherman and hooked fish. My forté is the quick cash deal with the minimum of paperwork. But if nothing else, I am a businessman, and I am an idea man. Old Honest Hal, sitting in his stocking feet in his $4,000-per-annum suite in the Parkman Towers in San Francisco, could have searched the world without finding a better man than me to start a new lot in Los Angeles. Except for one little thing:

I was bored. The excitement of having a large sum of money to play around with wore off quickly. The lot was established, my contacts were made, and the money was rolling in according to my predicted estimates. I enjoyed the $2,000 a month rolling in, but I banked most of it.

My expenses were small for my income. Ten years on an open lot in San Francisco had not only tanned my face; it had brought me a moderate fortune. In a checking account I kept a modest sum of $2,000 in order to avoid check charges. I had a savings account of $6,000, and $20,000 worth of US Savings Bonds buried away in a lockbox at the First National. I paid taxes every year on a pair of empty lots in Sausalito which were worth $1,500 apiece, and my 1940 Lincoln Continental, with its built-up engine, was a bonus gift from Honest Hal. By investing my money in stocks I could have made more money, but who can you trust these days? The simple truth: No one. With wheeler-dealers travelling around the country buying up proxies and selling off good companies for their own personal gains, a man who buys stock is a damned fool.

I knew how to spend money and I spent it. But I didn't know how to get *rid* of money. There's a difference. When I first began to get a few wads of the folding stuff I spent a lot of it on girls in San Francisco. I soon found out, however, that it was much cheaper and healthier to pay out twenty or fifty bucks for a call girl than it was to invest in a so-called decent girl who didn't always pan out after a considerable expenditure. Emotional entanglements are avoided, and one experienced call girl is worth ten amateurs looking for a husband.

My small apartment above the garage behind The House of Lumpy Grits was beautifully furnished with Herman Miller furniture and Henry Miller watercolors. My closet was jammed with clothes. My hi-fi was rigged by an expert and there were four speakers in various corners of the apartment. My record collection had been purchased intact from the estate of a Stockton, California music critic who had lost all in a divorce and drowned himself in Lake Tahoe.

I didn't own many books, however. But the books I owned were books I read, and I read them again and again. *Ulysses, The Trial, Practical Clinical Psychiatry, Crime and Punishment, Self Analysis, Seven Pillars of Wisdom;* and the collected poetry of Dylan Thomas, T. S. Eliot and Ezra Pound were my favorites. I was also fortunate enough to own a complete set of the works of Edgar Rice Burroughs which I had purchased from a soured science fiction fan

34

in San Francisco for only ten bucks. My favorite writer was F. Scott Fitzgerald, but not because of *The Great Gatsby* or *Tender is the Night*. I thought Fitzgerald was great because of the Pat Hobby – Screenwriter stories which had appeared in Esquire. And I must have read Fitzgerald's *The Last Tycoon* at least a dozen times. For lighter reading I purchased paperback books for two bits at drugstores, just like everybody else in America.

Almost every night before I fell asleep I watched the Late, Late movie on television, and when I slept I slept like a rock. In my way, I believe I was a moderate man, all of the way around, and I was contented with my lot. Except for one little thing:

I was bored.

My head was crammed with facts and figures, many of them useful. I knew the value, almost to the penny, of used cars dating from 1932 to the forward-looking, swept-back anythings. And I also knew, to the penny, how much more than the value I could obtain from anybody foolish enough to shop on my used-car lot.

Everything connected with the business was too easy and I was tired of it. I caught myself yawning as I filled in the papers with customers and asked the routine questions. I was due for a change, maybe a rest. After all, wasn't I now in the same position as Honest Hal?

All Honest Hal did for his take was to visit the lot once a day, scare the hell out of everybody by growling and moaning, and then he was off someplace in his little red Jaguar. His earnings were made for him by a capable manager. I needed a capable manager so that I could do the same. And I found him in the person of: MASTER SERGEANT WILLIAM CONAN HARRIS, US ARMY, (RETIRED).

Anytime an employer hires an ex-serviceman who has completed eight to ten years of service in any branch of the Armed Forces, and has quit for one reason or another, the employer is making a mistake. The new employee will be too independent, for one thing, and sooner or later the man will reenlist to complete his twenty years of service for retirement. While it is perfectly reasonable to hire a man who has completed only one enlistment, in most instances, the man who has done two hitches or more is a bad bet for any employer. He has too much time in the service to really give it up, and ten times out of ten he will return to the safe warm womb of service life. No employer in the United States today can offer the deal that the Armed Forces offers. At the completion of twenty years of active duty a Master Sergeant or Navy Chief can retire with a pension of $156 a month for the rest of his natural life. To meet this retirement plan a civilian employer would have to put approximately $5,000 a year into a trust fund for every one of his employees. Times are not *that* good!

However, any employer who fails to hire a retired Master Sergeant or Navy Chief who has completed the required twenty years is making a grave mistake. I mean retired enlisted men, of course. A retired officer is a different matter. Within five minutes a retired officer will attempt to tell you how to run your business. The fact that he doesn't know what he is talking about doesn't deter him at all; he believes he knows all there is to know about management. For some reason, no American male ever quite gets over having been an officer.

But a retired Master Sergeant is an uncut jewel, and I was lucky enough to hire one. I liked Bill Harris from the moment he stepped into my office. For two weeks I had run a carefully worded advertisement in the Los Angeles *Times*, and as a consequence I had interviewed and dismissed some mighty weird cats. Bill was different from his entrance, and on through his interview. Although the door was open, he knocked, and when I told him to come in he took his hat off without waiting to be told. And he said 'yes, sir' and 'no, sir' naturally, without obsequious deference.

I had brought a stack of the various office forms with me we had used in San Francisco, and I handed Bill a job application to fill in. It was a routine one-page form, but it covered a lot of territory. While Bill waited silently for me to talk to him I examined his completed form.

He was thirty-eight, married, the father of two children, and owned his own home in Fullerton (within the twenty-mile commuting distance). He had retired from the Army as a Master Sergeant, duty: first sergeant of infantry, and had been retired for three months.

Bill had never held a civilian job of any kind, having served twenty continuous years in the Army after graduating from high school in Santa Maria, California. During his twenty years he had managed to pick up approximately two years of college credits at various Army posts through college extension courses. His references included a major stationed in Japan, a captain in Europe, and a bird colonel at Fort Benning, Georgia. The lower half of the form, which provided space for the listing of previous employment, was blank. Bill's signature was noteworthy. Although the form only required first name, middle initial, the last name, Bill had signed his full name – William Conan Harris – in a freeswinging backhand scrawl, and he had underlined it to boot. When a man signs his full *middle* name it can mean only one thing: Narcissism. So what?

I gave Bill a little test. After digging into my pocket for some change, I tossed some coins on the desk. 'How about getting us a couple of Cokes out of the machine, Bill?'

'Yes, sir, Mr Hudson,' he replied. He used his own dimes, ignoring my change on the desk. After working the machine, he handed me an open bottle before he sat down with his own.

Respectful independence. What more can an employer desire?

Bill didn't have much hair, and he owned a well-developed paunch. His round face was unlined and closely shaved. He wore a constant smile with a fixed expression of happiness. His face, with its secret, knowing, covering smile, was a reflection of and on every commanding officer he had ever served. He had done their work for them, and he had received no credit, but he *knew*, and that was enough for him. There were hundreds like him in the Army, a not-so-secret society of non-commissioned officers who actually ran the Army year after year, watching tolerantly as the Reserve officers entered, served a couple of years, and departed in disgust with the system. As Bill once remarked when we were driving to Long Beach, 'Captains come and go, but the first sergeant stays forever.' A man like Bill Harris was blessed with a single virtue, and it was the only character trait the Army required from its professional soldiers: Loyalty.

'Do you know how to run an office, Bill?'

'Yes, sir. I was a sergeant major for three years, and a first sergeant for—'

'OK, then,' I cut him off. 'The office will be your baby. Hire yourself a good typist.' I tapped the folder containing the office forms and blank contracts. 'Read these. I'll explain the interview techniques to you, and the office will be your sole responsibility. I'll work the lot, along with the other salesmen, and when we bring a man or a woman through that door they'll be sold on an automobile. When they're turned over to you, all you have to do is keep them that way through the questioning and their signature on the dotted line. There are a lot of little tricks, and many of the buyers will be liars with rotten credit ratings, but these people you will have to spot and refuse. Do so diplomatically, but don't let a bad one get through. The way the Triple A Finance Company and I have it set up, I'm stuck for all repossesses. So naturally, I don't like to get any. Never give credit to a house painter, to a migrant agricultural worker or to any used-car salesman. Otherwise, except for these arbitrary rules, if they have a job of any kind, use your own judgment. Think you can handle it?'

'Yes, sir.' Bill nodded without hesitation.

'Fine. State your salary.'

'I thought you would do that,' Bill said worriedly, his set smile fading.

'No, Bill,' I said kindly, 'that isn't the American way. You are out of the Army now, and the time has come to decide what you're worth. If you want more than I can pay, I'll be sorry to see you go. I want you to work for me, but I think that any employer who sets a salary in this kind of business is wrong. You'll get no forty-hour work week from me. If you want time off, you'll have to work it out for yourself. Right now, I'm closed on Sundays, but the situation may change. If so, you'll have to be here.'

Bill set his lips grimly. 'All right, Mr Hudson. I want $400 a month. At the end of three months I'll want a raise. But I won't ask for it. If you don't give it to me of your own accord, I'll quit.'

'Fair enough,' I said. 'Take off your coat and let's get to work.'

RIPPLE

Four weeks later I raised Bill's salary to $600 a month. If he had asked for more I would have given it to him. But he didn't. I had forestalled him indefinitely by giving him such an unexpected raise. Bill was elated, of course, and I also added to his happiness by letting him put one of his ideas into effect. He wanted to give away free hot dogs at noon from a stand in the center of the lot. He had a grill set up, hired a kid to serve them, and as a consequence we got a hell of a lot of free publicity in the newspapers and a three percent increase in the turnover of old iron.

The office was a well-oiled machine. In one second flat Bill could put his fingers on any desired paper in the files. His weekly reports to Honest Hal, which I signed, were models of economy, accuracy and reportage. He had hired an old lady who typed about eighty words a minute, and she worked like a slave all day. When the typing was slack, Bill had her sweep the floor. He hired and fired salesmen until he had three of the best on the Boulevard. If he had started to give them a little close-order drill I wouldn't have been surprised. He became so adept at adding little extras to the contracts I had to slow him down.

It was my daily practice to arrive at the lot at 8 a.m., check the previous day's business, and then at nine, lecture my salesmen on salesmanship, techniques, and prices. Bill would arrive at nine thirty and I outlined what I wanted him to accomplish during the day, briefed him on the merchandise I wanted to push, and then we had coffee. If I didn't have anything else to do I spent the remainder of the morning on the lot, selling the tough ones, and adding the commissions to my monthly take. At noon I ate a hot dog from my own stand, drank a Coke, and hit the highways to Long Beach, San Pedro, Pasadena, Ontario and other nearby communities on buying sprees for myself and the San Francisco lot. I tried to keep at least seventy-five cars on my lot at all times, and my business was so good I had to keep buying almost every day. I used the lemons sent down from San Francisco as trading material. Not only did I sell to individual buyers, I did a nice business with other dealers. Although I didn't make as much on dealer sales, it was possible to sell in lots of five and ten cars, and it kept me from getting stuck with lemons on my inventory.

I took Bill on a few buying excursions and I gradually turned over some of the contacts to him. He was such a glutton for work I couldn't understand it. It came to me one day that this was the first time in his life that the poor bastard had ever earned any money, and he couldn't get over it.

I must get on with the story. As I stated in the beginning, this is mostly about myself and the movies. I enjoy putting down all of it in detail, every single thing, every scrap of conversation. But it is not relevant. There are no complications here. I am a competent, perhaps a brilliant, used-car salesman, but to embroider this narrative with my successes in this lucrative business makes for dull reading.

Just one more little detour, and then back on the track. Bill and Ray Moore, (the Asst Mgr for Triple A) had cooked up a little plan to get rid of some Triple A repossesses. It was all right with me, and I told Bill to go ahead. A finance company is hard put to get rid of repossessed cars. But the twenty didn't move, they were a hard-ridden bunch, without a single plum. It was the first day of August and the sun was beating down on my head unreasonably. But it melted through and gave me an idea. I left the sun, entered the air-conditioned office and sat on Bill's desk. The perspiration was rolling down my face, and my sport shirt was soaked through.

'Ah, me,' Bill sighed with mock sympathy through his secret, knowing smile, 'it's a pity that some people do not have administrative ability. I wouldn't trade places with you, Chief, for half your dough.'

'Never mind the pity,' I said. 'Lift the telephone, Cool One, and call a costume company.'

Bill opened the telephone book and riffled through the yellow pages. 'Any company in particular?'

'One that rents Santa Claus suits, complete with beards.'

'What sizes?'

'The sizes worn by Evans, Cartwell, and Jody-boy, our three star salesmen.'

'You shouldn't do it, Chief,' Bill said seriously, reading my mind. 'It's the middle of August. Those guys will melt out there.'

'It's the first of August, and they'll wear the suits every damned day until I tell them to take them off. What is more unusual than Santa Claus selling used cars in August?'

'You've got me for the moment.'

'Nothing. Honest Hal is now Santa Claus in the middle of summer, bringing the good people of the City of Angels goodies in the form of repos. *Your* repossesses,' I added. 'Now, get the suits and get our buddy boys into them. Take a half-page in the *News* and write some decent copy for a change. I don't want those repos on the lot by Saturday!'

Bill was dialing as I started for the door. At the doorway I turned and flashed him my most disarming smile. 'By the way, Cool One,' I said softly, 'you will inform our white-bearded salesmen that the Santy Claus suits are *your* idea.'

'What a bastard I work for,' Bill said bitterly. But he smiled beautifully as he said it, and I knew he would also take the blame with the same covering smile. How wonderful it must be to have the advantage of a military training!

I got into my convertible and drove to the beach.

BACKGROUND

This period of my life should have been a happy one, and I suppose it was, in a weird, unrealistic way. Wasn't I making money hand over fist, as the saying goes? And isn't the making of money the reason for existence? Isn't it?

I was beset with gloomy spells where I was really down, all the way down to the spelean depths, complete with self-directed stalactites of dissatisfaction. Under. But at these times I never felt sorry for Richard Hudson; it didn't work that way. I was sorry that things were the way they were, and for the people and the way they lived. And when I thought of people, the damned foolish people, and their prosperity that wasn't prosperity at all, the pit of my stomach ached. Their prosperity was something other than prosperity. But what? Why? I was a walking allegory looking for the hidden meaning in the life of others. Sometimes a wave of pity would hit me when I screwed some aircraft mechanic out of his money for a used car. But I did it. And at the same time I felt absolutely no pity for my three salesmen sweltering in Santa Claus suits beneath the August sun. I laughed instead; in their phoney, white cotton beards they were a very funny sight.

I tried to kid myself into believing I was at least enjoying my newfound home life.

Dinner with the family. Mother eating her small steak with tiny delicate bites, starving to death, and chewing each mouthful until it became water.

Becky eating cornflakes, Ritz crackers, spinach and tomato soup, a true confessions magazine propped in front of her against a vase containing imitation cornflowers.

Leo eating sparingly, but trying hard, and topping off his meagre repast of mush, soft-boiled eggs and orange juice with an eight-ounce glassful of Pepto-Bismol.

There was nothing wrong with my appetite. I ate more than the whole crew put together. I devoured sirloin steaks, baked potatoes, broccoli spears, great salads smothered in olive oil and stinking of bleu cheese, large chunks of garlic bread, and entire apple pies prepared by the black hands of Leona who loved to see me eat.

The dinner conversation was wonderful. I discoursed freely about art, literature, smog, television, traffic problems, the excellence of my steak, my new record album of *Waiting for Godot*, and gradually led up to the movies. Sooner or later I got to movies, and when Leo grabbed the conversational ball, goaded into talking at last, I listened and looked, looking for meaning in a drooping shoulder, lifted eyebrow, raised forefinger and twitching cheek. His gestures were punctuated with words of movie wisdom, and when he explained a particular scene he acted it out with calm deliberation. He had the ability to masterfully change his voice, his facial expressions, and he could project a character equally well in the throes of death or laughter. But when he really got going good, Mother would break in sharply: 'Don't get too emotional now, Leo. It isn't good for you.'

The spell broken, Becky would say, 'I think Rock Hudson is dreamy.'

And I would tell Leo: 'You really should be an actor, Pop. You really *should*, Pop! I mean it. Honest to God, you ought to talk to them down there. Jesus! I wish to hell I could do half the things you can do with your voice. There isn't another actor out there who can touch you, Pop. I mean it.'

'Hush, Richard, dear,' Mother said softly. 'You know that Leo is a director. You're embarrassing him.'

Leo would raise his narrow shoulders high, hold them there for a long moment, and then let them drop. His thin lips would curl into such a tender, melancholy smile it would damn near break my heart. I couldn't stand it, and I would have to leave the table and finish my coffee and pie in the living room.

'James Dean isn't really dead, you know,' Becky said shrilly, to no one in particular.

After dinner, Mother and I would sit together on the couch in the living room. Leo would enter his study and sit beneath his Rouault clown, which more and more he seemed to resemble. Sitting there like that, in semi-darkness, he seemed wise beyond eternity, with the accumulated wisdom of every Jew who ever died since time began.

The telephone was within easy reach of his hand, connected once again, but it never rang for Leo; the bell tolled only for me.

While Mother and I talked together, in remembrance of things past, Becky would do her homework and sing television cigarette commercials. Her favorite was 'Flavor, filter, flip-top box,' and she sang it over and over again until I was half-crazy with irritation. She knew them all. It is remarkable that the girl could know so many cigarette commercials when she didn't even smoke.

'I was thinking about Harry today,' Mother confided.

Flavor, filter, flip-top box.

'He was one of my favorite stepfathers,' I said.

Flavor, filter, flip-top box.

'He could have left a note, you know.' Mother pursed her lips disapprovingly.

Flavor, filter, flip-top box.

'He probably couldn't think of anything to say that rhymed,' I defended the dead songwriter.

Flavor, filter, flip-top box.

'He was a good man, Harry,' Mother sighed, remembering.

Flavor, filter, flip-top box.

'He sure did hate lumpy grits,' I said.

Flavor, filter, flip-top box.

'I liked the way he played the piano, but I could never dance to him.'

Flavor, filter, flip-top box.

'"Lumpy Grits" wasn't exactly ballet music, Mother dear.'

Flavor, filter, flip-top box.

'I mean other things.'

Flavor, filter, flip-top box.

'He made me a kite once,' I said.

Flavor, filter, flip-top box.

'Oh, he was good with his hands all right,' Mother agreed.

'Flavor, filter, flip-top box,' I said.

Flavor, filter, flip-top box.
'I think I'll run off to bed now.'
Flavor, filter, flip-top box.
'Good night, Mother dear.' And I kissed her good night.
Flavor, filter, flip-top box.
I helped Becky with her homework, checking it for accuracy. 'Didn't you learn anything at the New Jersey school except how to play with yourself?' I asked her bluntly, after correcting three wrong algebra problems in a row.

'We didn't,' she blushed primly. 'It wasn't allowed.'

'OK.' I handed back her papers. 'You probably won't get more than a B on this, but it's more than you deserve.'

'Thanks anyway, then.' Becky kissed me impulsively and leaped nimbly away from me to avoid being goosed. 'You need a shave,' she informed me. 'You always need a shave.' And then she departed for her room to watch the portable television set I had given to her for her seventeenth birthday.

A fine, normal, typical American family. A famous father, only thirty-seven years old, but already washed-up, and living in the past. A beautiful mother, who could have been famous, but who gave up a career to dance for herself in a mirror. A successful businessman for a son, living in the meaningless void of day-to-day business. And a sexy, dimwitted daughter, who would probably attend UCLA. for an entire semester before she married a creep of some kind with sideburns and a sports car.

But it was the only family life I had known in more than ten years, and I had a vague sense of contentment. I realized how lonely I must have been in my San Francisco apartment. The mere surface appearance of family life had some satisfaction. But if I allowed myself to think about our way of life and our tensions together, even for a second, I could sense impending disaster. So I didn't think about it.

Mother was gone. Becky was gone. Leona had finished the dishes and had departed for home and her unemployed husband. I made a cup of instant coffee in the kitchen and took it into Leo's study.

'How about a nice fresh cup of coffee, Pop?'

He wagged his head, smiled wanly. 'No thanks, Son.'

'Well, good night, Pop.' I left the house, and stumbled across the shaggy back garden to my garage apartment, wondering how much longer Leo would sit like that, deep into the night, night after night, day after day. What could I say to him? What could anybody say to him except, 'We need you at the studio. We have a new picture for you.'

I drank four ounces of gin and hit the sack.

GO TO BLACK

It may have been this night or another – it doesn't really matter – because it was during this restless period I have just outlined that the inevitable happened: *l'petite affaire* Becky Steinberg.

I had seen it coming for several weeks, and it wasn't really inevitable; I could have avoided easily the culmination of the affair. But I didn't, and the reason I didn't merely indicates the disturbed state of my restlessness during this transition period when my subconscious was searching for something – something, I knew not what . . .

At first our involvement, if I can call it that, was merely the Big Brother–Little Sister bit. Becky occasionally requested fraternal advice.

'How do you like my hair fixed this way?'

'It makes you look older, kid.'

'Anything wrong with looking older?'

'Nope. Not at your age.'

And then:

'I bought this new cashmere sweater at Bullock's today. How does it look on me?'

'The color you mean? Blue is blue, and it looks well on you.'

'No, no, not the color . . .'

'All right then.' I grinned. 'You've got breasts beneath that sweater – if they're real.'

'Oh, you!' She changed colors like a chameleon, but she was pleased. As she left the room she looked coyly over her shoulder. 'They're real, all right!' And when I laughed, she fled in confusion.

These were early signs, and they increased gradually. Almost every time we passed each other she managed to brush against me, or touch me in some way. I could have discouraged this schoolgirl crush, and it would have been a relatively simple matter to do so in the beginning. But I was playing 'house', pretending that ours was a normal American family, and that this was the way all families lived. I spoiled Becky. I gave her an extra ten dollars a week in addition to the five-dollar allowance her father gave her. Not wanting to embarrass Leo, I told Becky to keep her mouth shut about the extra money if she wanted the allowance continued. She did. But that was a shared secret between us and one secret leads invariably to another. She eventually got around to asking me about boys, but before I told her anything I pumped her to see how much she had found out on her own.

Little Becky was a wealth of misinformation.

Small wonder that every year in these United States the illegitimate birth rate goes up instead of down. Becky's knowledge of sex matters was an appallingly erroneous compilation of speculation (from girl-talk at the convent), innocuous advice on kissing and dating (learned from newspaper columns and articles in 'teen magazines, written by fuddy-duddy matrons), plus a very few red-hot particles of truly advanced items she had picked up from a hardened Hollywood High girlfriend who had been attending too many drive-in (passion pit) movies. I have known married women of ten years standing who haven't learned some of these spicy tidbits Becky had learned so innocently from her aberrant girl friend. And without making an issue out of it, I advised Becky to drop her friendship with this girl.

Becky was reluctant to ask her father about these (to her) burning questions, so she turned to me instead. The estranged years she had spent in the convent away from her father had erected a barrier between them. She considered Leo a brooding, forbidding stranger. If we had been a true brother and sister instead of the amused, mocking, nonrelated type, she probably wouldn't have come to me either. Looking back, and disregarding any consideration of the ethics involved, I believe it would have been a wiser move on my part if I had sent Becky to Mother for the answers to her eager questions. But as I said, this was the first taste of family life I had ever known, and I was more than a little flattered that Becky was not afraid to come to me with her frank inquiries.

Fortunately, everything worked out all right, but if Operation Becky had turned out messily, developing into a courtroom case of statutory rape, I would have been hard put to prove my innocence in answering questions slammed into me by a well-briefed district attorney:

'Did you or did you not—' The DA glances toward the jury to see if they are listening '—give your stepsister an allowance of ten dollars a week without the knowledge of her father?'

'Why, ah, yes, sir, I did, but—'

'Just answer the questions, Mr Hudson. What did you hope to gain by this weekly philanthropic gift?'

'Nothing, sir. I just thought that a young lady attending

high school needed more than five dollars a week for spending money.'

'I see. But you didn't find it expedient to tell her father about your weekly donation?'

'No, sir.'

'Why?'

'I just didn't, that's all.' I mutter lamely. (It would have been impossible for me to describe the state of Leo's financial affairs in an open courtroom.)

'I have a sworn statement here to offer into evidence from Rebecca Steinberg.' The DA holds up a thick sheaf of legal-sized papers for the judge and jury to see before he hands it to the Clerk. 'In this statement, Miss Steinberg claims that you, her brother—'

'*Step*brother by marriage only!' I remind him sharply.

'Her stepbrother – gave her a demonstration, utilizing the handle of a broom . . . a demonstration on how to put on and remove a contraceptive device; to wit, a condom! Is this statement true?'

'Yes, sir. It's true.'

'I'm truly bewildered, Mr Hudson. Why did you provide your sister—'

'Stepsister by marriage,' I break in wearily.

'A girl who had just turned seventeen; an *unmarried* teenaged girl attending high school, with this type of demonstration?'

'I didn't want her to get into trouble, that's why.'

The DA raises his eyebrows incredulously. 'It looks to me as if you were trying to get her *into* trouble!'

'I'm telling the simple truth,' I say indignantly. 'Admittedly, I don't know what is right and what is wrong for every young girl to know, but I know something about young men. And teenaged boys rarely learn the basic knowledge about contraceptives until they're taught about them during venereal disease lectures in the Army. And as a precautionary measure – there was no other motive

– I thought Becky should know about such things to protect herself. Just in case—'

'You also admit, then, that you explained to this young girl – the various venereal diseases? To a young teenaged girl?'

'Yes, sir. The schools don't teach them anything about it, and Becky is a big girl—'

'And if they're big enough,' the DA directs his gaze sympathetically toward the jury Foreman, an unemployed truck driver with three teenaged daughters, 'they're old enough for you! Is that right?'

'No, sir. It is not.'

And then the DA pulls the clincher. 'I have a receipted bill, and a cancelled check bearing your signature. The sum is seventy-five dollars. This evidence, in black and white, indicates that you paid Dr Rufus D. Featherstone, a gynecologist who practices in Venice, California, this sum of money to perform a minor operation on the person of Miss Steinberg. You directed Dr Featherstone to pierce this young lady's hymen with a scalpel, and—' he pauses for dramatic effect 'you also requested that this young virgin – at the time – be fitted with a contraceptive device commonly called a diaphragm! Is this evidence true or untrue?'

'It's true all right, but I only wanted to prevent her from getting into trouble with some thoughtless, teenaged boy.'

'I see!' His face turns white with righteous rage. 'So that you could get her into trouble yourself without danger!'

This weird scene isn't too far-fetched. I realize that a courtroom scene like this imaginary one *could* have happened – although it didn't – and yet I honestly believed that I was only being practical at the time. I had no designs on the girl; such thoughts never entered my mind. But if Becky had reported the sequence of these truthful events, and the resultant aftermath, to the District Attorney, there

51

isn't a jury alive that wouldn't have convicted me of statutory rape . . .

I had been sound asleep, for either hours or minutes, I couldn't tell, when I felt the persistent pressure of a bare, shivering body against mine.

I opened my eyes, blinking in the inky darkness, still partly asleep. The uninvited stranger in my bed was feminine; this much was obvious, even with the lights out. I had spent the night in bed with women before. A warm, well-rounded body next to mine was no novelty, but I had always selected my own companions. Few women, however, have ever said that I was inhospitable. I wasn't afraid; I was puzzled.

'Excuse me, Madame,' I said softly, without moving, 'but am I in the wrong bed perchance?'

Becky giggled. Her delighted, nervous gargle was unmistakable.

In a jumbled mish-mash, all of the frank talk, the advice, including the business with Dr Featherstone, of course, meshed through my mind with a dawning, unwilling comprehension. This clandestine visit was really my fault, not Becky's. I should have realized that her cat-like curiosity would cause her to come to my bed eventually. And now that she was in my bed (as though I had schemed and masterfully planned a deliberate assignation), how could I handle the situation diplomatically; without making an indignant issue out of it; without magnifying the event out of its true proportions?

Completely awake now, I reached up and switched on the headboard reading lamp.

Becky giggled girlishly again, and covered her head with the sheet. 'We don't need the light, do we?' Her shaky soprano was slightly muffled.

I raised myself on my elbows. Becky's black silk nightgown and scarlet dressing gown lay crumpled on the seat of the leather bedside chair. Her red satin mules, damp from the wet night grass separating my garage apartment from the big house, were beside the door to the down stairwell. I tried to reach across her huddled body to get the robe.

'All right, Becky,' I said calmly, 'the joke's over. Get into your things and run back to the house before Leo finds out about this little escapade.'

'Oh, no you don't!' She sat up boldly, a trifle desperately, in bed. She dug the fingers of both hands into the matted hair on my chest and pushed me down again.

'Ouch!' I grinned, without resisting, and she released her grip.

'Daddy's finally gone to bed,' she said excitedly, 'and he's asleep! I've waited a long time for this chance, and I'd never get up enough nerve to do it again. So you've got to go through with it, Richard! You've *got* to!'

'Go through with what?' I wet my lips as I looked at her. Her face was flushed feverishly; the delicate pinkness of her skin extended from her neck to her well-shaped breasts. Her breasts weren't full by any means, not yet; another year would be needed for complete maturity, but they were round and firm, with tender rose-colored nipples.

'Go ahead and look,' she said in a defiant whisper, tossing her black hair, ignoring my question. 'I don't care. I want you to see for yourself that they're real.'

She was a paradox, this girl. I had underestimated her, thinking that I knew her well, but this charming, naive combination of innocence and boldness fascinated me. Her red, inexpertly painted lips parted in a wet, provocative smile – undoubtedly practiced to perfection in a mirror. The smile was effective, too, but she spoiled the effect by batting her long, false eyelashes like an old-time silent movie queen – and the left eyelash was slightly askew.

I had to laugh; I couldn't help myself.

'Go ahead and laugh,' she said grimly, 'laugh all you want.' She managed to maintain her set, provocative smile. 'But you started it, and now you're going to finish it! Brother, dear!' she added sternly.

'Finish what?'

'You're going to make love to me, and I'm not leaving till you do!' she said determinedly.

'Suppose I don't want to?'

'Oh, you want to, all right,' she said firmly. 'I know!'

'All right.' I sighed. 'You win. But let me get up and smoke a cigarette first.' I was stalling for time, but she sensed it.

'I'll get you the cigarette!' She scrambled out of bed, and turned on the bright floorlamp. She shook a cigarette loose from the package on the end-table. I would have been less than human if I turned my eyes away from her creamy, nubile body. Her legs were long, and beautifully tapered down to her small bare feet. Her stomach was narrow with just the suggestion of a bulge at the navel, and her hips were wide and soft enough to avoid the unappealing boyish look so many young girls seem to have nowadays. As she lit the cigarette with the table lighter, tilting her small head to one side, and closing one eye against the smoke, the dormant juices stirred inside me – for the first time since I had discovered her beside me.

Yes, I did want to make love to her. And why not? Why in the hell shouldn't it be me? If I didn't, who would? Becky didn't have an adult, or physical need for love-making; she was merely curious; she wanted to find out for herself what it was all about.

Becky was a girl of average intelligence, not feebleminded by any means, but she wasn't too bright about people. And if it wasn't me it would soon be someone else, some unskilled but fast-talking high school boy who would make out with her by working the word 'love' into his pitch. An involvment of this kind would be sticky, unnecessarily

54

emotional, especially for an impressionable girl like Becky. No, I didn't want her to become involved in any shabby, back-seat affair with some excitable, immature male . . .

But if I was to be the one – and I had already made up my mind – I had to manage it bluntly, brutally, in fact. No tenderness, no subtlety, no shaded nuances or romance. I knew it would diminish my pleasure if I refused to be gentle and patient with her, but I didn't want her following me around like a dog afterwards either. I had to knock all notions of romance out of her head, once and for all. I hadn't had a girl since San Francisco – and although I wanted Becky, I only wanted her once!

'Never mind the damned cigarette!' I said roughly.

Startled by the gruffness in my voice, Becky dropped the cigarette into the ashtray. I kicked the covers down to the foot of the bed. Her dark eyes widened in sudden panic, and she made an audible gulping sound in her throat. My feet hit the floor, and I grabbed her thin wrist, jerking her onto the bed. I was more than brutal, savage really; I didn't even go through the preliminary of kissing the dumbfounded girl. The penetration was swiftly accomplished; the act itself hastily concluded. The cigarette Becky had lighted for me was still smouldering when I plucked it out of the ashtray and put it between my parched lips.

'OK, Becky,' I said flatly, with an indifferent yawn. 'You'd better get dressed and hustle back to the house before Leo finds out you're over here.'

I watched her out of the corner of my eye as she got up timidly, and quickly donned her nightgown. She slipped into her robe, and buttoned it with trembling fingers. Her lower lip quivered and her dark eyes were bright and shiny, on the near-verge of tears. She held onto the door for support as she dug her toes into the damp satin mules she had kicked off at the stairwell.

'Thanks for the party, kid,' I said callously. 'And any night you feel like you want it, come on over. Just be careful that no one sees you.'

She made a strangling noise, and fled down the stairs, without a backward glance.

Becky never came back again. But then, I never expected her back. After that experience, 'romance' was a dirty word to Becky. In fact, she studiously avoided brushing against me after that. We were still friends, of course; she wanted to be certain that I would continue to slip her the extra ten bucks every week. But the former intimacy was gone, and so was her schoolgirl crush . . . Justification on my part, or rationalization? It doesn't make any real difference, because a man can look at these things either way. But I solved Becky's problem and mine – at the time – and I saved the girl from an emotional and physical involvement with another male of *any* age for a long, long time!

WIPE

MORE BACKGROUND

Almost every idea I had ever had in my life leaped out of my head full blown and ready to be put into effect. But not my idea for the movie. This idea inched out, creeping into my conscious mind, darted back in fear, and then edged out again, getting bolder all of the time. My idea for the movie was like a column of surprises, each surprise camouflaged behind its own little tree. We relish these little surprises in our daily lives. If we were denied surprises we would all fold up into cataleptic balls and bounce only once on our way to our graves.

I was driving down Wilshire when the red signal flashed, following so quickly upon the yellow I had to jam on my brakes to stop in time. Squeal! Stop. Two inches short of the pedestrians' white line. A woman, blowsy, engulfed in a snot-green housecoat, with light frizzy hair, and well over 180 pounds, gathered a play of children about her billowing corduroy skirts. One, two, three, five of them altogether. All of them were yard-sized, tow-haired, with noses running in unison. The woman maintained a whining tirade, strident and nerveracking. 'Scoodie!' it sounded like, 'take aholt of Bubber's hand! Stay clost to me crossing the street! Melvin! Melvin! (shrilly delivered indeed) I said to wait! Now!' Still threatening loud admonitions and dire punishments she shooed the brood across the inter-section. The five children all held hands and completely encircled the woman. Here and there a grubby hand clung like death to the corduroy of her housecoat.

They all made it to the other side without trouble and then crowded like a mother hen and chicks through the double door of a supermarket. She would need, I added quickly in my head, about $47.85 worth of groceries for the weekend. Her husband, undoubtedly a stupid bastard, worked at Douglas. To support such a family he would have to work two shifts. To love such a family he would have to work three shifts. They would live in a project house, three bedrooms, but much too small. He would owe approximately twenty-seven more years of payments on the mortgage. At home he would be unable to sleep, rest, watch television, or even go to the bathroom comfortably. The children would all love him, and attempt to crawl into his lap. He would cuff them surlily out of the way, down his beer, and be grateful when it was time to go to work again at the plant. After eight hours at home with five brats, the strident wife, and the pile of bills on the Sears and Roebuck coffee table, the sound of riveting would be soothing to him.

Make a movie about this, my subconscious mind hinted. This is America. This is Mr and Mrs America. This is Mr and Mrs United States and the American way of life. Here is the new bourgeois with a home-freezer in every garage next to the cut-rate do-it-yourself workbench with the brand new power saw, power vise, and power Band-Aids. Well?

And then there were the Toastmasters.

I had joined one of the Toastmaster clubs in San Francisco and I was in full accord with its principles. There are no -isms in Toastmasters. Each club consists of a membership of thirty determined men, in various occupations, who gather together once a week at a luncheon or dinner meeting for the purpose of learning how to speak better. It is a practical organization. The man who is unable to talk to his fellow-American today is unable to eat. The better a man can speak, the better he can eat. It isn't what you say; it is how you say it. A simple, straightforward proposition. All of us are born with a tongue, but how many of us know how to use it effectively?

In the glove compartment of my car I carried a booklet listing all of the Toastmasters Clubs in the United States and their meeting places. It was a handy booklet to have. When I got the opportunity I dropped into a meeting, knowing that I would be welcomed as another Toastmaster in good standing. There were more than a dozen such clubs in Los Angeles; the thirty-member limit of each club and the dire need of ambitious men to make more money will increase the membership of Toastmaster's International a thousandfold in the next decade.

My day had been a dull one, and at five o'clock I had called the Sergeant-At-Arms of a Telephone Company Toastmaster's Club and asked him if I could attend their evening meeting. His friendly welcome chased away the cares of the day, and with my TM button on my lapel I entered the dining room of the Robert Fulton Hotel promptly at 7:30 p.m.

There were twenty members present and three guests, counting myself. After the brief invocation I was introduced to the club by the Sergeant-At-Arms, along with two aspirants for membership. Unlike many clubs, prospective Toastmasters are allowed to attend two meetings as guests before making up their minds – to join or not to join. Those who do not join sink back into the faceless mass and the chances are excellent that they will never be heard from again, at least in the competitive world of moneymakers.

With the arrival of tired salmon croquettes and Lyonnaise potatoes, the table topic began. Each one of us present was allowed one full minute to express our opinions, pro or contra, on the question of admitting a larger quota of immigrants into the United States. The members of this club were all employees of the Telephone Company, secure in their jobs, and the majority of the one-minute speakers were *for* the admission of more immigrants. In the majority opinion, 30,000 more people a year meant 30,000 more telephone installations. At the time, as I recall, I could not see how the running away from various countries could speed the freedom of the countries left behind. A minute passes quickly, and the chairman, a sonorous-voiced classified salesman, banged the gavel for me to sit down.

Three speeches were scheduled, and the first speaker was a bright young man making his initial speech to the club. This was called the 'Ice-breaker speech' and the speaker was quite nervous and ill at ease. As I listened to his pitiful five-minute autobiographical account of his last days at Manual Arts High School; his prowess with the tennis racket in the Exposition Park yearly tournaments, and his brilliant decision to join the National

Guard to avoid military service, I was touched. But I didn't know why.

Here was a young man who knew exactly where he was going. He was understandably nervous; it was his first speech. But the slight quaver in his voice would disappear with more practice. Within a few years he would be making $10,000 a year; he would be buying a house in San Fernando Valley; he would own a Beagle hound, and would undoubtedly have a pretty wife and two children; and planned children at that, so the wife wouldn't have to carry her babies in the hot summer. What was wrong then? I mean – what the hell? – here was the ideal American boy, an Eagle Scout, no less, and I was feeling sorry for him and everybody in the dining room. Looking around the U-table set-up I could see this boy in ten years, fifteen years, with a fine position in one of the best corporations to work for in the United States. He was off on the road to security with a flying start and smart enough to realize it. A pension plan, prompt and steady advancement, a chance to buy stock, and eventually, if he kept his shoes shined and developed the ability to get along with other people – which is all any corporation asks of their executives – he would be a top executive at the policy-making level. At fifty he would be keeping an eye out for promising youngsters like he was today so that the entire process could begin again. I didn't know! I just didn't *know!* By the time he had finished his speech my heart seemed to be twice as large as it should have been and I could feel the heat of sudden tears behind my eyes.

Quickly, I left my seat, slipped a five-dollar bill to the Sergeant-At-Arms, and excused myself. By the time I reached my car in the parking lot I was blubbering. These men were prisoners! And yet they were unaware of their plight because they were also their own jailers! A feeling of revulsion and terror swept through me. I sat in my car, hanging onto the steering wheel for dear life, and I let the salty tears flow. It was the first time I had cried like that since reaching manhood. It was the waste, I thought, the foolish waste, the dullness of their lives, the daily repetition of meaningless tasks, the stupidity of such an existence, and underlying everything – all of my thoughts were jumbled together – they didn't *know!* They knew instead that they had a good deal . . .

Our lives are so short and there is so little time for creativeness, and yet we waste our precious time, letting it dribble through our fingers like dry sand. But that was it. Creativeness. To create something. Anything. I pulled myself together, wiped my streaming eyes with my handkerchief. One thing. That was all. One little thing. And then, maybe two things. But above all, ONE THING! This was it. One creative accomplishment could wipe away the useless days and tie up in a single package our reason for being here, our reason for existence.

And I think then, at that very moment, I knew what I was going to do, but my thoughts were still hazy and I wasn't positive until the day I danced with Mother.

DISSOLVE TO:

I was looking for Mother, on some domestic errand concerning the house. I knew that she was in the basement rehearsal room, and I whistled as I descended the stairs so she would know that someone was coming. (Sometimes dancers, in performing various exercises, assume undignified or ungraceful positions, and I wanted to warn her.)

Mother's basement rehearsal hall was enormous, almost sixty-by-sixty feet in area, and for a basement room it had an unusually high ceiling. The floor was inlaid mahogany, and was kept in a high state of polish. An electric polisher sat in one corner, and Mother polished the floor herself. One entire wall was mirrored from the floor to the ceiling. Along the opposite wall there was a room-length exercise *barre*. Near the single doorway by the stairwell down from the living room, there was an upright piano, a huge Stromberg-Carlson hi-fi console, and a rack containing approximately 2,000 records, both LPs and ancient 78s. Four straight-backed Monterey chairs, painted a delicate beige, completed the furnishings.

Mother, her long black hair flowing down her back in a wild mane, and wearing a single-piece, white, form-fitting costume, stood in the third position in the center of the room. With her bright flushed face, perfect figure, and beaded upper lip, and the fine film of perspiration rolling down each temple, Mother didn't look more than eighteen years old. At the foot of the stairs I stopped and admired her beauty. On her pointes Mother skimmed across the floor, grasped both my hands and kissed me on the nose.

'You've come to dance with me!' Mother shouted gaily. 'Come on!' She dragged me to the console, pushed a button for the record player and the heavy opening bars of Bartok's *Miraculous Mandarin* jolted out of all five speakers and punched me in the solar plexus.

'All right. Why not!' I said, and the excitement in my voice surprised me. I kicked off my loafers, tossed my sport jacket, shirt and undershirt on a chair, and attempted a couple of low-key elevations. After a pretty fair *tour en l'air* I fled to the far end of the room, squealing like a schoolboy on the last day of school. I was almost out of breath already, and I leaned against the wall, looking sardonically at myself in the mirror.

Two hundred pounds, the beginnings of a paunch, big size eleven feet, more enormous yet in red-yellow-and-blue cashmere argyles, thick, hairy arms and basketball-player hands, a mat of blue-black chest hair; a sunburned grinning face, and a headful of dark unruly hair, badly in need of cutting. Some dancer! I laughed wildly. In the face of all maternal arguments I had quit taking ballet lessons when I turned fourteen and fell in love with baseball. The hell with it! I assumed an *attitude* and met Mother's charming *pas de Bourre* with outstretched arms and fingers.

The music from the suite of *The Miraculous Mandarin* can best be described as treacherous, and it fits the weird tale that goes with it beautifully. One of my favorite ballets, I remembered most of the tale as we danced. A young girl is used as a decoy by a band of forest thieves. She lures the victims into the forest and the thieves destroy them. But the Mandarin doesn't go for that crap. He goes for the girl, however, and she flees from his rapacious desires. The robbers get to him finally, choke him, run a sword through his guts, hang him to a tree, but he still won't join his ancestors until they cut him down and the girl takes him into her arms. The girl has broken down completely, cowed to submissiveness by his fierce devotion. When she kisses him at last, his wounds bleed, and he kicks off . . . The End. A wonderful story for a ballet.

I had listened to the music many times. I knew it for a savage, erotic, fierce succession of half-tones, with an odd waltz beat coming through from time to time, like the faraway sound of a radio in another room. The coda always brought to mind an evil memory of my childhood when I saw, or thought I saw, a double image of a man in a dressing room backstage at some theatre squash a lighted cigar out on the tip of a woman's breast. This terrible, half-lit scene stands out sharply in my mind, and whether I saw such a thing or merely dreamed it I do not know. But it could have happened, and it seems real enough when I think about it. I was backstage at many different theatres with Mother when I was a child. No matter.

And so we danced, my Mother and me, a half-remembered dream in my mind, a well-remembered story floating hazily on my conscious mind, and my reluctant, well-padded body coaxing almost forgotten dance sequences out of a pair of big and clumsy feet.

But I danced. And Mother danced. The longer I danced the better I became, and Christ almighty if I didn't become the Miraculous Mandarin himself, the damndest Chinaman anybody ever saw! I chased, I pursued, I made impossible leaps and came down as lightly as a wind-wafted cigarette paper. The things I accomplished were almost impossible for a man so long out of training. As the music swelled, yelled, jangled, soared to a half-tone above legal octave limits, and then dipped down to a foolish, single tootling oboe, I, me, Richard Hudson, pranced, cavorted, darted, turned, glided, bent, stretched, and did a mad *fouette* on one leg until I almost lost my reason. I even managed an *entrechat* and crossed my feet four times before I landed painfully on a big toe. Mother appeared to be having the time of her life, keeping well ahead of me, teasing, but all the same, her lips were set in a grim line, even though her eyes were sparkling with a wild merriment. She was an elusive white shadow beckoning me on with long pale arms, gracefully pirouetting away, forward, to the side, her flying feet like butterflies in an imaginative *suite de danses*. And mad Jack came tumbling after, loving every crazy moment of it.

Any balletomane in the world would have shelled out twenty bucks without a murmur to see the Steinburg-Hudson *divertissement* of *The Miraculous Mandarin*, and it was worth a hell of a lot more.

At last, at long, long last – the score ran for twenty-five minutes – the music ended with a fruity belch, and I was done – timed O so beautifully by Mother dear – and I held her lush body in my arms. She kissed me then, a sloppy tongue-tangling kiss, and yet so sweet and innocent my throat tightened with pain. Exhausted, I fell in my tracks to a prone position, my arms spread, my heavy, rasping breathing echoing in the enormous room.

'*Premier danseur noble!*' Mother hissed. She stood above me, still fresh and ready to continue, with only a quickened rise and fall of her bosom to show for her exertions. I looked at her through red cobwebs, and then I heard applause. Two hands smacking hard together like an over-paid clacque's. I got to all fours – I couldn't stand – and looked blearily toward the doorway. There was Leo; tears were coursing down his cheeks. He sniffled and smiled.

'It was so beautiful!' He said it over and over, 'So beautiful, so beautiful, so beautiful . . .'

Mother tossed a floor-length terry-cloth robe about her shoulders, and impatiently shook her black mane. 'Don't get so emotional, Leo,' she said fretfully. 'Why don't you take a Miltown, for Christ's sake!'

I dropped to my belly again, and in a moment I was asleep, flying tiptoe through an endless field of snowy, gold-flecked clouds, following a darting, jet black neutron into the sun . . .

CUT TO:

The next morning I did not go to the lot. I drove to Exposition Park, descended to the cool basement of the Los Angeles Museum, and spent a couple of quiet hours looking at Egyptian mummies. It was pleasant there, and except for the bored guard, I had the place to myself. There is something about mummies that comforts a man.

The time for fooling around was over. The time had come for me to create something, and at the same time, it was up to me to show the American people where they were headed before it was too late. I do not believe that I had a messianic complex or mad obsession. But perhaps I did. It does not make any real difference now. My primary desire was to create something with my own mind and hands. Firmly interlocked with this desire was the knowledge that nothing is truly creative unless it means something. Unless an art form contains a message or a universal truth it is meaningless.

As an artist I was limited as to what I could do. Painting, sculpture, music, architecture, the writing of a novel – all of these art forms take years of apprenticeship. And I didn't have time for any such apprenticeship; I had wasted too much of my life already.

But I knew I could write and direct a movie! (Italics mine.)

I *knew* it. For several months in 1953 I had been an active member of a little theatre group in Marin County, and I had directed a three-act play. I had performed as an actor in several plays. As a requirement for *Playwriting I* at Los Angeles Junior College I had written a one-act play, and received an A-minus for my effort. And certainly, I knew what movies were all about! I had seen thousands; well, hundreds, anyway.

Leo would help me. Hell, yes! I would talk to Leo.

Driving down Vermont toward home I began to chicken out. Just talking to Leo was not enough; I had to have an idea, something concrete I could present to him, a story line at least. And it had to be the type of story that would appeal to him. Reaching home, I parked, climbed the stairs to my apartment.

In my tiny kitchenette I reached for the jar with the stars on top, filled a teaspoon with thousands of tiny flavor buds, and made myself a cup of coffee with hot water from the kitchen tap. The telephone rang. It was Bill Hards.

'Our three salesmen quit,' Bill informed me.

66

'Why?' I was genuinely surprised.

'They didn't cotton to those Santa Claus suits.'

'Hire salesmen who *will* wear the suits.'

'If I do, they won't be worth a damn, Richard. It's pretty hot, but I think the main reason the boys quit was because they didn't like being laughed at.'

'I'm not interested in their reasons. I have other things on my mind. I hired you to keep things going when I wasn't there, and that's what I want you to do. And if you can't handle it, I'll get someone who can!'

'Yes, *sir!*'

'Wait a minute, Bill. I didn't mean what I said. Just do the best you can and it'll be good enough for me. But the Santa Claus suits are a good idea and I want them worn by our salesmen.'

'I'll see what I can do. There are other salesmen.'

'Fine, Bill. I know I can depend on you. I won't be down for a couple of days. Anything comes up sign my name. OK?'

'Sure. You need any help? If you're in trouble or anything—'

'No. Nothing like that. Sorry I blew up at you.'

I racked the receiver. That was that. Bill could handle things by himself for awhile. At least I was paying him a salary high enough to prevent him from stealing from me.

The apartment was too warm, and I turned on the air conditioner. Before sitting down with a tablet and pencil I put on some LPs and let June Christy sing to me. Within a few minutes it was pleasant in my living room. My apartment was well-shielded from street noises. Christy's voice was sweet and husky, and the coffee was strong. The atmosphere was conducive to creative thinking, and the summer day passed swiftly. By the time Leona shouted up the stairs that dinner was ready, I had an entire movie outlined in my mind, including the title; *The Man Who Got Away*.

During dinner I was quiet for a change; it was difficult for me to suppress my inner excitement. The dinner was excellent – pork chops, grits, cream gravy, and an abundant salad of lettuce, tomato, and avocado – but I couldn't eat much. Leona was disappointed in my appetite, and her mouth was poked out.

'You sick, Mr Richard? First time I ever seen you pass up my pork chops.'

'I had pork chops for lunch,' I lied.

Mumbling to herself, Leona took my barely touched plate into the kitchen. Leona was never sassy to me like she was to the rest of the family. I not only paid her salary; I had granted her 'carrying' privileges. Leona was from Anniston, Alabama, and she expected to take a few things home from time to time. Negroes never steal; they *carry* things away with them when they go home.

Now that dinner was over I was so keyed up I couldn't sit still. I left the table and fixed a gin and tonic. Mother and Becky lingered over their dinner, and Leo was unbearably long in finishing his glass of Pepto-Bismol. Three drinks later, Mother went to bed, and Becky left for the movies with three teenagers in a hot rod. After Leo retreated to his study I mixed another drink I didn't want. I drank it slowly, putting my thoughts in order, and then I bearded Leo in his den. I do not believe that I have ever been unduly sensitive, but I was afraid of being laughed at. This is a real fear, and I do not believe I could have taken it from Leo. The great respect I had for Leo frightened me, because if he had laughed at me, or even snickered, I would have killed him. No. I wouldn't have killed him, but I would have wanted to, and that was worse.

'Pop,' I began, using a flanking attack, 'what would you say the minimum cost is for producing a movie? I don't mean a color job now, or widescreen; I mean a plain old ordinary black-and-white movie. The very cheapest.'

'That depends on many things, Richard,' Leo said slowly. 'Stars, story, location, a lot of things.'

'Without stars. Using nobodies.'

'Well,' Leo shrugged, 'even without stars there's an actor's equity minimum. Ninety a week for speaking parts, I believe, and I would have to know the size of the cast. A director, even the worst you could find, should get $10,000 unless the studio is crazy. And stories run high, even rotten stories. Let's say you bought a magazine story, for instance. This story could cost as little as two hundred and fifty bucks. You would then have to pay a writer for a treatment, another for the scenario, maybe another to doctor the script, and yet another writer to put in some extra dialogue. To find a single writer capable of doing all of this, you would have to have Ben Hecht. And if you paid Ben Hecht for the scenario your movie would no longer be in the cheap class. I can't give you a snap answer to your question, Richard.'

'How much without the director's fee and the writers's fee? How much excluding them? And a small cast – say four or five principals and some extras, forty at the most.'

'What about locations, Richard? There were only a handful of actors in *The African Queen*, but when you count in the trip to Africa and the technical costs, a lot of money went down the river with that little boat.'

'The location is right here in California. San Francisco and Los Angeles. Most of the movie is a chase down Highway one-oh-one.'

'That would help considerably. In a chase every studio has a lot of stock film on hand; scenic views, stretches of beach, towns and so on down the coast. By filling with stock shots, the movie could be well-padded almost for free. But before I could give you an estimate, I would have to see the script. And the *stars*? One name star could kill a small budget. Why do you ask, anyway?'

'No, I mean without stars.'

'I don't really know, Richard.' Leo shrugged. 'I'd have to see the script.'

'Suppose I give it to you briefly, the story, I mean.' I sat down at Leo's desk and lit a cigarette. Although I had the story outlined in my head, it was difficult to put into words. But I tried.

'The title first,' I began. *The Man Who Got Away.*'

'I like the title,' Leo nodded.

'All right, here's the plot. Roughly, anyway.' I ran my fingers through my hair, trying to think of a good lead. Pop sat quietly in his chair, listening with half-closed eyes, and gently stroking his pointed chin with thumb and forefinger.

'The title is the clue to the whole damned movie. As far as the theme is concerned the movie is about Mr America, Mr Average American. The guy who has the job that's too good to quit, and yet a job where he can never go any higher. Most of the jobs in the United States fall into that category. The hero is a truck driver and he only makes ninety bucks a week, and to make that much he has to put in overtime.

'In the first part of the film his unhappiness is established, but he doesn't know he's unhappy. He's married to a sloppy broad; he lives in a project house, and has three children. His job is the dullest job imaginable. One day he drives his track from San Francisco to Los Angeles, and the next day he drives it back. Deadly. Twelve hours each way. The worst possible existence for anybody.

'Every fourth day the hero gets a day off, but he doesn't know what to do with it. The camera picks up his miserable home life – the bratty kids, the sloppy wife, television, the hero mowing the lawn, that kind of stuff. He is always glad to get back to his truck; at least he is alone in the cab. Of course, he feels guilty about wanting to be in his truck. But we show his mounting dissatisfaction. I have a wonderful scene in mind. He and his family are watching

70

a comedy on television. The camera pans, first on his laughing wife, back to the funny comedian on the set, then on the laughing, oldest daughter, back to the comedian, then to the two smaller children who are also laughing. Then the camera catches the hero. He is scowling. The camera dollies back for a group portrait. Everybody is laughing crazily except the hero.'

Leo smiled. He was interested. 'That could be a very effective scene if it was properly handled.'

'Right. That's the beginning. Then the first complication. The next day is supposed to be his day off, but the dispatcher asks him to take another run that's scheduled for another driver who is sick. The hero has already put in three twelve-hour days, and he refuses the run. He's tired and he wants his day off. But after a few hours at home in the kind of atmosphere it has, he calls the dispatcher and tells him he's changed his mind. He feels guilty about taking the run, but he justifies it to his wife by saying he needs the extra money. But the guy is really worn out, and the average moviegoer will recognize the foreshadowing. You know.'

'I know,' Leo nodded.

'The rest of the picture is down the highway. Atmosphere. Truck stops. Coffee. Messages on the blackboards. A weary, half-assed, unsuccessful flirtation with a waitress. These are all tired defeated men – the drivers, the swampers, hitch-hikers. There are the frustrations of the occupation, blowouts, vapor locks, weigh-in stations. A little bit of all of it is shown to more or less set the mood. Do you see it?'

'Montage effect.'

'Not exactly. At a much slower pace, a dull dragging pace. The second half of the movie is so fast, the first part will have to be that much slower by contrast. The hero's inner tension builds – a near fist fight, his disposition gets surlier, he buys a pint and takes a few drinks. This would

71

really tip off the audience and get them interested in what comes next. And then it happens. Bang!

'He is very tired and has had no sleep at all for twenty-four hours. And he's taken a few drinks. He's wheeling down the road like an automaton. He's driven the route so many times he doesn't even have to think about it. A child darts out on the highway in front of his truck. A little girl out picking wild flowers. That's as touching as hell, and she has her dog with her, a puppy. Bang! He runs over the little girl and squashes her flat. This scene could be sadder than a son of a bitch. The driver gets out of his truck, sees that the little girl is dead, and then he panics. He gets back in the cab and roars off down the highway.

'OK. Here he was, a nobody. But now, all of a sudden, he's the most important man in California! The entire state is interested in him. He's *done* something! The highway patrol is alerted, and the police of every town he has to pass through on the way to Los Angeles. The idea of deserting his big truck doesn't occur to him; the truck is his real home, you see. Radio stations are broadcasting; there are interruptions on television, everybody is interested in the mad dog. Roadblocks are erected and he ploughs right through them. He has this enormous monster of a semi- and nothing can stop him. A highway patrol car gets after him but he forces it off the road and the two patrolmen are killed. Now they are *really* after him! His route is plotted, the entire highway is cleared all of the way to Los Angeles. He is all alone on Highway one-oh-one – a good place to work in some symbolism – a man against the world.

'But down in Santa Barbara they are getting ready for the poor bastard. The people are working like mad at an old junkyard dragging old wrecks out and piling them on the highway to make a king-sized roadblock. Will they have it ready in time? Back and forth our camera goes – the driver's white and frightened face, the frenzied workers – boy oh boy! The police are lined up with rifles, machine guns; an enormous crowd has gathered to watch the kill. Tottering old men, rich old ladies; the principal even declares a holiday so the school kids can be in on it. A regular Roman holiday!

'And here he comes, barrelling down the highway to his doom. He doesn't know why he can't stop; he only knows he has to keep driving. And there is the roadblock ahead of him, hundreds of cars piled up across the four-lane highway, and a steep wall on each side. He can't go around or under it so he crashes into it. His truck tips over and catches fire. He catches on fire. He's burning. He stumbles blindly from the cab, a human torch. There is one good Samaritan in the crowd, and he rushes out and tries to throw an overcoat over the hero to put out the fire. The vicious crowd turns savagely on the Samaritan and knock the hell out of him. The police empty their pistols, rifles and machine guns into the burning body of the truck driver. It's all over.

'The final scene. The poor guy who tried to help the truck driver gets to his feet. His mouth is bleeding where someone hit him, and he's a trifle dazed. He asks one of the policemen, "Why did everybody turn on me? What did I do wrong, anyway?" The policeman is very serious. "You tried to help him. That's why."'

'Well, that's the end, Pop.' My face was perspiring, and I dabbed at it with my handkerchief.

'That's the end?'

'That's the end.'

Leo looked at the floor. He nodded his head up and down and his eyes were closed tight. He was attempting to visualize what I had told him, I supposed.

'Well,' I asked nervously, 'will it make a movie, Pop?'

'Yes, Richard,' Leo answered sincerely, looking me frankly in the eyes, 'it would make a movie.'

'Then how much would it cost? Rock bottom.'

'You're going to write the scenario?'

'Yes. And direct it. I want you to produce it, Leo. You're the producer and you can handle all the dough, the details, paperwork. It's a chance for you to get back on top again, Pop.'

'Let me sleep on it, do some figuring with a pencil. We'll talk some more in the morning. All right?'

'Tomorrow morning.' Without another word I left him sitting there and returned to my apartment. I had him hooked and I knew it.

I knew it!

DISSOLVE

At the first click of the alarm the next morning I caught it before it began to ring. A moment later I was out of bed and into the shower. After I shaved I slipped into gray Daks, a madras shirt and loafers, and prepared breakfast. A big slab of fried Swift's premium ham and a four-egg omelet, fluffed with plenty of whipping cream, three English muffins and four cups of coffee fortified me for the day. After breakfast I dumped the dirty frying pan and dishes into the sink for Leona. Although I was anxious to talk to Leo I waited until 9 a.m. before I went over to the house.

Leo had never left his study. Crumpled sheets of lined foolscap littered the floor. Leo was sitting at his desk studying a column of figures and sipping hot coffee. A pile of empty dishes on a tray indicated that he had eaten breakfast for a change.

'Jesus, Pop,' I greeted him. 'Did you stay up all night?'

Leo raised his right arm with the same gesture a fullback uses when he signals for a free catch.

'Sit down, Richard.' I sat down in the leather chair beside the desk. 'Listen to me for a few moments.' Leo spoke slowly, choosing his words with maddening deliberation. 'In these United States, Richard, there lives a nation of moviegoers. They have been conditioned to movies from the time they were able to clasp a dime in grubby fingers and walk unassisted to the corner theatre on Saturday mornings. As they are they all become experts on the movies. Sooner or later, but mostly sooner, they leave a Class B picture and say to themselves, "That was a lousy movie; I could write a better movie than that myself." But they're kidding themselves, Richard. They can't. I know.

'A lot of these people who think they are experts because they've seen a few hundred movies make their way out here to Hollywood. They give up good jobs in Peoria and the East Texas oilfields. They want to write movies. None of them have ever written anything except a letter to their parents asking for money, and yet they think they're writers. Now tell me: do you know what a movie is?'

'Of course I do. It's a three-act play without dialogue.'

'Very good. Now tell me the difference between movement and action.'

'Movement is just a bunch of crap; walking back and forth while talking, lighting a cigarette, opening a window and so on. Action shows the story instead of merely telling it; action moves the story ahead visually. In a perfectly done movie no dialogue would be needed. If it was my birthday, and you presented me with a birthday cake, I wouldn't need the words, "Happy Birthday" in green icing to tell me it was my birthday cake.'

'You surprise me, Richard,' Leo said warmly, 'A great many directors don't know that much.'

75

'You don't have to worry about me, Pop. I'm not from Peoria or East Texas. I was raised out here and I know damned well I can write and direct a movie.'

'What's the function of a director?'

'You may not agree with me here, Pop. I think it's the business of the director to put the story on the screen as the author wrote it, and to abstain from cuteness. When three or four writers work together on a script it is invariably lousy. When one writer writes a script, with minimum interference, he comes up with something good once in a while. Most movies are botched by too many people with too many ideas. What do you think of Piomkin as a director, Pop?'

'One of the few artists we have.'

'Right.' I grinned broadly. 'You just proved my point. When a person attends a Piomkin movie, he spends more time looking for the little tricks than he does at the story. That's the trouble with Piomkin; the story is subjugated to his artistry. He is, in effect, telling the moviegoer, "Never mind the story; look how clever I am!"'

Leo nodded. 'I've noticed that in Piomkin. But people like his movies.'

'No,' I disagreed. 'The *critics* like his movies. Sure, they make money on account of the build-up, the raving reviews, and because they're different. But they don't make as much as they should because people go to a movie to see a story. The best director, in my opinion, is the director the public doesn't know, the guy with the ability to put a story on the screen. Honestly, no frills or trick photography, and with enough artistic integrity and ability to faithfully interpret the script. It's simple; if nobody tampers with it a good script makes a good movie.'

'Fair enough, Richard. But what about acting? Do you think you can do your movie with nobodies?'

'To do my movie it has to be done with nobodies. I

want to do away with the movie personality for once. When people see James Stewart, they see James Stewart, regardless of the character he's portraying. Whether he's a ballplayer, a doctor, anything, he's still James Stewart. It kills the story. I want a real truck driver and a real housewife. If I can get actors nobody knows they'll believe in the characters as they see them on the screen.'

'I like it, Richard. We could make a movie that way, if we had the money.' Leo handed me the piece of paper with the figures on it. 'This is rough as hell.'

I didn't look at the figures; I looked at Leo. 'I have a lot of theories, Pop, and maybe I'm one of those Peoria moviegoers at that, and think I know more than I really do. But I'm counting on you to keep me on the right film track. Because when I don't know, you *do* know.'

Hiding my apprehension, I dropped my eyes to the column of figures. They weren't so bad.

Title: 'The Man Who Got Away'	
Producer: Leo Steinberg	
Director: Richard Hudson	
Writer: Richard Hudson	
Principals:	?
Est. days of Production:	28
Story:	0
Continuity:	0
Director:	0
Producer:	0
Principals:	$2,000
Extras:	$5,050
Bits:	$3,000
TOTAL:	$10,050.06
Director's Staff:	$4,000
Cameramen & Assts.:	$20,000

77

Sets, etc.	$20,000—?
Wardrobe, men & women	?
Makeup:	?
Props:	?
Location:	$18,000—?
Sound Recording:	$14,000
Stock shots:	0
Negative film:	$7,000
Positive film:	$2,250
Developing and Printing:	$10,000
Titles:	$4,000
Insurance:	$10,000
Casting, (including screen tests):	$2,000
Cutting, editing, projection:	$12,000
Music:	?
Social Security:	?
TOTAL:	$122,250
Ag. TOTAL:	$132,300
STUDIO OVERHEAD:	????

'I know how to work from a budget,' Leo said as I examined the figures, 'but preparing one is a different matter. I broke down every section as well as I could, pared it to the bone, and put down the closest round figure. Hidden costs, or exact costs rather, will bring the aggregate to about $200,000. A lot of money to you and me, Richard, but practically nothing for a studio. Take a look at the salary for the principals . . . I'm ashamed. Only one thousand apiece for a month's work. No actor would work for that—'

'You're wrong there, Pop. For a chance at a starring role, there are plenty of actors who would work for nothing. Leave it to me. After all, this is a good story, and it could make the right man.'

'What about music? Oy!' Leo rocked his head comically. 'The music alone could run as high as $25,000.'

I grinned. 'You're forgetting something, Pop. Mother owns 'Lumpy Grits' outright. Without the lyrics it's a damned good tune. I'll hire some son of a bitch with a guitar for ten bucks a day, and fill where I need music with 'Lumpy Grits'.'

'It's a solution maybe,' Leo agreed.

'If your budget is anywhere near being accurate, Pop, we can do it. I can dig up sixty thousand, twenty thousand of it in Honest Hal's dough. As long as he gets his checks every month, he won't investigate what I'm doing with the working capital in the bank down here.'

I looked at the Roualt clown on the wall. 'Right up there, Leo,' I said softly, 'is a clown worth thirty thousand on the hoof.'

'My clown?'

'Your clown. What the hell, Pop, you'll get it back! With ninety thousand dollars and a story you can talk to THE MAN at Mammoth. THE MAN isn't against independent producers on his lot. I've checked. Three independents are using his stages now. All you have to do is to talk THE MAN into putting up the rest of the dough we need and loan us some contract people he's paying anyway, whether they're working or not.'

'That's all I have to do?' Leo smiled.

'That's all,' I said firmly.

'I've got to see the script, Richard.'

'Never mind the script. I'll write the script. Can we do it?'

'We can do it.'

'Call THE MAN!' I handed Leo the telephone. He reached for it tentatively, and then withdrew his hand.

'THE MAN should really call me first, Richard.'

'I know that, Leo, but he doesn't know we have a story.

If you and I do this movie, Pop, we can split twenty-five percent off the top. One third apiece, and another third for Mammoth. With a budget as low as we've set it, we're bound to make money. And if we pull it off, and you know damned well we can, you can name your own contract at Mammoth or any other studio in Hollywood. Or we can make another movie on our own with the profits. This is opportunity, Leo. It's knocking on that bald head of yours! Call THE MAN!'

'It's crazy!'

'I know.'

'Give me the phone,' Leo said determinedly.

SYNOPSIS

There are several phases a movie script must pass through before it is completed, and the first phase is the synopsis. Story department readers leaf through magazines, novels, originals and submitted ideas daily in the search for material. Promising stories are condensed to synopses and routed to producers. Producers hate to read anything, but they will read synopses if they are not too taxing. If a synopsis takes their fancy, producers request a treatment. A treatment is longer, tells something about each character in the story, and tentatively outlines a couple of major scenes. If the treatment passes the producer's scrutiny, he requests a shooting script (temporary), and a writer is hired, or a contract writer goes to work.

Three writers later, ten shooting scripts (temporary) later, and a movie is sometimes made. This movie that is made will bear little resemblance to the original one-page synopsis which started the cycle in the first place.

The ideal synopsis is the shortest synopsis possible if it is to be read. A two- or three-page synopsis hasn't got a chance. My synopsis for *The Man Who Got Away* was only one paragraph.

THE MAN WHO GOT AWAY
Original: From Richard Hudson
Synopsis: From Richard Hudson

A truck driver driving from San Francisco to Los Angeles runs over and kills a child. He tries to get away. He doesn't.
THE END

Poor old Leo almost blew his top when he read it. He was less than an hour away from his appointment with THE MAN at Mammoth Studios when I handed him the neatly typed page. The way I figured it, the less THE MAN had to question, the more leeway Leo would have for his arguments. But Leo didn't see it that way.

'For three days now you tell me you're working on the story and then you hand me this!' Leo's bald head was a fiery red, and his hands were trembling.

'Take it easy, Pop,' I said calmly. 'Be sensible. You enter THE MAN's office with a treatment and he'll tell you to leave it so he can read it later. A nice quiet brush-off. This is one very short pungent paragraph and he will have to read it in your presence. He will be forced to ask questions, and then you've got him. You *sell* the story. We aren't beggars, for Christ's sake, we're putting up our own dough and your personal reputation as a movie maker. He'll buy the idea because it's cheap. He won't expect much, and he won't have to invest much to do you the favor you're entitled to. You've made a lot of money for Mammoth in your time.'

'And I've lost them plenty, too,' Leo said bitterly.

'Don't remind THE MAN of that. Come on, let's go.'
I drove Leo to Mammoth Studios in Culver City, and

81

dropped him at the gate.

For the next two hours I was miserable, nursing self-doubts. The front I had put on for Leo had disappeared at the gate to the studio. I sat in a Chinese restaurant two blocks away from Mammoth drinking hot tea and chain-smoking king-sized cigarettes. If we were in instead of out, my real troubles would begin. I was jettisoning everything I had worked for, and worked for hard, during the last ten years. My entire savings, and Honest Hal's dough, too. If the movie failed, I would not only be black-balled in the used-car business, I might end up in jail.

Self-doubt is the worst thing that can happen to a man. It tightens the stomach muscles, freezes the intellect. But worst of all it causes men to stay in dead-end jobs all of their lives because they are afraid to try anything else, afraid of failure, afraid to lose their stupid security. Afraid, period.

I remembered an advertisement that had appeared in all of the national magazines several years ago. Every time I happened to see it in a magazine it made me sick to my stomach.

A large Detroit automobile factory ran a photograph of three generations of a family at work. In the photo on a full page, the smiling faces of a grandfather, a father and a son gaped vacantly at each other, standing beside a machine of some kind in the factory. All of the men were in overalls, including the grandfather. Sixty years of employment in the same factory were represented by the three men, and not one of them had managed to get out of overalls. Three generations on the assembly line. It was one of the most pitiful photographs I have ever looked at; three smiling failures completely unaware of their plight! Instead of being ashamed, the automobile company was evidently proud of its three faithful workers; it proved their automobile was a good one, I supposed. But all the photograph meant to me, or to any other thinking

American, was that these assembly-line workers were doing the same thing, day after day, and were too stupid to realize that they were throwing their lives down the drain. It was hard to believe that the youngest worker couldn't see himself in thirty more years when he looked at his grandfather . . .

When I thought about this photograph, my confidence returned to me in force. If Mammoth Studios turned Leo down, I would take my movie elsewhere! There were other studios, and I could get more money, some way. One way or another, my movie would be produced!

My message was important! It had to be brought to the attention of the public! And once the movie was released, it would be easy to tie up the loose ends. I would ease Hal's dough back into the bank first and he would never know the difference. The movie would make some money, even if it was only used as the second half of a double feature. If we kept on schedule, cut every corner possible, I might even make a few dollars, fifty thousand or so. When Leo walked into the cafe, I was contemplating a very rosy future.

'We are in,' Leo announced triumphantly. 'THE MAN bought all of it. You to write and direct, me to produce. Mammoth will put up facilities and staff in lieu of cash, which is even better than I expected. We even have offices assigned to us and the name is being painted on the doors now. Elgee Productions!'

'Elgee?' I asked vacantly. 'What's that?'

'My own concoction,' Leo grinned. 'L. G. Lumpy Grits! It will be our own little secret, Mr Director. Let us eat. I want the most mixed-up concoction this Chinaman can prepare. Damn the ulcers, full speed ahead!'

I laughed so wildly, a patron at a nearby table was startled into dropping his fork.

MISS LAURA HARMON

There were twenty different film scripts on my desk, each of them bound in a blue manuscript cover. All of the manuscripts had been moneymakers for Mammoth, and I had read them all, looking for a basic approach, trying to learn how to write a script for my own movie. After a week of reading and study I still didn't know how to begin.

If I could only get started I knew it would be easy. But how could I get started . . . ?

Laura Harmon didn't help matters. She was a tall, heavily breasted young woman of twenty-four or -six, with strong white teeth, a dazzling smile, and fine ash-blonde hair hanging to her shoulders. The fuzzy sweaters she wore to the office each day were always two sizes too small for her, and she had the disconcerting habit of leaning periodically over my desk. For three days in a row, when Laura bent over my desk to ask a question, I shoved my chair back automatically. But on the fourth day I moved it forward instead and my chest almost made contact with those large breasts.

Laura had been assigned to me as a personal secretary, but she was evidently under the impression she could learn something from me about screenwriting. But after a few days in the same small office, looking at her, smelling her, and bored with old scenarios, I was tempted to teach her something I knew very well.

Laura backed away from the near-contact, smiling. 'I was going out for coffee, Mr Hudson,' she said uneasily, 'and I wanted to ask you if it was all right. That is, unless you want to dictate now.'

In four days she must have asked me twenty times if I wanted to dictate anything. My negative answers never seemed to register. I looked a her insolently, slowly, and approvingly. She was a bit hippy. Under my scrutiny Laura

84

wilted, retreating into a natural state of feminine inferiority women affect when they don't know what else to do.

I had worked too hard since my arrival in Los Angeles. Except for the single, highly unsatisfactory episode with Becky, there had been little time in my schedule for women. And once I became embarked in full-scale work on my movie, there would be even less time. Hurriedly, I made up my mind.

'Let's go to the beach, Laura.'

'Do you want to look for locations, Mr Hudson?' A bright, intelligent question.

'Not exactly. I have my locations pretty well in mind. We'll just take the afternoon off and go swimming.'

'I'll have to stop at my apartment for my suit . . .'

'Fine.'

We picked up Laura's suit and the other accessories women consider necessary for an afternoon at the beach, and drove to Laguna. I felt guilty about not working, or at least for not attempting to work, but I consoled myself with the thought that a day off and a little sex play would ease my inner tension. On the drive to the beach, with the top down, my worries about the script gradually deserted me.

When Laura came out of our rented cabaña in a white one-piece bathing suit, all extraneous thoughts not concerning the task at hand were dissipated into the ocean breezes. Why shouldn't a woman be a little hippy?

It was my turn to change. I entered the narrow cabaña and slipped into my trunks. Laura's clothes were scattered carelessly along the small bench against the wall and it was necessary to hang them up before I could sit down to remove my shoes. On an impulse, I squeezed Laura's panties, brassiere and slip into a small silky ball and buried my face into the softness, inhaling deeply of her delicious female fragrance. I had to laugh at myself. When a man starts doing weird things like that, he needs a woman in the worst way. In sudden disgust, I tossed her underthings on the floor, left the cabaña and joined Laura at the water's edge.

I grabbed Laura's hand and dragged her, squealing, into the cold purple water, and ducked her viciously beneath an incoming wave. We had a good time in the surf. Although the water was freezing at first, we got used to it, and both of us were exhilarated by the combination of holiday, sun and surf.

We whiled away the afternoon, baking in the sun or plunging into the surf. At five a cool wind came up and we took turns in the cabaña again, showering and changing back into our clothes. The long afternoon had made me ravenous.

'Could you eat a horse, Laura?'

'No,' she replied seriously, 'but I can eat a small Shetland pony.'

'Let's drive to the Hangover House instead, and settle for a prime sirloin.'

'That would be wonderful! Laura's face brightened, then fell. 'But my hair!' she wailed. 'It looks terrible!'

'The steak won't mind. Come on.'

It was a bad time of the day for driving. The beach road was crowded and I crawled through all of the popular beaches – Long Beach, Venice, Ocean Park, Santa Monica – before the traffic thinned out on 101. It was almost seven when we were seated at a table on the glass-enclosed loggia of Hangover House. The sun had disappeared, and instead of the usual view of the surf pounding against the rocks, we could only hear its crashing roar below us. We dived into our salads hungrily before finishing our martinis. And we made an elaborate joke of dividing the butter equally between us while we waited for the steaks. Away from the office, Laura had turned out to be good company. I was beginning to like her.

The steaks were excellent, medium rare, and we

consumed them in respectful silence, not talking until after the arrival of coffee and brandy.

'You seem a little too well-educated and intelligent, Laura,' I said, 'to be a writer's secretary. With, a degree from Stanford, it seems you could do better.'

'It's a start, Mr Hudson.'

'Richard.'

'Richard. But I hope to be a writer myself someday. I've done a few things already – at college – and a job with the studio, almost any kind of job connected with the movies, seemed like a good place to begin. And I can learn so much from writers like you! You don't know how glad I was to get out of that typing pool! For the last three months I've been typing contracts, contracts, contracts. It's the most boring work in the world.'

'I can imagine.'

'I'm really anxious to start work on the script. I read the synopsis you wrote, and there seems to be so much *leeway!* I mean,' Laura peered at me anxiously, 'it's a good story and all, I suppose, but there seems to be a million possibilities. It seems that way to me, I mean,' she finished lamely.

'I don't work like other writers,' I replied cryptically. 'Let's dance.'

It was best to get Laura off the subject of the movie. On the dance floor, with her well-cushioned breasts pressing hard against my chest, I wondered why this woman who was so obviously a woman wanted to be so intelligent. Women are made for bed, and men are made for war. Life would be so simple if both sexes could only remember these basic facts of life.

The table had been cleared by the time the music stopped. Over Laura's protest I ordered two double Scotch-and-sodas. I grabbed the conversational ball and pumped Laura with my practiced interviewer's technique.

She had been president of the drama dub, a member of the college debating team, and she had acted in a dozen plays. Two of her one-act plays had been produced at Stanford, and in the graduation yearbook she had been classified as: 'The all-around type, with teeth. Most likely to have her name on a theatre marquee.'

Very interesting, if true.

We had another for the road, and I paid the tab; a stiff one. We climbed into the Continental and at Malibu I took the cut-off for the Hollywood Hills and a well-remembered parking place. I cut the lights, and we could see the lights of Hollywood winking far below us.

Without a word I kissed Laura's full lips and she responded gallantly. It wasn't exactly a kiss; it was more like a saliva test. Then I met resistance; she pushed me away. Slightly miffed, but not impatient, I switched on the radio, watched Laura out of the corner of my eye. Music came in soldily, with a thick, pulsating boom from the bass. I lit a cigarette, tossed it away quickly.

Slowly and deliberately, Laura was dipping her tight sweater over her head. She folded it neatly, placed it on the seat. She leaned forward, unfastened her brassiere at the back, removed it, and folded it over the sweater. With her eyes closed, Laura leaned her head back against the seat, and dropped her arms listlessly. Her melon-shaped breasts loomed clearly in the yellow light from the radio dial.

I turned toward her eagerly—

'Just one minute, Richard,' Laura said quietly. The sharpness in her voice halted my mouth two inches from hers. My fingers trembled over her breasts.

'Before you get started,' she stated matter-of-factly, 'I'd better explain the rules.'

'Yeah,' I whispered huskily.

'Number one,' she recited, 'you can kiss me, but not too wet. I don't like it. Two, you can fondle my breasts if you like, but that is all. When you're ready, just tell me, and I'll . . . I'll relieve you.'

'You'll what?'

'I'll *relieve* you. You know what I mean. I'm a virgin, whether you believe it or not, and I intend to stay that way. On the other hand I owe you some kind of a good time for the afternoon on the beach, the steak, and the drinks. But I *don't* owe you my virginity.'

She was so calm, so schoolteacherish with her damned, preposterous rules that all of the desire I had kindled disappeared completely. I was more amused than angered. I could picture her at some college Lover's Lane, outlining these same rules to a panting, eager sophomore who had just blown his month's allowance on an evening's entertainment.

I laughed boisterously, moved back to my side of the seat, and ran my fingers through my hair.

'So you're one of those fellatio experts,' I laughed.

'What's that?'

'There's something wrong with your thinking,' I told her seriously. 'You majored in dramatics and minored in the humanities. It should have been the other way around.'

'I don't understand.' She was genuinely surprised. 'I've never had any objections before from anybody . . .'

'Don't worry about it, Laura. It's just that I'm not one of your schoolboy dates, that's all. I'll take you home.' I started the car, and Laura hastily donned her bra and sweater.

'One more thing,' I said, as I fought the wheel down the winding road, 'you'd better get a few medical texts and check the way you're heading. You're laying in a big stock of emotional grief for yourself.'

When I parked in front of her apartment house, a narrow three-story structure in pink stucco, I reached over into the back seat, retrieved Laura's swimming things and handed them to her.

'Good night, Laura.'

'Don't you want to kiss me good night?' Her lips were trembling and tears were very close behind her eyes.

'No thanks,' I said grimly. 'I kiss too wetly.' I pulled the door shut and drove away. In my rearview mirror I could see her watching the car, a forlorn figure with wet towel, bathing suit and beach bag clutched to her waist.

Tension gradually built inside my stomach as I drove directly home. After a lukewarm shower and change to pajamas I roamed my small apartment restlessly. Bored, I picked up a copy of T. S. Eliot's *Collected Poetry* and idly flipped the pages. I read sections from *Ash Wednesday*:

And I who am here dissembled
Proffer my deeds to oblivion, and my love
To the posterity of the desert and the fruit of the gourd.

These lines strangely excited me. Putting *Night on Bald Mountain* on the turntable, and after twisting up the volume, I turned to the beginning of the poem and began to read it aloud. I had to raise my voice against the weight of the stereo speakers until I was almost screaming the embittered lines. By the time I reached the end of the poem my eyes were streaming with self-pity, and my heart was full of compassionate love for Laura. Poor, poor, misguided young woman. I turned off the player and in the abrupt silence hurriedly pulled slacks on over my pyjama trousers. I was so choked with supercharged emotion my throat made funny noises and it was impossible to check the copious flow of tears.

I drove straight to Laura's apartment house, ignoring the red lights that blocked my way, driving mechanically. I parked, and locked the car before climbing the two flights to Laura's apartment. A trifle dazed, uncertain of myself, with no plausible or planned purpose in mind, I scratched apprehensively at her door.

The door was opened almost immediately. Laura, fresh and warmly pink from a long shower, her damp head wrapped turban-fashion in a white towel, and holding her robe closed with her left hand, stared at me with an expression of bewildered amazement on her pretty face.

I was still weeping helplessly, self-induced tears, yes, but they were real tears all the same. The combination of music and poetry had unlocked a hidden spring. And what can equal the tragedy of a strong man's tears? A moment later Laura was crying too, with sympathetic empathy. We clung to each other, desperately; Laura pulled me inside, and kicked the door closed. As I staggered weakly to the clean-smelling, pull-down Murphy bed, Laura ripped the thin silk pyjama jacket from my back, scraping my flesh with her sharp, impatient fingernails.

Her warm, soft mouth opened as I kissed her and she bit gently into my lower lip; caressed it soothingly with her tongue. Our breaths and tongues met and mingled. With our mouths locked together we fell back on the bed. Then I was on my back and Laura was kissing me all over as she tugged my belt loose with practiced hands. Her restless tongue, hot and hard, licked beneath my neck, at my armpit, stabbed wetly into my ear. Her trembling fingers danced like feathertips as they searched my body, exploring, tantalizing me until I wanted her with an urgency that could no longer be suppressed. Her nails raked cruelly across my shoulders, and she uttered incomprehensible animal sounds. Waves of feeling washed over me; she moaned, shuddered, and held me tighter—

'Dearest, dearest!' she cried happily (but unpractically for the moment). 'Again, again, again!'

This woman was a virgin? I thought with genuine inner amusement. Laura had merely proven the great value of a college education, that was all. The obscure tricks she knew couldn't be learned from books, but I didn't really care.

It may be fun to know, but it's even more fun to be fooled.

DISSOLVE

The next morning I was back in my own apartment and quite rational again. After getting a large breakfast under my belt I called Mammoth Studios and had the switchboard put me through to Mr Knowles, the personnel manager.

'This is Richard Hudson,' I told him. 'Elgee Productions.'

'Yes, sir.'

'Your office assigned a secretary to me, a Miss Laura Harmon.'

'Yes, sir. A very competent woman.'

'I agree,' I said, 'for typing maybe, but I'm afraid she isn't quite the type to work with a writer. She doesn't grasp the problems. I'm sending her back, and I recommend her for the typing pool. At any rate, I won't need a secretary for several days anyway. I'm going to work at home. But I'll let you know, Mr Knowles.'

'Fine, Mr Hudson, and I'm very sorry about Miss Harmon. But you never can tell how these girls will work out until you give them an opportunity. I knew she was inexperienced, but she has a fine background, and—'

'I feel the same way you do, Mr Knowles. Everybody is entitled to at least one chance, but Miss Harmon just doesn't have the personality to work with writers. I'm certain you can find her a suitable typing assignment. She's a very capable typist.'

'Thank you, Mr Hudson. I wish some of the other people here at the studio took as much interest in personnel problems as you do.' His voice sounded sincere, so I let it pass.

I racked the telephone, shrugged, and made another pot of coffee.

WIPE TO:

During my high school senior year I grabbed the lead in the senior play. The fact that I was handsome had nothing to do with my getting the part; it was Rostand's *Cyrano de Bergerac*, and I had to work like hell to win the lead. I knew my lines backward and forward, and each piece of stage business was engraved on my mind with blueprint accuracy. And yet, when opening night rolled around, I cowered in my dressing room with a dry mouth and sweat rolling down my back. I couldn't go on. I knew it!

Miss Hartwell, our English teacher, who also doubled as the director for school plays, and who acted as our Drama Club advisor, found me there. She was an old maid, but she was all business when it came to playacting and English composition, and she knew more about people than anyone I have ever met.

She squeezed my sweaty hand. 'It looks like our leading man has a slight case of stage fright.' She smiled kindly, but there was no sympathy in her voice.

'I can't go out there tonight, Miss Hartwell. I don't care what you call it. I simply can't face that stupid bunch of parents!'

'Stage fright is a wonderful thing, Richard,' Miss Hartwell said simply, 'as long as you can control it. And you can. The reason actors get stage fright, professionals as well as amateurs, is because they're afraid they will not be as good as they think they are. Now let that sink in.'

I let this statement sink in.

'But I *am* as good as I think I am,' I said with conviction.

'Of course you are.'

And I was, in the senior play, anyway.

But the writing of a scenario was a different matter.

For two days I had been holed up in a small suite in the Biltmore Hotel in downtown Los Angeles. The windows were closed and the venetian blinds were tightly shut. In the electric brilliance it could have been any hour of the day or night.

A new IBM electric typewriter sat on a typing table in the center of the sitting room humming away, ready to go, but still untouched by my fingers. There was a new tape recorder on the coffee table, loaded and ready with a full hour tape, but I hadn't even coughed into the microphone. If I wanted to dictate, all I had to do was push a button and start talking.

But I couldn't get started. I didn't know how to start. Maybe I wasn't as capable as I thought I was, but Leo expected a script and I had to produce one. A fresh sheet of paper was in the typewriter and the story was in my mind. I knew what I wanted and still I couldn't get started. I was beginning to get panicky. There was a knock on the door. A reprieve!

'Come in,' I shouted friendlily.

'It's me,' Bill Harris announced as he entered the door. He looked quizzically at the typewriter and tape recorder.

'How did you find me, Bill?'

'Your mother told me where you were.'

'You must have really snowed her to find out. I told her not to tell anybody.'

'I did,' he admitted with a smile, 'but it's important, Richard, or I wouldn't have bothered you.'

'What I'm doing is more important.' My voice lacked conviction.

'What are you doing, anyway? I haven't seen you in over a week. Things are really going to hell down at the lot. I wouldn't bother you with anything minor, but I just don't know enough about what I'm doing to run around half-cocked. The damned cars aren't moving; the two salesmen I finally hired to wear the Santa Claus suits couldn't sell newspapers if the headlines declared war on England.'

'I know, I know,' I said wearily.

'We need some new cars too. I thought at first I'd buy up some iron from Tone in Fullerton, but he's too sharp for me. I bought three '46 Fords from Barefoot Pete in Santa Monica, and when they were delivered Graphite Sam blew his top. One had a cracked block, and another had a hole the size of a dime in the gas tank. I feel like a damned fool.'

'Anybody who deals with Barefoot Pete *is* a damned fool.' I grinned.

'You used to buy from him—'

'That's different,' I snapped. 'I know the son of a bitch!'

'Well, I know him now,' Bill said sadly. 'But I still got stuck. What are you doing, Richard? If you don't want to tell me, OK. But problems are stacking up on me and business is off thirty-two percent this week.'

'Take some notes.' As Bill got his notebook and pencil ready I thought fast. When it came to used cars I knew what I was doing. There was no mental block here. When it came to used cars I could talk all day and all night and still have fresh ideas.

'Call Fred McCullers in Pasadena,' I said. 'He's a jobber and he's in the telephone book. Tell him you're working for me and that I need some creampuffs. He won't cheat you and he owes me a couple of favors. Get out on the lot yourself, Bill, and sell some cars. I know you can do it; let the clerk write contracts. If you're out there watching the salesmen, they'll produce, and if they don't, fire them and hire others. But the Santa Claus suits will be worn.

'Now, let's move the cars. Take a full-page ad in the morning and evening papers and list new, rock-bottom prices.

Cut down to exactly one hundred bucks profit on every car on the lot except the real creampuffs. Get rid of them. At that price all you have to do is get good credit risks; the selling will take care of itself. At those margins you can't take a chance on getting any repossess. Feel better?'

'A whole lot better.' Bill's smile had returned.

'How much dough in the bank?'

'About forty-four thousand. Something like that.'

'Withdraw a certified check made out to me for forty thousand, and bring it to me here.' I had already turned over twenty thousand in bonds to Leo, and Leo had sold his Roualt for $35,000. I had been reluctant to take $40,000 out of the Honest Hal account, but talking to Bill had restored some of my confidence.

'That's a lot of money, Richard.'

'Sure it is. You'll be short on capital, but hold up payment on your deliveries from McCullers for another week. You should have enough in by then to pay him. And then keep a week behind. Cut Honest Hal's take by fifty percent. Write in your next report that we're planning a big new campaign, and we need the cash to buy a lot of new stock from a lot that's closing down in San Diego. Tell him anything, but make it good.'

'Suppose he phones me and asks me about the campaign?'

'Think of a gimmick, for Christ's sake! You've got to do something for your six hundred a month!' I looked at the blank page in the typewriter in front of me for a moment, and then I smiled.

'Don't mind me, Bill,' I said winningly. 'I need your help, and I wouldn't ask you to do anything I didn't think you could do. Cover up all this cash business in the books some way. Work out something. If you need help, get a high school mathematics teacher to juggle the figures for you. For a hundred dollar bill a math teacher will do anything.'

'OK, Richard.' Bill made another note in his little book.

'Pour us a drink, Bill.' Harris filled two glasses with ice, added generous portions of Scotch. I sipped my drink, walked about the room aimlessly, and then sat down.

'I'm not on any secret project, Bill. The entire world will know about it soon enough, but right now, I don't want Hal to find out that I'm using his money. I'm writing a movie, and when I get it written I'm going to direct it.'

'I'll be goddamned!' Bill exploded admiringly. 'I'd never get to know you if I worked for you for a hundred years!'

'I'm out of my field all right,' I confessed, 'and I can't get started. Have you ever been in that situation? I have the story in my mind, the characters, everything. But I've been in this room for two days and I haven't written a single word. Not a word.' I drained my glass, poured more Scotch over what remained of the ice.

'That stuff won't help, Richard.' Bill said seriously. 'I don't even have a conception of what you're doing. And I wouldn't know how to begin either. But I know this much about writing. You have to write *something*. Anything. In the service I've written a hell of a lot of words. Nothing creative, nothing literary, nothing fancy, but communication – getting over ideas to others. When a captain of infantry tells you he wants to board a man out of the service, for instance, the first sergeant has to do the paper work. And the writing has to be effective, Richard, because the captain wants the man the hell out.

'It's up to the top kick to write up the facts in such a way that the board doesn't bounce – the paperwork has to get by a lot of lawyers in uniform. I don't know how many three-six-eight and three-six-nine boards I've written, but I've never had one bounce on me. It's hard work. You have to sit there filling paper in a convincing way. The first board I wrote almost drove me crazy, but

97

the guy was bounced out of the service. And I didn't have a damned thing to go on except that the captain didn't like the man.'

'What's the secret, Bill?'

'Rewriting. First, one word at a time. After you get enough pages done, you have something to read. If you can read it you can revise it. If you revise it enough times, you come up with something pretty good. All writing is like that; it couldn't be any other way. So if you know what your story is, go ahead and put it down as best you can. You can always revise the lousy draft. And you aren't going to get a perfect script the first time.' Bill finished his drink, got to his feet. 'I'd better get going.'

'OK. Get me that check before you do anything else, Bill. And keep things going down at the lot for me.'

'I'm on your side Richard. I don't know how you got into this movie business, but if anybody can come out on top, you can.'

'Thanks, Bill.'

In his bumbling way, Bill had hit my ego square in the middle. Fear had kept me from writing, just like the time I had stage fright in high school. I wanted and expected a masterpiece with my first draft. A perfect script I could toss on Leo's desk carelessly; a scenario so pure he would be unable to make any suggestions for improvement. I sat down at the typewriter, indented five spaces, and began to write.

One word at a time, one after the other, in script format. And it was far from a masterpiece. But gradually it began to take shape and form, roughly moulded, and with plenty of dangling loose ends. But here and there I had a strong scene, solid bits of dialogue, along with the weak scenes and stupid lines I could eliminate later. My first completed scenario was as rough as an unbarked tree on the rollers to the planing room.

When a man begins to write it is like discovering words for the first time. Each word as it appears on paper takes on a fresh meaning, a literal meaning that is often unnoticed when dropped from the lips in careless conversation. I had a good command of language; I worked with the spoken language every day. To convey spoken ideas is very simple. If you don't know the exact words, a gesture will sometimes take the place of the word you need, and the listener will get the gist of your idea. But on paper, the exact word is needed, and I meant to get through . . .

The next ten hours were the most gratifying hours, and the hardest hours I ever worked. I remember Bill bringing the check, and I remember calling room service and eating sandwiches and drinking many pots of coffee. But I don't recall the passage of time.

But ten hours after first talking to Bill I had a rough draft of a movie script. There were 148 numbered scenes, in sequence, and reading through them, they told a story. Most of the scenes were sketchy, and there was much too much dialogue. But my characters shone through the way I wanted them to, and I had something to work on.

I was proud of the people I had created on paper. They were composites of every buyer who had bought used cars from me during ten years of meeting the public on gravel lots. I had them!

I didn't worry too much about the rewriting. Within a few days I would have a script good enough to make pictures from, and wasn't I the director? In the final form, a movie is not a script, it is pictures, and it has to be seen to be believed. A script is merely a guide for the director, and the director, after all, was me.

I crawled into bed and slept for fourteen hours.

RIPPLE

The best I can say for my completed scenario is that it was beautifully typed and was colorfully bound in a bright yellow manuscript cover. The public stenographer at the Biltmore Hotel had done a wonderful job. But it was the best I could do at the time, and Leo was very happy when I tossed the script on his desk.

'There's too much dialogue,' he said as he riffled hurriedly through the pages.

'I know,' I said.

'Some of these directions are meaningless.'

'I know.'

'This set you have here for the cafe scene would cost more than the entire picture.'

'I know.'

'Then let's get to work.'

For the next three days we worked in Leo's study. Sometimes it was possible for me to force down a sandwich, but I subsisted mostly on coffee. Leo devoured tranquilizers like peanuts. But we worked and worked hard. Action was substituted for mere movement, and pregnant pauses for dialogue. Leo did most of the talking and I did the rewriting, scribbling with a soft No. 2 pencil, sitting at his desk. But I only made changes after he convinced me with irrefutable logic that the changes suggested were absolutely necessary.

When we finished our collaboration, it was a scenario any writer would be proud to have written. I was overjoyed, but sobered with apprehension and fear that THE MAN would not OK it for production. His OK was required. The completed scenario had been mimeographed at the studio, and fifty-nine scripts were locked in my desk at the studio. The single outstanding copy was in THE MAN'S office. We waited for either the 'OK' in blue grease pencil on the cover, or the 'X' in red grease pencil. If we got an 'OK' we would start casting; if the red 'X' criss-crossed the cover, we could start all over again . . .

We waited. One day.

'What do you think, Richard?' Leo asked, cracking his knuckles.

'I think THE MAN will buy it! I *really* do.' I said this so convincingly I almost believed it myself.

We waited. Second day.

'Damn it, Leo, he could read the script in a half-hour. What's the delay?'

'Now take it easy, Son. He may have a few suggestions, but I don't think he'll turn it down.'

'What do you think, Leo? The script is good, isn't it?'

'I'm not worried. He'll be crazy about it.'

We waited. Third day.

Instead of going to the studio we stayed at home, leaving word at our office where we were. Sitting around the cramped bungalow offices we had been assigned to all day long was getting on our nerves. But we hovered over the telephone in Leo's study, waiting, waiting, waiting. Periodically, my eyes kept returning to the empty space on the wall where Leo's Roualt had been. A guilty feeling would fill my stomach, and I would look at Leo with sudden compassion. He too, would be looking at the empty wall which had held his clown.

It did not console me that Leo had only put up $35,000 to my $60,000; I only felt worse. If everything was lost, I could start all over again. Leo couldn't.

Regardless of script, we had been committed, and THE MAN held the reins. It was THE MAN's final decision that mattered. If he so desired he could give the script to a Mammoth writer, assign his own director and producer, and produce the movie as a Mammoth

Production instead of an Elgee Production. This was the concession Leo had to make when he made the original deal. It was not unreasonable in view of my inexperience, and the amount of money we were investing compared to the studio's . . . but thinking about it could give me ulcers. If THE MAN did take over, we would get our money back, and then some, but that was not the idea, mine or Leo's. We wanted to make the movie ourselves; otherwise there was no point to knocking ourselves out in the first place.

A successful movie would assure Leo a place in the movie industry again, and I would . . . what would it do for me? I didn't think that far ahead. I was merely a man with a message, a man with something to say, and I knew that I could say it better than anyone else. And my message was *The Man Who Got Away!*

Why not get down to the damned nerve! I did not care about my money, Honest Hal's money, Leo's money, the studio's money, or anything else. If it was money I was interested in, I could have made all I wanted on my used car lot . . .

The telephone rang and both of us reached for it Leo won, listened for a moment, and then handed the telephone to me.

'Richard, darling,' a tearful voice queried. 'I've got to see you right away!' It was Laura Harmon, and her voice was tense with suppressed excitement.

'Get the hell off the line,' I said angrily, 'and don't call again. I'm expecting an important call.' I racked the telephone.

'Who was it Richard?'

'Laura Harmon, that sex-starved secretary I told you about.'

Leo nodded. We waited. One minute later the telephone rang and I let Leo take the call, thinking it was Laura again.

'Get rid of her,' I said.

'Yes,' Leo said strongly, 'this is Mr Steinberg.' He put his hand over the mouthpiece. 'THE MAN,' he said to me, and then he talked into the telephone, 'yes, sir . . . yes, sir . . . yes, sir.'

A thin smile played about the corners of Leo's lips as he hung up, following the short conversation. 'THE MAN wants to see us, Richard, both of us.'

'Then let's go.'

I had been my own man too long, and I didn't like myself very well during the next few minutes. Visiting the office of THE MAN was like being called to the principal's office at school, when you didn't know the reason. Fear, dread, and apprehension all mixed together, when there is not a valid reason.

We only waited in the outer office for two or three minutes, and then THE MAN'S secretary, an old white-haired man of about sixty-five, jerked his thumb for us to enter the inner sanctum. We waited at the massive door for the secretary to push a button under his desk to release the door lock. Two years before an actor had forced his way into THE MAN's office and fired three wild shots before he had been overpowered. The door-lock mechanism had been installed to prevent recurrences of similar events. Leo preceded me through the door, and it hissed shut behind me automatically.

As I surveyed the room, my confidence returned, and all apprehension left me. The room was lavish enough, much as I had pictured a famous movie executive's office in my mind. But it was in poor taste; the furniture was massive, the colors dashed, and the panelled walls, painted a stark white, gave an antiseptic look to the large room. It was as though a hospital dispensary was turned into a living room, with everything changed except the white walls. There were several framed black-and-white drawings on the walls, either

Matisse or James Thurber; it is hard to tell. But my eyes fell on a copy of *Newsweek* on the coffee table near the white-brick fireplace. I read *Time*! A vocabulary of only 20,000 words is required to read *Newsweek*, but the *Time* reader needs a vocabulary of 25,000 words. A little thing, maybe. But on such minutae rest the standards of culture in the United States, and in this one qualification, at least, Richard Hudson was a notch above THE MAN.

THE MAN did not rise to greet us. He sat behind his desk like a benign Buddha, impassive, fat, ancient, and completely hairless. His head was completely bald, and as brown as the rest of his face. Great dewlaps dangled on both sides of his round face. I have never seen him standing, and his shoulders were so narrow and his head was so large I do not know, and I cannot guess at his height. Perhaps he was a cripple; I do not know. But then, there are thousands of people in the United States who do not know that the late FDR was a cripple.

A stack of movie scripts was piled neatly on a corner of his enormous white desk. One of them was mine. I knew that much. I sat down, without being asked, in a red, womb chair and pulled out my cigarettes.

'I would rather you didn't smoke.' Although THE MAN'S voice was encompassed with suet, there was a sharp edge to his statement. I returned my pack to my coat pocket, and met Leo's reproving look with a soft smile. He had warned me about smoking, but I had forgotten.

'Did you hear the story about the director who took a vacation in Miami?' THE MAN asked flatly, addressing his question to no one in particular.

Leo, who was standing by the wall examining one of the framed drawings, answered for both of us. 'No, sir,' he said respectfully, 'we didn't.'

'Well, I think it goes something like this,' THE MAN began, which is no way to begin a story. 'The director flew to Miami one day ahead of his wife, leaving her to close their home in Beverly Hills. He checked into this year's hotel in Miami, and after being shown to his suite by the bellboy, he asked the bellboy to send up a little entertainment. Five minutes later a beautiful blonde arrived and the director asked her, "How much?" Her price was one hundred dollars and the director was indignant. "One hundred dollars!" he said. "I've never paid more than ten dollars in my life!" With that, he dismissed the blonde. Well, the next day his wife arrived and they went down to the beach. Pretty soon the beautiful blonde whore came along. She stopped, looked at the director, and then at his wife, and said: "See what you get for ten dollars!"'

THE MAN laughed heartily at his joke, if that is what it was, coughed up a big glob of phlegm, and spat into a piece of Kleenex. He examined the phlegm before tossing the wadded piece of tissue into a white leather waste-basket. Leo also laughed heartily, slapping his leg with exuberant amusement in an almost hysterical manner.

'That's rich,' Leo exclaimed, 'that's rich.' He repeated the tag aloud. 'See what you get for ten dollars! I'll have to remember that one!'

I didn't laugh. I wanted to laugh and I hated myself for wanting to laugh, but I couldn't, although I thought it would please THE MAN. The joke was not only stupid; it was pointless.

'What about the script,' I asked dryly, when the laughter had subsided.

THE MAN shifted his head in my direction and fixed me with a cold eye. It was almost a full minute before he spoke, and his voice was icy.

'I liked it, Hudson.' He shifted his eyes to Leo. 'Stop by the comptroller's office when you leave, Leo. He has the budget for your production.'

We were dismissed. I was suspicious and I didn't like the way THE MAN had handled the situation. It was too simple. Leo and I sat down on a bench in the patio, and he was angry with me.

'Couldn't you laugh?' Leo asked me seriously. 'THE MAN expected you to laugh at his joke.'

'The joke wasn't funny.'

'What the hell has that got to do with it? He's the head of the studio, for Christ's sake! I guess you still don't understand, Richard.' Leo had cooled off some. 'The joke was his way of telling us that we were in. Like an allegory. THE MAN is never blunt; he always uses an indirect approach, no matter what he does. It was very rude of you to ask about the script that way.'

'Rude? I'm a businessman. We were seat for to talk about the script He kept us sweating blood for three days—'

'That's the way he is.'

'And I am the way I am.'

'Forget it Richard. We're in business, so you might as well get with Milo and start casting. He's been assigned to us full-time, and you might as well put him to work.'

DISSOLVE

Milo Linder was a good man to have around. I had had lunch with him a couple of times in the studio commissary, and we got along well together. He was the type of man who could adapt himself to any director he happened to work with and that accounted for his popularity. Although it was doubtful whether he would ever become a full-fledged director, he was one of the best assistant directors at Mammoth Studios, and I was lucky Leo had managed to snag him for my picture.

So far, my time had been occupied with the script, but now that work was to begin on the production, Milo would be both my right and left hand man. He knew all of the shortcuts, and everybody at the studio. Only twenty-four, he had been at Mammoth for five years, and he had assistant director credits in more than fifty movies.

Milo Linder and I were closeted in my bungalow office with a copy of the budget, and the final version of the shooting script. Milo nervously patted the sharp spikes of his crewcut, and smiled ruefully. We had been discussing the movie for two hours, and Milo was enthusiastic about the script, but worried about the low budget.

'That budget is murder, Richard.'

'Not really. All we have to do is find the right principals, teach them how to act, and we'll be OK.'

'That won't be easy. The truck driver has got to be perfect or the whole picture will fall flat.'

'I know that. But the extras are provided for, and the bits. So all we need is our lead.'

'How about using Fred Bartell for the lead,' Milo mused. 'He's on contract.'

'I don't know him.'

'He's an atmosphere extra. I'll bet he's been in a thousand movies, at least, and he's never spoken a line.'

'The name doesn't ring a bell.'

'You've seen him, I know. He's the guy who stands there, or sits there in a scene, and never says anything. If you need five tough guys to sit in a car waiting to blast somebody coming out of a building, he's one of the five guys in the car. If some criminals are waiting to be tried by a judge in a courtroom scene, he's waiting to be tried and he always looks guilty. He stands by elevators, he eats lunch in restaurants. In westerns, he is the guy at the end of the bar drinking rye. Once in awhile he carries the rope at a lynching.'

'I've never heard of the bastard.'

'Nobody has, but you've seen him a thousand times. His face is sad, heavily lined, and his eyes can brim with tears at the snap of a director's fingers. On top of that he's a big son of a bitch, just right for a truck driver.'

'How come he never has any lines then? Maybe he's deaf and dumb?'

'I forgot,' Milo shook his head and snorted. 'He lisps, I'd forgotten about that. But we can use him as an atmosphere extra, anyway. In the cafe scene we can have him eat a hamburger. He looks like, a truck driver. It is always reassuring to an audience to see a familiar face or two in a low-budget movie.'

'Put him down then. We'll use him.'

And so it went. We discussed and covered the contract talent, and budding starlets, the extras, bit players, examining photograph after photograph, brought to the office from Casting by messenger girls wearing Wedgewood-blue uniforms. Milo's retentive memory was remarkable. We sat in comfortable chairs in dark projection rooms while five-minute screen tests of aspiring actors and actresses chased each other across the screen. The screen tests were on hand, and not on the budget; my only cost was the projectionist. It was discouraging to see so many untalented would-be actors and actresses, but I had to look. And I found the needed waitress for the cafe scene, so the time was not a total loss.

The minor roles, including the three children for the truck driver's family, were found among the photographs and the screen tests on file. They were all contract talent, and if they fitted the parts I had in mind, I relied on Milo's judgment for their ability to do the parts.

Three days of casting and it was completed except for the truck driver and his wife. We were stuck; the truck driver, my protagonist, had to be perfect. Once an actor was found, I could then select a wife to fit him from any one of a thousand housewives in the United States. But where could I find the defeated, cynical, sensitive face I needed . . . ?

Luckily, Milo Linder had a good memory.

CHET WILSON

Early one morning, just as the sun was coming up, Milo and I started out for Ojai Valley. Driving up the coast I asked Milo for details on this so-called actor he had dredged out of his memory.

'Actually, I don't know a damned thing about him, Richard. Even the way I happened to see him was an accident. I went to Santa Barbara a couple of years ago with Teddy Friedman to a sneak preview of *The Outrider*—'

'I remember it. Written by Jack Dover, produced by Teddy Friedman, directed by David Moore. Starred Buzz Canyon, Mary Marshman, and Pretty Boy, the Wonder Horse.'

'That's right. I don't know how you do it—'

'It's a gift. Go on.'

'Anyway, the preview didn't start until 11:30, following the last regular show, so we decided to take in a play at the Lobero Theatre. It was a community theatre thing, but it was something to do. Did you know that Santa Barbara, with only 45,000 population, has seven active theatre groups and a full-time drama critic on the newspaper?'

'No,' I said. 'Get to the play.'

'The play was a real weirdie; something in middle-English. Needless to say, we didn't have any trouble in getting seats to see a play in Middle English. Well, this guy, Chet Wilson, was playing the lead. No kidding, even in that medieval dialogue you could understand every thing he said. He had perfect enunciation and his face was as expressive as a caricature in iron filings. The play itself was nothing, some morality thing about witches and mountains, and the rest of the cast was half-assed. They do a lot of weird stuff in Santa Barbara anyway, and they don't give a damn whether they make any money or not. Believe it or not, Richard, some of these groups even do Saroyan.'

'That's hard to believe.'

'It's a fact. Mr Friedman was excited about Wilson and wanted to talk to him, but right after the play we had to hustle back to the movie theatre for the preview. The next day I made a call from the studio to the director of the play. All he could tell me was that Wilson had been in a hell of a lot of community plays in Santa Barbara and Ojai, and that he had a job watering an orange grove in Ojai.'

'If he was as good as you say, how come Friedman didn't give him a screen test?'

'I don't know. If nothing else the guy has a great potential. I told Mr Friedman what I found out, but he said he had thought it over, and he had the idea that Wilson looked good because the rest of the cast was so lousy.'

'Maybe he had a point there.'

'I don't think so, but it doesn't pay to argue with Mr Friedman.' Milo continued earnestly. 'If Chet Wilson fits your conception of the role, and I think he does, at least he'll work cheap.'

'He'll damned well have to – you've got the contracts with you haven't you, Milo?'

'Sure.'

'I think he'll grab it. A star in his first picture; how many actors get that kind of break? But the money isn't it. I've got to get the right man, and I can't quite picture him in my mind. Except for a bitterly twisted mouth, the rest of the face is a complete blank.'

Milo laughed. 'If Wilson is still watering orange trees for a living, and if he still has the acting ability I saw on the stage two years ago, he'll have a bitterly twisted mouth all right.'

When I reached the cut-off I turned away from 101 and took the narrow, winding road to Ojai. The road resembled an unstrung typewriter ribbon wadded and tossed on top of dirty brown foothills. It was desolate country. The bare foothills were covered with the twisted, blackened tendrils of manzanita, leftover chapparal of a year-old forest fire.

Ojai Valley was like a blast furnace, and at the first beer joint I came to on the narrow, dusty street, I pulled in fast, like a policeman going off-duty. It was much cooler in the dark barroom; there were a couple of overhead fans going, and someone had sprinkled water on the sawdust covered floor. The first beer sank in like a blotter, and when I ordered the second round I asked the bartender if he knew Chet Wilson.

'The actor? Sure, I know him. I saw him last month in *The Beautiful People*.'

'See!' Milo laughed gaily. 'I told you they did Saroyan!'

'Where can I find him?' I asked the bartender.

'Today's Tuesday, isn't it? He goes to art classes on Wednesday mornings, so I suppose he's at the grove today. But he might be hard to find though. Mrs Larson bought him a horse and he rides it all over hell and gone.'

'We'll look for him. Where's the grove?'

'What do you fellows want Chet for, anyway?'

'His aunt in Glendale died,' I said, 'and left him a million dollars.'

'He can sure use it,' the bartender said.

'Where's the grove,' I asked impatiently, as Milo laughed.

The directions were a bit complicated, but after a few wrong turns on sandy back roads we came to an orange grove covering about fifty acres. I parked the car well off the road under a tree. The irrigation ditches paralleling the trees were filling slowly with chocolate water and I knew that somebody had to be nearby in order to watch it. Milo remained in the car and I walked upstream, following the main ditch. In less than two hundred yards I spotted a horseman through the trees.

'Hey, Wilson,' I shouted. 'Over here! I want to talk to you!'

Wilson sat his mount well, and I studied him as he approached. He was letting the horse pick its way through the torn-up, freshly ploughed earth. Wilson was a thin, cadaverous man of about twenty-eight or -nine, and deeply tanned by the sun. His face was seamed and lined and an enormous hooked nose dominated his narrow face. He could have passed himself off as a Texan any day in the week. His mouth was so narrow it resembled a quick slash in a piece of saddle leather. The deep, tragic lines running from the thin wings of his preposterous nose to the corners of his twisted mouth made an almost perfect triangle. When he reined the bay horse to a halt on the opposite side of the three-foot irrigation ditch I looked directly into his eyes. They were a deep cobalt blue, but looked darker because of his lampblack brows. I was excited – it was a real discovery.

'You're Chet Wilson, aren't you?'

He cocked his head and spat. Wilson had an instinctive way of cocking his head as though he wanted to hear something he could take as an insult. He nodded curtly.

'I'm Richard Hudson from Mammoth Studios, and I want you to read for me.'

Watching me insolently from under his dark brows, Wilson removed a sack of Bull Durham from his blue work-shirt pocket and slowly rolled a thin cigarette. He puffed hungrily on the thin weed after lighting it with a kitchen match, and then flipped the spent cigarette into the muddy water of the ditch.

'Should I compare you to a f—— turd,' he began, and he added his own Anglo-Saxon adjectives as he went along, making the Shakespearean sonnet into an evil parody of a love song. The idea of love and tenderness was made obscene by his rich, baritone voice. The underlying bitterness in his throat reminded me of rusty razor blades. His perfect reading was a combination of the ludicrous and the tragic and I found myself grinning, and oddly touched at the same time.

'Climb down off your high horse,' I said when he had finished reciting the sonnet – his way – 'I want to see how tall you are out of the saddle.'

'Want to hear anything else?' he asked rudely. 'Richard the Third, Hamlet, King Lear, it don't make a damn to me. I know them all.'

'No,' I said. 'You'll do. I've got a part for you.'

'What part? I've been thinking about giving up acting altogether.'

'How long have you been thinking about it?'

'Ten years.' He laughed then, a rusty unused laughter, thick and pure.

'Think again then. You've got the starring role in *The Man Who Got Away*, an Elgee Production.'

'A movie?'

'That's right.'

Wilson dismounted, dropped the reins on the ground, waded through the ditch, and looked me squarely in the eyes. 'Now just who in the hell are you, anyway?' He asked belligerently.

'The writer and the director,' I said blandly, 'and you're the lead. Come on. I've got the contract in the car.'

Wilson followed me dumbly through the grove to the car, and I told Milo to dig out the contract. While Milo looked through his briefcase, I turned to Wilson. His body was shaking like a man with malaria, and his hands were trembling uncontrollably.

'You'd better sit down, boy,' I said.

Wilson sank to the ground, his legs crossed beneath him, and buried his face in his large, quivering hands. He sobbed once, wrenching the agonized sound up from deep in his body. A moment later his trembling lessened, and he shook his head back and forth, then tried his lips for a smile. It was more sneer than smile, but he meant the grimace as a smile.

'I knew it would happen like this, Mr Hudson,' Wilson said softly, with his rich, vibrant voice. 'A man all alone, riding around on a horse in the mountains, gets some pretty screwy ideas. But I guess they weren't so screwy after all.

'My entire life has been spent in preparation for this very moment, and now that it's here I can't believe it. It's too . . . unreal. I've always had this dream – a producer would come backstage after one of these lousy community plays and offer me a contract or it would happen like this – somebody would find me like you did. And it actually happened. Kind of shook me up for a minute. But you don't have to worry; I'll play your part for you, Mr Hudson! I'll *be* the part, I don't care what it is! I'm the best actor in the world!'

'Sure you are.' I patted him on the shoulder. 'That's why I came for you.' I shoved contract and pen into his eager hands and he signed his name without reading a word. I had to turn my head away. The beauty of his ugly, tragic face filled me with silent wonderment.

For a moment there, just for a moment, I felt like God.

MRS MILDRED CURRY SHANTZ

Milo Linder and I were shopping for an actress.

The Farmer's Market in Los Angeles splits the difference between Fairfax Avenue and the old Hollywood

Star's Baseball Park. It is a low, sprawling shopping area where a person can buy anything from a sack of Mexican jumping beans to a TV dinner for a child of five. Years ago, during the Great Depression, it was possible to actually obtain bargains at the Farmer's Market. No more. Small-time Japanese truck farmers from the Valley, and city residents on relief who grew a few tomatoes in their backyards, offered their produce for sale at cut-rate prices. But today, the shopping area is a highly commercialized center, with smart shops and stupid ones, huge parking lots, and any and all types of merchandise is for sale at today's prices.

The Farmer's Market was a likely place to shop for an actress who didn't know she could act – an American housewife to furnish the motivating force to my truck-driver hero, Chet Wilson.

Milo and I separated. He was searching under household wares, soap, and sundries, and I had stationed myself by the batteries of cash registers at the grocery checkout counters. There were at least thirty of the jangling cash registers, and I wandered from one to another as I examined the parade of housewives. A motley bunch, to say the least. In all shapes and sizes, determined women pushed metal carts loaded with children and groceries through the check stands where their purchases were toted to clanging bells. Long curling tapes erupted from the registers. It was a sight to make a man sick to his stomach.

For every one of these housewives, a man sweated somewhere to make the cash to buy these enormous baskets of groceries. In return for his labors he was fed a caloric horror consisting of fried hamburger, frozen peas, frozen chopped spinach, frozen peach pie, and instant coffee – that is – if his wife felt up to such wonderful culinary preparation. If she did not, he would feast on a commercial TV dinner: a dab of turkey meat, a small scoop of sage-saturated bread dressing, another dab of mealy, lumpy mashed potatoes, and thirty-seven large green peas. This tempting, appetizing delight would taste of aluminum foil, would be served on an aluminum plate, and would also be topped by the inevitable instant coffee. After a million cups of instant coffee, you cannot tell the difference.

These lovely ladies, these dazzling American beauties in shorts and halters, their gorgeous locks frozen stiff with home waves costing $1.75 per box, would prepare these delectable meals with loving care in houses smelling of baby pee on expensive pastel stoves which only added a few pennies a month to the cost of the house payments.

Yes, for his labors, the American male eats well, sires a family of three children, and lives in a $14,000 project house. And there were the marvelous creatures he slaved for, these brainless wonders standing in line repeating to each other with maddening accuracy what they all had seen and listened to on television the night before. In slacks, in shorts, in bermudas, in pedal pushers, they pushed their carts through the lines, accepting blindly the totals on the cash registers, and paying off with a smile . . .

After an hour I had enough. I felt smothered, and I resolved to select the next woman through the gate who had a bill of $49.00. It was easier that way; instead of looking at the women I could look at the cash register instead. Why I picked forty-nine as the magic number I do not know, perhaps because it was an uneven number. I never examine my motives too closely. I didn't have to wait much longer, at any rate.

This housewife was perfect. She was obviously tired, and harried by a four-year-old, red-haired little boy at the end of a leash. As the weary checker punched keys without looking at the register and shoved the grocery items to a pimply-faced stacker who was piling the stuff into a paper sack, the red-haired little monster took a swipe at a pyramid of canned milk cans and knocked them clattering to the floor. None of the women in the line, including the mother, paid any attention to this savage display of bad manners. Children must not be inhibited, don't you know. A tired old gentleman in a white smock patiently began to restack the pyramid, one can at a time.

The mother jerked the child through the turnstile and paid her tab. The total was $49.63, close enough for me. The housewife was somewhat different from the others in that she wore a flowered dress, instead of pants of some kind. Her dusty blonde hair was in curlers and her regular features were unmarred by beauty. She had one redeeming feature, a large front tooth made of solid, gleaming gold.

She sighed as she looked at the brimming cardboard box full of groceries and the sack beside it with celery balanced precariously atop two dozen eggs. As she reached for the sack, the child made two tight running circles around her legs and imprisoned her in the leash. She sighed again.

I left my place at the wall, hefted the heavy cardboard box to my shoulder and gave her my disarming smile.

'Lead the way to your vehicle, Madame,' I said courteously, 'and I shall follow.'

'Oh, thank you!' She flashed her golden smile. Wonderful! I followed the housewife and child to her parking place in the lot, and deposited the groceries on the front seat of her three-year-old Plymouth. Surreptitiously, I took a look at the registration slip on the steering column. Frank Shantz. I noted the Van Nuys address in my mind.

Turning toward the woman, I took the sackful of groceries she was carrying away from her and placed it next to the box. While she unharnessed the child I waited, eyeing her critically. The boy climbed noisily into the back

117

seat, and the woman fumbled in her purse, handed me a dime, and smiled kindly.

'God bless you, Madame,' I said, and I pocketed the dime. I left the parking lot, returned to the store and looked for Milo. As far as I was concerned, the search for a leading lady was over.

That evening Milo and I called on Mr and Mrs Frank Shantz at their Van Nuys home. Every house on the block looked alike with the exception of color and the care of the lawns. Next door to the Shantz's residence a sprinkler hissed, and three doors down a man clipped the edges of his lawn with manual clippers under the direction of his wife who shouted to him from their porch. This suburb of Van Nuys was the three-bedroom-den section, a step above the two-bedroom-den section, and way above the two-bedroom-no-den section.

'This may not be as easy as you think,' Milo said as I parked the car.

'Don't worry about it Just let me do all the talking,' I said. Milo looked very businesslike in a blue gabardine suit with his alligator briefcase under his arm. I was slightly concerned that Mr Shantz might take him for an insurance salesman.

A man of about forty, with thin brown hair, and a mole on his left cheek, opened the door to my ringing. He looked at us suspiciously with pale blue eyes.

'Yes?' His voice was high and querulous.

'Are you Mr Frank Shantz?' I asked politely. '*The* Mr Shantz, who sells air conditioners at Sears?'

'Why, yes. Yes, I am. Are you fellows police officers?'

'No,' I said. 'Are you expecting police?'

'No. Of course not!' He laughed nervously. 'I've been watching *Dragnet* and you look quite a bit like Sergeant Friday. Of course, you're a lot bigger than him.'

We all three laughed at this statement. 'No, Mr Shantz,' I grinned. 'We certainly aren't police officers. We're from

Mammoth Studios and we want to talk to your wife.'

'Did she win a prize? I guess it's about time she won. She's always sending in these crossword puzzles and things in the newspaper.'

'You might say it's some kind of a prize. We'd like to talk to her if she's home.'

'Sure. Come in. Come in.'

We entered the living room, and after I brushed some of the toys from an overstuffed chair I sat down. Milo sat on the couch, the briefcase across his knees. Mr Shantz shouted for his wife to come out of the kitchen. We had a minute or so to wait for Mildred Shantz to heed her husband's call, and while we waited we watched the television commercial – a man with a tattoo on his hand telling of the virtues of a certain cigarette. Mildred entered the room, quite flustered at the prospect of visitors, fluffing her short hair with fluttering fingers.

I got to my feet quickly, signaled Milo to do the same, and introduced myself. 'Good evening, Mrs Shantz. My name is Richard Hudson, and this is my associate, Mr Linder. We are from Mammoth Studios and we want to give you a screen test tomorrow.'

'A screen test? You mean, for the movies?'

'That's right. We have a particular part in mind for you, and if the screen test is all right, you'll be offered a contract.'

Mildred sank weakly into a chair and fixed me with big, blue unseeing eyes, a frozen smile upon her lips.

'You won that puzzle test, honey,' her husband said cheerily, 'and these gentlemen are going to put you in the movies.'

'Not exactly, Mr Shantz,' I explained. 'I'm directing a new movie, and your wife is merely one of the candidates for the part I have in mind.'

'You must have the wrong person, Mr Hudson,' Mildred said seriously. 'I've never done any acting at all, not even

119

in high school. Somebody must have given you the wrong Mildred Shantz,' she finished weakly.

'No. There's no mistake. I've had talent scouts watching you for a long time, and this morning, I took a look at you personally because of the many favorable reports. You should remember me – I was the man who carried your groceries for you this morning at the Farmer's Market. Remember?'

'Oh, no!' Mildred squealed, flushing to the roots of her dusty blonde hair. 'And I tipped you with a dime!' She covered her face with her hands, then peeped coyly through her fingers at me. 'It was all the change I had left,' she faltered. 'I always tip a quarter.'

This was a lie of course. Her bill had been $49.63; therefore she had at the very least thirty-seven cents in change left. Like most women, she was merely a cheap tipper.

'Do you want your dime back?' I smiled.

'No, no! You keep it!' This statement embarrassed her more than ever. 'I don't know what I'm saying, I'm so excited. In the movies! *Me!* I can't believe it.'

'It's true, however,' I said. 'Mr Linder has an appointment card for you which will pass you through the gate.' I jerked my head at Milo and he handed Mrs Shantz the appointment slip. 'We'll expect you at the studio for makeup at seven tomorrow morning. Don't dress yourself up, or do any home makeup – we'll take care of that end at the studio. Is seven too early for you? Can you make it all right?'

Mildred turned helplessly to her husband; there was a wild, desperate look on her face, and her mouth had dropped open.

'She'll be there, Mr Hudson,' Shantz stated firmly, 'with bells on. Even if I have to stay home from work and take care of the kids myself. But I won't. I'll call my sister right away, and she'll be over here in five minutes flat.'

Milo edged toward the door. I shook hands with Mr Shantz, patted Mildred on the shoulder reassuringly. 'Now don't worry about the test, Mrs Shantz,' I said. 'The best thing for you to do is go to bed now and get a good night's sleep.'

'Sleep!' she exclaimed humorously. 'I won't be able to sleep for a week!'

'Good night then. I'll see you in the morning.'

The typical American couple waved to us from their front porch as we drove away. Neither one of them was really surprised – or astonished. They had accepted Milo and myself as representing Mammoth Studios without question. Why? Because that is the way these things happen in the movies. That is why. This time it had merely happened to them.

That's all.

MONTAGE

I do not wish to minimize the role of the director in the production of a movie, because to do so would minimize my contribution as the director of *The Man Who Got Away*.

However, I now believe that almost anyone who has seen a couple of hundred movies, and who is furnished with the capable assistance that I had – Milo Linder, Leo Steinberg, and the production facilities and staff of a large studio, such as Mammoth, can direct a movie.

I do not say that anyone can direct a great movie, but almost anyone can, under the same circumstances that I had, direct a movie good enough to be distributed. And the chances are 50-50 that the movie will break even, no matter who directs it.

What bothered me most was the sense of unreality in what I was doing. I felt as though I was an unreal person

121

creating a reality that might become unreal if I didn't keep my eyes open every single second. The solemn deference paid to me on the set by assistants, cameramen, and people who drifted in and out from nowhere (I never discovered what half of the people were doing or why) added to my sense of unreality. I was the director – it said so on my canvas chair – but the director of what? And I knew that all of the frantic activity surrounding me had been directly caused by my initial idea for a movie, expressed extemporaneously to Leo Steinberg in his study.

A director is not an electrician; an electrician can pin his job down exactly. He furnishes light where it is required, and he knows exactly what he is doing. The cables in a movie studio may be heavier, and the lights a little brighter, but the electrician performs a task pertaining to electricity. If the electrician works in a movie studio or wires a housing project, his job is essentially the same.

I was working in the abstract with non-objective viewpoints toward a certain objective that was a nebulous idea. I was supposed to create something, and therefore I was in the middle, surrounded by technicians who knew what they were doing. Exactly. Once in awhile I would catch myself thinking about the differences, and then it would take great mental effort on my part to force such thoughts out of my mind. I was confused enough already; why add to my confusion by thinking about the unreality?

But unreality or not I had a schedule to go by. The schedule provided for every single minute once the shooting began and I had to adhere to it. The schedule was my lifeline to reality.

No matter how angry I was or dissatisfied with a scene, the budget did not allow for expensive retakes, tantrums, or kicking Mrs Shantz in the teeth. The schedule was too tight for such indulgences. In the making of a low-budget movie, the comptroller's word is law.

My use of film was limited to three takes of each scene. I had to rehearse the scene, and then a take; one more take to print, and then the last take as a cover in case the first two were no good. If all three were no good – tough. The scene was lost. And Leo assured me several times that there was no room in the budget for any retakes.

If there were any faults in the movie they were mine. The cameramen, grips, sound technicians, makeup men, sweepers, painters, everyone in fact, in the technical end, were experts at their jobs. They had all served apprenticeships, they were paid up in their union dues, and all of them were aware of the budget restrictions, and what had to be done. They helped me in every way they could, and I appreciated their help.

I had three weeks. That was all. Three weeks. A week on location, including two days in San Francisco, one day in Santa Barbara for background fills, and two days for all the highway scenes. The final scene of the crash into the pile of wrecked cars on the highway, which climaxed the movie, was supposed to be shot in Santa Barbara, but was changed to Burbank instead.

The remaining two-week period was spent on Sound Stage F, which wasn't quite large enough, but was used anyway. The sets were built while I was on location and were ready when I returned. Without a break, after the final location scene in Burbank was completed, the company moved to the Mammoth lot to shoot the beginning of the movie.

We finished on time due to Leo's genius for organization.

I didn't get much sleep. After a day of shooting, I watched the rushes from the day before. I then studied the script for the next day's shooting, discussing with Milo methods of getting the best out of Chet Wilson, Mildred Shantz, the bits and extras.

By midnight I was ready to talk interpretation with Chet. For two or more hours I would lecture Chet in his hotel room about the hero's personality and characterization. Chet would then go over his lines with me, if any, for the next day's scenes, and I would drive the poor bastard nuts in order to get a shaded nuance of a single word. I almost drove Chet crazy.

But my coaching produced the desired results. Chet was irritable, impatient, haggard, charged with emotion, fatigued, and he tossed his cookies two or three times a day. Wonderful! Just right for my truck-driving hero.

The scenes with Mildred almost drove *me* crazy. I was forced to turn her over to the Mammoth chief dramatic coach, an old lady from Lithuania, who had the patience of Job. The old girl accomplished a miracle with Mildred, teaching her how to say one word at a time, in the manner one would feed a parakeet a seed at a time from the lips. Mildred became bored, tired, disgusted, and developed a passionate hatred for Chet Wilson because he was so good. All of this came over in her 'acting' and was exactly what I wanted.

During the night, while I tossed fitfully on my cot in my bungalow office, little fairies in the forms of technicians made the sets ready for the next day. When I stepped through the doors of Sound Stage F, the properties were ready, the set was clean, the lighting plans had been worked out, the cameras were ready, the boom man was ready and the sound man was ready to mix the sound. The actors were in makeup, and the script girl had turned to the right page in my scenario. This was at 7 a.m.

I rehearsed the scene a couple of times, told Milo when I was ready, and he shouted 'Roll 'em' and 'Action.' The man slapped the blackboard in front of the camera and the actors went through the scene as we had rehearsed it. Once the sound of 'Action' went through the set I was committed, and I could only bite my fingernails, which I did. The scene was shot again after I pointed out things that were done wrong the first time, and then was shot once more for a covering take. It isn't hard to be a director. Not at all.

The entire crew, but especially Tommy Allison, the director of photography, thought I was the greatest director in the world. I adopted almost every suggestion Allison offered me – he, at least, knew what he was doing with the cameras.

It was one thing for me to have sat alone in a hotel room and put on paper:

TAKE 47 – LONG SHOT
Across the street from San Francisco truck lot. Semi-swings wide and enters the gate, stopping at Dispatch Office. Hero dismounts from cab.

It was something else to put this scene on film. There are a hundred ways to accomplish the same thing.

'Mr Hudson,' Allison would say, 'I've taken the liberty to change this a little. Instead of taking a long shot from across the street, let's take a medium from the dispatcher's sliding window as Chet pulls through the gate. This will help to emphasize the size and height of the truck. When Chet climbs out of the cab and we shoot up at him, it'll make the semi- look like a damned monster. OK?'

'OK.'

I was the man who made the decisions. And I made them quickly. Allison's plan was better than mine and yet it achieved the same end. When I didn't agree with him, we did it my way, and he never argued with me. I was the director.

There was a rather touching scene with Mildred and Chet; an attempt by both of them to make love to each other before Chet left on his run to Los Angeles. All love between the truck driver and his wife had disappeared years before, and their attempt to find it again in a half-hearted way, and their failure to do so, had to be shown to establish the pathos and futility of their lives. Mildred couldn't get it, and I had to get sloppy with her.

I took her into the dressing room, made love to her, patted her well-padded buttocks, told her how wonderful she was, kissed her and listened enraptured as she repeated her lines parrot-like, exactly as they had been fed to her by the dramatic coach. After she was sufficiently excited I ran her out on the set and shot the scene fast. The scene was as perfect as I could ever hope to get it.

The cafe scenes were the best in the movie; Mildred wasn't in any of them. Here I dealt with professional actors, and Chet Wilson, who had not lied to me – he was the best actor in the world. If there is such an animal as a creative actor, Chet Wilson is a creative actor. He created the part of the truck driver from somewhere deep within himself, and the remainder of the cast was inspired by his performance.

This is all a panoramic mish-mash, I know, but so was the three weeks of filming my picture. My original script sequence was not followed one, two, three; the picture was filmed according to Leo's schedule. Scene 14 could just as easily follow Scene 92, in fact it did. The movie was according to plan, location, and did not follow the strict continuity in numerical sequence.

The cafe scene, however, where Chet made a fumbling, amateurish attempt to date the waitress, was so moving and so well done, and so tender, that when Chet had finished talking to the girl and fled from the cafe with the tears streaming down his face, everybody on the set, including myself, gave him a round of applause that lasted for three full minutes.

Notwithstanding the end results – I shall never forget the three wonderful weeks I spent as a director.

I wish I could.

FADE TO:

There were four of us sitting in the dim projection room; Leo, Chet, Milo, and me – anyone could have picked me out by my heavy breathing. My movie – two hours and thirty-three minutes of unfinished film – had been put together in what I hoped would be some kind of sequence. Except for the dialogue there were no sound effects or music, and the titling hadn't been done either. It was just a movie in the raw state, but the shooting was completed and the four of us were having a little private preview before the editing.

'How about THE MAN,' I asked Leo, 'is he coming or not?'

'No.' Leo shrugged. 'He prefers to see the completed version. Movies in the rough make him stay awake at night worrying.'

'The hell with him,' I said, and I pressed the button on the floor to signal the projectionist. The film unrolled before us on the screen. Although I had a clipboard, pocket flashlight, and a ballpoint pen with me, and fully intended to take notes, I never got around to it during the first showing. I was too fascinated. For the first time in my life I had created something, and here it was, frozen in time before my eyes. The movie could not be changed or taken away from me. It could be shortened, but no rearrangement of scenes could change my basic story. My paper characters were flesh-and-blood, real live people, and what they said and did upon the screen could only be repeated exactly the same every time it was shown in a darkened room. And the first time through, I loved every minute of the 153 minutes.

The camera faded back from the silent crowd surrounding the smouldering body of Chet Wilson and the screen suddenly became a large white rectangle. The projectionist flipped the houselights on and the movie was over.

Leo looked at me for a long moment. 'How in the hell,' he asked admiringly, his eyebrows raised, 'did you ever get the expressions on the faces of that mob in the crash scene?'

Milo and I both laughed conspiratorily.

'It wasn't easy, Leo,' I admitted. 'It cost Milo twenty-five bucks out of his own pocket that wasn't on the budget.'

'And for once I don't want the money back,' Milo said virtuously. 'That scene was worth every penny.'

'Allison and I worked it out,' I explained further to Leo. 'We told the extras that there would be a slight delay in the shooting, and that we had provided some entertainment for them in the interim. Allison had the camera set up across the way – they didn't know he was shooting – and shot their faces with a zoom lense in a slow pan. Have you ever heard of Zelda?'

'Wow!' Milo laughed.

'She's a stripper from the Trinidad Club. She did her disrobement act among the piled up wrecks, and while the crowd watched we captured their faces.'

'It certainly worked.' Leo shook his head. 'I've got to hand it to you, Richard. Every face held a different reaction. Lust, greed, indignation, sheer joy, and yet they all managed to have a wet, shiny brightness in their eyes, regardless of facial expression.'

'Actually,' I said seriously, 'their faces would probably look the same way if they were really watching a body on fire.'

'No doubt at all.' Leo turned to Milo, clapped him on the shoulder. 'And you got stuck for Zelda's fee?'

'It was only twenty-five bucks.' Milo said modestly. 'It was worth that much for me to see her dance—'

'You'll get it back.' Leo pursed his lips. 'Now Richard, your real work begins. I know the saying is old, but it still holds true: Movies are made on the cutting room floor. You've got your work to be cut out for you, and you're the one who has to make the decisions.'

'I know, I know,' I said impatiently. 'Do you want to see it again?'

'I do!' Chet Wilson explained. 'It's the last chance I'll have to see it all before you get busy with the scissors.' Chet was like a small boy seeing his first movie. I couldn't blame him. During the shooting I hadn't allowed him to see any of the rushes.

Milo and Leo begged off, but Chet and I had the movie shown in its entirety three more times. With the second run through I began to make notes for editing.

The film did not excite me any longer; I was critical instead. For years I had watched movies with a critical eye, and in my second and subsequent viewings I managed to get my impersonal detachment back again. The pacing was way off. My original plan to pace the first half of the movie slow, and the second half fast, had been a good idea. But by not following the script sequence in the shooting the pacing had gotten away from me. Here and there it was much too erratic for good continuity and it was not possible to retake any scenes over again, so I had to cut. And cut I did.

Tom Ruggerio, a grizzled veteran of the movies, and the film editor for my movie, confirmed most of my convictions. We worked all day in the cramped editing room, minutely examining film and cutting ruthlessly. We patched in likely stock highway scenes, and chopped them out again. Ruggerio discovered a perfect shot of a police car going over a cliff, and patched it in expertly. I had taken the chase shot of Chet forcing the police car off the road, but Tom Ruggerio pieced in the car going over the cliff so skilfully it was impossible to determine any break in the continuity. Ruggerio was good at his work and I was critical enough to make him work.

It was too bad.

When I finished the editing the movie had perfect pacing, excitement, realism and beauty; but it was only sixty-three minutes long.

Tom and I had the completed film run off in the projection room – it was a work of art, and it contained my message in addition to being a good show. All the movie needed was guitar music, the titling, and the sound effects.

'What do you think, Ruggerio?' I asked the old man.

'Well, Mr Hudson, as it is, the movie is about as good as we can make it. With the sound effects and music dubbed in it will be a little masterpiece and I've never seen anything quite like it before. Unfortunately, we have to put back twenty-seven more minutes of film. Three minutes can be taken in titling, but the other twenty-four will have to be just plain old padding.'

'Can we pad twenty-four minutes and still maintain the pace I've set, the mood and so on?'

'Nope. As a matter of fact it would be better if we superimposed the titling and credits over the opening scene where Wilson pulls into San Francisco with the truck. But there's no choice. We've got to put in at least twenty-seven more minutes of film.'

'Why do we?'

'You know that as well as I do, Mr Hudson. A movie is ninety minutes long. It can be longer, but exhibitors insist on at least an hour and a half. Six full reels. That's the business.'

'But unnecessary padding will *ruin* my movie?'

'Not really. We can stretch the hell out of that chase down the highway. I've got stock stuff we haven't even looked at yet, reel after reel of it. Scenic views, wild flowers, traffic jams, all kinds of stuff, and we can fit it in fine. I remember a western once where I stretched a desert chase out twenty-five minutes with long shots of different guys on horseback. Nobody knew the difference. People like chases.'

'*The Man Who Got Away* isn't a western.'

'Yeah, but he doesn't really get away either. It's the same thing as a big chase—'

'God damn it, NO!' I shouted angrily. 'As far as I'm concerned my movie will run as it is, twenty-seven minutes short! Period. I'm not going to ruin my movie because of some stupid ruling that it has to be ninety minutes long. That's just like adding three more plates to the last supper, or an extra wing to the Pentagon.'

'That's up to you, Mr Hudson. If you can get it by THE MAN, it doesn't make a damn to me. But you can't. I wish you could. Right now, we've got something mighty fine in this movie of yours, and when we pad it out it will be just another movie. But that's the way it is. You can't fight the system.'

'All right, Ruggerio. Will you back me up in this thing? Will you go to THE MAN with me and insist that the movie should be left as is, at sixty-three minutes?'

'Nope. I'll tell him the truth if he asks me. The movie is too short. It's supposed to be ninety minutes long.'

'I think that you are a son of a bitch, Ruggerio. You tell me one thing, and yet you'll tell THE MAN another—'

'I'm not telling any lies, Mr Hudson. I've been working at Mammoth Studios for fourteen years, and that's the way things are. A movie is ninety minutes long.'

'How would you like an upper lip full of front teeth?'

'I wouldn't like it, Mr Hudson. But that wouldn't change anything either. If you want to take a swing at me, go ahead. But a movie is still ninety minutes long.'

'Mine won't be. Is that understood?'

'Yes, sir.'

'All right Attend to the titling and credits, the way I gave them to you, and keep your damned mouth shut over the length of my movie. Superimpose the titling over the opening scene. I'll have the music and sound effects put in myself.'

'You're the director, Mr Hudson.'

'You are damned right I am!'

CROSSFADE:

This is not a journal. There are not exact dates and the continuity is far from being constant – by any means. But it is my story, and what I have to put down here now is somehow relevant, although it pains me deeply to write it. In a way, this bare exposition throws a dark cloud over my manhood. Not exactly, once the explanation is heard and believed. But at the time, I worried enough about my manhood to talk to Leo about it. His glib explanation has never been fully accepted, but it sounded reasonable at the time and I accepted his version and went ahead with my work.

Laura Harmon had tried to telephone me many times, but I hadn't talked to her except that one time in Leo's study when I told her to get off the telephone. It was my practice, and a wise one, once I got underway with my movie, not to accept any unscreened telephone calls. I didn't want to be bothered.

During the shooting I slept in motels on location, and during the studio schedule I slept on a leather couch in my office. This is not a common practice for a director. Most directors look upon their work as a regular job, and leave their work when they leave the gate in the evening. Not me. When I am working I am so intent upon what I

132

am doing I have to be as close to my work as possible. When I first began to sell used cars in San Francisco I slept in a trailer at the back of the lot for almost a year. When I looked out of the trailer window at night and observed the row upon row of shiny unsold merchandise, it drove me wild with desire to get rid of them. Some of my best sales gimmicks came to me in the night when I studied the rows of automobiles.

In time, I outgrew this intensity of purpose. If I directed movies long enough I suppose I could eventually take them in stride too. In San Francisco I moved to an apartment befitting my increased income. But I also realize that my income would not have increased as quickly as it did if my intensity of single-minded purpose had not been as intense.

I am still skirting the subject, I notice, avoiding it.

To state it baldly, all desire for women, any woman, including Laura, left me abruptly the moment I got involved with the writing of my screenplay. Only recently has my desire returned, and now that I am not . . . but once again, I get ahead of myself.

After I began work on my movie I did not want to speak to Laura because to speak to her would have led to a rendezvous, and a rendezvous would have led to a romp in the hay, and I would have been inadequate. There it is. Bluntly.

And yet I caught myself, when every thought should have been directed solely on my movie, thinking about what happened to my desire – and would it ever return? and why did it actually repel me to think of getting into bed with a woman? and if my sexual ability was lost forever, what good was I now or forever? Stupid? Sure it was. But these thoughts were interfering with my work and I couldn't allow that to happen. So I spoke to Leo about it.

For two weeks I hadn't been near The House of Lumpy

Grits. But at midnight, with a sudden decision I left the studio and drove home, cornering Leo in his study. Leo was still awake, as usual, and was bent over some small models of the sets that were then under construction on Sound Stage F at the studio.

After a few minutes of discussing the sets with Leo, I blurted out my secret thoughts. His reaction to my deep-seated fears startled me, and filled me with a sudden, unreasoning anger. He laughed. The laugh was a thin, wailing type of laughter I had never heard him use before. Although it was difficult to suppress my embarrassment and chagrin, I forced a loose, comical smile, and said: 'I don't think it's funny, Pop.'

'Of course it isn't.' Leo wiped his streaming eyes with a violet-saturated handkerchief, and then sank weakly into his swivel chair.

'All of us, Richard,' Leo began seriously, 'men, I mean, because I don't know anything about women, have two drives deep within us. One is a sex drive, and the other is called the aggressive drive. These two drives are so closely meshed it is quite impossible to separate them. There is a little bit of pain in all types of love, and there is a little love in all types of pain. Do you agree?'

'Yes. So far, anyway.'

'This is very elementary psychology, but you'd be surprised at the number of people who don't know these things.'

'Well, I know something about psychology, Leo,' I said impatiently. 'I'd be a hell of a salesman if I didn't.'

'Right. But we're talking about you. For perhaps the first time in your life you find yourself deep in the throes of intense creative endeavor. Your desire to make good is so great that your aggressive drive has completely supplanted your sexual drive. This is not unusual. And it is perfectly normal. Painters, novelists, sculptors' – Leo laughed – 'and perhaps for the first time in the history of Hollywood, a combination writer-director, obtain their satisfaction, or whatever you want to call it, from their creative activity.

'A novelist finds release in the writing of his book, a painter in painting, and so on. But the sex loss is a temporary loss. When the painter completes his painting, or in your case, when the movie is finally over and done with, your natural sex drive will return in full force. Your aggressive drive will give up the ghost, and you'll probably go on a wild orgy of some kind.'

I smiled ruefully. 'You make it sound too simple.'

'That's the way it is. Believe me.'

'Do you know Lewis Carroll, Leo, as well as you know psychology?'

'Better.' Leo smiled.

'Then what happens if he doesn't find any?' I paraphrased the tale of the bread-and-butterflies.

'He dies of course,' Leo picked up the dialogue.

'Does it happen often?'

'It always happens,' Leo finished sternly.

After this talk with Leo I returned to the studio and slept like a stone right up until 5:30 a.m. the next morning. And I refused to allow my mind to dwell on sex again until the movie was over.

The movie, my movie, was much more important.

LAP DISSOLVE

'Are you ready?'

Flaps Heartwell nodded vigorously. He was a Negro guitar player, currently performing nightly at the Pampanga Club in Watts. I had hired him to play the music for my movie.

135

'Yes, *sir*, Mr Hudson. The juice is buzzin' in the box!' He meant his electric guitar and amplifier.

There was a slight sound in the rear of the studio as a metal chair was moved across the floor. I turned on the sound and angrily shouted, 'Shut up, back there!'

The six superfluous musicians, three with beards and three without, shifted nervously in their metal chairs, and eyed one another apprehensively. We had been forced to hire them as standby musicians although they contributed nothing; they didn't even have to take their instruments out of the cases to earn their daily wages. Such is the power of union. Every time I looked at them, and thought about the useless expenditure of funds from the meagre budget, I got sore.

'Just a second, Flaps,' I said.

I walked across the thickly carpeted floor and looked at the freeloading musicians. It would have given me great pleasure to knock their heads together.

'Before we start recording,' I said ominously, 'I want to impress upon you just how tough I can get. I was forced to hire you, even though I'm only using a guitar for the b.g. But one peep out of any of you during the recording and I'll sue your local for sabotage. I don't even want to hear a whisper. And if you think I'm going to pay you for sneaking out for coffee, or smoking cigarettes on my time, you are crazy. Anybody who absents himself from this studio for as long as ten minutes will be docked an hour's pay. Understood?'

Two of the men with spade beards nodded; the other four grinned sheepishly. I wanted to pitch into this nonproductive sextet with both fists flying. With all of the stumbling blocks in the way, it is a wonder that any art at all is ever produced in the United States. I returned to Flaps Heartwell, patted him gently upon his thin shoulder. Lighting a cigarette, I placed it between his lips.

'OK, Flaps,' I said softly, 'you've got the tune down fine, and I think you know all the cues. But once again; during the opening, play as mean and lowdown as you can, just the way we rehearsed it. And if you do everything right the ending will come out exactly even with the first line of dialogue spoken by the dispatcher. How do you like 'Lumpy Grits'?'

'I like it, Mr Hudson. I've had it in my repertoire for years. It's a mighty fine number.'

'How many times have you seen the movie now?'

'Five times. It's good, Mr Hudson.'

'Thank you. Would you like to see it cold again before we start?'

'No, sir. I'm ready to play.'

'Do you want another dry run?'

'No, sir, Mr Hudson. I'm ready. I'm ready!'

'How about questions? Do you have any questions at all. Any at all?'

'No, sir. The movie damned near broke my heart.'

'Well, play that way then, Flaps. When the movie starts I'll be in the booth and I'll give you the finger. Like this. You bang it out hard. Then through the rest of the movie you add the parts of 'Lumpy Grits' like we rehearsed it. Forget me, forget the other people in here, and everything else except what you see on the screen. Just play like you're all alone on a mountain back in Tennessee, playing for yourself. If you feel like humming parts of the song while you play, go ahead. I liked the way you did that last time.'

'I didn't mean to start hummin', Mr Hudson. Sometimes I hum that way because I can't help it.'

'That's all right, Flaps. I liked it. You are a true artist, Flaps, and I'm depending on you. We're only going to do this once and we're not breaking it up because I want the music to be spontaneous where it's needed.

Did you notice, on the last runthrough, your name sitting up there all by itself in a separate frame? *Music by Flaps Heartwell.*'

'I almos' fainted when I seen that, Mr Hudson.'

'The way you play when the movie starts will depend upon whether it stays there or not. Are you ready? Really ready?'

'Yes, sir. I'm ready.' By this time, Flaps' forehead was perspiring freely.

'That's the way I work, Flaps. Where credit is due, I give it. You deserve the credit for this music and I'm giving it to you. Millions of people all over the world are going to see your name on that screen. And when this movie is released you're going to have a towsack full of mail from people you never heard of.'

'It sure is an awful responsibility . . .' Flaps gulped. It was difficult for him to swallow.

'When the film starts, Flaps, you're on your own. I want to make that clear, and I won't be able to help you. You'll just have to watch and play, watch and play, and the emotion you feel—' I thumped his guitar, 'let it come out of this!'

'I'm ready! Gosh darn it, Mr Hudson I've done told you a hundred times I was ready!'

Flaps was so upset he was about to burst into tears. This was fine with me. This was the way I wanted him to be. Without another word I gravely shook hands with him and entered the control booth where the sound engineer was waiting. Flaps stood alone in the center of the studio, one foot on a chair, sweat glistening on his black face, the guitar trembling in his large hands. His eyes were glued on the white screen, he wet his lips with a pink tongue, and then he rolled his eyes wildly in my direction.

'OK,' I said to engineer and projectionist. 'Now.' I pointed my forefinger at Flaps.

The screen suddenly filled with an enormous truck

hurtling toward the audience of one, Flaps Heartwell, and angry guitar strings exploded in the control room. The music was vicious, savage, frightening, and barely under control. In other words, the music was perfect. The run-through was performed without a hitch and there was no necessity for any redubbing whatsoever.

The emotional effect the music produced in the completed movie was similar to wiring a Jackson Pollack painting for sound, if such a thing could be accomplished.

I cannot describe the music any better than that.

For his performance Flaps Heartwell received twenty bucks. The six musicians who did nothing received eight dollars an hour. The total for the sextet was $394.70. Luckily for me, Flaps didn't belong to a union.

FADE TO:

Three days after the recording session I entered Leo's office and plunked four cans of film down on his desk. I managed a good front but my insides were quivering with apprehension.

'Let's have the studio preview tonight, Leo. For a change I think *The Man Who Got Away* should be previewed in a drive-in.'

Leo looked at the four cans, raised his eyebrows quizzically, tapped the can with the end of a pencil. 'Where are the other two reels?'

'It just so happened that I didn't need six reels.' I smiled. 'Sixty-three minutes were all I needed.' This important tidbit of information had been withheld from Leo until music, titling and sound had been dubbed.

Leo wagged his head. 'I was under the impression that you would have trouble cutting to ninety minutes – but sixty-three . . .'

'I realize that it's a bit unorthodox, Pop, but I had to cut, that's all there is to it. I'm sorry, but that's the way it'll have to be.'

'You don't think that maybe you can add, say one more reel? Another fifteen minutes?'

'No. Nothing. I couldn't add another fifteen seconds. The movie is perfect as it is. I'll stake my reputation on it.'

'What about mine?'

'I'll stake yours too.'

Again, Leo tapped the top can with a pencil. 'THE MAN has to see this, you know, before there can be any preview.'

'Take it to him.' I said amply. 'It's ready.'

Leo gnawed on his lower lip for a long moment. 'I am worried about this, Richard. Really worried. I didn't have an inkling you were cutting so drastically. You should have told me. Maybe I could have helped you; it isn't too late anyway. Suppose we—'

'Don't worry about it, Pop. I'll take full responsibility.'

'As the producer *I've* already assumed full responsibility. Before I can show this to THE MAN I want to see it.'

'I want you to see it, Pop.'

After lunch, Leo and I saw the movie together, just the two of us, sitting in comfortable overstuffed chairs in the tiny Producer's Theatre next to Sound Stage A. Every time I saw my movie I liked it better. When it was over and the houselights were on, Leo pulled pensively at the lobe of his right ear.

'This isn't just another movie, Richard.'

'I know it isn't.'

'It will make people angry.'

'That's right.'

'There will be letters.'

'Bound to be.'

'That little girl . . . the tire marks across her white dress . . .'

'Too bad it isn't in color.'

'That little girl is very disturbing.'

'You're putting it mildly.'

'The music frightened me.'

'Good, isn't it?'

'Are we really honest, Richard? Is that bloodthirsty mob the American people?'

'For Christ's sake, Leo!'

'The ending then . . . there isn't any real answer.'

'Do you have the real answer? Does anybody? What the hell is the matter with you? We've gone over all of this before.'

'The movie isn't cynical, Richard. It's bitter.'

'Right. If that's the way you want to put it.'

'I don't believe in my heart, Richard,' Leo thumped his pigeon chest with an open palm, 'that the world is really like this. And yet your movie makes me believe it! Who did this to you? Why are you so unhappy?'

'Hell, I'm not unhappy, Pop. I'm the happiest man in the world.'

Leo sighed wearily and shook his head slowly back and forth.

DISSOLVE

KING OF THE MOUNTAIN

A By-Play in One Act

Scene: The office of THE MAN, Mammoth Studios, Culver City, California. Time: Day or night. Without windows, with air conditioning, and under brilliant electric illumination, who can tell the exact time? THE MAN is seated behind his huge, white desk; he wears a red linen sports jacket and a yellow sports shirt, open at the neck, exposing a sheaf of dirty-white chest hair at the V. On one corner of the great expanse of desk a milk-glass vase holds a dozen American Beauty roses. On the opposite corner of the desk, there is a stack of brightly bound manuscripts. LEO STEINBERG, wearing white trousers and a navy-blue jacket with brass buttons, is seated at the left of the desk. His eyes stare at the floor. By the bar, twenty feet away from the desk, RICHARD HUDSON shakes ice in a tall glass. His cold eyes shift back and forth from LEO to THE MAN, warily. Periodically he checks the zipper on his fly. It always seems to surprise him when he finds the zipper secured at the top of the fly. RICHARD'S plain charcoal suit, white shirt, maroon knit tie and plain black shoes are in sharp contrast to the yachting costume worn by Steinberg, and the sports apparel affected by THE MAN.

THE MAN: (*After an awkward silence*) Mr Steinberg told me that he didn't believe you would go along with my plan. But I can only believe that you really don't understand it. If you will please refrain from any more outbursts until I have completed, in detail, my plans for *The Man Who Got Away*, I am certain you'll see things my way.

RICHARD: Are you on *his* side or mine, Leo?

LEO: Can't you listen? For once in your life, listen!

RICHARD: (*Pours whiskey over his glassful of ice, recaps the bottle, and sets it on the bar.*) I'm listening.

THE MAN: My plan is not an idle whim or spur-of-the-moment decision, Mr Hudson. The inroads of television on the motion picture industry have been disastrous. Other studios have fought back by selling their movie backlogs, and producing their own series. Mammoth Studios can also make movies for television. The only reason I have held off so long as I have is I wanted the right format. Unwittingly, perhaps, your movie is

the right picture to start the series. The Mammoth
Hour will be a seasonal series of thirteen one-hour
filmed shows, and it will start with *The Man Who Got
Away*. The entire series will attack inequities in the
American way of life through adequate documentation.
I plan to document through dramatization the entire
range of public problems. Segregation, taxation, unions,
any and all problems of the day affecting the American
people. Your movie may well be a classic that can be
brought back every five years on television and reach
another appreciative audience.

LEO: It's a grand plan, Richard.

THE MAN: Mr Steinberg has agreed to be the executive
producer of the series, and will have a free rein. Nepo-
tism is not unheard of in Hollywood, Mr Hudson, and I
am certain that your stepfather will allow you to direct
some of the better scripts at $1,500 a show.

LEO: You'll have your choice, Richard!

RICHARD: I'm still listening.

THE MAN: I am positive that the combination of the
Steinberg name, along with this initial movie, will secure the top Trendex rating for The Mammoth Hour as
soon at it is launched. Your movie contains all of the elements I was looking for in a pilot film. A shocker! It's
controversial and it will cause angry comment, letters,
and editorials. You'll be the most talked-about writer-
director in television. (Pause.) Now tell me again that
you object.

RICHARD: How long is The Mammoth Hour going to
be? One hour or ninety minutes?

THE MAN: One hour.

RICHARD: All right. I've listened to you; how about
hearing my side?

THE MAN: Of course.

RICHARD: *The Man Who Got Away* is exactly sixty-three minutes long. It's as tight as a new goatskin bongo. In a one-hour television drama there is first the announcer. One minute. He announces the host. The host informs the audience that he is from Hollywood, that this is the first of a series, and of course he'll have to say something about the show the audience is going to see, something about the cast, and something about the entire forthcoming series. The announcer and the host, at the minimum, will consume four minutes. Then there will be the commercial. Two or three more minutes lost. The rest of the hour will be broken up three more times for commercials, not counting a one minute station break at the half-hour. And then the end. More host, telling the audience about next week's show, with a scene or two thrown in from the next show as a teaser.

THE MAN: You exaggerate, Mr Hudson.

RICHARD: No, I don't. All that would be left of my movie would be about forty minutes, cut up in such small segments it would take a genius to follow the continuity in his head from one commercial to the next. My movie is like a giant snowball going down hill, getting larger all of the time with suspense and danger until it explodes. A single break in the continuity and the effect is gone!

THE MAN: Mr Steinberg says that it can be done.

RICHARD: No. Anymore cutting and the movie would be as silly as cutting a condensed *Reader's Digest* novel.

THE MAN: I believe you are concerned more with your message than the dramatic effect. On television your movie will reach fifty million people.

RICHARD: But who could follow it? What more could be cut that wouldn't completely ruin it? Are you against me in this, Leo?

LEO: Part of what you say is true, Richard. There will be

144

a host, and commercials, but I will be the host, and I am positive that the movie can be cut in many places without the complete loss of continuity. Almost all of the long shots can be taken out, and they should be. Long shots are not good for television, and with your OK on each cut—

RICHARD: I won't OK anything! Evidently not a damned thing I've said the past few weeks has sunk into your pointed head! This isn't an ordinary movie or a dismembered television program. It is a movie! M-O-V-I-E! It was designed for a movie theatre, with a full audience in attendance. If it is projected in a theatre it'll tear the guts right out of the audience and spill them in the aisles. But it can't do that on television, chopped up with deodorant and sanitary pad commercials!

THE MAN: Exactly! (*The sharpness in THE MAN'S voice causes RICHARD to pause with another angry word on his lips.*) Do you think you're lecturing to a roomful of students? This series has been in the works for a long time. Studies have been made of every angle. On Leo's faith in your ability I took a chance, and it has paid off. Not only do I have a pilot film for The Mammoth Hour on television, I have a new star in Chet Wilson. Wilson alone will repay the studio many times over for my fiscal investment in the years to come. You had better wake up, Hudson. I'm in this chair to make money for Mammoth Studios, and for no other reason. Your piddling little one-hour movie would scare moviegoers to death in a movie theatre. It *has* to be broken up to destroy the realism! But there will be enough realism left for an artistic triumph. These are the facts. The simple facts.

LEO: Don't you think you're being a little unreasonable, Richard?

RICHARD: Not you, Pop? I can understand this stupid son of a bitch. He's only concerned with making money, but you, Leo . . . You!

LEO: You're only thinking about yourself. Try and understand my side. This is my opportunity. After your show there will be twelve more, and I'll have complete control over the stories, casting and direction. Don't you realize the wonderful things we'll be able to do together?

THE MAN: (*Slams his fist down hard on his desk.*) That's enough, Mr Steinberg! You're excused, Hudson!

RICHARD: (*Angrily.*) What do you mean, excused? I own a third of this movie and Leo owns another. Where does that leave you?

THE MAN: With two-thirds.

RICHARD: (*Turning to Leo.*) Is that true?

LEO (*With an elaborate shrug.*) It was part of the deal. In return for my rights I was given a seven-year contract and the new series. In my place, you would have done the same.

RICHARD: (*Quietly.*) I'll never sink low enough to be in your place. (*RICHARD throws his glass of ice and whiskey against the white wall of the office, and runs toward the door as THE CURTAIN FALLS.*)

One bright summer's day when I was fourteen years of age I pedaled my bicycle to Bimini Baths for a swim. This was long before the Palomar burned down, and Bimini was a block or so down from the dance hall right off Vermont Avenue. Bimini boasted of four separate swimming pools, three with hot water of different temperatures and one outside pool of cold water. I liked to go to Bimini in the summertime, all by myself, and plunge from very hot to slightly cooler than that, to the lukewarm, and then to the cold. It was a good way to kill a summer's day.

Leaping recklessly into the inside, lukewarm pool I

splashed water on a swimmer who turned out to be a girl named Frances – I never learned her last name.

'You rat,' she announced with a smile, rubbing water from her eyes.

'I'm sorry,' I said mockingly. 'How did I splash you – like this?' And I splashed more water into the girl's face. She splashed back, and for the next hour and a half we had a good time playing in the water. Racing each other, holding our breaths underwater, and diving from the three-foot springboard. When it came to diving I really showed off for my newly found girl friend by performing a half-gainer with a full twist, a dive I had never been able to do before.

We moved outside to the cold water pool, and after a couple of turns in icy water we stretched out on the tiles and sunned and smoked. Frances was a good-looking female with a small, almost delicate figure, short shapely legs, and a pretty – I hate to use the term – elfin face. Her eyebrows had been plucked away, the painted eyebrows washed away by the water, and her underarms had been depilated. A snug, white rubber swimming cap completely covered her hair. I was inquisitive.

'I've been trying to figure out what color your hair is,' I said, bending over her face.

Frances smiled, and looked at me boldly with frank blue eyes. She was lying flat on her back, and I was on my side in a half-reclining, half-sitting position.

'Where?' she said lazily.

At fourteen, I certainly knew 'dirty talk' when I heard it. I blushed, and blushing made me angry with myself. I thought Frances to be fourteen or fifteen, and no boy likes a girl to take the initiative at that age. At the same time I was excited by her offhand comment. Who could tell? Maybe this could lead to something? Boy-like, I tossed Frances into the pool because I couldn't think of a snappy comeback.

When we had had enough swimming and left the pool for our respective dressing rooms, I had a date to meet Frances outside for a hamburger and a Coke.

It didn't take me long to dress; I was barefooted, I didn't wear underwear in the summertime, and my outer garments consisted of yellow, bell-bottomed corduroy trousers and a well-worn T-shirt. At fourteen I was a husky kid, bronzed by the California sun, and tight black curls fell down beautifully over my forehead. A black fuzzy growth had sprouted on my chin, and I shaved once a week whether I needed it or not.

All in all, with my pants leg rolled up to my knee to avoid the bicycle sprocket, and with a fairly new bicycle, I pictured myself as a quite romantic figure, and a damned good catch for Frances. When Frances came out of the dressing room I planned to ride her on the handlebars up the street to the White Cabin where Cokes and hamburgers were only five cents apiece. One advantage to the Depression; if you had a quarter in your pocket it would buy something; and this was California before sales tax, and I had a quarter . . .

Frances appeared under the archway and the little bubbles in my head disintegrated. Frances wasn't a teenage girl; she was a woman of twenty-one or -two, dressed to kill in silk stockings, high heels, a tailored knee-length suit, and a tiny pink hat with a veil. Her eyebrows were now thickly pencilled arching curves of solid black, and her lips were painted with tantalizing Tangee. For a long horrible moment we stared at each other, our minds refusing to believe what our eyes perceived. Her chin dropped and so did mine.

What Frances expected me to be I do not know. Maybe she had figured me for a young man about town with a low-slung convertible, I do not know. I only knew that I was shocked into a dead silence by the appearance of this adult when I had been expecting a teenage girl!

Now that I am older I realize that Frances carried the situation off very well indeed. She let me down as gently as possible. She excused herself sweetly, stating it was much later than she had thought, and that she had to run. Maybe I would accept a rain check on our date – for another time perhaps.

I nodded dumbly and Frances tripped away toward the bus stop on her high heels, leaving me standing there, a barefooted young boy with too much cheek and a bicycle.

OK. I learned something. In one terrible moment I realized that I had reached a point of no return. In a pair of swimming trunks I was a man in the eyes of a woman. From that moment my childhood was over. I began to dress the part, act the part, and I moved into the adult world with its adult bedrooms.

But when I fled blindly from the office of THE MAN, almost in tears, I knew that I was still a child in an adult world, although I was thirty-one, and not fourteen. I had acted my part well. I had fooled Leo and I had fooled myself, but THE MAN and Leo Steinberg were adults, something I would never be. I didn't want to be an adult – I didn't want to lose my dream. Reality stinks. The dream is better; it makes the living worthwhile.

I can put it another way.

People like THE MAN and Leo Steinberg feed on men like me. They borrow our dreams for their own ends because they are too grown-up to have any dreams of their own. Like getting rid of a moth . . .

A moth will follow light. By turning out all of the lights in a house and by switching on a new one closer to the door each time as you switch off the light behind, you can lead a moth right out the front door. As the moth flaps out the front door to the porch light you slam the door behind it and the moth is outside. When the porch light is switched off the moth is out in the cold and cannot understand what happened to all of the pretty lights.

This is what THE MAN and Leo had done to me. As each door opened, I went through it blindly, following my dream. And now I was outside, a child in an adult world. They had my dream, and I had nothing.

The realization that I was as much a Feeb as any used-car buyer I had ever dealt with did nothing for my morale. I had been taken just like any clown who believes in the basic goodness of his fellow men. In my childlike thoughts I had built Leo into some kind of a tin god. To suddenly discover that he was merely another opportunist nauseated me.

It did not make me feel any better to confirm again what I already knew about people. Such knowledge had been confirmed too many times. Too many times.

I was out and there was no way to compromise. If I had only known – I mean, if my story had been planned from the beginning as a one-hour television show, there would have been a different ending; a different story. I could have written the story in three acts, with a logical cliffhanging suspense motif built into the end of the first two acts. Although the overly long commercials would still have affected the continuity, there could have been enough interest generated to keep itchy fingers away from the dial until the next act. I would have seen to that.

But the way my movie was in its completed form it was a runaway express train that couldn't allow for any stops or side trips. How utterly stupid of THE MAN not to see this!

Liquor helps. There may be some who will disagree. Let them. I know. Liquor helps. I had a drink at the first bar I came to after I left the studios. I drank my way through the long hot afternoon, sitting in a booth in the dark interior of a quiet saloon on Normandie. I didn't slug it down; that would have made me sick. I drank methodically, holding the Scotch for a long time in my mouth before swallowing, and gradually the pain in my heart began to disappear. My lips had a pleasant numbness and I raised my voice when I talked to the bartender. When I raised my voice I could hear better.

Night fell. I changed bars and picked up a female companion; an aged blonde old enough to be my mother. She had two front teeth missing and I was fascinated by her smile.

'Smile for me, baby,' I kept telling her, and she would scream with shrill, shrieking peals of laughter. O, it was great fun.

Somewhere along the way we picked up a Chief Petty Officer, US Navy. He and the blonde got along very well together and he wanted her for his very own. In an elaborate ceremony I sold her to him for fifty cents and four safety matches. It was all very funny. The woman shrieked with laughter, gasping for breath. The couple disappeared into the night. In an alley, I was very sick. Walking slowly for eight blocks in the cool night air cleared my head. I found my way back, on foot, to the dragon's mouth entrance of the Hong Kong Club. The bartender refused to sell me another drink. On general principles I put up a mild protest, but I didn't really want another drink. The only reason I had returned was because a parking stub in my pocket indicated that my car was parked in the Hong Kong Club's lot.

'You come back tomorrow, Mr Hudson,' the bartender humored me, 'and I'll sell you all you want. But I think you've had enough for one night.'

'All right.' I handed him my parking stub. 'Get somebody to drive me home then. If I'm too drunk to drink, I'm too drunk to drive.'

Smiling, the bartender nodded approvingly, and had one of the busboys drive me home to The House of Lumpy Grits. I gave the busboy a five-dollar bill for cab fare back to the Hong Kong Club, and climbed the stairs to my apartment.

Five minutes under a cold shower cleared my head. Without dressing I stood shivering in my tiny kitchen and downed three cups of instant coffee. Several layers of drunkenness had been peeled away. I felt mildly exhilarated, light, strong – and angry. In a sudden brilliant decision I made up my mind to punch Leo in the nose. The plans for my movie wouldn't be altered, but I would feel better.

I dressed with extreme care. Leo was, after all was said and done, a genius, and if he was to be punched in the nose it should be done respectfully and correctly. I slipped into a base of nylon underwear, black silk socks, garters, and inserted my big feet into patent leather pumps with black silk bows. This was the first time I had ever had the nerve to wear the patent leather dancing pumps. I had to paw through my shirts for ten minutes before I could find the white dress shirt with ruffles. Thirty dollars' worth of shirt, and I had never worn it. My fingers coped bravely with my onyx studs, and I managed them all right, but I couldn't tie the black bow tie. I settled for a black clip-on tie instead. I hoped that Leo would not notice this discourtesy. Fully dressed in my black mohair tuxedo, with my sunglasses on my nose, hiding my red-rimmed eyes, I surveyed myself in the full-length mirror. Very handsome. And I could stand perfectly straight without wavering, well, hardly wavering. I tried my voice for sound.

'Now is the time for all good men to come to the aid of their party,' I said to my reflection in the mirror.

'Righto, Mr Hudson,' I replied thickly.

There were some bad moments stumbling across the tangled growth of back garden before I reached the back door of the house and let myself in with my key. The house was dark and I flipped on lights in every room I passed through as I made my way to Leo's study. His study was dark, and I pressed the wall switch. It semed strange not to find Leo at his desk, but he wasn't there. But on the wall, mocking me, in blacks and reds, translucent whites and yellows, was Roualt's *clown*, Leo's clown, staring down at me with sad, sad eyes.

'He couldn't wait!' I thought. 'He couldn't wait to get his damned clown back! He couldn't wait to get back his artistic symbol!'

I hated the painting. Leo had bought the painting back to prove his mastery over me and THE MAN. No other reason. And I had nothing. Nothing! Without thinking any more about it I snatched a bronze letter-opener from the desk and slashed the clown across his heart. I slashed the painting diagonally from top to bottom. I slashed the other diagonal and the canvas shredded into tatters; chunks of flaky paint fluttered to the floor. I tore the mount from the wall and banged it on the desk. The heavy frame wouldn't break, but the canvas was ruined forever. I dropped the frame to the floor, Leo's foul soul, and left the house.

Thinking of nothing, I sat in the front seat of my car, bent over the steering wheel, attempting to make my mind a complete blank. I couldn't do it. Drooping gloops of Duco-red anger drooled past my eyes. I started the car, I drove directly to Mammoth Studios; I did not pass Go, and I didn't collect two hundred dollars. But I was going to win the Monopoly game my own way.

The night man at the gate didn't know me, but he let me in when I showed him my studio pass.

I parked in my reserved space in front of the bungalow office and carefully locked my car, reflecting that on the morrow another director would probably have the reserved space, the small office. When I inserted my key in the lock on the office door, the inside light switched on. I entered. Standing in the center of the room, Laura Harmon

153

waited for me. Evidently she had been asleep on the leather couch. There were deep creases on her left cheek. Her eyelids were swollen and I could see the pink membrane of her eyelids all of the way around her large red-veined eyes. Her thick hair was twisted and tangled. She wore no makeup, except for a trace of slightly smeared lipstick. Mrs Witch, meet The Devil.

'What are you doing in my office?' I asked coldly.

'I wanted to see you, Richard—'

'OK. You've seen me. Now get out.'

'Not until I've talked to you!' she said defiantly, holding her back stiff and thrusting out her great breasts. I shrugged indifferently.

'Go ahead and talk then.' I went directly to the file cabinet, and throughout her little speech I pulled out all of the mimeographed copies of *The Man Who Got Away* scripts and piled them on the desk. The scripts would make an excellent fire, I decided.

'I'm going to talk and you're going to listen,' Laura said, much in the manner of Bette Davis. 'You've managed to keep away from me and avoid every decent effort I've made to talk to you. But this time you're going to listen to me!'

'I'm listening,' I said flippantly. 'Talk fast, I'm leaving in a minute.'

'You aren't going anywhere!' Laura's voice was almost hysterical with anger. 'I'm pregnant!'

'Yeah. Go on,' I said. Emptying a large wastebasket onto the floor, I stacked scripts inside it as neatly as possible.

'You have to marry me, Richard!'

'No,' I informed her.

'I've been going crazy. I couldn't see you, I couldn't get you on the telephone. I even wrote you a letter—'

'We get a lot of crank letters at the studio. You ought to know that, working in the typing pool.'

'It's true, Richard! You don't seem to understand. I'm

154

going to have a baby . . . *our* baby, Richard!'

'Yours, you mean.' I laughed. 'Look, Laura, it's nice to talk to you and all that, but I have to go now—'

'You have to do something, Richard! If you won't marry me, maybe you can . . . I don't know what to do. I've been going crazy ever since I found out. I don't know where to turn.'

'If you don't want it, get rid of it.'

'That takes money, Richard, a great deal of money, and I don't know where to go, who to see. You've got to help me, Richard!' She began to cry.

'All right.'

The timing was terrible on Laura's part. At another time, another place, I would have handled the situation quite differently; given her a check, or I might have sent her to a doctor I know in Stockton. If she had wanted to keep the baby, I would have paid the bills, and maybe I would have set up a little monthly allowance for child support. I don't know exactly how I would have handled it. But this way . . . she picked a bad time.

As I straightened up, I brought my fist up hard. My fist caught Laura squarely in the soft part of her rounded belly and sank in wrist deep. Her breath whooshed audibly as it left her lungs. She bent over forward, almost falling, took two short backward steps and then sat down hard upon the floor. I lifted her to the couch, straightened her legs. Laura clutched her stomach with both hands and slowly began to breathe again. Tears of pain and anger flowed down her swollen cheeks.

'Breathing OK now?' I asked. Laura nodded her chin tremulously. 'You'll be all right now, kid. That ought to do it for you. There'll be a couple of bad days, I suppose, but they can't be helped. The next time you get layed, you'd better use some kind of precautions. I may not be around to help you.'

155

Shouldering the wastebasket full of scenarios I left the office. I stopped by Sound Stage F on my way to the film library to pick up a gallon of inflammable paint thinner. The film library, a small one-story building, was securely locked with a hasp and a Yale lock. I left the thinner and wastebasket by the door and returned to Stage F for a crowbar. Two or three minutes later I had the hasp pried off and the door open. Inside, I scattered the scripts in a messy pile by the librarian's desk. I tore open a few cans of film and let the film uncoil on top of the paper. Somewhere in this library, in four cans, my movie was filed away, but it would take too long to find it. It was much easier to burn the entire library.

Pouring liberal portions of thinner over the pile of paper and film, I made a trail of thinner to the doorway, tossed the empty can back into the room. Flipping my Zippo I attempted to light the trail of liquid thinner, but I couldn't get it going. I lighted the pile of paper without any trouble. The flames licked at the legs of the librarian's desk, the film smouldered and gave off a foul, acrid odor. Closing the door on the flames I returned to my office.

Laura was still in the same position on the couch, flat on her back, clutching her stomach, her eyes fixed on the ceiling.

'Do you want me to drive you home, Laura? Or do you want to stay here?'

'Don't touch me!'

'I wouldn't touch you for anything,' I laughed. 'I offered you a ride home. Do you want to go or not?'

'I don't want anything from you!' Laura said huskily. 'You're going to burn in Hell, Richard Hudson!'

'Then I'll be seeing you. Does the overhead light bother you? The studio has a campaign, you know, to save on electricity.'

Laura turned her head away from me toward the wall.

I switched off the light, closed the door gently, and got into my car. The fire would have anywhere from two to four hours, I thought, before it was discovered. And by that time, help would be too late.

As I drove out the gate I bade a cheery good night to the gatekeeper. Poor bastard. I doubt very much if he made more than a dollar an hour on his rotten job. Like most corporations and the US Government, Mammoth Studios was penny-wise and dollar foolish.

A few, just a few, well-paids guards would have saved Mammoth Studios a great amount of money . . .

WIPE

A telephone was ringing. A jangling, irritating, persistent, intermittent ringing that would not stop. I tried to ignore it by pulling the pillow over my head, but the noise came through the pillow, piercing my inner ears with sharp copper sounds. I opened my eyes, and tossed the pillow to one side. The telephone was a foot away from my head on the bedside stand.

'Good morning, Mr Hudson,' a female voice said cheerfully, as I picked up the receiver, 'it's eight o'clock.'

'I believe you.' I racked the receiver.

The roaring, crackling pains behind my forehead were at full volume. The back of my neck ached, and the tattoo needles behind my eyes were torturing me. Quite a normal hangover. I would have been disappointed without it.

There was a gasping snorting snore, followed by a creak of springs as the body beside me turned sideways. I groaned inwardly, but I didn't turn and look because I knew who it was. Unfortunately, I never blank out completely, no matter how much I drink. We were in a double room at the Biltmore, and I lay facing the polished mahogany dresser. The snoring woman's dark-blue uniform was draped neatly over a red-and-white candy-striped chair. Her navy-blue bonnet, with the streaming ribbons on it, and her battered tambourine were both on top of the dresser. But I didn't need the sight of this confirming evidence. It had been a hard-fought campaign against this seasoned soul saver, but I remembered winning the battle even though I had lost the war. In addition to my sick headache I now had an accompanying feeling of revulsion as I remembered the events of my busy night.

After leaving the studio I had driven into downtown LA and checked into the Biltmore, pausing only once on the drive to buy a bottle of Scotch in order to have some luggage.

My solitary company was terrible. Unable to drink alone I left the hotel and headed for one of the Hill Street bars on the other side of Pershing Square. By accident I happened to select a fairy hangout, but that didn't bother me. It wasn't that I wanted contact companionship, male, female, or in between; I just wanted to be near people instead of being alone. Never before had I felt so alone. I took an entire booth to myself, but no one bothered me. I was still wearing my tailored dinner jacket, and if my outward expression was as grim as my inner thoughts, I must have presented an unapproachably forbidding appearance. Except for a few surreptitious glances in my direction when I first entered, the gay ones avoided my eyes following the negative appraisal.

Two very young, importuning private soldiers sitting at the bar looked at me wonderingly for a moment, put their close-cropped heads together for a consultation, but they didn't join me either. I was mildly disappointed by their abrupt departure. My mood was meanness, and I had hoped, in a way, that they would come over to my booth with a proposition. I would have had an excuse to bang their shaven heads together, and I sorely needed something

158

to do; if not action, at least movement. Movement is always preferable to inaction.

A pale young man with overly long blond hair, wearing a flowered vest beneath a pink sport coat, joined the colored piano player on the tiny elevated stage at the far end of the bar. His voice was sweet and high, a contratenor (although he probably considered himself an alto), and he sang into the microphone. 'My Buddy'. The song, as it came over the cagily placed PA system speakers, drifting pure and incredibly high through the sentimentally silenced room, reminded me of *my* good old buddy – good old backstabbing Leo Steinberg. I signaled the waiter, ordered another drink, and gave him five dollars for the singer.

'Tell the boy to sing it again.'

'Yes, sir. It's a very popular song here.'

Listening to the song again in connection with Leo gave me a sardonic, bittersweet feeling of satisfaction. Perhaps, I thought, he would enjoy a recording of this buddy song as an artistic replacement for his damned Rouault . . . and at this moment the woman with the tambourine intruded upon my vengeful thoughts by shoving it in front of my face.

She was a woman in her late forties, short and hefty, plain-faced, freckled, and her well-tailored blue uniform was freshly pressed and immaculate. Her heavy eyebrows were solidly gray, and two strands of dark gray hair, one one each side of her high white forehead, were barely visible beneath her blue bonnet. There was a kindly, unfeigned smile on her bowed, unpainted lips. A blunt, nastily worded refusal or a graciously given donation were one and the same to this woman, I felt. From her manner, and she didn't say a word because her smile begged for her, I assumed that she would take either yes or no for an answer with true humility.

There was a one-dollar bill and some change on the table. I dropped the uncounted sum into her tambourine.

159

'Thank you, sir. And God bless you.' Her voice was deep and husky. It took many years of singing and sin-shouting on street corners to develop a voice so deep and strong.

'Just a minute, Captain,' I said.

'Yes, sir?'

'I want to give you some more money. But you'll have to wait until the waiter gets me some change.'

I beckoned to the waiter, handed him a twenty, and asked for one-dollar bills.

'Don't stand there, Captain,' I said smilingly. 'I can't get up in this booth for you, and besides, your feet hurt—'

'I don't think I'd better sit down.' She hesitated for a brief moment, and then sat down across from me with a deep sigh. 'My feet *are* tired, and for just a minute—' Her voice trailed away in a husky whisper.

'How long have you been doing this?' I asked politely.

'Almost twenty-five years now. But my husband had more than thirty years of service before he died.'

This remark appeared to be innocent enough on the surface, but I was suspicious; and although I could see how unreasonable my suspicions were I couldn't help having them. Why should she tell me indirectly that she was a widow? She had given me this unasked for information almost automatically, when I had merely asked an indifferent question to have someone to talk to for a couple of minutes. Why hadn't I ever suspected Leo, the way I suspected this poor, innocent woman for no reason at all? And then I had to know; I had to know if this woman had her price, just like everybody else in the world I had ever known. Like Leo, the one man in the world I had respected for incorruptible integrity! I had to make the test, and then I would truly know, once and for all. And if it were true I could learn – somehow – to live with it, to adjust to it for the remainder of my life. The nasty mood that I was in, in combination with the liquor I had put away that day, influenced my evil decision, but it certainly wasn't a valid excuse . . .

The waiter returned, and I gave him one of the bills as a tip.

'Would you like a cold drink, Captain?' I suggested.

'Oh, no! But thanks—'

'Bring the officer a Coke, and another one of these for me.'

Flustered, she started to slide out of the booth, but I stopped her by quickly dropping another bill into the tambourine. 'I've got a deal for you. You don't collect more than a dollar every five minutes as you make your rounds, do you?'

'No, sir. Not nearly that much.'

'All right, then. Keep your seat and be company for a while. And every five minutes I'll add another dollar to your collection.' I smiled, my boyishly winning smile.

'I shouldn't—'

'You're collecting for a worthy cause, aren't you?'

'Yes, sir, but it isn't that, Mr—'

'Hudson. You may call me Mr Hudson, but I'd rather you didn't tell me your name.'

'We aren't supposed to—' I dropped another dollar in the tambourine. 'I could get into trouble, sitting down in a bar this way, Mr Hudson, but I can stay for a few minutes, I guess.' She smiled. 'And my feet *do* hurt me.'

'Of course they do,' I said soothingly.

Now that I had a project in mind I nursed my drinks, spacing them to keep a sharp edge, but without drinking too much to dull it. I drew the woman out, encouraging her to talk about herself and her work, adding bills to the growing pile at untimed intervals. She had no children; she had spent five years in London, two in Hong Kong; and of all the places she had been stationed she liked Los Angeles best – because of the climate and all. And she hoped they would never send her back to Chicago again, even though that was her home town . . .

When the singles had all been transferred from my hand to her tambourine, she walked back to the hotel with me. I had more money in my room, I told her, and she came willingly enough when I promised to give her another twenty dollars.

There weren't many people in the lobby at this time of the night, but the few who were there didn't give us a curious glance. In Los Angeles the unusual is commonplace; not even the sight of a huge man wearing a dinner jacket, accompanied by a short woman in a Salvation Army uniform could raise a single eyebrow.

Once we were inside my room, she began to show a few signs of nervousness, but despite her obvious jumpiness I could perceive that she intended to remain until I gave her the promised money. I poured two stiff drinks in toothbrush glasses, and held one out to her.

'No thanks, Mr Hudson.' She shook her head, gnawed worriedly at her lower lip.

'You've had a drink before, haven't you?'

'Of course – it isn't that, Mr Hudson. After all, I'm forty-seven years old—'

'Then have one with me, one for the road,' I held out the glass again. 'I'll consider you rude and impolite if you don't join me. And I won't give you the other twenty until you do.'

'Good night, then, Mr Hudson.' Her plain face flushed, and she started for the door, but at the door she turned. 'But I want to thank you for the money you have already given me. Thank you very much.'

'That's quite all right, Captain,' I said coldly, narrowing my eyes. 'Good night'

She fumbled with the chain lock for fully twenty seconds before she turned around again.

'Would you mind,' she said timidly, examining the unpatterned pink carpet, and avoiding my eyes, 'putting a little water in mine, Mr Hudson?'

'Of course.' I grinned, but I didn't laugh. 'If that's the way you like it.'

After two more drinks apiece my patience was wearing thin and I propositioned her. After a summer stock exhibition of righteous indignation, we had an unduly prolonged bargaining session; and she settled for $150 in cash. The smallness of the sum was the only part about the acceptance that surprised me; I had no feelings of triumph, I would have gone higher, much higher. I had more than $400 in my wallet, and I could have had a check cashed for more money at the desk if I had needed it.

Her inhibitions left her one by one as she removed the various pieces of her uniform. Her body didn't go with her middle-aged face and long gray hair. Her plumpness was not that of a mature woman; it was more like that of a young fourteen-year-old girl who loves mashed potatoes and has never lost her baby fat. This illusion was heightened by the scattering of rusty freckles on her white shoulders, and the clean milky whiteness of her skin.

I undressed and sat down on the edge of the bed to kick off my pumps. My head reeled, but I watched Louise – she wanted me to call her by this name – pour two more drinks and add water to them, as she stood by the dresser. As she quacked away, loquacious with excitement and the unaccustomed liquor, she now reminded me of a tame white duck that was trying to tell me something, but I couldn't follow the gist of the monologue. And then we were both sitting side by side on the bed, the bottle on the floor between us. Her voice was a steady trade wind from the East; a muddy trickle of water that eventually turns into the Mississippi River if it runs long enough, and it began to sink into my consciousness that she was telling me the story of her life. Except that she was confessing to me – all of the little things she had done, the bad things; the sins of pride, of disliking someone and being unable to overcome it – and her monotonous, husky voice droned on and on. She had been bad with the innocent naughtiness of a four-year-old child who snooped through a mother's purse when the mother wasn't looking. All at once I knew I couldn't go through with it. Making love to Louise would be the same thing as owning a sports car. The analogy was a good one – I had once owned an MG in San Francisco. I had enjoyed driving it while I was driving, but I was always a little ashamed of having such a small car.

Unwilling, mentally and physically, to possess this little woman, now that I had proven a needlessly proven point, I kept refilling her glass instead to keep her talking. Half asleep I tried to smoke, and the cigarette would drop from my numb fingers to the carpet, but I outlasted her somehow.

'I'm sleepy,' she said in midsentence, and she fell backwards, snoring before her head reached the mattress. I had tugged her into a more comfortable position, and before going to sleep myself I had had enough presence of mind to call the desk and leave an eight o'clock call.

And now, using raw courage, I swung my feet to the floor. Louise was another stone added to my guilty load. The recollection that I hadn't made love to her physically was no consolation to me; it is the intent that counts. I was as guilty as a burglar captured inside a store before he has filled his bag – and with this good woman I didn't even have the excuse of telling myself that if it wasn't me it would have been someone else.

I groaned with pain. Inadvertently, I had shaken my head remorsefully, and it almost fell off. With my eyes barely opened and squinting against the brilliant sunlight streaming in through the window, I made my way into the bathroom, shoved an index finger down my throat, and tickled. After the deluge I washed my face in cold water, gasping for breath, my burning eyes starting from their sockets. I got under the needle shower of icy water. For fifteen minutes I alternated from water as hot as I could stand it to water as cold as it would get. Massaging the back of my neck under the hot water the pain in my head gradually left. I knew that as long as I stayed under the shower I would feel all right, but the moment I left it the pain would return. To think is difficult when standing beneath a hot waterfall, and it is doubly hard to think with a hangover. I switched abruptly to cold, stuck it out as long as I could, turned off the tap and briskly toweled myself. Shivering and cursing I struggled into my clothes.

My headache returned full force. To pull on my clammy socks was disgusting, but I was dressed again. As I combed my hair I looked closely at my face in the mirror above the dresser. Not the face of a failure, surely. Some dark stubble on the meaty chin, and red-rimmed eyes, but it wasn't a beaten face. I had plenty of fight left in me.

My military companion of the night slept on. Her mouth was open, and her long, tangled gray hair straggled out on the pillow. Uncovered, flat on her back, with her short fat legs spread apart, she didn't look as attractive as I had remembered. For a moment, but only for a moment, I thought about picking up the money I had paid her for an unrendered service. Trustingly, the innocent woman had left all of the bills in her tambourine. But it was only money, and I had enough reasons for feeling sorry for myself without adding another one to my back. But no man can afford the luxury of self-pity – not when he has work to do!

I left the room, feeling conspicuous in my tux, and waited in the corridor for the elevator.

'Straight down to the barber shop,' I ordered. The elevator operator accepted two crumpled one-dollar bills and dropped directly to the basement, bypassing five floors.

I was shaved, enjoyed three hot towels, but skipped the massage I really wanted. My head wasn't in any shape for rough handling. After I turned in my key at the desk and paid my bill, I waited outside for my car to be brought around. I tipped the boy who brought my car a dollar, circled Pershing Square, and headed for Crenshaw Boulevard and my used-car lot. The movies were not for me, Richard Hudson. My kind of artistry was salesmanship, the selling of used cars. Somehow I had gotten reality mixed up with a dream, a bad dream. Now that the dream was all over I had to get back to work, sell cars, and as many of them as possible so I could get even again, get Honest Hal even again. Old Hal would be mighty sad about the loss of forty thousand bucks! I laughed at a sudden thought. The film library was insured and I'd get every cent of my money back!

All I had lost in the struggle was the integrity of my self-expression. And what did that mean? Words. I could express myself much better as a salesman.

I turned into the alley behind the lot and parked beside the small maintenance shed where Graphite Sam kept his paint and tools. After locking the car I climbed over the chain and walked between the rows of cars toward the stucco office. The two salesmen were standing outside the office flipping quarters. One was wearing the red jacket to his costume, but not the beard. The other salesman wore the tasseled red cap, the red pants and boots, but sported a blue plaid sport shirt instead of the Santa Claus jacket He, too, was minus the white beard.

'Bill,' I screamed angrily. 'Come out here!'

The screen door flew open and Bill came running out of the office, a worried expression on his round face.

When he saw me, he smiled. I wiped the smile off in a hurry with my first question.

'Are these men supposed to be salesmen?'

'Sure, Richard. They're working for us.'

'Not any more. Tell them to turn in their suits and head for the showers. Pay 'em off!'

I brushed by Bill and entered the office. The walls were covered with several charts and graphs prepared by Bill during my absence. There was a chart on fuel and oil consumption, a chart on employee relationships, a bar graph and legend concerning the number of cars bought and sold, and many others. I studied the sales chart closely. Bill Harris had learned how to make charts and graphs while he was in the Army, I supposed. With nothing else to do, the peacetime army attends management schools and the soldiers work like hell keeping up charts instead of doing any real work. Eyewash. All of it. When Bill re-entered the office with the two Santa Claus costumes draped over his arm, I was boiling with anger.

'Did you pay them off?'

'They didn't have any dough coming.'

'I thought as much. Where's the typist?'

'I had to let her go, Richard. There wasn't enough doing to keep her busy.'

'I see. What have you been doing? How many cars have you sold this morning?'

'Well, none. Yet.'

'How many yesterday?'

'Two.'

'The day before?'

'Two.'

'I've been looking at your charts. You haven't done a goddamned thing all the time I was gone.'

'I've tried, Richard,' Bill said earnestly. 'Really tried. But everything seems to go wrong. I can't seem to find

167

any decent salesmen and the ads don't seem to pull anybody in any more. I've wanted to call you several times, but you said not to bother you, and—'

'Never mind. You're fired. Get out.'

'You mean I'm fired? Just like that?'

'That's right. Get off my lot.'

'OK.' Bill's set secret smile returned. 'I guess the only difference between the Army and civilian life is that in the Army you take any job they give you, and in civilian life you take any job you can get.'

'I don't want to listen to any of your cheap enlisted-man philosophy either,' I said angrily. 'Just get out!'

'There's one advantage to civilian life – I don't have to take any crap!'

The slight movement of Bill's right shoulder telegraphed his punch, and I caught him in the crotch with my knee by moving in fast. Bill doubled over and screamed sharply. Picking up the marble base of the pen holder on the desk, I shook the two pens loose, and hit Bill squarely between the eyes as he started to unwind from his crouched position. Blood spurted brightly from his slashed forehead and nose. I dropped the pen holder to the floor, spun Bill around with one movement and threw him through the screen door. He landed sprawling on the gravel of the lot. I leaned in the doorway, breathing heavily from the sudden exertion, looking down at him.

'Get off my lot,' I said through my teeth.

Bill got slowly to his feet straightened to a half-crouch, and took about ten steps away from the office, clutching his groin with both hands. His smile was a painful grimace.

'There are other ways, Mr Hudson,' he said bravely. 'I still happen to have Hal Parker's telephone number. He might be interested in a little transaction of forty thousand dollars!'

I started for Bill with my fists doubled, but he hobbled swiftly away from me to the curb and climbed into his parked car. When he rolled up the windows and locked the doors from inside I was forced to laugh. He put his head over the steering wheel and remained that way for several minutes. Until he drove away I watched him from the doorway, and then I re-entered the office. I felt sorry for Bill Harris, and yet I was happy for him, in a way. He had discovered that loyalty was not enough. Loyalty may be fine for the Army, but it has no place in the outside world. Bill would have a few bad nights after he called Honest Hal, but eventually his guilty feeling would disappear and he would become a responsible citizen. Responsible to himself, the way all of us are. I didn't worry about his telephone call to San Francisco; I knew how to handle Honest Hal . . .

Stripping off my tuxedo I changed into a Santa Claus costume. I adjusted the cotton beard under my chin, donned the red cap with its white tassle and settled my sunglasses over my nose. A Santa Claus outfit is not becoming, but it is a much better costume for selling used cars than a tuxedo. I picked up a cowbell from the small table beneath the window and sallied forth into the world of my used-car lot, swinging the bell merrily back and forth. I resolved to sell the first person who stepped on my lot an automobile whether I lost money or not. In my mind I set a goal of ten cars for the day . . .

And then I heard the siren.

I didn't have to be told that the siren was for me. I knew it. Instinctively. I didn't attempt to run away. Instead I felt a welcome sense of relief combined with a feeling of dark depression and failure. I walked to the curb and waited. Unwilling tears rolled down my cheeks and were quickly absorbed by the white cotton beard.

The police car stopped, and the policeman sitting next to the driver got out of the sedan and held the door open for me without a word. Leo Steinberg and Laura Harmon were in the back seat of the car. Leo refused to look at me, but Laura stared at me defiantly, her lips set in a tight, grim line. Twice I rang the cowbell.

'God rest you merry gentlemen!' I exclaimed. 'Ho, ho, ho,' I laughed, deep in my chest. Then I climbed into the front seat of the police car.

MUSIC: SNEAK IN LONG SHOT – FINAL TAKE

The police car sounds its siren again. As the volume of the siren increases the north and south bound automobiles pull over reluctantly to their respective curbs and stop. The black-and-white police car, containing two uniformed policemen, Leo Steinberg, Laura Harmon, and Richard Hudson, leaves the curb, makes an illegal U-turn and heads south. The volume of the siren decreases gradually as the police car disappears from view. Slowly, the heavy traffic begins to flow again on Crenshaw Boulevard, 873 cars one way every fifteen minutes; 927 the other way every fifteen minutes, toward Hollywood.

SUPERIMPOSE: 'The End'
MUSIC: UP FULL FOR CREDITS

Written, Produced, and Directed

By

RICHARD HUDSON

BOOK TWO

Cockfighter

What matters is not the idea a man holds,
but the depth at which he holds it.

Ezra Pound

For Mary Jo

Chapter One

First, I closed the windows and bolted the flimsy aluminium door. Then I flicked on the overhead light and snapped the Venetian blinds shut. Without the cross ventilation, it was stifling inside the trailer. Outside, in the Florida sunlight, the temperature was in the high eighties, but inside, now that the door and the windows were locked, it must have been a hundred degrees. I wiped the sweat away from my streaming face and neck with a dishcloth, dried my hands, and tossed the cloth on the floor. After moving Sandspur's traveling coop onto the couch, I checked the items on the table one more time.

Leather thong. Cotton. Razor blade. Bowl of lukewarm soapy water. Pan of rubbing alcohol. Liquid lead ballpoint pencil. Sponge. All in order.

I lifted the lid of the coop, brought Sandspur out with both hands, turned the cock's head away from me, and then held him firmly with my left hand under his breast. I looped the noose of leather over his dangling yellow feet, slipped it tight above his sawed-off spur stumps, and made a couple of turns to hold it snug. Holding the chicken with both hands again, I lowered him between my legs and squeezed my knees together tight enough to hold him so he couldn't move his wings. Sandspur didn't like it. He hit back with both feet four times, making thumping sounds against the plastic couch, but he couldn't get away.

I pinched off a generous wad of cotton between my left thumb and forefinger and clamped my fingers over his lemon-yellow beak. There was just enough of a downward

175

curve to his short beak so he couldn't jerk his head out of my fingers. He couldn't possibly hurt himself, as long as the cotton didn't slip.

Impatient knuckles rapped on the door. Dody again. A vein throbbed in my temple. At that moment I would have given anything to be able to curse.

'How long you gonna be, Frank?' Dody's petulant voice shrilled through the door. 'I gotta go to the bathroom!'

I didn't answer. I couldn't. She rapped impatiently a couple of more times and then she went away. At least she didn't holler anymore.

My right hand was damp again, and I wiped my fingers on my jeans, still holding Sandspur's beak with my left thumb and forefinger. I picked up the razor blade and cut a fine hairline groove across his bill as high up as possible. This was ticklish work and I cut a trifle too deep on the right side. I dropped the razor blade back on the table and released the cock's head. I picked up the ballpoint lead pencil with my left hand and rubbed the point across my right fingertip until it was smeared with liquid lead. Pinching off more cotton with my left hand, I caught Sandspur's beak again and rubbed the almost invisible groove with my lead-smeared forefinger. I took my time, and Sandspur glared at me malevolently with his shiny yellow eyes.

As soon as I was satisfied, I unloosened the thong around his feet and put the bird on the table, washed his legs with lukewarm soapy water, and rubbed his breast and thighs. I repeated the rubdown with alcohol. I was particularly careful with his head and bill, only using cotton dipped in the pan of alcohol.

Finished, I returned the items to my gaff case and dumped the used soapy water and alcohol into the sink. Sandspur was a fine-looking cock, and after his light rubdown he felt in fine feather. Holding his head high he strutted back and forth on the slick Masonite table. He was a Whitehackle cross in peak condition, a five-time winner, a real money bird. I knew he would win this afternoon, but I also knew he *had* to win.

I stepped in close to the table, made a feinting pinch for his doctored beak and he tried to peck me. I examined his beak, and even under close scrutiny the bill looked cracked. The liquid lead inside the hairline made the manufactured crack look authentic even to my expert eyes. As a longtime professional cocker I knew the crack would fool Mr Ed Middleton, Jack Burke, and the accordion-necked fruit-tramp bettors. I picked Sandspur up and lowered him gently into his coop.

I opened the door, but Dody was nowhere in sight. She was probably visiting inside one of the other trailers in the camp. After sliding up all the windows again I lit a cigarette and sat down. What I had done to Sandspur's bill wasn't exactly illegal, but I didn't feel too proud about it. I only wanted to boost the betting odds and my slender roll.

Although I knew I couldn't possibly lose, I was apprehensive about the fight coming up. Everything I had, including my old Caddy and my Love-Lee-Mobile Home, was down on this single cockfight. And Sandspur was the only cock I had left. In my mind, I reviewed my impulsive bet. I had been a damned fool to bet the car and trailer.

At four that morning I had slid out of bed without waking Dody and switched on the light. Dody slept like a child, mainly because she was a child. The girl was only sixteen. I had picked her up in Homestead, Florida, three weeks before at a juke joint near the trailer camp where I had been staying. Her parents had their trailer in the Homestead camp, and Dody was only one out of their five children. It was a family of fruit tramps, and I doubt very much if they even missed her when I took her away with me. I wasn't the first man to sleep with Dody, not by any means. There had been dozens before me, but seeing her asleep and vulnerable that morning made me feel uneasy about our relationship. She was awfully damned young. At thirty-two, I was exactly twice as old as Dody.

It was too hot in Belle Glade to have even a sheet over you, and Dody lay on her back wearing a flimsy cotton shorty nightgown. She slept with her mouth open, her long taffy-coloured braids stretched out on the pillow. Her face was flushed with sleep, and she didn't look twelve years old, much less sixteen. Her body was fully mature, however, with large, melon-heavy breasts, and long tapering legs. In her clumsy, uninhibited way she was surprisingly good in bed. She was as strong as a tractor, but not quite as intelligent.

I felt sorry for Dody. She didn't have much to show for her life so far. With her parents, she had followed crops all over the country – staying locked in a car by a field someplace until she was big enough to carry baskets – and this constant exposure to the itinerant agricultural worker's lackadaisical code of living had made her wise beyond her age. After spending the night with me in my trailer in Homestead, she had begged to be taken along, and I brought her with me to Belle Glade. Why I weakened I don't know, but at the time I had been depressed. I had lost four birds in the Homestead fighting, and if Sandspur hadn't won his fight, the Homestead meet would have been a major disaster. But three weeks is a long time to live with a young, demanding girl – and a stupid, irritating girl, at that.

Anyway, it was 4 a.m. I dressed and took Sandspur outside and around to the back of the trailer.

It was still dark and I wanted to flirt him for exercise. A cooped bird gets stale in a hurry. I sidestepped the chicken six times, gave him six rolls, and let him drink a half dip of water. He would get no more water until after the fight. When the sky began to lighten I released him. Sandspur lifted his head and crowed twice. I lit my first cigarette of the day. As I watched the cock scratch in the loose sand, a shadow fell across my face. I looked up and there was Jack Burke, a wide grin splitting his homely face. I scooped Sandspur up quickly, dropped him into the coop and closed the lid. Burke had seen him, but there still wasn't enough light for a close look.

'That the mighty Sandspur?' Burke said.

I nodded.

'He don't look like no five-time winner to me. Tell you what I'll do, Mr Mansfield,' Burke said, as though he were doing me a big favor, 'I'll give you two to one.'

When Burke made this offer, I had just started to get to my feet. But now I decided to remain in my squatting position. Burke is a man of average height, but I am a full head taller than he is, and my eyes are bluer. My blond hair is curly, and his lank blond hair is straight. Looking down on me that way gave him a psychological advantage, a feeling of power, and I wanted him to have it – hoping that his overconfidence would help me get even better odds that afternoon.

Burke had written me a postcard to Homestead, challenging Sandspur to the fight at even money. I had accepted by return mail, glad to get a chance at his Ace cock, Little David. Little David wasn't so little in his reputation. He was an eight-time winner and had had a lot of publicity. When my Sandspur beat Burke's Little David, his value would be doubled, and my chances for taking the Southern Conference championship would be improved.

On the drive from Homestead to Belle Glade, I had thought of the crack-on-the-bill plan, and now I didn't want even money or two to one either. After the bettors looked at the birds before the pitting, I expected to get

179

odds of four to one, at least. I had eight hundred and fifty dollars in my wallet and I didn't want to take Burke's offer, but after accepting an even-money fight by mail, I couldn't legitimately turn down the new odds.

I snapped my fingers out four times, folded in my thumb, and held up four fingers. I nodded twice.

'You mean you've only got a hundred dollars to bet?' Burke said, with a short angry laugh. 'I figured on taking you for at least a thousand!'

I pointed to the coop and lifted a forefinger to show Burke I only had the one cock. He knew very well I had lost four birds at Homestead. By this time, everybody in Florida and half of Georgia knew it.

Jack Burke followed the Cocker's Code of Conduct, and he was honest, but he disliked me. Although my luck had been mostly bad for the last three years, four years before at Biloxi my novice stag, Pinky, had killed his Ace, Pepperpot. He would never be able to forgive or forget that beating. Pinky had won only one fight against five for his cock, and Burke had taken a terrific loss at five-to-one odds. More than the money he had lost, he had resented my winning. A columnist in *The Southern Cockfighter* had unfairly blamed his conditioning methods for the loss. Actually, Pinky had only made a lucky hit. A man is foolish to fight stags, but I had needed the young bird to fill out my entry for the main – not expecting to clobber Pepperpot.

Burke studied the ground, rubbing his freshly shaven chin. He was in his middle forties, and he wore his pale, yellow hair much too long. He paid considerable attention to his clothes. Even at daybreak he was wearing a blue seersucker suit, white shirt and necktie, and black-and-white shoes. Two-toned shoes indicate an ambivalent personality, a man who can't make up his mind.

'Okay, Mr Mansfield,' Burke said at last, slapping his leg. 'I'll take your hundred dollars and give you a two-to-one. I know damned well Sandspur can't beat Little David, but your cock always has a chance of getting in a lucky hit . . . the way Pinky did in Biloxi, for instance. So let's say you really get lucky – what do you have? Two hundred dollars. To give you a fighting chance to get on your feet again after Homestead, I'll put up eight hundred bucks against your car and trailer. Even money.'

I chewed my lower lip, but the bet was fair. My battered Caddy was worth at least eight hundred, but I didn't know what the trailer was worth. Secondhand trailers bring in peculiar prices, and mine was fairly small, with only one bedroom and one door. If I unloaded the car and trailer through a newspaper advertisement, I could've probably sold them both together for at least a thousand. Burke wanted to beat me so bad he could taste it. And if Little David won, I'd be out on the highway with my thumb out.

I stuck out my right hand and Burke grabbed it eagerly. The bet was made.

'Too bad you haven't got anything else to lose,' Burke laughed gleefully. 'I'd like to make another bet that you just made a bad bet!'

My lips curved into a broad smile as I thought of Dody sleeping peacefully inside the trailer. In the unlikely event that Burke's cock did win the fight, he would also be stuck with Dody. When I pictured Burke in my mind stopping at every gas station on the road to buy Dody ice cream and Coca-Colas it was impossible to suppress my smile. On the way up from Homestead she had damned near driven me crazy.

But now the bet was made.

I consulted my wristwatch. 2:30 p.m. It was time to go. Bill Sanders was going to meet me outside the pit at three to pick up my betting money. I stashed a hundred dollars in the utensil cupboard to cover my two-to-one

181

bet with Burke, counted the rest of my money, and it came out to an even seven hundred and fifty dollars. That was everything, except for a folded ten-dollar bill in my watch pocket. This was my getaway bread – just in case.

I put my straw cowboy hat on my head to protect my face from the Florida sun, picked up the aluminium coop and my gaff case, and stepped outside. There were fourteen trailers in Captain Mack's Trailer Camp, including mine, and if you had touched any one of them, you would have burned your hand. In the distance, across the flat, desolate country, I could see Belle Glade, three miles away. The heat waves rising off the sandy land resembled great sheets of quivering cellophane. I turned away from the trailers and started toward the hammock clump a mile away where the pit had been set up. As hot as it was, I was in no mood to unhitch my car from the trailer and work up a worse sweat than I had, and the walk was only a mile.

There was a wire gate behind the camp, with an old-timer collecting an entrance fee of three dollars. I raised my coop to show him I was an entrant, and he let me through without collecting a fee. As I passed through the gate, Dody came flying up the trail, pigtails bouncing on her shoulders. She was barefooted, wearing a pair of red silk hotpants and a white sleeveless blouse. Her big unhampered breasts jounced up and down as she ran.

'Frank!' she called out before she reached the gate. 'Take me with you! Please, Frank!'

The gateman, a grizzled old man in blue overalls, raised his white brows. I shook my head. He closed and latched the gate as Dody reached it.

'Damn you, Frank!' Dody shouted angrily. 'You don't let me do nothin'. You know I've never seen you cockfight. Please let me go!'

I ignored her and continued up the trail. I had enough to worry about, without her yammering around the pit and asking questions.

Captain Mack, who had made all the arrangements for the Belle Glade pitting, was talking earnestly to a Florida trooper when I reached the parking area. The trooper's state patrol car was parked directly behind a new convertible with a Dade County plate. The right door of the convertible was open, and a pretty blonde woman sat in the front seat. Her face was pale, and she had her eyes closed, breathing deeply through her open mouth. There was a wet spot in the sand outside the door. I supposed the girl had watched a couple of fights inside the pit and got sick as a consequence. Not many city women have the stomach for watching cockfights.

The pit was surrounded on four sides by a green canvas panorama made from army surplus latrine screens. There were about thirty cars in the parking area, not counting the trucks. I set down my gaff case and coop in the sparse shade of a melaleuca tree, and leaned against a parked Plymouth, watching Captain Mack argue with the trooper. Captain Mack shrugged wearily, took his wallet out of his hip pocket, and handed two bills to the trooper. Through a gap in the canvas wall, they went inside the pit. Although cockfighting is legal in Florida, betting is not, so Captain Mack had been forced to pay out some protection money.

There was excited shouting from inside the pit, followed by several coarse curses, and then the voices subsided. Mr Ed Middleton's baritone carried well as he announced the winning cock.

'The winner is the Madigan! One minute and thirty-one seconds in the third pitting!'

Again there were curses, followed by the derisive sound of laughter. I lit a cigarette, took my notebook out of my shirt pocket, and wrote the essential information concerning

183

Sandspur on a fresh sheet of paper. A few minutes later Bill Sanders came outside and joined me beneath the tree. I handed him my roll of seven hundred and fifty dollars and he counted it. Bill put the money in his trousers and watched my fingers. I held up four fingers on my left hand and my right forefinger.

'I doubt if I can get you four to one, Frank.' Bill shook his head dubiously. 'Your reputation is too damn good. You could show up with a battered dunghill, and if these redneckers thought you fed it, they'd bet on it. But I'll try.'

If anybody could get good odds for me, Sanders could, and I knew he would certainly try. When I was discharged from the Army, I had spent two months in Puerto Rico with Sanders, living in the same hotel; and we had attended mains at all the best game clubs – San Juan, Mayagüez, Ponce, Arecibo, and Aibonito. I had steered Sanders right on the betting, after I had gotten accustomed to the fighting techniques of the Spanish slashers, and both of us had returned to Miami with our wallets full of winnings. Bill Sanders was not a professional cockfighter like myself, he was a professional gambler. He had lost his share of the money he won in Puerto Rico at the Miami horse and dog tracks. A little bald guy with a passion for high living, he lived very well when he had money and even better when he had none. He was that kind of a man, and a good friend.

I took Sandspur out of his coop and pointed out the 'cracked' beak. Bill whistled softly and his blue eyes widened.

'If that bill breaks off, you've had it, Frank.' He shrugged. 'But that mutilated boko should get me the four-to-one odds.'

Sanders hit me lightly on the shoulder with his fist and returned to the pit.

I held Sandspur with my left hand, filled my mouth with smoke, and blew the smoke at his head. He clucked angrily, shaking his head. Blowing tobacco smoke at a cock's head irritates it to a fighting pitch, and I was smoking a mild, mentholated cigarette. I enveloped the cock's head with one more cloud of smoke and returned him to his coop. Too much smoke could make a cock dizzy.

I opened my gaff case and removed two sets of heels. I put a pair of short spurs in my left shirt pocket and a pair of long jaggers in my right shirt pocket. After shutting my gaff case, I picked up the coop and case and entered the pit.

There were only about sixty spectators inside, but this was a fairly good crowd for September. The Florida cockfighting season didn't start officially until Thanksgiving Day, when an opening derby was held in Lake Worth. And Belle Glade isn't the most accessible town in Florida. The canvas walls successfully prevented any breeze from getting into the pit, and it was as hot inside as a barbecue grill.

I recognized a couple of Dade County fanciers and nodded acknowledgments to them when they greeted me by name. There was a scattering of Belle Glade townspeople, two gamblers from Miami who probably owned the blonde and the convertible, Burke and his two handlers, and two pregnant women I had seen around the trailer camp. The remainder of the crowd was made up from the migrant agricultural workers' camp on the other side of town.

The cockpit was made of rough boards, sixteen inches high, and about eighteen feet in diameter. The pit was surrounded on three sides by bleachers, four tiers high. Under an open beach umbrella on the fourth side of the pit, Mr Middleton sat at a card table with Captain Mack. Behind the table there was a blackboard. I noted that Jack Burke had won both of the short-entry derbies, the first, four-one, and the second, three-two. That accounted for the glum expressions on the faces of the two Dade County breeders. Not only had they made a poor showing, their one-hundred-dollar entry fees, less Captain Mack's ten percent, had wound up in Burke's pocket as prize money.

Two men in the bleachers I didn't know called out my name and wished me good luck. I waved an acknowledgment to them, and joined Ed Middleton and Captain Mack. I removed Sandspur from the coop and handed the slip of paper to Mr Middleton. Jack Burke and his handler, Ralph Hansen, came over. The handler was carrying Little David. Mr Middleton produced a coin.

'Name it, gentlemen,' he said.

'Let Mr Mansfield call it,' Burke said indifferently.

I tapped my forehead to indicate 'heads.' Mr Middleton tossed the half dollar into the air and let it land with a thump on the card table. Heads, I reached into my left shirt pocket, pulled out the short gaffs, and held them out in my open palm. They were hand-forged steel gaffs, an inch and a quarter in length. Burke nodded grimly and turned to his handler.

'All right, Ralph,' he said bitterly. 'Short spurs, but set'em low.'

Burke was a long gaff man, but I preferred the short heels. Sandspur was a cutter and fought best with short gaffs. Little David was used to long three-inch heels. Winning the toss had given Sandspur a slight advantage over Little David.

The cockfight between Sandspur and Little David was an extra hack, and I had not, of course, been required to post any entry fee. However, Mr Middleton examined both cocks with minute attention. He was acting as judge and referee and had received at least a minimum fee of one hundred and fifty dollars, plus expenses, from Captain Mack. The judge of a cockfight has to be good, and Ed Middleton was one of the best referees in the entire South. His word in the pit was law. There is no appeal from a cockfight judge's decision. As sole judge-referee, Ed

Middleton's jurisdiction encompassed spectator betting as well. The referee's job has always been the most important at a cockfight. As every cocker knows, for example, honest Abe Lincoln was once a cockpit referee during his lawyer days in Illinois. Hard and fair in his decisions, and as impersonal as doom, Ed Middleton was fully aware of the traditional responsibilities of the cockpit referee.

After completing his examination of the cocks to see that they were not soaped, peppered or greased and that they were trimmed fairly, Mr Middleton stepped back to the table.

'Southern Conference rules, gentlemen?' he asked.

'What else?' Burke said.

I nodded my head in agreement.

'Forty-minute time limit, or kill?'

I closed my fist, jerked my thumb toward the ground.

'What else?' Burke said.

Captain Mack held Sandspur while Jack Burke examined him, and I took a close look at Little David. Burke's chicken was a purebred O'Neal Red and as arrogant as a sergeant major in the Foreign Legion. Although I had never seen Little David fight before, I had followed his previous pittings in *The Southern Cockfighter*, and I knew that he liked aerial fighting. But so did Sandspur fight high in the air, and my cock was used to short gaffs. The three additional wins Little David had over Sandspur didn't worry me when I had such an advantage.

Burke tapped me on the shoulder and grinned. 'If I'd known your chicken had him a cracked bill, I'd have given you better odds.'

I shrugged indifferently and sat down on the edge of the pit to arm my cock. I opened my gaff case, removed a bottle of typewriter cleaning solvent and cleaned Sandspur's spur stumps. Most cockers use plain alcohol to clean spurs, but typewriter solvent is fast-drying and, in my opinion, removes the dirt easier. After fitting tight chamois-skin-coverings over both spurs, I slipped the metal sockets of the short heels over the covered stumps and tied them with waxed string, setting them low and a trifle to the outside. The points of the tapered heels were as sharp as needles, and a man has to be careful when he arms a cock. I had a puckered puncture scar on my right forearm caused by a moment of carelessness seven years before, and I didn't want another one.

The betting had already started, but the crowd quieted down when Mr Middleton stepped into the pit. They listened attentively to his announcement.

'This is an extra hack, gentlemen,' he said loudly. 'Little David versus Sandspur. Southern Conference rules will prevail. No time limit, and short gaffs. Little David is owned by Mr Jack Burke of Burke Farms, Kissimmee, Florida. He's an Ace cock, with eight wins and will be two years old in November. Little David will be handled by Mr Ralph Hansen of Burke Farms.'

The crowd gave Little David a nice hand, and Mr Middleton continued.

'Sandspur is owned by Mr Frank Mansfield of Mansfield Farms, Ocala, Florida, and he will handle his own chicken. Sandspur is a five-time winner and a year-and-a-half old. Both cocks will fight at four pounds even.'

Sandspur got a better hand than Little David, and the applause was sustained by the two Dade County breeders who wanted him to beat Burke's cock. Mr Middleton examined Sandspur's heels and patted me on the shoulder. Many cockers resent the referee's examination of a cock's heels, but I never have. A conscientious referee can help you by making this final check. Once the fight has started and your cock loses a metal spur, it cannot be replaced.

As Mr Middleton crossed the pit to examine Little David, I watched the flying fingers of the bettors. The majority of the betting at cockfights is done by fingers

– one finger for one dollar, five for five dollars, and then on up into the multiples of five – and I was an expert in this type of betting. I had learned finger betting in the Philippines when I was in the army and didn't understand Tagalog, and I had also used the same system in Puerto Rico, where I didn't understand Spanish very well. Little David was the favorite, getting two-to-one, and in some cases three-to-one odds.

Bill Sanders, Jack Burke and the two Miami gamblers were in a huddle next to the canvas wall. Both gamblers were staring across the pit at Sandspur while Sanders and Burke talked at the same time. Sanders had a roll of money in his hand and was talking fast, although I couldn't hear his voice from where I was sitting beside the pit.

A fistfight broke out on the top tier of seats between two fruit tramps, and one of them was knocked off backward and fell heavily to the ground. Before he could climb back into the stands, the state trooper had an armlock on him and made him sit down on the other side of the pit. When I looked back to Bill Sanders, he was smiling and holding up three fingers.

So Bill had got three-to-one. That was good enough for me. When Sandspur won, I'd be $2,250 ahead from the Miami gamblers, plus $1,500 more from Jack Burke. $3,250. This would be more than enough money to see me through the Southern Conference season, and enough to purchase six badly needed fighting cocks besides.

'Get ready!' Mr Middleton yelled. I stood up, stepped over the edge of the pit, and put my toes on the back score. The backscore lines placed us eight feet away from each other. Ralph Hansen, holding Little David under the chest with one hand, called impatiently to the referee.

'How about letting us bill them first, Mr Middleton?'

Billing is an essential prelude to pitting. Ed Middleton didn't need the reminder. 'Bill your cocks,' he growled.

We cradled our fighters over our left arms, holding their feet, and stood sideways on our center scores, two feet apart, so the cocks could peck at each other. These cocks had never seen each other before, but they were mortal enemies. Ed allowed us about thirty seconds for the teasing and then told us to get ready. Ralph backed to his score and I returned to mine. I squatted on my heels and set the straining Sandspur with his feet on the score. The cocks were exactly eight feet apart.

I watched Mr Middleton's lips. This was a trick I had practiced for hours on end and I was good at it. Before a man can say the letter 'P' he must first compress his lips. There isn't any other way he can say it. The signal to release the cocks is when the referee shouts 'Pit' or 'Pit your cocks!' The handler who releases the tail of his cock first on the utterance of the letter 'P' has a split-second advantage over his rival. And in the South, where 'Pit' is often a two-syllable word, 'Pee-it', my timing was perfect.

'Pit!' Mr Middleton announced, and before the word was out of his mouth Sandspur was in the air and halfway to Little David. The cocks met in midair, both of them shuffling with blurred yellow feet, and then they dropped to the ground. Neither cock had managed to get above the other.

With new respect for each other, the two birds circled, heads held low, watching each other warily. Little David feinted cleverly with a short rush, but Sandspur wasn't fooled. He held his ground, and Burke's cock retreated with his wings fluttering at the tips.

As he dropped back, Sandspur rose with a short flight and savagely hooked the gaff of his right leg into Little David's wing. The point of the heel was banged solidly into the bone and Sandspur couldn't get it dislodged. He pecked savagely at Little David's head, and hit the top of the downed cock's dubbed head hard with his bill open . . . too hard.

The upper section of Sandspur's bill broke off cleanly at the doctored crack I had made. A bubble of blood formed, and Sandspur stopped pecking. Both cocks struggled to break away from each other, but the right spur was still stuck and all Sandspur could do was hop up and down in place on his free leg. I looked at Mr Middleton.

'Handle!' the judged shouted. 'Thirty seconds!'

A moment later I disentangled the gaff from Little David's wing and retreated to my starting line. I put Sandspur's head in my mouth and sucked the blood from his broken beak. I licked the feathers of his head back into place and spat as much saliva as I could into his open mouth. For the remaining seconds I had left I sucked life into his clipped comb. The comb was much too pale . . .

'Get ready!' I held Sandspur by the tail on the line. 'Pit your cocks!'

Instead of flying into the air, Sandspur circled for the right wall. Little David turned in midair, landed running, and chased my cock into the far corner. Sandspur turned to fight, and the cocks met head on, but my injured bird was forced back by the fierceness of Little David's rush.

On his back, Sandspur hit his opponent twice in the chest, drawing blood both times, and then Little David was above him in the air and cutting at his head with both spurs. A sharp gaff entered Sandspur's right eye, and he died as the needle point pierced his central nervous system. Little David strutted back and forth, pecked twice at my lifeless cock, and then crowed his victory.

'The winner is Mr Burke's Ace,' Mr Middleton announced, as a formality. 'Twenty-eight seconds in the second pitting.'

All I had left was a folded ten-dollar bill in my watch pocket and one dead chicken.

Chapter Two

There was a burial hole in the marshy ground, about four feet square and three feet deep, on the far side of the parking area. Water was seeping visibly into the mucky pit, and the dead roosters in the bottom had begun to float.

I removed the gaffe from my dead cock's spurs and added his body to the floating pile of dead chickens. As I put the heels away in my gaff case, Bill Sanders joined me at the edge of the communal burying pit.

'I just wanted to let you know that I got all your dough down, Frank,' he said. 'Every dollar at three-to-one, and there's nothing left.'

I nodded.

'Tough, Frank, but my money was riding on Sandspur with yours.'

I shrugged and emptied the peat moss out of the aluminium coop into the hole on top of the dead chickens.

'You're going to be all right, aren't you? I mean, you'll be on the Southern Conference circuit this year, and all?'

I nodded and shook hands with Sanders. As I looked down at Bill's bald head, I noticed that the top was badly sunburned and starting to peel. The little gambler never wore a hat.

'Okay, Frank. I'll probably see you in Biloxi.'

I clapped Bill on the shoulder to squeeze out a farewell. He went over to the blue Chrysler convertible and started talking to the blonde. She had evidently recovered from her upset stomach. She had remade her face, and she now listened with absorbed attention to whatever it was Bill Sanders was telling her.

I removed the bamboo handle from the aluminium coop, collapsed the sides, and made a fairly flat, compact square out of the six frames. After locking them together with the clamps, I attached the handle again so I could carry the coop folded. A machinist in Valdosta had made two of the traveling coops for me to my own specifications and design. At one time I had considered having several made, and putting them up for sale to chicken men traveling around the country, too, but the construction costs were prohibitive to make any profit out of them. My other traveling coop was at my farm in Ocala.

Carrying my gaff case and coop, I walked back to the trailer camp. Dody met me at the door of the Love-Lee-Mobile Home with a bright lopsided smile. Her lipstick was on crooked, and there was too much rouge on her cheeks. She wanted to look older, but makeup made her look younger instead.

'Did you win, Frank?'

I leaned the folded coop against the side of the trailer and pointed to it with a gesture of exasperation.

'Oh!' she said. Her red lips were fixed in a fat, crooked 'O' for an instant. 'I'm real sorry, Frank.'

I placed my gaff case beside the coop and entered the trailer. There was a dusty leather suitcase under the bed, and I wiped the scuffed surfaces clean with a dirty T-shirt I found on top of the built-in dresser. I unstrapped the suitcase, opened it on the bed, and began to pack. There wasn't too much to put into it. Most of my clothes were on the farm. I packed my clean underwear, two clean white shirts, and then searched the trailer for my dirty shirts. I found them in a bucket of cold water beneath the sink. Dody had been promising to wash and iron them for the past three days, but just like everything else, she hadn't gotten around to doing it. I couldn't very well pack wet shirts in the suitcase on top of clean dry clothing, so I left the dirty shirts in the bucket.

In the tiny bathroom I gathered up my toilet articles and zipped them into a blue nylon Dropkit. When I packed the Dropkit into the suitcase, Dody began to evidence an avid interest in my actions.

'What are you packing for, Frank?' she asked.

Despite the fact that I had never said as much as a single word to her in the three weeks we had been living together, she persisted in asking questions that couldn't be answered by an affirmative nod, a negative waggle of my head, or an explanatory gesture of some kind. If I had answered every foolish question she put to me in writing, I could have filled up two notebooks a day.

I tossed two pairs of clean blue jeans into the open suitcase, and then undressed as far as my shorts. I pulled on a pair of gray-green corduroy trousers, and put on my best shirt, a black Oxford cloth Western shirt with white pearl buttons. The jodhpur boots I was wearing were black and comfortable, and they were fastened with buckles and straps. I had ordered them by mail from a bootmaker in El Paso, Texas, and had paid forty-five dollars for them. They were the only shoes I had with me. I untied the red bandana from around my neck and exchanged it for a square of red silk, tying a loose knot and tucking the ends inside my collar before I buttoned the top shirt button. It was much too hot to wear the matching corduroy coat to my trousers, so I added it to the suitcase. The coat would come in handy in northern Florida.

'You aren't leaving, are you, Frank?' Dody asked worriedly. 'I mean, are we leaving the trailer?'

I nodded impatiently, and searched through a dozen drawers and compartments before I found my clean socks. There were only three pairs, white cotton with elastic tops. I usually wear white socks. Colored socks make my feet sweat. I put the socks into the suitcase.

'Where're we going, Frank? I can get ready in a second,' the girl lied.

There were five packages of Kools left, a half can of lighter fluid and a package of flints. I put a fresh pack of Kools in my pocket, and tossed the remaining packs, fluid and flints into the suitcase. After one last look around I closed the lid and buckled the straps. To get my guitar from under the bed I had to lie flat on the floor and reach for it. The guitar was now the substitute for my voice, and my ability to play it was what had attracted Dody to me in the first place. When I needed a woman again, the guitar would help me get one.

I carried the guitar case and suitcase into the combination kitchen-living-dining room.

'Why don't you answer me!' Dody yelled, pounding me on the back with her doubled fists. 'You drive me almost crazy sometimes. You pretend like you can't talk, but I know damned well you can! I've heard you talking in your sleep. Now answer me, damn you! Where're we going?'

I drank a glass of water at the sink, set the glass down on the sideboard, and pointed in a northerly direction.

'I don't consider that an answer! North could be anywhere. Do you mean your farm in Ocala?'

Dody had an irritating voice. It was high and twangy, and there was a built-in nasal whine. I certainly was sick of listening to her voice.

The pink slips for the Caddy and the mobile home were in the drawer of the end table by the two-seater plastic couch. I opened the drawer, removed the pink slips and insurance papers and put them on the Masonite dinette table. In the linen cupboard of the narrow hallway I found a ruled writing pad and a dirty, large brown Manila envelope. I took the five twenty-dollar bills out of the utensil cupboard and sat down at the table. Now that I had lost, I was happy about having had the foresight to hide the money from Dody to cover my bet with Burke.

Standing at the sink, her arms folded across her breasts, Dody glared at me with narrowed eyes. Her lips were poked out sullenly and drawn down at the corners. I put the insurance policies, pink slips and money into the envelope. With my ballpoint lead pencil I wrote out a bill of sale on the top sheet of the ruled pad.

To Whom It May Concern
I, Frank Mansfield, hereby transfer the ownership of a 1963 Cadillac sedan, and one Love-Lee-Mobile Home to Jack Burke, in full payment of a just and honorable gambling debt.

(Signed) Frank Mansfield

That would do it, I decided. If Burke wanted to transfer the pink slips and insurance to his own name, the homemade bill of sale would be sufficient proof of ownership.

'Is that note for me?' Dody asked sharply.

Although I answered with a short, negative shake of my head, Dody rushed across the narrow space, snatched the pad from the table and read it anyway. Her flushed face paled as her lips moved perceptibly with each word she read.

'Oh, you didn't lose the trailer?' she exclaimed.

I nodded, curiously watching her face. The girl was too young to have control over her features. Every emotion she felt was transmitted to her pretty, mobile face. Her facial expressions underwent a rapid exchange of dismay, anger, frustration and fear, settling finally on a fixed look of righteous indignation.

'And, of course,' she said, with an effort at sarcasm, 'you lost all your money, too?'

I nodded again and held out a hand for the pad. She handed it to me, and I ripped off the top sheet and added it to the contents of the bulging envelope.

'You don't give a damn what happens to me, do you?'

I shook my head. I felt sorry for her, in a way, but I didn't worry about her. She was pretty, young and a good lay. She could get by anywhere. Twisting in the seat, I reached into my pocket for my key ring. I unsnapped the two car keys and the door key for the trailer. After dropping them into the envelope, I licked the flap, sealed it and squared it in the center of the table.

There was a rap on the door. I jerked my head toward the door, and Dody opened it, standing to one side as Jack Burke came inside.

'Afternoon, ma'am,' Burke said politely, removing his hat. He turned to me. 'I'm sorry, Mr Mansfield, but I made the bet in good faith and sure didn't know Sandspur had him a cracked hill. But if you'd won, I know damned well you'd've come around for eight hundred dollars from me. So I'm here for the car and trailer.'

Still seated, I shoved the envelope toward him. Burke unfastened the flap, which hadn't quite dried, and pawed through the contents. He put the hundred dollars into his wallet before he read the bill of sale. His face reddened, and he returned the bill of sale to the envelope.

'Please accept my apology, Mr Mansfield. I don't know why, but I guess I expected an argument.'

Either he was plain ignorant or he was trying to make me angry. A handshake by two cockfighters is as binding as a sworn statement witnessed by a notary public, and he knew this as well as I did. For a long moment I studied his red face and then concluded that he was merely ill at ease on account of Dody's presence and didn't know what he was implying.

197

Dody leaned against the sink, glaring angrily at Burke. 'I never heard of nobody so lowdown mean to take a family's home away from them!' she said scathingly.

Her remark was uncalled for, but it caused Burke a deeper flush of embarrassment. 'I reckon you don't know Mr Mansfield, little lady,' he said defensively, 'and not overmuch about cockfighting neither. But a bet is a bet.'

'For men, yes! But what about me?' Dody patted her big breasts several times with both hands and looked beseechingly into Burke's eyes. He was troubled and he scratched his head, slanting his wary eyes in my direction.

I stood up, smiled grimly, and holding out my hands with the palms up, I made an exaggerated gesture of presentation of Dody to Jack Burke. There could be no mistake about the meaning.

'Well, I don't rightly know about that, Mr Mansfield.' Burke scratched his head. 'I already got me a lady friend up Kissimmee way.'

I stepped out from behind the table and put on my cowboy hat. Dody came flying toward me with clawing nails. The space was cramped, but I sidestepped her rush and planted a jolting six-inch jab into her midriff. Dody sat down heavily on the linoleum floor and stayed there, gasping for breath and staring up at me round-eyed with astonished disbelief.

There are three good ways to win a fight: A blow to the solar plexus, *first*, an inscrutable expression on your face, or displaying a sharp knife blade to your opponent. Any of these three methods, singly or in combination, will usually take the bellicosity out of a man, woman or child.

The swift right to her belly and the sight of my impassive face were enough to take the fight out of Dody. Burke tried to help her to her feet, but she shrugged his hands away from her shoulders as she regained her lost breath.

'You – can – go – to – hell, Frank Mansfield!' Dody said in gasps. 'I can take care of myself!' However, she prudently remained seated, supporting herself with her arms behind her back.

Burke said nothing. He ran his fingers nervously through his long hair, looking first at me and then at Dody and back to me again. He wanted to say something but didn't know what he wanted to say. I sat down at the table again and scratched out a short note.

Mr Burke – If your Little David is still around, I challenge you to a hack at the Southern Conference Tournament—

I pushed the straw cowboy hat back from my forehead and handed him the note. After reading the message, Burke crumpled the paper and looked at me thoughtfully.

'You don't have any fighting cocks left, do you, Mr Mansfield?'

I shook my head, and moved my shoulders in a barely perceptible shrug.

'Do you honestly believe you can train a short-heeled stag to beat Little David, a nine-time winner' – he counted on his fingers – 'in only six-months' time?'

In reply, I pointed to the crumpled challenge in his hand.

'Sure, Mr Mansfield. I accept, but it'll be your funeral. And I expect you to put some money where your mouth is when the hack's held.'

We shook hands. I picked up my suitcase and guitar and went outside. As I collected my gaff case and coop together, trying to figure out how I could carry everything, Burke and Dody followed me outside. The four odd-sized pieces made an awkward double armload.

'I'll give you ten bucks for that coop,' Burke offered.

The suggestion was so stupid I didn't dignify it with so much as a shrug. If Burke wanted a coop like mine, he could have one made.

Ralph Hansen had Burke's Ford pickup parked on the road about twenty yards away from the trailer. Burke strolled over to his truck to say something to Ralph. The other handler was in the truck bed with Burke's fighting cocks. The truck bed had steel-mesh coops welded to the floor on both sides, with solid walls separating each coop so that none of the cocks could see each other. A nice setup for traveling, with plenty of space down the center to carry feed, luggage and sleeping bags. I walked down the sandy road toward the open gate and the highway.

A moment later Dody caught up with me and trotted along at my side.

'Please, Frank,' she pleaded, 'take me with you. I don't want to stay with Mr Burke. He's an old man!'

Burke was only forty-five or -six and not nearly as old as Dody thought. I shook my head. Dody ran ahead of me then, and planted herself in my path, spreading her long bare legs, and holding her arms akimbo. I stopped.

'I'll be good to you, Frank,' she said tearfully. 'Real good! Honest, I will! I know you don't like them TV dinners I been fixin', but I'm really a good cook when I try. And I'll prove it to you if you'll take me with you. I'll wash your clothes and sew and everything!' She began to blubber in earnest. Juicy tears rolled out of her moist brown eyes and flowed over her smooth round cheeks, cutting furrows in her pancake makeup.

I jerked my head for her to get out of my way. Dody moved reluctantly to one side and let me pass. At the open gate to the highway I put my luggage down and lit a cigarette. Ralph stopped the white pickup at the gate.

'I can carry you up as far as Kissimmee, Mr Mansfield,' he offered. 'Mr Burke is going to bring your Caddy and trailer up tomorrow, he said.'

I shook my head friendlily, and waved him on his way. I didn't want any favors from Jack Burke. After Ralph made his turn onto the highway, I looked back toward my old trailer. Jack Burke and Dody had their heads together, and it looked like both of them were talking at the same time. A moment later, Burke held the trailer door open for Dody and then followed her inside.

It occurred to me that I didn't know Dody's last name. She had never volunteered the information and, of course, I had never asked her. I hate to write notes, and I only write them when it is absolutely necessary. What difference did it make whether I knew her last name or not? But it *did* make a difference, and I felt a sense of guilty shame.

The long blue convertible came gliding down the trail from the cockpit. The driver stopped at the gate. The blonde sat between the two Miami gamblers on the front seat, and Bill Sanders, puffing a cigar, was sitting alone in the back.

'Do you want to go to Miami, by any chance?' Sanders asked.

I shook my head and smiled.

'We've got plenty of room,' the driver added cheerfully. 'Glad to take you with us.'

I shook my head again and waved them on. Sanders raised a hand in a two-finger 'V' salute, and the big car soon passed out of sight.

I didn't want to go to Miami, and I had turned down a free ride to Kissimmee. Where did I want to go? The lease on my Ocala farm had two more years to run, and it was all paid up in advance. But without any game fowl, and without funds to buy any, there was no point in going there right now. The first thing on the agenda was to obtain some money. After I had some money, I could start worrying about game fowl.

Doc Riordan owed me eight hundred dollars. His office was in Jacksonville, and he was my best bet. My younger brother, Randall, owed me three hundred dollars, but the chances of getting any money from him were negligible. Doc Riordan was the man to see first. Even if Doc could only give me a partial payment of two or three hundred, it would be a start. With only a ten-dollar bill in my watch pocket, and a little loose change, I felt at loose ends. After collecting some money from Doc I could make a fast trip home to Georgia and see my brother. I couldn't go home completely broke. I never had before, and it was too late to start now.

As I thought of home I naturally thought of Mary Elizabeth. My last visit had been highly unsatisfactory, and I had left without telling her good-bye.

On my last trip home two years before, I had been driving a black Buick convertible, and I had worn an expensive white linen suit. Although I looked prosperous, most of it was front. My roll had only consisted of five hundred dollars. That was when Randall had nicked me for the loan of three hundred. In the rare letters I had received from him since – about one every four or five months – he had never once mentioned returning the money.

Jacksonville it would be then. If nothing else, I could pick up my mail at the Jacksonville post office.

Two ancient trucks rolled through the gate loaded down with fruit tramps. They were returning to the migrant camp on the other side of Belle Glade. A couple of the men shouted to me, and I waved to them. There was a maroon Cadillac sedan about two hundred yards behind the last truck, hanging well back out of the dust. This was Ed Middleton's car. As he came abreast of the gate, I grinned and stuck out my thumb. Mr Middleton pressed a button, and the right front window slid down with an electronic click.

'Throw your stuff in the back seat, Frank,' Ed Middleton said. 'I don't want to lose this cold air.' The window shot up again.

I opened the back door, arranged my luggage on the floor so it would ride without shifting, slammed the door, and climbed into the front seat. A refreshing icy breeze filled the roomy interior from an air-conditioning system that actually worked.

I settled back comfortably, and Ed pointed the nose of the big car towards Orlando.

Chapter Three

Ed Middleton is one of my favorite people. He is in his early sixties, and if I happen to live long enough, I want to be exactly like him someday. He is a big man with a big voice and a big paunch. Except for a bumpy bulbous nose with a few broken blood vessels here and there on its bright red surface, his face is smooth and white, with the shiny licked look of a dog's favorite bone.

Against all the odds for a man his age, Mr Middleton still has his hair. It is a shimmering silvery white, and he always wears it in a thick bushy crew cut. A ghost of a smile – as though he is thinking of some secret joke – usually hovers about the corners of his narrow lips. In southern cockfighting circles, or anywhere in the world where cockers get together for chicken talk, his name is respected as the man who bred the Middleton Gray. Properly conditioned, the purebred Middleton Gray is a true money bird.

Despite his amiable manner, Ed can get as hard as any man when the time to get tough presents itself, and he wears the coveted Cocker of the Year medal on his watch fob.

'Lost your car and trailer, eh Frank?'

I nodded. Bad news has a way of traveling faster than good news.

'Tough luck, Frank.' Mr Middleton laughed aloud. 'But I don't worry about you landing on your feet. If I know you, you've probably got a rooster hidden away somewhere that'll give Jack Burke his lumps.'

I smiled ruefully, made an 'O' with the thumb and forefinger of my left hand and showed it to him.

'I sure didn't suspect that, Frank,' Mr Middleton said sympathetically.

I opened a fresh package of cigarettes, offered them to Ed and he waved them away. He was silent for more than ten minutes, and then he fingered his lower lip and squirmed about slightly in the seat. The signs were easily recognized. He wanted to confess something; a problem of some kind was on his mind. Two or three times he opened his mouth, started to speak his mind, and then shook his head and clamped his lips together. But he would get it out sooner or later, whatever it was. Since my vow of silence I had become, unwillingly, a man who listened to confessions. Now that I couldn't talk, or wouldn't talk – no one, other than myself, knew the truth about my muteness – people often told me things they would hesitate to tell to a priest, or even to their wives. At first, it had bothered me, learning things about people I didn't want or need to know, but now I just listened – not liking it, of course, but accepting the confessions as an unwelcome part of the deal I had made with myself.

We sailed through the little town of Canal Point and hit Highway 441 bordering Lake Okeechobee.

From time to time, when the roadbed was higher than the dike, I got a glimpse of the calm mysterious lake, which was actually a huge inland sea. Small herds of Black Angus cattle were spotted every few miles between the lake and the highway, eating lush gama grass, but there were very few houses along the way. Lake Okeechobee, with its hundreds of fish and clear sweet water, is a sportsman's paradise, but the great flood of the early twenties, when thousands of people were drowned, had discouraged real-estate development, I supposed. No plush resort hotels or motels had ever been built near its banks.

'Frank,' Ed Middleton said at last, lowering his voice to conspiratorial tones, 'today's pitting at Belle Glade was my last appearance at a cockpit. Surprises you, doesn't it?'

It did indeed. I reached up and twisted the rearview mirror into position so Ed could look at my face without taking his eyes off the highway too much. I looked seriously into the mirror and widened my eyes slightly.

'Nobody can keep a secret long in this business, Frank, but I've kept my plans to myself to avoid the usual arguments. I've argued the pros and cons of cockfighting thousands of times, and you know I've always been on the pro side. If there's a better way of life than raising and fighting game chickens, I haven't found it yet,' he said grimly. 'But I'm a married man, Frank, and you aren't. That's the difference. I'm happily married, and I have been for more than thirty years, but I can still envy a man like you. There aren't a dozen men in the United States who've devoted their lives solely to cockfighting like you have, that is, without earning their living in some other line of business.

'I suppose I've known you for ten years or more and, as a single man, you've got the best life in the world. You've earned the admiration and respect of all of us, Frank.'

I was embarrassed by the praise.

'That was a clever trick you pulled this afternoon, Frank!'

I started with surprise, and Mr Middleton guffawed loudly.

'I haven't seen anyone pull that stunt with the cracked bill to raise the odds in about fifteen years. Don't blame yourself for losing the fight. Write it off to bad luck, or face up that Jack Burke had the better chicken. But that isn't what I wanted to talk about.

'Martha has been after me to quit for years, and I finally gave in. I'm not too old, but I certainly don't need the money. I've got enough orange trees in Orlando to take care of my wants for three lifetimes. If Martha shared my enthusiasm for the game, it would be different. But she won't go on the road with me. This business of living alone in motel rooms doesn't appeal to me anymore. The two months I spent refereeing in Clovis, New Mexico, last spring were the loneliest weeks of my entire life.

'Anyway, I've sold all my Grays. Made a deal for the lot with a breeder in Janitzio, Mexico, and shipped out the last crate of April trios last week. If he fights my Grays as slashers, he'll lose his damned *camisa*, but at any rate, they won't be fighting in the States.

'If you wonder why I refereed today's fight, it was because I promised Captain Mack a year ago. But that was my last appearance in the pit, and you won't see me in the pits again, either as a referee or spectator.' Ed sighed deeply, his confession completed. 'Like the lawyer feller says, Frank, "Further deponent sayeth not."'

Several dissuading arguments came immediately to my mind, but I remained silent, of course. As far as I was concerned, what Ed Middleton did was his business, not mine, but his loss to the game would be felt in the South. We needed men like him to keep the sport clean and honest. But I didn't say anything because of my self-imposed vow of silence.

Up to this moment I've never told anyone why I made the vow. What I do is my business, but the silver medal on Ed Middleton's watch fob held the answer. Money had nothing to do with my decision to keep my mouth shut.

All of us in America want money because we need it and cannot live without it, but we don't need as much money as most of us think we do. Money isn't enough. We must have something more, and my *something more* was the Cockfighter of the Year award.

The small silver coin on Ed's watch fob was only worth, in cash, about ten or fifteen dollars, but a lot of men have settled for lesser honors. A man may refuse a clerk's job with a loan company, for instance, for one hundred dollars a week. But if this same man is put in charge of three typists and is given the exalted title of office manager, the chances are that he will work for ninety dollars a week. In business, this is a well-known 'for instance.'

Unlike Great Britain, we don't have any peerages to hand out, or any annual Queen's Honour List, so most of us settle for less, a hell of a lot less. In large corporations, the businessman has reached his goal in life when he gets a title on his door and a corner office with two windows instead of one. But I'm not a businessman. I am a full-time cockfighter.

My goal in life was that little silver coin, not quite as large as a Kennedy half dollar. On one side of the medal there is an engraved statement: *Cockfighter of the Year*. In the center, the year the award is given is engraved in Arabic numerals. At the bottom of the coin are three capital letters: SCT These letters stand for Southern Conference Tournament.

To a non-cocker, this desire might sound childish, but, to a cockfighter, this award is his ultimate achievement in one of the toughest sports in the world. The medal is awarded to the man Senator Jacob Foxhall decides to give it to at the completion of the annual SCT held in Milledgeville, Georgia. However, Senator Foxhall doesn't always see fit to award the medal. In the last fifteen years he has only awarded the medal to four cockfighters. Ed Middleton was one of them.

In addition to the medal there is a cash award of one thousand dollars. In effect, the cocker who wins this award has the equivalent of a paid-up insurance policy. He can demand a minimum fee of one hundred and fifty dollars a day as a referee from any pit operator in the South, and the operator considers it an honor to pay him. To a cocker, this medal means as much as the Nobel Prize does to a scientist. If that doesn't convey an exact meaning of the award, I can state it simpler. The recipient is the best damned cockfighter in the South, and he has the medal to prove it.

For ten years this medal has been my goal. The SCT is the toughest pit tourney in the United States, and a cockfighter can't enter his game fowl without an invitation. Only top men in the game receive invitations, and I had been getting mine for eight years – even during the two years I was in the army and stationed in the Philippine Islands.

A vow of silence, however, isn't necessary to compete for the award. That had been my own idea, and not a very bright idea either, but I was too damned stubborn to break it.

Three years before I had been riding high on the list of eligible SCT cockfighters. In a hotel room in Biloxi, I had gotten drunk with a group of chicken men, and shot off my big mouth, boasting about my Ace cock, a Red Madigan named Freelance.

Another drunken breeder challenged me, and we staged the fight in the hotel room. Freelance killed the other cock easily, but in the fight he received a slight battering. The next day at the scheduled SCT pitting, I had been forced to pit Freelance again because I had posted a two-hundred-dollar forfeit, and I had been too ashamed to withdraw. Freelance lost, and I had lost my chance for the award.

A few weeks later, while brooding about this lost fight, a fight that had been lost by my personal vanity and big mouth, I made my self-imposed vow of silence. I intended to keep the vow until I was awarded that little silver medal. No one, other than myself, knew about my vow, and I could have broken it at any time without losing face. But *I* would know, and I had to shave every day. At first it had been hell, especially when I had had a few drinks and wanted to get in on the chicken talk in a bar or around the cockhouses at a game club, but I had learned how to live with it.

On the day Mr Middleton picked me up in his Cadillac at Captain Mack's Trailer Court in Belle Glade, I hadn't said a word to anyone in two years and seven months.

'You're a hard man to talk to since you lost your voice!' Ed Middleton boomed in his resonant baritone.

With a slight start, I turned and grinned at him.

'I mean it,' he said seriously. 'I feel like a radio announcer talking into a microphone in a soundproof room. I know I must be reaching somebody, but I'll be damned if I know who it is. You've changed a lot in the last two or three years, Frank. I know you're working as hard as you ever did, but you shouldn't take life too seriously. And don't let a run of bad luck get you down, do you hear?'

I nodded. Ed jabbed me in the ribs sharply with his elbow.

'You've still got a lot of friends, you big dumb bastard!' he finished gruffly. With a quick movement he snapped on the dash radio, twisted the volume on full and almost blasted me out of my seat. He turned the volume down again and said bitterly: 'And on top of everything else, there's nothing on the radio these days but rock 'n' roll!'

He left the radio on anyway, and said no more until we reached Saint Cloud. We pulled into the parking area of a garish drive-in restaurant and got out of the car. It was only six thirty, but the sun had dropped out of sight. There were just a few jagged streaks of orange in the western sky, an intermingling of nimbus clouds and smoke from runaway muck fires. As we admired these fiery fingers in the sky, Mr Middleton smacked his lips.

'How does a steak sound, Frank?'

I certainly didn't intend to spend my remaining ten dollars on a steak. In reply, I emptied my pockets and showed him a double handful of junk, and some loose change.

'I didn't expect you to pay for it,' he said resentfully. 'Let's go inside.'

The sirloin was excellent. So was the baked potato and green salad and three cups of coffee that went with it. After three weeks of Dody's halfhearted cooking, I appreciated a good steak dinner. On regular fare, such as greens, pork chops, string beans, cornbread and so on, I'm a fairly good cook, and I enjoy the preparation of my own meals. But I never prepare food when I have a woman around to do it for me. As I ate, I wondered vaguely how Jack Burke was making out with the girl. Although I was broke, the steak restored my good spirits, and I felt a certain sense of newfound freedom now that I no longer had Dody to worry about.

We lingered over dinner for more than an hour and didn't arrive at Mr Middleton's home until after nine. His ranch-style, concrete brick and stucco house was about three miles off the main highway on a private gravel road and completely surrounded by orange groves. An avid fisherman, Ed had built his home with the rear terrace overlooking a small pond. He parked in a double carport, set well away from the house, backing in beside a blue Chevy pickup.

Before we crossed the flagstone patio, Ed flipped a switch in the carport and flooded the patio and most of the small lake with light. The pond was about forty yards in diameter, and there was an aluminium fishing skiff tied to a concrete block pier at the edge of the gently sloping lawn.

'I've stocked the damned lake with fish four different times,' Ed said angrily, 'but they disappear someplace. Hide in the muck at the bottom, I suppose. Anyway, I've never been able to catch very many.'

When the lights were turned on, Mrs Middleton opened the back door and peered out. Her dark hair, shot through with streaks of gray, was coiled in a heavy round bun at the nape of her neck.

'Who's that with you, Ed?' she asked.

We crossed the patio to the door and Ed kissed his wife on the mouth. He gripped my upper arm with his thick fingers and pulled me in front of him.

'Frank Mansfield, Martha. You remember him, I'm sure. He's going to spend the night with us.'

'Of course,' Martha said. 'Come on inside, Frank, before the mosquitoes eat you alive!'

We entered the kitchen and I blinked uncomfortably beneath the blue-and-yellow fluorescent lights. I shook hands with Mrs Middleton after she wiped her hands unnecessarily on her clean white apron. She was a motherly woman, about ten or fifteen years younger than her husband, but without any children to 'mother.'

'Have you boys had your dinner?' she asked.

'We had a little something in Saint Cloud,' Ed admitted.

'Restaurants!' she said. 'Why didn't you bring Frank on home to dinner when you were that close?' she scolded. 'Sit *down*, Frank! How've you been? Could you eat a piece of key lime pie? Of course you can. I know you both want coffee.'

As we sat down at the breakfast nook together, Ed winked at me. Mrs Middleton bustled around in her bright and shiny kitchen, banging things together, just as busy as she could be.

'Force some pie down anyway, Frank,' Mr Middleton said in a loud stage whisper. 'I'm going to eat a piece even though I hate it.'

'Ha!' Martha said from beside the stove. 'You hate it all right!'

After we were served and eating our pie, there was nothing else Mrs Middleton could do for us. She stood beside the table with her hands clasped beneath her apron, working her pursed lips in and out. I had the feeling that she wanted to ask me questions, but out of consideration for my so-called affliction, she wanted to phrase her questions so that I could answer them yes or no, and yet she couldn't manage any questions of that kind. I hadn't seen Mrs Middleton or talked to her for at least four years. As I recalled, the last time I had seen her was at a banquet held following the International Cockfighting Tournament in Saint Petersburg. My 'dumbness' had been a subject that she and her husband had undoubtedly discussed between them.

'Sit down, Martha,' Ed said. 'Have a cup of coffee with us.'

'And stay awake all night? No thanks.' She sat beside her husband, however, and smiled across the table. 'Do you like the pie, Frank?'

I kissed my fingertips and rolled my eyes toward the ceiling.

'Lime is Ed's favorite.' She put a hand on her husband's sleeve. 'How was the trip, Ed?'

Ed Middleton put his fork crosswise on his empty plate, wiped his lips with a napkin, and looked steadily at his wife. 'The trip doesn't matter, Martha,' he said, 'because it was the last, the very last.'

For a long time, a very long time it seemed to me, the elderly couple looked into each other's eyes. Mr Middleton smiled and nodded his head, and Martha's lower lip began to tremble and her eyes were humid. An instant later she was crying. She hurriedly left the table, put her apron to her face and, still crying, ran out of the room.

Mr Middleton crumpled the square of linen and tossed it toward the stove. The napkin fluttered to the floor, and he smiled and shook his head.

'She's crying because she's happy,' he said. 'Well, dammit, I promised to give up cockfighting, and a promise is a promise!' He got up from the table, doubled his right fist, and punched me hard on the shoulder. 'Pour yourself some more coffee, eat another piece of pie. I'll be back in a minute.'

He pushed through the swinging door and disappeared.

The lime pie was tart, tasty, with a wonderful two-inch topping of snow white, frothy meringue. I ate two more pieces, drank two more cups of coffee. I smoked two cigarettes. Just as I was beginning to wonder whether Ed was going to come back to the kitchen or not, he pushed through the door.

'Come on, Frank,' he snapped his fingers, 'Let's go get your suitcase.'

We went out to his Caddy, and after he unlocked the doors, I got my suitcase out of the back. When we returned to the kitchen, he switched off the patio lights. I followed him through the living room and into his study.

'This was supposed to be a third bedroom,' he explained. 'Actually, it was designed as the master bedroom, and it's a lot larger than the other two bedrooms in the back. But Martha and I decided to each take a small bedroom apiece so our snoring wouldn't bother each other. And besides, I needed a large room like this as an office. A big man needs a big room.' He opened the door leading to the bathroom. 'Here's the can, Frank. Take a shower if you want to. There's always hot water, and these towels are all clean in here. I'll get you some sheets.'

Ed left the room and I could hear him clumping down the hallway, yelling to his wife and asking her where she kept the clean sheets hidden.

The Middletons' ranch-style home was so modern in design and color that the old-fashioned furniture in the study was out of place. The walls were painted a bright warm blue, and there were matching floor-to-ceiling drapes over both windows. The floor was black-and-white pebbled terrazzo, and there the modernity stopped. The floor was covered with an oval-shaped hooked rag rug. There was an ugly, well-scratched, walnut rolltop desk against one wall, and there was an ancient horsehair-stuffed Victorian couch against the opposite wall. Beneath one window there was a scuffed cowhide easy chair, and a shiny black steamer trunk under the other window. A red-lacquered straight chair, with a circular cane seat, stood beside the desk. Three heavy wrought-iron smoking stands completed the furnishings.

I was attracted to the framed photographs on the walls. Each photo was framed in a cheap glass-covered black frame, the type sold in dime stores. Most of the glossy photos were of gamecocks, but there were several photos of Ed Middleton and his cronies. An old cover page of *The Southern Cockfighter*, with a four-color drawing of Ed Middleton's famous cock Freddy, held the place of honor above the desk. Freddy had won nineteen fights and had died in his coop ten years before. Anywhere chicken talk is held, Freddy's name comes up sooner or later.

Mr Middleton re-entered the room, carrying sheets, a blanket and a pillow under his right arm, and a portable television set in his left hand. He tossed the bedcovers on the couch, placed the portable set on the seat of the red straight-backed chair, and plugged the cord into the wall socket.

'I told Martha you wouldn't need a blanket, but you know how women are.'

I nodded. I knew how women were. I began to make up the lumpy couch with the sheets.

'To give you something to do, I brought in the TV. It isn't much good but you can get Orlando, anyway. I'd stay up and keep you company for a while, but I'm pretty tired. This has been a long day for an old man.'

I soon had the couch made up, but Mr Middleton lingered in the room. He studied a photograph of a framed cock on the wall, and beckoned to me as I started to sit down.

'Come here, Frank. Take a look at this cock. It's a phenomenon in breeding and you'll never see another like it. A bird called Bright Boy, one of the most courageous birds I ever owned. Yet it was bred from a father and a daughter. By all the rules, a cock bred that way usually runs every time, but this beauty never did. He was killed in his second fight in a drag pitting. Sorry now I didn't keep him for a brood cock to see what would have happened. I suppose there are similar cases, but this is the only one I really know is true. Did you ever hear of a real fighter bred of father and daughter?'

I shook my head. If true, and I doubted Ed's story, this was an unusual case. When it comes to cocks of the same blood, those bred from mother and son have the biggest heart for fighting to the death. Somebody had probably switched an egg on old Ed.

'Every time a man thinks he's got the answers on cock-breeding, something like this happens to teach him something new. I'm going to be pretty well lost without my chickens, Frank, but I've got a lot of stuff stored away in that trunk, old game-strain records and so on. Maybe I could write a useful book on breeding.' He shook his head sadly. 'I don't know. I suppose I'll find something to do with my time.'

To get rid of him, I clapped him on the shoulder, sat down, and unbuckled my jodhpur boots.

I was growing weary of always being on the receiving end of personal confidences and long sad stories. The man who is unable to talk back is at the mercy of these people. He is like an inexperienced priest who listens tolerantly to the first simple confessions of impure thoughts, and then listens with increasing horror as the sins mount, one outdoing the other until he is shocked into dumbness. And, of course, the sinner takes advantage of a man's credulousness, loading ever greater sins upon him to see how far he can really go now that he has found a trapped listener who is unable to stop him. My ears had been battered by the outpourings of troubles, tribulations, aspirations, and the affairs of broken hearts for two years and seven months. Only by being rude enough to leave the scene had I evaded some of my confessors.

But Ed Middleton was wise enough to take the hint.

'Good night, Frank,' he said finally, 'I'll see you in the morning,' and the door closed behind him.

After taking a needed shower I switched on the little television set and sat on the couch to watch the gray, shimmering images. There was a lot of snow, and jagged bars of black appeared much too often. In less than five minutes I was forced to turn it off. I'm not overly fond of television anyway. Traveling around so much I have never formed the habit of watching it. And I've never owned a set.

I was impressed by this pleasant room of Ed Middleton's. It was a man's room, and if he really wanted to write a book about cock-breeding, it was certainly quiet enough. I doubted, however, that he would ever write one. What Ed Middleton did with his remaining years was no concern of mine, and yet I found myself worried about him. He had been fighting game fowl and refereeing pit matches for thirty-odd years. Without any birds to fool around with, what could he possibly do with his time? I felt sorry for the old man.

He had a nice home, his wife was a wonderful woman, and the Citrus Syndicate took care of his orange groves. He had turned over the operation of his groves to the Central Citrus Syndicate some years back. In return, they paid him a good percentage on the crop each year, and now he didn't have to do anything with his trees except to watch them grow. By giving up cockfighting he was giving up his entire existence, and, like most elderly men who retire, he probably wouldn't live very long – with nothing to do. Martha was wrong, dead wrong, in forcing Ed to give up his game chickens.

Mary Elizabeth's opposition to the sport was the major reason we had never gotten married. Why can't the American woman accept a man for what he is instead of trying to make him over into the idealized image of her father or someone else?

There was no use worrying about Ed Middleton. I had problems of my own that were more pressing. But with a little pushing from me, my problems would somehow take care of themselves. All I knew was that I had to do what I knew best how to do. Nothing else mattered.

I switched off the light and, despite the lumpiness of the beat-up old couch, fell asleep within minutes.

Chapter Four

It seemed as if I had only been asleep for about five minutes when the lights were switched on and Ed Middleton yelled at me to get up.

'Are you going to sleep all day?' he shouted gruffly. 'I've been up for more than an hour already. Come on out to the kitchen when you get dressed. I've got a pot of coffee on.'

Reluctantly, I sat up, kicked off the sheet, and swung my feet to the floor. The door banged shut and I looked at my wristwatch. 5:30 a.m. It was pretty late to be sleeping. No wonder Ed had hollered at me. I stumbled into the bathroom. After a quick shave I dug some clean white socks out of my suitcase, and put on the same clothes I had worn the day before. I joined Ed in the kitchen, and sat at the breakfast nook.

'We can eat breakfast later, Frank,' he said, pouring two cups of coffee. 'Coffee'll hold us for a while. I want to show you something first.'

I drank the coffee black, and it was thick enough to slice with my knife.

'You want a glass of orange juice?'

I held up a hand to show that coffee was enough for now.

Ed refilled my cup, set the pot back on the stove, and paced up and down on the shiny terrazzo floor. He wore an old pair of blue bib overalls and an expensive, embroidered short-sleeved sport shirt. The bottoms of the overalls were tucked into a pair of ten-inch, well-oiled engineer boots. His great paunch stretched the middle of the overalls tight, but the bib on his chest flapped loosely as he walked.

The second cup of coffee seemed hotter than the first, and I was forced to sip it slowly. Ed snapped his fingers impatiently, pushed open the back door, and said over his shoulder, 'Come on, Frank. We can have breakfast later, like I told you already.'

I gulped down the remainder of the coffee and followed him outside to the patio. The sun was just rising, and the upper rim could be seen through the trees. The tops of the orange trees across the pond were dipped in molten, golden-green fire. The oranges on the darker green lower limbs of the trees looked as if they had been painted on. A mist rose from the tiny lake like steam rising from a pot of water just before it begins to boil. Ed Middleton sat down in the center of the little skiff tied to the concrete pier, and fitted the oars into the locks. I sat forward in the prow.

'Untie the line, Frank, and let's cast off.'

Mr Middleton rowed across the lake – all forty yards of it. It would have been less trouble to take the path that circled the pond, but if he wanted to use the skiff, it didn't make any difference to me.

When we reached the other side of the pond, I jumped out, held the skiff steady for Mr Middleton, and then both of us pulled the boat onto dry land. There was a narrow path through the grove, and I trailed the old man for about five hundred yards until we reached his chicken walks. There was a flat, well-hidden clearing in the grove, and about a dozen coop walks, each separated by approximately twenty yards. The walks were eight feet tall, about ten feet wide by thirty feet in length, with the tops and sides covered with chicken wire. The baseboards were two feet high, and painted with old motor oil to keep down the mite population.

Seeing the empty walks reminded me of my own farm in Ocala, although I had a better setup for coop-walked birds than Ed Middleton. At one time, many years before, long before he had converted his land to orange trees, he had had the ideal setup for a country-walked rooster. A pond, gently rolling terrain, and enough trees for the chickens to choose their own limbs for roosting. We walked down the row of walks to the end coop. As the rooster crowed, Ed turned around with a proud expression and pointed to the cock.

If there is anything more beautiful than the sight of a purebred gamecock in the light of early morning I do not know what it is. This fighting cock of Ed's was the most brilliantly colored chicken I had ever seen, and I've seen hundreds upon hundreds of chickens.

Middleton had devoted sixteen years and countless generations of game fowl to developing the famous Middleton Gray, and there were traces of the Gray in the cock's shawl and broad, flat chest. But the cock was a hybrid of some kind that I couldn't place or recognize. He walked proudly to the fence and tossed his head back and crowed, beating the tips of his long wings together. The tips of his wings were edged with vermilion. The crow of a fighting cock is strong and deep and makes the morning sounds of a common dunghill barnyard rooster sound puny in comparison.

The same flaming color that tipped his wings was repeated in his head feathers and thighs, but his remaining feathers, including the sweep of his high curving tail, were a luminous peacock blue. Ed was planning – or had planned – to keep him for a brood cock, because his comb and wattles hadn't been clipped for fighting. His lemon beak was strong, short and evenly met. His feet and legs were as orange and bright as a freshly painted bridge.

The floor of the cock's private walk was thickly covered with a mixture of finely ground oyster shells and well-grated charcoal, essential ingredients for a fighter's diet. The oyster shells were for lime content, and the charcoal for digestion, but against this salt-and-pepper background, the cock's colorful plumage was emphasized.

Unfortunately, coloring is not the essential factor for a winning gamecock. Good blood *first*, know-how in conditioning, and a good farm walk are the three essentials a pit bird needs to win. I knew that thirty years of cock-breeding knowledge had found its way into that cock. I could see it in every feather, and his good blood was assured by the pleased smile on Ed Middleton's thin lips.

'Except for a couple of battered Grays and an old Middleton hen I've kind of kept around for a pet, this is the only cock I've got left. I've never pitted him, and he's overdue, but I was afraid to lose him. Not really, Frank. I know damned well he can outhit any other cock in the South!'

I agreed with him, at least in theory. I spread my arms, grinned, and shook my head with admiration. Ed nodded sagely with self-satisfaction, and I didn't blame him. A flush slowly enveloped his features until his entire face was as red as his bulbous nose.

'He's got a pretty damned fancy handle, Frank,' Ed said. 'I call him Icarus. You probably remember the old legend from school. There was a guy named Daedalus, who had a son named Icarus. Anyway, these two – Greeks they were – got tossed into jail, and Daedalus made a pair of wings out of wax for his boy to escape. This kid, Icarus, put on the wings and flew so damned high he reached the sun and the wings melted on him. He fell to the ground and was killed. No man has ever flown so high before or since, but, anyway, that's the handle I hung on the chicken. Icarus.'

Ed Middleton cracked his knuckles and clomped away from the walk and entered the feed shack. I gripped the chicken wire with my fingers and turned my attention to

Icarus. For a rugged character like Ed Middleton, the highbrow name and the story that went with it were fairly romantic, I thought. Most cockers who fight a lot of cocks don't get around to naming them in the first place. A metal leg band with the cock's weight and owner number usually suffices for identification. Of course, a favorite brood cock, or a bird that has won several battles, is frequently named. But I went along with Ed all the way. As far as looks were concerned the fancy name fitted the chicken to a T. However, if I had owned the bird, I would have called him Icky, and kept the private name to myself.

I entered the feed shed, dipped into the open sack of cracked corn in the corner, and picked out a dozen fat grains. I returned to the cock's walk, opened the gate and entered. As the cock watched me with his head to one side I lined up the grains of corn on the ground about six inches apart. The cock marched toward me boldly, eating as he came, and pecked the remaining grain of corn out of my outstretched palm. He wasn't a man fighter. Ed had probably spent a good many hours talking to the cock and gently handling him. I picked Icarus up with both hands, holding him underhanded, and examined the cock's legs and feet.

They hung down in perfect alignment with his body. If a cock's legs are out of line with the direction of his body, he is called a dry-heeled cock, because he can't hit and do much harm. But if the legs are in perfect direction, the cock stands erect, and he rises high. And usually he's a close hitter. This cock's legs were perfect.

I lowered the cock to the ground, released him and opened the gate. The cock tried to follow me out, and I liked that, for some reason. Ed came out of the feed shack, and showed me the bird's weight chart, which was attached to a clipboard.

Icarus was seventeen months old and weighed 4:03 pounds. He had maintained this weight fairly well for the past three months, within two ounces either way. For a cock that wasn't on a conditioning diet, this even weight indicated that the bird was healthy enough. He was fed cracked corn twice a day, barley water, and purged twice a week with a weak solution of one grain of calomel and one grain of bicarbonate of soda dissolved in water.

The flirting and exercising sections on the chart were empty. I tapped them with a forefinger and looked questioningly at Mr Middleton.

'I haven't done any conditioning, Frank. But as you can see, I've watched his weight closely. He should go to 4:05, maybe, or 4:07 at most – under training. That's my opinion, anyway,' he qualified his estimate. For a full minute, Ed looked through the fence at the cock, and I returned the weight chart to the hook on the wall inside the shack.

'Do you want this cock, Frank?' Ed asked fiercely, when I rejoined him.

What could I say? I stretched out the fingers of my left hand and made a sawing gesture on my right forearm. I shook my head, then made the sawing motion higher up, at the shoulder.

'Okay, Frank. You can have him for five hundred dollars. I told Martha last night you'd come home with me to buy the last of my chickens. So that's the price. Pay me and take him!'

The old cock fancier dug his hands into his pockets and walked away from me, unable, for the moment, to look me in the face.

He knew perfectly well I didn't have five hundred dollars, and he also knew that the cock wasn't worth that much. For fifty dollars apiece I could purchase country-walked gamecocks, with authenticated bloodlines, from almost any top breeder in the United States. And fifty dollars was a good price. The average for a purebred cock was thirty-five, and I could buy stags for ten and fifteen dollars apiece. I've seen Ace cocks sell for a hundred, and sometimes for one hundred and fifty – but never for five hundred.

No breeder wants to sell any of his fighters to another cocker he may meet at the same pit someday. The cock he sells or gives away may possibly kill some of his own birds in a pitting. On the other hand, the breeders who raise game fowl to sell would be thought ridiculous if they attempted to peddle an untested cock for five hundred dollars!

The answer was simple. Ed Middleton didn't want to sell Icarus. He was looking for an out to keep his pet. After I left he could tell Martha I had made an offer and that he had promised to sell it to me. Anybody else who came around to buy it could be legitimately refused. 'I'd be glad to sell it,' he could truthfully say to a prospective buyer, 'but I've promised the cock to Frank Mansfield. Sorry . . .'

The old bastard was trying to renege on his promise to his wife. Knowing that I didn't have his price and was unlikely to pay it if I did, he planned on keeping his pet cock until it died of an old age. One thing I did know. If I showed up with the money, he would have to sell it. And I wanted that bird. I seemed to sense somehow that this was the turning point in my run of bad luck at the pits . . . Little Icky.

Standing by an orange tree, Ed jerked a piece of fruit from a lower limb and threw it in a looping curve over the trees, I could hear the mushy thud of the orange as it landed deep in the grove. I crossed the space separating us with an outstretched right hand.

Ed grimly accepted my promise to buy his cock with a strong handshake.

While Mr Middleton made a mixture of barley water, I leaned against the door of the feed shack and finished my cigarette. Somehow, I was going to get the money to buy that cock. Now my impending trip to Jacksonville had a sharpened point to it. If Doc Riordan had any money at all, I intended to get it.

Ed measured out the cracked corn and fed his pet, the two battered Gray roosters, and the old hen. Although I could feel some sympathy for Martha in not wanting her husband out traveling the cockfight circuits, I could not understand her desire to make him give up cock-breeding. If she considered cock-breeding morally wrong, she could have consoled herself with the idea that Ed was doing the breeding, not her. A man like Ed Middleton could never give up his love of the game. Perhaps she was going through her menopause and, as a consequence, was losing her mind.

'Let's go get us some breakfast, Frank,' Ed said, as he locked the feed shack door. Ed started down the path toward the lake, and I lingered for a last look at Icarus. He pecked away at his grain hungrily. I could see the fine breeding of the cock in his stance and proud bearing. The cock had shape, health, and an inborn stamina. Through proper conditioning I could teach him responsiveness, alertness, improve his speed, and sharpen his natural reflexes. Other than that, there wasn't much else I could do for the cock. His desire to fight was inherited. And the only way his gameness could be tested truly was in the pit.

I turned away from the walk and ran down the path to catch up with Ed.

When we entered the kitchen Martha greeted us cheerfully and began to prepare our breakfast. Ed and I sat down across from each other at the breakfast nook and I inhaled the delicious fragrance of the frying bacon. It was quite a breakfast: crisp bacon, fried eggs, hot biscuits, grits and melted butter, orange juice, and plenty of orange-blossom honey to coil onto the fluffy biscuits.

As I sat back with a full stomach to drink my after-breakfast coffee, Ed told his wife that I was going to buy his remaining chickens.

226

'That's wonderful, Ed,' Martha said happily. She smiled at me and bobbed her chin several times. 'You know Ed wouldn't sell those old birds to just anybody, Frank. But Ed has always had a lot of respect for you, and I know you'll take good care of them.'

I nodded, finished my coffee, and slid out of the booth.

'Frank isn't taking the cocks today, Martha,' Ed said, getting up from the table. 'He'll be back for them later on.'

'Oh, I didn't know that! I thought he was taking them now.'

'These deals aren't made in an instant, sweetheart,' Ed said sharply. 'But we've shaken hands on the deal, and Frank'll be back, all in good time.' He forced a smile and turned toward me. 'Come on, Frank. I'll drive you into Orlando.'

'Where're you going, Frank?' Martha asked.

I shrugged indifferently and returned her smile. This was the kind of question that could only be answered by writing it down, and I didn't feel that it required an answer. Where I was going or what I was going to do couldn't possibly have any real interest for the old lady.

'Frank can't answer questions like that without writing them down,' Ed reminded his wife. 'But you know we'll be reading about him in the trade magazines.'

'Well, I'll pack a lunch for you anyway. Wait out on the patio. Take some more coffee out there with you. It'll only take a minute and you can surely wait that long.'

While she fixed a lunch for me, I repacked my suitcase and took it out to the car. Ed unlocked the door, and I removed the coop and handed it to him before I tossed the suitcase on the floorboards.

'Sure, leave the coop with me if you like,' he said, leaning it against the concrete wall.

When I returned for Icky, I could use the coop to carry him, and I didn't feel like lugging it along to Jacksonville, not hitchhiking, anyway.

227

A few minutes later Martha joined us on the patio and handed me a heavy paper bag containing my lunch.

'I used the biscuits left from breakfast,' she said, 'and made a few ham sandwiches. There's a fat slice of tomato on each one and plenty of mayonnaise. There wasn't any pie left, but I put in a couple of apples for dessert.'

Rather than simply shake hands with her, I put an arm around her narrow shoulders and kissed her on the cheek. Mrs Middleton broke away from me and returned to the safety of her kitchen. Ed called through the door that he would be back from Orlando when he got back.

We drove down Ed's private road to the highway. I didn't know where he was taking me, but I hoped he wouldn't drop me off in the center of town. With the baggage I was carrying, the best place to start hitchhiking was on the I-4 Throughway on the other side of Winter Park. Several years had passed since I had been forced to use my thumb, and I wasn't too happy about the prospect.

Orlando is a fairly large city and well spread out. The streets that morning were crowded with traffic. Ed drove his big car skillfully, and when he hit the center of town, he made several turns and then stopped in front of the Greyhound bus station. I took my baggage out of the back and started to close the door, but held it open when Ed heaved himself across the seat. He got out on my side, reached in his wallet, and handed me a twenty-dollar bill.

'You can't hitchhike with all that stuff, Frank. You'd better take a bus.'

I nodded, accepted the bill and buttoned it into my shirt pocket. That made five hundred and twenty dollars I owed him, but I was grateful for the loan.

We shook hands rather formally, and Ed plucked at his white chin with his puffy fingers. 'Now don't worry about Icarus, Frank,' he said with an attempt at levity. 'I'll take good care of him whether you come back for him or not.' His eyes were worried just the same.

I held up two spread fingers in the 'V' sign. It was a meaningless gesture in this instance, but Ed smiled, thinking I meant it for him. I remained at the curb and waved to him as he drove away.

I picked a folder out of the rack, circled Jacksonville on the timetable with my ballpoint pencil, shoved the folder and my twenty under the wicket, and paid for my ticket. After slipping the ticket into my hatband, I gathered my baggage around me and sat down on a bench to wait for the bus.

I thought about Icky. In reality, five hundred dollars wasn't even enough money to get started. I needed a bare minimum of one thousand five hundred dollars to have at least a thousand left over after paying for the cock. Two thousand was more like it.

Somehow, I had to get my hands on this money.

Chapter Five

I didn't arrive in Jacksonville until a little after three that afternoon. Instead of waiting for an express, I had taken the first bus that left Orlando, and it turned out to be the kind that stops at every filling station, general store and cow pasture along the way. A long, dull ride.

After getting my baggage out of the side of the bus from the driver I left the station and walked three blocks to the Jeff Davis Hotel, where I always stayed when I was in Jax. On the way to the hotel I stopped at a package store and bought a pint of gin.

Perhaps the Jeff Davis isn't the most desirable hotel in Jax, but it is downtown, handy to everything, the people know me there, and crowded or not I can always get a room. The manager follows cockfighting, advertises in the game fowl magazines, and there is usually someone hanging around the lobby who knows me. The daily rate is attractive, as well – only three dollars a day for cockers, instead of the regular rate of five.

As soon as I checked in at the desk and got to my room, I opened my suitcase and dug out my corduroy coat. In September, Jacksonville turns chilly in the afternoons, and the temperature drops below seventy. Not that it gets cold, but the weather doesn't compare favorably with southern Florida. The long pull of gin I took before going out on the street again felt warm in my stomach.

I walked briskly through the streets to the post office, entered, and twirled the combination dial on my post-office box. It didn't open, but I could see that there was mail inside the box through the dirty brown glass window. I searched through my wallet, found my box receipt for the rental, and shoved it through the window to the clerk. He studied the slip for a moment, and called my attention to the date.

'You're almost ten days overdue on your quarterly box payment, Mr Mansfield,' he said. 'Your box was closed out and rented to somebody else. I'm sorry, but there's a big demand for boxes these days and I don't have any more open at present. If you want me to, I'll put your name on the waiting list.'

I shook my head, pointed to the rack of mail behind him. This puzzled him for a moment, and then he said: 'Oh, you mean your mail?'

I nodded impatiently, drumming my fingers on the marble ledge.

'If you have any, it'll be at the general-delivery window.'

I picked up my receipt and gave it to the woman at the general-delivery window. She handed me two letters and my current *Southern Cockfigher* magazine. I shoved the letters and magazine into my coat pocket and filled in change-of-address cards to transfer the magazine and post-office-box letters to my Ocala address. After mailing one card to the magazine and turning in the other to the woman at the window I returned to my hotel room.

The first letter I opened was from a pit operator in Tallahassee inviting me to enter a four-cock derby he was holding in November. I tossed the letter into the wastebasket. The other letter was the one I had been expecting. It was from the Southern Conference Tournament committee, and contained my invitation, the rules, and the schedule for the SCT season.

I studied the mimeographed schedule, but I wasn't too happy about it. There wasn't a whole lot of time to obtain and keep gamecocks for the tourney.

SCHEDULE
SOUTHERN CONFERENCE

Oct. 15 – Greenville, Mississippi
Nov. 10 – Tifton, Georgia
Nov. 30 – Plant City, Florida
Dec. 15 – Chattanooga, Tennessee
Jan. 10 – Biloxi, Mississippi
Jan. 28 – Auburn, Alabama
Feb. 24 – Ocala, Florida
Mar. 15 – 16 – SCT – Milledgeville, Georgia

I was already too late for Greenville, Mississipi. The SCT
was unlike other invitational mains and derbies, both in
rules and gamecock standards. When Senator Foxhall had
organized the SCT back in the early thirties, his primary
purpose had been to improve the breeds and gameness in
southern cockfighting. The hardest rule of the tourney
was that all the cocks entered in the final round at
Milledgeville had to be four-time winners. A cock can win
one or sometimes two fights with flashy flies in the first
pitting, and some good luck. But any cock that wins four
in a row is dead game. Luck simply doesn't stretch through
four wins. This single SCT rule, more than any other, had
certainly raised breeding standards in the South, and it
kept out undesirables and fly-by-night cockers looking for
a fast dollar. All the pit operators on the SCT circuit were
checked from time to time by members of the committee,
and if their standards of operation dropped, they were
dropped, in turn, by the senator.

Like the other big-time chicken men, I had fought
cocks in the highly competitive six-day International
Tournament in both Orlando and Saint Pete, and I
intended to enter it again someday, but I preferred the
more rigid policies of the SCT. It was possible to enter

the annual International Tournament by posting a preliminary two-hundred-dollar forfeit, which was lost if you didn't show up and pay the three-hundred-dollar balance. The winning entries made big money at the International, but I could make just as much at SCT pits and at the final Milledgeville meet. And the wins on the SCT circuit really meant something to me.

At that moment, however, I didn't feel like a big-time cockfighter. I was at rock bottom and it was ironical to even think about fighting any cocks this season. All I had in my wallet was eighteen dollars, plus some loose change in my pockets. I owned a thirty-dollar guitar, a gaff case, a few clothes in a battered suitcase, and a lease on a farm.

Of course, the contents of my gaff case were worth a few hundred dollars, but I needed everything I had to fight cocks. I sat down on the edge of my bed, and opened my gaff case to search for the last letter Doc Riordan had sent me. I opened the letter, but before reading it again, I made a quick inventory of the gaff case to see if there was anything I could do without. There wasn't. I needed every item.

There were sixteen sets of gaffs, ranging from the short one-and-one-quarter-inch heels I preferred, up to a pair of three-inch Texas Twisters. I even had a set of slashers a Puerto Rican breeder had given me one afternoon in San Juan. With slashers, the bird is armed on one leg only. I don't believe in fighting slashers for one simple reason. When you fight slashers, the element of chance is too great, and the best cock doesn't always win. With a wicked sharp blade on a cock's left leg, the poorest cock can sometimes get in a lucky hit. Pointed gaffs, round from socket to point, are legitimate. Once a cock's natural spur points have been sawed off, the hand-forged heels fitted over the half-inch stumps are a clean substitute for his God-given spurs, and they make for humane fighting. Two cocks meeting anywhere in their natural state will fight to the death or until one of them runs away. Steel spurs merely speed up the killing process, and a cock doesn't have to punish himself unnecessarily by bruising his natural spurs.

Of course, I had fought slashers when I was a soldier in the Philippines because I had to, and I knew how to fight them. But I had never considered them altogether fair because of that slight element of chance. Cockfighting is the only sport that can't be fixed, perhaps the only fair contest left in America. A cock wouldn't throw a fight and couldn't if he knew how.

Every pair of my sixteen sets of heels was worth from twenty to thirty-five dollars, and I needed them all. The correct length of heels is a common argument, but what really determines the right length for any given cock is the way it fights. And even though I favor short heels, like they use in the North, or 'short-heel country' as the North is called, I would never handicap a cock by arming him with the wrong spurs out of vain, personal preference. It is a crime not to arm a cock with the spurs which will allow him to fight his very best.

In addition to my heel sets I had a spur saw, with a dozen extra blades, moleskin heeling tape, blade polishers, gaff pointers, a set of artificial stubs for heeling slip-leg cocks, two pairs of dubbing shears, one curved and the other straight, and two new heeling outfits, each containing pads, tie strings and leather crosspieces. There was also a brand new roll of Irish flax, waxed tie string, some assorted salves and a few gland stimulation capsules. To anybody except a cocker, this collection of expensive equipment was worthless junk. If I pawned the entire contents of my case, a pawnbroker wouldn't give me more than forty dollars for the lot.

For a few thoughtful moments I clicked the dubbing shears in my hand, and then picked up Doc's letter. I'd been carrying it around in my case for more than three months.

Dear Frank,

I haven't written you for some time, but I wanted you to know your investment is as good as gold. Don't be surprised if you get a stock split one of these days soon and double your eight hundred dollars. Next time you get to Jax, drop in and see me and I'll give you the details.

Very truly yours,

Doc Riordan

To anyone who didn't know Doc Riordan, this letter would have sounded encouraging indeed. But the letter was more than three months old and, unfortunately, I knew Doc too well. I liked the man for what he was and respected him for what he was trying to be. But unlike me, Doc lived with a big dream that was practically unattainable. All I wanted to be was the best cockfighter who ever lived. Doc, who had already reached his late fifties, wanted to be a big-time capitalist and financier.

He wasn't a real doctor, I knew that much. He was a pharmacist, and a good one, and somewhere along the years he had added Doc to his name. I had met him several years before at various Florida cockpits, and I had bought conditioning powder and ergot capsules from him when he still had his mail-order business. Conditioning powder can be made up by any pharmacist who is given the formula, but Doc was dependable, well liked by cockers, and he had also invented a salve that was a quick healer for battered cocks. However, there are a lot of businessmen who advertise the same types of items in the cocker journals. There wasn't enough big money in cocker medical supplies for Doc, and he dropped out of the field. However, he would still supply a few friends like myself when we wrote to him.

Some four years before, Doc had caught me in an amiable mood and with more than five thousand dollars in my pockets. I had put eight hundred dollars into his company – The Dixie Pharmaceutical Company – and I had never received a dividend. I had had several glowing letters from him, but not a cent in cash. In fact, I didn't even have any stock certificates to show for my investment. It was one of those word-of-mouth deals so many of us enter into in the South. A handshake is enough, and I knew my money would be returned on demand . . . providing Doc had it. But whether he had it or not was something else altogether.

It was five o'clock and I decided to wait and see him in the morning. Feeling as low as I did, I didn't want to return to my room with a turndown that evening.

I left my room, walked down the street to a café and ate two hamburgers and drank two glasses of milk. When I returned to my room, I nipped at the gin and read my new *Southern Cockfighter* magazine. The magazine had been published and mailed out before the Belle Glade derby, but there was a short item about the Homestead pitting, and my name was mentioned in Red Carey's column, 'On the Gaff.'

Looks like bad luck is still dogging Silent Frank Mansfield. His sad showing at Homestead makes us wonder if his keeping methods are off the beam. Another season like his last three, and we doubt if he'll still be on the SCT rolls.

The item should have irritated me, but it didn't. A columnist has to put something in his column, and I was fair game. There was nothing wrong with my conditioning methods. They had paid off too many times in the past. My problem was to get the right cocks, and when I got Icky from Mr Middleton, I would be off to a good season. I finished the rest of the gin and went to bed.

As far back as 320 BC an old poet named Chanakya wrote that a man can learn four things from a cock: To fight, to get up early, to eat with his family, and to protect his spouse when she gets into trouble. I had learned how to fight and how to get up early, but I had never gotten along too well with my family and I didn't have any spouse to protect. Fighting was all very well, but getting up early was not the most desirable habit to have when living in a big city like Jacksonville.

The next morning I was up, dressed and shaved, and sitting in the lobby by five thirty. I bought a morning *Times-Union*, glanced at the headlines and then went out for breakfast because the hotel coffee shop didn't open until seven thirty. I lingered as long as I could over coffee, but it was still only six thirty when I returned to the hotel. I was too impatient just to sit around, and I soon left the dreary lobby and walked the early morning streets. The wind off the river was chilly and it felt good to be stirring about. A sickly sun rode the pale morning sky, but after an hour passed it began to get warm and promised to be a good day.

Promptly at eight I entered the Latham building to see if Doc Riordan had arrived at his office. The Latham building was an ancient red-brick structure of seven stories built in the early 1900s. Nothing had been done to it since. The entrance lobby was narrow, grimy and filled with trash blown in from the street. There was a crude, hand-lettered sign on the elevator stating that it was out of order. Doc's company was on the sixth floor.

The stairwell up was unlighted and without windows. I climbed the six flights only to discover that his office was closed. The office was two doors away from the far end of the hallway, and the frosted glass top half of the door had gold letters painted on it four inches high:

THE DIXIE PHARMACEUTICAL CO.

Dr Onyx P. Riordan

PRESIDENT AND GENERAL MANAGR.

I tried the door and found it locked. Rather than descend the stairs and then climb up again I leaned against the wall and smoked cigarettes until Doc showed up.

The wait was less than twenty minutes and I heard Doc huffing up the stairs long before I could see him. He entered the hall, red-faced, carrying a large cardboard container of coffee. The container was too hot for him to hold comfortably, and as he recovered his breath, he kept shifting it from one hand to the other as he fumbled with his key in the door lock.

'Come on in, Frank,' Doc said, as he opened the door. 'Soon as I set this coffee on the desk I'll shake hands.'

I followed Doc into the tiny office, and we shook hands. Doc wiped his perspiring bald head and brow with a handkerchief and cursed angrily for two full minutes before he sat down behind his desk.

'I've told the superintendent before and I'm going to tell him one more time,' Doc said as he ran down, 'and if he don't get that damned elevator fixed, I'm moving out! That's a fact, Frank, a fact!'

I sat down in a straight-backed chair in front of Doc's desk, and surveyed his ratty little office. A single dirty window afforded a close-up of the side of a red-brick movie theater less than three feet away, and the proximity of the building didn't allow much light into the room. Doc probably had to burn his desk and ceiling lights even at midday. Doc's desk was a great, wooden, square affair, and much too large for the size of the room. In front of the fluorescent desk lamp was his carved desk sign: *Dr*

Onyx P. Riordan, Pres. (and a beautifully carved ornate job it was, too). In addition to his desk there was a low two-drawer filing cabinet, the swivel executive chair he was sitting in, and two straight-backed chairs. These simple furnishings made the room overly crowded. On the wall behind his desk was a hand-lettered, professionally done poster in three primary colors praising the virtues of a product called Licarbo. After reading the poster I studied Doc's face. He had taken two green dime-store cups out of his desk and was filling them with black coffee.

With his bald head and tonsure of thin, fine gray hair, Doc looked his fifty some-odd years, all right, but there was a certain youthfulness about his face that denied those years. His features were all small, gathered together in the center of a round, bland face. His mouth and snubby nose were small. His blue eyes were ingenuously wide and revealed the full optic circle. With his round red cheeks and freshly scrubbed look, Doc could probably have passed for thirty if he wore a black toupee and dyed his eyebrows to match.

'It's been a long time, Frank,' Doc said sincerely, 'and I'm really glad to see you again.' He sat back with a pleased smile. 'I want to show you something!'

He began to rummage through his desk. I sipped some coffee and lit another cigarette from the butt of the one I was smoking. The sight of this little hole-in-the-wall office had dashed any hopes I might have had about getting even a portion of my money back from the old pharmacist.

'Read this, Frank!' Doc said eagerly, sliding a letter across the broad surface of the desk. I read the letter. It was from a drug laboratory in New York.

President
Dixie Pharmaceutical Co.
Latham Building
Jacksonville, Florida

Dear Dr Riordan:

We have made exhaustive tests of your product,
LICARBO, at your request, and we agree that it is
nontoxic, and that it will provide nonharmful relief to
certain types of indigestion, such as overeating, overindul-
gence, etc.

However, we are not in the market for such a product at
this time. Thank you for letting us examine it. Best wishes.

Very truly yours,

The signature was indecipherable, but vice-president was
typed beneath the inked scribble. I put the letter down
on the desk.

'Do you realize what that letter means, Frank?' Doc
said excitedly. 'They're interested, definitely interested!
They couldn't find a single fault, and do you know why?
Licarbo doesn't have any, that's why! I've dealt with
companies like that before. They think I'll sell out for
little or nothing, but if they want Licarbo, and you can
read between the lines of the letter that they're dying to
get it, it'll cost them plenty!'

Doc sat back in his big chair, steepled his fingers
together, and attempted to look shrewd by narrowing his
eyes. His narrowed eyes only made him look sleepy,
however.

'Not only do I want a flat ten thousand for my rights,
Frank, I'm also holding out for a percentage on every
package sold. Now what do you think of that?'

I admired Doc's spirit, but, evidently, he refused to
recognize a politely worded turndown when he saw it. I
shrugged my shoulders noncommittally.

'By God, I forgot!' Doc snapped his fingers. 'You haven't
tried Licarbo yet, have you?'

I shook my head. Doc opened the top right drawer of his desk and removed three flat packets approximately the size and shape of restaurant-size sugar packets. The name Licarbo was printed in red ink on each packet, including directions to take as needed, with or without water, following overindulgence, overeating or for mild stomach distress.

'Go ahead, Frank, open one up and taste it. There isn't a better relief for indigestion in the world than Licarbo! Take it with a glass of water and you'll belch every time. What more does a man want than a big healthy belch when his belly hurts him? Right? In the South we like our medicines in powder and liquid form. No self-respecting Southerner will take a fancy capsule for belly pains, no matter how many colors it's got.'

I ripped open a packet and spilled some of the mixture into my hand. Licarbo resembled gunpowder, or a mixture of salt and black pepper, heavy on the pepper. I put my tongue to the mixture. It tasted like licorice, not an unpleasant taste at all.

'Mix it in with your coffee, Frank. Licarbo will dissolve almost instantly.'

I shuddered at this suggestion, shook my head and smiled.

'Tastes good, don't it?' Doc beamed proudly, folding his short arms across his chest. 'All it is, Frank, is a mixture of licorice root, bicarbonate of soda, a few secret ingredients and some artificial coloring. But the formula will make me rich, and you too, Frank. It takes time, however, to invent and develop a new product and get it out to the waiting market. The New York company isn't my only prospect, not by any means. I've got feelers out all over the nation. This is the *big* one, Frank, the one I've been working up to through thirty years in practical pharmacy. I've invented other products and sold them too, but this time I'm holding out to the last breath. Why, if I only had the capital I could manufacture Licarbo myself and literally make a fortune. A fortune!'

Doc turned in his chair, sighed deeply, and looked out the window at the rusty wall of the theater.

'People just don't have faith no more, Frank. People today don't recognize a commercial drug when they see and taste it, damn them all, anyway! But this product has got to go over, it *has* to!' Doc dropped the level of his voice, and said softly, as if to convince himself, 'It's only a matter of time, Frank. Only a matter of time . . .'

I slipped the two unopened packets of Licarbo into my jacket pocket. At least I had something to show for my eight-hundred-dollar investment. Doc swiveled his chair and faced me with a bright smile.

'I made this first batch up myself, Frank, and had the sample packages printed up here in town. It costs a lot of money to get started, but you've got to admit the product is good, don't you?'

I nodded, pursing my lips. As far as I was concerned, Licarbo was as good as any one of a hundred similar products on the market. Plain old bicarbonate of soda will make you belch if a belch is required, and that was Doc's main ingredient.

'You'd like to have your eight hundred dollars back just the same. Am I right?' Doc said hesitantly.

I spread my hands, palms up, and nodded.

'Well, I just don't have it right now, Frank.' Doc wet his thumb. 'I just don't have it. But you'll get it back one of these days soon, every damned dime, and with plenty of interest. To be honest, I'm just hanging on these days. Don't even have a phone anymore in the office, as you can see. I've got a part-time pharmacist's job at night in a drugstore near my rooming house, and every cent I make goes into office rent, promotion of Licarbo, and I'm barely getting by on what's left. I've dropped everything else to concentrate on Licarbo, but when it hits, and it's going to, it'll be big, really big!'

Old Doc Riordan was another man like myself, riding along on an inborn, over-inflated self-confidence and a wide outward smile. Deep inside, I knew he was worried sick about being unable to write me a check for my money. Well, I could relieve him from that worry in a hurry. Whether his product ever went over big or not was no concern of mine. I wasn't about to ride another man's dream; I had a big dream of my own. It was time to get the hell off Doc's back.

There was a writing tablet on his desk. I reached for it, took my ballpoint lead pencil out of my coat pocket and wrote on the pad:

President, Dixie Pharm. Co.
In return for a ten-year supply of conditioning powder and other medicinal aids for poultry at the Mansfield Farms, the undersigned hereby turns over all his existing stock in the Dixie Pharm. Co. to the President.

After signing my name with a flourish, I smiled, and handed Doc the tablet. He read the note and frowned.

'Don't you have any faith in Licarbo, Frank?'

I looked at him expressionlessly and nodded slowly.

'Then why are you pulling out?'

I got to my feet, leaned over the desk and underlined 'ten-year supply' on the note I had written.

A knowing smile widened Doc's tiny mouth, and he nodded sagely.

'You're a mighty shrewd businessman, Frank. Why, if you ever expand your farms you'll double your eight hundred dollars in five years easily! But damn your eyes, anyway!' He laughed gleefully. 'I'm just going to take you up on this proposition! Whether Licarbo hits big or not,

I'll either have my own lab or work in a pharmacy some-place where I can get wholesale prices on drugs. So on a deal like this, neither one of us can lose!'

We shook hands, and I turned to go. Doc stopped me at the door by putting his hand on my arm. 'Just a minute, Frank. As soon as I can afford it, I'm moving to a better office. And, of course, when I get enough capital, I'm going to build my own laboratories. But meanwhile, here's the address of the drugstore where I work.' He handed me a card and I slipped it into my wallet. 'I'm on duty there every Friday, Saturday and Sunday night from six to midnight. And almost every Wednesday from noon till midnight. I relieve the owner, you see. So when you need anything, drop me a line there, or come by and see me yourself.'

I opened the door, and returned my wallet to my hip pocket.

'You going to put an entry in the Orlando tourney, Frank?'

I shook my head and pointed north.

'Southern Conference then?'

I nodded.

'Well, I'll probably see you in Milledgeville, then. I haven't missed an SCT in ten years and I don't intend to now. And when you see any of the boys on the road, say hello for me, and tell them I still send out a few things when they write.'

I winked, clapped him on the shoulder, and we shook hands again. I started down the hallway toward the stair-well and Doc watched me all the way. When I reached the stairs, he called good-bye to me again. I waved an arm and descended the stairs. At the drugstore on the corner I had a cup of coffee at the counter and then returned to my room at the Jeff Davis Hotel. Fortunately, I had kept my morning newspaper.

I turned to the classified ads and looked under the Help Wanted, Male section to see what I could do about getting a job.

Chapter Six

It is a funny thing. A man can make a promise to his God, break it five minutes later and never think anything about it. With an idle shrug of his shoulders, a man can also break solemn promises to his mother, wife or sweetheart, and, except for a slight, momentary twinge of conscience, he still won't be bothered very much. But if a man ever breaks a promise he has made to himself he disintegrates. His entire personality and character crumble into tiny pieces, and he is never the same man again.

I remember very well a sergeant I knew in the army. Before a group of five men he swore off smoking forever. An hour later he sheepishly lit a cigarette and broke his vow to the five of us and to himself. He was never quite the same man again, not to me, and not to himself.

My vow of silence was much harder to maintain than a vow to quit smoking. It was a definite handicap in everything I did. I read through the want ads three times, studying them carefully, and there wasn't a single thing I could find to do. A man who can't, or won't, talk is in a difficult situation when it comes to finding a job in the city. Besides, I had never had a job in my life – except for my two years in the service.

Of course, during my year of college at Valdosta State I had waited tables in the co-op for my meals, but I didn't consider that as a job. Growing up in Georgia, I had done farm work for my father when I couldn't get out of it, such things as chopping cotton, milking a cow, and simple carpentry repair jobs around the farm. There were a good many things

I was capable of doing around a farm without having to talk. But the want ads in the newspaper were no help to me at all. Unwilling to use my voice, I couldn't even ask for a job unless I wrote it down. The majority of the situations that were open in the agate columns were for salesmen. And a man who can't talk can't sell anything. I wadded the newspaper into a ball, and tossed it into the wastebasket.

One thing I could always do was walk and condition cocks for another breeder. There were plenty of chicken men in the South who would have jumped at the chance to pay me five dollars apiece for every game fowl I conditioned for them. But for a man who was still considered a big-time cockfighter throughout the South, it would be too much of a comedown to work for another cock breeder. I had never worked for anybody else in my thirty-two years on this earth, and it was too late to start now. By God, I wasn't that desperate!

Sitting in that hotel room, with only a few loose dollars in my pocket, I was beginning to feel sorry for myself. My eyes rested on my guitar case.

My guitar was an old friend. During the first few months of my self-enforced silence, the days and nights had almost doubled in length. It is surprising how much time is killed everyday in idle conversation. Just to have something to fill in time I had purchased a secondhand Gibson guitar for thirty dollars in a Miami pawnshop. The case wasn't so hot – cheap brown cardboard stamped to resemble alligator leather – but the guitar was a good one, and it had a strong, wonderful tone. The guitar served as a substitute for my lost voice, and I don't know what I would have done without it.

I opened the guitar case, removed the instrument and ran through a few exercises to limber my fingers. I hadn't played the guitar for five or six days, but the calluses on my fingers were still hard and tough. The Uncle who sold me the Gibson had also thrown in a free instruction booklet, but I had never learned how to play any regular songs. After learning most of the chords and how to tune and pick the strings, I had tossed the booklet away.

I only knew three songs, and they were tunes I had made up myself, sitting around, picking them out until they sounded like the mental images I wanted them to resemble. One was 'Georgia Girl.' This was a portrait in sound of Mary Elizabeth, my fiancée. The second tune I had composed I called 'Empty Pockets.' My pockets had been empty many times in my life, and in making up this song I had discovered a way of getting a hollow sound effect by banging the box near the hole and playing a succession of fast triplets on the lower three strings at the same time. Despite the hollow sounds, this was a gay, fast tune and I was rather fond of it. The remaining song was merely my impression of an old patchwork quilt Grandma had made many years ago, and that's what I called it – 'Grandma's Quilt.' I had tried to duplicate the colors and designs of that old patchwork, faded quilt in chord patterns, and I had been fairly successful.

My repertoire, then, consisted of three highly personal songs. If it was music, it was reflective music made up for my own personal enjoyment, and not for the general public. But I had to get a few dollars together, and soon, and maybe my guitar was the way? I could have pawned the Gibson for twenty dollars or so, and this sum would pay a week's rent, but if I pawned the guitar, where would I be then?

I decided to take a chance and temporarily invade the world of music. As a last resort, when push came to shove, I could pawn the instrument. I removed my wristwatch, waited until the sweep hand hit twelve, picked up my guitar and played my three songs in succession all the way through. Time elapsed: seventeen minutes, fourteen seconds. Not a lot of time for a guitar concert, but I had nothing to lose by trying, and the songs were all different. Perhaps some bar owner would put me on for a few dollars in the evening.

I shucked out of my black cowboy shirt, which was getting dirty around the collar, even though it didn't show very much, and changed into a clean white shirt. I retied my red silk neckerchief, slipped into my corduroy suit and looked at myself in the dresser mirror. I looked clean and presentable. The red kerchief looked good with a white shirt and my gray-green corduroy suit. The cheap straw cowboy hat pushed back from my forehead was just the right touch for a would-be guitar player. I had burned my name into the yellow box of my guitar with a hot wire two years before, so all I had to do was write something simple on a piece of paper and get going.

I took a fresh sheet of paper out of my notebook, sat down at the desk and looked at it, trying to figure out a strong selling point for my slender abilities. At last it came to me, a simple straightforward statement of fact. In large capital letters I wrote JOB on the page, and put the slip of paper in my shirt pocket. If a prospective owner was interested in the word JOB he would give me an audition. If I got an audition, my guitar would have to talk for me.

I checked the little square felt-covered box inside the case, and there were plenty of extra plastic picks and two new strings wrapped in wax paper. As I started toward the door, carrying my guitar, I caught a glimpse of my grim, determined expression in the mirror. I almost laughed, I made an obscene gesture with my thumb at my grinning reflection and left the room.

The time was only ten thirty. There were dozens of bars, cabarets and beer-and-wine joints in Jacksonville, and I decided to cover them all, one by one, until I found a job.

I entered the first bar I came to down the street and handed the slip of paper to the bartender. He glanced at it, gave it back and pointed to the door.

At the bar on the next corner I tried a different tactic. I had learned a lesson in the first bar. Before presenting my slip of paper to the man in the white jacket, I made the sign of the tall one, and put change on the bar to pay for the beer. Beer is the easiest drink there is to order, whether you can talk or not. No matter how noisy a place is you can always get a bartender's attention by holding stiff hands out straight, the right hand approximately one foot above the left. This gesture will always produce a beer, draft if they have it, or a can of some brand if they do not.

'Sorry, buddy,' the bartender returned my slip of paper, 'but I don't have a music and dancing license. I couldn't hire you if I wanted to.'

I finished my glass of beer and returned to the sidewalk. A license for music and dancing had never occurred to me, but that simple requirement narrowed my search. I decided to become more selective. After bypassing several unlikely bars, and walking a half-dozen blocks, I came to a fairly nice-looking cabaret. There was a small blue winking neon sign in the window that stated Chez Vernon. The entranceway was between a men's haberdashery and a closed movie theater. To the left of the bar entrance another door opened into the package store, which was also a part of the nightclub, and there was a sandwich board on the sidewalk announcing that the James Boys were featured inside every night except Sunday.

There were four eight-by-ten photos of the James Boys mounted on the board, and I studied them for a moment before I went inside. They wore their hair long, almost to the shoulder, but they had on Western-style clothes. They were evidently a country music group. In the smiling photos two of them had Spanish guitars like mine, one held an electric guitar and the remaining member peeped out from behind a bass. I entered the bar.

The bar was in a fairly narrow corridor – most of the space it should have had was crowded out by the partitioning for the package store – but there were approximately twenty-five stools, and a short service bar at the far end. Only one bartender was on duty, and there was only one customer sitting at the first stool. The customer sat with his arms locked behind his back glaring down distastefully at a double shot of whiskey. At night, with a fair-sized crowd, a bar this long would require at least two bartenders.

Beyond the bar there was a large square room with a small dance floor, a raised triangular platform in the corner for the musicians and two microphones. There were about thirty-five small circular tables, with twisted wire ice-cream parlor chairs stacked on top of them. The walls of the large room had been painted in navy blue. Silver cardboard stars had been pasted at random upon the wall and ceiling to simulate a night sky. The ceiling was black, and the scattered light fixtures on the ceiling were in various pastel colors.

Between the bar and the nightclub section there were two lavatories, with their doors recessed about a foot into the wall. A crude effort at humor had been attempted on the restroom doors: One was labeled SETTERS and the other POINTERS. After sizing the place up, I sat down at the far end of the bar and made the sign of the tall one. As I reached for the stein with my left hand, I handed the bartender the slip of paper with my right.

'I only work here,' he said indifferently, eyeing my guitar. 'The James Boys are supposed to play out the month, but the boss is in the back.' He pointed to a curtain covering an arched doorway near the right corner of the bandstand. 'Go ahead and talk to him if you want to.' His face colored slightly as he realized I couldn't talk, but he smiled and shrugged his shoulders. 'His name is Mr Vernon. Lee Vernon.'

As soon as I finished my beer, I picked up my guitar, dropped a half dollar on the bar and headed for the back, pushing the curtain to one side. The hallway was short. There was a door leading to an alley, and two doors on either side. I opened the first door on the right, but it was a small dressing room. I knocked at the door opposite the dressing room and didn't enter until I heard 'Come in.'

For a nightclub owner, Lee Vernon was a much younger man than I expected to meet. He was under thirty, with a mass of black curls, a smiling well-tanned face, and gleaming china-blue eyes. There were three open ledgers on his gray metal desk and a few thick Manila folders. He tapped his large white teeth with a pencil and raised his black eyebrows. I removed my guitar from the case before I handed him the slip of paper.

Lee Vernon laughed aloud when he saw the word JOB and shook his head from side to side with genuine amusement. 'A non-singing guitar player!' he exclaimed, still smiling. 'I never thought I'd see the day. Go ahead' – he looked at my name burned into the guitar box – 'Frank, is it?'

I nodded, and wiped my damp fingers on my jacket so the plastic pick wouldn't slip in my fingers. I put my left foot on a chair, and cradled the instrument over my knee.

'Play anything, Frank,' Vernon smiled. 'I don't care. I've never turned down an excuse to quit working in my life.'

I vamped a few chords and then played 'Empty Pockets' all the way through. Mr Vernon listened attentively, tapping his pencil on the desk in time with the music. This was the shortest of my three songs, but it sounded good in the tiny office. The ceiling was low and there was a second listen effect reverberating in the room, especially during the thumping part.

'I like the sound, Frank,' Vernon said. 'You're all right. All right. But I don't think I can use you right now. I'm trying to build the Chez Vernon into a popular night spot, and the James Boys pretty well fill the bill. I pay them eight hundred a week and if I pay much more than that for music, I'll be working for them instead of myself. Do you belong to the union, Frank?'

I shook my head. The idea of any free American male paying gangsters money for the right to work has always struck me as one of the most preposterous customs we have.

'Tell you what,' Vernon said reflectively. 'Do you really need a job?'

I nodded seriously.

'Okay, then. The James Boys play a forty-minute set, and then they take a twenty-minute break. They play from nine till midnight, an extra hour if the crowd warrants it, and till 2 a.m. on Saturday nights. In my opinion, a twenty-minute break is too long, and I lose customers sometimes just because of it, but those were the terms I hired them under. If you want to sit in by yourself on the stand to fill the breaks I'm willing to try it for a few nights to see how it goes. I can give you ten bucks a night, but that's the limit.'

For a few moments I thought about it, but ten dollars was too much money to give me when I only knew three songs. I held up five fingers.

'You want fifty dollars?' Vernon asked incredulously.

I shook my head and snapped out five fingers.

'You're a pretty weird cat,' Vernon laughed. 'Not only do you not sing, you're honest. Five bucks a night it is, Frank. But I'll tell Dick James to clean out his kitty between his sets, and any tips you get on the breaks belong to you. You'll pick up a few extra bucks, anyway.'

I nodded, shook hands with my employer and returned my guitar to its case.

'Come in about eight thirty, Frank,' Vernon concluded the interview, 'and I'll introduce you to the James Boys.'

I returned to the hotel and stretched out on my bed for a nap. Although I had taken a lower figure than the ten he offered, I still felt a little uneasy. After Lee Vernon heard me playing the same songs all evening he wouldn't be too happy about it. But during the days, maybe I could make up a few more. If so, I could ask for a raise to ten. The immediate problem was remedied. I could pay my room rent of three dollars a day, and eat on the other two until I could work my way out of the hole with an ingenious plan of some kind.

A few minutes later I was asleep.

Chapter Seven

The James Boys were very good. If Lee Vernon was paying them eight hundred dollars a week, they were worth every cent of it.

I sat at the end of the bar where I could take in the entire room, enjoying the music and the singing, and the antics of the patrons at various tables. Not many of the couples danced. It wasn't the smallness of the floor that prevented them from getting to their feet, it was just that the James Boys were more amusing to watch than they were to dance to. They wore red Western shirts with white piping on the collars and cuffs, but they didn't restrict their playing to Western music. They seemed to be equally at home with calypso and rock 'n' roll. Each of the boys, in turn, sang into the microphone, and they all had good voices.

Dick James was at the microphone, and his face had a mournful expression. He said, 'It is now my sad duty to inform you, ladies and gentlemen, that for the next twenty minutes we will be absent from the stand.'

He held up a hand to silence the murmurs of disappointment. 'We don't want to go. Honest! It's just that we can't afford to drink here. We have to go down the street to a little place where the drinks are cheaper. And I might add,' he said disingenuously, 'unwatered!'

A very small ripple of laughter went through the room. Perhaps the patrons of the Chez Vernon thought their drinks were watered.

'But during our brief absence, the management has obtained for your listening pleasure, at *great* expense, one of the world's greatest guitarists! Ladies and gentlemen, I give you Frank Mansfield!'

I had been so engrossed in watching and listening, and drinking a steady procession of beers, I hadn't realized how quickly the time had passed. To a burst of enthusiastic applause, led by the four James Boys, I threaded my way through the close-packed tables to the stand. As I sat down in a chair on the stand and removed my guitar from its case, Dick James lowered the microphone level with my waist.

'Good luck, Frank,' he said, and followed the other members of the group into the hallway leading to the dressing room. I was in shirtsleeves, but wore my hat. I wished that I could have gone with them, picked up my coat in the dressing room, and made a getaway through the back door to the alley. In anticipation of fresh entertainment, the audience was fairly quiet. I felt like every eye was on me as I sat under the baby spot on the small, triangular stand.

I delayed as long as I could, well aware that I had twenty full minutes to fill before the James Boys returned, and not enough music to fill it with. I vamped a few chords, tuned the 'A' string a trifle higher, and then played 'Empty Pockets.' The moment I hit the last chord, I got to my feet and bowed from the waist to the thin, sporadic applause. Before playing 'Grandma's Quilt,' I went through the motions of tuning again, and slowed the tempo of the song as I picked through it. The applause was stronger when I finished. By this time the crowd realized that my music was unusual, or, at least, different. My last number was the best, my favorite, and my nervousness had disappeared completely. There was hardly a sound from the audience as I played 'Georgia Girl,' but when I finished and stood up to take a bow, the applause was definitely generous.

'I could take lessons from you,' Dick James said, as he climbed onto the stand. 'You make some mighty fine sounds, Frankerino.'

I nodded, smiled and wet my lips. The James Boys were also unaware that my repertoire only consisted of three homemade numbers. Lee Vernon, a tall drink in his hand, crossed the room and congratulated me. He whispered something to Dick, and readjusted the microphone. I had returned my guitar to the case and was halfway to the bar when Vernon's voice rasped out of the speakers in the ceiling.

'Ladies and gentlemen, there's something you don't know about Frank Mansfield!' His voice stopped me, and I looked down at the floor. 'In view of his great manual dexterity, it may be difficult to believe, but Frank Mansfield is the only deaf-and-dumb guitar player in the world! Let's give Frank another big hand? Let him feel the vibrations through the floor!'

As the drunken crowd applaused wildly and stomped their feet on the floor, I ran across the room, pushed aside the curtain to the hallway, and rushed blindly into the dressing room. I supposed Lee Vernon meant well, but I was angered by his announcement. Not only did I want to quit, I wanted to punch him in the nose. In view of his stupid announcement, he would be damned well embarrassed when I played the same three songs forty minutes later.

There was an open bottle of bourbon on the dressing table. I hit it a couple of times and smoked five cigarettes before my next appearance on the stand. Tiny James, the bass player, came and got me.

'You're on, Mansfield.' He jerked his thumb. 'Dick's announced you already.'

I returned to the stand and got out my guitar. The room had twice as many patrons and the air was blue with smoke. Vernon's announcement had created a morbid interest. The bar crowd had pushed their way in and standees blocked the way to the service bar. The moment I picked up my instrument and strummed a few riplets, there were shushing sounds from the tables and the room was silent.

Indifferently, expertly, I played through my three numbers without pause. The applause was generous. I put the guitar back in the case and made my exit to the dressing room. When the door closed on the last James Boy I took a pull out of the open bottle of whiskey. Lee Vernon entered the room. His face was flushed and he was laughing. He held out a hand for the bottle and, when I handed it to him, freshened the drink in his left hand.

Watching him sullenly, I took another drink out of the bottle. Vernon let loose with a wild peal of happy laughter.

'Those are the only three songs you know, aren't they?' he said.

I grinned and took another short drink.

'That's wonderful, Frank,' he said sincerely. 'Really wonderful!' He smiled broadly, showing his big white teeth. 'Did you make them up yourself?'

I nodded.

A frown creased Vernon's flushed face, and he placed his glass down carefully on the narrow ledge in front of the mirror. He's going to fire me, I thought. The moment I put the five-dollar bill in my pocket I'm going to knock his teeth out.

'I think that's terrific, Frank. I really do. Any fool can take a few lessons and play ordinary songs on a guitar. Hell, I can play a little bit myself, and if I sing while I'm playing, I can drown out the mistakes I make. But you . . .' He shook his head comically. 'To deliberately master the damned guitar the way you have and compose your own songs – well, I can only admire you for it.' He picked up his glass and raised it. 'To Frank Mansfield! You've got a job at the Chez Vernon for as long as you want to keep it!'

He drained his glass and opened the door. His shoulder hit the side of the door as he left, and he staggered slightly as he walked down the hall.

I closed the door and sat down, facing the back of the chair. If a man accepts life logically, the unexpected is actually the expected. I should have known he wouldn't fire me. A nightclub owner, by the fact that he is a night-club owner, must necessarily accept things as they are. Vernon had accepted the situation cheerfully, like a peace-time soldier who finds himself suddenly in a war. There was nothing else he could do.

I had wanted to quit, but now I was unable to quit. I was in an untenable position. I had only one alternative. Every time I played my twenty-minute stint, I would have to improvise something new. If I couldn't do it, I would have to walk away and not even stop to collect the five dollars I had coming to me. It was unfair to keep playing the same three songs over and over.

I took another drink, a short one this time. I was begin-ning to feel the effects of the whiskey on top of the beers I had had earlier. I made my decision. When my turn came to play again I would improvise music and play something truly wonderful.

After Dick James announced me, I sat quietly in my chair, the guitar across my lap, a multicolored pick gripped loosely between my right thumb and forefinger. The room was filled to capacity. Under the weak, colored ceiling lights I could make out most of the faces nearest the stand. There was a hint of nervous expectancy in the room. Here is a freak, their silence said, a talented, deaf-and-dumb freak who plays music he cannot hear, who plays for applause he can only feel. This was the atmosphere of the Chez Vernon, caused in part by Lee Vernon's earlier announcement, and by my last session on the stand when the listeners had heard a different kind of music. Vernon sat at a table close to the platform, his face flushed with liquor, a knowing smile on his lips. On his left was a young man with long blond hair, dressed in a red silk dinner jacket, white ruffled shirt, and plaid bow tie. On Vernon's right, a tall pink drink before her, was a woman in a low-cut Kelly green evening gown. She was in her early forties, but she was the type who could pass easily for thirty-nine for a few more years.

Her lips were wet and shiny, and her dark eyes were bright with excitement as I caught them with mine and held them. She nodded politely, put long tapering fingers to her coal-black hair. The woman and the young man at Vernon's table stood out from the crowd. Most of the patrons were wearing short-sleeved sport shirts. Only the younger men with dates wore coats and ties. Lee Vernon raised his glass and winked at me.

The microphone was less than a foot away from my guitar. I tapped the pick on the box. The sound, amplified by six speakers, sounded like knocking on a wooden door. Scratching the wooden box of the Gibson produced a sound like the dry rasping of locusts. The locusts reminded me of the long summer evenings in Mansfield, Georgia, and I thought about the bright silvery moths circling the lamp on the corner, down the street from Grandma's house.

I played their sound, picking them up and flying and flickering with them about the streetlight, teasing them on the 'E' string.

Down the block, swinging to and fro on a lacy, metal porch swing, the chains creaking, complaining, a woman laughed, the joyful, contented laughter of a well-bred Southern woman, a mother perhaps, with two young children, a boy and a girl, and the little boy said something that amused her and she laughed and repeated what the child said to her husband sitting beside her.

I played that.

And I repeated the solid rumbling laugh of her husband, which complemented her own laughter, and then my fingers moved away from them, up the staff to pick out the solid swishing whispering smack of a lawn sprinkler and a man's tuneless humming a block away. And there came a boy in knickers down the sidewalk, walking and then running, dancing with awkward feet to avoid stepping on a crack, which would *surely* break his mother's back! He bent down and picked up a stick and scampered past a white picket fence, the stick bumping, rattling, drowning out a man's lecture to a teenage girl on the porch of that old white house two doors down from the corner, the house with the four white columns.

And I played these things, and then the sounds of supper and the noises, the fine good clatter in the kitchen when Grandma was still alive, and Randall and I sent to wash up before dinner in the dark downstairs bathroom where the sound of water in the pipes made the whiney, sharp, unbearable spine-tingling noise and kept it up until the other tap was turned on and modulated it, turning the groaning into the surreptitious scraping of a boy's finger on a blackboard, and sure enough, we had the school-teacher for dinner that night and she was talking with Mother, monotonously, like always, and I hated her, and the dry, flat registers of her authoritative voice would put you to sleep in the middle of a lesson if you didn't keep pinching yourself, and Daddy pulled out his watch with the loud ticks and it was suppertime, the solid ring of the good sterling silver, the tingle-tinkle of the fine crystal that pinged with a fingernail and listen to the echo! and the rich dark laughter of Aimee, our Negro cook in the kitchen, and after supper I was allowed to go to the movie but Randall wasn't because he was three years younger and had to go to bed so I played these things and what a wonderful movie it was! Young Dick Powell, handsome, in his West Point uniform, and the solid ranks of straight tall men marching in the parade and only vaguely did the old songs filter through the story, *Flirtation Walk*, and the lovely girl under the Kissing Rock, and then the movie was over but I stayed to see it again, and repeated it very quickly because nothing is ever any good the second time and I was late, it was dark, and I was running down the black narrow streets, the crickets silenced ahead of my slapping feet, and the grim and heavy shadows of the great old pecan trees on our black, forbidding block. As I reached our yard, safe at last from whatever it was that chased me, Mother was on the front porch waiting with a switch in her hand, and she intended to use it, I know, but I began to cry and a moment later she pulled me in close to her warm, wonderful, never-changing smell of powder, spicy lilac and cedar and sweet, sweet lips kissing me and chiding and kissing and scolding and damned if the 'G' string didn't break.

The pick fell from my fingers and I looked numbly at the guitar. The room was as silent as death. A moment later, like an exploding dam, the room rocked with the sound of slapping hands and stomping feet. I fled into the dressing room with the guitar still clutched by the neck in my left hand. The James Boys, who had been listening by the arched, curtained doorway to the hall, followed me into the small room, and Dick handed me the bottle.

'I'll be a son of a bitch, Frank,' he said warmly. 'I never heard finer guitar in my life. You can be a James Boy anytime you want. Go ahead, take another snort!'

I sat down, lit a cigarette and studied my trembling fingers. My throat was dry and tight and for the first time in my life I felt lonely, really lonely, and I didn't know why. I had buried all those memories for so many years, it was frightening to know that they were still in my head.

The James Boys returned to the stand, leaving the door open, and I could hear the heated strings of their first number, 'The Big D Rock.'

'Mr Mansfield—' I looked up at the sound of Lee Vernon's voice, and got to my feet quickly as he ushered in ahead of him the young man and the woman who had been sitting at this table out front. 'I want to introduce you to Mrs Bernice Hungerford and Tommy Hungerford.' He turned and smiled at the woman. 'Mr Frank Mansfield.'

'Tommy is my nephew,' Bernice Hungerford said quickly, holding out her hand. I shook it briefly, and then shook hands with her nephew. His expression was studiedly bored, but he was slightly nervous.

Mrs Hungerford was a truly striking woman, now that I could see her under the bright lights of the dressing room. A white cashmere stole was draped over her left arm, and she clutched a gold-mesh evening bag in her left hand. Her burnt sienna eyes never left my face. I was amused by the scattering of freckles on her straight nose. The freckles on her face and bare shoulders belied her age sure enough.

With a straight face, Vernon said: 'Mrs Hungerford was very impressed by your concert, Mr Mansfield. When I told her that you had studied under Segovia in Seville for ten years, she said she could tell that you had by your intricate fretwork.'

Bernice Hungerford bobbed her head up and down delightedly and shook a teasing forefinger at me. 'And I recognized the tone poem, too.' She winked and flashed a bright smile. Her teeth were small, but remarkably well matched and white. 'You see, Mr Mansfield,' she continued, 'I know a few things about music. When I hear Bach, it doesn't make any difference if it's piano or guitar, I can recognize the style. That's what I told Mr Vernon, didn't I, Lee?' The woman turned to the implacable Lee Vernon who was covering his drunkenness masterfully. Only the stiffness of his back gave him away.

'You certainly did, Bernice. But I had to tell her, Mr Mansfield. She thought you were playing a Bach fugue, but it was a natural mistake. She didn't know that it was a special Albert Schweitzer composition written on a theme of Bach's. Quite a natural mistake, indeed.'

'If we don't get back to your guests, their throats will be dreadfully parched, Auntie dear,' Tommy said lazily. 'We've been gone, you know, for the better part of an hour, and that's a long time just to refurbish the liquor supply.' The careless elisions of his voice were practiced, it seemed to me.

'But if we take Mr Mansfield back with us, we'll be forgiven.' Mrs Hungerford patted her nephew's arm.

'I don't want to hold you up any longer, Mrs Hungerford,' Vernon said. 'Why don't you and Tommy wait in the package store. Your liquor is ready, and I'll do my best to bring Mr Mansfield along in a minute. All right?'

'But you will persuade him, won't you?' Mrs Hungerford said.

'I'll certainly try,' he replied cheerfully.

As soon as they had gone, Vernon closed the door, leaned against it and buried his face in his arms. His shoulders shook convulsively, and for a moment I thought he was crying. Then he let out a whoop of laughter, turned away from the door and sat down. Recovering, he wiped his streaming eyes with a forefinger and said, 'I'm sorry, Frank, but the gag was too good to resist. When she started that talk about Bach and Segovia at the table, I had to go her one better. But it's a break for you. She has a few guests at her house, and only stopped by here to pick up some Scotch. I told her that she mustn't miss your performance, and when you came out with that tricky, weird chording and impressed her so much, I thought it might be a break for you. Anyway, the upshot is that she wants you to go home with her and play for her guests. Should be worth a twenty-dollar bill to you, at least.'

I shrugged into my corduroy jacket. All through the talk about Bach and Segovia I had thought they were attempting some kind of joke at my expense, but apparently Mrs Hungerford actually believed I had studied under the old guitarist. Vernon had gone along with the gag, which was a break for me, although I detested the condescending son of a bitch. If she wanted to pay me twenty dollars I would accept it, play my three songs, and then get out of her house. I had already made up my mind not to return to the Chez Vernon. A final concert for a group of rich people who could afford to pay for it and wouldn't miss the money would be a fitting end to my short, unhappy musical career.

'By the way, Frank,' Vernon said, as soon as I was ready to go, 'don't get the idea that I was trying to make fun of you by falling in with the gag. If I'd been strictly sober, I might have set her straight, but basically I poured it on so you could pick up a few extra bucks. No hard feelings?'

I ignored the outstretched hand, and brushed by him, carrying my instrument. Vernon followed me out into the club. As I stopped at the stand, to put the guitar in the case, be handed me a ten-dollar bill.

'Hell, don't be sore about it, Frank.'

There was a black silhouette cutout of a plyboard cat at the end of the stand. I wadded the bill in my fist and shoved it into the open mouth of the kitty before crossing the dance floor and entering the inside door to the package store. If Lee Vernon had followed me into the package store, I would have knocked his teeth out, even if he was drunk. Although I wasn't the butt of the joke, I didn't like to be patronized by a man I considered an inferior. But Vernon was wise enough not to come outside, and I've never seen him since.

Tommy drove the Olds and Mrs Hungerford sat between us on the wide front seat. With the guitar case between my legs, my left leg was tight against her right leg, and I could feel the warmth of her body through my corduroy trousers.

'This isn't exactly a party, Mr Mansfield,' she explained, as we drove through the light traffic of the after-midnight streets. 'We all attended the Jacksonville Little Theater to see *Liliom*, and I invited the bunch home for a cold supper and a few drinks. It was a real *faux pas* on my part. There's plenty of food, but I didn't realize I was out of Scotch. But bringing you home to play will more than make up for my oversight, I'm sure. Don't you think so, Tommy?'

'If they're still there,' he observed dryly.

'Don't worry,' Mrs Hungerford laughed pleasantly, 'I know my brother!' She turned toward me and put her hand lightly on my knee. 'There are only two couples, Mr Mansfield. Tommy's father and mother, and Dr Luke McGuire and his wife. Not a very large audience, I'm afraid, after what you're accustomed to, is it?'

In reply, I spat out the window.

'But I know you'll find them appreciative of good music.'

A few minutes later we turned into a driveway guarded by two small concrete lions. Tommy parked behind a Buick on the semicircular gravel road that led back to the street. The two-story house was of red brick. Four fluted wooden columns supported a widow's walk directly above the wide, aluminium-screened front porch. The lawn slanted gradually to the street for almost a hundred yards, broken here and there with newly planted coconut palms. The feathery tips of the young trees rattled in the wind. She was wasting money and effort attempting to grow coconut trees as far north as Jax. The subtropics start at Daytona Beach, much farther downstate.

Mrs Hungerford rushed ahead of us after we got out of the car. Tommy, carrying two sacked fifths of Scotch under his left arm and a six-pack of soda in his right hand, hurried after her. As I climbed the porch steps, Mrs Hungerford switched on the overhead lights and opened the front doors. She held a finger to her lips, as she beckoned me into the foyer with her free hand.

'Now, you stay right here in the foyer,' Mrs Hungerford whispered excitedly, 'so I can surprise them!'

Closing the front door softly, she followed her nephew into the living room. The voices greeting them contained a mixture of concern over the prolonged absence, and happiness at the prospect of a drink. Above the sound of their conversation, the clipped electronic voice of a newscaster rattled through his daily report of the late news.

The foyer was carpeted in a soft shade of rose nylon. The same carpeting climbed the stairway to the walnut-balustraded second floor. A giant split-leaved philodendron sat in a white pot behind the door. There was a spindly-legged, leather-covered table beneath a gilded wall mirror, and a brass dish on the table held about thirty calling cards. Out of long-forgotten habit I felt a few of the cards to see if they were engraved. They were. I turned my attention to a marble cherub mounted on a square ebony base. It was about three feet high, and the well-weathered cherub looked shyly with its dugout eyes through widespread stubby fingers. A lifted, twisted right knee hid its sex, and three fingers of the left hand were missing. I removed my cowboy hat and hung it on the thumb of the mutilated hand.

The bored announcer was clicked off in mid-sentence, and Mrs Hungerford came after me a moment later.

'They're all tickled to death, Mr Mansfield,' she said happily. 'Come on, they want to meet you!'

In one corner of the large living room, Tommy was engaged behind a small bar. Two middle-aged men got out of their chairs and crossed the room to greet me. Dr McGuire was a thickset man without a neck, and his gray hair was badly in need of cutting. Mr Hungerford, Sr., Tommy's father, was an older edition of his blond son, except that he no longer had his hair and the top of his head was bronzed by the Florida sun. Both of the men wore white dinner jackets and midnight blue tuxedo trousers. I acknowledged the introductions by nodding my head and shaking hands. The two wives remained seated on a long, curving white sofa, and didn't offer their hands to be shaken.

'I know you're all eager to hear Mr Mansfield play,' Bernice announced to the room at large, 'but you'll have to wait until he has a drink first.'

Welcome news. After dropping my guitar case on the sofa I headed for the bar.

'There's plenty of gin if you don't want Scotch,' Tommy suggested.

I poured two ounces of Scotch into a tall glass in reply, and added ice cubes and soda. An uneasy silence settled over the room as I hooked my elbows over the bar and faced the group. Bernice, or Tommy, one, had evidently informed them about my inability to talk, and they were disturbed by my silence. The two matrons, bulging in strapless evening gowns, had difficulty in averting their eyes from my face. I doubt if they meant to be rude, but they couldn't keep from staring at me. Dr McGuire, standing with his back to the fireplace, lit a cigar and studied the tip through his bifocals. Only Bernice was at ease, sitting comfortably on the long bench in front of the baby grand piano, apparently unaware of her guests' discomfort. Mr Hungerford, Sr., cleared his throat and set his glass down on a low coffee table.

'Bernice tells us you studied under Segovia, Mr Mansfield,' he said.

'Yes,' Bernice replied for me. 'That's what Mr Vernon told us, didn't he, Tommy?'

'That's right. And he played a beautiful thing written by Dr Albert Schweitzer. I hope he'll play it again for us.'

'African rock 'n' roll, I suppose,' Dr McGuire chuckled from the fireplace. 'That would be a treat!' When no one joined him in his laughter, he said quickly, 'We're very grateful you came out to play for us, Mr Mansfield.'

I finished my drink, lifted my eyebrows for Tommy Hungerford to mix me another. I took my guitar out of the case, and started to restring it with another 'G' string to replace the broken one. While I restrung the guitar, Mrs Hungerford asked her brother and the doctor to move chairs into the center of the room and form a line. She then had her guests sit in the rearranged chairs facing me, as I stood with one foot on the piano bench. Tommy Hungerford, smiling at the new seating arrangements, remained standing at the bar. I plucked and tightened the new string, and Bernice hit the 'G' on the piano for me until I had the guitar in tune. Satisfied, I put the guitar on the bench and returned to the bar for my fresh drink. The small audience waited patiently, but Dr McGuire glowered when Tommy insisted that I have another before I began. I shook my head, picked up my guitar and played through my three-song repertoire without pause.

The moment I hit the last chord I smiled, bowed from the waist and put the guitar back in the case. Bernice Hungerford, who had hovered anxiously behind the row of chairs during my short concert, led the applause.

'Is that all he's going to play, Bernice?' the doctor asked. 'I'd like to hear more.'

'I think we all would,' his fat wife echoed.

I shrugged, and joined Tommy at the bar for another drink.

'No, that's enough,' Bernice said. 'Mr Mansfield has been playing all evening and he's tired. We shouldn't coax him. The concert is all over. Go on home. You've been fed, you've had your drinks, now go on home.'

Bernice herded the two wives out of the room to get their wraps, and their husbands joined Tommy and me at the bar for a nightcap.

'You play very well, young man,' Dr McGuire said. 'Did you ever play on television?'

I shook my head, and added Scotch to my glass to cut the soda.

'I think you should consider television, don't you, Tommy?'

'Not really, sir,' Tommy wrinkled his brow. 'I'm not so sure that the mass audience is ready for classical guitar music. I'm trying to recall, but I can't remember ever hearing or seeing a string quartet on television. If I did, I can't remember it.'

'By God, I haven't either!' the doctor said strongly. 'And certainly the string quartet is the most civilized entertainment in the world! Don't you agree, Mr Mansfield?'

I shrugged my shoulders inside my jacket, and lit a cigarette.

He didn't want a reply, anyway. 'But there's a definite need for serious music on TV,' he continued. 'And, by God, the public should be forced to listen! No matter how stupid people are today, they can be taught to appreciate good music.' He banged his fist on the bar.

The two middle-aged men drained their glasses quickly as Bernice came into the room, and turned to join their wives in the foyer. Bernice crossed the room, and placed a hand on my arm. So far, she had never missed a chance to touch me.

'Mrs McGuire would like to know if you'd consent to play for her guests next Saturday night. She's giving a party, quite a large one, and she's willing to—'

I shook my head, and crushed out my cigarette in a white Cinzano ashtray.

'It's "no", then?'

I nodded. She smiled, turned away and returned to the foyer to say good night to her guests and break the news to Mrs McGuire.

'Tell me something, Mr Mansfield,' Tommy said hesitantly. 'Did you really study under Segovia?'

I grinned, and shook my head. After setting my glass down, I picked up my guitar case. Tommy laughed, throwing his head back.

'I didn't think you did, but I'll keep your secret till the day I die.'

Bernice Hungerford returned with a smile brightening her jolly face. I didn't know why, but I was attracted to this graceful, pleasant woman. She appeared to be so happy, so eager to please, and yet, there were tiny, tragic lines tugging at the corners of her full lips.

'I'll drive Mr Mansfield back into town, Auntie,' Tommy said.

'Oh, no you won't!' Bernice said cheerfully. She took the guitar case out of my hand and placed it on the couch. 'I'll drive him back myself. You can just run along, Tommy. I'm going to fix Mr Mansfield something to eat – you could eat something, couldn't you?'

I shrugged, then smiled. She hadn't paid the twenty dollars yet, and I could always eat something. The cold buffet supper, however, didn't appeal to me. There were several choices of lunch meat, cold pork, three different cheese dips and pickles. I looked distastefully at the buffet table.

'Now, don't you worry,' Bernice said, patting my arm with her small, white hand. 'I won't make you eat the

270

remains of the cold supper. I'll fix you some ham and eggs.'

'Me, too, Auntie dear?' Tommy grinned.

'No, not you. Don't you have a job of some kind to report to in the morning?'

Tommy groaned. 'Don't remind me. Well, good night, Mr Mansfield.' He shook hands with me, brushed his lips against his aunt's cheek and made his departure from the room. A few moments later the lights of his Olds flashed on the picture window as he made the semicircle to the street.

Now that we were alone in the big house, Bernice's composure suddenly disappeared. She blushed furiously under my level stare, and then took my hand. 'Come on,' she said brightly. 'You can keep me company in the kitchen while I cook for you.'

I followed her into the kitchen, and sat down at a small dinette table covered with a blue-and-white tablecloth. There were louvred windows on all three sides of the small dining alcove, but the kitchen itself, like those of most depression-built homes, was a large one. The cooking facilities were up to date, however. In addition to a new yellow enameled electric stove, there was a built-in oven with a glass door, and a row of complicated-looking knobs beneath it.

'There's coffee left, but it's been sitting on the warm burner so long it's probably bitter by now. I'd better make fresh coffee, if you don't mind waiting awhile, but by that time I'll have the other things ready. I think that coffee setting too long gets bitter, don't you? I've got some mashed potatoes left over from dinner, and I'll make some nice patties to go with your ham.'

Bernice kept a running patter of meaningless small talk going as she cooked, and I listened thoughtfully and smoked, watching her deft, efficient movements from my

271

chair. She had tied a frilly, ruffled white apron about her waist, and it looked out of whack with her Kelly green evening gown. She kept talking about pleasant things to eat, and I got hungrier by the second.

She wanted to please me, even though she didn't know why. She knew she was a good cook, and by cooking a decent meal for me, she knew I would be pleased. If I was pleased with her, I'd take her to bed. These thoughts probably never entered her conscious mind, but I sensed this, and knew instinctively that she was mine if I wanted her. As she chattered away, gaily, cheerfully, I learned that I did want her, very much so. She was a damned attractive woman, a little heavy in the thighs, perhaps, but I didn't consider that a detriment. I like women a little on the fleshy side. Skinny, boyish-type figures may be admired by other women, but not by most men.

I smiled appreciatively, showing my teeth, when she set the huge platter before me. The aroma of the fried ham steak, four fried eggs, and fluffy potato pancakes all blended beautifully as they entered my nose. Bernice poured two steaming cups of fresh coffee and sat down across from me to watch me eat, her face flushed from recent exertion and pleasure as I stowed the food away.

'I should have made biscuits,' she said, 'but I could tell you were too hungry to wait, so I made the toast instead. Would you like some guava jelly for your toast?' She started to get up, but I shook my head violently, and she remained seated.

A minute later she smiled. 'I like to see a man eat,' she said sincerely.

I've heard a lot of women make that trite remark: Grandma, Mother, when she was still alive, and a good many others. I believe women really do like to see men eat, especially when they're fond of the man concerned, and he's eating food they have prepared for him. I have never denied any woman the dubious pleasure of watching me eat. Outside of taking care of a man's needs, women don't get very much pleasure out of life anyway.

When I finished eating everything in sight, I pushed the empty platter to one side, and wiped my mouth with a square of white damask napkin. Smiling over the lip of her cup, Bernice nodded with satisfaction. I winked slowly, returned her smile, and she blushed and lowered her eyes.

'My husband's been dead for five years, Mr Mansfield,' she said shyly. 'You don't know how nice it is to cook a meal for a man again. I'd almost forgotten myself. I loved my husband very much, and still do, I suppose. My brother's always telling me how foolish I am to keep this big house and live here all alone. An apartment would be easier to keep, I know, and give me more free time, but I don't know what I'd do with more free time if I had it. I don't know what to do with myself half the time as it is.

'This old house has a lot of pleasant memories for me, and I'd miss them if I ever sold it. I can see my husband in every room. Sometimes, during the day, I pretend he isn't dead at all. He's at the office, that's where he is, working, and when six o'clock comes he'll be coming home through the front door like always, and . . .' Her voice trailed away, and two tears escaped into her long black eyelashes.

Bernice wiped them away, tossed her head impatiently and laughed.

'Morbid, aren't I? How about some more coffee?'

I nodded, took my cigarettes out of my shirt pocket, and offered them to her. She put the cork tip in her mouth, and when I flipped my lighter, she held my hand with both of hers to get a light. This was unnecessary. My hand was perfectly steady. After refilling the cups she sat down again and described circles on the tablecloth with a long red fingernail.

'I know that you want to go, Mr Mansfield,' she said at last, 'but I'm finding this a novel experience. It's a rare instance when a woman can pour her troubles into a man's receptive ear without being told to shut up!' She laughed, and shrugged comically.

'But I really don't have any troubles. As far as money goes, I'm fixed forever. My husband saw to that, God bless him. I own the house, and my trust fund is well guarded by the bank trustees. And I have a circle of friends I've known most of my adult life. So where are my troubles?' She sighed audibly and licked her lips with the point of her tongue like a cat.

'I should be the happiest woman in the world. But once in a while, just once in a while, mind you, Mr Mansfield, I'd like to go into my bathroom and find the toilet seat up instead of down!' Color flooded into her face, and the freckles almost disappeared. She got up from the table hastily and pushed open the swinging door leading to the living room. 'I'll get your money for you, Mr Mansfield.'

She had aroused my sympathy. I wondered what her husband had been like. An insurance executive probably. Every time he had gotten a promotion he had used the extra money for more protection, more insurance. It must have cost her plenty to keep up this big house. And it was a cinch she didn't have any children, or she would have talked about them instead of a man five years dead. If I could have talked, I would have been able to kid her out of her mood in no time. My sex life had really suffered since I gave up talking. Not completely, because money always talks when words fail, but a lot of women had gotten away during the last couple of years because of my stubborn vow of silence.

As I pondered the situation, how best to handle it, Bernice returned to the kitchen. She placed a fifty-dollar bill on the table. The fifty ruined everything for me.

I could have accepted a twenty, because Lee Vernon had set the fee, but I couldn't, with good conscience, accept *fifty* dollars. My concert wasn't worth that much. I knew it, and Bernice Hungerford knew it. She was trying to buy me and I resented it. I folded the bill into a small square, placed it on the edge of the table and flipped it to the floor with my forefinger. I got up from the table and left the room.

I picked up my guitar in the living room and had almost reached the foyer when Bernice caught up with me. She tugged on my arm, and when I stopped, got in front of me, looking up wistfully into my face. My jaws were tight and I looked over her head at the door.

'Please!' she said, stuffing the folded bill into my shirt pocket. 'I know what you're thinking, but it isn't true! The only reason I gave you a fifty was because I didn't have a twenty. I thought I had one, but I didn't. Please take it!'

I dropped my eyes to her face, looked at her steadily, and she turned away from me.

'All right. So I lied. Take it anyway. Fifty dollars doesn't mean anything to me. I'm sorry and I'm ashamed. And if you want to know the truth I'm more ashamed than sorry!'

I retrieved my hat from the marble angel's thumb and put it on my head. But I didn't leave. I reconsidered. Damn it all anyway, the woman was desirable! I removed my hat, replaced it on the angel's thumb and dropped my guitar case to the carpeted floor. Bernice had started up the stairs, but I caught up with her on the third step, lifted her into my arms and continued up the stairs. She buried her face in my neck and stifled a sob, clinging to me with both arms like a child. As I climbed I staggered beneath her weight – she must have weighed a solid one hundred and forty-five pounds – but I didn't drop her. When I reached the balcony I was puffing with my mouth open to regain my wind.

Bernice whispered softly into my ear, 'The bedroom's the first door on the right.'

The first time was for me. As nervous as Bernice was, at least at first, it could hardly have gone any other way. But I was gentle with her, and providing me with satisfaction apparently gave her the reassurance she needed. There was none of that foolishness about wanting to turn off the bedside lamps, for example, and when she returned from the bathroom, she still had her clothes off.

I had propped myself up on both pillows, and I smoked and watched her as she poured two small snifters of brandy. The cut-glass decanter was on a side table, beside a comfortable wing chair. It was unusual, I thought to keep a decanter of cognac in a bedroom, but having a drink afterward was probably a postcoital ritual that she and her late husband had practiced.

Although Bernice was a trifle on the chunky side, she had a good figure. Her heavy breasts had prolapsed slightly, but the prominent nipples were as pink as a roseate spoonbill. Her slim waist emphasized the beautiful swelling lines of her full hips, and her skin, except for a scattering of freckles on her shoulders, was as white as a peeled almond. With her thick black hair unloosened, and trailing down her back, Bernice was a very beautiful woman. To top it off, she had a sense of style. I wanted to talk to her so badly I could almost taste the words in my mouth, and it was all I could do to hold back the torrent that would become a flood if I ever let them go.

After Bernice handed me my glass, she sat cross-legged on the bed, facing me, swirling her brandy in the snifter she held with cupped hands. Her face was flushed slightly with excitement. She peered intently into her brandy glass, refusing to meet my level stare.

'I want to tell you something, Frank,' she said in a soft contralto, 'something important. I'm *not* promiscuous.'

She said this so primly I wanted to laugh. Instead, I grinned, wet a forefinger in my brandy and rubbed the nipple of her right breast.

'And no matter what you may think, you're the first man I've let make love to me since my husband died.'

I didn't believe her, of course, not for an instant. But that is the way women are. They always feel that a man will think less of them if they act like human beings. What did it matter to me whether she had slept with anyone or not for the last five years? What possible difference could it make at this moment? Now was now, and the past and the future were unimportant.

As the nipple gradually hardened beneath my circling finger she laughed, an abrupt, angry little laugh, and tossed off the remainder of her brandy. I took her glass, put both of them aside, pulled her down beside me, and kissed her.

The second time was better and lasted much longer. Although I was handicapped by being unable to issue instructions, Bernice was experienced, cooperative and so eager to please me that she anticipated practically everything I wanted to do. And at last, when I didn't believe I could hold out for another moment, she climaxed. I remained on my back, with Bernice on top of me, and she nibbled on my shoulder,

'I could fall in love with you, Frank Mansfield,' she said softly. 'If there were only some way I could prove it to you!'

Suddenly she got out of bed, grabbed my undershirt and shorts from the winged chair, and entered the bathroom. I raised myself on my elbows, and watched her through the open door as she washed my underwear in the washbowl. She hummed happily as she scrubbed away. My underwear wasn't dirty. I had put it on clean after a shower at the hotel before reporting in at the Chez Vernon at eight thirty that evening. Women, sometimes, have a peculiar way of demonstrating their affection.

Five o'clock finally rolled around, but I hadn't closed my eyes. Bernice slept soundly at my side, a warm heavy leg thrown over mine, an arm draped limply across my chest. She breathed heavily through her open mouth. I eased my leg out from beneath hers and got out of bed on my side. The sheet that had covered us was disarranged, kicked to the bottom of the bed. I pulled it over her shoulders, before taking my clothes from the chair into the bathroom. My underwear was still dripping wet and draped over the metal bar that held the shower curtain. I pulled on my clothes without underwear. As soon as I was dressed, I raised the toilet seat, switched off the bathroom light and tiptoed out of the bedroom, closing the door softly behind me.

At the foot of the stairs, I retrieved my hat and guitar, and made my exit into the dawn. The sky was just beginning to turn gray. I opened the guitar case, removed the instrument, and tried to scrape off my name with my knife. It was burned in too deeply, but Bernice would be able to see that I had tried to scrape it off. Then I put the neck of the guitar on the top step, and stomped on it until it broke. After cutting the strings with my knife, I placed the broken instrument on the welcome mat.

There was an oleander bush on the left side of the porch. I tossed the guitar case into the bush. Now I could keep the fifty-dollar bill in good conscience. The guitar had been worth at least thirty dollars, and the fee for the private concert was twenty dollars. We were even. The message was obscure, perhaps, but Bernice would be able to puzzle it out eventually.

I walked down the gravel driveway to the street, and noticed the number of the house on a stone marker at the bottom of the drive. 111. I grinned. I would always remember Bernice's number.

Carrying my wet underwear, I had to wander around in the strange neighborhood for almost five blocks before I could find a bus stop and catch a bus back to downtown Jacksonville.

Chapter Eight

All day long I stayed in my room. Ideas and plans circulated inside my head, but none of them were worthwhile. One dismal thought kept oozing to the top, and finally it lodged there.

I had been cheated out of my inheritance.

This wasn't a new thought by any means. I had thought about it often in the five years since Daddy died, but I had never considered seriously doing anything about it before. The telegram informing me of Daddy's death had reached me one day too late to allow me to attend the funeral. I had immediately wired Randall and given him the circumstances. Two weeks later I had received a letter from Judge Brantley Powell, the old lawyer who handled the estate, together with a check for one dollar. He had also included a carbon copy of Daddy's will. Randall, my younger brother, had inherited the four-hundred-acre farm, seven hundred dollars in bonds, and the bank account of two hundred and seventy dollars. The check for one dollar was my part of the inheritance.

With plenty of money in my pockets at the time, I had dismissed the will from my mind. After all, Randall had stayed home, and I had not. He had gone to college, earned a degree in law and passed the Georgia bar exams, returning home ostensibly to practice. I had attended Valdosta State College for one year only and had quit to go to the Southwestern Cocking Tourney in Oklahoma City. I had never returned to college and Daddy had never gotten over it. He had always wanted to keep both of us under his thumb, but no man can tell me what to do with my life.

What had happened to the lives we lived?

I had gone on to make a name for myself in cockfighting. Sure, I was broke now, but I had firmly established myself in one of the toughest sports in the world. And what did Randall have to show for his fine education? What had he done with his inheritance?

When he was accepted for the bar he went to work as a law clerk for Judge Brantley Powell. Six months later, claiming that he was doing most of the work anyway, he asked for a full partnership in the firm. When the judge turned him down, he had quit, and he hadn't done much of anything since. He hadn't even hung out his own shingle. All day long he sat in the big dining room at home, looking for obscure contradictions in his law books, occasionally having an article published on some intricate point of law in some legal quarterly nobody had ever heard of before. To get by, he sold off small sections of the farm to Wright Gaylord, my fiancée's brother. He had also married Frances Shelby, a dentist's daughter from Macon. I suppose she had some dowry money and a few dollars from her father once in a while, but Randall's total income from tobacco, pecans and land sales was probably less than three thousand dollars a year. He was also writing a book – or so Frances said.

By all rights, Daddy should have left the farm to me. There were no two ways about it. I was the oldest son, and there wasn't a jury in Georgia that wouldn't award the farm to me if I contested the will. They read the Bible in Georgia, and in the Holy Bible the eldest son always inherits the property.

By four that afternoon I had made up my mind. I would go home and press Randall for the three hundred dollars he owed me. If he paid me, I'd forget about the farm and never consider taking it away from him again. If he didn't, I'd see Judge Powell and do something about it. I needed money, and if I didn't get some soon I'd miss out on the cockfighting season.

I checked my bag and gaff case at the desk, wrote a message for the desk clerk to hold any mail that came for me, paid my bill, and headed for the bus station. I only planned to stay overnight at home, so my shaving kit was enough baggage. If my black shirt got too dirty, I could have my sister-in-law wash and iron it for me.

The bus pulled out at 4:45. There was a one-hour layover in Lake City to change buses, and I arrived in Mansfield, Georgia, at 3:30 a.m. The farm was six miles out of town on the state highway. I could either wait for the rural route postman and ride out with him or I could walk. After being cramped up in the bus for such a long time, I decided to stretch my legs.

I enjoyed the walk to the farm. When I had attended school in town the county had been too poor to afford a school bus. I had walked both ways, winter and summer, over a deeply rutted red dirt road, muddy when it rained, and dusty when it hadn't rained. The road was paved now, and had been since right after the Korean war. Soldiers from Fort Benning had used a lot of the county as a maneuver area. When the war was over the county had sued the United States Army for enough money to blacktop most of the county roads.

I reached the farm a little after six. I passed Charley Smith's house first, the only Negro tenant Randall had left, but I didn't stop to see the old man, even though a coil of black smoke was curling out of his chimney. Charley was much too old to do hard farm work any longer, but his wife, Aunt Leona, helped Frances around the house four or five days a week, and she was still a good worker.

The old homestead was a gray clapboard two-story structure set well back from the road. Randall hadn't done
anything to improve the looks of the place in the five years
he had owned it. The ten Van Deman pecan trees, planted
between the house and the road some sixty years before,
had been the deciding factor when Daddy first bought the
place. In another month or so, Charley, Aunt Leona and
Frances would be under the trees gathering nuts. If Randall
hit a good market, he would realize three or four hundred
dollars from the pecans before Christmas, but I couldn't
wait that long to get the money he owed me.

Old Dusty was lying on the long front gallery near the
front door, but he didn't bark or lift his head when I
entered the yard through the fence gate. He could neither
see nor hear me. The old dog was almost sixteen years
old, blind and stone-deaf. When I reached the steps,
however, he felt the vibration, snuffled, and began to bark
feebly. His hind legs were partially paralysed. When he
tried to struggle to his feet, I patted his head and made
him lie down again. The hair of his great head was white
now. Unable to hear himself, he would have continued to
bark indefinitely, so I closed his mouth with my hand to
shut him up. He recognized me, of course, and licked my
hand, his huge tail thumping madly on the loose floorboards of the gallery. He had been a good hunting dog
once, and despite his infirmities, I was grateful to Randall
for not putting him away. I hadn't expected to see Old
Dusty again.

Instead of entering by the front door, I took the brick
walk around the house to the back. I opened the screen
door to the kitchen, leaned against the doorjamb, and
grinned at the expression of surprise and chagrin on my
sister-in-law's face.

But I believe I was more shocked than Frances. She had
begun to put on weight the last time I had seen her, but

in two years' time she had gained another forty pounds. She must have been close to one hundred and eighty pounds. Her rotund body was practically shapeless under the faded blue dressing gown she wore over her nightgown. Frances's face was still young and pretty, but it was as round and shiny as a full moon. Her short brown hair was done up tight with a dozen aluminium curlers. With a grimace of dismay, Frances put a chubby hand to her mouth.

'You would catch me looking like this!' she exclaimed. 'Why didn't you let us know you were coming?'

I put an arm about her thick waist and kissed her on the cheek.

'Well,' she said good-naturedly, 'you can stop grinning like an ape and sit down at the table. The coffee'll be ready in a minute. I was just fixing to start breakfast.'

I sat down at the oilcloth-covered kitchen table. Frances lifted the lid of the coffee pot to look inside, and clucked her tongue disapprovingly. 'You may have lost your voice, Frank,' she scolded, 'but you can still write! We haven't heard from you in more than six months.'

I spread my arms apologetically.

'I guess I'm a fine one to talk,' she said, smiling, 'I never write myself, but we do enjoy hearing from you once in a while.' Frances filled two white mugs with coffee, put the sugar and cream where I could reach it easily, and sat down across from me.

'Randy'll be down pretty soon. He was up late last night working on an article, and I didn't have the heart to wake him. He likes to work at night, he says, when it's quiet. But if it was any quieter in the daytime I don't know what I'd do. We never go anyplace or do anything anymore, it seems to me.' She sipped her hot coffee black and then fanned a dimpled hand in front of her pursed lips. 'This isn't getting your breakfast ready now, is it?'

Because Frances knew how fond I was of eating, or because she used my visit, as an excuse, she prepared a large and wonderful breakfast. Fried pork chops, fried eggs, grits, with plenty of good brown milk gravy to pour over the grits, and fresh hot biscuits. I ate heartily, hungry after walking out from town, listening with stolid patience to the steady flow of dull gossip concerning various kinfolk and townspeople. I was finishing my third cup of coffee when I heard Randall on the stairs. As he entered the room, I got up to greet him.

'Well, well,' he said with false heartiness, holding onto my hand and grinning, 'if it isn't the junior birdman!'

He patted his wife on her broad rump, crossed to the sideboard and poured a shot glass full of bourbon. He swiftly drank two neat shots before turning around.

'Welcome home, Bubba,' he said, 'how long are you going to stay?'

He sat at the table, and I dropped into my seat again. Randall looked well. He always did, whether he had a hangover or didn't have one. His face was a little puffy, but he was freshly shaven, and his curly russet hair had been cut recently. His starched white shirt, however, was frayed at the cuffs. The knot of his red-and-blue striped rep tie was a well-adjusted double Windsor, and his black, well-worn Oxford flannel trousers were sharply creased.

When I managed to catch his eyes with mine, I shrugged.

'I see,' he nodded, 'the enigmatic response. Before I came downstairs I looked outside, both in front and out back, and didn't see a car parked. Until I realized it was you, I thought Frances was merely talking to herself again. But if you're broke, you're welcome to stay home as long as you like and close ranks with me. I've never been any flatter.'

'I saved two pork chops for you, Randy,' Frances said quickly.

'No, thanks. Just coffee. Save the chops for my lunch.' Randall smiled abstractedly, clasped his fingers behind his head and studied the ceiling. 'It isn't difficult to divine the purpose of your visit, Bubba,' he continued. 'When you're flush, you wheel up in a convertible, your pockets stuffed with dollar cigars. When you're broke, you're completely broke, and on your uppers. But if the purpose of your visit is to collect the honest debt I owe you, you're out of luck. Three hundred dollars!' He shook his head and snorted. 'Frankly, Bubba, I'd have a hard time raising twenty!'

He leaned forward in his chair and said derisively, 'But you can live here as long as you like. We can still eat, and thanks to Daddy there's a wonderful roof over our heads. And whether we pay our bills in town or not, the Mansfield credit is still good.'

To drink the coffee Frances set before him, Randall gripped the large white mug with both hands. His fingers didn't tremble, but it must have taken a good deal of concentrated effort to hold them steady.

'Going to see Mary Elizabeth?' he asked suddenly.

I shrugged and lit a cigarette. I offered the pack to my brother. He held up a palm in refusal, changed his mind and took one out of the pack. He held both of his hands in his lap, after putting the cork tip in hs mouth, and I had to lean across the table to light it for him.

'You kind of believe in long engagements, don't you, Bubba?' he said, smiling sardonically. 'It's been about seven years now, hasn't it?'

'Eight,' Frances amended. 'Eight years come November.'

'Well, you can't say I haven't done my part to bring you together,' Randall said wryly, watching my face closely. 'Five years ago our farms were almost three miles apart. But thanks to selling land to Wright Gaylord, we're less than a mile away from them now!' He laughed with genuine amusement.

I was unable to listen to him any longer. He made me feel sick to my stomach. I rose from the table, and picked up my shaving kit from the sideboard.

'There's plenty of hot water upstairs if you want to shave, but not enough yet for a bath. Lately I've taken to turning the heater off at night and not lighting it again till I get up,' Frances said. 'Your room is dusty, too, but when Leona comes over this morning I'll have her do it up and put fresh sheets on the bed.'

I nodded at my sister-in-law and left the room. As I climbed the stairs to the second floor, Randall said, 'Maybe you'd better scramble me a couple of eggs, hon. But don't put any grease in the skillet, just a little salt . . .'

Not only was Randall weak, he was a petty tyrant to his long-suffering wife. Before she could scramble eggs she would have to pour the good milk gravy into a bowl, and wash and dry the frying pan.

My old room was at the very end of the upstairs hallway, next to the bathroom. When Daddy bought the farm and moved us out from town, I had been elated about the move because it meant having a room to myself. And somehow, Daddy had made a go of the farm when many other good farmers were half starving in Georgia. He had earned a fair sum by *not* planting things and by collecting checks from the government. But even when times were excellent, he had never made any real money out of the farm. He was a fair farmer, but a poor businessman. Daddy had only been good for giving Randall and me advice, cheap advice, and he had never found anything in either one of us except our faults.

My room was dusty all right, as Frances had said. It had also been used as a catchall storeroom during the two years I had been away. The stripped double bed had been stacked with some cardboard cartons full of books, two shadeless table lamps and two carelessly rolled carpets. Extra pieces of dilapidated furniture had been tossed haphazardly into the room, and the hand-painted portrait of Grandpa was lying flat on top of my desk. A thick layer of dust was scattered over everything. When I opened the window, dust puffs as large as tennis balls took out after each other across the floor.

For a moment or two I looked out the window at the familiar view, but it didn't seem the same. Something was missing. And then I noticed that the ten-acre stand or slash pine had disappeared – cut down and sold as firewood probably, and not replanted.

I lifted the stern-faced portrait of Grandpa off the desk and leaned it against the dresser. I wiped the surface of the desk with my handkerchief. After rummaging through the drawers, I found a cheap, lined tablet with curling edges. Sitting down at the desk, I took out my ballpoint.

It took approximately half an hour to write out a list of instructions for Judge Brantley Powell. I wanted to be sure that I covered everything completely so he wouldn't have any questions. After rereading the list, and making a few interlinear corrections, I folded the sheaf of papers and stuffed them into my hip pocket.

I went into the bathroom and shaved, planning on an immediate departure for town in order to catch the judge in his office before he went home for the day. After returning to my room, I was rebuttoning my shirt when a soft rap sounded at the door.

'Bubba,' Randall's voice called through the door. 'How long're you going to be?'

I opened the door and looked quizzically at my brother. He was smiling a sly, secretive smile. Whenever Mother had caught him smiling that way, she slapped his face on general principles, knowing instinctively that he had done something wrong, and also knowing that she would never find out what he had done.

'Come on downstairs,' he said mysteriously. 'I've got a surprise for you.' Still smiling, he turned away abruptly and descended the stairs.

I slipped into my corduroy jacket, put my hat on and followed him.

The surprise was Mary Elizabeth, the last person I wanted to see right then, standing at the bottom of the stairs, cool and crisp in a wide-necked white blouse, blue velvet pinafore and white sling pumps. Ordinarily, I would have stopped to see Mary Elizabeth first, before coming home, but I didn't want to see her at all when I was broke and without a car. My last visit home, when I had first made my vow of silence, had been a strained, miserable experience for both of us.

'Hello, Frank,' Mary Elizabeth said shyly, 'welcome home.'

She hadn't changed a fraction in two years. She was every bit as beautiful as I remembered. Mary Elizabeth had pale golden hair, and dark blue eyes – which often changed to emerald green in bright sunlight – a pink-and-white complexion, fair, thick, untouched pale brows, and long delicate hands. Her figure was more buxom than it had been ten years before, but that was to be expected. She was no longer a young girl. She was a mature woman of twenty-nine.

A moment later Mary Elizabeth was in my arms and I was kissing her, and it was as though I had never been away. There was a loud click as Randall closed the double doors to the dining room and left us alone. At the sound, Mary Elizabeth twisted her face to one side. I released her reluctantly and stepped back.

'Your voice still hasn't come back.' It was a statement, not a question.

Slowly, regretfully, I shook my head.

'And you haven't been to a doctor, either, have you?' she said accusingly.

Again the negative headshake, but accompanied this time with a stubborn smile.

'I've had a lot of time to think about it, Frank,' she said eagerly, 'and I don't believe your sudden loss of speech is organic at all. There's something psychological about it.' She dropped her eyes demurely. 'We can discuss it later at The Place. Randall's telephone call caught me just as I was leaving for school, and I don't think Mr Caldwell liked it very well when I called him at the last minute that way. When I take a day off without notice, or get sick or something, he has to take my classes.

'But I've packed a lunch, and it's still warm enough to go for a swim at The Place . . .' She colored prettily. 'If you want to go?'

I opened the front door and took her arm. As we climbed into her yellow Nova, she was over her initial nervousness, and she began to scold me.

'Did it ever occur to you, Frank, that even a picture postcard mailed in advance would be helpful to everybody concerned?' I rather enjoyed the quality of Mary Elizabeth's voice. Like most schoolteachers of the female sex, she had an overtone of fretful impatience in her voice, and this note of controlled irascibility amused me.

I grinned and tweaked the nipple of her right breast gently through the thinness of her white cotton blouse.

'Don't!' The sharp expletive was delivered furiously, and her blue-green eyes blazed with sudden anger. She set her lips grimly and remained silent for the remainder of the short drive to her farm, where she lived with her brother. As she pulled into the yard and parked beneath a giant pepper tree, I noticed that she had cooled off. The moment she turned off the engine, I pulled her toward me and kissed her mouth softly, barely brushing her lips with mine.

'You *do* love me, don't you, Frank?' she asked softly, with her eyes glistening.

I nodded, and kissed her again, roughly this time, the way she liked to be kissed. One day, when we had first started to go together, Mary Elizabeth had asked me thirty-seven times if I loved her. At each affirmative reply she had been as pleased as the first time. Women never seem to tire of being told, again and again and again.

'Here comes Wright,' Mary Elizabeth said quickly, looking past my shoulder. 'We'd better get out of the car.'

We got out of the car and waited beneath the tree, watching her brother approach us from the barn with his unhurried, shambling gait. Wright Gaylord hated me, and I was always uneasy in his presence because of his low boiling point. He worshipped his little sister and had put her through college. Now in his late forties, Wright was still unmarried. He had never found a woman he could love as much as he loved his sister. He hated me for two reasons. One, I could sleep with Mary Elizabeth and he couldn't. After all these years he was bound to know about us, or at least suspect the best. And two, when I married Mary Elizabeth, he knew that I would take her away and he would never see her again. When our engagement had been announced and published in the paper, he had locked himself in his bedroom for three days.

'I didn't get sick or anything,' Mary Elizabeth said as Wright came within earshot. 'Frank came home, so I took the day off for a picnic.'

Wright glared at me. His face reminded me of a chunk of red stone, roughly hewn by an amateur sculptor, and then left in the rain to weather.

'When are you leaving?' Wright asked rudely, shoving both hands into his overall pockets deliberately, to avoid shaking hands.

'Now, that's no way to talk, Wright,' Mary Elizabeth chided. 'Frank just got home this morning.' She patted her brother's meaty arm. 'We're going to The Place for our picnic. Why don't you come with us?'

'I ain't got time for picnics,' he said sullenly. 'I got too much work to do. Anyway, I've been meanin' to go to

291

town all week. Give me the keys, and I'll take your car instead of the pickup.'

Mary Elizabeth handed him her keys. 'It might do you good to take a day off and come with us.'

Wright grunted something under his breath, got into the car, and slammed the door. We entered the house, picked up a quilt and the lunch basket to take with us, and then cut across the fields for The Place.

We had called it The Place for as long as I could remember. The tiny pool in the piney woods wasn't large enough to be called a swimming hole. Fed by an underground spring that bubbled into a narrow brook about fifty yards up the pine-covered slope, the pool was only big enough for two or three people to stand in comfortably, and the water was only chest deep. The clear water was very cold, even on the hottest days. On a cruel summer day, a man could stand in the pool, his head shaded by pines, and forget about the heat and humidity of Georgia.

The Place had other advantages. There was a wide flat rock to the right of the pool, with enough room for one person at a time to stretch out on it and get some dappled sunlight. To the left of the pool, facing up the steep hill, there was a clearing well matted with pine needles. For two people, the clearing was the perfect size for an opened quilt and a picnic. Best of all, The Place was secluded and private. Located on the eastern edge of the Gaylord farm, the wooded section merged with a Georgia state forest. The only direct access to The Place was across Wright Gaylord's property, and nobody in his right mind would have trespassed on Wright's land.

Two hours before, Mary Elizabeth and I had arrived at the pool, hot and dusty from trudging across the cultivated fields. We had stripped immediately and jumped into the water. After splashing each other and wrestling playfully in the icy water, we had allowed the sun to dry us thoroughly before we made love on the quilt stretched flat on the bed of pine needles. There had been no protest from Mary Elizabeth, despite my long absence. Her natural, animal-like approach to sex was really miraculous in view of her strong religious views. I sometimes wondered if she ever connected the physical act of love with her real life.

I don't believe she thought consciously of sex at all. If she did, she must have thought of it as 'something Frank and I do at The Place,' but not connected with conjugal love or as something out of keeping with her straitlaced Methodist beliefs. Perhaps it was only habit.

I had never managed to make love to Mary Elizabeth anywhere else. She had been seventeen the first time, with just the two of us at The Place. It had been an accident more than anything else. Afterward I had been ashamed of myself for taking advantage of her innocence. But the first time had led to the second, and all during that never-to-be-forgotten summer we had made daily pilgrimages to The Place.

I have never underrated Mary Elizabeth nor underestimated her intelligence, but the situation was unusual. After all, Mary Elizabeth was a college graduate now, and a teacher of high school English – she surely must have known what we were doing. But we had never discussed sex. I had an idea that the subject would be distasteful to her, and she had never brought it up on her own. And yet, every time I came home we headed for The Place like homing pigeons long absent from their coop. I had a hunch, and I had never pressed my good fortune, that as long as Mary Elizabeth never thought about it, or discussed it, we could continue to make love at The Place forever.

Once, and only once, I had asked Mary Elizabeth to drive to Atlanta with me for a weekend. She had been shocked into tears by my reasonable proposition.

'What kind of girl do you think I am?' she had asked tearfully.

Completely bewildered by her reaction, I had been unable to come up with a ready reply. I had never brought up the subject again. And besides, there wasn't a better spot in the world for making love than The Place.

Mary Elizabeth sat up suddenly, swung her long bare legs gracefully around, and sat on the rock facing me, dangling her feet in the water. I was in the pool, chest deep, and I had been studying her body as she lay flat on her back. Spreading a towel across her lap, but leaving her breasts uncovered, Mary Elizabeth looked at me sternly, and then wet her lips.

'What about us, Frank?' she said at last. 'How long do we go on like this?' The tone of her voice had changed. It wasn't harsh, but it wasn't feminine either. It was more like the voice of a young boy, on the near verge of changing.

I raised my eyebrows, watching her intently.

She cupped her breasts and pointed the long pink nipples toward the sky. She narrowed her eyes, no longer greenish, but now a dark aquamarine, and caught mine levelly.

'Are they still beautiful, Frank?' she asked in this strange new voice.

I nodded, dumbly, trying to figure out what she was driving at.

'You're wrong.' She smiled wanly, dropped her hands, and her plump breasts bobbed beautifully from their own momentum. 'You haven't noticed, but they're beginning to droop. Not much, but how will they look in five years? Ten years? Nobody's ever seen them except you, Frank, but how much longer will you be interested? All I've ever asked you to do is quit cockfighting so we could get married. We've drifted along in a deadlock too long, Frank, and it's impossible for me to accept your way of life. I thought that as you got older, you would see how wrong it is, but now you seem to be entangled in a pattern. And cock-fighting is wrong, morally wrong, legally wrong, and every other kind of wrong! You're a grown man now, Frank!'

I sloshed forward in the tiny pool, put my arms around her hips, warm from the sun, and buried my face in her lap.

'Yes, you big, dumb child,' she said softly, running her fingers through my damp hair, 'but I can't meet you halfway on an issue like cockfighting. My roots are here and so are yours. Give it up, please, give it up, and marry me. Can't you see that you're wrong, wrong, wrong!' She gripped my hair with both hands and tugged my head gently from side to side.

'I can't exist on postcards any longer, Frank. *'Dear M.E. I'm in Sarasota. Won the derby 4–3. I love you. Will write from Ocala. F.!'* In a few more weeks, I'll be thirty years old. I want to be married and have children! I'm tired of people snickering behind my back at our engagement. Nobody believes it any more. If you loved me only half as much as I love you, you'd give it up. Please, Frank, stay home, marry me—'

There was a catch in her voice, and I lifted my head to look at her face. She wasn't crying, far from it. She was trying to beat me down again with an emotional appeal to my 'reason'. I had explained patiently to Mary Elizabeth, a dozen times or more, that cockfighting was not a cruel sport, that it was a legitimate, honorable business, and I had asked her to witness one fight, just one fight, so she could see for herself instead of listening to fools who didn't know what they were talking about. She had always refused, falling back on misinformation learned from reformers, the narrow-minded Methodist minister, and the shortsighted laws prohibiting the sport that were pushed through by a minority group of do-gooders. If she wouldn't see for herself, how could I persuade her?

'You're a brilliant man, Frank,' Mary Elizabeth continued earnestly. 'You could make a success out of anything you went into in Mansfield. This farm is half mine, you know, and when we're married, it'll be half yours. If you don't want to farm with Wright, I've got enough money saved that you can open a business of some kind in town. I've saved almost everything I've earned. Wright doesn't let me spend a penny, and I've been teaching for six years. And I'll help you get your voice back. We'll work it out together, you and I, Frank. We can get a book on phonetics and you—'

As she constructed these impossible feminine castles I got restless. I pulled away from her, clambered up the opposite bank and began to dress, without waiting to get dry.

'What are you doing?' she said sharply.

As she could see for herself, I was putting my clothes on.

'You haven't listened to a single word, have you?'

I grinned, and buckled the straps on my jodhpur boots.

'If you leave now,' she shouted, 'you needn't come back! We're through, d'you hear? Through! I won't be treated this way!'

When a woman starts to scream unreasonably, it's time to leave. I snatched a cold fried chicken leg out of the basket, draped my coat over my arm and started down the trail. Mary Elizabeth didn't call after me. Too mad, I reckoned.

Mary Elizabeth was stubborn. That was her problem. Anytime she truly wanted to get married, all she had to do was say so. But it had to be on my terms. I loved her, and she was a respectable woman with a good family background. I knew she would make me a good wife, too, once she got over this foolishness of wanting me to give up cockfighting and settle down in some dull occupation in Mansfield. We had been over this ground too many times, and I had a new season of cockfighting to get through. Nothing would have pleased me more than to have Mary Elizabeth as a bride at my Ocala farm, preparing meals and keeping my clothes clean. And, until she became pregnant, what would keep her from teaching school in Ocala, if that was what she wanted to do? As soon as she came around to seeing things my way, and quit trying to tell me what I could and couldn't do, we'd be married quick enough. And she knew it.

I grinned to myself, and tossed the chicken bone in the general direction of an ant nest. Mary Elizabeth had a sore point on those postcards. I'd have to do better than that. When I got back to Ocala, I'd write her a nice, interesting letter, a long newsy one for a change.

When I crossed through Wright's yard to the state road, I looked about apprehensively to see if he had returned, but he hadn't come back from town. Every time Wright caught me alone, he attempted to goad me into a fight. For Mary Elizabeth's sake, I had always refused to fight him. It would have given me a good deal of pleasure to knock a little sense into his thick head, but I knew that as soon as we started fighting he would whip out his knife, and then I would have to kill him.

I walked down the asphalt road. My biggest problem now was how to retrieve my shaving kit from the dresser in my room. If I returned to the house to get it, Randall would be curious as to why I was leaving so soon. If I wrote a note informing him I was going to take my rightful property and have him and Frances tossed out, he would attempt, with his trained lawyer's logic, to argue me out of my convictions. As I remembered, I had never really bested him in an oral argument. The only way I had ever won an argument with Randall was by resorting to force. And besides, Frances would bawl and carry on like crazy.

By the time I was level with the house, I decided to hell with the shaving kit, and continued on down the road.

It would be less trouble all the way round if I bought another razor and toothbrush when I got back to Jacksonville.

I walked about four miles before I was picked up by a kid in a hot rod and taken the rest of the way into Mansfield. When he let me out at a service station, I walked through the shady residential streets to Judge Brantley Powell's house on the upper side of town. He only went to his office in the mornings, and I was certain I could catch him at home. When I rapped with the wrought-iron knocker, I only had to wait a minute before Raymond, his white-wooled Negro servant, opened the door. Raymond peered at me blankly for a moment or so before he recognized me, and then he smiled.

'Mr Frank,' he said cordially, 'come in, come in!'

It was dark in the musty hallway when he closed the door. Raymond took my hat, led the way into the dim living room and raised the shades to let in some light.

'The judge he takin' his nap now, Mr Frank,' he said uneasily. 'I don't like to wake him 'less it's somethin' important.'

I considered. What was important to me probably wouldn't be considered important by the old judge. I waved my right hand with an indifferent gesture, and settled myself in a leather chair to wait.

'You goin' to wait, Mr Frank?'

I nodded, picked up an old *Life* magazine from the table beside the chair and leafed through it. Raymond left the room silently, and returned a few minutes later with a glass of ice cubes and a pitcher of lemonade. A piece of vinegar pie accompanied the lemonade. Firm, tart and clear, with a flaky, crumbly crust, it was the best piece of vinegar pie I had ever eaten.

It was almost five before the judge came downstairs. Evidently Raymond had told him I was waiting on him because he addressed me by name when he entered the room and apologized for sleeping so late. Judge Powell had aged considerably in the four or five years that had gone by since I had last talked to him. He must have been close to eighty. His head wobbled and his hands trembled as he talked. I handed him the list of instructions I had written, and he sat down in a chair close to the window to read them. He looked through the papers a second time, as if he were searching for something, and then removed his glasses.

'All right, Frank,' he said grimly. 'I'll handle this for you. Your Daddy was a stubborn man, and I told him he was wrong when he changed his will.'

I picked up my hat from the table where Raymond had placed it.

'One more thing, Frank. How long do you expect to be at the Jeff Davis Hotel in Jax?'

I shrugged, mentally totaled my remaining money, and then held up four fingers.

'You'll hear from me before then. And when you get your money, Frank, I hope you'll settle down. A dog has fun chasing his own tail, but he never gets anywhere while he's doing it.'

I shook hands with the old man and he walked me to the front door. 'Can you stay for dinner, son?'

I shook my head and smiled my thanks, but when I opened the door he grasped my sleeve.

'There're all kinds of justice, Frank,' he said kindly, 'and I've seen most of them in fifty years of practice. But poetic justice is the best kind of all. To measure the night, a man must fill his day,' he finished cryptically.

I nodded knowingly, although I didn't know what he meant, and I doubt very much whether he did either. When a man manages to live as long as Judge Powell has, he always thinks he's a sage of some kind.

I cut across town to the US Highway and ate dinner in a trucker's cafe about a mile outside the city limits.

Two hours later I was riding in the cab of a diesel truck on my way back to Jacksonville. I had the feeling inside that I had finally burned every bridge, save one, to the past. But I didn't have any regrets. To survive in this world, a man has got to do what he has got to do.

Chapter Nine

I was tired when I reached Jacksonville, but I wasn't sleepy. I had hoped to get some sleep in the cab of the truck on the long drive down, but the driver had talked continuously. As I listened to him, dumbly, my eyes smarting from cigarette smoke and the desire to close them, he poured out the dull, intimate details of his boring life – his military service with the First Cavalry Division in Vietnam, his courtship, his marriage and his plans for the future (he wanted to be a truck dispatcher so he could sit on his ass). He was still going strong when we reached Jax. To finish his autobiography, he parked at a drive-in and bought me ham and eggs for breakfast.

After shaking hands with the voluble truck driver, who wasn't really a bad guy, I caught a bus downtown and checked into the Jeff Davis Hotel. One look at the soft double bed and I became wide awake. If my plan was successful, I would know within three days, and I didn't have time to sleep all day. I had to proceed with a confidence I didn't actually have, as though there could be no doubt of the outcome.

After I shaved, I prepared a list for Doc Riordan. These were supplies I would need, and I intended to take advantage of our agreement. It would take a long time to use up eight hundred dollars' worth of cocker's supplies.

One. Conditioning powder. Doc made a reliable conditioning powder – a concoction containing iron for vigor, and Vitamin Bl. This powder, mixed with a gamecock's special diet, is a valuable aid to developing a bird's muscles and reflexes. I put down an order for three pounds.

Two. Dextrose capsules. A dextrose capsule, dropped down a gamecock's throat an hour before a fight, gives him the same kind of fresh energy a candy bar provides to a mountain climber halfway up a mountain. On my list I put down an order for a twenty-four-gamecock season supply.

Three. Doc Riordan's Blood Builder. For many years Doc had made and sold a blood coagulant that was as good as any on the market. If he didn't have any on hand he could make more. This was a blood builder in capsule form containing Vitamin K, the blood coagulating vitamin, whole liver and several other secret ingredients. Who can judge the effectiveness of a blood coagulant? I can't. But if any blood coagulants worked, and I don't leave any loopholes when it comes to conditioning, I preferred to use Doc Riordan's. Again I marked down enough for a twenty-four-gamecock supply.

Four. Disinfectants. Soda, formaldehyde, sulfur, carbolic acid, oil of tansy, sassafras, creosote, camphor and rubbing alcohol. Insects are a major problem for cockfighters. Lice are almost impossible to get rid of completely, but a continuous fight against them must be fought if a man wants to keep healthy game fowl. *Give me a plentiful supply of all these*, I wrote on my list.

Five. Turpentine. Five gallons. The one essential fluid a cocker must have for survival. God has seen fit to subject chickens to the most loathsome diseases in the world—pip, gapes, costiveness, diarrhea, distemper, asthma, catarrh, apoplexy, cholera, lime legs, canker and many others. Any one of these sicknesses can knock out a man's entire flock of game fowl before he knows what has happened to him. Fortunately, a feather dipped in turpentine and shoved into a cock's nostrils, or swabbed in his throat, or sometimes just a few drops of turpentine on a bird's drinking water, will prevent or cure many of these diseases. When turpentine fails, I destroy the sick chicken and bury him deep to prevent the spread of his disease.

When I completed my list I sealed it in a hotel envelope, wrote Doc Riordan's name on the outside, and headed for the drugstore where he had part-time work. Doc wasn't in, but the owner said he was expected at noon. Figuring that Doc would freely requisition most of the items on my list from the owner, I decided not to leave it, and to come back later.

I walked to the Western Union office and sent two straight wires. The first wire was to my neighbor and fellow cocker in Ocala, Omar Baradinsky:

HAVE LIGHTS AND WATER TURNED ON AT
MY FARM. WILL REIMBURSE UPON ARRIVAL.
F. MANSFIELD.

I knew Omar wouldn't mind attending to this chore for me in downtown Ocala and inasmuch as I didn't know what day or what time I would arrive at the farm, I wanted to be certain there was water and electricity when I got there.

The other wire was to Mr Jake Mellhorn, Altamount, North Carolina. Jake Mellhorn bred and sold a game strain called the Mellhorn Black. It was a rugged breed, and I knew this from watching Blacks fight many times.

These chickens fought equally well in long and short heels, depending upon their conformation and conditioning, but they were unpredictable fighters – some were cutters and others were shufflers – and they had a tendency to alternate their tactics in the pit. As a general rule I prefer cutters over shufflers, but I needed a dozen Aces and a fair price. Jake Mellhorn had been after me for several years to try a season with his Blacks, and I knew that he would give me a fairly low price on a shipment of a dozen. If I won with his game strain at any of the major derbies, he would be able to jack the price up on the game fowl he sold the following season to other cockers. I could win with any hardy, farm-walked game strain that could stand up under my conditioning methods – Claret, Madigan, Whitehackle, Doms – but the excellent cocks I would need would cost too much, especially after putting out five hundred dollars for Icky. It wouldn't hurt anything to send a wire to Jake and find out what he had to offer anyway.

> TO: JAKE MELLHORN, ALTAMOUNT, N.C.
> NEED TWELVE FARM-WALKED COCKS. NO
> STAGS. NO COOPWALKS WANTED. PUREBRED
> MELLHORNS ONLY. NO CROSSES. SEND PRICE
> AND DETAILS C/O JEFF DAVIS HOTEL,
> JACKSONVILLE, FLA. F. MANSFIELD.

If I knew Jake Mellhorn, and I knew the egotistic, self-centered old man well, I'd have a special delivery letter from him within a couple of days. And on my first order, at least, he would send me Aces.

I paid the girl for the wires, and then ate a hamburger at a little one-arm joint down the street before returning to Foster's Drugstore.

Now that the wires were on their way, I felt committed, even though they didn't mean anything in themselves. I felt like I was getting the dice rolling by forcing my luck.

I couldn't pay for the Mellhorns, no matter how good a price Jake gave me. I couldn't even repay Omar Baradinsky the utilities deposit money he would put up for me in Ocala – and yet I felt confident. Surely Judge Powell would come through with one thousand five hundred dollars now, because I had acted as though he would. It was a false feeling of confidence, and I knew that it was bogus in the same way a man riding in a transatlantic airplane knows that there cannot possibly be a crack-up because he bought one hundred dollars' worth of insurance at the airport before the plane took off.

Doc Riordan was sitting at the fountain counter, wearing a short white jacket, when I entered the drugstore. I eased onto the stool beside him and tapped him on the shoulder.

'Hello, Frank,' he said, smiling. In the cramped space, we shook hands awkwardly without getting up. 'Mr Foster said there was a big man with a cowboy hat looking for me. Inasmuch as I don't know any bill collectors who don't talk, I figured it was you.'

I handed Doc the envelope. He studied the list, and whistled softly through closed teeth. 'That's a mighty big order on short notice, Frank,' he said, frowning. 'I don't have any conditioning powder made up, and there's been so much flu going around Jax lately, I've got sixty-three prescriptions to fill before I can do anything else.' He tapped the list with a forefinger. 'Can you let me have a couple of days?'

I had to smile. At that stage I could have let him have a couple of months. I clapped him on the shoulder and nodded understandingly.

'Good. Come in day after tomorrow and it'll be waiting for you. All of it.' He smiled. 'Kinda looks like you've got your chickens for the season, and I hope you'll have a good one. Anytime you need something fast, just drop me a card here at Foster's. I know damned well I'll make the Milledgeville Tourney, but that'll be the only one this year. I've got too many feelers out on Licarbo to go to chicken fights. But then, I might get a chance to run down to Plant City—'

He had work to do, so I slid off the stool and left abruptly while he was still talking.

For the rest of the afternoon I prowled used-car lots as a tire-kicker, trying to locate a pickup truck of some kind that would hold together for four or five months. Around four o'clock I discovered an eight-year-old Ford half-ton pickup that looked suitable, and the salesman rode around the block with me when I tried it out. All afternoon my silence had unnerved talkative used-car salesmen. After five minutes of my kind of silence, they usually gave up on their sales talks and let me look around in peace. This fellow was more persistent. After reparking the truck in its place on the fourth row of the lot, I looked at the salesman inquisitively.

'This is a real buy for one fifty,' he said sincerely. He was a young man in his early twenties, with a freckled earnest face. His flattop haircut, and wet-look black leather sports jacket, reminded me of a Marine captain wearing civilian clothes for the first time. For all I knew, he was an ex-Marine.

I looked steadily into his face and he blushed.

'But old pickups don't sell so well these days. Too many rich farmers buying new ones. So I'll let you have it for a hundred-dollar bill.'

I studied him for a moment, maintaining my expressionless face, and then got out of the cab of the truck. I started toward the looping chain fence that bordered the sidewalk, and he caught up with me before I reached the first line of cars. He put a freckled hand on my arm, but when I dropped my eyes to his hand, he jerked it away as though my sleeve were on fire.

'I'll tell you what I'll do, sir,' he said quickly. 'Just to move the old Ford and get it off the lot, I'll give up my commission. You can have the truck for eighty-five bucks. Give me ten dollars down, and drive it away. Here're the keys.' He held out the keys, but I didn't look at them. I kept my eyes on his face.

'All right,' he said nervously. 'Seventy-five, and that's rock bottom.'

I nodded. A fair price. More than fair. The truck had had hard use, and most of the paint had been chipped off in preparation for a new paint job. But no one had ever gotten around to repainting it. I pointed to the low sun above the skyline, and he followed my pointing finger with his pale blue eyes. To catch his wandering attention again I snapped my fingers and then held up three fingers before his face.

'Three suns?' he asked. 'You mean three days?'

I nodded.

'Without a deposit, I can't promise to hold it for you, sir.'

I shrugged indifferently and left the lot. I had a hunch that the pickup would still be there when I came back for it.

When I got back to my hotel room I counted my money. Twenty-three dollars and eighty-one cents. Money just seems to evaporate. I had no idea where all of it had gone, but I had to nurse what was left like a miser. Twelve dollars would be needed to pay four days' rent on the hotel room, and I would have to eat and smoke on the remainder. If I didn't get a letter from Judge Powell within three days, or four at the most, I would have to make other plans of some kind.

I spent the next three days at the public library. There was a long narrow cafe near the hotel that featured an 'Eye-Opener Early-Bird Breakfast,' consisting of one egg, one slice of bacon, one slice of brushed margarine toast and a cup of coffee – all for forty-two cents. After eating this meager fare, I walked slowly to the library and sat outside on the steps until it opened, thinking forward to lunch. I read magazines until noon in the periodical room, and then returned to the hotel and checked the desk for my mail. I then returned to the library. By two o'clock I was ravenous, and I would eat a poor boy sandwich across the street, and drink a Coca-Cola. The poor boy sandwich had three varieties of meat, but not much meat. I then returned to the library and read books until it closed up at nine.

My taste in reading is catholic. I can take Volume III of the *Encyclopedia Americana* out of the stacks and read it straight through from Corot to Deseronto with equal interest, or lack of interest, in each subject. *Roget's Thesaurus* or a dictionary can hold my attention for several hours. I don't own many books. There were only a few on poultry breeding at my Ocala farm and a first edition of *Histories of Game Strains* that I won as a prize one time at a cockfight. And I also owned a beat-up copy of *Huckleberry Finn*. I suppose I've drifted down the river with Huck Finn & Co. fifty times or more.

When the library closed at nine, I ate a hamburger, returned to the hotel and went to bed.

Three days passed quickly this way. On the morning of the fourth day, however, I didn't leave the hotel. My stomach was so upset I didn't even feel like eating the scanty 'Eye-Opener Early-Bird Breakfast', afraid I couldn't hold it. I sat in the lobby waiting apprehensively for the mail.

There were two letters for me, both of them special delivery. One was a thick brown envelope from Judge Powell, and the other was a flimsier envelope from Jake Mellhorn. I didn't open either letter until I reached my room. My fingers were damp when I opened the thick envelope from Judge Powell first, but when I emptied the envelope onto my bed, the only thing I could see was the gray-green certified check from the Mansfield Farmer's Trust, made out to my name for one thousand five hundred dollars!

My reaction to the check surprised me. I hadn't realized how much I had counted on getting it. My knees began to shake first, and then my hands. A moment later my entire body was shivering as though I had malaria, and I had to sit down quickly. I was wet from my hair down to the soles of my feet with a cold, clammy perspiration that couldn't have been caused by anything else but cold, irrational fear. Of course, I hadn't allowed my mind to dwell on the possibility of failure, but now that I actually had the money, the suppressed doubts and fears made themselves felt. But my physical reaction didn't last very long. I stripped to the waist and bathed my upper body with a cold washrag, and dried myself thoroughly before reading Judge Powell's letter. It was a long letter, overly long, typed single spaced on his law firm's letterhead, watermarked stationery:

Mr Frank Mansfield
c/o The Jeff Davis Hotel
Jacksonville, Florida

Dear Frank:

I handled this matter personally, following your desires throughout, feeling you knew your brother Randall better than me. You did. When I called on him and informed him that you intended to break the will of your father, he laughed. If it hadn't been for your copious notes, his laughter would have surprised me.

'Is Frank willing to fight this in court?' he asked me.

'No,' I told him (again following your instructions). 'Your brother Frank said it wouldn't be necessary. "When Randall sees that he is in an untenable position, he will sign a quitclaim deed immediately and move out."'

Again your brother laughed as you predicted. 'Do you think I'm in an untenable position, Judge?' he then asked.

'Yes, you are,' I told him. 'That's why I brought a quitclaim deed for you to sign.'

He laughed and signed the deed. 'In New York,' he said, 'you wouldn't have a chance, Judge.' I remained

309

silent instead of reminding him that the case, if brought to a trial, would be held in Georgia. 'When does Frank want me to leave?'

'As soon as the property is sold.'

'Does Frank have a buyer in mind?'

'He recommended that I try Wright Gaylord first,' I said.

This statement gave your brother additional cause for merriment, because he laughed until the tears rolled down his face.

'Frank only wants a profit of one thousand, five hundred dollars,' I told your brother. 'He instructed me to give you any amount over that, after deducting my fee, of course.'

'That's generous of Frank,' he said, 'but there are some taxes due, about seven hundred dollars.'

'I'm aware of the taxes,' I said.

'All right, Judge. You've got your quitclaim deed. Continue on down the road and sell the property to Wright Gaylord. I'll be ready to leave tomorrow morning when you bring me my share, if there's anything left over.'

Wright Gaylord gave me a check the same afternoon for three thousand five hundred dollars, which I accepted reluctantly. Given more time I am positive that your property would have sold for eight or possibly ten thousand dollars. But the sum adequately covered your required one thousand five hundred and my fee of five hundred dollars, so I closed the sale then and there. You didn't mention it in your notes, but I realize the astuteness of selling to Mr Gaylord, although I doubt if he did. Upon your marriage to his sister you will automatically get half your farm back and half of his as well. Mr Gaylord is also a client of mine, and this was a fine point of legal ethics, but inasmuch as he is certainly aware of your engagement to his sister, I did not deem it necessary to remind him.

Enclosed is a certified check for one thousand five hundred dollars. My fee of five hundred dollars has been deducted, the taxes have been paid, plus stamps, and miscellaneous expenses. I gave your brother a cheque for seven hundred and sixty-eight dollars and fifty cents. Randall and his wife left yesterday on the bus for Macon.

Mr Gaylord has already begun to tear down your father's farmhouse and the outlying buildings. He hired a wrecking crew from Atlanta, and I saw some of their equipment moving through town yesterday. However, he agreed to keep your Negro tenant on the place if he wanted to stay, per your request. But he would not consent to keep him on shares because Charley Smith is too old. Your main concern, I believe, was to maintain a home for Charley and his family, so again, in lieu of instructions to the contrary, I agreed to this condition.

There are also some papers enclosed for you to sign on the places marked with a small X in red pencil. They have been predated, including the power of attorney, in order to send you the money without undue delay. Please return them (after you have signed them) as quickly as possible.

If your father were alive, I know he would want you to use your money wisely, so I can only say the same. 'A rolling stone gathers no moss' is an old saying but a true one nevertheless. If I can help you further do not hesitate to ask me.

Very truly yours,

BRANTLEY POWELL

BP/bj

Attorney-at-Law

I didn't mind the moralizing of the windy old man, because he didn't know what I planned to use the money for, but I was irritated because he had dictated the letter to his big-mouthed old maid secretary, Miss Birdie Janes. The small initials 'bj' in the lower left-hand corner of the letter meant that my business would be spread all over the county by now. I realized that it was a long letter, and I appreciated the details, but the old man should have written the letter personally. When I returned to Mansfield, eventually, sides would be taken – some for Randall and some for me, but the majority would take Randall's side, even though I was legally and morally right about taking what rightfully belonged to me.

The letter from Jake Mellhorn was more pressing:

Dear Frank,

Glad to see you're getting sense enough to know that the Mellhorn Black is the best gamecock in the world, bar none!!! And you're lucky you wired me just when you did. I just brought in twenty-two cocks, but if you only want a dozen country-walked roosters, you can have the best of the lot, which is plenty damned good!!! I can ship you six Aces, two to three years old. The other six are brothers, five months past staghood, but all are guaranteed dead game, and they'll cut for you or your money back. As you know, I ship them wormed, in wooden coops, but they'll need watering upon arrival. Don't trust the damned express company to water birds en route – they'll steal the cracked corn out of the coops and make popcorn out of it. As a special price – TO YOU ONLY!!! One dozen Mellhorn Blacks for only seven hundred dollars. That's much less than seventy-five apiece. Let me know by return wire, because I can sell them anywhere for one hundred to one hundred and twenty-five dollars each.

For a good season,

JAKE MELLHORN

An outlay of seven hundred dollars, although it was an exceptionally fair price for Ace Mellhorns, would make a deep dent in my one thousand five hundred dollars, but I had little choice. I had to have them, or others just as good. Another five hundred to Ed Middleton, seventy-five dollars for the truck, and I'd be down to only two hundred and twenty-five. Luckily, I had feed at Ocala left over from last year, and the older Flint corn is, the better it is for feeding. And within two weeks I could win some money at the Ocala cockpit. At least two, or possibly three birds could be conditioned for battle by that time.

After packing and checking out of the hotel, I cashed the check at the bank. I wired seven hundred dollars to Jake Mellhorn immediately with instructions to ship the cocks to my farm. I mailed the signed papers back to Judge Powell special delivery, and headed for the used-car lot to buy the staked-out pickup truck.

Within two hours, I was driving out of Jacksonville. The cocker's supplies from Doc Riordan were in the truck bed, along with my suitcase and gaff case, covered by a tarp. The remainder of my money, in tens and twenties, was pinned inside my jacket pocket with a safety pin.

As I turned onto Highway 17 I thought suddenly of Bernice Hungerford. She had been in my thoughts several times during the last three days, especially late at night when I had been trying to sleep, with hunger pangs burning at my stomach. In fact, I had considered seriously going out to her house and chiseling a free meal. But I had felt too guilty to go. Leaving a broken guitar on her front porch hadn't been a brilliant idea.

313

There was a filling station ahead, and I pulled onto the ramp and pointed to the regular pump.

'How many sir?'

I pulled a finger across my throat.

'Filler up? Yes, sir.'

While I was still looking at the large city map inside the station, the attendant interrupted me to ask if everything was all right under the hood. The question was so stupid I must have looked surprised, because he blushed with embarrassment and checked beneath the hood without waiting for a reply. How else can a man discover whether oil and water are needed unless he looks?

I traced the map and found Bernice's street. Her house was about three miles out of my way. I didn't really owe her anything, but I knew my conscience would be eased if I repaid the woman the thirty dollars she had advanced me when I had needed it. I turned around, and drove slowly until I reached a shopping center that had a florist's shop. I parked, entered the shop, and selected a dozen yellow roses out of the icebox. The stems were at least two feet long.

'These will make a beautiful arrangement,' the gray-haired saleswoman smiled. 'Do you want to include a card?'

When I nodded she gave me a small white card and a tiny envelope that went with it. I scrawled a short note:

Dear Bernice:

Drop me a line sometime. RFD # 1. Ocala, Fla.

Frank Mansfield

Whether Bernice would write to me or not I didn't know. I did feel, however, that the roses and thirty dollars in cash would make up for my abrupt leave-taking without

314

saying good-bye. And I did like the woman. I tucked the money inside the little envelope, together with the card, and licked the flap.

'And where do you wish these delivered, sir?' the saleswoman asked, handing me a pink bill for twenty-five dollars and fifty cents. I put the money on the counter, and tugged at my lower lip. By having them delivered I could save time.

'We deliver free, of course,' the woman smiled.

That settled it. I had to deliver the roses and the note myself. The woman was too damned anxious. Her gray hair and kindly, crinkle-faced smile didn't fool me. I had selected the twelve yellow roses with care. If I had allowed them to be delivered she would have either switched them for older roses, or changed them for carnations or something. After pocketing my change, I pointed to the stack of green waxed paper and made a circular motion with my hand for the woman to wrap them up.

When I reached 111 Melrose Avenue, I rang the bell several times, but there was no one at home. I waited impatiently for five minutes, and then left the flowers at the door. I slipped the note containing the money under the door. Maybe it was better that way.

The next move, if any, would be up to Bernice. If she had been home, I probably would have stayed overnight with her and lost another day. There was too much work ahead of me to waste time romancing a wealthy widow.

The old pickup drove well on the highway, but I was afraid to drive more than forty miles an hour. When I revved it up to fifty, the front wheels shimmied. Long before reaching Orlando I was remorseful about the grand gesture of giving the roses and thirty bucks to Bernice Hungerford. It would have been wiser to wait until I was flush again. The damned money was dripping through my fingers like water, and I'd have to win some fights before any more came in. But when I pictured the delighted expression on Bernice's jolly face when she discovered the flowers at her front door, I felt better.

I reached Orlando before midnight. I saved eight dollars by driving through town to Ed Middleton's private road, and by sleeping in the back of the truck in his orange grove. The excitement had drifted out of my mind, and, as tired as I was, I slept as well in the truck as I would have slept in a motel bed.

The next morning, when I parked in his carport, and knocked on his kitchen door at 6 a.m., Ed wasn't happy to see me. Martha Middleton, however, appeared to be overjoyed by my early morning appearance. She cracked four more eggs into the frying pan and decided to make biscuits after all.

'I didn't expect you back so soon,' Ed said gruffly, after he filled my cup with coffee.

I grinned at his discomfiture, took the money out of my jacket, and peeled off five hundred dollars on the breakfast-nook table. Ed glared at the stack of bills. Martha stayed close to her stove, pursing her lips. I drank half my coffee, and started in on my fried eggs before Ed Middleton said a word. In the back of my mind, I was more or less hoping he would change his mind and renege on the deal. Icarus was a mighty fine rooster, but five hundred dollars was a lot of money, and I needed every cent I could get at that moment.

'Well,' Ed said thoughtfully. He counted the money twice, removed the top five twenty-dollar bills and shoved the remaining four hundred dollars back across the table.

'Here!' he said angrily. 'I won't hold you to the ridiculous price we agreed on, Frank. I'll just take a hundred as a token payment. Besides, I'm sick of looking at game chickens. I'm tired of the whole business! Come on, let's go get your damned rooster!'

By the time Ed had finished talking, he was almost shouting and out of the nook and fumbling at the doorknob.

'Can't you wait until Frank finishes his breakfast?' Martha said, with quiet good humor.

'Sure, sure,' Ed managed to get the door open. 'Take your time, Frank,' he said contritely. 'I'll go on out to the runs and put Icarus in your aluminium coop. Also, those two battered Grays are in good shape again. You can have them and the game hen, too. I'll have them all in coops by the time you finish eating.' The door banged shut.

I wiped some egg yolk off the top twenty with a napkin and returned the money to my inside jacket pocket. The kitchen door opened up again, and Ed stuck his head in. 'Can you use some corn? Barley?'

I nodded.

'Good. There's about three or four partly used sacks of both in the feed shack. But if you want 'em, you'll have to carry 'em to the truck yourself. I'll be goddamned if *I'm* going to do it!' The door slammed again.

I wanted to follow him out the door but thought it best to finish my breakfast and let Ed cool off a little bit. He had never really expected me to show up with five hundred dollars for his pretty pet gamecock. But his astonishment was in my favor. He had been shamed into returning four hundred dollars, and now I was way ahead of the game. The Middleton Gray game hen was valuable for breeding, and the two Gray gamecocks were worth at least fifty dollars apiece.

'Don't you pay any mind to Ed's bluster, Frank,' Martha said gently. 'He's just upset and doesn't mean half of what he says. I know how much store he sets by those chickens. Someday, he'll thank me, Frank. You think I'm unreasonable, I know, making him give up his chickens and stopping him from following fights all over the country, but I'm not really. Ed's had two heart attacks in the last eighteen months. After the last one he was in bed for two weeks and the doctor told him not to do anything at all. Nothing.' She shook her head.

'He isn't supposed to pick so much as an orange up off the ground. Why, the last time the doctor came out and saw that the roosters were still out there he had a fit! Now go out and get your chickens, Frank, and don't let Ed help you lift anything.'

I slid out from the table and patted Martha on the shoulder. Ed Middleton certainly knew how to keep a secret. I hadn't known anything about his ailing heart.

'I know you won't say anything, Frank,' Martha said, smiling, 'but don't *look* anything, either!' Despite her smile and the humor in her voice, there were sparks of terror in her eyes. 'Ed hasn't told a soul about his bad heart, and I know he wouldn't want me to tell you. He tries to pretend he's as strong as he ever was.'

I wanted to say something, anything that would comfort the woman, but I couldn't. He was going to die soon. I could tell by her eyes.

I smiled, nodded and left the kitchen. The moment I was outside, I lit out around the little lake at a dead run to get my prize rooster before Ed Middleton could change his mind.

Chapter Ten

The scarlet cock, my lord likes best,
And next to him, the gray with thistle-breast.
This knight is for the pile, or else the Black.
A third cries no cock like the dun, yellow back.
The milk-white cock with golden legs and bill.
Or else the Spangle, choose as you will.
The King he swears (of all), these are the best.
They heel, says he, more true than all the rest.
But this is all mere fancy, and no more,
The color's nothing, as I've said before!

This anonymous English cocking poem was thumbtacked to the wall beside my bed. I had copied it in longhand and stuck it there as a reminder that experience, rather than experiment, would be my best teacher. This poem must have been more than two hundred years old, and yet it still held a sobering truth. The best gamecock has to be of a proven game strain. Crossed and recrossed, until the color of the feathers resemble mud, if a cock can be traced to a legitimate game strain on both sides, he will fight when he is pitted and face when he is hurt. This old poem contained a particularly worthwhile truth to remember, now that I possessed Icky, the most gaily plumaged cock I had ever owned. The bettors at every pit on the circuit would be anxious to back him because of his bright blue color, and he would have to be good, because of the odds I'd be forced to give on him.

While I poured coffee into cups at the gate-legged table,

Omar Baradinsky, his hairy fingers clasped behind his back, studied the poem on the wall. He must have read it three or four times, but if he moved his lips when he read, I wouldn't have known about it. Omar's pale face, which no amount of exposure to the Florida sun could tan, was almost completely covered by a thick, black, unmanageable beard. This ragged hirsute growth, wild and tangled, began immediately below his circular, heavily pouched brown eyes, and ended in tattered shreds halfway down his chest. A thick, untrimmed moustache, intermingled with his beard, covered his mouth completely. When he talked, and Omar liked to talk, his mouth was only a slightly darker hole in the center of the jet-black tangle of face hair. Out of curiosity, I had asked Omar once why he wore the beard, and his answer had been typical of his new way of life.

'I'll tell you, Frank,' he had boomed. 'Did you ever eat baked ham with a slice of glazed pineapple decorating the platter?'

When I admitted that I had, he had pulled his fingers through his beard fondly and continued. 'Well, that's what my face looked like when I went to the office every day in New York. Like a slab of glazed, fried, reddish pineapple! For me, shaving once a day wasn't enough. The whiskers grew too fast. I shaved before leaving home in the morning, again at noon, and if I went out again at night, I had to scrape my jowls again. For as long as I can remember, my face was sore, raw in fact, and even after a fresh shave people told me I needed another. So, I no longer have to shave and I no longer shave, and I'll never shave again!'

To see Omar Baradinsky now, standing in my one-and-a-half-room shack near Ocala, wearing a pair of faded blue denim bib overalls, a khaki work shirt with the sleeves cut off at the shoulders, scuffed, acid-eaten, high-topped work shoes, and that awe-inspiring growth of black hair covering his face – no one in his right mind would have taken him for a once successful advertising executive in New York City. A closer look at his clothes, however, would reveal that Omar's bib overalls and shirt were expensive and tailored – which they were. He ordered his clothes from Abercrombie & Fitch up in New York, and they would wash and dry without needing to be ironed. In the beginning, I suspect that he had probably started to wear bib overalls as a kind of uniform, to fit some imaginary role he had made up in the back of his mind. But now they had become a part of him, and I couldn't picture Omar wearing anything else.

But Omar had been an advertising man four years before. Not only had he been a successful executive with a salary of thirty-five thousand dollars a year, he had also owned a twenty-unit luxury apartment house in Brooklyn. He was now a breeder and handler of gamecocks in Florida, keeping Claret crosses and Allen Roundheads, and after four experimental years, slowly beginning to pull ahead. The one remaining tie Omar had with New York was his wife. She visited him annually, for one week, when she passed through central Florida on her way to Miami Beach for the winter season. So far, she had been unable to make him change his mind and return to New York. Omar's wife wasn't the type to bury herself on an isolated Florida chicken farm, so they were stalemated.

Unlike most American sportsmen, the cockfighting fan has an overwhelming tendency to become an active participant. There is no such thing as a passive interest in cockfighting. Beginning as a casual onlooker, a man soon finds the action of two gamecocks battling to the death a fascinating spectacle. He either likes it or he doesn't. If he doesn't like it, he doesn't return to watch another fight. If he does like it, he accepts, sooner or later, everything about the sport – the good with the bad.

As the fan gradually learns to tell one game strain from another, he admires the vain beauty of a game rooster. Admiration leads to the desire to possess one of these beautiful creatures for his very own, and pride of ownership leads to the pitting of his pet against another gamecock. Whether he wins or loses, once the fan has got as far as pitting, he is as hooked as a ghetto mainliner.

Of course, not every beginner embraces the sport like Omar Baradinsky – to the point of quitting a thirty-five-thousand dollar-a-year position, and leaving wife, family and friends to raise and fight gamecocks in Florida. The majority of fans are content to participate on a smaller scale – as a handler, perhaps, or as an owner of one or two gamecocks, or as a lowly assistant holding a bird for a handler while he lashes on the heels. Many spectators, unfortunately, are interested in the gambling aspects of cockfighting to the exclusion of everything else. But even gamblers must learn a lot of information about game fowl to win consistently. Whether he wins or loses, the gambler still has the satisfaction of knowing that a cockfight cannot be fixed, and not another sport in the United States will give him as fair a chance for his money.

Omar Baradinsky, however, had gone all the way, caught up in the sport at the dangerous age of fifty, the age when a man begins to wonder just what in the hell he has got out of his life so far, anyway? Omar was still as bewildered by his decision to enter full-time cockfighting now as he had been when he started.

'I can't really explain it, Frank,' he had told me one idle morning, after we got to know each other fairly well, right after he had first moved to Florida. 'I had done a better than average job on one of my smaller advertising accounts, and the owner invited me to his home in Saratoga Springs for a weekend. Smelling a little bonus money in the deal, you see, something my firm wouldn't know anything about, I accepted and drove to this fellow's place early on a Saturday morning.

'Just as I anticipated, he presented me with a bonus check for a thousand clams. And we sat around his swimming pool all afternoon – which was empty by the way – drinking Scotch and water and talking business. Out of nothing, he asked me if I'd like to see a cockfight that night.

'"Cockfight!" I said. "They're illegal, aren't they?" "Sure, they are!" he laughed. "But so was sleeping with that blonde you fixed me up with in New York. If you've never seen a cockfight, I think you might get a kick out of it."

'So I went to my first cockfight. I'll never forget it, Frank. The sight of those beautiful roosters fighting to the death, the gameness, even when mortally wounded, was an exciting, unforgettable experience. Before the evening was over, I knew that that's what I wanted to do with my life: breed and fight game fowl. It was infantile, crazy maybe, I don't know. My wife thought I'd lost my mind and wouldn't even listen to my reasons. Probably because I couldn't give her any, not valid, reasons. I *wanted* to do it and that was my sole reason!

'I was fed up to the teeth with advertising, and I had saved enough money to quit. I was only fifty, and although my future still glimmered on Madison Avenue, I didn't really need any more money than I already had. Still, I played it pretty cagy with the firm. I made a secret deal with one of the other vice-presidents to feed him my accounts in return for supporting my resignation on the grounds of ill health. That way, I picked up twenty-five thousand dollars in severance pay. I sold my apartment house and set up a trust fund for my wife to take care of her needs in New York. Besides, she has money of her own. Her father was a proctologist, and he left her plenty when he died. And for the first time in my life, I'm happy, really happy. Funny, isn't it?'

This was Omar Baradinsky, who owned a game farm only three miles away from mine. So far, he hadn't even prospered in his adopted profession, but he was breaking even by selling trios and stags to other cockers. His game-cocks usually lost when he fought them in Southern pits. He must have been hard enough to succeed in the business world, but the stubborn streak of tenderness in his makeup didn't give him enough discipline to make Aces out of his pit fowl. He overfed them, and he didn't work them hard enough to last.

Turning away from the poem, Omar turned his huge brown orbs on me and jerked a thumb at the wall.

'Did you write that, Frank?'

I shook my head and pulled out a chair for him to sit down.

'Then what about your new cock, Icky? If that chicken wasn't bred purely for color I've never seen one.'

I shrugged. Icky had been bred for color, certainly, but from a pure game strain, and his conformation was ideal for fighting. In a few days I'd see whether he could fight or not when I gave him a workout with sparring muffs in my training pit.

'Anyway, I like the look of those Mellhorn Blacks, and especially your two Middleton Grays.'

So did I. Buford, my part-time Negro helper, had gone downtown to the depot with me the night before when I picked up my shipment of Mellhorn Blacks. After helping me put the dozen cocks away in their separate stalls in the cockhouse, he had driven by Omar's place and told him about them. Omar had arrived early that morning for a look at the Mellhorns and a long admiring examination of Icky. Buford had undoubtedly given Icky a big buildup, but Omar hadn't been impressed until he saw the cock for himself.

'Tell me something, Frank, if you will,' Omar said, when he finished pouring some condensed milk into his coffee.

'Did you get an invitation to the Southern Conference Tourney at Milledgeville?'

In reply, I got up from the table, rummaged in the top drawer of my dresser until I found the invitation and the schedule for the SC pit battles, and passed them to Omar. He glanced at the forms, pulled on his shaggy beard a couple of times, and returned the papers.

'I just don't understand you people down here,' he said. 'It may be partly my fault, because I wrote Senator Foxhall a personal letter asking for an invitation and enclosed a two-hundred-dollar forfeit. Three days later I got the check back in the mail and no invitation. Not a damned word of explanation. What in the hell's the matter with me? I've got more than fifty birds under keep, and last season my showings hit fifty-fifty. Maybe I'm not in the same class with the SC regulars, but if I'm willing to lose my entry fee why should Senator Foxhall care? And here you are – I saw the date on your invitation – you didn't own a single gamecock when you got that invite! I'm not belittling your ability, Frank. I know you're a top cocker and all that, but how did the senator know you'd be able to attend? How did you receive an invitation without asking for one when I couldn't get one when I did?

'I've never attended the Milledgeville meet, and I want to go, even as a spectator. But after fighting at all the other SC pits this season, I'd be embarrassed to attend the tournament without an entry. Do you know what I mean?'

I knew what he meant, all right. Omar had done the normal, logical thing, and the turndown had hurt his feelings. Most of the US derbies and tourneys get their entries through fees. The man who sends in a two- or three-hundred-dollar forfeit either shows up or he loses his money. A contract is returned to him by mail. When the list is filled, no more entries are accepted. I didn't really know why Omar had been turned down by Senator Foxhall. It wasn't because he was a Pole or a New Yorker.

Members of the cockfighting fraternity are from all walks of life. There are men like myself, from good Southern families, sharecroppers, businessmen, loafers on the county relief rolls, Jews, and Holy Rollers. If there is one single thing in the world, more than all the others, preserving the tradition of the sport of cocking for thousands of years, it's the spirit of democracy. In a letter to General Lafayette, George Washington wrote, 'It will be worth coming back to the United States, if only to be present at an election and a cocking main at which is displayed a spirit of anarchy and confusion, which no countryman of yours can understand.' I carried a clipping of this letter, which had been reprinted in a game fowl magazine, in my wallet. I had told Mary Elizabeth once that George Washington and Alexander Hamilton had both been cockfighters during the colonial period, but she had been unimpressed. Nonetheless, cockfighters are still the most democratic group of men in the United States.

But the Milledgeville Tourney was unlike other US meets. Senator Foxhall had his own rules, and he made his own decisions about whom to invite. I had earned my right to fight there, and I suppose the old man knew that I would be there if it was physically possible to be there. Maybe he didn't think Omar was ready yet. I didn't know. Surely Omar's fifty-fifty showing didn't put him into the top cocker's class. He still had a lot to learn about game fowl if he wanted to be a consistent winner.

I looked at Omar and smiled. There wasn't any use to write a note for him telling him what I thought was the reason for his turndown. His feelings would be hurt more than they were already. By writing to the senator, he had made a grave error, a social error. It was like calling a host of a party you were not invited to and asking point blank for an invitation!

326

I had finished my coffee, and I had work to do. I got up from the table and clapped Omar on the shoulder. Before leaving the shack, I took a can of lighter fluid off the dresser and slipped it into my hip pocket. Omar sighed audibly and decided to follow me out.

When we got to the cockhouse, I removed the Mellhorn Blacks one at a time from their separate coops, showing off the good and bad points to Omar as well as I could before putting them back. For a shipment of a dozen, they were a beautiful lot. As Jake had promised in his letter, six were full brothers, a few months past staghood, and the other six were Aces, two to three years old, with one or more winning fights behind them. Each cock was identifiable by its web-marking, and the cardboard record sheet of each bird had been enclosed in its shipping crate when Jake had expressed them down from North Carolina. Before putting them away the night before, I had purged them with a mild plain-phosphate mixture, and they were feeling fine as a consequence.

As a conditioning bench, I used a foam-rubber double mattress stretched fiat on a wooden, waist-high platform Buford and I had knocked together out of scrap lumber when I had first leased the farm. I had one of the older Mellhorn cocks on the bench showing it to Omar. The cock was a one-time winner, but he must have won by an accident. His conformation was fair, but the bird was high-stationed, with his spurs jutting out just below the knee joint. He would miss as often as he hit. A low-stationed cock would have greater leverage and fight best in long heels, but a high-stationed cock like this one would never make a first-class fighter. Jake Mellhorn hadn't gyped me on the sale. He was truly bred, and in small-time competition against strainers, the cock could often win. It had weight in its favor and was close to the shake class, but the chicken couldn't really compete in SC competition unless it got lucky. Luck is not for the birds. The element of chance must be reduced to the minimum if a cocker wants to win the prize money. In a six-entry derby, for instance, when the man winning the most fights takes home the purse put up by all the entries, the odd fight often provides the verdict. I couldn't take a chance with this one.

After pointing out the high spurs to show Omar what was wrong with the Black, I picked up my hatchet and chopped off the rooster's head on the block outside the doorway.

'I see,' Omar said thoughtfully, as he watched the decapitated chicken flop about in the dusty yard. 'You don't like to pit high-stationed cocks.'

I clipped the hatchet into the block so it stuck.

'Some cockers prefer high-stationed birds,' Omar said argumentatively. 'And a seventy-five dollar chicken is damned expensive eating.'

True, the plateful of fried chicken I would eat that night would be a costly meal, but it would have been much more expensive to pit the cock when he would probably lose. And an owner should only bet on his own gamecock – not against it. I shrugged indifferently.

'I suppose you know what you're doing,' Omar said. 'But he was a purebred Mellhorn and could have been kept as a brood cock.'

Except on a small scale, I've never done much breeding. I prefer to buy my gamecocks. Conditioning and fighting them are what I do best, but I would never have bred the high-stationed Black. Like begets like, and the majority of the chicks sired would have been high-stationed.

I shook my head and grinned at Omar. He was well aware of the heredity factor – his head was crammed with breeding knowledge he had learned through reading and four years' experience. Omar was still sore about the Milledgeville Tourney.

'What about the six brothers? How do you know they're game? The Aces have been pit-tested, but if one of the brothers is a runner they all may be runners.'

Unfortunately, there is no true test for gameness. Only a pit battle can decide gameness. There are various tests, however, a cocker can try which will give him an indication of a cock's gameness. In the case of the six brothers, I was stymied by a lack of knowledge concerning the father and mother. If the father had been a champion, Jake Mellhorn would have said so, and charged a higher price for them. The six cocks were obviously Mellhorn Blacks. I could tell that by looking at them. But only one drop of cold blood from a dunghill will sometimes cause a cock to run when it is hurt. One of the young cocks had to be tested for gameness, and I had planned on doing it this morning before Omar came over. If the cock I tested proved to be game, I could then assume that the others were equally game. But in the testing I would lose the gamecock. Another seventy-five bucks shot.

One rigid test for gameness is to puncture a cock all over his body with an ice pick, digging it in for a quarter to half an inch. If the injured cock will still attempt to fight another cock the next morning, even if all he can do is lie on his back and peck, it is considered game. The ice-pick method of testing is fairly popular with cockers because they can usually salvage their bird after it recovers from its injuries. I don't consider this test severe enough. The Roman method I use is more realistic than a half-hearted jabbing with an ice pick, even though the cock is lost during the process.

For the test, I selected one of the brothers with the poorest conformation. The choice was difficult because all of the brothers were fine Mellhorn Blacks. For an opponent, I used the largest of the two Middleton Grays. Omar held the Gray when I heeled it with sparring muffs.

The Black would be practically helpless, and I didn't want him killed until he had suffered sufficiently to determine his gameness.

My homemade pit is crudely put together with scrap lumber, but it meets the general specifications. I've also strung electric lights above it in order to work my birds at night, and it's good enough for training purposes. Omar put the Gray under one arm, after I completed the heel-tying of the muffs, and headed for the training pit in front of my shack.

The young Black was a man fighter and pecked my wrist twice before I could get a good grip around his upper legs with my left hand. A moment later I had his body held firmly against my leg where he couldn't peck at me anymore. In this awkward position, I stretched his legs out on the block outside the cockhouse and chopped them off at the knee with the hatchet.

When I joined Omar at the pit, his brown eyes bulged until they resembled oil-soaked target agates. 'Good God, Frank! You don't expect him to fight without any legs, do you?'

I nodded and stepped over the pit wall. I cradled the Black over my left arm, holding the stumps with my right hand, and raised my chin to indicate that we should bill them. Omar brought the Gray in close and the Black tore out a beakful of feathers.

We billed the cocks until their ingrained natural combativeness was aroused, and then I set the Black down on the floor of the pit and took the Gray away from Omar. The Gray was anxious to get to his legless opponent, but I held him tightly by the tail and only let him approach to within pecking range. When the Black struggled toward him, I pulled him back by his tail. Without his feet, the Black was unable to get enough balance or leverage to fly, and his wildly fluttering wings couldn't support him in an upright position. He kept falling forward on his chest, and after a short valiant period of struggling, he gave up altogether. I let the Gray scratch into range, still holding him by the tail. The Black pecked every time, although he no longer tried to stand on his stumps. Finally, I let the Gray go, and he described a short arc in the air and landed, shuffling, in the center of the Black's back. Getting a good bill hold on the prostrate cock, the Gray shuffled methodically in place, hitting the padded muffs hard enough to make solid thumping sounds on the Black's body. This was the first time I had seen the Gray in action. I realized that Ed Middleton had really done me a favor when he gave me the once-battered fighter. Any cock that could shuffle with the deadly accuracy displayed by the Middleton Gray would win a lot of pit battles.

The Black was too helpless to fight off the Gray, so I picked up the muff-armed bird and gave him to Omar to hold for a moment. I took the can of lighter fluid out of my hip pocket, and sprinkled the liquid liberally over the Mellhorn Black. Flipping my lighter into action, I applied the lighter to the cock, and his feathers blazed into oily flames.

When Omar returned the Gray I pitted him against the burning bird from the score on the opposite side of the pit. He walked stiff-winged toward the downed Black with his long neck outstretched, holding his head low above the ground. The fire worried and puzzled him, and he was afraid to hit with his padded spurs. The Gray pecked savagely at the Black's head, however, even though it was on fire, and managed to pluck out an eye on his first bill thrust.

The Black tried to stand again, fluttering his smoldering wings, but his impassioned struggles only succeeded in increasing the flames. The smell of scorching feathers filled the air with a pungent, acid stench. As I grabbed the Gray's tail with my right hand, I held my nose with my left. As the flames puffed out altogether, the Black lay quietly. The charred quills resembled matchheads or cloves dotting his undressed body, and for a moment I thought he was dead. But as I allowed the straining Gray to close the gap between them, the dying Mellhorn raised his head and pecked blindly in the general direction of the approaching Gray. With that last peck, a feeble peck that barely raised his head an inch above the ground, he died.

I put the Gray under my arm and turned around to see what Omar thought of this remarkable display of gameness. But Omar had gone inside the shack. I cut the sparring muffs away from the Gray's spurs and returned him to his coop.

Omar sat at the table, staring at his open hands, when I joined him inside the shack. I opened a pint of gin I had stashed away behind the dresser – because of Buford – and put the bottle on the table. Omar took a long pull, set the bottle down, and I took a long one myself. I needed that drink and felt a little sick at my stomach. And I knew that Omar felt as badly as I did. But what else could I do? I had lost a wonderful gamecock, but I could now assume that his five brothers would be as game as he had been. The unfortunate part of the testing was that I didn't really know if the brothers were equally game. But I could now *assume* they were.

'I couldn't treat a gamecock like that, Frank,' Omar said, without looking at me, keeping his eyes on his open hands. 'Sure, I know. A chicken is supposed to be an insensitive animal and all that crap. But *I* couldn't do it! I could no more set a cock on fire than I could—' His mind searched for something he could no more do, and then he shrugged his heavy shoulders and took another shot of gin.

I took another short one myself.

'Was he game, Frank? It was too much for me. I couldn't stick around to see.'

332

I nodded glumly and lit a cigarette.

'Unbelievable, isn't it! Burning like a damned torch and still trying to fight! A man couldn't take that kind of punishment and still fight. Not a man in this world could do it.'

I stubbed out the cigarette. It tasted like scorched feathers, despite the menthol and filter tip.

'Well, Frank,' Omar said pensively, 'there're a lot of things I don't like about cockfighting, but a cocker's got to take the bad with the good.'

I nodded in agreement and pushed the bottle toward him.

Omar studied my face and, ignoring the bottle, leaned forward.

'You and I need each other, Frank,' he said suddenly. 'Why don't we form a partnership for the season?'

For some reason his suggestion startled me, and I shook my head automatically.

'Don't decide so hastily,' he continued earnestly, leaning over the table. 'I've picked up twenty cocks already, and I've still got better birds to pick up on walks in Alabama. Between the two of us, if you conditioned and handled, and I took charge of the business end, we could have one hell of a season. I know how tough it's been since you lost your voice. I still remember how you used to holler and argue and knock down the odds before the fights. What do you say, Frank?'

I was tempted. Two of my cocks were gone before I started. I only had thirteen birds left for the season, and my cash was low. If we combined our gamecocks we could enter every money main and derby on the circuit, and if Omar didn't interfere with my conditioning—

'Let it go for now,' Omar said carelessly, getting to his feet. 'Just think about it for a while. I don't like to mention my money, but I'm lousy with capital. I've got

333

a lot more than you have, and if you had a partner putting up the forfeits, entry fees, and doing all the betting, you could concentrate on conditioning and handling. And on a partnership we can split everything we take in right down the middle.'

He turned in the doorway and his shadow fell across my face. 'No matter what you decide,' he said cheerfully, 'come over to my place for dinner tonight. I'll take that high-stationed Mellhorn home with me. I've always wanted to eat a Mellhorn Black with dumplings.' He laughed. 'Chicken and dumplings for two! That's about thirty-seven fifty a plate, isn't it?' Omar waved from the door and disappeared from sight.

I remained seated at the table. A few minutes later I heard the engine of his new Pontiac station wagon turn over, and listened to the sounds as he drove out of the yard. The pot of coffee on the hot plate burbled petulantly. I poured another cup, and a cock crowed outside, reminding me of all the work still to be done that morning. I couldn't put off the dubbing of Icky any longer.

Ordinarily, the deaf ears, wattles and comb are trimmed away when the bird is a young stag of six or seven months. Ed Middleton, for reasons known only to himself, had failed to dub Icky. He probably meant to keep Icky as a pet and brood cock and had never intended to pit him. But I was going to pit him, and he had to be dubbed for safety in battle. With his lovely free-flowing comb and dangling wattles, an opposing cock could get a billhold and shuffle him to death in the first pitting. I had been putting off the dubbing, afraid that he might bleed to death. With a stag the danger is slight, but Icky was fully matured, more than a year-and-a-half old. And it had to be done.

I got my shears, both the straight and the curved pairs, and went outside to Icky's coop room.

He was a friendly chicken, used to kindness and handling, and ran toward me when I opened the gate. I picked him up, sat on the bench in front of the shack, and went to work on his comb. With my experience I don't need a man to hold a chicken for me. I've dubbed as many as fifty stags in a single morning, all by myself, and I've never had one die from loss of blood yet. But I was extra careful with Icky.

Gripping his body firmly between my knees, and holding his head with my left hand, I clipped his comb with the straight shears as close to the head as possible. Many cockers leave about an eighth of an inch, believing erroneously that the slight padding will give the head protection from an opponent's pecking. But I've never known a cock to be pecked to death. I trim right down to the bone because the veins are larger close to the head and there isn't as much bleeding. I cut sharply, and with solid, quick snips, so the large veins were closed by the force of the shears. Luckily, Icky's head bled very little. I then cut away the wattles and deaf ears with the curved shears, again taking my time, and did a clean job. As an afterthought I pulled a few short feathers out of the hackle and planted them in Icky's comb. The little blue feathers would grow there and ornament his head, until they were billed out by an irate adversary.

When I completed the dubbing I turned him loose in his coop. He had held still nicely, and because he had been so good about it, I caught the Middleton Gray game hen running loose in the yard, and put her into his coop. The dubbing hadn't bothered him. He mounted the hen before she had taken two steps. A moment later he flew to his roosting pole and crowed. Within a week his head would be healed completely, and he would be ready for conditioning.

Omar had taken the decapitated Ace Black with him, but the charred Mellhorn was still in the pit. I buried the dead chicken and the other cock's severed head in the sand before eating lunch.

If I had been completely broke, or without any game-cocks of my own, I wouldn't have considered a partnership with Omar. But I had enough Ace chickens to hold up my end. Omar had excellent, purebred gamecocks. All he needed was a man like me to work the hell out of them. The idea of forming a partnership with anybody had never occurred to me before, although partnerships were common enough in cockfighting circles. Besides, I had a good deal of affection for Omar, almost a paternal feeling toward him, despite the fact that he was more than twenty years older than me. He wanted success very much, and there were many things he had to learn. And there was a lot that I could teach him.

After feeding the chickens that evening, I drove to Omar's farm for supper. His farm was on the state road, and his house was a two bedroom-den structure with asphalt-tile floors. It was a luxurious house compared to my one-and-a-half room shack. There was an arch above the entrance gate, and a sign painted with red letters on a white background stated:

THE O.B. GAME FARM

'Our Chickens Lay Every Night!'

Omar had been in advertising too many years to pass up a good slogan. In addition to the arch sign, there was a smaller sign nailed to the post of the gate at the eye level of passing motorists.

EGGS. $15 PER DOZEN

At least once a week, some tourist driving down the highway toward Santos or Belleview would stop and attempt to buy eggs from Omar, thinking that the sign was in error and that the eggs were fifteen cents a dozen. Omar enjoyed the look of surprise on their faces when he told them that there was indeed no mistake. Of course the eggs were fifteen dollars a dozen and worth a hell of a lot more! And of course, Allen Roundhead and Claret setting eggs were a bargain indeed at fifteen dollars a dozen.

Smiling at the sign, I turned into Omar's farm. A man like Omar Baradinsky would be a good partner for me. Why not? I couldn't think of a single valid objection.

That evening after supper, when Omar brought out the bottle of John Jameson, a partnership was formed.

Chapter Eleven

For the next three days Omar and I lived out of his station wagon, driving through southern Alabama and picking up his country-walked roosters from various farmers. The back of the station wagon had been filled with young stags before we left, each of them in a separate coop. Every time we picked up a mature cock we left a stag to replace it.

Omar paid these Alabama farmers ten dollars a year for the privilege of leaving one of his gamecocks with the farmer's flock of hens. In addition to the board bill, he also had to buy up and kill all the farmer's stags each year. Selecting the right farm walk for a fighting cock is an art, and Omar had done a careful, thorough job. All his Alabama walks were more than adequate.

A gamecock is a bird that loves freedom of movement. With his harem at his heels, a cock will search for food all day long, getting as far as three or more miles away from his chicken house on the farm. The more difficult his search for food, the greater his stamina becomes. At night, of course, once the chickens are asleep, the farmer must sneak out and scatter enough corn in the yard to supplement the diet. But he must never put out enough feed to completely satisfy the chickens. Like members of a welfare state, chickens who don't have to get the hell out and scratch for their living will soon learn to stand around waiting for a free handout, getting fat and useless.

The hillier the farmland, the better it is for the cock's legs. Trees to roost in at night, green fields, and, whenever possible, a fast-flowing brook for fresh water are the requisites for a good walk. Florida is too flat for good walks, and Omar had been wise to put his roosters out in southern Alabama.

To assist us in picking up the half-wild, country-walked gamecocks, I had brought along my big Middleton Gray. He had a deep, strong voice and an exceptionally aggressive disposition. We had little difficulty in getting the half-wild cocks to come back to the farmyards.

First, we drove into a farmer's yard, and Omar told him we were there to pick up the rooster, and that we had another to replace him.

'Well, now, Mr Baradinsky,' the farmer said, invariably scratching his head, 'I ain't seen your rooster for two or three days now.'

'Don't worry,' Omar would laugh. 'He'll be here in a minute.'

By that time, I would have the big Gray heeled with a pair of soft sparring muffs. As soon as I dropped the Gray in the yard, he would begin to look for hens, crowing deep from his throat. Within seconds, an answering crow would echo from the fields or woods a mile away. As we watched, the cock we came for would be running toward us as fast as his strong legs could carry him, his harem scattered and trailing out behind him. He often crowed angrily as he ran – *Who is this threat to my kingdom? This interloper who would steal my hens?* – he seemed to say. When he reached the yard, he attacked immediately, and the Gray, seeing all those pretty hens, piled right into him with the sparring muffs. Omar would catch the wild country-walked cock, and I'd put the Gray back into his coop.

After closely examining the wild gamecock, I'd saw off his natural spurs a half inch from the leg, and arm him with the other pair of sparring muffs. We pitted the two cocks then and there to see how the bird fought. It is very difficult to spot a runner on his own domain – often a useless dunghill rooster will fight to protect his own hens – but I could always get a fair idea of the bird's fighting ability. If the cock was satisfactory, we left a young stag to take over the harem and placed the cock in the stag's coop. Before leaving, Omar would pay the farmer ten dollars in advance for the next year's board and warn the man against clipping the new stag's wings. We never took the farmer's word either. Before leaving we always checked personally to see that there weren't any other full-grown roosters, turkeys, or guinea fowl around. A stag must be in complete control of the yard. If there was a mature rooster on the farm, dunghill or otherwise, the stag might have been intimidated and gone into hack, submitting to the dunghill's rule.

Omar had developed a firm, gruff manner with these farmers who loaned their farms for walks. Despite his strong New York accent, which rural Southerners distrust instinctively, he had won them over completely during four years of contact. He didn't merely leave a stag and forget about it until the following season. He wrote letters periodically during the year, asking how his rooster was getting along, enclosing a stamped, self-addressed postcard to make sure he would get a reply. The farmers responded cheerfully to Omar's active interest, and, if nothing else, they were awed by his impressive jet-black beard.

Most farmers, once they accept the idea of having a gamecock instead of a dunghill ruling their hens, are well pleased by the setup. Why shouldn't they be? The eggs they obtain are bigger and better-tasting, the offspring of a gamecock have more meat, and the small payment of ten dollars a year is money from an unexpected source. And any farmer who keeps a few hens has to have a rooster. Why not a game rooster?

Every time we picked up another country-walked rooster my heart swelled with pleasure. Their feathers were tight and their yellow eyes were bright and alert. Their exercised bodies were firm to the touch, and their dubbed combs usually had the dark red color of health. Out of the twenty-eight cocks Omar had on country walks, we picked up twenty-one. The other seven, in my considered opinion, needed another full year of exercise in the country.

I was happy to get back to Ocala and anxious to get to work. The little town of Ocala has always been my favorite Florida city, combining, as it does, the best aspects of Georgia and the worst side of Florida. A small city, of about twenty thousand permanent residents, and some one hundred miles below the Georgia state line, Ocala is where the state of Florida really begins.

As a driver enters town on the wide island-divided highway, the first sight that hits his eyes is the banner above the road: OCALA – BIRTHPLACE OF NEEDLES! This famous racehorse will be remembered by the Ocala townspeople forever.

To his left, six miles away, is Silver Springs, one of the most publicized tourist attractions in the world. On either side of the highway there are weird attractions, displays and souvenir shops. Commercial Florida also begins at Ocala. But the town itself is like a small Georgia town. Decent, respectable and God-fearing. The townspeople are good Southerners – they provide their services to the rural residents and to themselves, and take only from the vacationing tourists with cameras dangling from their rubber necks.

Two miles outside the city limits in gently swelling country is my small leased farm of twenty-three acres, a small house to live in, an outhouse and outside shower, a well-constructed concrete brick cockhouse and some thirty-odd coop walks. My shack, as I called it, was unpainted but comfortable. The man who built it had started with concrete bricks, but ran short before the walls

341

had reached shoulder height. The remainder of the house had been completed with rough, unfinished pine, and roofed over with two welded sheets of corrugated iron. In a downpour, the heavy pounding of raindrops on the corrugated iron had often driven me out of the shack.

Omar dropped me off first and then drove to his own farm. He had much better facilities to take care of the cocks than I had, and, upon his suggestion, I had agreed to alternate between our farms for conditioning purposes.

Buford ran out of the cockhouse as I entered the yard, a big white smile shining in the middle of his ebony face.

'Mr Frank,' he said happily, taking my bag. 'I sure is happy to see you! My curiosity's been drivin' me near crazy for two days. Just wait till you see them big packages I put in the house!'

I entered the shack, followed closely by Buford, and the first thing I did was reach behind the dresser for my pint of gin. As I had suspected, the bottle contained less than two ounces, and it had been almost half full when Omar had picked me up three days before. I looked sternly at Buford, but he was pointing innocently to the two large cardboard boxes on my bed.

'I don' know what they is, Mr Frank,' he said quickly. 'The man from the express brought 'em out day before yesterday, and I signed your name. What do you reckon's in there?'

I finished the gin, and handed the empty to Buford. Buford had had his share while I was gone – the man had an unerring instinct for discovering where I hid my bottle. He thought that finding my bottle was some kind of game.

I took out my knife and slit open the two cardboard boxes. One box contained a speaker, and the long box held an electric guitar. But *what* a guitar! The instrument was fashioned out of some kind of light metal, painted a bright lemon yellow and trimmed in Chinese red. On the box, above the strings, there were two sets of initials, encircled by an outline of a heart.

If I thought I had made the grand gesture when I sent Bernice a dozen yellow roses, she had certainly topped me. The electric guitar and its matching yellow amplifying speaker must have set her back four or five hundred dollars. I searched through the excelsior in both cartons for a note of some kind, but there wasn't even a receipt for the instrument. The initials inside the heart contained her message.

Buford looked admiringly at the guitar, shaking his head with feigned amazement. As soon as I looked at him he laughed the professional laugh of the American Negro.

'Whooee!' he exploded with false amusement. 'You got yourself a guitar now for sure, Mr Frank!'

I pointed to the door. Out in the yard I gave Buford a ten-dollar bill in payment for looking after the place for three days. Buford had his own farm, a wife and four children, but he spent more time with me than he did with his family. When I happened to think about it, I'd slip him a five or a ten, but I didn't keep him on a regular salary because I didn't need him around in the first place. He knew as much about the raising and handling of game-cocks as any Negro in the United States, if not more. Unfortunately, because of his color, he was barred from almost every white cockpit in the South. He would have been an invaluable assistant for me on my trips to circuit cockpits, but I couldn't take him along. However, he helped me out around the place, handled opposing cocks in my own training pit and made himself fairly useful during conditioning periods. He loved gamecocks. That much I knew about him. And I believe he would have sacrificed an arm or a leg for the opportunity to fight them. Because I knew this much about the man, I was well aware that his rich and easy laughter was insincere.

What in the hell did Buford have to laugh about?

'I fixed up all them sun coops the way you showed me, Mr Frank,' Buford said. 'And I put some new slats in the cockhouse stalls. But they ain't much else to do, so I won't be back around till Saturday.'

I nodded, and Buford climbed into his car.

'Whooee!' he laughed through his nose. 'You got you a git-fiddle now, sure enough! Will you play some for me come Saturday?'

Again I nodded. As Buford made a U-turn onto the gravel road toward the highway, I entered the shack.

The wonderful and unexpected gift had made my heart sing with delight, although I had controlled my inner excitement from Buford. As soon as he was gone, I connected the various electrical cords, following the directions in the illustrated instruction booklet. I plugged the cord into the wall outlet and tuned the strings. The full tones, amplified by the speaker set at full volume, reverberated in the small room and added a new dimension to my playing. After experimenting with several chords, banging them hard and listening to them echo metallically against the iron ceiling, I tried a song.

Halfway through the song I stopped playing and placed the guitar gently on the floor. Unconsciously, I had played 'Georgia Girl' first. The rich amplified tones brought suppressed visions of Mary Elizabeth flooding into my mind, and I dropped the plastic pick.

In the sharp silence, following so closely on the sound of the echoing song, I pictured Mary Elizabeth in my mind, still in the same position where I had left her at The Place. She sat quietly, feet below the surface of the pool, and with dancing dappled sunlight reflecting on her pale nude body. Her blue-green eyes looked at me reproachfully, and her ordinarily full lips were set in a tight grim line.

To make her disappear I shook my head.

This was a recurrent vision of Mary Elizabeth. Whenever I happened to think of the woman, a guilty, sinking feeling accompanied the thought. She was always nude, always at The Place. I never thought of her as fully clothed – that was a Mary Elizabeth I didn't want to think about – the spinsterish, schoolteacherish, Methodist kind, with a reproving expression on her face. As a rule, when I hadn't seen Mary Elizabeth for several months, her features became indistinct, except for her hurt blue? green? eyes. But her body was always as clear in my mind as a Kodachrome color print. I remembered every anatomical detail, the way her right shoulder dipped a quarter of an inch lower than her left, the round, three-eyed shape of her button navel, and every golden pubic hair.

I loved her and I had always loved her and I always would love her, and the dark guilty shadows erased her pink-and-white body from my mind. No man had ever treated a woman any shabbier than I had Mary Elizabeth!

Suppose, I thought blackly, she just says the hell with you, Frank Mansfield, and marries a nice stay-at-home Georgia boy . . . a bloated bastard like Ducky Winters, for instance, the manager of the Purina Feed Store? Why not? He's single and over thirty. What if his bald head does look like a freshly washed peach and the roll of fat around his waistline resembles a rubber inner tube half filled with water? He's got a good job, and he's a member of the Board of Stewards of the Methodist church . . . well, isn't he? His mother can't live forever, and he did pinch Mary Elizabeth on the ass at the box social that time . . . remember? You wanted to take him outside, but Mary Elizabeth wouldn't let you.

How many good prospects does she have? Ducky Winters, no matter what you may think, is one of the *better* prospects. Suppose she marries one of those red-necked woolhat cronies of her brother's? Wright doesn't want her to get married, but he would approve of some farmer who would keep her close to home, just so he would be assured of seeing her every day. What if she married Virgil Dietch, whose farm is only three miles down the road? Virgil's only forty, a widower with two half-grown boys, and he'd be damned happy to marry a woman like Mary Elizabeth. With his growling German accent – despite three generations in Georgia – and his lower lip packed chock-full of Copenhagen snuff, she wouldn't be able to understand half of what he said, but Wright liked Virgil and ran around with him. And Wright wouldn't object to a marriage between them.

For more than an hour I tortured myself, mulling over the list of eligible suitors in the county Mary Elizabeth could marry if she wanted to spite me. There weren't many left. Most of the men in rural Georgia get married young, and divorces are rare. The remaining eligibles were a sorry lot, especially when I considered the widowers who had worked their wives into an early grave.

It was exquisite torture to consider these ignorant wool-hatters who shaved only on Saturday, who wore a single suit of long johns from October to May, and who didn't take a bath until the Fourth of July. And yet, as far as husbands were concerned, every one of these men would make a better husband than I would. As a woman, she was entitled to a home and children and a husband who stayed with her at all times.

I had provided Mary Elizabeth with eight years of nothing. A quickly scrawled line on the back of a picture postcard, and on one of my rare, unscheduled visits, a quick jump in a woodland glen. To make matters worse, I hadn't even talked to her on my last two visits. But I had never been able to talk to her anyway. She had consistently resisted every explanation I had tried to give her concerning my way of life and had never consented

346

to share it with me. Perhaps I could write her a letter, a really *good* letter this time, a letter that would make her think?

This year was going to be my year. I could sense it, and my new partnership with Omar was the turning point in my run of ill fortune. I knew this. My prospects had been as good before, but they had never been any better. I couldn't continue through life silent and alone, and I couldn't keep Mary Elizabeth dangling on a thread – the thread would break, and both of us would be lost. If there was to be a break, it would have to be now – Her way or My way – and *she* could make the choice!

I sat down at the table to write Mary Elizabeth a letter:

Dearest Darling,

I love you! How inadequate are written words to tell you of my feelings! To be with you and yet to be unable to speak, to tell you again and again that I love you is unbearable. To leave without saying good-bye, as I did, hurt me more than you can ever know. And yet, I had to leave silently, like a thief in the night. If I had written you a note with a bare 'Good-bye', you would have rightfully demanded an explanation I couldn't give because I couldn't speak! But an explanation is due, my love, and on the blankness of this page I shall attempt the impossible. Never, never doubt my love!

First, I was home to obtain my rightfully owned property. You know this now, of course, because your brother bought my farmhouse and land from me. What you don't know is that Judge Powell was instructed to sell only to Wright. Whether I was right or wrong in turning Randall out of his home depends upon how you want to look at it. In the Holy Bible the eldest son gets the inheritance of his father, as you know. In the eyes of the Lord, and I recognize no other Master; I was right. But even so, I only sold my land because I had to.

For ten years my goal has been to be the best cockfighter in the United States. Several, not many, times I've tried to explain cockfighting and my ambitions to you, but you have never listened. Read this, now, and then decide. Our future happiness, yours and mine, depends upon your decision. Closing your ears to all rational argument, you have always said that cockfighting was cruel and therefore wrong. But you have never SEEN a cockfight, and you said that you never intended to. At last I say you must!

The only way that you can find out that cockfighting is not a cruel sport is to see for yourself. I am now engaged in my very last try to reach the top. To continue fighting year after year without success is no longer possible. If I don't win the two-day Milledgeville Tourney this year, I promise you that I'll quit forever! We will be married immediately, and I'll enter any profession or endeavor YOU decide upon!

However, if I do win, and I want you physically present at the Milledgeville pit, win or lose, I intend to follow cockfighting as a full-time profession for the rest of my natural life. If you can accept this way of life, we will get married immediately and go to Puerto Rico on our honeymoon.

The remaining alternative, of course, is to tear this letter to bits and put me out of your mind forever. If this latter course is your decision, I'll abide by it, and I'll never, I promise, write or see you again, but my heart will be completely broken!

Don't write and tell me what your decision is. If you do write, I won't open your letters. Two seats will be reserved in your name at the Milledgeville Tourney (bring your brother if you like) from 15 March to 16 March. I won't write again, and will pray daily to the good Lord *above that you will TRY – and please let your heart decide – to be there at Milledgeville.*

I love you. I always have and always will!

Frank

I read the letter twice before sealing it into an envelope, and I thought it was a damned good letter. The little religious touches were particularly well done, and so was the part about going to Puerto Rico for our honeymoon. There are many luxury hotels in San Juan, and March is a good time to see slasher fights at the Valla Piedros. The pit opens daily at 2 p.m. and the cockfights are continuous until the cocktail hour. After dinner we could hit the casinos, shoot craps or even play a little blackjack.

Of course, there was always the chance that Omar and I wouldn't win the tourney. With ten entries scheduled, a lot of things could happen, but the main idea of the letter was to ensure Mary Elizabeth's physical presence at the pit. Once she saw for herself how well organized the tourney was, and how fair the pit decisions were, I was positive she would like the sport. A lot of ministers follow cockfighting zealously without conflict with their religious beliefs. After all, the cock that crowed after Peter denied Jesus Christ thrice was a gamecock! That was right in the Bible and a damned good point.

I considered rewriting the letter and mentioning this fact to Mary Elizabeth, but it was too late. I had already sealed the envelope. A better idea, perhaps, would be to introduce her to a couple of the ministers who attended the Milledgeville Tourney every year and let them talk to her. I knew little about the Bible and hadn't read any scripture in fifteen years, maybe more.

Suppose she didn't show up? My stomach tightened at the thought. I had to risk it. If she couldn't see my side of things after reading a letter like that, there was no hope left for the two of us anyway. Feeling better about our relationship than I had in months, I picked up the guitar again and strummed it gently, enjoying the amplified sounds.

The tablet was still on the table, and I decided to write Bernice Hungerford a letter. She was entitled to a thank-you note after giving me such an expensive gift. A letter was the least I could do. Perhaps Bernice would like to see the tournament? She thought I was some kind of modern-day minstrel. What a terrific surprise it would be for her to learn that I was a professional cockfighter!

Dear Bernice:

What a wonderful surprise, what a wonderful guitar! There is only ONE way you could have pleased me more, and I intend to get into that later. This may come as a shock to you, but I'm a professional cockfighter, not a musician. For the next few months I'll be out on the circuit and won't be able to see you, but two seats will be reserved for you at the Milledgeville, Georgia, S.C.T., 15–16 March. Please come. Bring your nephew, Tommy, along to keep you company, because I'll be too busy during the meet to sit with you. I know it's a long time off and I don't know how I'll be able to wait that long without seeing you again, but I must.

I have reason to hope that my voice will come back within the next few months. A letter is not the best way to tell you how I feel about you – I would prefer to tell you in person, whispering in your pretty ear! Perhaps I've written too much already, but you should have a FAIR idea of how I feel about you. All my love – till 15 March.

Frank

P.S. The Milledgeville pit is north of town. Check at any gas station in town for directions.

After sealing and addressing the envelope to Bernice, it occurred to me that she might not know anything about cockfighting or what the initials SCT stood for – most of the people in the US thought that because cockfighting was illegal it had been abolished. I should have spelled it out in detail, I supposed. But if she made any inquiries at all, she could find out about it easily enough. Her nephew could do the investigating for her, and my name was certainly well known in cockfighting circles. The letter was better this way. If she attended the Milledgeville meet, I'd be able to determine if she was as interested in me as she appeared to be.

I walked down the gravel road to the highway and put the two letters and some change for stamps into my RFD mailbox. The night was warm and soft for late September, and a gentle breeze blew steadily across the fields. There was a steady hum from a million insects communicating with each other in their own little ways.

When I switched on the overhead lights in the cockhouse to check the chickens, the Mellhorn Blacks jumped up and down nervously in their coops, clucking and crowing almost in unison. They were all hungry, and I intended to keep them that way. I filled the water dips with water and returned to my shack. Without turning on the lights again, I sat in the dark strumming away on my new guitar until way past midnight.

This was one of the most pleasant evenings I have ever spent by myself. Although I was tired after three hectic days on the road with Omar, I was much too happy to sleep.

Chapter Twelve

We were unable to make the first Southern Conference meet, 15 October, at Greenville, Mississippi, but there was ample time to prepare our gamecocks for the six-cock, 10 November derby in Tifton, Georgia.

During the interim, Omar wrote to Pete Chocolate at Pahokee and arranged a hack match at the Ocala cockpit to be held on a Sunday afternoon in two weeks. Pete Chocolate was a worthy opponent, although he was eccentric in many ways. He was a top cockfighter and a longtime Southern Conference regular and usually fought Spanish game fowl and Spanish crosses. He also had the distinction of being the first Seminole Indian to graduate from the University of Florida with a master's degree in Asian Studies. I don't know why he wanted a degree in Asian Studies, but I know how he got it. A rich Chinese pawnbroker who had made all his money in Miami left an annual scholarship to the university in Asian Studies for any Seminole who wanted to take it. The Chinaman had been dead for more than fifteen years, and Pete Chocolate had been the first and only Seminole to take advantage of the free degree.

Another peculiarity about Pete was his habit of wearing a black tuxedo suit at all times, even when he handled in the pit. He didn't always wear a white shirt and black tie with the tuxedo. Sometimes he did, but he occasionally wore a sport shirt, a blue work shirt, or, as often as not, no shirt at all.

His master's degree and tuxedo had nothing to do with

his ability as a cockfighter. He was a top handler and feeder, and a tough opponent to face in the pit.

The check weights for the hacks were 4:02, 5:00, 5:06 and 5:10. This early in the season, Pete only wanted to fight these weights, and we had to meet them in order to get the match. Each hack was to be a separate pit battle, and we were to put up fifty dollars a fight. With the wide selection of cocks we had, it was easy to meet the weights. I selected two of Omar's Roundheads, one Ace Mellhorn Black, and my 5:00 Middleton Gray. Although Icky's weight was only 4:02, I put him on the conditioning program too, in case I could get an extra hack for him. Before I could enter Icky in the Milledgeville Tourney against my old rival Jack Burke, he had to win at least four fights. In my opinion, Icky was the cock to beat Burke's Little David. With this eventual goal in mind, I intended to select Icky's four preliminary matches with care.

For the first few days of our partnership, Omar was often sullen, but he gradually came around to my way of conditioning. To prepare a gamecock for the pit is tough enough if he is in good feather already, but if the conditioner has to work off excess fat at the same time, his task is doubly difficult. When I worked out a regular diet for Omar's flock of Roundheads and Clarets, he objected bitterly.

'Damn it, Frank,' he said, shoving my list of feeding instructions back into my hand, 'I feed my cocks three times as much as that!'

We were looking over Omar's chickens at the runs on his farm, so I tried to show him why the new feeding schedule was necessary. I picked one of his Claret roosters out of a nearby coop, felt his meaty thighs with a dour expression on my face, handed him to Omar, and nodded for him to do the same.

'He's hard as a brick,' Omar said defensively, squeezing the Claret's legs.

I shook my head, picked up a stick and printed FAT! on the ground with the point of it. Omar rubbed out the word with his toe, returned the cock to the coop, and pawed through his beard.

'All right. If you say so, Frank. But he doesn't feel fat to me!'

Although Omar had been fighting cocks for four years, it was evident that he had never 'felt' a truly conditioned gamecock. The right *feel* of a gamecock is indescribable. Maybe it is an instinct of some kind, but if a man ever gets the right feel of a perfectly conditioned gamecock in his fingers, his fingers never forget. The exact right *feel* is an incorporeal knowledge, and once the fingers memorize it, they are never satisfied until they find it again. When a gamecock has the right feel, it is ready for the pit. Omar thought my regular diet was drastic, but I had to get the excess fat off his birds before I could put them on my special conditioning diet.

I checked the list again: *1 tablespoon of ⅔ cracked corn and ⅓ whole oats, once a day, tossed into scratch pen. One-fourth of an apple every four days. Two ounces of hamburger every ten days. Plenty of grit and oyster shells available at all times. Keep the water cups full.*

This was a good diet, a practical feed I had learned through long apprenticeship. The chickens wouldn't starve, and they wouldn't get fat. If they had any fat when they were put on it, they would lose it in a hurry. And as long as this diet was maintained, any cock could be switched to a battle-conditioning diet and be ready to fight within ten days. By weighing them daily, any sudden, dangerous weight loss would be detected, and the feed could be increased slightly. But Omar had to begin somewhere, and the new diet was the first step forward in his professional education. I returned the list to my unhappy partner and this time he accepted it. The Claret crowed deeply, anxious to get some more attention.

'You'd better crow now,' Omar shouted at the game-cock. 'By this time next week you'll be too damned hungry to crow!'

The conditioning of game fowl is not a job for a lazy man. To condition five gamecocks for the hack coming up was easy for me, but I don't think Omar had ever worked as hard in his life. The way he groaned and complained was downright funny. Just wait, I thought, until we start conditioning twenty or thirty at a time. In order to get six cocks ready for the Tifton derby, we would have to condition at least twenty.

After I rousted Omar out of bed at his farm at four thirty two mornings in a row, he brought a cot and his sheets over to my shack and bunked there. There was an old Negro couple, Leroy and Mary Bondwell, who looked after Omar at his farmhouse. During the two weeks Omar lived with me, Leroy fed Omar's cocks with the new diet. Every afternoon Omar drove home to check and weigh his birds, returning to my place for the evening conditioning sessions.

Buford dropped by for an hour or so every day, and I would put him to work changing straw in the coops, painting coop walks with creosote, or give him some other kind of odd job. But Omar and I, on a strict time schedule, did everything else.

I wakened Omar daily at five. I shaved and Omar fixed breakfast. By five thirty, at the latest, we were in the cockhouse.

During the entire conditioning period, the cocks were each kept in a separate stall in the cockhouse. The wooden slats on each door were close enough together so the chicken couldn't stick his neck between them and jump up and down. They were so hungry, they thought they were going to be fed every time a man entered the cockhouse. If they were allowed to bounce up and down, with their necks between the slats, they would bruise the top of their dubbed heads.

While Omar crushed two hard-boiled eggs, shells and all, into the feed pan, I measured out cracked Flint corn and pinhead oats. When the mixture was blended, each of the five cocks got one heaping teaspoonful. We never mixed more than enough for one feeding, and they all got a second feeding that night. Every other morning I tossed three or four large chunks of marble grit on the floor of their stalls.

When the chickens finished eating, and they ate fast, a cup of water was put in each coop. As long as they were drinking they were left strictly alone, but the moment they quit drinking or lost interest in the water, the cup was removed.

By six thirty they were ready for the foam-rubber mattress workbench. It was firm and only slightly springy, and it was covered with an Army surplus shelter half. I ran the cocks first, one at a time, of course, from one end to the other, and then back again, twenty times the first day, thirty the second day, increasing the number of runs each day until they reached a hundred. A cock fights fast so I ran them as fast as I could up and down the workbench.

Following the runs, the cocks were flirted. Flirting forces a cock to flap his wings to maintain his balance, and his wing muscles are strengthened. Like the runs, they started with twenty flirts the first day, and were increased ten flirts every day until they reached a hundred. Once a man gets the hang of it, flirting isn't really difficult. A conditioner must remember to always be as careful as he can so the cock won't get bruised. If a cock is flirted roughly, he will soon get stiff, even if he doesn't get bruised. Omar was good at flirting so I usually took the runs and let him fly them back and forth between his big hands. It was a pleasure to relax with a cigarette and watch Omar work.

With his left hand on the cock's breast, he would toss the bird deftly back for about a foot and a half, catch him with his right hand, and then toss him back. Omar started slowly, but once he caught the rhythm the cock was flying back and forth from one hand to the other so fast it looked like the cock was running in place. He had a definite flair for careful flirting, and he was proud of his ability.

Every other day, following the flirting period, we heeled a pair of the cocks undergoing conditioning with sparring muffs, and let them fight each other in the pit for about a minute and a half.

If one of the cocks appeared to be too tired, I didn't spar him. There is always risk involved in sparring. Even when a bird is armed with soft chamois muffs he can get hurt. But by watching two sparring cocks closely, I can observe how well their stamina is building up.

After the sparring period, the cocks were allowed to rest for fifteen minutes, and then we washed them with warm soapy water. To help relieve soreness, I rubbed their legs down gently with a sponge dipped in rubbing alcohol. When the birds were all washed and rubbed down, they were placed in separate sun coops for twenty minutes. There was a roosting pole in each sun coop, and if the cocks were still active enough to have a fine old time jumping up to the pole and then down again with animated eagerness, I made a note to increase their runs and flirting for the next day.

The drying-off period gave Omar and me enough time to have a coffee break.

Before we returned the cocks to the cockhouse for the day, each bird was given two flies. Two daily flies not only bring out the aggressive spirit of a gamecock, they get him used to the idea that the best way to reach his opponent is to use his wings and fly to him. For the fly, Omar held out one of the cocks with his arm extended, with the tail of the bird facing me. I held the flying cock on the ground until Omar was ready, and then I'd let him go. When I released his tail he would take to the air, but before he could reach the bird Omar was holding out toward him, Omar would twist slightly to one side, causing the flying bird to extend himself to fly higher. After a few days of flying, a mature cock could rise eight or ten feet into the air from a standing position. If a cock could remember that he knew how to fly this well, it could save his life when pitted.

The flies completed the morning conditioning. A record sheet was kept on a clipboard beside each coop, and I filled in the cock's weight, number of runs, flirts, flies, and made a note of his color. The well-conditioned cock has a dark red face and comb. When the color turns pinkish something is wrong. In the space for comments I jotted down any observed weaknesses, or changes to be made in the diet due to gains or losses that were unexpected.

Like people, every gamecock has to be handled a little differently. A chicken's brain is about the size of a BB, but within those tiny brains there is an infinite variety of character and personality traits. I've seen personalities that ranged from lassitude to zealousness, from anarchy to obedience, from friendliness to indifference. Luckily, a chicken can't count. If they could count, they would have resented the daily rising of the number of flirts and runs we gave them.

A gamecock is the most stupid creature on earth and, paradoxically, the most intelligent fighter.

When my chart notations were completed, I dropped a canvas cover over the slatted doorway of each coop, and the darkness kept the birds quiet until it was time for the evening training periods.

The other cocks, not under conditioning, were fed, watered, examined and weighed, and I was through for the morning. Omar and I would then play chess until time for lunch. When Buford was around, I drove to Omar's farm for lunch, and inspected his gamecocks before returning home. If Buford failed to drop by, I would cook either a potful of canned beef stew or pork and beans and fix a pan of hoecakes.

'How come you've never gotten married, Frank?' Omar asked me one day, as he looked unhappily at his heaping platter of hot pork and beans. 'By God, if I didn't eat something else besides stew or beans every day, I'd marry the first woman who came along!'

Omar was so used to my silence by now that he answered his own questions. 'I don't suppose many women would want to marry a professional cockfighter, though. Most of the women I've known want their husband home every night, whether they like him or not, just so they can have somebody to complain to. But canned beans – ugh!'

In the afternoon, after Omar went home, I took a walk with one of my gamecocks that wasn't undergoing conditioning. When taken out of their runs, some of the cocks would follow me around. They liked attention, but they also hoped that I would drop a grain of corn on the ground now and then. And sometimes I did.

Mary Bondwell either fixed supper for us at four thirty at Omar's farm, or we drove into Ocala for a steak or barbecued ribs. By five thirty, we were ready to start the conditioning all over again – the feeding, weighing, flies, flirts, runs and recording. Not many game strains can stand up to the hard conditioning I give them, but my two cocks – the Mellhorn and the Gray – came along fast, and Icky thrived on it. Omar's Roundheads had a tough time for the first three days, but as soon as their excess fat disappeared, they came up nicely.

At night, to get our gamecocks used to lights and noise, because they would be fighting at night later on in the season, I turned on the overhead lights of the cockpit, and played sound-effects records on a portable phonograph. The records weren't loud enough to suit Omar. He charged around the outside of the pit, shouting out bets at the top of his voice.

'Hey! Who'll give me an eight to ten! I got a blinker here, half dead already! Who'll lay twenty to ten!'

He then accepted preposterous bets in a mincing falsetto, managing to make enough noise for a major cockpit. It was comical to watch his wild antics, charging around the pit, flopping his big bare arms loosely, his black beard glistening under the lights. I could never picture Omar in a homburg and gray flannel suit walking down Madison Avenue. He fitted in with a cocker's life as though he had been born to it.

After only a few nights of noise and lights, every one of the cocks could stand quietly and patiently in the center of the pit, and pay no mind either to the records or Omar.

And of course, we had a bottle every night, either gin or bourbon, and we passed it back and forth. Omar would tell me stories about New York, the advertising business, or anecdotes about radio and television people he had known.

Quite suddenly he would stop relating a story in mid-sentence — 'Frank, do you want to know something? You and I, you big, dumb, silent son-of-a-bitch, we've got the best life in the entire world! I wouldn't trade my life now if I was given every filter-tip account in the United States and fifty percent of the stock!'

He would reach for the bottle, take a healthy swig and pass it to me.

'I know you're tired of listening to me ramble on. Why don't you get out that electronic monster of yours and play us something?'

I had rigged an extension cord from the shack, and I would play for an hour or so, sitting on the bench beside the lighted cockpit. I never played songs, I more or less played with the guitar instead, trying out chord progressions, or attempting to express a mood of some kind. Omar never said whether he liked my music or not, but he listened attentively.

One night Buford drove over with a big pot of greens his wife had cooked for me. Omar told Buford to get his enamel cup from the hook above the faucet where he kept it, and then filled it with whiskey. Before Buford had finished the cupful of whiskey he got mellow and sang for us – old-time blues and field hollers. When he held a note long enough for me to catch it, I would hit the corresponding chord on my guitar. I might have been a little drunk, but I thought Buford had the greatest voice I had ever heard.

These were all pleasant evenings for me. I have always guarded my aloneness jealously. But Omar didn't encroach on my solitude, he complemented it. For the first time in my life, I realized that companionship between two kindred spirits is not impossible – as long as each man respects the other's rights.

On the eighth day of conditioning, the exercising of each cock was cut in half. On the morning of the ninth day my Mellhorn Black got moody and refused to eat. He wasn't sick, he was mean and sulky. I put the Gray game hen in his coop with him for a couple of hours and he snapped out of his lethargy. When I removed the hen and dumped a spoonful of feed on the floor of his coop, he gobbled it up in no time.

Omar thought this was funny. 'Maybe that's what's wrong with me, Frank,' he laughed. 'If somebody dropped a blonde into my bed for two hours every night, I could probably eat those beans of yours and like them.'

On the twelfth day, the cocks were taken off exercise and food together. They weren't given any water, but they didn't want water. This was a good sign, and meant they were ready for the pit. They would fast right up until pit time. All five cocks were in the peak of condition. I made Omar 'feel' every one of them, and his fingers learned the difference.

'If I didn't know better, Frank,' he said, 'I'd think these cocks were made out of stone.'

Sunday afternoon we put the cocks into traveling coops and drove to the cockpit in Omar's station wagon. The Ocala Game Club wasn't really in Ocala – it was closer to Martel, eight miles west of the city. But it was called the Ocala pit because out-of-town cockfighters stayed in Ocala motels when the 24 February SC derby was held. During the entire season, the pit operator, an old retired farmer named Bandy Taylor, held hack matches almost every Sunday.

Bandy Taylor was in his late sixties, with brown leathery skin and enough deep wrinkles on his face to resemble a relief map. His legs were so bowed, he couldn't have caught a pig in a trench.

Although Bandy's pit was not an elaborate setup, all of the Lownes County cockfighters liked to meet there. His wife maintained a small stand outside the pit area, where she sold coffee, Coca-Colas and hamburgers, and Bandy charged a reasonable, one-dollar admission fee. The old man, an authorized SCT referee, never bet on the fights, but he made enough money on admission fees and the food his wife sold to get by. Any wins I had there could be signed by Bandy on the official records, and they would be acceptable by the Milledgeville judges for qualifying purposes.

The crowd was small, considering that four hacks between Pete Chocolate and our new partnership had been scheduled. There were thirty-some-odd spectators, including a nervous Yankee tourist from Silver Springs.

There were only a half dozen other cockers, looking for extra hacks. I wanted to get an extra hack for Icky, but the prospects weren't too good. I wrote my name and Icky's weight on the blackboard and hoped for the best.

Pete Chocolate won the toss and decided to fight from bottom weights up. His fighters were all Spanish crosses, and they were in fine feather. Omar held for me while I heeled the 4:02 Roundhead, and then he tried to rustle up a few bets in the bleachers. I considered fighting Icky against the other 4:02 opponent, but the Spanish Ace looked too formidable. I had made a good decision. Omar was also lucky in the stands, because the only bet he could get was a ten-dollar even money wager.

The Spanish cock uncoupled my Roundhead, breaking his spine, in the first pitting. He was counted out, paralyzed and unable to move a feather. Omar paid Pete Chocolate the fifty-dollar loss, and paid off the fan in the stands. Because of our quick loss in the first fight, Omar was able to lay a thirty-dollar bet on the outcome of the second hack.

In the second fight, I showed the 5:00 Middleton Gray, and he finished his opponent in the fourth pitting. My Gray shuffler got above the Spanish every time.

The third battle was one of those fights that never appear to get anywhere. The two cocks were evenly matched, and very little damage was done until the eighteenth pitting. By the twenty-third pitting we were alternating on calling for the count. On my count, however, the Spanish developed a rattle from an earlier wound, refused to face, and the hack was mine. Our Roundhead was well battered and wouldn't be able to fight again for at least two months.

The fourth hack was a miracle win. My 5:10 Mellhorn Black had been in fights before, and he smothered the Spanish in the first two pittings. In the third pitting, the

Black attacked furiously the moment I released his tail. The Spanish was bowled over and fell back close to the wall. He leaped high into the air, and landed on the ground outside the pit. The Spanish was game – he wasn't a runner by any means – but he was outside the pit and my Black was still inside.

It was a tense moment. I held my breath, and none of the spectators made a sound. If Pete's Spanish had jumped back into the pit, the fight would have been continued. He didn't. Confused, twisting his head about in search of my gamecock, the Spanish darted under the bleachers in bewildered retreat. The hack was mine by default.

I had known Pete Chocolate for several years, but this was the first time I ever saw him get really angry. He caught his gamecock, removed the heels, and swung the cock's neck against an upright post. He then jerked off the cock's head. This isn't easy. It takes a strong man to pull a chicken's head off with his bare hands. He tossed the dead chicken on the ground and came back to the pit.

'That's the first runner I ever had, Frank,' Pete said blackly. 'A Spanish don't run! That same cock won two fights before. Is that a runner? D'you ever hear of me showing a runner?'

I shook my head solemnly. Blood had dripped from the dead chicken's neck onto the white polo shirt Pete was wearing with his tuxedo, and his white tennis shoes were splashed with blood.

'He didn't run, Pete,' Omar said. 'He was confused and didn't remember where the pit was, that's all.'

'He won't get confused again!' Pete said with satisfaction. He whipped out his wallet and paid Omar off. We were ahead one hundred dollars from Pete Chocolate, and Omar had won eighty dollars more in side bets. We had lost one cock, and our Roundhead had been battered so badly he might not ever win another fight. We were just about even.

A good first day, I thought, as Omar joined me at the lunch stand.

'Frank,' he said, 'there's a kid at the cockhouse with a Gray cross of some kind who wants to fight Icky. His name is Junior Hollenbeck. D'you know him?'

I nodded and finished my Coke. I didn't actually know Junior, but his father, Rex Hollenbeck, was a real-estate man in Ocala. He had introduced himself to me one day in town. Mr Hollenbeck was a fan, he said, and he had seen me handling at the Orlando International Tourney.

'Do you want to fight him, Frank? The kid's only about nineteen, and his Gray shades Icky two full ounces.'

I started toward the cockhouse to see whether I did or not. Junior was waiting in front of Icky's coop, cradling his Gray gamecock in his arms. He was a well-dressed young man, wearing buckled shoes, charcoal-flannel Daks, and a gaily colored body shirt. His tangled chestnut hair was worn long, all the way to his shoulders, and his face was sunburned. He had a sparse straggly moustache, and the pointed chin whiskers of a young ram goat. Evidently his nose had peeled, because it was smeared with a thick covering of white salve.

'This is Mr Mansfield, Junior,' Omar introduced us.

'I know. I saw the 4:02 weight on the blackboard, Mr Mansfield,' Junior said, all business, 'and thought I'd challenge you. My cock's won two fights this year and has a couple of ounces over yours, but I'm willing to cut away some feathers for the chance to fight you.'

I stared impassively at the kid, and he blushed through his sunburn.

'That is,' he added, 'the man I bought him from *said* he won two fights in Tallahassee.'

I took the Gray out of Junior's arms and felt him. The bird went in and out like an accordion. I turned to Omar, winked, and moved my chin down a fraction of an inch.

'You've got a hack, Junior,' Omar said. 'And you don't have to cut any feathers. The Southern Conference allows a two-ounce leeway either way on hacks. But you'll have to fight short heels. Got any?'

'No, sir. I don't have any heels at all. I thought I might borrow a set. And I want to bet twenty-five dollars, even money.'

'Fair enough. I'll lend you a pair. D'you want me to heel him for you?'

'I know how to heel him,' Junior said defensively. 'I've heeled cocks plenty of times. Just lend me the heels and hold him for me.'

Omar laughed good-naturedly. 'Sure. Wait'll I tell Bandy there's an extra hack, before his crowd gets away.'

There had been two hacks held before the four between Pete Chocolate and me. After our last hack, a few of the spectators had departed, including the nervous tourist, but there were still a dozen or more standing around discussing the fights. When Bandy announced that there was going to be another hack, they scrambled hurriedly into the bleachers and began making bets.

We heeled with inch-and-a-quarter gaffs. To my surprise, Junior did a good job of heeling his Gray. By the way he handled his chicken, I could see he knew his way around the pit, and I felt a little better about the fight coming up.

While Bandy examined both cocks prior to the fight, I listened to the bettors. Although the Gray was announced as a two-time winner, and the Blue – as Icky was called – was announced as a short-heel novice in his first fight, most of the bettors were taking Icky and offering five to one. The odds were caused, in part, by my reputation, but they really preferred my gamecock because of his color. This kind of thinking was like betting on the color of a jockey's eyes instead of on the record of the horse at a racetrack. At any rate, Omar had a hard time getting bets.

Even with the high odds, only a few men were willing to back the Gray. But Omar finally managed to lay three ten-dollar wagers.

Junior was nervous during the billing, but he handled fairly well.

When Bandy told us to 'get ready' in his reedy old man's voice, Junior squatted behind his score, and held the Gray's tail like a professional.

'Pit!'

Icky took two short steps forward and then flew six feet into the air. The Gray ran forward on the ground at the same time, and Icky landed behind him. They wheeled simultaneously and mushed, breast against breast, engaged in a shoving contest. The Gray backed off, and then tried a short rushing feint that didn't work. Icky got above him, shuffled, and the two went down with Icky's right gaff through the Gray's left wing.

'Handle!'

Junior disengaged the heel from the Gray's wing bone, and we retreated to our respective scores for a thirty-second rest. The boy worked so furiously over the Gray I had to grin. He blew on the cock's back, stretched and jerked the neck, spat into its mouth, rubbed the thighs vigorously between his hands, and licked the head feathers and hackles with his tongue.

These were all legitimate nursing techniques, but to use them, any of them, after the first pitting was ridiculous. Over-nursing does more harm than good. Unless a game-cock is in drastic need of help, the handler can help him best by letting him rest between pittings. I laced Icky away from the Gray and let him stand quietly so he could get the maximum benefit from the rest period.

'Get ready,' Bandy said, watching his wristwatch sweep-hand.

'Pit!'

We dropped them on their scores. Because of rough over-nursing, more than for any other reason, the Gray was slow in getting started. Icky made a forward dash with raised hackles, took off in a low, soaring flight, fanning in midair, and cut deeply into the Gray's neck with blurred gaffs. The left heel stuck, and the two cocks tumbled over, coupled.

'Handle!' Bandy said quickly.

The instant Junior moved Icky's gaff from the Gray's neck, his gamecock strangled. When a cock's neck fills with blood, the strangling sound is unmistakable. Except for going through the motions in accordance with the rules, the fight was over. Until the Gray actually died, or refused to fight through three twenty-second counts, or unless his handler picked him up and carried him out, we still had to go through the routine pittings and counts.

Junior had heard the strangle, but he nursed the Gray furiously. He sucked blood out of the Gray's throat and rubbed its chest hard enough to dislodge the tight feathers. He held the feet, placed the cock on its chest and pressed his mouth against the back, blowing his breath noisily into the feathers to warm the Gray's circulation. The Gray was down, his neck stretched flat, and his eyes were glazed. Blood bubbled from his open beak, but he wasn't dead. And then, right before my astonished eyes, Junior inserted his right forefinger into the downed Gray's vent and massaged the cock's testicles!

I snapped my fingers in Bandy's direction, but he had witnessed the foul as soon as I had.

'Foul!' Bandy yelled. 'The Blue wins in the second pitting!'

I picked Icky up and held him tail first toward Bandy so he could cut the tie strings away from the heels with his penknife. None of the spectators complained about the ruling. The Gray had obviously lost before the foul was called anyway. With his sunburned face redder than it had been before, Junior pushed between us.

'What do you mean, foul!' he shouted at Bandy.

'Mr Mansfield and I both saw you put your finger in the vent, son,' Bandy said quietly. 'And so did everybody else, if they had any eyes.' Omar joined me in the pit and I handed Icky over to him.

'That's no foul,' Junior protested. 'Nursing's allowed, ain't it?'

'Legitimate nursing, yes. Not that kind!'

'I was told if you rubbed the balls with your finger you could put new life in your chicken—' Junior argued futilely.

'Who told you that, son?' Bandy cut him off.

'My dad told me,' Junior replied. We were all three staring at him now, and he looked at us worriedly. 'Is that considered a foul?'

'Your daddy told you wrong, Junior,' Bandy said quietly. 'You rub a cock's balls and you take every speck of fight right out of him. It's a deliberate way of throwing a fight.'

'Well, I didn't know it,' Junior said. 'I want to apologize, Mr Mansfield,' he said, with evident sincerity.

'Too late for that now,' Bandy told him. 'You're through. I got to send in a report on this to the Southern Conference. As of now, you're blacklisted at every cockpit in the SC I reckon that's what your daddy wanted or he wouldn't have told you no lie. But you've pitted your last gamecock at this game club, Junior.'

Junior's sun-reddened face was reduced to a pink glow. 'How long's the blacklist last, Mr Taylor?' he asked.

'Forever. Whether you knew what you were doing or not don't make no difference. You threw the fight and there was people with bets on your Gray. I don't want you comin' out here no more, and you tell your daddy that he ain't welcome out here neither!'

369

Bandy turned away, his speech over, but Omar took a grip on his arm. 'Now, just a minute, Bandy,' Omar said good-humouredly, 'aren't you carrying this thing too far? The kid said he didn't know about the rule, and he apologized. Isn't that enough? The Gray had strangled anyway.'

'Are you arguing with me, Mr Baradinsky?' Bandy said testily. 'You'd better read up on the rules before you try! My decision's final, and if you want to argue you just try it! I'll suspend you from this pit for thirty days so fast your head'll spin!'

Omar started to say something else. I managed to catch his eye, and put a finger to my lips. Bandy turned away and headed for the cockhouse, walking as dignified as a bandy-legged man is capable of walking. I took out my notebook and pencil, scribbled the word *Apologize!* and handed the open notebook to Omar.

'The hell with that crusty old bastard,' he said, returning my notebook. 'Why should I apologize?'

'Please don't get into trouble on my account, Mr Baradinsky,' Junior said humbly. 'I've learned a lesson today I'll remember all my life.'

'I agree. But it's a hard lesson. Bandy meant what he said, you know. You're washed up when it comes to cockfighting.'

'I know it, sir. But I still want to apologize to you both.' Junior hung his head, and started to leave the pit. I snapped my fingers, and held out my hand, palm up.

'Oh, that's right!' Junior smiled winningly. 'I owe you twenty-five dollars, don't I? Well, to tell you the truth, Mr Mansfield, I don't have any cash with me. I was so sure I'd win I didn't think I'd need any. But I've got some money at home, and just as soon—'

I grabbed Junior's wrist, twisted his arm behind his back and put some leverage on it. He bent over with a sharp cry of pain, and then whimpered. I took his wallet

370

out of his right hip pocket with my left hand and passed it to Omar who promptly put Icky on the ground. Omar opened the wallet and counted seventy-eight dollars. After taking twenty-five dollars from the sheaf of bills, he returned the remainder and threw the wallet disgustedly on the floor of the pit.

As I released Junior's wrist, I coordinated nicely and booted him with the pointed toe of my jodhpur boot. He sprawled awkwardly on the hard ground, and his head made a solid 'thunk' when it bounced against the low pine wall of the cockpit. Without a word of protest, Junior picked up his wallet and broke for his car in the parking lot at a dead run. I picked Icky up and grinned.

For a moment, Omar stared at the bills in his hand, and then cleared his throat. 'Well, Frank,' he said, 'I guess I'd better find old Bandy Taylor and apologize. If anybody learned a lesson today, it was me.'

Omar headed reluctantly toward the cockhouse, his hands shoved deep in his pockets. Omar might have been a big shot in the advertising business, but he certainly had a lot to learn about people if he wanted to make a name for himself in cockfighting.

Chapter Thirteen

To prepare our cocks for the six-cock Tifton derby, I found it more practical to move myself and my game-cocks to Omar's farm. I was made comfortable there. I had my own bedroom, there was an inside shower and bathroom, and the meals prepared by Mary Bondwell were a lot tastier than the bachelor meals I had been cooking for myself.

I was so anxious to win the Tifton meet, I put thirty cocks into conditioning just to shape up six top fighters. Working thirty cocks daily rarely gave me a free hour to myself during the day, and I was usually asleep by eight thirty. Sunday is not a holiday for a cockfighter when he has birds to condition for a derby. There were too many things I had to do on Sunday to fight at the Ocala pit, but I sent Omar to the pit to fight some of the cocks that peaked fast. He didn't lose a single hack out of the eight battles he fought.

Our wallets were growing fatter.

On the morning of 9 November, we left for Tifton, Georgia, at five, and arrived at the Tifton game club at three the same afternoon. We signed the derby contracts and were assigned to a cockhouse and given a padlock for the door.

Jack Burke was an entry in the Tifton derby, and he looked me up that evening after supper. Omar had stayed in our motel room to watch television, but I was edgy and drove out to the pit to take a final look at the twelve cocks we had brought along. The birds were roosting all right. As I locked the door and lit a cigarette, Jack Burke approached me through the dusk.

'Evenin', Frank,' he greeted me cordially. 'It's nice to see you again.' Jack looked prosperous in a double-breasted blue worsted suit, a wide paisley necktie, and black-and-white shoes.

I shook hands with the man. Jack rubbed his chin nervously, and I could sense that something was on his mind. He fixed his eyes on an imaginary point to the left of my head.

'I don't suppose you heard the good news,' he said, smiling bleakly.

I waited patiently for him to tell it.

'I got married!' He laughed. 'Bet that surprises you, don't it? Yes, sir! Sooner or later they catch up with the best of us, Frank!' He hesitated. 'I married Dody White, Frank,' he added softly.

I felt sorry for Jack, but I shook hands with him again anyway. So White was Dody's last name. I had wondered about that. And now she was Mrs Dody Burke.

'I wanted to bring Dody along to the derby, Frank, but she wouldn't come because you were here. I tried to tell her you weren't the kind who would rake up the past, but she wouldn't believe me. She seems to have the idea that you can talk, and she's afraid you'll say something about her. I know you can't talk, but I couldn't convince Dody.' He hesitated.' Can you use your voice, Frank?'

I smiled and flipped the butt of my cigarette in an arc to the ground. The idea that I would ever say anything about Burke's wife whether I could talk or not was patently ridiculous. And Burke knew it. Dody had undoubtedly forced him to ask me to keep quiet about our former alliance. For an instant I felt sorry for him, and then despised him for being so damned weak and pussy-whipped.

'I feel like a fool!' Burke blushed. For a man in his mid-forties, the ability to blush is quite a feat.

'Well,' Burke said, 'I'll bring her along to the Plant City derby, and introduce you all just like you'd never seen each other before. That way, Dody's mind'll be at ease. All right?'

I nodded and looked away. I could almost smell the rancorous acid burning Jack's insides. What a comedown for Jack Burke, to let a little tramp like Dody humiliate him this way.

'Now to business!' Jack said briskly, in his regular voice. 'D'you think you and that new partner of yours can show enough cocks after the Plant City meet to fight me in an old-fashioned main?'

The decision was up to me. I was positive Omar wouldn't object to the challenge. Burke fed almost twice as many cocks as we did, but I had a fierce hankering to beat him in a two-entry main. I lowered my chin a fraction and spat between his feet.

'Good! I'll make the necessary arrangements to get the pit on the thirty-first, the day after the derby. How does two hundred dollars a fight sound, with a thousand on the odd fight?'

For the third time in as many minutes, I shook hands with Burke.

He started to say something else, changed his mind, and walked away through the deepening dusk toward the parking lot. Burke was still a damned good man. In time he would learn how to handle Dody. But the memory of this humiliating episode would rankle him forever. I knew this, and I knew just as well that he would eventually blame me instead of himself. That's the way men are.

The next day we lost only one fight in the six-cock derby, but it was one fight too many. Jack Burke didn't lose a single fight, and picked up the thousand-dollar purse.

Getting close only means something when it comes to pitching horseshoes. But despite the lost fight, Omar had placed enough judicious bets to add nine hundred dollars to our bankroll.

The money was welcome, of course, but the Tifton loss was made even more depressing by the sad news that Martha Middleton, Ed Middleton's wife, had died of a heart attack. Her obituary appeared in the same issue of *The Southern Cockfighter* that carried the announcement of Ed Middleton's retirement from the sport.

I had liked the old lady, and I tried to write Ed a letter of condolence. But after a futile attempt to write a decent letter that didn't sound banal or morbid, I gave up on the idea and sent him a commercial condolence card by special delivery. Not much of a writer himself, Ed Middleton acknowledged receipt of my condolences by thanking me on the back of a picture postcard of Disney World. His card was waiting for me when I returned to Ocala.

There was also a letter waiting for me in my mailbox from Frances, my fat sister-in-law. Frances was the last person I ever expected to hear from. After two stiff drinks and a wait of one hour, I made myself open the letter.

Dear Frank,

Only a few short weeks ago I hated you and would have been glad to shoot you. But now I see your wisdom in getting Randall out of the terrible rut he was in. He won't write you, because he's too proud. But he loves you and he's your very own brother and I want you to write him soon.

It was an awful shock to move out of what I considered my home for life, especially knowing that wreckers were going to tear it down the next day.

But I forgive you, Frank, for what it did for Randy.

We could have moved in with Daddy in Macon, but Randy wouldn't do it. We rented a room in a boarding-house in Macon instead – and Frank, Randy hasn't had a single drink since the morning we left the farm!

He found a position right away. You remember how he used to dig through those law books day after day? Well, he took some of his findings down to the White Citizen's Council and they were actually amazed at some of the loopholes he found in the new bussing laws. Anyway, they hired him as a full-time WCC counselor with a retainer of eight thousand dollars a year! And it's all been so wonderful for me, too. Randy takes me to all the meetings and I've met ever so many nice new people! His speeches are just wonderful, Frank, and he gets one hundred dollars and expenses every time he talks. Next Monday, we're going to the WCC rally in Atlanta and Randy is going to talk about the black-power movement. I'm proud enough to bust and his picture will be in the paper! Next Monday, in the Constitution, but I'll cut it out and send you a copy.

I can't tell you how happy I am about Randy's success. Make up with your brother, Frank. Please?

He loves you and so do I!

All my love, Frances

I had no intention of writing Randall and making up with him. But I appreciated the news from Frances. I had feared that the two of them would appear at my Ocala farm some morning, begging to be taken in – and I would have been forced to shelter them. Now that Randall was finally on his own, he could go his way and I would go mine. I didn't answer Frances either, but I saved the envelope because it had their Macon address.

When Christmastime came, I would send them a card. *Peace on Earth. Good Will toward Men!* Anytime Randall really wanted to make up with me, all he had to do was to send me the three hundred dollars he owed me.

It was my fault that we lost the Plant City derby, although no one can win them all, no matter how good his gamecocks are. But I had concentrated on the selection and the conditioning of the cocks for the post-derby main with Jack Burke, and Omar had done most of the conditioning for the derby. I can't blame Omar for the loss. He did a good conscientious job. I did feel, however, that if I had helped him more we would have come out better than third place. There was some consolation in the fact that Jack Burke finished fourth. Like me, Jack had undoubtedly concentrated his efforts on preparing for our main.

The Texas entry of Johnny McCoy and Colonel Bob Moore were the winners of the derby, and it was no disgrace to lose to them. These partners are two of the biggest names in US cockfighting.

Like a bridge player, who can remember every important hand he held in a rubber of bridge five or ten years back, a cockfighter can remember the details of every pitting in an important cockfight. The details of the two-entry main between Jack Burke and myself are still as vivid in my mind as if it were held ten minutes ago. But I like the way Tex Higdon reported the event in *The American Gamefowl Quarterly*.

Tex had been reporting cockfights for game fowl magazines for twenty years or more, and he's a topflight pit reporter. And yet, hardly a season goes by when Tex doesn't get into one or two fistfights for his pains. His way of writing rubs a lot of high-strung cockfighters the wrong way, especially when they are on the receiving end of his sarcasm. But his reporting is conscientious when it comes to accuracy. It takes a damned good eye to catch fast action in the pit. The following is a tear sheet of his article from *The American Gamefowl Quarterly*:

Red Heels At Plant City?

by Tex Higdon

Plant City Florida, 31 November – if you're looking for the results of the Southern Conference Plant City Derby, held 30 November, you'd better look elsewhere in these pages. This Texan is reporting the Main between the two master cockers, Jack Burke and silent Frank Mansfield. By the way, folks, Frank has gone out and got himself a partner after all these years, a New York country boy with the worst-looking black beard your reporter has seen in a month of Sundays. It's a good thing Frank don't talk anymore. His new sidekick, Omar Baradinsky, does enough talking for *three* cockfighters!

The Main was a real old-fashioned-type event, well worth staying over for in Plant City another day. I wish we had more mains like this one, or at least more mains. This is an old cockpit, but there's plenty of room for three hundred people. The main pit is below ground, the way they ought to be; there are plenty of cockhouses, and clean latrines for visitors, plus a drag pit that's better than most regular pits I've seen at supposedly high-class game clubs. Pit operator-referee Tom Doyle sells toasted cheese sandwiches for a dollar apiece, and that's an outrage, but as long as people buy them, he'll probably keep the same price. Next time I visit Plant City, this Texas boy will bring his own lunch!

Referee Tom Doyle announced right off: 'If you people violate our rules, have yourself a few too many drinks and get tough, you're just right for me to handle!' Tom Doyle is big enough for the crowd to believe him. They were downright cowed, and hip pints were well hidden.

There were three checkweights, 5:00, 6:05, and shake, as set up by Jack Burke. Mansfield won the toss and decided to fight from bottom weights up. Twenty-six cocks were shown by both cockers and thirteen fell in.

No. One. Both show 5:00 cocks, Burke a Brady Roundhead, Mansfield an Allen Roundhead. Mansfield broke through early and then slowed up about the 12th pitting. He was blinded in the 20th right after they went to breast on the time call. The Brady was a hardhead that kept trying, took plenty of punishment, and broke counts as fast as the Allen Roundhead took them. In the 48th pitting Jack Burke won with a down cock that got the count and kept it while his opponent breathed gently down his neck but quit pecking.

No. Two. Burke a 5:01 Claret cross; Mansfield a 5:02 Mellhorn Black. This was a bang-up 1st pitting, followed by a dozen dirty buckles in the 2nd. Mansfield had the best cutter, and in the 18th Burke stayed put on his score. When they went to breast in the 25th the Mellhorn Black kicked like a taxpayer and won in the 30th when Burke carried his bird out.

No. Three. Burke showed an Alabama Pumpkin (if I ever saw one) bred by his brother Freddy in Vero Beach. 5:08. Mansfield a Middleton Gray, 5:06. Mansfield had a great shuffler that wasn't even touched. He was over the Burke chicken in the 1st pitting like a short-circuited electric blanket, uncoupled him in the 2nd, and won in the 5th when Burke carried out a dead one. This made the Gray a five-time winner, according to Mr Baradinsky – who made a special trip to the press box to relieve me of fifty dollars – and I could very well believe it.

No. Four. Burke showed a 5:08 Blackwell Roundhead, Mansfield a 5:07 Claret. This was the most even and best match so far. The two cocks mixed like sand and cement every time they met until the 10th when Burke got tired. The Roundhead was down on his score in the 18th, and taken out in the 19th unable to face.

No. Five. Burke a Blue-Spangle cross, Mansfield a green-legged Allen Roundhead with the widest wing-spread I've seen outside of Texas. Both scaled 5:09. Two ring-wise roosters met in this battle and it was truly the best fight of the whole Main. Mansfield rattled in the 6th and then came back strong after I don't know how many changed bets. Burke was killed in the 19th after the Roundhead regained vigor and shuffled all over the Cross a dozen times. Folks, there was *money* lost on this fight!

No. Six. Both showed 5:10 cocks. Burke a Tulsa Red and Mansfield a Claret cross. The light-footed Tulsa Red was truly a great cutter that uncoupled the Claret in the 2nd pitting. Mansfield carried him out in the 3rd.

No. Seven. Both showed 5:12 cocks. Burke an O'Neal Red. Mansfield a low-stationed Mellhorn Black. Burke was rattled in the 3rd and down on his score in the 14th. The Mellhorn Black who spiked the steel with unerring accuracy in every pitting won for Mansfield in the 20th.

No. Eight. Both showed 5:13 cocks. Burke a Butcher Boy and Mansfield an Allen Roundhead. The steel was tossed from every angle in the 1st and 2nd pittings as sudden squalls hit Middle Florida. The Butcher Boy weakened in the 3rd but grew stronger in the 7th and hurt the Roundhead in the next two pittings. In the 9th the Roundhead slowed and the Butcher Boy put him out of the running. Mansfield carried him out after the 10th.

No. Nine. Both showed 5:14 cocks. Burke a battle-wise Whitehackle, Mansfield a fine-colored Claret. Mansfield was smiling all over the place up to the 8th pitting when the Whitehackle got down to business and changed his smile to a frown. His Claret was counted out in the 12th.

No. Ten. Both showed six-pounders. Mansfield a side-stepping Mellhorn Black that skipped constantly to the right, and Burke a black-and-white Spangle. The Black broke the Spangle's leg in the 3rd and Burke carried his cock out. Mansfield had a real Ace here, and his way of fighting bewildered the Spangle. This was the sidestepper's fourth win this season.

No. Eleven. Two more six-pound cocks, Burke with an Ace Kansas Cutter, and Mansfield with a three-year-old Alabama-walked Claret. The Kansas chicken hung every time he got close to the Claret, and Mansfield had to take him out in the 9th.

No. Twelve. Burke showed a 6:02 Sawyers Roundhead and Mansfield gave him two ounces with the Claret he showed. These cocks came out with plenty of gas, and buckled hard for the first five pittings. An even match, one in and then the other. Mansfield was cut down on his score in the 13th. A few fast shuffles by the Sawyers Roundhead and the blood-sodden Claret was carried out helpless.

The score was tied six to six!

Odd fight. Shakes. No weights were given, of course. Burke looked determined to win the odd fight when he showed an enormous Shawlneck. My educated guess gave the Shawlneck at least ten ounces over Mansfield's over-sized Roundhead. But Jack needed more than weight. In Mansfield's hands the Roundhead showed a furious style of fighting that befuddled the heavier bird. Burke was down in the 18th with a broken leg and Mansfield won in the 23rd.

But there was an even better fight to come!

As Jack Burke, great sportsman that he is, was counting out the greenbacks into Mansfield's eager hand, Mrs Dody Burke, Jack's beauteous young bride, decided to put on a hack of her own! Weighing approximately 125 pounds, and armed with red shoes (with three-inch heels), she flew across the pit and gaffed silent Mansfield in the shins. She also tried a right-cross to Mansfield's jaw with a free-swinging red leather purse, but was blocked by her handler, Jack Burke, and carried out of the pit screaming. A fine ending to a fine main! We wonder what kind of conditioning Mr Burke is giving his new bride?

Chapter Fourteen

'When the pressure's on, a promoter's got to do the best he can,' Fred Reed said petulantly for the fourth time during his sales talk. He ought to make a recording, I thought to myself.

Fred Reed had done the best he could all right, but I didn't like the setup, not any part of it. Including Mr Reed, there were nine of us sitting around in the plush pink-and-white bridal suite of the new Southerner Hotel in Chattanooga. Johnny Norris, Roy Whipple, Omar and myself were all Southern Conference regulars, but the other entries were not, although they had paid their fees for the Chattanooga derby.

Except for promoter Fred Reed, who wore a suit and necktie, the rest of us were either in sports clothes or blue jeans, and we looked as out of place in the mid-Victorian decor of the bridal suite as a honeymoon couple would have looked bedded down in a cockpit. My pictur-esque partner, with his wild beard and bib overalls, sat uneasily on a fragile gilded chair by the door to the bath-room. I was sharing a blue velvet love seat with Old Man Whipple, a gray-stubbled cockfighter from North Carolina whose odor would have been improved by a couple of quick runs through a sheep dip.

Mr Reed wiped his sweaty brow with a white linen handkerchief and continued: 'Boys, when the SRCA really puts their foot down, the sheriff has to go along with 'em, that's all there is to it!

'Elections are coming up, and I just couldn't pay nobody

off. But I did get to the city officials and we can stage the derby right here in this suite without interference. I know you men have all fought cocks in hotel rooms before, but you've never had a better one than this! Just take a look at this wonderful floor.' Mr Reed bent down with a broad smile on his face and rubbed the blue nylon carpet with his fingers. 'Why, a carpet like this makes a perfect pit flooring for chickens! And don't worry about damages. The manager has been tipped plenty, and I promised him I'd pay any cleaning charges on the carpets. You've all got reserved rooms on this floor, and we've got the exclusive use of the service elevator to bring the cocks straight up from the basement garage.

'Frankly, boys, I think the Chattanooga derby is better off here than it is at my pit outside of town. There won't be as many spectators because of the space limitations, but I've invited some big money men, and you'll be able to place bets as high as you want to on your birds.'

Old Roy Whipple, sitting beside me on the love seat, spat a stream of black tobacco juice onto the nylon carpet and then cleared his throat. 'Where're we goin' to put the dead chickens, Mr Reed?'

'That's an excellent question, Mr Whipple,' Reed replied pompously. 'I'm glad you asked it. The dead cocks will be stacked in the bathtub. Are there any other questions?'

'Yes, sir. I have one,' Johnny Norris said politely. 'The action will be slowed down considerably, won't it, if we have to bring the cocks up from the basement before every fight? It'll take forever to finish the derby. And what do we use for a drag pit?'

'That's another good question, Mr Norris,' Reed replied, with the deference in his voice that Johnny Norris usually received. 'But these matters have all been taken into account. Except for the traveling pit, the rest of the furniture in here will be removed, and folding chairs will be

384

set up. You'll heel the cocks in the bedroom, and the weights'll be announced far enough in advance so that there'll always be another pair waiting to pit. There's another connecting door through the bedroom to the next suite – the VIP suite, the hotel calls it – and the living room of the next suite'll be used as a drag pit. With two referees, I can assure you, gentleman, that the fighting will be as fast here as anywhere else. Are there any more questions, anything at all?'

There were no more questions.

'All right then, gentlemen. The fighting starts at 10 a.m. tomorrow morning. Mimeographed schedules will be run off tonight and will be slipped under the doors to your rooms. If you'll all give me a list of your weights, I'll get started on the matching right away. By the way, gentlemen, if you don't want to dress up for dinner, you can have your meals served in your rooms. Otherwise, the hotel's got a rule about wearing coats and ties in the dining room. Your meals have been paid for, too, including tips.'

Discussions began among the other cockfighters, and they started to work on their weight lists. I caught Omar's eye and jerked my head for him to follow me out into the hall. When Omar joined me in the corridor, I led the way to our room. I wrote a short note to my partner on a sheet of hotel stationary:

No good, partner. Deputies understand agrarian people and cockfighters, but city cops have a bad habit of not staying bought There'll be a lot of drinking and a lot of money changing hands. That means women present and women mean trouble. We've got thirty of our best cocks in the basement and a confiscation raid would ruin us for the season. Get our entry fee back from Mr Reed.

Omar read the note and then stared at me morosely with his large brown eyes. The corners of his mouth were probably turned down as well, but I couldn't see his mouth beneath his heavy moustache. 'Damn it, Frank,' he said, 'I'm inclined to go along with you, but we'll be passing up a whole lot of easy money. Fred Reed told me personally that there were two big-money gamblers flying in from Nashville tonight, and we get fat. Really *fat!* The only entry we really have to worry about is Johnny Norris from Birmingham.'

I took the note out of his hands and ran a double line under every word in it to emphasize the meaning, and passed it back.

'I'm with you, all right. Don't worry,' he said earnestly. 'But don't forget those eight cocks we selected to enter. They're trimmed mighty fine. If we don't fight them tomorrow they're likely to go under hack.'

I nodded, thinking about the problem.

If we didn't fight our eight conditioned gamecocks, we would have to put them back on a regular maintenance diet and then recondition them all over again for the 10 January Biloxi meet. Even if they were reconditioned, they would be stale. And stale, listless cocks aren't winners.

I opened my suitcase, remembering the four-cock derby scheduled at Cook's Hollow, Tennessee. I flipped through the pages of my current *Southern Cockfighter* magazine until I found Vern Packard's advertisement for the meet. As I recalled, the derby was scheduled for the next day, 15 December, at the Cook's Hollow Game Club. Vern Packard was a friend of mine, although I hadn't fought at his pit for more than four years. I circled Vern's telephone number in the advertisement, and wrote on the margin of the magazine:

Call Packard. We're too late for the derby, but I can fight our cocks in post-and pre-derby hacks. Vern's a friend of mine. You take the truck and the rest of the cocks on to Biloxi like we planned.

Omar, cheered considerably, laughed and said: 'I'll buy that, Frank. And raid or no raid, the idea of fighting cocks in a bridal suite doesn't appeal to me anyway.'

Omar picked up the telephone and called Vern Packard. As I thought, I was too late to enter Vern's derby, but there were only three entries instead of four, and Vern planned 'feathering the pit' hacks as well as post-derby hacks. He was happy to have me, and told Omar that he would put me up in his spare bedroom and have some coops readied for my eight cocks.

While Omar looked for Fred Reed to get our entry money back, I packed both our bags. Ordinarily, we would have had to forfeit the two hundred dollars we put up, because we had already signed the contracts and mailed them in from Ocala. But we had contracted to fight at the Chattanooga Game Club, five miles out of the city, not in a hotel suite. It was Fred Reed's hard luck that the sheriff had padlocked his pit, not ours. I repacked our bags, and by the time Omar returned to the room we were ready to leave.

As we entered the elevator, Omar said: 'Fred was mighty unhappy about our withdrawal, Frank. We were the only entry to pull out. He tried his damndest to talk me out of it. There's going to be a bar with free drinks and sandwiches all day, he said, which only proves that we're doing the right thing. By one tomorrow afternoon that suite'll be so full of smoke and drunks you won't be able to see the chickens.'

Although I couldn't have agreed with Omar more, I hated to leave. There was something exciting about fighting cocks in a hotel and the prospect of winning large sums of money. It's almost impossible to resist free drinks, and there would be some beautiful women around to spend some money on. And when it comes to good-looking women, Chattanooga has got prettier girls than Dallas, Texas.

I had written to Dirty Jacques Bonin in Biloxi and arranged a deal to put Omar and me and our gamecocks up at his game farm. When he came to fight his chickens at the Ocala derby in February, we would fix him up with like facilities either at my place or Omar's.

We shook hands and parted in the basement garage of the hotel. Omar headed for Biloxi in the pickup with twenty-two gamecocks, and I drove to Cook's Hollow with Icky and the derby-conditioned birds in the station wagon.

In the heat of the fighting the next day at Vern Packard's pit, I realized how much I had depended upon Omar to look after things during the season so far. If Omar hadn't done a good portion of my talking for me, I would have had a rough time getting matches. But thanks to Omar's efforts, I managed to fight five of my eight cocks, and I won every hack. By picking the winning derby entry, and laying even money with a local gambler, I won four hundred dollars. My five hack wins added two hundred and fifty dollars more to my roll, and I was well satisfied with the outcome of the side trip to Cook's Hollow. This was a small sum compared to what we might have won at Chattanooga, but it was enormous compared to winning nothing at all.

By four that afternoon the fighting was over, and I hadn't been able to get a match for Icky. Icky scaled now at a steady 4:02 and was too light for derby fighting in the Southern Conference. All of the SC derby weights began at 5:00, and the only way I could fight Icky was in hack battles. In New York and Pennsylvania, where the use of short heels is preferred and smaller gamecocks are favored, I could have had all the fights I wanted. So far, Icky had only had two fights. Before he met Jack Burke's

Little David at Milledgeville, I wanted him to win at least three more. He would need all of the pit experience he could get to win over Burke's Ace.

The Cook's Hollow Game Club was similar to a hundred other small Southern cockpits. The pit was on Vern Packard's rocky farm, adjacent to his barn, and covered with a corrugated iron roof. There were three-tier bleachers on three sides, and the fourth side was the barn wall. A double door in the barrier provided an entranceway inside, and two-by-two coops were nailed to the interior walls of the barn to serve as cockhouses for visitors.

There was a large blackboard nailed to the outside of the barn. The fans could follow the running results of the derby as they were chalked up by the referee following each battle. Cockfighters looking for individual hacks also used the blackboard. I had written my name and the weights of all my cocks in square letters, hoping for a challenge. When three-quarters of the crowd had left, I decided to quit myself.

I was inside the barn, transferring my birds into my traveling coops, when Vern Packard introduced me to an old farmer and his son.

'Frank,' Vern said, 'this is Milam Peeples, and his son, Tom.'

I shook hands with both men. Milam Peeples was in his late fifties, tanned and well weathered by his years of outside labor. The yellow teeth on the left side of his mouth, I noticed, were worn down almost to the gum line from chewing on a pipe. The son was a full head taller than his father, with long thick arms and big raw-looking hands. He had a lopsided smile, a thick shock of wheat-colored hair, and he wore a gauze pad over his left eye. His right eye was blue. A thin trickle of spit ran down his chin from the left corner of his slack mouth. Either it didn't bother him or he didn't notice it. I noticed it, and it bothered me.

'Glad to meet you, Mr Mansfield,' Tom Peeples said.

'I saw on the blackboard out there' – his father made a sweeping gesture with his malodorous briar pipe – 'that you got a 4:02 lookin' for a fight. If you don't mind givin' me an ounce, I got a 4:03 out to my place that can take him.'

'He's my cock, Mr Mansfield,' Tom broke in. 'Little Joe. You ever hear of him?'

'Mr Mansfield hasn't fought in this neck of the woods for some years, Tom,' Vern answered for me. 'I doubt if he has.

'Little Joe's a six-time winner, Mr Mansfield,' the old man continued, 'but I've never fought him here in Vern's pit. He's crowd shy and can't be conditioned to people or noise. But if you want to drive on out to my farm, maybe we could have us a little private hack.'

I nodded sympathetically. Often a gamecock is crowd shy. But I wasn't too anxious to pit Icky against a six-time winner.

'I'll tell you what,' Milam Peeples said generously, 'I'll give you two-to-one odds, and you can name the amount. After all, you got to fight at my place instead of here, and I want to be fair.'

I agreed, holding up five fingers.

'Nope,' Milam Peeples shook his head. 'I ain't fightin' Little Joe for no fifty dollars. Ain't worth the risk.'

I had meant five hundred dollars. I grinned and opened and closed my fist five times, as rapidly as I could.

'Five hundred dollars?' Mr Peeples took the pipe out of his mouth.

When I nodded, he hesitated.

'Now that's getting mighty steep. If I lose, you win yourself a thousand dollars.'

'You offered Frank two to one,' Vern Packard reminded the old man.

'Little Joe can take him, Daddy!' Tom said eagerly.

'All right.' Peeples agreed to the bet and we shook hands. 'When you're ready to go you can follow us on out in your car.'

'Why don't you load Mr Mansfield's coops in his station wagon, Tom,' Vern suggested. 'And I'll take him up to the house to get his suitcase.'

'Yes, sir,' Tom said.

As soon as Vern and I entered the back door of his house into the kitchen, he dropped into a chair beside the table where we had eaten breakfast. There was an amused smile on his friendly, open face. Vern was a short, wiry little man with a sparse gray moustache, and he had been a good host.

'Just a second, Frank,' Vern's voice stopped me as I started for the bedroom. 'It's a trick. Old Man Peeples has never heard of you, Frank, and he's taken you for a sucker. I've seen him take itinerant cockers before, and I've never said anything. Why not? Peeples is a local cocker, and most of the drifters who fight here don't come back anyway. But I don't feel that way about you. Because the local gamblers didn't know your reputation I won six hundred bucks today on your hacks.' Vern laughed with genuine amusement.

'You wouldn't fight the old man anyway, once you saw his setup. He's got a square chunk of waxed linoleum in his barn for the floor of his cockpit. And that cock of his hasn't won six fights, he's won at least *eighteen* fights! He rubs rosin on Little Joe's feet, and on that slick waxed floor the opposing cock doesn't have a chance. But if you really think your cock can take him, now that you know their game, I'll give you a chunk of rosin. That way, you'll both start even.'

I got my suitcase out of the bedroom. Vern rummaged through the drawers of the sideboard.

'Here,' he handed me an amber chunk of rosin the size of a dime-store eraser. 'You don't need very much, Frank.

But don't fight him on that waxed linoleum unless you use it. If you want my advice, you're a damned fool to fight him at all!'

I winked, shook hands with Vern and crossed the yard toward the station wagon. These two peckerwoods had a lesson coming, and I had made up my mind to teach it to them. Icky was in peak condition, as sharp as a needle. They would be counting on their trick to win. With the rosin safe in my pocket, the odds were in my favor. I couldn't believe that Little Joe, despite his eighteen wins, was in proper condition to beat Icky in an even fight.

I put my suitcase in the back, checked Tom's loading of my coops, climbed into the front seat, and honked my horn to let Peeples know that I was ready to go. I followed his vintage black car out of the parking lot. The Peeples farm was some six miles out in the country, and to get there I had to follow the lurching car over a twisting, rock-strewn, spring-breaking dirt road. When the old cock-fighter stopped at the entrance to his dilapidated barn, I parked beside him.

I could see the cockpit without getting out of the station wagon. The linoleum floor was a shiny, glistening design in blue-and-white checkered squares. The glassy floor was such a flagrant violation of pit regulations – anywhere – that I began to wonder if there wasn't more going on here than Vern Packard had told me. But Vern had advised me *not* to fight, so I decided to go ahead with it and see what happened.

When I leaned over the seat to pull out Icky's coop, Tom opened the front door and offered his help.

'I'll hold him for you, Mr Mansfield.'

I took my blue chicken out of the coop and passed him to Tom Peeples. He smiled, hefting Icky gently with his big raw hands.

'He feels jes' like a baseball!' Tom said, as I opened my gaff case. 'Sure does seem a shame to see Little Joe kill a pretty chicken like this one.'

I cleared Icky's spur stumps with typewriter-cleaning fluid, and heeled him low with a set of silver one-and-a-quarter-inch gaffs. Holding the cock under the chest with one hand, Tom passed him back to me.

'By the way,' he said, snapping his fingers, 'Little Joe always fights in three-inch heels, if you want to change.' Tom had waited patiently until I had finished heeling before providing me with this essential information. Another violation of form. Of course, he had no way of knowing that I wouldn't have changed to long heels anyway.

I shook my head indifferently, and he ran to meet his father who was rounding the corner of the barn. Mr Peeples had gone to the rows of chicken runs behind the barn to get Icky's opponent while Tom had helped me heel. I took a good look at Little Joe from the front seat.

The cock had been so badly battered I couldn't determine his game strain. His comb and wattles were closely cropped for fighting, and most of his head feathers were missing, pecked out in earlier battles. Instead of the usual graceful sweep of arching tail feathers, the Peeples cock had only three broken quills straggling from his stern. Both wings were ragged, shredded, in fact. Both wings had been broken in fighting, and although they had knitted, they had bumpy leading edges. As Milam Peeples sat down on a sawhorse beside the pit and turned the cock on its back for Tom to heel him, I noticed that Little Joe's left eye was missing. A blinker on top of everything else. If Little Joe had won eighteen fights, and from his appearance he had been in many battles, Icky was in for the toughest fight of his life.

Maybe his last.

Under cover from Milam and Tom Peeples, I sat in the front seat of the station wagon holding Icky in my lap and briskly rosined the bottom of his feet. I was still rubbing the feet when the old man called out that he was ready. There was only a sliver of rosin left, but I put it in my shirt pocket and joined Milam and his son at the pit.

'I'm goin' to handle,' the old man said. 'And if you don't have no objections, Tom here can referee.'

I nodded, stepped over the low wooden wall of the pit, and took my position on the opposite score. The waxed floor was so slick my leather heels slipped on it slightly before I got to the other side. Although I figured Mr Peeples was expecting an argument of some kind about the illegal flooring, I kept a straight face. I wondered, though, what kind of an explanation he used to counter arguments about the pit. It must have been a good one.

'Better bill 'em, Mr Mansfield,' Tom said.

We billed in the center, and Icky got the worst of the prefight session. The bald head of Little Joe and shortage of neck feathers didn't give him a mouthful of anything. The Peeples cock was the meanest and most aggressive biller I'd seen in some time. I dropped back to my score. Both sets of scores, the eight and the two feet, had been straightedged onto the linoleum with black paint. As I squatted behind my back score, Tom asked me if I was ready, and I pointed to his father.

'Get ready, then,' Tom said to the old man.

Milam was forced to hold the straining Little Joe under the body with both hands. There weren't enough tail feathers for a good tail hold – and I watched Tom's lips.

'Pit!'

The fight was over.

The battle ended so quickly, all three of us were stunned. I've seen hundreds of cockfights end in the first pitting, a great many of them in fewer than fifteen seconds. But the fight between Icky and Little Joe didn't last two seconds.

I was aware that Little Joe's feet were rosined as well as Icky's. Mr Peeples had coated them surreptitiously when he got the chicken from its coop run behind the barn. So the only way I can account for the quick ending is by crediting Icky's superior speed and conditioning and my long-time practice of releasing him first. The old man was hampered when the time came to let go, because of the manner in which he had to hold the Ace cock.

Tom's sharp order to pit was still echoing in the rafters of the barn when I released my Blue. Icky, with his sticky feet firmly planted, didn't take the two or three customary steps forward like he usually did. He flew straight into the air from a standing takeoff. Old Man Peeples scarcely had time to pull his hands away from beneath Little Joe's body when Icky clipped twice and cut the veteran fighter down on its score. It happened that fast. *Click! Click!* One heel pierced Little Joe's head, and the other heel broke his neck.

As the three of us watched in silent stupefaction, Icky strutted proudly to the center of the pit, leaving white gummy footprints in his wake, and issued a deep-throated crow of victory. The expressions on the faces of Milam Peeples & Son were truly delightful to see. And then Tom Peeple's face changed from milky white to angry crimson.

'You killed my Little Joe!' he shouted.

I was still squatting on my heels when he yelled, and I was totally unprepared for the enormous fist that appeared from nowhere and caught me on the temple. I crashed sideways into the left pit wall and it was smashed flat under the weight of my body. My eyes blurred with tears. All I could see were dark red dots unevenly spaced and dancing upon a shimmering pink background. I must have sensed the darker shadow of Tom's heavy work shoe hurtling toward my head. I rolled over quickly, and his kick missed my head. Two more twisting evasive turns, and I was in the empty horse stall next to the pit. As I scrambled to my knees, my fingers touched the handle of a heavy grooming brush. I regained my feet and swung it in an arcing loop from the floor. Tom saw the edge of the weighted brush ascending, tried to halt his rushing lunge, and half turned away. The brass-studded edge caught him on his blind side, on the bump behind his left ear. As Tom fell, his arms held limply at his sides, the opposite wall of the pit collapsed under him. He was out cold.

I could see all right now, but I kept a firm grip on the brush handle as I watched Milam Peeples to see what his reaction was going to be. The old man shook his head sadly, and removed an old-fashioned snap-clasp pocket-book from his front pocket.

'You didn't have no call to hit the boy that hard, Mr Mansfield,' he said. 'Little Joe was Tom's pet. He was bound to feel bad about losin' him so quick.'

I tossed the brush back into the empty horse stall and rubbed my sore side. My bruised ribs felt like they were on fire. My head was still ringing, and I probed my throbbing temple gingerly with a forefinger. There was a marble-sized knot beneath the skin, and it was swelling even more as I touched it.

'Now, I'm a little short of a thousand dollars in cash, Mr Mansfield,' Milam Peeples said plaintively, standing on the other side of Tom's felled body, 'but here's three hundred and fifty-two dollars in bills. You're goin' to have to take the rest of the debt out in game fowl. We'd best go on down to the runs and you can pick 'em out. I figure six gamecocks'll make us even.'

I didn't. I counted the bills he handed me, shoved the wad into my hip pocket, and then held up ten fingers.

'Most of these cocks are Law Grays, Mr Mansfield,' Peeples protested. 'And three are purebred Palmetto Muffs. You know yourself there ain't no better cocks than

Palmetto Muffs! Take a look first, and you'll see what they're worth. I only got ten gamecocks altogether.'

I followed the old man out of the barn.

Professional cockers frequently pay off their gambling debts with gamecocks instead of cash. But this kind of payoff is normally agreed upon before a fight – not afterward. I had no objection to taking game cocks instead of money this late in the season. Some hard-hitting replacements would be useful before we entered the Milledgeville Tourney, and I was on the high side of the hog when it came to settling up with Peeples.

On the way to the coop walks, Peeples stopped at the watering trough to light his pipe and to do some preliminary dickering.

'Now you seen them three Grays I fit this afternoon, Mr Mansfield. Aces every one. You take them, and any five more of the lot and we'll be fair and square. Countin' the cash I gave you already, you're gettin' the best end and you know it.'

Giving Peeples more credit than he probably deserved, I figured his gamecocks were worth about fifty dollars a head. According to my arithmetic I would be short about two hundred and fifty dollars if I only took eight cocks. Even if I took all of them I would be one hundred and fifty dollars short of the thousand dollars he had bet me. I shook my head with a positive-negative waggle.

Feet pounded on the hard-packed ground behind me. I turned. Less than twenty feet away Tom Peeples was charging toward me with a hatchet brandished in his upraised right hand. His red face was contorted and his angry blue eye was focused on infinity.

Without taking time to think I jumped toward him instead of trying to dodge his rush, twisted my body to the left, and kicked hard at his right shinbone. Tripped neatly, he sprawled headlong in the dirt. The hatchet flew out of his hand and skittered for a dozen yards across the bare ground. Before he could recover himself I had a handgrip in his thick hair and another hold on his leather belt. With one jerk as far as my knees, followed by a short heave, Tom Peeples was in the water trough. I shifted my left hand from his belt to his hair and held him beneath the water with both hands. His legs thrashed the scummy water into green foaming milk, but he couldn't get his head up. I watched the popping bubbles break at my wrists and held him under until his feet stopped churning.

'You'd best not hold his head under too long, Mr Mansfield,' his father said anxiously. 'He'll be drownded!'

That was true enough. I didn't want to drown the man. I only wanted to cool him off so I could complete my business with Mr Peeples and get back to Cook's Hollow. When I let go of Tom's head, he broke free to the surface, blubbering. He had lost the bandage in the water, but both eyes were closed. He took handholds on both sides of the tin-lined trough and brought his body up to a crouched position. He stayed that way, half in the water, and half out, his chin on his chest, weeping like a child. But he wasn't a child. He was at least twenty-two years old, and he had tried to kill me.

Mr Peeples and I continued our walk toward his chicken runs. Although the old cockfighter complained, he helped me put the seven mature cocks into narrow traveling coops that were in the runs, and brought the three Grays that were already in coops over to my station wagon from his old car. It was easy to catch Icky, who was scratching in a horse stall. After cutting off the heels, I put him back in his coop.

'I suppose you're goin' to tell Vern Packard how you beat me,' Mr Peeples said, as I slipped behind the wheel and slammed the door.

Looking him directly in the eyes, I nodded my head.

'If you do, Mr Mansfield,' he begged, 'me or Tom neither'll be ashamed to show our faces down to the pit for two or three years.'

I shrugged, and let out the clutch.

As I drove out of the barn lot, Tom Peeples was still hunkered down dejectedly in the water trough like an old man washing his privates in a bathtub.

On the return drive to Vern Packard's house I missed one of the turns and had to redouble twice before I found the way back to the main road. It was dark when I wheeled into his driveway. Vern switched on the yard lights and came outside to meet me.

'Who won?' he asked excitedly, as I got out of the station wagon.

I handed him the fragment of rosin, took the wad of bills out of my pocket and counted off one hundred dollars. Grinning, I pushed the hundred dollars into his hand. He kissed the bills, and returned the sliver of rosin.

'You keep it, Frank,' he said happily. 'You paid me enough for it. Come on inside and eat. I was looking for you to get back an hour ago, but I've been waiting supper on you. It's still warm though.'

As soon as I was seated at the kitchen table, Vern served the plates and turned the burner up higher under the coffee to reheat it. There were rolls, baked ham and candied sweet potatoes. Vern put enough food on my plate for three men, but I dug into it.

As he poured the coffee, Vern said jokingly, 'What do you carry, Frank? A rabbit's foot, a lucky magnet or do you wear a bag of juju bones around your neck?'

I stopped eating and looked at him.

Vern laughed. 'Your partner telephoned about twenty minutes after you left. Mr Baradinsky. First, he wanted to know how you made out, and I told him. Then he had some news for you about the Chattanooga derby in the Southerner Hotel.'

I put my knife and fork down and waited, trying to hide my impatience at the way he was dragging out the story.

Again Vern laughed. 'No,' he said, 'it isn't what you're thinking, Frank. They weren't raided. The pit was hijacked, and the thieves got away with about twenty-five thousand bucks, according to your partner. He got the information secondhand, and it won't be in the papers. No chickens were lost, but everybody there – cockers, gamblers and even Mr Reed himself – lost their pants. There were three holdup men, all with shotguns, and they knew exactly what they were doing. They made everybody take off their pants and throw them in the middle of the pit. Then one of them filled up a mattress cover with all the pants and they left the hotel suite. They didn't fool with rings or watches. Just the pants' – Vern laughed heartily – 'but the *money* was in the pants! That closed the Chattanooga meet. I'll bet Fred Reed has a tough time getting an okay from Senator Foxhall for a SC derby next year!'

I pursed my lips thoughtfully, nodded my head, and started eating again. My swollen temple was throbbing, and I wanted to put an ice pack on it.

The next morning I left Cook's Hollow to join Omar in Biloxi, with a standing invitation to fight at Vern Packard's game club any time I felt like it. I had added $902 to my bankroll and ten purebred fighting cocks to our stake in the SC Tourney. But no matter what Vern Packard thought, I wasn't lucky.

At long last, my experience and knowledge of cock-fighting were beginning to pay off. That, and the fact that I was using the good sense God gave me.

Chapter Fifteen

I have back issues of all five game fowl magazines covering the Southern Conference derbies held at Biloxi, Auburn and Ocala, but I don't have to dig through them to find the results. I remember them, all of them, perfectly.

In Biloxi, we fought in the cockpit established in a warehouse near the waterfront, and we won the derby 6-3, plus three thousand five hundred dollars in cash. Icky also won his fourth hack at Biloxi over a Hulsey two-time winner entered by Baldy Allen from Columbus, Georgia. Omar, who was spelling me on handling in the pit from time to time, was awarded a wristwatch by the pit officials as the Most Sportsmanlike Handler in the Biloxi derby. My partner was as pleased with this award as I was, but he wouldn't admit it. I knew that Omar was proud of the award because he put his Rolex away, and, from that day forward, wore the wristwatch he was given at Biloxi – a cheap, $16.50 Timex.

My partner didn't attend the Alabama meet with me. The meet at Auburn on 29 January coincided with his wife's annual visit to Florida. I never met the woman, but I had seen a half-dozen snapshots she had mailed to him that had been taken at Fire Island. In the photos, all six of them taken in a crocheted bikini, she looked brittle, thin and febrile-eyed. She didn't look particularly sexy to me, but inasmuch as it was costing my partner more than twelve thousand a year to keep her in New York City, I couldn't begrudge him a week in bed with her. He was entitled to that much, I figured.

Johnny Norris of Birmingham won the Auburn derby, and I came in third. Four of my Allen Roundheads were killed during the meet, but I won two thousand five hundred dollars. A carload of arsenal employees drove over from Huntsville, Alabama, and I won most of my money from them. When it came to cockfighting, these rocket makers didn't know which way was up. In a post-derby hack, I pitted Icky against an Arkansas Traveler that ran like a gazelle in the second pitting.

Our veterans took every fight in 24 February Ocala derby. They fought in the familiar pit as though they were defending their home territory and hens against invaders from outer space. Out of fourteen pit battles, I only carried out one bird. In order to get bets, Omar was forced to give three-to-one odds on every fight, but we still made eighteen hundred dollars on the Ocala derby and hacks.

As the weeks passed, I kept as busy as possible. My personal life, perhaps, may have seemed dull, but I loved the way I lived. On my way home at night, after a day of conditioning at Omar's farm, I often selected a book out of my partner's library. Like a lot of businessmen in New York, he had always wanted to read books, but never had enough time. When he moved permanently to Florida, he ordered a complete set of the Modern Library, including the Giants. Starting at the lowest number, I was gradually working my way through them. By March, I was up to *The Plays of Henrik Ibsen.*

Not only did I get up with the chickens, I went to bed with them as well, but I still had time for reading and for playing my guitar. My partner had asked me to stay at his house, but I declined. I liked Omar, everybody did, but we were together all day, and that was enough. Both of us were entitled to privacy, and I think he was relieved when I decided to sleep at my own farm.

Omar Baradinsky, like any man who has strong opinions, liked to talk about the things he was interested in. This was understandable, and most of the time I enjoyed the insight he revealed on many subjects. However, to listen to him every night, especially when he got a little high on John Jameson, was too much. Unable to talk back, I had to grit my teeth sometimes to prevent myself from setting him straight when he got off the track.

Against the day when my vow was over and I could talk again, I made little entries in a notebook. Someday, Old Boy, I thought, I'm going to set you straight on every one of these topics. If we hadn't separated every evening, our partnership probably wouldn't have lasted the entire season. As it happened, we were still friends after more than five months. Because we were friends, I was worried. We were leaving the next morning and I didn't want to hurt my partner's feelings or interfere in any way with his individuality. But when it came to the Milledgeville Tourney, Omar had a serious problem, and it was up to me to explain it to him.

On the afternoon of 13 March we sat across from each other at the big oak table in Omar's living room going over the ledger and our accumulated records in preparation for the tourney. We had received a telegram the week before from Senator Foxhall reconfirming our joint entry in the tournament and acknowledging receipt of our five-hundred-dollar entry fee. The wire also told us that there would be only eight entries instead of the ten originally scheduled. Two entries had forfeited.

'It's going to make a big difference, Frank,' Omar said, rereading the telegram for the tenth time that day. His initial delight over our joint acceptance – which in my mind had never been in doubt – had gradually turned to concern about whether we would win the tourney or not.

'I know we won't need as many cocks as we figured on,' he continued, 'but neither will the other seven entries. Every cock in the tourney will be a topflight Ace.'

I nodded understandingly. Omar's concern was justified. With only eight entries instead of ten the competition would be a lot stiffer. In comparison with a derby, a major tournament is a complicated ordeal. The matchmaker for a tourney has a compounded headache. In setting up the matches for a derby, the matchmaker only has to match the cocks to be shown at the closest possible weights.

In a tournament, every entry must meet each other at least once. Not only is the matchmaking more complicated, each tourney entry must have an Ace for every weight – that is, if he expects to win.

I wanted to win the tourney just as much as Omar did, but this was my fifth try against my partner's first, and I refused to worry about winning. There was nothing more either one of us could do except pray. We had to fight the gamecocks we had, and they were in the peak of condition. To worry needlessly about winning was foolhardy.

'Do you think we've selected the right cocks?'

I nodded.

'That's it, then.' Omar closed the ledger. 'I'm not taking our entire bankroll, Frank. Four thousand is in the bank, and I'm leaving it there. That way, if we lose, we'll still have two thousand apiece to show for the season. I'm taking eight thousand in cash to the tourney, and I'm going to lay it fight by fight instead of putting it all down on the outcome. No matter what happens, we'll still have a fifty-fifty chance of coming home with a bundle. Now, just in case we win the tourney, how much do we stand to win?'

I wrote the information on a tablet, and shoved it across the polished table.

8 entries @ $500 each	*$4,000*
Sen. Foxhall purse	*$2,000*
Total	*$6,000*

If I win the Cockfighter of the Year Award, that'll be another $1,000—

Omar dragged a hand through his beard as he looked at the figures. 'Doesn't Senator Foxhall take a percentage of the entry fees like the derby promoters?' he asked.

I shook my head and smiled. The senator wasn't interested in money. He had more money than he knew what to do with, but he would still come out even and probably ahead. There would be at least four hundred spectators at the two-day tourney paying a ten-dollar admission fee each day. And the senator would make a profit from his restaurant, too. The Milledgeville cockpit was seven miles out in the country. Where else could the visitors eat?

'Do you have to win the tourney to get the Cockfighter of the Year Award, Frank?' Omar asked me.

I spread my arms wide and shrugged my shoulders. I didn't really know. Senator Foxhall hadn't given the award to anybody in three years, and it was possible that he wouldn't give the medal again this year. All I knew was that the senator awarded the medal to the man he thought deserved it. I didn't want to think about it.

I studied my partner across the table. If anything, his beard was blacker and more unkempt than it had been at the beginning of the season. He still wore his bib overalls, short-sleeved work shirt and high-topped work shoes. During our association, I had never seen him dress differently. He was a free American and entitled to dress any way he pleased. Once a week, when he took a bath, he changed his overalls, but he wore them everywhere he went, to dinner when we ate in Ocala, and downtown when we had fought in Biloxi. Everywhere. This was my problem, and I had to tell him. I pulled the tablet toward me and began to write.

Here are some things about the tourney I have to tell you. As official entries, we'll be put up in Senator Foxhall's home, and eat our meals there. We don't have to wear tuxes for dinner; but we do have to wear coats and ties. Entries and spectators alike are not admitted to the pit unless they wear suits and ties. This is a custom of the tourney out of respect to Senator Foxhall.

But he's really a good man. He was never a real senator; I mean in Congress. He was a Georgia state senator in the late twenties. But for whatever it means, he's a gentleman of the old school and we have to abide by the customs. I don't mind wearing a suit and tie in the pit and you shouldn't either; because it's an honor to fight at Milledgeville.

I also have a personal problem, two of them. I've made seat reservations for four people. My fiancée and her brother, and for Mrs Bernice Hungerford and her nephew. This was several months ago. I don't know if they're coming – neither woman has written or wired me. I don't care. Well, I won't lie. I DO care. If they come, help me entertain them. I'll be handling most of the time, and you'll have to give them some attention for me. Neither woman has seen a cockfight before. My fiancée's name is Mary Elizabeth Gaylord . . .

I looked over the message, which had taken two sheets of tablet paper, and then passed it to Omar. He scanned it slowly, folded the two sheets, put them carefully in his shirt pocket and entered his bedroom.

He slammed the door behind him.

I wanted to damn Omar's sensitive soul, but I couldn't. The custom of the cockpit wasn't my doing, but I felt ashamed. To dictate a person's wearing apparel is a violation of every human right, but I had been forced to tell my partner about the custom or he wouldn't have been allowed through the gate.

After fifteen minutes had passed, and Omar still didn't reappear, I got out of my chair and knocked softly on his door.

'I'll be out in a minute,' he called out. 'Fix yourself a drink!'

I measured three ounces of bourbon into a six-ounce glass. Every time I wrote a note of any kind, I always felt that I was circumventing my vow in an underhanded way, but I was sorry I hadn't written a more detailed explanation about the suit business. But I needn't have worried.

Two drinks later the bedroom door opened. I set my glass on the table, grinned at my partner and shook my head in disbelief.

Omar had cut his beard off square at the bottom with a pair of scissors, and evenly trimmed the sides. His newly cropped beard was as stiff as the spade it resembled. His heavy black moustache had been combed to both sides, and the ends were twisted into sharp points. The white smiling teeth in the dark nest of his inky beard were like a glint of lightning in a dark cloud. He wore a pearl-gray homburg over his bushy black hair, a dark gray double-knit suit, a white shirt and cordovan shoes. Hanging out for two or three inches below his beard, a shimmering gray silk necktie was clipped to his shirt by a black onyx tie bar. He looked like a wealthy Greek undertaker.

'I was saving this costume as a surprise for you tomorrow,' Omar said with a pleased laugh. 'My new suit arrived from my New York tailor three days ago. How do I look?'

I clasped my hands over my head like a boxer, and shook them.

'Do you know what makes my beard so stiff?' Omar said, as he mixed a drink at the table. 'Pommade Hongroise. And just in case you don't know what that means, it's imported moustache wax from France.'

Omar added more whiskey to my glass.

'You Southerners don't have a cartel on manners, Frank. It may come as a shock to you, partner, but I even know the correct tools to use at a formal dinner.' He raised his glass. 'A toast, Mr Mansfield!'

I grinned and clinked my glass against his.

'To the All-American cockfighters, the English-Polish team of Mansfield and Baradinsky! Gentlemen, gamblers, dudes and cocksmen, each and every one!'

We drank to that.

We left Ocala at three o'clock, but it was almost two in the afternoon before we reached Milledgeville. I should have traded my old pickup in for a newer truck, but I had never gotten around to it. For Omar, trailing me all the way, the slow rate of speed on the highway must have been maddening.

When we reached Milledgeville, I waved for Omar to follow me out, and drove on through without stopping.

Milledgeville isn't much of a city – a boy's military academy, a girl's college and a female insane asylum – but it's a pretty little town with red cobblestoned streets lined with shade trees.

Once we were out of town and drawing closer to the cockpit, I didn't mind driving so slowly because I liked the familiar scenery. During the summer, the highway would be bordered on both sides with solid masses of blackberry bushes draped over the barbed-wire fences. In the middle of March, the fields were iron-colored and bare. The tall Georgia slash pines were deep in rust-colored needles. The sky was a watercolor blue, and tiny tufts of white clouds were arranged on this background like a dotted-swiss design. The sun was smaller in March, but the weather wasn't cold. The clear air was sharp, tangy and stimulating, without being breezy.

Like Omar, in his new double-knit suit, I was dressed up, and we both had a place to go. I wore a blue gaberdine suit that I had had for two years, but it was fresh from the cleaners. Well in advance of the tourney, I had ordered a white cattleman's Town and Country snap-brim hat from Dallas, and a new pair of black jodhpur boots from the Navarro Brothers, in El Paso. For the past seven nights I had shined and buffed the new boots until they gleamed like crystal. I wore yellow socks with my suit, and I had paid forty dollars in Miami Beach for my favorite yellow silk necktie, with its pattern of royal blue, hand-painted gamecocks.

I wasn't dressed conservatively, but a lot of my fans would be at the tourney, and they expected me to look dashing and colorful. Press representatives from all five game fowl magazines would be present, and Omar and I were bound to get our photos printed in two or three magazines whether we won the tourney or not.

A Georgia state highway patrolman waved us through the gate to the senator's plantation without getting off his motorcycle. Seeing the back of the pickup and the station wagon both loaded with chicken coops, he didn't need to check our identification cards. A mile down the yellow-graveled road, I took the fork toward the cockpit and cockhouses to weigh in and put our gamecocks away before signing in at the senator's house.

Peach Owen met us in the yards, assigned us to a cock-house, and gave us our numbers to wear on the back of our coats. We were No. 5, and before we did anything else we pinned on our numbers.

Mr Owen was the weight-and-time official for the tourney, and president of the Southern Conference Cockfighting Association. He was a well-liked, friendly man in his mid-thirties who had given up a promising career in cockfighting to work full time for the senator and the Southern Conference. Senator Foxhall, who was getting too old now to do much of anything, paid Peach ten thousand dollars a year to breed and take care of his flock of fancy game fowl.

'Do you want to weigh in now or wait till morning?' Peach asked.

'Let's get it over with,' Omar said, handing Peach our record sheets.

'I don't need both of you,' Peach winked at me. 'There's a fellow up at the house who wants to see you, Mr Mansfield.'

He didn't say who it was so I stayed for the weighing-in, an almost useless precaution at a professional meet like the SC Tourney.

At the majority of US tournaments, cocks are weighed and banded upon checking in. This banding procedure is supposed to ensure that each entry will fight only the cocks he has entered. Before each fight, weight slips are called out, and the entrants heel the cock from their assigned cockhouse according to the exact weight on the slip. If they fail to show a cock making the weight within the check margin, that fight is forfeited to the other cocker who can. The metal band on the leg of the heeled cock is checked by the weight-and-time official immediately prior to the fight and then removed. If the cock wasn't banded by one of the tourney officials upon arrival, the cock is a ringer. In theory, banding upon arrival at a tourney appears to be a sound practice, but bands can be purchased from a dozen or more manufacturers of cocking supplies by anybody who wants to pay for them. The man who wants to cheat by entering a sure loser, for instance, instead of a legitimate fighter, can buy all the metal leg bands he wants to, and clamp one on a ringer in a couple of seconds.

Banding had been eliminated at the SC Tourney. Every cock pitted at the SC Tourney was a four-time winner at an authorized cockpit or game club. And all the wins were entered upon an official record sheet and initialed by the pit operator. Weighing-in at the tourney consisted of checking each gamecock against his record sheet and description and weighing the gamecock itself. Minor weight variations were taken into account by the official.

The system wasn't foolproof. It was still possible to substitute a runner for one of the checked-in fighters, but a man would be a fool to try it. Among the spectators were most of the SC pit operators who could recognize at sight the gamecocks that had fought in their pits earlier in the season. If one of them or one of the other entries spotted a ringer, the man who tried to pull a fast one was through with cockfighting. His name went out on a black-list to every US pit operator, and the blacklist of crooked cockfighters was published annually in the April issue of every US game fowl magazine.

The four-win stipulation was a tough rule, but I was all for it because it separated the amateurs from the professionals and raised the breeding standards of game fowl. This single rule had been the biggest advance in US cock-fighting since the late Sol P. McCall had originated the modern tournament. Many of the fans and gamblers who attended the two-day event traveled thousands of miles to see it, but they knew they would get their money's worth. The fighting would be fast, and every cock shown had proven himself to be dead game.

After completing the weighing-in, which took about an hour, our thirty-one gamecocks were transferred to their stalls inside the cockhouse. We gave each bird a half dip

411

of water, and I scattered a very small portion of grain on the moss-packed floor of each coop to give them some exercise after the long trip. We dropped the canvas covers over the coops to keep the birds quiet, locked the door, and drove the short distance to the senator's home to sign the guest register.

I believe that Omar was impressed by the senator's home. I had been the first time I stayed there, and it still gave me a warm feeling to see the big house as we topped the rise and parked in front of the wide veranda. The mansion was one of the better Southern examples of modified English Georgian. There are many great homes like it in the southern states, but not many of them are as well tended as they should be. It takes a lot of money. Good craftsmanship had been insisted upon when the house had been constructed. All the doors, and even the windows, had ornate, carved designs. The great balustrade that led from the downstairs hall to the upstairs bedrooms had been formed and curved for the purpose from a single tree. There was enough room to sleep thirty guests, but except for the official entries, their wives, and pit officials, spectators attending the meet had to find accommodations in a hotel or motel in Milledgeville.

As we climbed the steps to the veranda, the front door opened and Ed Middleton came out and grabbed my hand. He laughed at my expression and said fondly in his deep, booming voice: 'You didn't expect to see me here, did you? How's my pretty blue chicken getting along?'

In a lightweight gray linen suit, with a pink-and-gray striped tie, Ed didn't look like a sick man to me, but the brown circles under his eyes were a little darker on his pale face. He looked happy, however, and he hadn't been happy when I last saw him in Orlando. Despite his appearance of well-being, he was still liable to have a heart attack at any moment.

Still gripping Ed's hand, I jerked my head for Omar to come forward and introduce himself.

'How do you do?' Omar said. 'I've seen you referee, Mr Middleton, but I've never had the pleasure of meeting you.'

'Glad to meet you at last then, Mr Baradinsky. Evidently you've been a settling influence on my boy here. When I heard about the holdup in Chattanooga, I checked right away, and don't think I wasn't surprised when I learned that you two had pulled out before the meet! The *old* Frank Mansfield I knew would've been right in there, reaching for the ceiling with the rest of 'em.'

Omar laughed. 'If there's any influencing going on, Mr Middleton, it's Frank working on me, not the other way around.'

'Well, come on in,' Ed entered the hall ahead of us. 'I'm not the official greeter here, Mr Baradinsky, I'm only filling in for Mrs Pierce. She had to go downtown for something or other.' Ed snapped his fingers at a grinning Negro boy of fourteen or fifteen in a white short jacket. 'Take the bags out of the station wagon to Number Five upstairs.'

'Yes, sir!' the boy said quickly. He had been eager enough to get our luggage, but the three of us had blocked his way.

While Omar and I signed the guest register, Ed Middleton surprised me again.

'I'm not here as a spectator, Frank,' he explained. 'I'm the referee, and don't think I won't be watching every move you make in the pits.' He turned to my partner. 'I retired a while back from active cockfighting, Mr Baradinsky, but I decided later that I was too young to quit.'

Ed laughed, and then he looked at me, staring directly into my eyes, 'I promised Martha I'd quit, as you know, Frank' – he shrugged – 'but now the promise doesn't mean anything – now that she's passed away. And I know damned well she wouldn't want me sitting around all by myself.'

I nodded sympathetically and smiled. Two full and active days on his feet could very well kill Ed Middleton. And yet, I was still glad to see him and delighted to learn that he was the Number One pit official. Suppose he did keel over dead? That was a much better way to go than eating his guts out with boredom while he stared at a grove of orange trees.

'Say, Frank,' Ed snapped his fingers as we started to go upstairs, 'did your partner ever see the senator's flock of fancy chickens?'

'No, I haven't, Mr Middleton,' Omar said, 'although I've heard enough about them.'

'Good! Mrs Pierce'll be back soon, and I'll take you on the ten-cent guided tour.'

We climbed the stairs to the second floor to where the Negro boy held the door open. I gave him a five-dollar bill, which was plenty, but Omar gave him a five as well. The boy was so astonished by the size of the two gratuities, he returned to our room in less than three minutes with four additional bath towels, a bowlful of icecubes and a pitcher of orange juice.

Omar glanced critically around the room and eyed the cut-glass chandelier in the high ceiling. 'I'll say this much, Frank,' Omar said, 'the rag rug on the floor isn't made of rags, the furniture wasn't made in Grand Rapids, and that calendar on the wall above my bed wasn't placed there by any Baptist.'

I opened my suitcase on my bed and unpacked, putting my extra black button-down shirts and white socks into the high walnut dresser between our beds. Omar pushed open the double French windows and looked out, his hands clasped behind his back.

'There's a good view of the cockpit from here, Frank,' he said. 'The dome has turned rose in the afternoon sun. Take a look at it.'

I joined him at the window. A half mile away, the dome was pink on one side, and on the other side, away from the sun, the shadows were a dark purple. The twenty separated concrete cockhouses formed a U on the southern side of the circular pit. The Atlanta architect who had built the cockpit had settled for concrete blocks, but had incorporated many of the features of the Royal Cockpit at Whitehall Palace into the structure. The long narrow windows, recessed deeply into the walls, were traditional, but they didn't let in enough light. The five strong electric lights over the pit had to be turned on for both day and night fighting.

The square, squat, ugly restaurant, with a white asbestos tile roof, had been added ten years after the cockpit had been finished and was connected to the pit by a screened-in breezeway. The restaurant was entirely out of keeping with the general design, and I had always thought it a pity that it hadn't been built in the first place by the original architect.

The interior of the two-story pit held circular tiers rising steeply to the rim of the dome, and seated four hundred people. The judge's box was to the right of the connecting hall to the drag pit, and the press box was directly above this exit. Including the new doorway that had been cut through the wall leading to the restaurant, there were five arched doorways to the pit.

I finished my unpacking, and slipped on my jacket again in preparation to go out. Omar turned away from the windows, and poured a glass of orange juice.

'I want to tell you something, Frank.' The husky tone of his voice stopped me before I reached the door. 'Whether we win the tourney or not, I want you to know that I'll always be grateful to you for getting me this far. This is truly the greatest experience of my life.'

He said this so warmly that I hit him fondly on the arm with my fist. I was tempted to tell my partner about

415

my vow of silence, but this wasn't the time to tell him. If he knew that my voice was riding on the prospect of being awarded the Cockfighter of the Year award, he would have gotten more nervous about the outcome than he was already.

'Well,' he said cheerfully, clearing his throat, 'isn't it about time to take a look at those fancy chickens?'

I wagged my chin and pointed to his chest. I couldn't go with him, but I knew he would enjoy seeing them. Senator Foxhall had one of the finest collections of fancy game fowl in the world. He had turned fancier, after getting too old to fight chickens in the pit. He raised purebred Gallus Bankivas, the original wild jungle fowl from which all game fowl are descended, Javanese cocks, with tails ten feet long, miniature bantams from Japan – beautiful little creatures not much larger than quail – and many other exotic breeds. If Mary Elizabeth came to the meet, I intended to show them to her. But I couldn't go with Ed and Omar right then. I had to drive into Milledgeville.

I had wired the Sealbach Hotel and reserved four rooms, but with the crowd of visitors expected the next day I knew the manager wouldn't hold them for me unless I paid for them in advance. I wrote a short note for Omar, telling him where I was going and why.

'If you want me to, I'll go with you.'

I shook my head.

'Okay. But rest easy about your guests, Frank. I'll see that they're well taken care of, don't worry. Didn't I ever tell you that I was once a vice-president in charge of public relations?'

I waved a hand in his direction, and drove into town.

By seven thirty that evening all the official entries had signed in, and the great downstairs hall was crowded as we waited for Senator Foxhall to come downstairs to lead the way into the dining room. On time, the old man came down

416

the wide stairs, clutching his housekeeper's arm tightly for support. A slight, spare man, not much taller than a fifteen-year-old boy, he still managed to hold himself rigidly erect. In his old-fashioned, broad-lapeled dinner jacket and white piqué vest, he had an almost regal appearance. His pale blue eyes, deeply recessed now in his old age, were still alert and friendly behind his gold-rimmed glasses as he passed through the crowd. Somehow, he had preserved his hair, and his ivory mane was combed straight back from his high forehead in a well-groomed pompadour.

Ed Middleton, my partner and I were standing together. When the senator reached us, Ed introduced the old man to Omar.

'Oh, yes. Baradinsky? You're a Russian, aren't you?'

'No, sir,' Omar replied. 'Polish.'

'You look like a Russian.'

'It's probably the beard,' Omar said self-consciously.

'Maybe so. Anyway, you're in good hands with Frank Mansfield.' The senator smiled in my direction, exposing his blue-gray false teeth. 'You'll teach him our American ways, won't you, son?'

Smiling in return, I nodded my head. Omar's great-great-grandfather had emigrated to the United States, but it would have been useless to explain this fact to the senator.

Senator Foxhall nodded his head thoughtfully about twenty times before speaking again.

'Frank is a good man, Mr Baradinsky. I knew his grand-daddy. You listen to Frank and you'll learn something about gamecocks. Did you ever hear of Polish poultry?'

'Yes, sir.'

'Well, they don't come from Poland! I'll bet you didn't know that, did you?'

'No, sir, I didn't.'

'I didn't think you did,' the old man said gleefully. 'Not many people do. Did you know that, Ed?'

'I sure did, Senator,' Ed said, with a rueful laugh. 'I once tried to cross some frizzle-haired Polish cocks, and after losing three in the pit, I found out that they wouldn't face when they were hurt.'

'You should've come to me,' the old man said. 'I could've told you that and saved you some money.' He turned back to Omar. 'Cockfighting in Poland has never been up to standard, Mr Baradinsky. They don't feed them right. Same thing with Ireland. Gamecocks can't fight on raw potatoes, Mr Baradinsky.'

'I'll remember that,' Omar said blandly.

Mrs Pierce, the senator's housekeeper for more than thirty years, tugged on the old man's arm. 'We'd better go in to dinner now,' she reminded him. As the old couple turned away from us to lead the way into the dining room, Omar shrugged his shoulders helplessly, and winked at me. I grinned and nodded my head. Actually, my partner had shown considerable restraint. The senator had been correct in everything he said. If Omar had tried to argue with him, the old man would have cut him to shreds.

Except for Omar and myself, the guests seated around the dinner table were a rather eccentric group. I had known most of them for years, but even to me it seemed like an unusual gathering of people. All of us wore our entry numbers on the back of our coats. We needed these numbers in the pit as identification for the benefit of the spectators. But we also had to wear them at all times for Senator Foxhall. He knew our names, and he knew them well, but sometimes he had a tendency to forget them. When he did forget, he checked his typewritten list of entries against our numbers so he could address any one of us by name without embarrassment.

Senator Foxhall sat at the head of the long table, and Mrs Pierce was seated at the opposite end. Ed Middleton and Peach Owen were seated on either side of the senator.

Next to Ed was Buddy Waggoner, the second referee, who would preside over the drag pit.

By their entry numbers, the remaining guests were seated around the table, clockwise from Buddy Waggoner.

No. 1. Johnny McCoy and Colonel Bob Moore, USAF (Retired). Johnny McCoy and his partner, Colonel Bob, flew to meets all over the US from their fifty-thousand-acre ranch near Dan's Derrick, Texas, in a Lear jet. Colonel Bob, although he had been retired for at least ten years, still wore his Air Force blue uniform at all times. Only two days before, this Texas partnership had fought in the Northwest Cockfighting Tourney in Seattle, Washington. From there, they had flown back to Dan's Derrick and picked up fresh, newly conditioned gamecocks. They then had flown in to Macon. The senator's limousine and private game-fowl trailer had brought them from Macon to Milledgeville.

No. 2. Pete Chocolate, Pahokee, Florida. Except for the senator, Pete Chocolate was the only male guest wearing dinner clothes. He had spoiled the effect, however, by wearing a blue-and-white T-shirt under his black tuxedo jacket. And around his neck he wore an immaculate cream-colored ascot scarf.

No. 3. Dirty Jacques Bonin, Biloxi, Mississippi. There was nothing 'dirty' about Jacques Bonin's appearance. His suit was flawlessly tailored, and his spatulate nails were freshly manicured. Clean shaven and soberly attired, he looked like, and was, a church deacon. He had earned the appellation of Dirty Jacques during World War II when he had organized the gang of strikebreakers who killed or maimed eighty striking long-shoremen on the Mobile docks. He had never lived the name down, although his full-time occupation was now the breeding and fighting of Louisiana Mugs.

No. 4. Jack Burke. Dody sat beside her husband, and I sat next to her – one of Mrs Pierce's ideas. Dody spoke to me once, and only once, during dinner.

419

'Jack told me to apologize for kicking you at Plant City,' she whispered.

I waited politely for her to continue, but that was all she said.

Jack Burke also spoke to me during dinner, leaning forward in his chair and twisting his head in my direction.

'Let's make it an even thousand bet between Little David and your chicken, Frank. I've okayed it with Ed and Peach to have the hack immediately after the last tourney fight while the judges tote up the final scores. All right?'

When I nodded in agreement, he sat back in his chair.

No. 5. The English-Polish team of Mansfield and Baradinsky.

No. 6 Roy Whipple and his son, Roy, Jr. Mr Whipple was the old cockfighter who had shared the velvet love seat with me in the bridal suite of the Southerner Hotel in Chattanooga. He had lost a bundle in the holdup, but it hadn't dented his bankroll. The man owned three Asheville, North Carolina, resort hotels. Roy, Jr, was a senior at the University of North Carolina, Chapel Hill, and had obtained special permission from the dean of men to assist his father at the meet.

No. 7. Baldy Allen, of Columbus, Georgia, was the owner of several liquor stores. Breeding and fighting milk-white Doms was not only a sideline for Baldy, it was a profitable enterprise. His gregarious wife, Jean Ellen, who did his betting for him, accompanied Baldy everywhere.

No. 8. Johnny Norris, Birmingham, Alabama. Johnny was famous as a conditioner of game fowl, but I didn't consider him a first-rate handler. For fifteen years he had conditioned cocks for the late Ironclaw Burnstead. When Mr Burnstead died, he left Johnny three hundred thousand in cash and his entire flock of game fowl. In the past three years, Johnny had gained a reputation as an all-around cocker, and this was his first entry in the SC Tourney.

During dinner, I listened attentively to the conversation. All I heard was 'chicken talk.' The only subject that any of us had in common was cockfighting, and the love of cockfighting was the distinguishing feature of every entry. Every man present had the game fowl, the knowledge, the ability and the determination to win the tourney, but only one of us could win.

I intended to be that one.

Chapter Sixteen

Out of long habit more than anything else, I drank a quick cup of coffee in the dining-room the next morning and was in the cockhouse by five thirty. Gamecocks cooped for long periods in a small two-by-two stall have a tendency to get sleepy and bored. Too much lassitude makes a cock sluggish when pitted. To wake them up, I took each cock out of its coop and washed its head with a damp sponge dipped in cheap whiskey. By the time I finished the sponging at seven thirty, our game-cocks were skipping up and down inside their stalls with rejuvenated animation and crowing and clucking with happiness.

Omar joined me at eight, and a few minutes later Doc Riordan showed up at the cockhouse to wish me luck in the tourney. The pharmacist and my partner hit it off well together from the moment they met.

'I never miss the Southern Conference Tourney,' Doc told Omar, 'but all season long I've been chained to my desk. I'm the president of the Dixie Pharmaceutical Company, as Frank may have told you, and this year our firm is launching a new product.' He reached into his coat pocket and handed Omar a small white packet. 'Licarbo!' he said proudly. 'Advertising is our biggest head-ache, although the raising of capital isn't the simple matter it used to be.'

'Who handles your advertising?' Omar asked, tearing open the sample and cautiously tasting the product with the tip of his tongue.

'Unfortunately,' Doc sighed, 'I have to handle it myself. That's been my main trouble. But I'm a registered pharmacist, and most of the drugstores in Jax have allowed me to put my posters in their windows.'

'I think you've got a good idea here in Licarbo,' Omar said sincerely. 'After the tourney I won't have too much to do until April, and maybe you and I can get together on this product. I used to be in advertising in New York. Perhaps Frank told you?'

'No, he didn't.' Doc looked at me reproachfully. 'I didn't know Frank had himself a partner until I read the account of the Plant City Main between you-all and Jack Burke. Now, that was a main I wish I'd seen! That reminds me, Frank—' Doc took a small bottle of black-and-gray capsules out of his pocket and placed it on the workbench. 'These are energy capsules. I made 'em up for Mr Burke from a formula he gave me, and they should be good. They take about an hour for the best results, but when I made 'em up for Mr Burke's chickens, I said to myself: "While I'm at it, I'll just make up a batch for Frank Mansfield."'

'We appreciate it, Doctor,' Omar said – and then to me, 'The restaurant should be open by now. Let's get some breakfast.'

Shaking my head, I opened my gaff case on the workbench and started to polish gaffs with my conical grinding stone.

'I'll have some coffee with you, Mr Baradinsky,' Doc offered.

'Fine, I'd like to find out more about Licarbo.'

'Right now,' Doc said, 'advertising isn't quite as important as raising a little capital. However, I'd appreciate any advice you'd—'

'I'll bring you some coffee, Frank,' Omar said over his shoulder. 'Capital, Doctor, is simply a matter of devious stratagems worked out through a mathematical process known as pressure patterns peculiar to pecuniary people.'

As soon as they were out of earshot I opened the small bottle of energy capsules Doc had given me, dumped them on the floor, and crushed them into powder with my heel. The capsules might have been wonderful, but I wouldn't take any chances with them. Jack Burke knew that Doc Riordan was a friend of mine, and that fact alone was enough to make me distrust the medicine. Perhaps Jack Burke didn't have enough brains to plan anything so devious, but I wouldn't have used a strange product on my chickens whether Burke's name had been mentioned or not. A major tournament is not the place for experimentation.

As the parking lot filled slowly, I leaned against the locked door of our cockhouse and watched the arriving cars as they pulled in and parked under the directions of the attendants. By 9 a.m., when the time came for Omar and me to go over to the pit for the opening of the tourney, there was still no sign of either Bernice or Mary Elizabeth.

Tension was building up inside me, as it always does just before a meet, and I was happy when Peach Owen disengaged the mike, and handed it to Senator Foxhall. Peach played out the extra cord behind the senator as the old man marched stiffly to the center of the pit. The senator waited for silence, which didn't take very long. This early in the morning, there were only about two hundred spectators, but by two in the afternoon, the place would be jammed.

'Ladies and gentlemen,' Senator Foxhall said in his high reedy voice, 'welcome to the Southern Conference Tourney! We sincerely hope that all of you will have a good time. There is only one rule that you must observe during the meet.' He paused. 'Conduct yourselves like ladies and gentlemen.'

(Applause.)

'Before the tourney is over,' he said wryly, licking his thin lips, 'some of you may desire to place a small wager or two—'

(Laughter.)

'If you do, make certain you know the man you're betting with – there *may* be Internal Revenue agents in the crowd!'

(Laughter.)

The old man turned the hand microphone over to Peach Owen and returned to his chair beside the judge's box. For the remainder of the tourney he would sit there quietly, watching everything that went on with his deep-set, cold blue eyes. With those experienced eyes watching me, I knew I couldn't make a single mistake when I was in the pit.

I was elated when Peach Owen called over the PA system for entry Number Two and entry Number Five to report to the judge's box to pick up their weight slips. My tension disappeared. Now I could be busy.

The first match was 5:00 cocks. After getting our weight-slip, Omar and I double-timed back to the cock-house to heel our chicken. Time was going on from the second we received our weight slip, and only fifteen minutes were allowed to heel and be ready for the pitting. If an entry failed to make it on time, he forfeited that fight, and the next waiting, heeled pair was called. The fifteen-minute time limit kept the fights moving along fast. Where a match was even, or after ten minutes of fighting in the main pit, the two cocks were sent to the drag pit and a new pair was started in the center pit.

From the first pitting, I knew that the fight was going to be a long-drawn-out battle. Pete Chocolate matched a Spanish cross against my Mellhorn Black, and both birds were wary and overcautious. They did little damage to each other by the fourth pitting, and just before the fifth, when Ed Middleton saw that Roy Whipple and Baldy Allen were heeled and ready, he signaled for second referee Buddy Waggoner to start the next match and ordered us to follow him into the drag pit.

In the thirty-first pitting we went to breast after the third count of twenty, one hand under the bird only, at the center score.

'Get ready,' Ed Middleton said.

Pete and I faced each other across the two-foot score, both holding weary fighters with our right hand, and one foot above the ground. That's when the Indian made his first mistake.

'Pit!'

I dropped on signal and so did Pete, but Pete pushed, causing his Spanish to peck first because of the added impetus. I saw him plainly, but Ed missed it. Snapping my fingers I made a pushing gesture with my right palm and pointed to the straight-faced Seminole.

'I'm refereeing this fight, Mr Mansfield!' Ed snapped angrily. 'Handle!'

We picked up the cocks for the short rest period. I couldn't argue, but Ed had been alerted and he watched Pete closely during the next actionless pittings. There are no draws at the SCT, and I was beginning to think the fight was going to last all day when Pete just barely pushed his bird on the forty-fifth pitting. This time, Ed caught him at it.

'Foul! The winner is Number Five!'

'Foul?' Pete asked innocently. 'I committed a foul of some kind?'

'Pushing on the breast score. Are you trying to argue, Mr Chocolate?'

'I'm afraid I must, Mr Middleton,' Pete said with feigned bewilderment. Spreading his arms widely, Pete turned to the crowd of a dozen or so spectators who had followed the first fight into the drag pit. 'Did any of you gentlemen see me pushing?'

'That's a fifty-dollar fine for arguing. Anything else to say, Pete?'

Pete glowered at Ed for about ten seconds, and then shook his head. We carried our birds out, returning to our respective cockhouses. The door was open and my partner was attempting frantically to heel a 5:02 Roundhead by himself when I entered.

'Take over, Frank!' Omar said excitedly. 'Your drag lasted almost an hour, and we've got less than five minutes to meet Roy Whipple with a 5:02!'

I put the battered Mellhorn away, and while Omar held, I finished heeling the Roundhead. We made it to the weighing scales with two minutes to spare. During the long drag battle with Pete, three fights had been held in the main pit.

From the word 'Pit!' my Allen Roundhead lasted exactly twenty-five seconds with the Whipple cock before it was cut down in midair and killed.

The fighting was just as fast for the rest of the morning. If I didn't lose during the first three or four pittings I usually won the battle. My tough, relentless conditioning methods paid off with stamina. In a long go, my rock-hard gamecocks invariably outlasted their opponents. Every fight at Milledgeville was a battle between two Aces, however, and during the first three to five pittings, when both cocks were daisy fresh, it was anybody's fight. At 1 p.m., when a one-hour break for lunch was called, I had lost two and won three.

Omar and I left the pit together, planning to eat at the senator's house rather than wait for service in the crowded restaurant. As we left by the side entrance, a parking attendant came running over and caught up with us.

'Mr Mansfield, there's a lady down in the lot who asked me to find you.'

'Shall I go with you, Frank?' Omar said.

I nodded, and we followed the attendant into the parking lot.

It was Bernice Hungerford. As we approached her car, she got out, slammed the door and waited. Bernice looked much prettier than I remembered. Either she wore a tight girdle, or she had lost fifteen pounds. A perky, wheat-straw, off-the-face hat was perched atop a brand new permanent, and her dark hair gleamed with some kind of spray. She wore a mustard-colored tweed suit, softened at the throat by a lemon-yellow silk scarf. The air was chilly, but it wasn't cold enough for the full-length sheared beaver coat she held draped over her left arm.

When I accepted her white-gloved extended right hand, I noticed that it was trembling.

'I had to send for you, Frank,' she apologized, lifting her face to be kissed. I brushed her lips with mine, and she stepped back a pace, blushing like a girl. 'I've been here for more than an hour,' she said with a shy laugh. 'But when I went up to the entrance and saw all those men standing around – and no women – I was afraid to go inside!'

'You'll find a lot of ladies here, once you get inside, Miss—'

'Mrs Hungerford,' Bernice said self-consciously.

'Mrs Hungerford,' Omar said, 'I'm Frank's partner, Omar Baradinsky. And I'm glad the boy caught us in time. We were just leaving for lunch, and now you can join us.'

'I feel better already.' Bernice smiled. 'I started not to come, Frank.' She took my arm, and Omar relieved her of her heavy coat. 'Tommy couldn't get away, and I dreaded coming by myself, but now . . . Mr Baradinsky,' she turned impulsively to Omar on her left. 'Is there such a thing as a powder room around here?'

Omar laughed. 'If you can hold out for about five hundred more yards, Mrs Hungerford, you'll be made comfortable at the house.'

'Thank you. How do I look, Frank? How *does* a lady dress for a cockfight?'

'A woman as beautiful as you,' Omar said, 'could wear a sackcloth and still look like a queen.'

'Now I do feel better!' Bernice laughed gaily. 'What does one *do* at a cockfight!'

'At first, I'd advise you merely to watch. But if you decide to place a wager, let me know. Frank and I will be busy, but one of us will look after you when we're free.'

Thanks to my partner, the luncheon was a success. He was gracious and paternal toward Bernice, without being patronizing, and before we returned to the pit, she was no longer ill-at-ease or prattling with nervousness. When the fighting began, I rarely sat with her. Most of Omar's time was taken up with the placing of bets, payoffs and collections, but he joined her as often as he could.

There was another one-hour break at seven, and then the fights were to continue until midnight. According to the schedule – if everything went according to plan – the tourney would be completed by 3 p.m. the following afternoon. After the prizes and purses were awarded, the senator always held a free barbecue for everybody on the park-like lawn between his house and the cockpit.

We ate dinner, all three of us, in the restaurant. After dinner, Bernice begged off as a spectator from the evening fights. She was tired and bored from watching them. Without a basic understanding or knowledge of what to look for, Bernice's boredom was not unreasonable. Women rarely find cockfighting as exciting as men do.

Although I missed her friendly white-gloved wave and cheery cry of 'good luck' each time I entered the pit, I wasn't sorry to send her to the hotel in town. She promised to meet us at noon the following day, and I was relieved that I didn't have to entertain her until then.

The night fighting got bungled up.

There were two forfeits in the 5:12 weights, when Dirty Jacques Bonin and Jack Burke weren't heeled and ready on time, plus long technical arguments on both sides. To return to the cockpit after heeling, it was necessary to cross through the parking lot. Jack Burke claimed – and I think he had a reasonable point – that automobiles leaving the area after the ten-thirty fight had held him up. He failed to see why he should be penalized for a parking attendant's failure to control the traffic properly. Peach Owen brought out the rules and read them aloud. The rules stated clearly that the handler was to be ready for pitting within fifteen minutes after receiving his weight slip. No provisions had been written concerning interference, so Jack forfeited the fight after being promised by Peach Owen that this provision would be discussed by the S.C.T. committee before the next season.

Due to these delays, it was after one o'clock before Omar and I got back to our room in the mansion. I had lost four fights out of twelve, but my partner, who had placed shrewd bets on every match held during the day, had added two thousand eight hundred dollars to our bankroll.

'Are we going to win the tourney, Frank?' Omar said, as we undressed for bed.

Down to my underwear, I sat on the edge of my bed and checked over the official scorecard. Jack Burke, Roy Whipple and Johnny Norris were ahead of us, but they weren't so far ahead that we couldn't catch up with them the next day. I drew a large question mark on the blank side of the scorecard, sailed the square of cardboard in Omar's general direction and got wearily into bed. With a full day of fighting to go, the top three could just as easily be the bottom three when the points were tallied at the end of the meet.

Before Omar finished counting and stacking the money into neat piles on top of the dresser and switched off the overhead chandelier, I was sound asleep.

The next morning at eleven – during my third match of the second day – soft-spoken Johnny Norris was no longer a contender. His name was stricken from the lists, and he was barred forever from Southern Conference competition for ungentlemanly conduct.

At most Southern pits, the sidewalls are constructed of wood, but the sunken pit at Milledgeville has concrete walls. At a wooden-walled pit, when two cocks are fighting close to the barrier, it isn't unusual for one of the fighters to jab one of his gaffs into a board and get stuck.

Because of this possibility, cockpits with sixteen-inch wooden walls have a ground rule to 'handle' when an accident like this happens. The handler then pulls the gaff loose from the wall and, following a thirty-second rest period, the birds are pitted again.

There was no such rule at Milledgeville.

With a concrete pit, this ground rule was considered unnecessary. Unfortunately for Johnny Norris, after many years of operation, there were hairline cracks in the concrete wall. In the sixth pitting, my Claret drove Johnny's spangled Shuffler into the wall. During a quick flurry, the Shuffler hung a gaff into one of the narrow cracks. The long three-inch heel was wedged tight. The Shuffler was immobilized, with his head dangling down, about ten inches above the dirt floor of the pit.

Johnny looked angrily at Buddy and said: 'Handle, for Christ's sake!'

'No such rule at this pit.' Buddy shook his head stubbornly.

My Claret had backed away and was eyeing the upside-down bird, judging the distance. Advancing three short steps, he flew fiercely into the helpless Shuffler with both heels fanning. The fight was mine.

Johnny swung a roundhouse right and broke Buddy Waggoner's jaw.

After a near riot, order was restored when Senator Foxhall announced that he would stop the tourney and clear the pit if everybody didn't quiet down. Johnny Norris was taken off the SCT rolls and banished back to Birmingham. Because of Johnny's forced withdrawal, the remaining seven entries had to be reshuffled and rematched by the officials. This administrative work took more than an hour.

At one o'clock, when the lunch break was called, Mary Elizabeth still hadn't put in an appearance. I had made a nuisance out of myself by writing notes and checking periodically with the box office and parking attendants, but by 1 p.m. I had resigned myself that she wouldn't come.

I took Bernice to the house for lunch.

The rematching delay ruined the planned schedule. The last match between Roy Whipple and Colonel Bob Moore didn't start until three thirty. The moment the two cock-fighters entered the pit, Omar and I raced for our cock-house to heel Icky for the last hack between my bird and Burke's Little David.

When we returned to the pit, Jack Burke was already heeled and waiting. As the three of us stood in the doorway, watching the fight in progress, Jack looked contemptuously at Icky and said, 'Let's raise the bet to two thousand, Frank.'

Omar bridled. 'One thousand is the bet, Mr Burke. You've had Little David on a country walk all season, and Icky's had to fight to qualify. If there's any bet-changing to be done, you should give us some odds.'

'Are you asking for odds, Frank?' Burke challenged, ignoring my partner.

I shook my head. Holding Icky under my left arm, I pointed to the pit with my free hand. Colonel Bob was carrying out a dead chicken, and Ed Middleton was cutting the gaff tie strings away from Whipple's winner with his knife.

We reported to the judge's booth and weighed in. Icky was at fighting weight, an even 4:02. The freedom of the long rest on a farm walk had brought Little David's weight up from four pounds to 4:03. Omar protested the one-ounce overweight immediately, and Peach Owen ordered Burke to cut away feathers until his cock matched Icky exactly.

'While the results of the tourney are being tabulated and rechecked,' Peach drawled into the microphone with his deep southern voice, 'there'll be an extra hack for your pleasure. The weight is 4:02, short heels, between entries four and five!'

A murmur of approval and a scattering of applause encircled the packed tiers. The majority of the people in the audience were aware of the extra hack before the announcement. Omar had laughingly told me about some of the rumors he had heard. Some people thought that the hack was a simple grudge match, while others claimed that several thousand dollars had been bet between us. The reported incident at Plant City, when Dody had kicked me in the shins, had also caused a great many rumors. Supposedly, I had made a pass at Jack's wife, or Jack Burke had taken Dody away from me, or – wildest of all – Dody had been my childhood sweetheart. How man of thirty-three could possibly have had a childhood sweetheart of only sixteen didn't prevent the rumors. What Jack had spread about himself, or what people said about me, didn't matter. My only concern was to win the hack.

Ed Middleton examined both cocks, returned them to us, and told us to get ready.

'I've *been* ready!' Jack said.

I bobbed my head, and Ed said, 'Bill 'em!'

We billed the cocks on the center score.

'That's enough,' Ed said, when he saw how quickly the combativeness of both cocks was aroused. 'Pass 'em once and get ready.'

Holding our gamecocks at arm's length, we passed them in the air with a circling movement and retreated to our respective eight-foot scores.

'Pit!'

As usual, by watching the referee's lips, I let Icky go first, beating Burke off the score. I needed the split second. The O'Neal Red, with its dark red comb, and fresh from a country walk, was faster than Icky. Despite his superb condition, the days and nights in a narrow coop walk had slowed my Blue chicken down. Icky missed with both spurs as Little David side-stepped, and my cock wound up on his back with a spur in his chest.

'Handle!'

The second I disengaged the spur from Icky's breast, I retreated to my side of the pit and examined the wound. It wasn't fatal. Using the cellulose sponge and pan of clean water furnished by the pit, I wiped away the flowing blood, and pressed my thumb against the hole to stop the bleeding until the order came to get ready.

'Pit!'

Little David was overconfident and Icky was vigilant. The Red tried three aerial attacks and failed to get above my pitwise Blue. With mutual respect, they circled in tight patterns, heads low above the floor, hackles raised, glaring at each other with bright, angry eyes. Icky tried a tricky rushing feint that worked. As Little David wheeled and dodged instead of sidestepping, Icky walked up his spine like a lineman climbing a telephone pole. There was an audible thump as Icky struck a gaff home beneath Little David's right wing.

'Handle!'

Burke removed the gaff with gentle hands. The O'Neal Red had been hurt in the second pitting. The wound in Icky's chest no longer bled, but I held my thumb over the hole anyway, and made him stand quietly, facing him toward the wall where he couldn't see his opponent.

The third, fourth and fifth pittings were dance contests that could have been set to music. The two colorful game-cocks maneuvered, wheeled, sidestepped, feinted and leaped high into the air as they clashed. When one of them did manage to hang a heel, first one and then the other, the blow was punishing.

Prior to the sixth pitting, I held Icky's legs tight under his body to rest them, facing him toward the wall. I raised my eyes for a moment, and there sat Mary Elizabeth, not six feet away from me. I almost didn't recognize her at first. She was wearing a light blue coat with raglan sleeves, and she had a pastel-blue scarf over her blonde hair, tied beneath her chin. She sat in the second row – not in the seat I had reserved for her. Her skin was pale, and her expression was strained. As I smiled in recognition, Ed called for us to get ready, and I had to turn my back.

'Pit!'

For the first time in months I was second best in releasing my gamecock's tail. Little David outflew my Blue and fanned him down. On his back, Icky shuffled his feet like a cat. Both birds fell over, pronged together with all four gaffs, like knitting needles stuck into two balls of colored yarn.

'Handle!'

It took Burke and me almost a full minute to disengage the heels. Both cocks were severely injured and my hands were red with blood as I sponged my battered bird down gingerly with cold water. During the short rest period I didn't have time to exchange any love glances with my fiancée in the stands. Thirty seconds passed like magic.

'Get ready . . . Pit!'

Both gamecocks remained on their scores as we released them.

'Count!' Burke ordered.

'One, two, three, four, five, six, seven, eight, nine and one for Mr Burke. Handle!' Ed said, looking up from his wristwatch.

Both of us needed the additional thirty-second rest period. I sucked Icky's comb to warm his head, held his beak open wide and spat into his open throat to refresh him. I was massaging his tired legs gently when Ed told us to get ready.

'Pit!'

Stiff-winged, the two cocks advanced toward each other from their scores and clashed wearily in the center. Too sick and too tired for aerial fighting they buckled again and again with weakened fury. Little David fell over limply, breathing hard, and stayed there. Grateful for this respite, Icky also stopped fighting, standing quietly with his head down, bill touching the dirt.

'The count is going on,' Ed announced, watching his wristwatch and the two cocks at the same time. At the silent count of twenty seconds, when neither bird had tried to fight, Ed ordered us to handle.

I wanted to work feverishly, but I was unable to do the nursing needed to help my fighter. Rough nursing could put Icky out of the fight for good. I sponged him gently and let him rest. Icky had recovered considerably by himself from the twenty-second count.

When the order to pit was given again, he crossed the dirt floor toward his enemy on shaky legs. Little David squatted on his score like a broody hen on eggs, with his beak wide open, and his neck jerking in and out.

Icky pecked savagely at the downed cock's weaving head. An instant later, the maddened Little David bounced into the air as though driven by a compressed spring and came down on Icky's back with blurring, hard-hitting heels. My cock was uncoupled by a spine blow, paralyzed, and unable to move from the neck down. Little David's right one-and-a-quarter inch heel had passed cleanly through Icky's kidney and the point was down as far as the caeca. On the order to handle, I disengaged the gaff and returned to my score.

I didn't dare to sponge him. There was very little I could do. Water would make him bleed more rapidly than he was bleeding already. I held him loosely between my hands, pressing my fingers lightly into his hot body, afraid he would come apart in my hands. Fortunately, Little David was as badly injured as Icky. His last desperate attack had taken every ounce of energy he had left.

After three futile counts of twenty, Ed Middleton ordered us to breast on the center score, one hand only beneath the bird.

Which gamecock would peck first?

Which gamecock would die first?

It was an endurance test. Little David had been the last chicken to fight. If Icky died first, Little David would be declared the winner by virtue of throwing the last blow. On the third breast pitting, Icky stretched out his limp neck and pecked feebly. The order to handle was given. Again we pitted, and again Icky pecked, and this time he got a billhold on the other cock's stubby dubbed comb. Little David didn't feel or notice the billhold. Little David was dead. And so was Icky, his beak clamped to the Red's comb to the last.

'I'll carry my bird out,' Jack Burke said.

'You're entitled to three more twenty-second counts,' Ed reminded him, going by the book.

'What's the use?' Burke said indifferently. 'They're *both* dead, now.'

'Dead or not,' Ed said officially, 'you're entitled by the rules to three counts of twenty after the other cock pecks.'

Without another word Jack Burke picked up his dead gamecock and left the pit. I picked up the Blue and held him to my chest. His long neck dangled limply over my left arm. My eyes were suddenly, irrationally, humid with tears.

'That's what I call a dead-game chicken, Frank!' Senator Foxhall called out from the judge's box.

I nodded blindly in his general direction and then turned my back on the old man to look for Mary Elizabeth. She wasn't in her seat. I caught a glimpse of her blue topcoat as she hurried out through the side entrance to the parking lot. I ran after her and caught up with her running figure just beyond the closed, shuttered box office.

'Mary Elizabeth!' I said aloud. My voice sounded rusty, strangled, different, nothing at all like I remembered it.

She stopped running, turned and faced me, her face like a mask. Her lips were as bloodless as her face.

'You've decided to talk again? Is that it? It's too late now, Frank. And I know now that it was always too late for us. You aren't the man I fell in love with, but you *never* were! If I'd seen you in the cockpit ten years ago, I would've known then. I didn't watch those poor chickens fight, Frank, I watched your face. It was awful. No pity, no love, no understanding, nothing! Hate! You hate everything, yourself, me, the world, everybody!'

She closed her eyes to halt the tears. A moment later she opened her purse and wiped her eyes with a small white handkerchief.

'And I gave myself to you, Frank,' she said, as though she were speaking to herself. 'I gave you everything I had to offer, everything, to a man who doesn't even have a heart!'

I didn't know this woman. I had never seen her before. This was a Mary Elizabeth I had hidden from myself all these years.

I dropped my dead Blue chicken to the ground, put my left heel on its neck, reached down, and jerked off his head with my right hand. I held the beaten, bloody, but never, never bowed head out to Mary Elizabeth in my palm. I had nothing else to say to the woman.

Mary Elizabeth licked her pale lips. She took Icky's head from my hand and wrapped it in her white handkerchief. Tucking the wrapped head away in her purse, she nodded.

'Thank you. Thank you very much, Frank Mansfield. I'll accept your gift. When I get home, I'll preserve it in a jar of alcohol. I might even work out some kind of ritual, to remind myself what a damned fool I've been.'

Her emerald eyes burned into mine for a moment.

'My brother's been right about you all along, but I had to drive up here to find out for myself. You're everything he said you were, Frank Mansfield. A mean, selfish son of a bitch!'

Turning abruptly, she headed toward the rows of parked cars. After only a few steps, she broke into a wobbling, feminine run. I don't know how long I stood there, looking after her retreating figure, even after she had passed from sight. A minute, two minutes, I don't know.

A voice blared over the outside speakers of the PA system: 'MR ROY WHIPPLE AND MR FRANK MANSFIELD. REPORT TO THE JUDGE'S BOX, PLEASE!' The announcement was repeated twice, and I heard it, but I didn't pay any attention to the amplified voice. I was immobilized by thought. I've grown up, I reflected. After thirty-three years, I was a mature individual. I had never needed Mary Elizabeth, and she had never needed me. Finally, it was all over between us – whatever it was we thought we had. My last tie with the past and Mansfield, Georgia, was broken. From now on I could look toward the future, and it had never been any brighter—

He must have made some noise, but I didn't hear Omar's feet crunching on the gravel until he grabbed my arm.

'For God's sake, Frank,' Omar said excitedly. 'What the hell are you standing out here for? Senator Foxhall's awarding you the Cockfighter of the Year award! Let's go inside, man! As your partner, I'm entitled to a little reflected glory, you know.'

Now that he had my attention, he smiled broadly, his white teeth gleaming through his black moustache. 'Of course,' he shrugged, 'Old Man Whipple won the tourney, but what do we care? Thanks to Icky's victory, we're loaded!' He patted his bulging jacket pockets. 'We've got so damned much money, I'm almost afraid to count it.'

Smiling, I gestured for him to go on ahead of me. Omar turned toward the entrance and trotted down the short hallway to the pit.

When I reached the doorway, I paused. After the barbecue was over, I would ask Bernice to go to Puerto Rico with me for a month or so. If it got dull in Puerto Rico, we could swing on down to Caracas, and I might be able to pick up some Spanish Aces for next season. Omar could put our proven birds out on their Alabama walks without any assistance from me. And then, if I returned from South America by the middle of April, I would be back in plenty of time to start working with the spring stags.

Across the pit, standing behind the referee's table in front of the judge's box, the two greatest game fowl men in the world were waiting for me. Senator Foxhall and Ed Middleton. To the left of the table, Peach Owen was holding the leather box that contained my award.

Well, they could wait a little longer.

As I neared her seat in the front row, Bernice smiled and said, 'Congratulations, Frank!'

'Thanks,' I replied.

'Oh!' she said, her eyes widening with astonishment. 'You – you've got your voice back!'

'Yeah,' I said, grinning at her expression, 'and you'll probably wish I hadn't.'

'I – I don't know what you mean.'

'You'll find out that I'm quite a talker, Bernice, once I get wound up. How'd you like to go to Puerto Rico for a few weeks?'

'Right now,' she said, 'I'm so confused that the only answer I can think of on the spur of the moment is "Yes."'

I laughed and turned away, joy burbling out of my throat. How good to talk again, to *laugh* again!

I jerked my jacket down in back and pushed my white hat back on my head at a careless angle. Then, squaring my shoulders, I crossed the empty pit to get my goddamned medal.

BOOK THREE

The Burnt Orange Heresy

Nothing exists,
If anything exists, it is incomprehensible,
If anything was comprehensible,
it would be incommunicable.

Gorgias

For the late, great Jacques Debierue, c. 1886–1970
Memoria in aeterna

PART ONE

Nothing exists

Chapter One

Two hours ago the Railway Expressman delivered the crated, newly published *International Encyclopedia of Fine Arts* to my Palm Beach apartment. I signed for the set, turned the thermostat of the air conditioner up three degrees, found a clawhammer in the kitchen, and broke open the crate. Twenty-four beautiful buckram-bound volumes, eggshell paper, deckle edged. Six laborious years in preparation, more than twenty-five hundred illustrations – 436 in full-color plates – and each thoroughly researched article written and signed by a noted authority in his specific field of art history.

Two articles were mine. And my name, James Figueras, was also referred to by other critics in three more articles. By quoting me, they gained authoritative support for their own opinions.

In my limited visionary world, the world of art criticism, where there are fewer than twenty-five men – and no women – earning their bread as full-time art critics (art reviewers for newspapers don't count), my name as an authority in this definitive encyclopedia means Success with an upper-case S. I thought about it for a moment. Only twenty-five full-time art critics in America, out of a population of more than two hundred million? This is a small number, indeed, of men who are able to look at art and understand it, and then interpret it in writing in such a way that those who care can share the aesthetic experience.

Clive Bell claimed that art was 'significant form.' I have no quarrel with that, but he never carried his thesis out to its obvious conclusion. It is the critic who makes the form(s) significant to the viewer! In seven more months I will reach my thirty-fifth birthday. I am the youngest authority with signed articles in the new *Encyclopedia*, and, I realized at that moment, if I lived long enough I had every opportunity of becoming the greatest art critic in America – and perhaps the world. With tenderness, I removed the heavy volumes from the crate and lined them up on my desk.

The complete set, if ordered by subscribers in advance of the announced publication date – and most universities, colleges, and larger public libraries would take advantage of the prepublication offer – sold for $350, plus shipping charges. After publication date, the *Encyclopedia* would sell for $500, with the option of buying an annual volume on the art of that year for only $10 (same good paper, same attractive binding).

It goes without saying, inasmuch as my field is contemporary art, that my name will appear in all of those yearbooks.

I had read the page proofs months before, of course, but I slowly reread my 1,600-word piece on art and the preschool child with the kind of satisfaction that any well-done professional job provides a reader. It was a tightly summarized condensation of my book, *Art and the Preschool Child*, which, in turn, was a rewritten revision of my Columbia Master's thesis. This book had launched me as an art critic, and, at the same time, the book was a failure. I say that the book was a failure because two colleges of education in two major universities adopted the book as a text for courses in child psychology, thereby indicating a failure on the part of the educators concerned to understand the thesis of the book, children, and psychology. Nevertheless, the book had enabled me to escape from the teaching of art history and had put me into full-time writing as an art critic.

Thomas Wyatt Russell, managing editor of *Fine Arts: The Americas*, who had read and understood the book, offered me a position on the magazine as a columnist and contributing editor, with a stipend of four hundred dollars a month. And *Fine Arts: The Americas*, which loses more than fifty thousand dollars a year for the foundation that supports it, is easily the most successful art magazine published in America – or anywhere else, for that matter. Admittedly, $400 a month is a niggardly sum, but my name on the masthead of this prestigious magazine was the wedge I needed at the time to sell freelance articles to other art magazines. My income from the latter source was uneven, of course, but with my assured monthly pittance it was enough – so long as I remained single, which was my avowed intention – to avoid teaching, which I despised, and enough to avoid the chilly confinement of museum work – the only other alternative open to those who selected art history as graduate degrees. There is always advertising, of course, but one does not deliberately devote one's time to the in-depth study of art history needed for a graduate degree to enter advertising, regardless of the money to be made in that field.

I closed the book, pushed it to one side, and then reached for Volume III. My fingers trembled – a little – as I lit a cigarette. I knew why I had lingered so long over the preschool child piece, even though I hated to admit it to myself. For a long time (I said to myself that I was only waiting to finish my cigarette first), I was physically unable to open the book to my article on Jacques Debierue. Every evil thing Dorian Gray did appeared on the face of his closeted portrait, but in my case, I wonder sometimes if there is a movie projector in a closet somewhere whirring away, showing the events of those two days of my life over and over. Evil, like everything else, should keep pace with the times, and I'm not a turn-of-the-century dilettante like

Dorian Gray. I'm a professional, and as contemporary as the glaring Florida sun outside my window.

Despite the air-conditioning I perspired so heavily that my thick sideburns were matted and damp. Here, in this beautiful volume, was the bitter truth about myself at last. Did I owe my present reputation and success to Debierue, or did Debierue owe his success and reputation to me?

'Wherever you find ache,' John Heywood wrote, 'thou shalt not like him.' The thought of Debierue made me ache all right – and I did not like the ache, nor did I like myself. But nothing, nothing in this world, could prevent me from reading my article on Jacques Debierue . . .

Chapter Two

Gloria Bentham didn't know a damned thing about art, but that singularity did not prevent her from becoming a successful dealer and gallery owner in Palm Beach. To hold her own, and a little more, where there were thirty full-time galleries open during the 'season', was more than a minor achievement, although the burgeoning art movement in recent years has made it possible to sell almost any artifact for some kind of sum. Nevertheless, it is more important for a dealer to understand people than it is to understand art. And Gloria, skinny, self-effacing, plain, had the patient ability to listen to people – a characteristic that often passes for understanding.

As I drove north toward Palm Beach on A1A from Miami, I thought about Gloria to avoid thinking about other things, but without much satisfaction. I had taken the longer slower route instead of the Sunshine parkway because I had wanted the extra hour or so it would take to sort out my thoughts about what I would write about Miami art, and to avoid, for an additional hour, the problem – if it was still a problem – of Berenice Hollis. Nothing is simple, and the reason I am a good critic is that I have learned the deep, dark secret of criticism. Thinking, the process of thinking, and the man thinking are all one and the same. And if this is true, and I live as though it is, then the man painting, the painting, and the process of painting are also one and the same. No one, and nothing, is ever simple, and Gloria had been anxious, too anxious, for me to get back to Palm Beach to attend the preview of her new show. The show was not important, nor was the idea unique. It was merely logical.

She was having a tandem showing of naive Haitian art and the work of a young Cleveland painter named Herb Westcott, who had spent a couple of months in Pétionville, Haiti, painting the local scene. The contrast would make Westcott look bad, because he was a professional, and it would make the primitives look good, because they were naively unprofessional. She would sell the primitives for a 600 percent markup over what she paid for them and, although most of the buyers would bring them back after a week or so (not many people can live with Haitian primitives), she would still make a profit. And, for those collectors who could not stand naive art, Westcott's craftsmanship would look so superior to the Haitians that he would undoubtedly sell a few more pictures in a tandem exhibit than he would in a one-man show without the advantage of the comparison.

By thinking about Gloria I had avoided, for a short while, thinking about Berenice Hollis. My solution to the problem of Berenice was one of mild overkill, and I half-hoped it had worked and half-hoped that it had not. She was a high school English teacher (eleventh grade) from Duluth, Minnesota, who had flown down to Palm Beach for a few weeks of sun-shiny convalescence after having a cyst removed from the base of her spine. Not a serious operation, but she had sick leave accumulated, and she took it. Her pale pink skin had turned gradually to saffron, and then to golden maple. The coccyx scar had changed from an angry red to gray and finally to slightly puckered grisaille.

Our romance had passed through similar shades and tints. I met Berenice at the Four Arts Gallery, where I was covering a traveling Toulouse-Lautrec exhibit, and she refused to go back to Duluth. That would have been all right with me (I could not, in all honesty, encourage anyone to return to Duluth), but I had made the mistake of letting her move in with me, a foolish decision which had seemed like a great idea at the time. She was a large – strapping is a better word – country girl with a ripe figure, cornflower-blue eyes, and a tangle of wheat-colored hair flowing down her back. Except for the thumbtack scar on her coccyx, which was hardly noticeable, her sun-warmed sweet-smelling hide was flawless. Her blue eyes looked velvety, thanks to her contact lenses. But she wasn't really good-natured, as I had thought at first, she was merely lazy. My efficiency apartment was too damned small for one person, let alone two, and she loomed in all directions. Seeing her dressed for the street or a party, no one would believe that Berenice was such a mess to live with – clothes strewn over every chair, wet bath towels, bikinis on the floor, the bathroom reeking of bath salts, powder, perfume, and unguents, a tangy mixture of smells so overpowering I had to hold my nose when I shaved. The state of the pullman kitchen was worse. She never washed a cup, dish, pot, or pan, and once I caught her pouring bacon grease into the sink.

I could live with messiness. The major problem in having Berenice around all the time was that I had to do my writing in the apartment.

It had taken all of my persuasive abilities to talk Tom Russell into letting me cover the Gold Coast for the season. (The official 'season' in Palm Beach begins on New Year's Eve with a dull dinner-dance at the Everglades Club, and it ends fuzzily on 15 April). When Tom agreed, finally, he refused to add expenses to my salary. I had to survive in Palm Beach on my monthly stipend, and pay my air fare down out of my small savings (the remainder of my savings bought me a $250 car). By sub-letting my rent-controlled Village pad for almost twice as much as I was paying for it myself, I could get by. Barely.

I worked twice as hard, writing much better copy than I had in New York, to prove to Tom Russell that the Gold Coast was an incipient American art center that had been neglected far too long by serious art journals. Such was not truly the case, as yet, but there were scattered signs of progress. Most of the native painters of Florida were still dabbing out impressionistic palms and seascapes, but enough reputable painters from New York and Europe had discovered Florida for themselves, and the latter were exhibiting in galleries from Jupiter Beach to Miami. Enough painters, then, were exhibiting during the season to fill my *Notes* column on new shows, and at least one major artist exhibited long enough for me to honour him with one of my full-length treatments. There is money in Florida during the season, and artists will show anywhere there is enough money to purchase their work.

With Berenice around the tiny apartment all the time, I couldn't write. She would pad about barefooted, as quiet and as stealthy as a 140-pound mouse – until I complained. She would then sit quietly, placidly, not reading, not doing anything, except to stare lovingly at my back as I sat at my Hermes. I couldn't stand it.

'What are you thinking about, Berenice?'

'Nothing.'

'Yes, you are, you're thinking about me.'

'No, I'm not. Go ahead and write. I'm not bothering you.'

But she did bother me, and I couldn't write. I couldn't hear her breathing, she was so quiet, but I would catch myself listening to see if I *could* hear her. It took some mental preparation (I am, basically, a kind son of a bitch), but I finally, in a nice way, asked Berenice to leave. She wouldn't go. Later I asked her to leave in a harsh and nasty way. She wouldn't fight with me, but she wouldn't leave. On these occasions she couldn't even talk back. She merely looked at me, earnestly, with her welkin eyes wide open – the lenses sliding around – tears torrenting, suppressing, or making an effort to hold back, big, blubbery, gasping sobs – she was destroying me. I would leave the apartment, forever, and come back a few hours later for a reconciliation replay and a wild hour in the sack.

But I wasn't getting my work done. Work is important to a man. Not even a Helen of Troy can compete with a Hermes. No matter how wonderful she is, a woman is only a woman, whereas 2,500 words is an article. In desperation I issued Berenice an ultimatum. I told her that I was leaving for Miami, and that when I came back twenty-four hours later I wanted her the hell out of my apartment and out of my life.

And now I was returning seventy-two hours later, having added two extra days as insurance. I expected her to be in the apartment. I wanted her to be there and, paradoxically, I wanted her to be gone forever.

I parked in the street, put the canvas top up on the Chevy – a seven-year-old convertible – and started across the flagged patio to the stuccoed outside staircase. Halfway up the stairs I could hear the phone ringing in my apartment on the second floor. I stopped and waited while it rang three more times. Berenice would be incapable of letting a phone ring four times without answering it, and I knew that she was gone. Before I got the door unlocked the ringing stopped.

Berenice was gone and the apartment was clean. It wasn't spotless, of course, but she had made a noble effort to put things in order. The dishes had been washed and put away and the linoleum floor had been mopped in a half-assed way.

There was a sealed envelope, with 'James' scribbled on the outside, propped against my typewriter on the card table by the window.

Dearest dearest James—

You are a bastard but I think you know that. I still love you but I will forget you – I hope I never forget the good things. I'm going back to Duluth – don't follow me there.

B.

If she didn't want me to follow her, why tell me where she was going?

There were three crumpled pieces of paper in the wastebasket. Rough drafts for the final note. I considered reading them, but changed my mind. I would let the final version stand. I crumpled the note and the envelope and added them to the wastebasket.

I felt a profound sense of loss, together with an unreasonable surge of anger. I could still smell Berenice in the apartment, and knew that her feminine compound of musk, sweat, perfume, pungent powder, lavender soap, bacon breath, Nose-cote, padded sachet coat hangers, vinegar, and everything else nice about her would linger on in the apartment forever. I felt sorry for myself and sorry for Berenice and, at the same time, a kind of bubbling elation that I was rid of her, even though I knew that I was going to miss her like crazy during the next few terrible weeks.

There was plenty of time before the preview at Gloria's Gallery. I removed my sport shirt, kicked off my loafers, and sat at the card table, which served as my desk, to go over my Miami notes. My three days in Dade County hadn't been wasted.

I had stayed with Larry Levine, in Coconut Grove. Larry was a printmaker I had known in New York, and his wife Paula was a superb cook. I would reimburse Larry with a brief comment about his new animal prints in my *Notes* column.

I had enough notes for a 2,500-word article on a 'Southern Gothic' environmental exhibit I had attended in North Miami, and an item on Harry Truman's glasses was a good lead-off piece for my back-of-the-book column. Larry had steered me to the latter.

A mechanic in South Miami, a Truman lover, had written to Lincoln Borglum, who had finished the monumental heads on Mount Rushmore after his father's death, and had asked the sculptor when he was going to add Harry Truman's head to the others. Lincoln Borglum, who apparently had a better sense of humor than his late father, Gutzon, claimed, in a facetious reply, that he was unable to do so because it was too difficult to duplicate Harry Truman's glasses. The mechanic, a man named Jack Wade, took Borglum at his word, and made the glasses himself.

They were enormous spectacles, more than twenty-five feet across, steel frames covered with thickly enameled ormolu. The lenses were fashioned from twindex windows, the kind with a vacuum to separate the two panes of glass.

'The vacuum inside will help keep the lenses from fogging up on cold days,' Wade explained.

I had taken three black-and-white Polaroid snapshots of Wade and the glasses, and one of the photos was sharp enough to illustrate the item in my column. The spectacles were a superior job of craftsmanship, and I had suggested to Mr Wade that he might sell them to an optician for advertising purposes. The suggestion made him angry.

'No, by God,' he said adamantly. 'These glasses were made for Mr Truman, when his bust is finished on Mount Rushmore!'

The phone rang.

'Where have you been?' Gloria's voice asked shrilly. 'I've been calling you all afternoon. Berenice said you left and that you might never come back.'

'When did you talk to Berenice?'

'This morning, about ten thirty.'

This news hit me hard. If I had returned in twenty-four hours, in forty-eight, or sixty – I'd still have Berenice. My timing had been perfect, but a pang was there.

'I've been in Miami, working. But Berenice has left and won't be back.'

'Lovers' quarrel? Tell Gloria all about it.'

'I don't want to talk about it, Gloria.'

She laughed. 'You're coming to the preview?'

'I told you I would. What's so important about second-hand Haitian art that you've had to call me all day?'

'Westcott's a good painter, James, he really is, you know. A first-rate draughtsman.'

'Sure.'

'You sound funny. Are you all right?'

'I'm fine. And I'll be there.'

'That's what I wanted to talk to you about. Joseph Cassidy will be there, and he's coming because he wants to meet you. He told me so. You know who Mr Cassidy is, don't you?'

'Doesn't everybody?'

'No, not everybody. Not everybody needs him!' She laughed. 'But he's invited us – you and me and a few others – to supper at his place after the preview. He has a penthouse at the Royal Palm Towers.'

'I know where he lives. Why does he want to meet me?'

'He didn't say. But he's the biggest collector to ever visit *my* little gallery, and if I could land him as a patron I wouldn't need any others—'

'Don't sell him any primitives, then, or Westcotts.'

'Why not?'

'He isn't interested in conventional art. Don't try to sell him anything. Wait until I talk to him, and then I'll suggest something to you.'

'I appreciate this, James.'

'It's nothing.'

'Are you bringing, Berenice?'

'I don't want to *talk* about it, Gloria.'

She was laughing as I racked the phone.

Chapter Three

As much as I dislike the term 'freeloader,' no other word fits what I had become during my sojourn on the Gold Coast. There are several seasonal societal levels in Palm Beach, and they are all quite different from the social groups, divided uneasily by the Waspish and Jewish groupings found in Miami and Miami Beach. In Lauderdale, of course, the monied class is squarely WASP.

I belonged to none of the 'groups,' but I was on the periphery of all of them by virtue of my calling. I met people at art show previews, where cocktails are usually served, and because I was young, single, and had an acceptable profession, I was frequently invited to dinners, cocktail parties, polo games, boat rides, late supper, and barbecues. These invitations, which led to introductions to other guests, usually produced additional dinner invitations. And a few of the Gold Coast artists, like Larry Levine, for example, were people I had known in New York.

After two months in Florida I had many acquaintances, or connections, but no friends. I did not return any of the dinner invitations, and I had to avoid bars, night clubs, and restaurants where I might get stuck with a check. The man who never picks up a check does not acquire friends.

Nevertheless, I felt that my various hosts and hostesses were recompensed for my presence at their homes. I put up genially with bores, I was an extra man at dinners where single, heterosexual young men were at a premium, and when I was in a good mood, I could tell stories or carry conversation over dead spots.

I had two dinner jackets, a red silk brocade and a standard white linen. There were lipstick mouthings on the white jacket, where a tipsy Berenice had bitten me on the shoulder while I was driving back from a party. I was forced, then, to wear the red brocade.

As I walked the six blocks from my apartment to Gloria's gallery, I speculated on Joseph Cassidy's invitation to supper. A social invitation wasn't unusual, but she had said that he wanted to meet me, and I wondered why. Cassidy was not only famous as a collector, he was famous as a criminal lawyer. It was the huge income from his practice in Chicago that had enabled him to build his art collection.

He had one of the finest private collections of contemporary art in America, and the conclusion I came to, which seemed reasonable at the time, was that he might want to hire me to write a catalogue for it. And if he did not want to see me about that (to my knowledge, no catalogue had been published on his collection), I had a good mind to suggest it to him. The task would pay off for me, as well as for Cassidy, in several ways. I could make some additional money, spend a few months in Chicago, do some writing on midwestern art and artists, and my name on the published catalogue would enhance my career.

The more I thought about the idea the more enthusiastic I became, but by the time I reached the gallery my enthusiasm was tempered by the knowledge that I could not broach the suggestion to him. If he suggested it, fine, but I could not ask a man for employment at a social affair without a loss of dignity.

And what else did I have to offer a man in Cassidy's position? My pride (call it *machismo*) in myself, which I overrated and which I knew was often phony, was innate, I supposed – a part of my heritage from my Puerto Rican father. But the pride was there, all the same, and I had passed up many opportunities to push myself by considering first, inside my head, what my father would have done in similar circumstances.

By the time I reached the gallery, I had pushed the idea out of my mind.

Gloria forced her thin lips over her buck teeth, brushed my right sideburn with her mouth, and, capturing my right arm in a painful armlock, led me to the bar.

'Do you know this man, Eddy?' she said to the bartender.

'No,' Eddy shook his head solemnly, 'but his drink is familiar.' He poured two ounces of Cutty Sark over two ice cubes and handed me the Dixie cup.

'Thanks, Eddy.'

Eddy worked the day shift at Hiram's Hideaway in South Palm Beach, but he was a popular bartender and was hired by many hostesses during the season for parties at night. I usually ran into him once or twice a week at various places. Everybody, I thought, needs something extra nowadays. A regular job, and something else. Gloria, for example, wouldn't have been able to pay the high seasonal rent on her gallery if she didn't occasionally rent it out in the evenings for poetry readings and encounter-group therapy sessions. She detested these groups, too. The people who needed to listen to poetry, or tortured themselves in encounter-group sessions were all chain smokers, she claimed, who didn't use the ashtrays she provided.

Eddy worked at a sheet-covered card table. There was Scotch, bourbon, gin and vermouth for martinis, and a plastic container of ice cubes behind the table. I moved back to give someone else a chance, and picked up a mimeographed catalogue from the table in the foyer. Gloria was greeting newcomers at the door, bringing them to the table to sign her guest book, and then to the bar.

Her previews were not exclusive by any means. In addition to her regular guest list for previews, she gave invitations to Palm Beach hotel PR directors to hand out to guests who might be potential buyers. The square hotel guests, 'honoured' by being given printed preview invitations to a private show, and thrilled by the idea that they were seeing 'real' Palm Beach society at an art show preview, occasionally purchased a painting. And when they did, the publicity director of the hotel they came from received a sports jacket or a new pair of Daks from Gloria. As a consequence, the preview crowd at Gloria's gallery was often a weird group. There were even a couple of teenage girls from Palm Beach Junior College peering anxiously at the primitives and writing notes with ballpoints in Blue Horse notebooks.

Herbert Westcott, I learned from the catalogue, was twenty-seven years old, a graduate of Western Reserve who had also studied at the Art Students League in New York. He had exhibited in Cleveland, the Art Students League, and Toronto, Canada. A Mr Theodore L. Canavin of Philadelphia had collected some of his work. This exhibit, recent work done in Haiti during the past three months, was Westcott's first one-man show. I looked up from the catalogue and spotted the artist easily. He was short – about five seven – well tanned, with a skimpy, light brown beard. He wore a six-button, powder blue Palm Beach suit, white shoes, and a pale pink body shirt without a tie. He was eavesdropping on a middle-aged couple examining his largest painting – a Port-au-Prince market scene that was two-thirds lemon sky.

He drew well, as Gloria had said, but he had let his colors overlap by dripping to give the effect of fortuitous accident to his compositions. The drips – a messy heritage from Jackson Pollock – were injudicious. He had talent, of course, but talent is where a painter starts. His Haitian men and women were in tints and shades of chocolate instead of black, something I might not have noticed if it

465

had not been for the Haitian paintings on the opposite wall, where the figures were black indeed.

The dozen Haitian paintings Gloria had rounded up were all suprisingly good. She even had an early Marcel, circa 1900, so modestly different from the contemporary primitives, with their bold reds and yellows, it riveted one's attention. The scene was typically Haitian, some thirty people engaged in voodoo rites, with a bored, comical goat as a central focusing point, but the picture was painted in gray, black, and white – no primary colors at all. Marcel, as I recalled, was an early primitive who had painted his canvases with chicken feathers because he could not afford brushes. It was priced at only fifteen hundred dollars, and someone would get a bargain if he purchased the Marcel . . .

'James,' Gloria clutched my elbow, 'I want you to meet Herb Westcott. Herb, this is Mr Figueras.'

'How do you do?' I said, 'Gloria, where did you get the Marcel?'

'Later,' she said. 'Talk to Herb.' She turned away, with her long freckled right arm outstretched to a tottering old man with rouged cheeks.

Westcott fingered his skimpy beard. 'I'm sorry I didn't recognize you before, Mr Figueras – Gloria told me you were coming – but I thought you wore a beard . . .'

'It's the picture in my column. I should replace the photo, I suppose, but it's a good one and I haven't got another one yet. I had my beard for about a year before I shaved it. You shouldn't tug at your beard, Mr Westcott . . .'

He dropped his hand quickly and shuffled his feet.

'I worked it all out, Mr Westcott, and found that a beard would add about six weeks to my life, that is, six full weeks of shaving time saved in a lifetime, seven weeks if one uses an electric razor. But it wasn't worth it. Like you, I could hardly keep my fingers off the damned thing, and my neck itched all the time. The secret, they say, is never to touch your beard. And if you've already got that habit, Mr Westcott, your beard is doomed.'

'I see,' he said shyly. 'Thanks for the advice.'

'Don't worry,' I added, 'you probably look handsomer without one.'

'That's what Gloria said. Here,' he took my empty Dixie cup – 'let me get you a fresh drink. What are you drinking?'

'Eddy knows.'

I turned back to examine the Marcel again. I wanted to leave. The small high-ceilinged room, which seemed smaller now as it began to get crowded, was jammed with loud-voiced people, and I did not want to talk to Westcott about his paintings. That's why I got off onto the beard gambit. They were all derivative, which he knew without my telling him. The entire show, including the Marcel, wasn't worth more than one column inch (I folded the catalogue and shoved it into my hip pocket), unless I got desperate for more filler to make the column come out to an even two thousand words.

Gloria was standing by the bar, together with a dozen other thirsty guests. Poor Westcott, who was paying for the liquor, hovered on the outskirts trying to get Eddy's attention. I took the opportunity to slip into the foyer and then out the door. I was on Worth Avenue in the late twilight, and heading for home. If Mr Cassidy wanted to meet me, he could get my telephone number from Gloria and call for an appointment.

Twilight doesn't last very long in Florida. By the time I reached my ocherous pre-depression stucco apartment house – a mansion in the twenties, now cut up into small apartments – my depression was so bad I had a headache. I took off my jacket and sat on a concrete bench beneath a tamarisk tree in the patio and smoked a cigarette. The ocean wind was warm and soft. A few late birds twittered angrily as they tried to find roosting places in the crowded tree above my head. I was filling with emptiness up to my eyes, but not to the point of overflowing. Old Mrs Weissberg, who lived in No. 2, was limping down the flagstone path toward my bench. To avoid talking to her I got up abruptly, climbed the stairs, heated a Patio Mexican Dinner for thirty minutes in the oven, ate half of it, and went to bed. I fell asleep at once and slept without dreams.

Chapter Four

Gloria shook me awake and switched on the lamp beside the Murphy bed. She had let herself in with the extra key I kept hidden in the potted geranium on the porch. She had either witnessed Berenice using the key or heard her mention that one was there. I blinked at Gloria in the sudden light, trying to pull myself together. My heart was still fluttering, but the burbling fear of being wakened in the dark was gradually going away.

'I'm sorry, James,' Gloria said briskly, 'but I knocked and you didn't answer. You really ought to get a doorbell, you know.'

'Try phoning next time. I almost always get up to answer the phone, in case it might be something unimportant.' I didn't try to conceal the irritation in my voice.

My cigarettes were in my trousers, which were hanging over the back of the straight chair by the coffee table. I slept nude, with just a sheet over me, but because I was angry as well as in need of a smoke, I threw the sheet off, got up and fumbled in the pockets of my trousers for my cigarettes. I lit one and tossed the match into the stoneware ashtray on the coffee table.

'This is important to me, James. Mr Cassidy came and you weren't there. He asked about you and I told him you had a headache and left early—'

'True.'

Gloria wasn't embarrassed by my nakedness, but now I felt self-conscious, standing bare-assed in the center of the room, smoking and carrying on a moronic conversation.

Gloria was in her late forties, and had been married for about six months to a hardware-store owner in Atlanta, so it wasn't her first time to see a man without any clothes on. Nevertheless, I took a terry-cloth robe out of the closet and slipped into it.

'He wants you to come to supper, James. And here I am, ready to take you.'

'What time is it, anyway?'

'About ten forty.' She squinted at the tiny hands on her platinum wristwatch. 'Not quite ten forty-five.'

I felt refreshed and wide-awake, although I had only slept two hours. Being awakened that way, so unexpectedly, had stirred up my adrenalin.

'I think you're overstating the case, Gloria. What, precisely, did Mr Cassidy say to make you so positive he wanted me – in particular – to come to his little gathering?'

She rubbed her beaky nose with a skinny forefinger and frowned. 'He said, "I hope that Mr Figueras' headache won't keep him from coming over this evening for a drink." And I said, "Oh, no. He asked me to pick him up later at his apartment. James is very anxious to meet you."'

'I see. You turned a lukewarm chunk of small talk into a big deal. And now I have to go with you to get you off the hook.'

'I wouldn't put it that way. He bought a picture from me, James, one of the primitives – the big one with the huge pile of different kinds of fruit. For his colored cook to hang in the kitchen.'

'No Westcotts?'

'He didn't like Herb's pictures very much. I could tell, although he didn't say anything one way or another.'

'I think he did. Buying a Haitian primitive for his cook says something, don't you think? Do I need another shave?'

She felt my chin with the tips of her fingers. 'I don't think so. Brush your teeth, though. Your breath is simply awful.'

'That's from the Mexican dinner I had earlier.'

I dressed in gray slacks, a white shirt, and brown leather tie, dark brown loafers, and a gray-and-white striped seersucker jacket, resolving to take my soiled dinner jacket to the cleaner's in the morning. I remember how calm I was, and how well my mind seemed to be functioning after only two hours of sleep. All of my muscles were loose and stretchy. There was a spring to my step, as though I were wearing cushioned soles. I was in a pleasant mood, so much so that I pinched old Gloria through her girdle as we left the apartment.

'Oh, for God's sake, James!'

As we drove toward the Royal Palm Towers, a seven-story horror of poured concrete, in Gloria's white Pontiac, I found myself looking forward to meeting Mr Cassidy and to seeing his paintings. He was bound to have a few pictures in his apartment, although his famous collection was safe in Chicago. I wondered, as well, why he had elected to live in the Royal Palm Towers, which overlooked Lake Worth instead of the Atlantic. He would be able to see the Atlantic from his rooftop patio, but only from a distance, and that wasn't the same as being on the beach.

The Towers was a formless mixture of rental apartments, condominium apartments, hotel rooms, and rental suites. The corporation that owned the building had overlooked very little in the way of income-producing cells. There were rental offices on the mezzanine (Cassidy also had a suite of offices there), and on the ground floor the corporation leased space for shops of all kinds, including a small art gallery. The coffee shop, the lounge bar, and the dining room were all leased to various entrepreneurs. The corporation itself invested nothing in services and took from everybody. Cassidy probably maintained the penthouse, I decided, because the Royal Palm Towers was one of the few apartment hotels in Palm Beach that remained open all year round.

Many New Yorkers, who didn't like Florida for its climate, loved the state because there was no state income tax. By maintaining a residence for six months and one day in Florida they could beat New York's state income tax. An ignoble but practical motive for moving one's residence and business headquarters to Florida.

'Where,' I asked Gloria, 'did you get the Haitian primitives?'

'A widow in Lauderdale sold them to me,' she giggled. 'For a song. Her husband just died, and she sold everything – house, furniture, collection, and all. She was moving back to Indiana to live with her daughter and grandchildren.'

'You priced the Marcel too low, baby. You can get more than fifteen hundred for it.'

'I doubt it, and I can't lose anything – not when I only paid twenty-five dollars for it.'

'You're a thief and a bitch.'

Gloria giggled. 'You're a blackguard. What have you done with Berenice?'

'She went back to Minnesota. I don't want to talk about her, Gloria.'

'She's an awfully nice girl, James.'

'I said I don't want to talk about her, Gloria.'

We took the elevator to the penthouse, but the door didn't open automatically. There was a small one-way window on the steel door (a mirror on our side), and the Filipino houseboy checked us out before pressing the door release from his side. There was probably a release button concealed somewhere within the elevator cage. There had to be. Cassidy couldn't keep someone in his penthouse at all times, just to push a button and let him in – or could he? The very rich do a lot of strange things.

The party was not a large one. Seven people counting Mr Cassidy. Gloria and I brought the total to nine. It was the kind of party where it was assumed that everyone knows one another and therefore no one is introduced. There are many parties like that in Palm Beach. The main idea is to eat first, and then drink as much as possible before the bar is closed or the liquor runs out. If one feels the need to talk to someone, he introduces himself or starts talking to someone without giving his name. It makes very little difference. Mr Cassidy had to know everyone there – at least slightly – to brief the Filipino houseboy on the person's credentials for admittance.

Sloan, the bartender (he wore a name tag on his white jacket), poured us Cutty Sarks over ice cubes. I trailed Gloria toward the terrace, where Mr Cassidy was talking to a gray-haired man who was probably a senior officer in some branch of the armed forces. He wore an Oxford gray suit with deeply pleated trousers. The suit was new, indicating that he didn't wear it often. This meant that he wore a uniform most of the time. A suit lasts army and navy officers for eight or nine years. Pleats were long out of fashion and Oxford gray is the favorite suit color for high-ranking officers. They lead dark, gray lives.

'I appreciate that, Tom,' Cassidy said, sticking out his hand, and the gray-haired man was dismissed.

I watched the old-timer head for the elevator. I could have confirmed, easily enough, whether the man was in the service by asking, 'Isn't that General Smith?' In this case, however, I believed that I was right and didn't feel the need of confirmation.

Joseph Cassidy was short, barely missing squatness, with wide meaty shoulders and a barrel chest. His tattersall vest was a size too small and looked incongruous with his red velvet smoking jacket. He needed the vest for its pockets – pockets for his watch and chain, and the thin gold chain for his Phi Beta Kappa key. He had a tough Irish face, tiny blue eyes, with fully a sixteenth of an inch of white exposed beneath the irises, and square white teeth. His large upper front teeth overlapped, slightly, his full lower lip. His high forehead was flaking from sunburn. He wore a close-cropped black moustache, and his black hair, which was graying at the sides, was combed straight back and slicked down with water. Cassidy was a formidable man in his early fifties. He carried himself with an air of authority, and his confident manner was reinforced by his rich, resonant bass voice. And his gold-rimmed glasses – the same kind that Robert McNamara wore when he was Secretary of Defense – were beautifully suitable for his face.

Gloria introduced us and started toward the indoor fountain to look at the carp. The pool was crowded with these big fish, and I could see their backs, pied with gold and vermilion splotches, from where I stood, some fifteen feet away from the pool. A concrete griffin, on a pedestal in the center of the pool, dribbled water from its eagle beak into the carp-filled pool. It was a poorly designed griffin. The sculptor, who probably knew too much about anatomy, had been unable to come to terms with the idea of a cross between an eagle and a lion. Medieval sculptors, who knew nothing about anatomy, had no trouble at all in visualizing griffins and gargoyles. Cassidy took my arm, grasping my left elbow with a thumb and forefinger.

'Come on, Jim,' he said, 'I'll show you a couple of pictures. They call you "Jim," don't they?'

'No,' I replied, hiding my irritation. 'I prefer James. My father named me Jaime, but no one ever seemed to pronounce it right, so I changed it to James. Not legally,' I added.

'It's the same name.' He shrugged his meaty shoulders. 'No need for a legal change, James.'

I smiled. 'I didn't ask for that advice, Mr Cassidy, so please don't bill me for it.'

'I don't intend to. I was just going to say that you don't look like a man named Jaime Figueras.'

'Like the stereotype Puerto Rican, you mean? The peculiar thing is that my blond hair and blue eyes come from my father, not my mother. My mother was Scottish-Irish, with black hair and hazel eyes.'

'You don't have a Spanish accent, either. How long have you lived in the States?'

'Since I was twelve. My father died, and my mother moved back to New York. She never liked Puerto Rico, anyway. She was a milliner, a creative designer of hats for women. You can't sell original hats to Puerto Rican women. All they need is a mantilla – or a piece of pink Kleenex pinned to their hair – to attend mass.'

'I've never met a milliner.'

'There aren't many left. My mother's dead now, and very few women wear originals nowadays, even when they happen to buy a hat.'

'Are hats worth collecting?' he asked suddenly, moistening his upper lip with the tip of his pink tongue. 'Original hats, I mean?'

I knew then that Mr Cassidy was a true collector, and, knowing that, I knew a lot more about him than he thought I knew. In general, collectors can be divided into three categories.

First, the rare patron-collectors who know what they want and order it from artists and artisans. This first category, in the historical past, helped to establish styles. Without the huge demand for portraits in the sixteenth and seventeenth centuries, for example, there would have been no great school of portrait painters.

Second, the middle-ground people, who buy what is fashionable, but collect fashionable art because they either like it without knowing why (it reflects their times is why) or have been taught to like it.

In the third category are the collectors for economic reasons. They buy and sell to make a profit. That is, in a tautological sense, they are collectors because they are collectors, but they enjoy the works of art they possess at the moment for their present and future value.

The one trait that all three types of collectors have in common is miserliness. They write small, seldom dotting 'i's or crossing 't's and they are frequently costive. Once they own something, *anything*, they don't want to give it up.

The collector's role is almost as important to world culture as the critic's. Without collectors there would be precious little art produced in this world, and without critics, collectors would wonder what to collect. Even those few collectors who are knowledgeable about art will not go out on a limb without critical confirmation. Collectors and critics live within this uneasy symbiotic relationship. And artists – the poor bastards – who are caught in the middle, would starve to death without us.

'No.' I shook my head. As we crossed through the living room toward his study I explained why. 'Hats are too easy to copy. Original hats, during the twenties and thirties, were expensive because they were made specifically for one person and for one occasion. As soon as a new hat was seen on Norma Shearer's head, it was copied and mass-produced. The copy, except perhaps for the materials, looked about the same. Some of the hats worn during the Gilded Age, when egret feathers were popular, might be worth collecting, but I doubt if restoration, storage, and upkeep costs would make it worthwhile to collect even those.'

'I see. You have looked into it then?'

'Not exhaustively. Fashion isn't my field – as you know.'

We entered his study, which was furnished in black leather, glass, and chrome. Cassidy sank into an audibly cushioned chair while I looked at the three pictures on the apple-green wall. There was an early Lichtenstein (a blown-up Dick Tracy panel), an airbrush Marilyn Monroe, in pale blue, from the Warhol series, and a black-and-white drawing of a girl's head by Matisse. The latter was over the ebony desk, in quiet isolation. The drawing was so bad Matisse must have signed it under duress. I sat across from Cassidy and put my empty glass on the rosewood coffee table. The Filipino houseboy appeared with a fresh drink on a tray, picked up my empty glass, and handed me the drink and a cocktail napkin.

'You wish something to eat, sir?'

'I think so. A turkey sandwich, all white meat, on white toast. With mayonnaise and cranberry sauce, and cut off the crusts, please.'

He nodded and left.

'You don't like the drawing, do you?'

I shrugged, and sipped from my glass. 'Matisse had a streak of meanness in him that many Americans associate with the French. When he went out to a café – after he became well known – he would often sketch on a pad, or sometimes on a napkin. Then, instead of paying his tab in cash, he'd leave the drawing on the table and walk out. The proprietor, knowing that the drawing was worth a good deal more than the dinner, was always delighted. A man full of rich food and a couple of bottles of wine doesn't always draw very well, Mr Cassidy.'

He nodded, relishing the story, and looked fondly at his Matisse. A bad drawing is a bad drawing, no matter who has drawn it. But my little story – and it was a true one – had merely enhanced the value of the Matisse for Cassidy. An ordinary person, if he had purchased a bad Matisse, would have felt gypped. But Cassidy wasn't an ordinary person. He was a collector, and not an ordinary collector.

'An interesting story.' He smiled. 'I don't have much here, and I haven't decided what to bring down from Chicago.'

Here was a natural opening, and I took it. 'I'd like to see the catalogue of your collection some time, Mr Cassidy.'

'Don't have one yet, but I've got a good man at the University of Chicago working on it. Dr G. B. Lang. D'you know him?'

'Yes, but not personally. He wrote an excellent monograph on Rothko.'

'That's Dr Lang. It isn't costing me a dime, either – except for the printing costs. Dr Lang teaches at the university, and one of my clients is on the Board of Trustees. Through him, my client, I managed to get Lang a reduced teaching schedule. He teaches two courses, and the rest of his load is research, the research being my catalogue. Dr Lang's happy because he'll get another publication under his belt and, if he does a bang-up job, the University of Chicago Press will probably publish it.'

When Cassidy smiled, exposing his teeth, his canines made little dents in his bottom lip. He stared at me for two long beats. His eyes, behind the gold-rimmed glasses, were flat and slightly magnified. He leaned forward slightly. 'When men of good will get together, some sort of deal can be worked out to everyone's satisfaction. Isn't that right, James?'

'If they're "men of good will," yes. But my own experience has led me to believe that there aren't many of them around.'

He laughed, as though I had said something funny. The houseboy brought my sandwich. I took a bite and called him back before he got out the door. 'Just a minute! This isn't mayonnaise, this is salad dressing.'

'Yes, sir.'

'Don't you have any mayonnaise?'

'No, sir. May I bring you something else, sir?'

'Never mind.'

In his own way, Joseph Cassidy was as famous as Lee Bailey. In court Cassidy was certainly as good a lawyer, but he wasn't as flamboyant with reporters outside of court as Bailey, nor did he take cases for sheer publicity value. He was a cash-in-advance, on-the-line lawyer. No one had written a biography on Cassidy yet, but he had socked away a lot more money than Bailey. His shrewdness in buying the right painters at the right time and at rock-bottom prices had made him another fortune – if he ever decided to put his collection on the market.

The houseboy still hovered about, wanting but unwilling to leave. He was upset because I didn't eat the sandwich.

'Close the bar, Rizal,' Cassidy ordered quietly, 'and tell Mrs Bentham that I'll see that Mr Figueras gets home all right.' He exposed his toothy smile. 'You don't mind sticking around for a while, do you, James?'

'Of course not, Mr Cassidy.'

Because of my upbringing, which has been on the formal side – insofar as observing the amenities was concerned – I resented the easy use of my first name by Mr Cassidy without my permission or invitation. But I knew that he wasn't trying to patronize me. He was attempting to put me at my ease. Nevertheless, although I considered the idea, I couldn't drop to his level and call him Joe. There's too much informality in America as it is, and in Palm Beach, during the season, it is often carried to ridiculous lengths.

Rizal left to close the bar, which meant that the party was over. The guests would depart without saying goodbye to their host, and that would be that. Not out of rudeness, but out of deference. If Cassidy had gone out for a series of formal good-nights they would have adjusted to that kind of leave-taking just as easily.

After Rizal closed the door, Cassidy took a cigar out of his desk humidor, lighted it, and sat down again. He didn't offer me one.

'James,' Cassidy said earnestly, 'I know a lot more about you than you think I do. I rarely miss one of your critical articles, and I think you write about art with a good deal of insight and perception.'

'Thank you.'

'This is all straight talk, James. I'm not in the habit of handing out fulsome praise. A second-rate critic doesn't deserve it, and a first-rate critic doesn't need it. In my opinion, you're well on the way to becoming one of our best young American critics. And, according to my investigations, you're ambitious enough to be *the* best.'

'By investigations, if you mean you've been talking to Gloria about me, she isn't the most reliable witness, you know. We've been friends for several years now, and she's prejudiced in my favor.'

'No, not only Gloria, James, although I've talked to her, too. I've talked to dealers, to some of my fellow collectors, and even to Dr Lang. You might be interested to know that Dr Lang's highly impressed with your work, and he knows more about art history and criticism than I'll ever know.'

'I'm not sure about that, Mr Cassidy.'

'He should. That's his business – and yours. I'm an attorney, not an art historian. I don't even intend to write a foreword to my catalogue – although Lang suggested it to me.'

'Most collectors do.'

He nodded, and waved his right hand slowly so the ash wouldn't fall off the end of his cigar. 'In the art world, you happen to have a reputation for integrity. And I've been informed that you're incorruptible.'

'I'm not getting rich as an art critic, if that's what you mean.'

'I know. I also know how to make inquiries. That's my business. The law is ninety-five percent preparation, and if a man does his homework, it's easy to look good in the courtroom. To return to corruption for a moment, let me say that I respect your so-called incorruptibility.'

'The way you say it makes me feel as if I've missed some opportunity to make a pile of dough or something and turned it down. If I have missed out on something, I sure don't know about it.'

'If you want to play dumb, I'll spell it out for you. Number one – free pictures. That kid's show this evening, ah, Westcott. Suppose you had said to Gloria that you would give Westcott a nice buildup in return for a couple of free pictures, what would have happened?'

'In Westcott's case, she'd have given *all* of them to me.' I grinned. 'But you aren't talking about integrity now, Mr Cassidy, you're talking about my profession. I've never taken a free picture. The walls of my apartment in the Village are bare except for chance patterns of flaking paint. But if I ever took one picture, just one, that I could resell for two or three hundred bucks, the word would be out that I was on the take. From that moment on I would be dead as a critic. And a good review for pay, which is still being done in Paris, has damned near ruined serious art criticism in France.

'There are some exceptions, naturally, and those of us in the trade know who they are. So the way things are, I can't even afford to take legitimate art gifts from friends, even when I know that there are no strings attached. The strings would be there inadvertently. The mere fact that I took the gift might influence my opinion if I ever had to cover the man's show. By the same token, I don't buy anything either. And I've had some chances to buy some things that even I could afford. But if I owned a painting, you see, there might be a temptation on my part to push the artist beyond his worth – *possibly* – I don't know that I would – in order to increase the value of my own painting. I don't mean that I am completely objective either. That's impossible. I merely try to be most of the time, and that allows me to go overboard and be subjective as hell when I see something I really flip over.'

I finished the last of my drink and set the glass down a little harder than I had intended. When I looked up, there was a smile on Cassidy's Irish face. Perhaps he had been baiting me, but I had been through this kind of probing before. It was natural, in America, for people to think that a critic had been paid off when he gave some artist a rave write-up, especially when they didn't know anything about art. But Cassidy knew better.

'You know all this, Mr Cassidy, so don't give me any undeserved credit for integrity. I like money as much as anyone, and I made more money when I taught art history at CCNY than I do now. I'm ambitious, yes, but for a reputation, not for money. When I have a big enough reputation as a critic, then I'll make more money, but never a huge amount. That isn't the game. The trick – and it's a hard one – is to earn a living as an art critic, or, if you prefer, art expert. If you want me to authenticate a painting for you, I'll charge you a fee. Gladly. If you want to ask my advice on what to buy next for your collection, I'll give you suggestions free of charge.' I held up my empty glass. 'Except for another drink. Or is the bar closed for me, too?'

'I'll get the bottle.' Cassidy left the room and returned almost immediately with an open bottle of Cutty Sark and a plastic bucket of cubes. I poured a double shot over two ice cubes and lit a cigarette. Cassidy picked up a yellow legal pad from his desk, sat down with it, and unscrewed the top from a fountain pen.

'I don't have any pictures for you to authenticate, James. And I didn't intend to ask you for any advice on collecting, but since you made the offer, what do you have in mind?'

I decided to tell him about my pet project.

'*Entartete Kunst.* Degenerate art.'

'How do you spell that?'

I told him and he wrote it on the pad.

'It's a term that was used by Hitler's party to condemn modern art. At the time, Hitler was on an ethnic kick, and the official line was folk, or people's, art. Modern art, with its subjective individualistic viewpoint, was considered political and cultural anarchy, and Hitler ordered it suppressed. Even ruthlessly. Then, as now, no one was quite sure what modern art was, and it became necessary to make up a show of "degenerate art" so that party men throughout Germany would know what in the hell they were supposed to prevent. So, in July 1937, they opened an exhibit of modern art in Munich. It was for adults only, so no children would be corrupted, and the exhibit was called *Entartete Kunst*. It was supposed to be an example, a warning to artists, and to people who might find such art attractive. After the Munich showing, it traveled all over Germany.'

I leaned forward. 'Listen to the names of the painters represented – Otto Dix, Emil Nolde, Franz Marc, Paul Klee, Kandinsky, Max Beckmann, and many more. I have a copy of the original catalogue in New York, locked away in the bottom drawer of my desk at the office.'

'Those paintings would be worth a fortune today.'

'The paintings are all a part of art history now – and any of, say, Marc's paintings are expensive. But suppose you had every painting in this particular show? Every German museum was "purified". That was the term they used, "purified". And the painters represented by the show, if the museum happened to have any of their work, were removed. Some were destroyed, some were hidden, and some were smuggled out of the country. But to have the *original* traveling exhibit, and it would be *possible* to obtain these pictures . . .'

Cassidy drew a line through the two words on his pad and shook his head. 'No, I could never swing anything like that by myself. I'd have to get a group together to raise the money, and – no, it wouldn't be worth it to me. Any more ideas?'

'Sure, but you didn't ask me here for my ideas on collecting.'

'That's right. Basically, James, you and I are honest men, and, in our own ways, we are equally ambitious. One dishonest act doesn't make a person dishonest, not when it's the only one he ever performs. That is, a *slightly* dishonest act. A little thing, really. Suppose, James, that you were given the opportunity to interview' – he hesitated, moistened his lips with his tongue – 'Jacques Debierue?'

'It would merely set me up with the greatest exclusive there is! But Debierue is in France, and he's only given three interviews in forty years – no, four – and none since his home burned down a year or so ago.'

'In other words,' he chuckled, 'you would be somewhat elated if you could look at his new work and talk to him about it personally?'

'Elated isn't the word. *Ecstatic* isn't strong enough. Now that Duchamp is dead, Debierue is Mr Grand Old Man of Modern Art.'

'Don't go on, I know. Just listen. Suppose I told you that I could make arrangements for you to see and talk with Debierue?'

'I wouldn't believe you.'

'But if it was true – and I am now telling you that it *is* true – what would you do for me in return?'

My throat and mouth were suddenly dry. I tipped the plastic ice bucket and poured some ice water into my empty glass. I sipped it, and it tasted almost warm. 'You have something dishonest in mind. Isn't that what you implied a moment ago?'

'No. Not dishonest for you, dishonest for me. But even so, Debierue is in debt to me, if I want to look at it that way, and I do. I don't want money from him, I want one of his paintings.'

I laughed. 'Who doesn't? No individual, and not a single museum, has a Debierue. If you had one, you'd be the only collector in the world to have one! As far as I know, only four critics have been privileged to see any of his work. A servant or two has seen his paintings, probably, I don't know – maybe some of his mistresses a few years back, when he was still young enough to have them. But no one else—'

'I know. And I want one. In return for the interview, I want you to steal a picture for me.'

I laughed. 'And then, after I steal it, all I have to do is smuggle it back here from France. Right?'

'Wrong. And that's all I'll tell you now until I get a commitment from you. Yes or no. In return for the interview, you will steal a picture from Debierue and give it to me. No picture, no interview. Think about it.'

'Hypothetically?'

'Not hypothetical. Actual.'

'I'd do it. I *will* do it. That is, I'll steal one if he has any paintings to steal. Everything he had went up in smoke with his house, according to the reports. And if he hasn't painted anything since, well . . .'

'He has. I know that he has.'

'You've got a deal. But I don't have the money for a round-trip air fare to France, not even for a slow freighter.'

'Let's shake hands on it.'

We got to our feet and shook hands solemnly. The palms of my hands were damp, and so were his, but we both gripped as hard as we could. He got the humidor and offered me a cigar. I shook my head and sat down. I started to pour another drink, but decided I didn't need it. My head was light and close to swimming. My heart was fluttering away as if I had swallowed a half-dozen butterflies.

'Debierue,' Cassidy laughed, a snort rather than an actual laugh, 'is here in Florida, thirty-odd miles south,

485

via State Road Seven. And that is my so-called dishonest act, my friend. I have just betrayed a client's confidence. A counselor isn't supposed to do that, you know. But now that I have, I'll tell you the rest of it.

'Arrangements were made for Debierue to come to Florida more than eight months ago, and I was the intermediary here. The emigration was set up by a Paris law firm, who contacted me, and I handled the matter on a no fee basis, which I was glad to do. I rented the house – a one year lease – hired a black woman to come in and clean it for him once a week, bought his art supplies at Rex Art in Coral Gables, and picked him up at the airport. The whole thing. He's a poor man, as you know.'

'And you're supporting him now?'

'No, no. The money comes from *Les Amis de Debierue*. You are—'

'I send them five bucks a year myself.' I grimaced. 'It's tax deductible, if I ever make enough money to list it among my many charities.'

'Right. That's it. The Paris *Amis*, through the law firm, send me small sums more or less regularly, and I see that the old man's bills are paid – such as they are – and keep him in pocket money. He doesn't need much. The house is cheap, because of the rotten location. It was built by a man who retired to raise chickens. After six months of trying, and not knowing anything about poultry, he went back to Detroit. He's been trying to sell the house for two years, and was happy as hell to get a year's rent in advance.' Cassidy smiled. 'I even selected the old man's phoney name for him – Eugene V. Debs. How do you like it?'

'Beautiful!'

'Better than beautiful. Debierue never heard of Gene Debs. And that's about it.'

'Not quite. How did he get into the States without reporters finding out?'

'No problem. Paris to Madrid, Madrid to Puerto Rico, through the customs at San Juan, then on to Miami – and he came in on a student visa. J. Debierue. Who's going to suspect a man in his nineties on a student visa? And Debierue is a common enough name in France. There are about sixty flights a day from the Caribbean coming into Miami International on Sundays. It's the busiest airport in the world.'

I nodded. 'And the ugliest, too. So he's been right here in Florida for eight months?'

'Not exactly. The negotiations started eight months ago, and it took some time to set everything up. The funny thing is, the old man will actually be a student. I mentioned my connections at the University of Chicago – well, starting in September, Debierue will be taking twelve hours of college credit, by correspondence, from Chicago.'

'What's his major?'

'Cost accounting and management. I've got a young man working for me who can whip through those correspond-ence courses with his left hand, and he'll probably get the old man an A average. On a student visa, you see, you have to carry twelve hours a semester to stay in the country. As long as you're making good grades with the college, you can stay as long as you like.'

'I know. But why me? Why don't *you* steal a picture from Debierue?'

'He'd know it was me, that's why. After I got him settled, he told me he didn't want me to visit him. For the sake of secrecy. I went down a couple of times anyway and pestered him for a painting. He got good and angry the last time, and his studio is kept padlocked. I want one of his paintings. I don't care what it is, or whether anyone knows that I have one. *I'll* know, and that's enough. For now. Of course, if you manage to get a successful interview – and that's your problem – and you write about his new work – he hasn't got *too* many years to live – then I can bring my painting out and show it. Can't I?'

'I understand. You'll have pulled off the collector's coup of this decade – but what happens to me?'

'You'll stand still for it, no matter what happens. I've checked you out, I told you. You're ambitious, and you'll be the first, as well as the *only*, American critic to have an exclusive interview with the great Jacques Debierue. After you steal one of his pictures, he sure as hell won't talk to anyone else.'

'What time is it set up for, and when?'

'It isn't. That's up to you.' He wrote the address on the yellow pad, and sketched in State Road Seven and the branch road leading into it from Boynton Beach. 'If you happen to drive past the turnoff, and you might miss Debierue's road because it's dirt and you can't see the house from the highway, you'll know you missed it when you spot the drive-in movie about a half mile farther on. Turn around and go back.'

'Does he know I'm coming?'

'No. That's your problem?'

'Why did he decide to come to Florida?'

'Ask him. You're the writer.'

'He might slam the door in my face, then?'

'Who knows? We made a deal, that's all, and we shook hands on it. I know my business, and you should know yours. Any more questions?'

'Not for you.'

'Good.' He got to his feet, an abrupt signal that the discussion was finished. 'When are you driving down?'

'That's my business.' I grinned, and stuck out my hand.

We shook hands again, and Cassidy asked kindly if he could telephone for a taxi. Sending me home in a cab at my own expense was his method of 'seeing that I got home all right.'

I declined, and rode down in the elevator. To clear my head, I preferred to walk the few blocks to my apartment. As I walked the quiet streets through the warm soft night, a Palm Beach police car, staying a discreet block behind, trailed me home. I wasn't suspected of anything. The cops were merely making certain that I would get home all right. Palm Beach is probably, together with Hobe Sound, the best-protected city in the United States.

Now that I was alone, I was so filled with excitement I could hardly think straight. Dada, first, and Surrealism, second, were my favourite periods in art history. And because of my interest in these movements when I had been in Paris, I knew the Paris art scene of the twenties better, in many respects, than most of the people who had participated in it. And Debierue – Jacques Debierue! Debierue was the key figure, the symbol of the dividing line, if a line could be delineated, in the split between Dada and Surrealism! In my exhilarated state, I knew I wouldn't be able to sleep. I was going to put on a pot of coffee and jot down notes on Debierue from memory in preparation for the interview. Tomorrow, I thought, *tomorrow*!

I turned the key in the door and opened it to unexpected light. The soft light streamed in from the bathroom. Silhouetted in the bathroom doorway, wearing a gray-blue shorty nightgown, was my tawny-maned schoolteacher. Her long, swordlike legs trembling at the knees.

'I – I came back, James,' Berenice said tearfully.

I nodded, dumbly, and lifted my arms so she could rush into them. After she calms down, I thought, I'll have her make the coffee. Berenice makes much better coffee than I do . . .

Chapter Five

Debierue is a difficult artist to explain, I explained to Berenice over coffee:

'*No pido nunca a nadie* is a good summary of the code Debierue's lived by all his life. Translated, it means, "I never ask nobody for nothing."'

'I think that's the first time I've ever heard you talk in Spanish, James.'

'And it might be the last. It didn't take me long to quit speaking Spanish after we moved to New York from San Juan. And as soon as I wised up to how they felt about Puerto Ricans, I got rid of my Spanish accent, too. But the Spanish *No pido nuncia a nadie* sounds better because the reiterated double negatives don't cancel each other out as they do in English. And that's the story of Debierue's life, one double negative action after another until, by not trying to impress anybody, he ended up by impressing everybody.'

'But why did you give up speaking Spanish?'

'To prove to myself, I suppose, that a Puerto Rican's not only as good as anybody else, he's a damned sight better. Besides, that's what my father would've done.'

'But your father's dead, you told me—'

'That's right. He died when I was twelve, but technically I never had a father. He and my mother separated before I was a year old, you see. They didn't get divorced because they were Catholics, although my mother made semiofficial arrangements with the church for them to live apart. There was no money problem. He supported us until he died, and then we came up to New York, Mother and I, with the insurance and the money from the sale of our house in San Juan.'

'But you saw him once in a while, didn't you?'

'No. Never. Not after their separation – except in photographs, of course. That's what made things so tough for me, Berenice. What I've had instead is an imaginary father, a father I've had to make up myself, and he's what you might call *un hombre duro* – a hard man.'

'What you mean, James, you've deliberately made things hard on yourself.'

'It isn't that simple. A boy who doesn't have a father around doesn't develop a superego, and if you don't get a superego naturally you've got to invent one—'

'That's silly. Superego is only a jargon word for "conscience," and everybody's got a conscience.'

'Have it your way, Berenice, although Fromm and Rollo May wouldn't agree with you.'

'But *you've* got a conscience.'

'Right. At least I've got one intellectually, if not emotionally, because I was smart enough to create an imaginary father.'

'Sometimes I don't understand you, James.'

'That's because you're like the little old lady in Hemingway's *Death in the Afternoon*.'

'I've never read it. That's his book on bullfighting, isn't it?'

'No. It's a book about Hemingway. By talking about bullfighting he tells us about himself. You can learn a lot about bullfighting in *Death in the Afternoon*, but what you learn about life and death is a matter of Hemingway.'

'And the little old lady . . . ?'

'The little old lady in *Death in the Afternoon* kept asking irrelevant questions. As a consequence, she didn't learn much about bullfighting or Earnest Hemingway and toward the end of the book Hemingway has to get rid of her.'

'I'm not a little old lady. I'm a young woman and I can learn. And if I want to understand you better, I should listen to what you have to say about art because it's a matter of life and death to you.'

'You might put it that way.'

'I am putting it that way.'

'Would you like to hear about Jacques Debierue?'

'I'd love to hear about Jacques Debierue!'

'In that case, I'll begin without the overall frame of reference and fill in the necessary background as I come to it. I said, I'll begin without the – I see, you don't have any relevant questions and you've decided to remain silent until you do? Fine. You'll understand my exhilaration about my opportunity to meet Jacques Debierue, then, when I tell you that I've read all, as far as I know, that's been written about him. The scope is wide, but the viewpoint is narrow.

'Only four other critics, all Europeans, have actually seen and written about his work at firsthand. I'll be the first American critic to examine his work, and it'll be new, original painting that no one else has ever seen before. For the first time in my critical career, I'll see the most recent Nihilistic Surrealistic paintings by the most famous artist in the world. It will also be possible, afterward, for me to evaluate and compare my opinions with the critiques of those critics who've written about his earlier work. I'll have a broad view of Debierue's growth – or possible retrogression – and historical support, or better yet, nonsupport, for my convictions.

'The incidental factors that led to Debierue's fame during the course of contemporary art history are marvelous. His silent, uphill fight against improbable odds appears, on the surface, to be effortless, but such was not the case. Mass hostility is always omnipresent toward the new, especially in art. Hundreds of books, as you know,

492

have been filled with exegetical opinions about the Impressionists, Expressionists, Suprematists, Cubists, Futurists, Dadaists, and Surrealists of the early years of this century. All of the major innovators have been examined in detail, but there were many other painters who received no recognition at all. And there were smaller movements that were formed and then dissolved without being mentioned. How many, no one knows.

'But it was these minor movements that I was interested in during my year in Europe. It was a way to earn a reputation, you see. And if I could've pinned *one* of them down, one that got away, a movement that I could've written about and established as an important but overlooked movement in art history, I could've started my critical career immediately instead of teaching art survey courses to bored accountants at CCNY.

'Paris seethed with new developments in art before, during, and after the First World War. Hardly a day passed without a new group being formed, a new manifesto being drafted, followed by polemics, fistfights, dissolvements.

'Three painters would meet in a café, argue affably among themselves until midnight, and decide to form their own little splinter group. Then, as wine and arguments flowed for the remainder of the night as they scribbled away at a new manifesto, they detested each other by dawn.

'White-faced with anger and lack of sleep, they'd march off to their studios in the nacreous light of morning, their new movement junked before it was begun.

'A few of these lesser movements caught on, however, lasting for a few days or weeks after a scattered flurry of press publicity, but most of them died unheralded, unnoticed, for want of a second – or for no discernible reason. The fortunate, well-publicized movements lasted long enough to influence enough imitators to gain solid niches

493

in art history. Cubism, for example, a term that pleased the reading public, was one of them.

'Paris, of course, was the center of the vortex during the early twenties, but forays into new and exciting art expressions were by no means confined to France.

'During my single year in France, as I tried to track down tangible evidence of these minor movements without success, my side trips to Brussels and Germany were even more tantalizing.

'In Brussels, the Grimm Brothers, Hal and Hans, who called themselves "The Grimmists," spent months in dark mines collecting expressive lumps of coal. These were exhibited as "natural" sculptures on white satin pillows. Within two days, however, shivering Belgians had pilfered these exposed lumps of coal, and the exhibit closed. The Belgians are a practical people, and 1919 was a cold winter. In their own way, the Brothers Grimm had originated "Found" art—'

'James – when you say that you have no superego, or conscience, does that mean that you've never done anything *bad*, anything you've ever been sorry for, later?'

'Yeah. Once. There was an assistant professor I knew at Columbia, an anthropologist, whose wife died. He had her cremated, and bought a beautiful five-hundred-dollar urn to keep her ashes in. He used to keep the urn on his desk at home, as a *memento mori*. Anthropologists, as you know, are pretty keen on ritual, burial ceremonies, and pottery – things of that nature. His wife died of tuberculosis.

'I never knew his first wife, but I met his second wife, who was one of his graduate students. Men, like women, are usually attracted to the same type of person when they remarry—'

'That isn't true! I've never known anyone like you before—'

'But then you've never been married, Berenice. And I'm talking about a widower who married again. His name doesn't matter to you, but it happened to be Dr Hank Goldhagen. Anyway, his second wife, Claire, was *also* susceptible to respiratory infections. Sometimes, when they got into an argument, Hank would point to the urn of ashes, and say, "My first wife, in that urn, is a better woman and a better wife to me than you are, right now!"'

'What a terrible thing to say!'

'Isn't it? I sometimes wonder what she said to him to provoke it. But the marriage didn't last long. Following a weekend skiing trip to New Hampshire, Claire developed lumbar pneumonia and died. To save Hank money, I advised him to put Claire's ashes in the same expensive urn with his first wife.'

'But why . . . ?'

'There was ample room in the urn, and why not? Did it make any sense to buy a second expensive urn? And if he bought a cheaper one, that would've indicated to his friends that he thought less of Claire than he did of his first wife. But my practical suggestion backfired. Hank got so he was staring at the urn all the time brooding over and about the mixed ashes of these two women, and eventually he cracked up. And because it was my fault, I felt bad about it for weeks.'

'That isn't a true story, is it? Is it, James?'

'No, it isn't a true story. I made it up to please you, because, it seems, you're a little old lady who likes stories.'

'No, I'm not – and I don't like stories like that!'

'I'm leading up to Debierue, and I promise you that it's much more interesting than the story of Dr Goldhagen's two wives.'

'I'm sorry I interrupted, James. May I pour you another cup of coffee?'

'Please. Let me tell you first about the *Scatölögieschul* that was formed by Willy Büttner in Berlin, during the post-war years of German political art. The *Scatölögieschul* probably holds the European record for short-livedness. It opened and closed in eight minutes flat. Herr Büttner and his three defiant fellow exhibitors, together with their cretin model – who denied her obvious presence in every painting – were carted off to jail. The paintings were confiscated, never to be seen by the public again. According to rumor, these ostensibly pornographic paintings wound up in General Göering's private collection. They're now believed to be in Russia, but no one really knows. I couldn't find a single eyewitness who had seen the pictures, although a lot of people knew about the exhibit. This was another frustrating experience for me in Europe.

'By the early sixties the trail was too cold for valid, documentary evidence. I was too late. The European Depression and World War Two had destroyed the evidence. I still feel that the critical neglect of these so-called minor movements may prove to be an incalculable loss to art history. Then, as now, critics only choose a very small number of painters to be *the* representatives of their times. And we only remember the names of those who come in first. Any sports writer can recall that Jesse Owens was the fastest runner in the 1936 Olympics, but he won't remember the names of the second and third place runners who were only split seconds behind him.

'Therefore, it's almost miraculous that Jacques Debierue was noticed at all. When you think about the peculiar mixture of hope and disillusionment of the twenties, he seems to be the most unlikely candidate of all the artists of the time to be singled out for fame. And he was studiously indifferent to the press.

'One painter, a true archetype, can hardly be said to constitute a movement, but Debierue rose above the

Parisian art world like an extended middle finger. Paris critics found it embarrassing to admit that none of them knew the exact date his one-man show opened. The known details of the discovery of Debrierue, and the impact of his influence on other painters, has been examined at some length by August Hauptmann in his monograph entitled *Debierue*. This isn't a long book, not for the work of a German scholar, but it's a well-documented study of Debierue's original achievement.

'There isn't any mass of published work on Debierue, as there is on Pablo Picasso, but Debierue's name crops up all the time in the biographies and autobiographies of other famous modern painters – usually in strange circumstances. The frequent mention of his name isn't surprising. Before Debierue was in the art world, he was of it. Because he framed their paintings, he knew personally, and well, most of the other firsts of the war and postwar years.'

'He was a picture framer?'

'At first, yes. Miró, De Chirico, Man Ray, Pierre Roy, and many other painters found it expedient to visit him in his tiny framing shop. He gave them credit, and until they started to make money with their work, they sorely needed credit. Debierue's name is brought up in the studies published on every important postwar development because he was there – and because he knew all the artists involved. But his only commonality with other innovators is the fact that he was a first in his own right as the acknowledged father of Nihilistic Surrealism. Debierue, by the way didn't coin this term for his work.

'The Swiss essayist and art critic, Franz Moricand, was the first writer to use this term with reference to Debierue's art. And the label, once attached, stuck. The term appeared originally in Moricand's essay, "*Stellt er nur?*" in *Mercure de France*. The article wasn't penetrating, but other critics were quick to snatch the term "Nihilistic

Surrealism" from the essay. An apt and descriptive bridge was needed, you see, to provide a clear dividing line between Dada and Surrealism. Both groups have attempted at various times to claim Debierue, but he was never in either camp. Dada and Surealism both have strong philosophical underpinnings, but no one knows what Debierue's leanings are.

'Chance is an important factor in the discovery and recognition of every artist, but what many modern critics fail to accept is that Debierue's many artist-friends paid him off by sending people to see Debierue's one-man show. In his Montmartre hole-in-the-wall framing workshop he had mounted many paintings at cost, and others absolutely free, for poor young painters whose work sold a few months later for high prices. Those "crazy boatloads" of Americans, as Fitzgerald called them, coming to France during the boom period, always carried more than fifty dollars in cash on their person. They bought a lot of paintings, and the selling painters didn't forget their obligations to Debierue.

'Despite Hauptmann's book, an aura of mystery about Debierue's first and only one-man show remains. No invitations were issued, and there were no posters or newspaper ads. He didn't even mention the show to his friends. One day, and the exact date is still unknown, a small, hand-lettered card appeared in the display case behind the street window of his framing shop. "Jacques Debierue. *No. One.* Shown by request only." It was spelled Capital N-o-period. Capital O-n-e.'

'Why didn't he use the French *Nombre une?*'

'That's a good point, Berenice. But no one really knows. The fact that he used the English *No. One* instead of *Nombre une* may or may not have influenced Samuel Beckett to write in French instead of English, as the literary critic Leon Mindlin has claimed. But everyone concerned agrees that it was an astute move on Debierue's part when American tourists, with their limited French, began to arrive on the Paris scene. Using a number as a title for his picture, incidentally, was another first in art that has been indisputably credited to Debierue. Rothko, who uses numbers exclusively for his paintings, has admitted privately, if not in writing, his indebtedness to Debierue. The point's important because several art historians falsely attribute the numbering of paintings as a first for Rothko. Debierue hasn't said anything one way or another about the matter. He's never commented on his picture, either.

'This much is certain. *No. One* postdated Dada and predated Surrealism, thereby providing a one-man bridge between the two major art movements of this century. And Debierue's Nihilistic Surrealism may, in time, turn out to be the most important movement of the three. In retrospect, it's easy enough for us to see how Debierue captured the hearts and minds of the remaining Dadaists who were gradually, one by one, dropping out of Dada and losing their hard-earned recognition to the burgeoning Surrealists. And you can also realize, now, why the Surrealists were so anxious to claim Debierue. But Debierue stood alone. He neither admitted nor denied membership in either movement. His work spoke for him, as a work of art is supposed to do.

'*No. One* was exhibited in a small and otherwise empty room – once a maid's bedroom – one short flight of stairs above Debierue's downstairs workshop. An environment had been created deliberately for the picture. The visitor who requested to see it – no fee was asked – was escorted upstairs by the artist himself and left alone with the picture.

'At first, as the viewer's eyes became adjusted to the murky natural light coming into the room from a single dirty window high on the opposite wall, all he could see was what appeared to be an ornate frame, without a picture in it, hanging on the wall. A closer inspection, with the aid of a match or cigarette lighter, revealed that the gilded frame with baroque scrollwork enclosed a fissure or crack in the gray plaster wall. The exposed wire, and the nail which had been driven into the wall to hold both the wire and the frame, were also visible. Within the frame, the wire, peaking to about twenty degrees at the apex – at the nail – resembled, if the viewer stood well back from the picture, a distant mountain range.'

Berenice sighed. 'I don't understand it. The whole thing doesn't make any sense to me.'

'Exactly! No sense, but not nonsense. This was an irrational work in a rational setting. Debierue's Nihilistic Surrealism, like Dada and Surrealism, is irrational. That's the entire point of Dada, and of most of the other postwar art movements. Distortion, irrationality, and unlikely juxtaposition of objects.'

'What did the reviewers say about it?'

'What the reviewers said in the newspapers isn't important, Berenice. There's a distinction between a reviewer and a critic, as you should know. The reviewer deals with art as a commodity. He's got three or four shows a week to cover, and his treatment of them is superficial, at best. But the critic is interested in aesthetics, and in placing the work of art in the scheme of things – or even as a pattern of behavior.'

'All right, then. What did the critics say about *No. One*?'

'A great many things. But criticism begins with the structure, and often ends there, especially for those critics who believe that every work of art is autotelic. Autotelic. That means—'

'I know what autotelic means. I studied literary criticism in college, and I've got a degree in English.'

'Okay. What does it mean?'

'It means that a work of art is complete in itself.'

500

'Right! And what else does it mean, or imply?'

'Just that. That the poem, or whatever, should be considered by itself, without reference to anything else.'

'That's right, but there's more. It means that the artist himself should not be brought into the criticism of the work being considered. And although I'm a structuralist, I don't think that any work – poem, painting, novel – is autotelic. The personality of the artist is present in every work of art, and the critic has to dig it out as well as explicating the structure and form. Take pro football—'

'I'd love to. It's more interesting than painting.'

'To you, yes, but I want to make an analogy. A good critic's like a good football announcer on television. We see the same play that he does, but he breaks it down for us, reveals the structure and the pattern of the play. He explains what went wrong and what was right about the play. He can also tell us what is likely to come next. Also, because of the instant tape replay, he can even break down the play into its component parts for us to see again in slow motion. We do the same thing in art criticism sometimes, when we blow up details of a painting in slides.'

'Your analogy doesn't explain the "personality" in the football play.'

'Yes it does. This is the quarterback, who caused the play in the first place. That is, if the quarterback called the play. Sometimes the coach calls every play, sending in the new play every time with a substitute. If the announcer doesn't know what the coach is like, what he has done before, *or* the quarterback, I'll say, his explanation of the structure of the play is going to be shaky, and any prediction he makes won't be valid. Do you follow me?'

'I follow you.'

'Good. Then you shouldn't have any trouble in understanding the success of *No. One*. Only one person at a time was allowed to examine the picture. But there was no time limit set by the artist. Some visitors came down-stairs immediately. Others remained for an hour or more, inconveniencing those waiting below. The average viewer was satisfied by a cursory inspection. But according to Hauptmann, there were a great many repeats.

'One old Spanish nobleman from Seville visited Paris a half-dozen times for the sole purpose of taking another look at *No. One*. No visitor's log was kept, but the fact that a vast number of people visited Debierue's shop to see the picture is a matter of public record. Every Parisian artist of the time made the pilgrimage, usually bringing along some friends. And *No. One* was widely discussed.

'Sporadic newspaper publicity, the critical attention Debierue provoked in European art reviews, and word-of-mouth discussion of the exhibit, brought a steady stream of visitors to his gallery until 25 May, 1925, when he sold his shop for the purpose of painting full time.

'*No. One*, naturally, was a picture that lent itself to varied, conflicting opinions. The crack enclosed by the mount, for example, might've been on the wall before Debierue hung the frame over it – or else it was made on purpose by the artist. This was a basic, if subjective, deci-sion each critic had to make for himself. The conclusions on this primary premise opened up two diametrically opposed lines of interpretive commentary. The explicit versus the implicit meaning caused angry fluctuations in the press. To hold any opinion meant that one had to see the picture for himself. And the tiny gallery became a "must see" for visiting foreign journalists and art scholars.

'Most of the commentators concentrated their remarks on the jagged crack within the frame. But there were a few who considered this point immaterial because the crack couldn't be moved if the frame were to be removed. They were wrong. A critic has to discuss what's there, not something that may be somewhere else. And he never exhibited it anywhere else after he sold his shop. The consensus, including the opinions of those who actually detested the picture, was an agreement that the crack represented the final and inevitable break between traditional academic art and the new art of the twentieth century. In other words, *No. One* ushered in what Harold Rosenberg has since called 'the tradition of the new'.

'Freudian interpretations were popular, with the usual sexual connotations, but the sharpest splits were between the Dadaists and the Surrealists concerning the irrational aspects of the picture. Most Surrealists (Buñuel was an exception) held the opinion that Debierue had gone too far, feeling that he had reached a point of no return. Dadaists, many of them angered over the use of a gilded baroque mounting, claimed that Debierue hadn't carried irrationality out far enough to make his point irrevocably meaningless. Neither group denied the powerful impact of *No. One* on the art of the times.

'By 1925 Surrealism was no longer a potent art force – although it was revived in the thirties and rejuvenated in the early fifties. And the remaining Dadaists in 1925, those who hadn't joined André Breton, were largely disorganized. Nevertheless, Debierue's exhibit was still a strong attraction right up until the day it closed. And it was popular enough with Americans to be included on two different guided tours of Paris offered by tourist agencies.

'Once Nihilistic Surrealism became established as an independent art movement, Debierue was in demand as a speaker. He turned these offers down, naturally—'

'Naturally? Doesn't a speaker usually get paid?'

'Yes, and he would've been well paid. But an artist doesn't put himself in a defensive position. And that's what happens to a speaker. A critic's supposed to speak. He welcomes questions, because his job is to explain what the artist does. The artist is untrained for this sort of thing, and all he does is weaken his position. Some painters go around the country on lecture tours today, carrying racks of slides of their work, and they're an embarrassed, inarticulate lot. The money's hard to turn down, I suppose, but in the end they defeat themselves and negate their work. A creative artist has no place on the lecture platform, and that goes for poets and novelists, as well as painters.'

'So much for the Letters section of *The New York Review of Books*.'

'That's right. At least for poets and novelists. The nonfiction writer is entitled to lecture. He started an argument on purpose when he wrote his book, and he has every right to defend it. But the painter's work says what it has to say, and the critic interprets it for those who can't read it.'

'In that case, you're responsible to the artist as well as to the public.'

'I know. That's what I've been talking about. But it's a challenge, too, and that's why I'm so excited about interviewing Debrierue. When Debierue was preparing to leave Paris, following the closing of his shop and exhibit, he granted an interview to a reporter from *Paris Soir*. He didn't say anything about his proposed work in progress, except to state that his painting was too private in meaning for either his intimate friends or the general public. He had decided, he said, not to show any of his future work to the general public, nor to any art critic he considered unqualified to write intelligently about his painting.

'For the "qualified" critic, in other words, if not for the general public, the door was left ajar.

'The villa on the Riviera had been an anonymous gift to the artist, and he had accepted it in the spirit in which it was offered. No strings attached. He wasn't well-to-do, but the sale of his Montmartre shop would take care of his expenses for several months. The *Paris Soir* reporter then asked the obvious question. "If you refuse to exhibit or to sell your paintings, how will you live?"

'That,' Debierue replied, 'isn't my concern. An artist has too much work to do to worry about such matters.' With his mistress clinging to his arm, Debierue climbed into a waiting taxi and was off to the railroad station.

'Perhaps it was the naiveté of his reply that agitated an immediate concern among the painters he had known and befriended. At any rate, an organization named *Les Amis de Debierue* was formed hastily, within the month following his departure from the city. It's never disbanded.'

'There was an organization like that formed for T. S. Eliot, but it disbanded. The purpose was to get Mr Eliot out of his job at the bank.'

'I know. But Eliot took another job in publishing. Debierue, so far as we know, never made another picture frame, except for his own work. *Les Amis* held its first fundraising banquet in Paris, and through this continuing activity enough money was collected to give the artist a small annual subsidy. Other donations are still solicited from art lovers annually. I've been giving *Les Amis de Debierue* at least five bucks a year since I left graduate school.

'During World War Two, the Germans let Debierue alone. Thanks to two critical articles that had linked his name with Nietzsche, he wasn't considered as a "degenerate" French artist. And apparently they didn't discover any of his current work to examine for "flaws."

'When the Riviera was liberated, it was immediately transformed into an R and R area for US troops, and he was soon visited by art students, now in uniform, who'd read about him in college. They mentioned him in their letters home, and it didn't take long for American art groups to begin a fresh flow of clothing, food, art supplies, and money to his Riviera outpost.

505

'Debierue had survived two world wars, and a dozen ideological battles.

'The first three reviews of Debierue's Riviera works, with a nod to *symbolisme*, are self-explanatory. "Fantasy," "Oblique," and "Rain" are the names given to his first three "periods" – as assigned by the first three critics who were allowed to examine his paintings. The fourth period, "Chironesque," is so hermetic it requires some amplification.'

Berenice nodded in assent.

'A paucity of scholastic effort was put into the examination of these four important essays. Little has been published, either in book or monograph form as in-depth studies of each period – the way Picasso's Rose and Blue periods have been covered. This is understandable, because the public never saw any of these pictures.

'The established critic prefers to examine the original work, or at least colored slides of that work, before he reaches his own conclusions. To refute or to agree with the critic who's seen the work puts a man on shaky ground. Each new article, as it appeared, however, received considerable attention. But writers were chary of making any expanded judgements based upon the descriptions alone.'

'Yes, I can understand that.'

'This general tendency didn't hold true for Louis Galt's essay, "Debierue: The Chironesque Period," which appeared in the Summer 1958 edition of *The Nonobjectivist*. It was reprinted in more than a dozen languages and art journals.

'Galt, you see, was known as an avowed purist in his approach to nonobjective art, and that's why he published his article in *The Nonobjectivist* when he could've had it published by *Art News* for ten times as much money. Galt had once gone so far as to call Mondrian a "traitor" in print when the Dutchman gave up his black-and-white palette to experiment with color in his linear paintings. I didn't agree with him there, but he made some telling points. But with so many able critics available, all of them anxious to see Debierue's post-World War Two work, it was considered a damned shame that he'd chosen a purist who would only look at the new work from a prejudiced viewpoint.

'The appellation "Chironesque" was considered as a derogatory "literary" term. It was deeply resented by Susan Sontag, who said so in *The Partisan Review*. The Galt essay wasn't, in all fairness, disrespectful, but Galt stated bluntly that Debierue had retrogressed. He claimed that "bicephalous centaurlike creatures" were clearly visible in the dozen paintings Debierue had shown him. And this forced Galt to conclude that the "master" was now a "teacher", and that didacticism had no place in contemporary art. The "purist" view, of course.'

'Of course.' Berenice nodded.

'At any rate – and here he was reaching for it – because Chiron the centaur was the mythical teacher of Hercules, and other Greek heroes, Galt christened the period "Chironesque." This was a cunning allusion to the classicism Galt destested, elements Galt would've considered regressive in any modern painter.

'Debierue, of course, said nothing.'

Berenice nodded and closed her eyes.

'The controversial Galt essay was well timed. It rejuvenated interest in the old painter, and the "bicephalous centaur-like creatures," as described by Galt, made the new work resemble – or appear to resemble – Abstract Expressionism. Some wishful thinking was going on. Nineteen fifty-eight wasn't an exciting pictorial year. Except for a handful of New York painters, called the "Sidney Janis Painters", after their dealer, the so-called New York School was undergoing a transitional phase. And Debierue was news, of course, because he'd received so little public notice in recent years.'

Berenice dropped her chin. 'Uh huh.'

'One New York dealer cabled Debierue an offer of fifty thousand dollars for any one of the Chironesque paintings, sight unseen. Debierue acknowledged it by sending back a blank cablegram – with just his type signature. The dealer took advantage of the publicity by blowing up a copy of his offer and Debierue's reply and by placing the photo blow-ups in the window of his Fifty-seventh Street gallery. Other dealers, who aped and upped the original offer, didn't receive any replies.

'How I'll manage it, I don't know, Berenice. I know only that I'm determined to be the first critic to see Debierue's American paintings, and I've already decided to call it his "American Period"!'

But I was talking to myself. Berenice, I noticed, with some irritation, had fallen asleep.

Chapter Six

Despite her size, and she was a large woman, Berenice, curled and cramped up in sleep, looked vulnerable to the point of fragility. Her unreasonably long blonde lashes swept round flushed cheeks, and her childish face, in repose and without makeup, took several years from her age. Her heavy breasts and big round ass, however, exposed now, as the short flimsy nightgown rode high above her hips, were incongruously mature in contrast with her innocent face and tangled Alice-in-Wonderland hair. As I examined her, with squinted-eyed, ambivalent interest, a delicate bubble of spit formed in the exact center of her bowed, slightly parted lips.

Oh, I had put Berenice to sleep all right, with my discursive discussion of Jacques Debierue. With an impatient, involuntary yawn of my own I wondered how much she had understood about Debierue before she had drifted off completely. She had been attentive, of course, as she always was when I talked to her, but she had never asked a serious question. Not that it made much difference. Berenice had a minimal interest in art – or in anything that bordered on abstract thought – and for some time I had suspected that the slight interest she was able to muster occasionally was largely feigned. An effort to please me.

Except for her adhesive interest in me as a person, or personality, and in matching sexual frequencies, I wondered if anything else had ever stimulated her intellectually. For a woman who had majored in English, and taught the subject (granted, she taught on a high school level), she was surprisingly low on insight into the nature of literature.

No one could accuse her of being well read, either. Her insights into literature when I had, on occasion, attempted to draw her out, were either sophomoric or parroted generalities remembered from her college English courses. She had an excellent memory for plot lines and the names of characters, but for little else.

She was probably a poor classroom teacher, I decided. She had such a lazy, good-natured disposition she could not have been any great shakes as a disciplinarian. But she would have few disciplinary problems in a city like Duluth, where teenagers were polite incipient Republicans. New York high school students would have had a gentle woman like Berenice in tears within minutes.

But how did I know? I didn't. In a power situation, with children, she might inspire terror, fear, and trembling. She never talked about her work and, for all I knew, she might be an expert in grammar and a veritable hotshot in the classroom.

The persona of a woman in love is highly deceiving.

Did she feign sentimentality as well as other things? She cried real tears one night when Timmy Fraser sang 'My Funny Valentine' at the Red Pirate Lounge – stretching out the song in the mournful way that he does for fully ten minutes. Any woman who fails to recognize the inherent viciousness of Lorenz Hart's 1930s lyrics has a head filled with cornmeal stirabout instead of brains. She also mentioned once that she had cried for two days over Madame Bovary's suicide. Fair enough. Flaubert had earned those tears, but she had no insight into the style of the novel, nor did she analyze how Flaubert had maneuvered her emotionally into weeping over the death of that poor, sick woman.

Knowing this much, and after thinking about it, I realized that I knew very little about her, it was unreasonable of me to expect a wakeful interest from Berenice in Jacques Debierue. Berenice was a funny valentine, that is what she was, and her chin was a little weak, too. In a vague abstract way I loved her. At the same time, I wondered what to do with her. She had been a sounding board to diminish some of the excitement inside me, but now it was 2 a.m. and I was going to be busy today. Busy, busy. Perhaps if I used her right, she would be an asset. Wouldn't it help to have a beautiful woman in tow when I called on Debierue? He would hardly slam the door in the face of a strikingly attractive woman. A Frenchman? Never . . .

The bubble of spit ballooned suddenly as she exhaled, and inaudibly popped. Berenice whimpered in her sleep and tried, wriggling, to find a more comfortable position in her chair. This was impossible. With her long legs cramped up under her rear and in a tight-fitting canvas officer's chair, it was miraculous that she could fall asleep in the first place.

I stopped rationalizing, recognizing what I was doing – rationalizing – and prodded Berenice's soft but rather flat belly with a stiff forefinger.

'Wake up, Audience,' I said, not unkindly.

'I wasn't asleep,' she lied. 'I just closed my eyes for a second to rest them.'

'I know. I forgot to ask, but where have you been the last couple of days?'

'Here.' Her eyes widened. 'Right here.'

'Not today you weren't.'

'Oh, you mean today?'

'Yes. Today.'

'I was at Gloria's apartment. Honestly, I got so blue just sitting around here all alone waiting for you to come back that I called her. She drove over for me and took me in.'

'I thought as much. Gloria tried to pump me on the phone when I got back. I thought something was odd about her phony laughter, but couldn't figure it out. If you didn't intend to go back to Duluth, why did you take your bags and leave that weird note for me?'

'I tried to go, I really did, but I just couldn't!' Her eyes moistened. 'I want to stay with you, James . . . don't you want me to?'

I had to forestall her tears. Why can't women learn how to say 'Goodbye' like a man?

'We'll see, baby, we'll see. Let's go to bed now. We'll talk about it in the morning, much later *this* morning.'

Berenice rose obediently, crossed her arms, and with a sweeping graceful movement removed her shorty nightgown. No longer sleepy, she grinned wickedly and crawled into the tumbled Murphy bed, shaking her tremendous stern as she did so. I smiled. She was amusing when she tried to be coy because she was so big. I undressed slowly and crawled in beside her. The air conditioner, without enough BTUs to cool the apartment adequately, labored away – uh uh, uh uh, uh uh . . . As a rule I could shut the sound out, but now it bothered me.

I was tense, slightly high from drinking four cups of black coffee, and overstimulated by my ability to recall, with so little effort, the details of Debierue's career. Three, no, four days had passed since the last time, and yet, strangely, I wasn't interested in sex. To make love now would be to initiate a new beginning to a something I had written 'ending' to – perhaps that was the reason. That, or my unresolved feelings about Berenice now that I was on the verge of a future – if everything worked out all right – that held no place for a woman who was interested in me as a person. Any relationship between a man and a woman that is based upon bodies and personalities alone can lead only to disaster.

It was a premonition, or some kind of precognitive instinct for self-preservation, I should have heeded. But at two in the morning, with my mind still reeling with matters intellectual, I was physically unable to muster enough brute bellicosity to toss Berenice and her suitcase down the stairs. She was loving, too loving.

The inchoate premonition, or whatever it was, of some disaster, froze my body as well as my mind into a state of flaccid inaction. Berenice was puzzled, I know. When none of her usual tricks worked, she climbed over me suddenly, got out of bed, and switched off the floor lamp. Except for the tiny red light on the electric coffee pot, which was not a red, baleful staring eye, but merely an effective reminder that the coffee was hot if I was not, the room was as dark as my thoughts. We had never made love in the dark before. I didn't know about Berenice, but such a peculiar idea had never occurred to me in my lifetime. It is too impersonal to make love in the dark. Your partner could be *anyone*, anyone at all.

How she knew this I don't know, but the gimmick worked. As Berenice whipped her head back and forth, stinging first my chest and then my stomach with her long hair, my doubts disappeared. And because this unseen woman became any woman, and was no longer a problem named Berenice Hollis, I became rigid with the pain of need, and mounted her savagely. Savagely for me, because I am usually methodical in sexual relations, knowing what I like and dislike. Being flagellated with long hair was a new experience for me as well, and I favored Berenice with the best ride she had ever had. She climaxed as I entered, then twice, and we made the final one together. She bit my shoulder so hard to keep from mewing (knowing how irritated I get when she makes animal noises) she left the marks of her teeth in my skin.

Euphoric, my tenseness dissipated, the thought of sending this big, marvelous woman back to Minnesota became intolerable. She turned on the floor lamp and rummaged around in her suitcase for douching equipment.

'Hang up that yellow linen suit of yours, baby,' I told her, 'so the wrinkles will shake out.'

'Why?' she asked, doing as she was told. 'It isn't wrinkled.'

'Because I want you to wear it tomorrow. I'm taking you with me.'

'Where are we going? Are we going to have fun?'

'To call on M. Debierue.' I sighed. 'I'll try to explain it again tomorrow – in one-syllable words.' With the light on, Berenice Hollis was a problem again.

'We'll have fun, though, won't we?'

'Sure,' I replied glumly. 'Fun, fun, fun.'

I closed my eyes as she went into the bathroom. I remember dimly being washed with a warm washrag, but I was sound asleep before she finished.

PART TWO

If anything exists, it is incomprehensible

Chapter One

The apartment looked terrible, as if a small whirlwind had been turned loose for a few minutes, but Berenice, in her lemon linen suit, with its skimpy micro-skirt, was beautiful. At my request she wore stockings, sheer enough to enhance the sienna brown of her deeply tanned legs. The skirt was so short, when she sat or leaned over, the white metal snaps that held up her stockings were exposed slyly enough to make her as sexy as a Varga drawing.

Instead of a blouse she wore a filmy blue-and-red scarf around her neck. The two loose ends of the scarf were tucked crosswise beneath the lapels of the square-cut double-breasted jacket. Very few women would dare to wear such a severely cut suit, but the square straight lines of the jacket exaggerated the roundness of Berenice's lush figure. With the supplement of a rat she had put up her hair, and the ample mound of tawny hair, sun-tinged with yellow streaks, piled on top of her head, together with her childish features, gave her an angelic expression.

There was, I think, too much orange in her lipstick, but perhaps this slight imperfection was the single needed touch that made her so lovely as a whole.

I had shaved and showered before Berenice took over the bathroom for an hour, and I had trimmed my Spanish Don sideburns neatly with scissors. Nevertheless, I looked incongruously raunchy beside Berenice in my faded blue denim, short-sleeved jumpsuit, especially when she slipped on a pair of white gloves. It was too hot outside for a jacket, and I needed the multiple pockets in the jumpsuit to carry all my paraphernalia.

I had three pens, a notebook, my wallet and keys, a handkerchief, two packs of Kools, and my ribbed-model Dunhill lighter (one of the few luxuries I had treated myself to when I had a regular teaching salary coming in), a tiny Kodak Bantam in my right trousers pocket, some loose change, a pocket magnifying glass in a leather case, fingernail clippers, and a two-inch piece of clammy jade, with indentations for a finger grip. Except for the well-concealed Kodak Bantam, loaded with color film, I carried too much crap around with me, but I had gotten used to carrying it and could hardly do without it.

We had slept late and had a leisurely breakfast. After getting dressed, I had jotted down a few questions in my notebook. I would not refer to the questions, but the act of writing them down had set them in my mind. This was an old reporter's trick that worked, and I always took my Polaroid camera along, loaded with black-and-white, and extra film. Professionals sneer at Dr Edwin H. Land's Polaroids, but I was an expert with them and rarely snapped more than two shots before getting what I wanted. I had learned, too, that people will okay without argument almost any picture that they have seen, but will refuse to allow photos to be published when they haven't seen everything on the roll.

By 1:30 p.m. we were ready to go. I preceded Berenice down the stairs into the glare of the breaktaking Florida sunlight. The humidity was close to ninety, although the temperature wasn't quite eighty-five. There were threatening nimbus clouds farther south, but the sky was clear and blue above Palm Beach. It doesn't always rain in South Florida when the humidity hits 100 percent, although technically it is supposed to, but inasmuch as we were heading toward the dark sky above Boynton Beach, I decided not to put the canvas top back. Inside the car, on burning leatherette seats, we sweltered.

We had hardly crossed the bridge into West Palm when Berenice pointed to a blazing orange roof and said, 'Let's stop at Howard Johnson's.'

'Why? We just finished breakfast an hour ago.'

'I have to widdle. That's why.'

'I told you to pee before we left.'

'I did, but I have to go again.'

It was partly the heat, but I jerked the car into the parking lot, thinking angrily that it wasn't too late. I could call a cab and send Berenice back to the apartment.

But once inside the cave-cold depths and booth-seated, I ordered two chocolate ice-cream sodas, waited for them and Berenice, and smoked a Kool. Because the service was seasonal, Berenice joined me at the table long before the sodas arrived. She picked up my cigarette from the ashtray, took a long drag, replaced the cigarette exactly as she found it, held the inhaled smoke inside her lungs like a skin diver trying to break the hold-your-breath-underwater record, and finally let what was left of the smoke out. I had noticed, during the three days I was in Miami, when Berenice had not been with me, that her so-called efforts to quit smoking caused three packs a day to go up in smoke instead of my usual two. She had merely quit buying and carrying them. She smoked mine instead – or took long drags off the cigarette I happened to be smoking. She hated mentholated cigarettes, or so she claimed, but not enough, apparently, to give them up altogether.

'If you want a cigarette,' I said, pushing the pack toward her, 'take one. When you drag mine down a quarter of an inch that way, I finish the cigarette unsatisfied because I didn't have the exact ration of smoke I'm accustomed to. Then, because I feel gypped out of a quarter inch, I light another one, only to find that an entire cigarette, smoked too soon after the one I just finished, is too much. I butt it, replace it in the pack, and when I finally get around to lighting the butt the next time I want a smoke, it tastes too strong and it still isn't a regular-length smoke. If I throw the butt away, with only a couple of drags gone, it's a waste, and—'

Berenice put a cool hand over mine. There were faint crinkles in the corner of her guileless cornflower blue eyes. Her bowed lips narrowed as they flickered a rapid smile.

'What's bothering you, James?'

I shrugged. 'I don't know. I took an up with my third cup of coffee, and the combination of a benny with too much coffee makes me talk too much. As I told you last night, Berenice, this is a one-of-a-kind opportunity for me. And I'm apprehensive, that's all.'

She shook her head. The smile appeared and disappeared against so fast I almost missed it. 'No, James, you told me so much about this painter last night I got confused, bogged down in details so to speak. Something is either missing or you didn't tell me everything.'

'You fell asleep, for Christ's sake.'

'No, I didn't. Well, maybe toward the end. But what I don't understand is how this painter, this Debierue, can be such a famous painter when no one has ever seen any of his paintings. It doesn't make sense.'

'What do you mean, no one has seen his paintings? Thousands of people saw his first one-man show, and his subsequent work has been written about by Mazzeo, Charonne, Reinsberg, and Galt, who all studied his paintings. These are some of the most famous critics of this century, for God's sake!'

She shook her head and pursed her lips. 'I don't mean them, or even you – that is, if you get to see what he's painted since coming to Florida. I mean the public, the people who flock to museums when a traveling Van Gogh

520

show comes in, and buy all kinds of Van Gogh reproductions and so on. I had seen dozens of Van Gogh paintings in books and magazines long before I ever saw one of his originals. That's what I mean by famous. How can I be impressed by Debrierue's fame when I've never seen any of his work and can't judge for myself how good he is?'

Our ice-cream sodas arrived. I didn't want to hurt Berenice's feelings, but I was forced to because of her ignorance.

'Look, baby, you aren't qualified to judge for yourself. Now keep quiet, and drink your nice ice-cream soda – there's a good girl – and I'll try and explain it to you. Did you ever study cetology?'

'I don't know. What is it?'

'The scientific study of whales. A cetologist is a man who studies whales, and he can spend an entire lifetime at it, just as I've spent my life, so far, studying art – as have the critics who wrote about Debierue. Now, let's suppose that you pick up a copy of *Scientific American* and read an article about whales written by a well-known cetologist—'

'Are there any well-known cetologists?'

'There are bound to be. I don't have any names to rattle off for you – that isn't my racket. But I haven't finished yet. All right, you're reading this article by a cetologist in *Scientific American* and he states that a baby sperm whale is a tail presentation.'

'What does that mean?'

'It means that a baby whale, unlike other mammals, is born tail first.'

'How do you know that?'

'I read a lot. But the same would hold true even if the cetologist said that it was a cephalic presentation. The point I'm making is this: The article is written by a cetologist and published in *Scientific American*, and you will accept an expert's word for it. You aren't going to get yourself a god-damned boat and sail around the seven fucking seas trying to find a pregnant whale, are you? Just so you can check on whether a baby whale is born head first or tail first?'

Berenice giggled. 'You're cute when you're stern. No . . . I guess not, but art, it seems to me, is supposed to be for everybody, not just for those critics you mentioned . . .'

I put down the spoon and wiped my lips on a paper napkin. '*Whales* are for everybody, too, sweetheart. But not everybody studies whales as a lifetime occupation. That's the big difference you don't seem to understand.'

'All right.' She shrugged. 'I still think there's something you haven't told me about all this.'

I grinned. 'There is. In return for Debierue's address I've got to do a favor for Mr Cassidy—'

'The lawyer who told you about Debierue?'

'Yeah.' I nodded. 'And what I'm telling you is "privileged information", as Cassidy would put it. It's between you and Mr Cassidy and these ice-cream sodas.'

'You can trust me, James.' Her face softened. 'You can trust me with your life.'

'I know. And in a way it *is* my life. Anyway, Mr Cassidy gave me privileged information – where Debierue is living – and all I have to do in return is to steal a picture for him.'

'Steal a picture? Why can't he buy one? He's rich enough.'

'Debierue doesn't sell his pictures. I explained all that. If Cassidy gets a picture, even one that's been stolen, he'll be the only collector in the world to have one, you see.'

'What good will it do him? If it's a stolen picture, Debierue can get it back by calling the police.'

'Debierue won't know he has it, and neither will anyone else – until after Debierue's dead, anyway. Then the picture will be even more valuable.

'How're you going to steal a picture without Debierue knowing it was you?'

'I don't know yet. I'm playing things by ear at the moment. It might not be a picture. If he's working with ceramics, I can slip a piece in my pocket while you distract him. Maybe there are some drawings around. Mr Cassidy would be satisfied with a drawing. In fact he'd be delighted. But until I find out what Debierue has been doing, I won't know what to do myself.'

'But you want me to help you?'

'If you want to, yes. He can't watch both of us at the same time, and he's an old man. So when a chance comes, and it will, I'll give you the high sign and then I'll snatch something.'

'It's awfully haphazard, James, the way you say it. Besides, as soon as we leave, he'll know that you're the one who stole it – what*ever* it is.'

'No.' I shook my head. 'He won't know. He'll *suspect* that I took it, but he won't be able to prove it. I'll deny everything, if charged, and besides it'll never get that far. Meanwhile, Mr Cassidy will have the painting, chunk of sculpture, drawing, or whatever, hidden away where Jesus Christ couldn't find it. See?'

'Do you realize, James,' she said, rather primly, 'that if you ever got caught stealing a painting from anybody that your career would be over?'

'Not really, and not, certainly, from Debierue. His work, as you mentioned before about Van Gogh, belongs to the world – and if I were ever tried for something like that, which I wouldn't be – I'd have a defense fund from art lovers and art magaínzes that would make me look like a White Panther. Anyway, that's the plan – in addition to somehow getting an interview, of course.'

'It isn't much of a plan.'

'True. But now that you know what I have to do, you might get an idea once we're on the scene. The important thing is this: don't take anything yourself. I'll take it when the time is propitious. I have to get the interview before anything else is done.'

'I understand.'

The rain caught us before we reached Lake Worth.

There were torrents of it, and I could hardly see to drive. Berenice, because of her suit, had to roll up her window, but it was too hot for me to roll up mine. My left shoulder and arm got soaked, but with the humidity I would have been just as wet inside the car with the window rolled up. The rain finally came down so hard I had to pull over to the curb in Lake Worth to wait for a letup.

Berenice was frowning. 'How much,' she asked, 'does a baby whale weigh when it's first born?'

'One ton. And it's fourteen feet long.' I lit a cigarette and passed it to Berenice. She shook her head and handed it back. I took a long drag. 'One ton,' I said solemnly, 'is two thousand pounds.'

'I *know* how much a ton is!' she said angrily. 'You – you – you damned intellectual, you!'

I couldn't contain myself. I had to laugh and ruin my joke.

Chapter Two

I could have taken State Road Seven straight away by picking it up west of West Palm Beach, but because the old two-lane highway was used primarily by truck traffic barreling for Miami's back door, into Hialeah, I stayed on US 1 all the way to Boynton Beach before searching for a through road to make the cutover. I got lost for a few minutes and made several aimless circles where new black-tops had been crushed down for a subdivision called inappropriately Ocean Pine Terraces (miles from the ocean, no pines, no terraces), but when I finally reached the state highway, it was freshly paved, and the truck traffic wasn't nearly as bad as I had expected.

The rain, mercifully, had stopped.

My crude map was clear enough, but I had zipped past Debierue's turnoff to the Dixie Drive-in Movie Theater before I realized it. The mixed dirt-and-gravel private road leading to Debierue's home and studio was clearly visible from the highway, and on the right of the highway about three hundred yards before the drive-in entrance, but I had failed to notice it. I made a crimped circle in the deserted drive-in entrance and this time, from the other side of the highway, it was easy to spot the break.

Thick gama grass had reclaimed the deep wheel ruts of the road, and I crawled along in first gear. The bumpy, rarely used trail straight-lined through a stand of second-growth slash pine for about a half mile and then made a sigmoid loop to circumvent two stinking stagnant ponds of black swamp water. On the right of the road, abandoned chicken runs stretched into the jungly mass of greenery, and weeds had grown straight and tall along the sagging chicken-wire fences. The unpainted wooden chicken-houses had weathered to an unpatterned dirty gray, and most of the roofs had caved in. The narrow road petered out at an open peeled-pine gate. I eased into the fenced area, with its untended, thickly grassed yard, which resembled a huge, brown bathmat, and pulled up in front of the screened porch of the house.

Paradoxically, I was awed by my first sight of the old painter. I switched off the engine, and as it ticked heatedly away, I sat and stared. I say 'paradoxically' because Debierue in person was anything but awe-inspiring.

He resembled any one of a thousand, no literally tens of thousands, of those tanned Florida retirees one sees on bridges fishing, on golf courses tottering, and on the shuffleboard courts of rest homes and public parks shuffling. He even wore the uniform. Green-billed khaki baseball cap, white denim Bermuda shorts, low-cut Zayre tennis shoes in pale blue canvas, and the standard white, open-necked 'polo' shirt with short sleeves. The inevitable tiny green alligator was embroidered over the left pocket of the shirt, an emblem so common in Florida that any Miami Beach comedian could get a laugh by saying, 'They caught an alligator in the Glades the other day, and he was wearing a shirt with a little man sewn over the pocket . . .'

But unlike those other thousands of old men who had retired to Florida in anticipation of a warm death, men who had earned their dubious retirement by running shoe stores, managing light-bulb plants in Amarillo, manufacturing condoms in Newark, hustling as harried sales managers in the ten western states, Debierue had served, and was still serving, the strictest master of them all – the self-discipline of the artist.

Debierue, apparently unperturbed by the arrival of a strange, beat-up convertible in his yard, sat limberly erect in a green-webbed aluminium patio chair beside the porch door, soaking up late afternoon sun. I was pleased to see that he was allowing his white beard to grow again (for several years he had been clean shaven), but it was not as long and Melvillean as it had been in photos of the old artist taken in the twenties.

Physically, Debierue was asthenic. Long-limbed, long-bodied, slight, with knobbly knees and elbows. Advanced age had caused his thin shoulders to droop, of course, and there was a melony potbelly below his belt. His sun-bronzed skin, although it was wrinkled, gave the old man a healthy, almost robust appearance. His keen blue eyes were alert and unclouded, and the great blade of his beaky French nose did not have those exposed, tiny red veins one usually associates with aged retirees in Florida. His full, sensuous lips formed a fat grape-colored 'O' – a dark, plump circle encircled by white hair. His blue stare, with which he returned mine, was incurious, polite, direct, and distant, but during the long uncomfortable moment we sat in silent confrontation, I detected an air of vigilance in his sharp old eyes.

As a critic I had learned early in the game how unwise it was to give too much weight or credence to first impressions, but under his steady, unwavering gaze I felt – I *knew* – that I was in the presence of a giant, which, in turn, made me feel like a violator, a criminal. And if, in that first moment, he had pointed to the gate silently – without even saying 'Get out!' – I would have departed without uttering a word.

But such was not the case.

Berenice, her hands folded in her lap over her chamois drawstring handbag, sat quietly, and there she would sit until I got out of the car, walked around it, and opened the door on her side.

I was uninvited, an unexpected visitor, and it was up to me to break the frozen sea that divided us. Apprehensively, and dangling the Land camera from its carrying strap on two fingers, I got out of the car and nodded politely.

'Good afternoon, M. Debierue,' I said in French, trying to keep my voice deep, like Jean Gabin, 'at long last we meet!'

Apparently he hadn't heard any French (and mine wasn't so bad) for a long time. Debierue smiled – and what a wonderful, warmhearted smile he had! His smile was so sweet, so sincere, so insinuating that my heart twisted with sudden pain. It was a smile to shatter the world. His age-ruined mouth, purple lips and all, was beautiful when he smiled. Several teeth were missing, both uppers and lowers, and those that remained gave a jack-o'-lantern effect to his generous mouth. But the swift transformation from mournful resignation to rejuvenated, unrestrained happiness changed his entire appearance. The grooved down-pointing lines in his face were twisted into swirling, upswept arabesques. He rose stiffly from his chair as I approached, and shook a long forefinger at me in mock reproach.

'Ah, Mr Figueras! You have shaved your beard. You must grow it back quickly!'

His greeting me by name that way brought sudden moisture to my eyes. He pumped my hand, the single up-and-down European handshake. His long spatulate fingers were warm and dry.

'You – you *know* me?' I said, in unfeigned astonishment.

He treated me to the first in a series of bona fide Gallic shrugs. 'You, or another—' he said mysteriously, 'and it is well that it is you. I am familiar with your work, naturally, Mr Figueras.

I gulped like a tongue-tied teenager, abashed, not knowing what to say, and then noticed that he was looking past my shoulder toward Berenice.

'Oh!' I said, running around the car, and helping Berenice out the door. 'This is my friend, M. Debierue, Mlle Hollis.'

Berenice glared at me when I pronounced her name 'Holee,' and said, 'Hollis, Mr Debierue,' in English, 'Berenice Hollis. And it's a pleasure to meet you, sir.'

Debierue kissed her hand, and I thought (I was probably oversensitive) he was a little uneasy, or put off by her presence. He didn't know – and there was no unawkward way for me to enlighten him – whether she was truly just a friend, my mistress, my secretary, or a well-heeled art patron. I decided to say nothing more. He would be able to tell for himself by the way she looked at me and touched my arm from time to time that we were on intimate terms. It was best to let it go at that.

The old man's English was adequate, despite a heavy accent, and as we talked in French, that beautiful late April afternoon, he or I occasionally translated or made some comment to Berenice in English.

'I'm one of those obscure journalists who presume to criticize art,' I said modestly, with a nervous smile, but he stopped me by raising a hand.

'Non, no, no' – he shook his head – 'not obscure, Mr Figueras. I know your work well. The article you wrote on the California painter . . . ?' He frowned.

'Vint? Ray Vint, you mean?'

'Yes, that's the name. The little fly. That was so droll.' He chuckled reflectively. 'Do not feel guilty, Mr Figueras.' He shrugged. 'The true artist cannot hide forever, and if not you, another would come. Now, come! Come inside! I will give you cold orange juice, fresh frozen Minute Maid.'

I was flattered that he knew my work as well as my name, or at least *one* article – I checked myself – written in English, at that, and not to my knowledge translated into French. But why did he mention this particular article on Vint? Ray Vint was an abstract painter whose paintings sold sparsely – for a dozen good reasons I won't go into here. Vint was an excellent craftsman, however, and could get all the portrait work he desired – more, in fact, than he wanted to paint. He needed the money he made from portraits to be able to work on the abstracts he preferred to paint. But because he hated to do portraits, he also hated the people who sat for them and provided him with large sums for flattering likenesses. He got 'revenge' on the sitters by painting a fly on them.

In medieval painting, and well into the Renaissance, a fly was painted on Jesus Christ's crucified body: the fly on Jesus's body was a symbol of redemption, because a fly represented sin and Jesus was without sin. A fly painted on the person of a layman, however, signified sin *without* redemption, or translated into 'This person is going to Hell!' Ray Vint painted a trompe-l'oeil fly on every portrait.

Sometimes his patrons didn't notice the fly for several days, and when they did they were unaware of its significance. They were usually delighted when they discovered it. The fly became a conversational gambit when they showed the portrait to their friends: 'Notice anything unusual there about my portrait?'

Artists, of course, when they saw the fly, laughed inwardly, but said nothing to the patrons about the meaning of the Vintian trademark. I had hesitated about whether to mention Vint's symbolic revenge when I wrote about him, not wanting to jeopardize his livelihood. But I had decided, in the end, to bring the matter up because it was a facet of Vint's personality that said something implicit about the emotionless nature of his abstracts.

As I guided Berenice into the house in Debierue's wake, holding her left elbow, I became apprehensive about the old painter's offhand remark and dry, brief chuckle. A chuckle, unlike a sudden smile or a sincere burst of laughter is difficult to interpret. Whether a chuckle is friendly or unfriendly, it merely serves as a nervous form of punctuation. But to mention one particular incident, or paragraph, out of the thousands I had written, and the 'fly' symbol at that, caused the knot of anxiety in the pit of my stomach to throb. The fact that he had read my piece on Vint (not a hack job, because I don't write hack pieces, but it certainly wasn't one of my best articles – Vint's work simply hadn't been good enough for a serious in-depth treatment) could be a hindrance to me.

No one knew, because Debierue had never commented, what the old man had thought about Galt's article, with its fanciful 'Chironesque' interpretations, but writers with reputations much greater than mine had been turned down subsequently when they had asked the painter for interviews. After the Galt article, Debierue had every right to distrust critics.

Damn Galt, anyway, I thought bitterly. Then I saw the gilded baroque frame on the wall and pointed to it.

'That isn't the famous *No. One*, is it?'

Debierue pursed his lips, and shrugged. 'It was,' he answered lightly, and entered the kitchen.

The moment I examined the picture I knew what he meant, of course. There was no crack on the wall behind the mount. The frame, without the crack, and not hanging in its original environment, was no longer the fabled *No. One*. My exultation was great nevertheless. It was something I had never expected to see in my lifetime. Berenice, after a quick glance at the empty frame, seated herself in a Sears-Danish chair and asked me for a cigarette.

I shook my head impatiently. 'Not till we ask permission,' I told her.

There was a narrow bar-counter built into the wall. It separated the kitchen from the living room. There was no dining room, and the living room was furnished spartanly. The chicken farmer-tenant who had built the house had probably intended, like many Floridians, to use the large screened porch as a dining area. There was a square, confirming pass-through window from the kitchen to the porch.

There were no other pictures on the walls, and the living room was furnished cheaply and austerely with Sears furniture. Mr Cassidy had certainly spared expense in furnishing the house for the famous visitor. There wasn't a hi-fi stereo, a radio, or television set, and there were no drapes to mask the severe horizontal lines of the Venetian blinds covering the windows. Except for two Danish chairs, a Marfak-topped coffee table, a black Naugahyde two-seater couch and one floor lamp – all grouped in a tight oblong – the huge living room, with its carpetless terrazzo floor, was bare. A *Miami Herald* and a superclick copy of *Réaltiés* were on the coffee table. There were two tall black wrought-iron barstools at the counter. Debierue either had to have his meals at this bar-counter or take his food out to the porch and eat on a Samsonite card table.

Mr Cassidy would not, I knew, tip Debierue off that I was coming, but if the old painter asked me how I had found him, what could I say? He didn't appear surprised by my sudden appearance. If he asked, I would say that my editor had told me and that he sent me down on an assignment. These thoughts nagged at my mind as Debierue prepared the frozen orange juice. He placed an aluminum pitcher on the table, opened the frozen can with an electric can opener, and then made three trips to the sink to fill the empty can with tap water.

He worked methodically, with great concentration, adding each canful of water to the pitcher like a chemist preparing an experiment. With a long-handled spoon he stirred the mixture, smiled, and beckoned for us to come and sit at the bar. Berenice and I climbed onto the stools, and he filled three plastic glasses to their brims.

Without touching his glass he looked beyond me to *No. One* on the wall. 'This is the new world, M. Figueras, and there are no cracks in the wall of the new world. Here the concrete, brick, and stucco walls are hurricane-proof. My insurance policy guarantees this.'

This might be a good opening or closing sentence for my article, I thought. I leaned forward, prepared to explore his thinking on the New World in more detail, but he shook his head as a signal for me to remain silent.

'I will not suggest to you that only M. Cassidy could have directed you here, M. Figueras. It is unimportant now that you are here, and we are both aware that M. Cassidy is, like all collectors, a most peculiar man.'

Grateful for the easy out, I asked for permission to smoke. Debierue took a saucer from the cabinet, set it between us, and waited until I lighted Berenice's cigarette and mine before he continued. He refused a cigarette by waving his hand.

'What can I say to you, M. Figueras, that would dissuade you from writing about me for your magazine?'

'Nothing, I'm afraid. You make me feel like a complete bastard, but—'

'I'm sorry for your feelings. But as a favor to me, do you have so much zeal that you must tell my address in your magazine? Much privacy is needed for my work, as it is for all artists. Every day I must work for at least four hours, and to have frequent interruptions—'

'That's no concession at all, sir. I'll dateline my piece "Somewhere in Florida." I know how you feel, of course. The Galt article was damned unfair to you, I know—'

'How do you know?' Again the sad, sweet smile.

'I know Galt's attitude toward art, that's how I know. He's got a one-track mental set. He invariably puts

533

everything he sees into a highly subjective pattern – whether it fits or not.'

'Is not all art subjective?'

'Yes.' I grinned. 'But didn't Braque say that the subject was not the object?'

'Perhaps. I don't know whether Braque said this himself, or whether some clever young man – a man like yourself, M. Figueras – *said* that he said it.'

'I – I don't recall,' I replied lamely, 'where the quote originated, not at the moment, but he is supposed to have said it himself. And if not . . . well . . . the play on words has a subtle validity, for . . . the art of our times. Don't you think?'

'The word "validity" cannot be used validly for the art of any time.'

I hesitated. He was testing me. By going into theoretical entelechy I could have answered him easily, but I didn't want to argue with him – I shrugged and smiled.

'By validity,' he smiled back, 'do you mean that the eye contains the incipient action?' The corners of his eyes wrinkled with amusement.

'Not exactly, sir. Cartesian dualism, as an approach to aesthetics, no longer has intrinsic value – and that's Galt's fault. He has never been able to transcend his early training. Not to be summational is the hardest task facing the contemporary critic. To see the present alone, blocking out the past and future, calls for optic mediation.' My face grew warm under the force of his steady blue eyes. 'I don't mean to run Galt down, sir, or to give you the impression that I'm a better critic than he is. It's just that I'm twenty-five years younger than Galt, and I've looked at more contemporary art than he has—'

'Do not be so nervous, M. Figueras. *¿Debemos dar preferencia al hablar del español?*'

'No. I think in Spanish when I speak it, and I prefer to think in English and talk in French—'

534

'What are you talking about?' Berenice said, sipping from her glass.

'The difference between Spanish and English and French,' I said.

'I hate Spanish,' Berenice said, winking at me. 'It's got too many words for bravery, which makes a person wonder sometimes about the true bravery of the Spanish character.'

'And French, I think,' Debierue said in English, 'has too many words for love.' He reached over and touched my hair. 'You have nice curly yellow hair, and she should not tease you. Come now, drink your orange juice.'

The paternal touch of his hand unknotted my inner tenseness, and I realized that the old artist was trying to make things easier for me. At any rate, my guilty feelings had been dissipated by his casual acceptance of both me and my professionalism. My awe of the old painter was also going away. I was still mightily impressed by him, and I felt that our conversation was going well.

Any writer who is awed in the presence of the great or the near-great cannot function critically. I respected Debierue enough to be wary, however, knowing that he was not an ingenuous man, knowing that he had survived as an individual all of these years by maintaining an aloof, if not an arrogant, silence, and a studied indifference to journalists. Debierue realized, I think, that I was on his side, and that I would always take an artist's viewpoint before that of the insensitive public's. He had read my work and he remembered my name. I could therefore give him credit for knowing that I was as unbiased as any art critic can ever be. To see his paintings, which was the major reason for my odyssey, I now had to gain his complete confidence. I had to guard against my tendency to argue. Nor should I bait him merely to obtain a few sensational opinions about art as 'news'.

'I am curious about why you immigrated to Florida, M. Debierue.'

'I almost didn't. For my old bones, I wanted the sun. When more than fifty years of my work was burned in the fire – you knew about the fire?'

'Yes, sir.'

'A most fortunate accident. It gave me a chance to begin again. The artist who can begin again at my age is a very fortunate man. So it was to the new world I turned, the new world and a new start. Tahiti, I think at first, would be best, but my name would then be linked somehow to Gauguin.' He shook his head sadly. 'Unavoidable. Such comparisons would not be fair, but they would have been made. And on the small island, perhaps the bus would pass my studio every day with American tourists to stare at me. Tahiti, no. Then I think, South America? No, there is always trouble there. And then Florida seems exactly right. But I did not come right away. I knew about the war in Florida, and I have had enough war in my lifetime.'

'The war?' I said, puzzled. 'The war in Vietnam?'

'No, no. The Seminole War. It is well known in Europe that these, the Florida Seminole Indians, are at war with your United States. Is it not so?'

'Yes, I suppose so, but only in a technical sense. The Seminoles are actually a very small Indian nation. And it's not a real war. It's a failure on the part of the Indians to sign a peace treaty with the US, that's all. Once in a while there's a slight legal flare-up, when some Florida county tries to force an Indian kid to go to school when he doesn't want to go – although a lot of Indians go to school now voluntarily. But there hasn't been an incident with shots fired for many years. The Seminoles have learned that they're better off than other Indian nations, in a legal way, by not signing a treaty.'

'Yes.' He nodded. 'I learned this from M. Cassidy, but I wrote some letters first to be certain.' He pursed his lips solemnly and looked down at the countertop. 'I will die in Florida now. This much I know, and a Frenchman does not find it so easy to leave France when he knows he will never see it again. There are other countries in the world that would have welcomed me, M. Figueras. Greece, Italy. The world is too good to me. I have always had many good friends, friends that I have never met. They write me letters, very nice letters from all over the world.'

I nodded my understanding. It was perfectly natural for strangers in every country to write to Debierue, although it had never occurred to me to write him myself. The same thing had happened to Schopenhauer in his old age, and he had been as pleased as Debierue to receive the letters. Any truly radical artist with original ideas who lives long enough will not only be accepted by the world at large, he will be admired, if not revered, for his dogged persistence – even by people who detest everything he stands for.

But there was a major difference between the old German philosopher and this old French painter. Schopenhauer had accepted the flood of congratulations on his birthdays during his seventies as a well-deserved tribute, as a vindication. Debierue, on the other hand, while grateful, seemed bewildered and even humbled by the letters he received.

'But I am not sorry I came to Florida, M. Figueras. Your sun is good for me.'

'And your work? Has it gone well for you, too?'

'The artist' – he looked into my eyes—'can work anywhere. Is it not so?'

I cleared my throat to make the pitch I had been putting off. 'M. Debierue, I respect your stand on art and privacy

537

very much. In fact, just to sit here talking to you and drinking your fresh orange juice—'

'The fresh *frozen*,' he amended.

'. . . is an honor. A great honor. I'm well aware of your reluctance to show your work to the public and to critics, and I can't say that I blame you. You have, however, on occasion, permitted a few outstanding critics to examine and write about your work. You've only been in Florida for a few months, as I understand it, and I don't know if you've completed any paintings you'd be willing to show an American critic. But if you have, I would consider it a privilege—'

'Are you a painter, M. Figueras?'

'No, sir, I'm not. I had enough studio courses in college to know that I could never be a successful painter. My talent, such as it is, is writing, and I'm a craftsman rather than an artist, I regret to say. But I am truly a superior craftsman as a critic. To be frank, in addition to the personal pleasure I'd get from seeing your American paintings, an exclusive, in-depth article in my magazine would be a feather in my cap. The sales of the magazine would jump, and it would be the beginning for me of some very lucrative outside assignments from other art journals. As you know, only *one* photograph of any single one of your paintings would be art news big enough to get both of us international attention—'

'Do you sculpt? Or work with collage, ceramics?'

'No, sir.' I tried to keep the annoyance I felt out of my voice. 'Nothing like that. I'm quite inept when it comes to doing work with my hands.'

'But I do not understand, M. Figueras. Your critical articles are very sensitive. I do not understand why you do not paint, or—'

'At one time this was a rather sore point with me, but I got over it. I tried hard enough, but I simply couldn't draw well enough – too clumsy, I guess. If I didn't have a well-developed verbal sense I'd probably have a tough time making a living.'

'I've got to go to the restroom, Mr Debierue,' Berenice said shyly.

'Certainly.' Debierue came around the bar and pointed down the hallway. 'The door at the far end.'

I climbed off the stool when she did and looked down the hallway past Debierue's shoulder. Berenice was undoubtedly bored, but she also undoubtedly had to go to the can. At the end of the short hallway there were two more doors *en face*, in addition to the door to the bathroom straight ahead. One door was padlocked, and one was not. The padlocked door, with its heavy hasp, was probably Debierue's studio and formerly the master bedroom of the original owner.

I took the Polaroid camera out of its leather case, and checked to see if there was an unused flashbulb in the bounce reflector.

'This camera,' I said, 'is so simple to operate that an eight-year-old child can get good results with it almost every time. It's that simple.' I laughed. 'But before I learned how to work the damned thing I ruined ten rolls of film. It's ridiculous, I know. And with typing, which I had to learn, I was equally clumsy. I took a typing course twice, but the touch system was too much for me to master.' I held up my index and second fingers. 'I have to type my stuff with these four fingers. So you can see why I quit trying to paint. It was too frustrating, so I quit trying before I suffered any emotional damage.'

He looked at me quizzically, and stroked his hooked nose with a long finger.

'I guess I sound a little stupid,' I said apologetically.

'No, no. The critic – all critics – arouses my curiosity, M. Figueras.'

'It's quite simple, really. I'm purported to be an expert, or at least an authority, on art and the preschool child. And what it boils down to is this. Most motor activity is learned before the age of five. A preschool child can only learn things by doing them. And if you have a mother who does everything for you – little things like tying shoelaces, brushing your teeth, feeding you, and so on, you don't do them yourself. After five or six, when you *have* to do them yourself, in school, for example, it's too late ever to master the dexterity and motor control a painter will need in later years. Overly solicitous mothers, that is, mothers who wait on their children hand and foot, inadvertently destroy incipient artists.'

'Have you ever written about this theory?'

I nodded. 'Yes. A short book entitled *Art and the Preschool Child*, and I'll mail you a copy. It explains, in part, why men who are psychologically suited to becoming painters turn out so much bad art. It isn't a theory, though, it's a fact. A neglected point that I made is that such people are not lost to the world as artists. If their problem is recognized, they can be rechanneled into other artistic activities that do not call for great manual dexterity.'

'Like what?' Debierue appeared to be genuinely interested.

'Writing poetry, composing electronic music. Or even architecture. The late Addison Mizner, who couldn't draw a straight line in the sand with a pointed stick, became an important South Florida architect. His buildings in Palm Beach – those that remain – are beautifully designed, and his influence on other Florida architecture has been considerable, especially here on the east coast.'

I stopped before I got wound up. Debierue was pulling on me – on *me*! – one of the oldest tricks not in the book, and here I was, falling for it, just like the rawest of cub reporters. It is a simple matter for the person who is wise with the experience of being interviewed to learn the interests of the interviewer. Then, all he has to do is to keep feeding questions to the interviewer and the interviewer will end up with an interview of himself! Naively happy with a long and pleasant conversation, the interviewer will leave the subject in a blithe mood, only to learn later, when he sits chagrined at his typewriter, that he has nothing to write about.

The toilet flushed. Debierue waited politely for me to continue, but I swirled the juice in my glass, sipped the rest of it slowly until Berenice rejoined us, and then excused myself on the pretense that I also had to use the facility.

I still carried my camera, of course, and I quickly opened the door on the left of the hall, across from the padlocked door. I closed it softly behind me and took the room in rapidly. If one of Debierue's paintings was on the wall, I was going to take a picture of it. But there was only one painting on the wall, a dime-store print in a cheap black frame of *Trail's End* – the ancient Indian sitting on his wornout horse. In the 1930s almost every lower-middle-class home in America contained a print of *Trail's End*, but I hadn't expected to find one in Debierue's bedroom. Either Cassidy, in his meanness, had hung it on the wall, or it had been left there by the owner of the house. But I still couldn't fathom how Debierue could tolerate the corny picture, unless, perhaps, he was amused by the ironic idea behind the print. Of course, that was probably the reason.

The bedroom was austere. A Hollywood single bed, made up with apple-green sheets – and no bedspread – an unpainted pine highboy, a wrought-iron bedside table with a slab of white tile for a top, and a red plastic Charles Eames chair beside the bed made up the inventory. There was a ceiling light, but no lamp. Debierue was a nihilist and stoic in his everyday life as well as in his art, but I felt a wave of sympathy for the painter all the same. It was a shame, I felt, that this great man had so few creature comforts in his old age. There was no need for me to slide open the closet door, or to search the drawers of the highboy and paw through his clothing.

I took a nervous leak in the bathroom, and turned on the tap to wash my hands in the washbowl. I opened the mirrored cabinet to see what kind of medicines he kept there. If he had any diseases, or an illness of some kind, the medicines he used would furnish a valid clue, and that might be worth writing about. Except for Elixophyllin-K1 (an expectorant that eases the ability to breathe for persons with asthma, emphysema, and bronchitis) and three bars of Emulave (a kind of 'soapless' soap, or cleansing bar for people with very dry skin – and I had noted the dryness of the painter's hands already), there was nothing out of the ordinary in the cabinet. A pearl-handled straight razor, a cup with shaving soap and brush, a bottle of blue-green Scope, a half-used tube of Stripe toothpaste, a green plastic Dr West toothbrush, a 100-tablet bottle of Bayer aspirin, with the cotton gone, and that was it. There wasn't even a comb, although Debierue, with a bald head as slick as a peeled almond, didn't need a comb. As bathroom medicine chests in America go, this was the barest cabinet – outside of a rented motel room – I had ever seen.

I returned to the living room in time to hear Berenice say, 'Don't you get lonely, Mr Debierue, living way out here all alone?'

He smiled, patted her hand, and shook his head.

'It's the nature of the artist to be lonely,' I answered for him. 'But the painter has his work to do, which is ample compensation.'

'I know,' Berenice said, 'but this place is a million miles from nowhere. You ought to get a car, Mr Debierue. Then you could drive over to Dania for Jai-alai at night or something.'

'No, no,' he protested, still patting her hand, 'I am too old now to learn how to drive an automobile.'

'You could take some students,' Berenice said eagerly. 'There would be a lot of students who would like to work with you in your studio! And I bet they'd come with cars from all over' – she turned to me— 'wouldn't they, James?'

Debierue laughed, and I joined him, although I was laughing more at Berenice's droll expression – half anger and half bewilderment – because we were laughing at her. For any other painter of equal stature, Picasso, for instance, the suggestion of a student working with a master was valid enough. But for Debierue, who showed his work to no one, the idea was absurd. Debierue had sidetracked me neatly. It was time to get back to business.

I put an affectionate arm around Berenice's waist and squeezed her as a signal to keep quiet. 'You didn't answer my question a while ago, M. Debierue,' I said soberly. 'You have been very nice to me – to us both – even though we've invaded your privacy. But I would like to see your present work—'

He sighed. 'I'm sorry, M. Figueras. You have made your visit without reason. You see,' he shrugged, 'I have no work to show you.'

'Nothing at all? Not even a drawing?'

The corners of his mouth drooped morosely. 'Work I have, yes. But what things I have done in Florida are not deserving of your attention.'

'Why don't you let me be the judge of that?'

His strained half-smile was weary, but his features stiffened with a mask of discernible dignity. His voice dropped to a husky whisper. 'The artist alone is a final judge of his work, M. Figueras.'

I flushed. 'Please don't misunderstand me,' I said quickly. 'I didn't mean what I said to come out that way.

What I meant was that I don't intend to criticize your work, or judge it in any way. I meant to say that I would prefer to be the judge of whether I'd like to *see* it or not. And I would. It would be an honor.'

'No. I am sorry but I must refuse. You are a critic and you cannot help yourself. For you, to see a picture is to make a judgment. I do not want your judgment. I paint for Debierue. I please myself and I displease myself. For a young man like you to say to me, "Ah, M. Debierue, here in this corner a touch of terracotta might strengthen the visual weight," or "I like the tactile texture, but I believe I see a hole in the overall composition . . ."' He chuckled drily. 'I must say no, M. Figueras.'

'You are putting me down, sir,' I said. 'I know there are critics such as you describe, but I'm not one of them.' My face was flaming, but my voice was under control.

'With the art of Debierue, one man is a crowd. Me. Debierue. Two people are a noisy audience. But to have one spectator with a pen, the critic, is to have many thousands of spectators. Surrealism does not need your rationale, M. Figueras. And Debierue does not paint "bicephalous centaurs."'

'He won't let you see his pictures, will he?' Berenice guessed, looking at my face.

I shook my head.

'Maybe,' she turned and looked coyly at Debierue, 'you'll let me see them instead, Mr Debierue?'

He stepped back a few feet and examined her figure admiringly. 'You have a wide pelvis, my dear, and it will be very easy for you to have many fine, beautiful babies.'

'By that he means no for me too, doesn't he?'

'What else?' I shrugged, and lit a cigarette.

As I had suspected, Debierue had disliked Galt's criticism. I could have begged, but that would have been abhorrent to me. If this was the way he felt there was no

544

point in pursuing the matter anyway. In one way, he was right about me. It would have been impossible for me to look at his work without judging it. And although I would not have said anything derogatory about his work, no matter how I felt about it, there was bound to be some indication of how I felt – pro or con – reflected in my face. If he didn't actually believe that his paintings were worthy (although his faculty for criticism was certainly not as good as mine), all I could do now was take him at his word. I felt almost like crying. It was one of the greatest disappointments of my life.

'Perhaps another time, then, M. Debierue,' I said.

'Yes, perhaps.' He stroked his beaked nose pensively and studied my face. Not rudely, but earnestly. He glanced toward the hallway leading to his padlocked studio, looked back at me, smiled at Berenice, and tugged pensively at his lower lip. I suspected that he had expected me to put up a prolonged, involved argument, and now he didn't know whether to be grateful or disappointed by my failure to protest.

'Tell me something, M. Figueras. I am called *the* Nihilistic Surrealist, but I have never known why. Do you see much disorder here, in my little house?'

'No, sir.' I looked around. 'Far from it.'

For an artist, the lack of clutter was most unusual. Painters, as a 'class', are a messy lot. They collect things. An old board, with concentric swirls, a rock, with an intriguing shape, jumbles of wire, seashells, any and all kinds of things that have, to them, interesting shapes or colors. A chunk of wood, for example, may gather a heavy patina of dust for years before a sculptor finally detects the shape within the object and liberates it into a piece of sculpture.

Painters are even messier, in most instances, than sculptors. They stick drawings up here and there. Pads with sketches are scattered about haphazardly, and they clutter their quarters with all kinds of props and worthless junk. Things are needed for visual stimulation and possible ideas. This clutter is not confined to their studios either. It generally spills over into their everyday habitat, including the kitchen and bathroom.

And a Surrealist, like Debierue, dealing in the juxtaposition of the unlikely, would ordinarily require a great many unrelated objects in his home and studio to nudge his subconscious. But then, Debierue was an anomaly among painters. My experience with the habits of other painters could hardly apply to him. Besides, I had not, as yet, seen the inside of his studio . . .

'As you see, I am an orderly, clean old man. Always it was so, even as a young man. So it may be, after all, that I am not the Surrealist. Is it not so?' The grooved amusement lines crowding his blue eyes deepened as he smiled.

'It's a relative term,' I said politely. 'A convenient label. "Surrealist" or "Subrealist" would both have served as well. The term "Dada" itself was just a catchall word at first, but the motto "Dada *hurts*," when it was truly followed or lived up to in plastic expression, was quite important to me. In fact it still is, but I've always considered "Surrealism" as a misnomer.'

'Debierue does not like any label. Debierue is Debierue. Marcel Duchamp I admired very much, and he too did not like labels. Do you remember what Duchamp did when a young writer asked him for permission to write his biography?'

'No, sir.'

'When Duchamp was asked for the quite personal information about himself he said nothing. He did not have to think. He emptied all of the drawers from his desk onto the floor and walked out of the room.'

'An existential act.' The story was one I hadn't heard.

'Another label, M. Figueras?' He clucked his tongue. 'So now on the floor are odds and ends, little things saved in the desk for many years for no good reason. Snapshots, little notes one receives or makes for himself. Old letters from friends, enemies, ladies. And, what is it? – the *doodles*, little pencil squigglings. And pretty canceled stamps saved because they are exotic perhaps. Stubs from the theater.' He shrugged.

'It sounds like my desk in New York.'

'But this was the Duchamp biography. The clever young man picked up everything from the floor and went away. He pasted all of the objects in a big book, entitled it *The Biography of Marcel Duchamp* and sold it for a large sum of dollars to a rich Texas Jew.'

'It's funny I never heard about it. I thought I knew practcally everything about Duchamp there was to know . . .'

'And so did the young man who "wrote" the biography about Duchamp out of odds and ends from a desk.'

'Nevertheless,' I said, 'I'd like to take a look at that book. Every scrap of information about Duchamp is important because it helps us to understand his art.'

The artist shrugged. 'There is no such book. The story is apochryphal – I made it up myself and spread it to a few friends many years ago to see what would happen. And because it is something Duchamp might do, many believed it as you were prepared to do. The chance debris of an artist's life does not explain the man, nor does it explain the artist's work. The true artist's vision comes from here.' He tapped his forehead.

Debierue's face was expressionless now, and I was unable to tell whether he was serious, teasing me, or getting hostile. He turned to Berenice and smiled. He took her right hand in both of his and spoke in English.

'If a man had a wife and children, perhaps a short biography to leave his family, a record for them to remember

547

him . . . but old Debierue has no wife, children, no relatives now living, to want such a book. The true artist, my dear, is too responsible to marry and have a family.'

'Too responsible to fall in love?' Berenice asked softly.

'No. Love he must have.'

I cleared my throat. 'The entire world is the artist's family, M. Debierue. There are thousands of art lovers all over the world who would like to read your biography. Those who write to you, I know, and those who—'

He patted my arm. 'Let us be the friends. It is not friendly to talk about nothing with such seriousness on your face. It is getting late, and you will both stay to dinner with me, please.'

'Thank you very much. We would like very much to stay.' He had changed the subject abruptly, but the longer I stayed the better my chances became to gain information about the old man. Or did they?

'Good!' He rubbed his dry hands together and they made a rasping sound. 'First I will turn on my electric oven to four-two-five degrees. I do not have the printed menu, but you may decide. There is the television turkey dinner. Very good. There is the television Salisbury steak. Also very good. Or maybe, M. Figueras, you would most like the television patio dinner? Enchilada, tamale, Spanish rice, and refried beans.'

'No,' I said. 'I guess I'll have the turkey.'

'I'd rather have the Salisbury steak,' Berenice said. 'And let me help you—'

'No. Debierue will also have the turkey!' He smiled happily, and turned toward the stove. Relenting, he changed direction, went to the sideboard and got out a box of Piknik yellow plastic forks and spoons. There was a four-mat set of sticky rubber yellow place mats in the drawer. He handed the mats and the box of plastic utensils to Berenice and asked her to set the card table on the porch.

So far, I thought bitterly, as I glumly watched this bustling domestic activity, except for a few gossipy comments on a low curiosity level, I had picked up damned little information of any real interest from the old artist. If anything, he had learned more about me than I had about him. He had refused to let me see his work, and just as he had started to open up he had slammed the lid on what might have been an entire trunkful of fascinating material. He was a bewildering old man, all right, and I couldn't decide whether he was somewhat senile (no, not that), putting me down, with some mysterious purpose in mind, or what . . .

Working away, stripping the cardboard outer covers from the aluminum TV dinners he had taken from the freezer compartment of the purple Kentone refrigerator, Debierue sang a repetitive French song in a cracked falsetto.

No matter how he downgraded himself, false modesty or not, he was the world's outstanding Nihilistic Surrealist. That was the reason I wasn't getting anywhere with him. I was trying to talk to him as if he were a normal person. Any artist who has isolated himself from the world for three-fourths of his life either has to be a Surrealist or crazy. But Debierue was as sane as any other artist I had ever met. Even the fact that he denied being a Surrealist emphasized the fact that he was one. What else could he be? This was the rationale of the purposeful irrationality of Surrealism. The key. But the key to what?

How could a man live all alone as he did – without a phone, a TV, a radio – for months on end without going off his rocker? Even Schweitzer, when he exiled himself to Africa, took an organ along, and surrounded himself with sick, freeloading black men . . .

From this desperate brooding, my pedestrian mind came up with one of the best original ideas I ever had, an idea so simple and direct I almost lost it. The thought was still

549

formless, but I didn't let the idea get away from me. Berenice put three webbed chairs up to the table on the porch. She re-entered the living-room, and I clutched her wrist.

'I'm going to do something strange,' I whispered. 'But don't let on, no matter what happens. Understand?'

She nodded, and her blue eyes widened.

Debierue came out of the kitchen and tapped my wrist-watch. 'Sometimes I do not hear so well the timer on the oven, so you will please watch the time for us. And in thirty-five minutes when you say "Now," we will have the dinner all ready to eat!' He beamed his jack-o'-lantern smile at Berenice. 'So simple. The television dinner is the better invention for wives than the television itself. Is it not so, my dear?'

'Oh, absolutely,' Berenice said cheerfully.

'Look, M. Debierue,' I said, taking my Polaroid from the bar, 'I know it's a lot to ask, at least from your viewpoint, but I've got this Polaroid here, and you can see the results for yourself in about ten seconds. While we wait for dinner, let me take a few shots of you, and until we get one that you think is all right, you can just tear them up. Fair enough?'

'In only ten seconds? A picture?'

'That's all. Maybe fifteen seconds inside the house here, for a little extra snap and contrast.'

He frowned slightly, and fingered his white whiskers. 'My beard isn't trimmed . . .'

'In a photo, it doesn't matter. No one can tell from a black-and-white picture.' I promised recklessly.

He hesitated. His eyes were wary, but he was wavering. 'Should I put on a necktie?'

'No, not for an informal picture,' I said, before he could change his mind. Taking him by the arm, I guided him to a point in front of the coffee table. I picked up the *Miami Herald*, flipped through it to find the classified ad section, opened it and thrust the paper into his hands.

'There. Just spread the paper, and pretend to read it. You can smile if you feel like it, but you don't have to.'

A trifle self-consciously, he followed my simple directions. After focusing the camera on him, and setting it for 'dark', I asked him to lower his arms slightly to make certain his face and beard would be in the picture. The flag of the *Miami Herald* and *Classified* could both be read through the viewfinder. I moved forward and touched his hand.

'No,' I admonished, 'please don't move or look up at me. I'll take the photo from back there.'

This was the last moment to take my premeditated chance, and one chance was all I could expect to get. I forced a loud cough to cover the slight click of my Dunhill, and ignited the paper at the bottom. A moment later, six feet back, I was squinting through the viewfinder. The timing was perfect. The bounce flashbulb worked, and it was only a split second after I snapped the shutter that the flames burst through the paper on his side and he dropped it with an astonished yelp. Berenice, who had been watching with bulging eyes and with her right hand clamped over her mouth, moved forward squealing, and began to stamp on the burning paper. I helped her, and it only took us moments to crush out the flames on the terrazzo floor.

I had expected an angry reaction from Debierue, but he was merely puzzled. 'Why,' he asked mildly, 'did you light the paper? I don't understand.' He looked about bewilderedly as the charred bits of newsprint, caught by the slight breeze coming through the jalousied door, fluttered over his clean floor.

I grinned and held up a forefinger. 'Wait. Give me ten seconds, and then you'll see the picture.'

I was all thumbs with excitement, but I took my time, being careful as I jerked out the strip of prepared paper that started the developing process and, instead of guessing,

I watched the sweep-second hand on my watch, allowing exactly twelve seconds for the developer to work.

As curious as a child, the old artist was brushing my shoulder with his as I opened the back of the camera to remove the print. When I turned the photo face up on the bar, his jarring burst of jubilant laughter startled me.

'Don't touch it!' I said sharply, sliding the print out of the reach of his clutching fingers. 'I've got to coat it first.' I straightened the print on the edge of the counter and then gave it eight precise sweeps with the gooey print coater. It was the best photo, absolutely the finest, that I had ever taken.

Perfectly centered, the old man wore his wise, beautiful, infectious smile. He appeared to be reading the want ads in the *Herald* as if he didn't have a care in the world. His face was purely serene, and the deeply etched lines in his face were sharp, clear-cut, and as black as India ink. He had been completely unaware of the blazing newspaper when I snapped the picture, but no one who saw the paper would ever guess that. The entire lower half of the paper blazed furiously away. No professional model could have posed knowingly with a flaming newspaper without a slight twinge of anxiety showing in his face. But the old man, with his skinny legs exposed beneath the flames, with his bland innocent face and the wonderful smile flowing through his downy white beard, appeared as relaxed as a man who had spent a restful night in a Turkish bath.

Debierue watched me coat the print, but he kept reaching for it impatiently. I guarded it with my arm so it could dry.

'Let me see,' he said childishly.

'If you touch it now,' I explained patiently, 'it'll pick up your fingerprints and be ruined.'

'Very well, M. Figueras,' he said good-naturedly. 'I want this photo. It's the most formidable *surréalité* I've ever seen!'

His exuberance was as great as my own. 'You'll have it, all right,' I said happily. 'In fact, when I get back to New York, I'll send you fifty copies of the picture if you want them, and a copy to every friend on your mailing list.'

Chapter Three

When Debierue granted his permission for me to keep and publish the photograph, I hurried out to the car and got one of our magazine's standard release forms out of the glove compartment. The mimeographed form (large-circulation magazines have them printed) is a simple agreement between subject and magazine to make publication legal, to protect one party from the other. There is nothing underhanded about a signed photo release. Debierue could read English, of course, but the involved legalese the form was couched in forced me to explain the damned thing at some length before he would sign it. Debierue wasn't stupid or willful. He believed naively that his oral okay was enough.

Because of this discussion, the dinners were ready before we knew it. I forgot to look at my watch, and it was Berenice who heard and recognized the faint buzzing in the kitchen as the oven timer.

It was almost pleasant on the screened porch. A light breeze came up, and although the wind was hot, it was relatively comfortable in the darkening twilight as we sat at the candlelit card tabletop to eat the miserable off-brand TV dinners.

The dinners had been purchased by the Negro maid who came every Wednesday to take care of the old man's laundry and to do his difficult cleaning. She also brought his other weekly food supplies. By buying these cheap TV dinners, she was probably knocking down on the food money. I didn't suggest this to him, but I discussed brand names, the brand-name fallacy, and wrote out a short list of worthwhile frozen food buys he could depend upon. He had a delusion that frozen foods were better, somehow, than fresh. Berenice started halfheartedly to tell him otherwise, but when she saw me shake my head she changed the subject to domestic wines. Debierue distrusted California wines, but I added the brands of some Napa Valley wines to the frozen food list, and he said he would try them. Other than tap water, all he drank, because French wines were too dear, was frozen orange juice.

The Gold Coast for some twenty miles inland, from Jupiter downstate to Key Largo, is tropical – not *subtropical*, as so many people erroneously believe. The tropical weather is caused by the warmth of the Gulf Stream, less than six miles off the coast. There is little difference between the weather in Miami and that of Saigon. Debierue's house, on a hammock with a black swamp and the Everglades for a backyard, was depressingly humid. After eating the dry turkey dinner, my mouth felt as if it were dehydrated, and I couldn't drink enough fluid to unparch my throat. I poured another glass of orange juice (my fourth) and sensed, as I did so, a certain anxiety or impatience developing in the old man. As an experienced dinner guest, I have picked up an instinct about wearing out welcomes.

The sky had darkened from bruise blue to gentian violet, and it was only a few minutes after six thirty. It was much too early for him to go to bed, but even Berenice, who was not particularly observant, became aware of the old painter's restlessness. She winked across the table, tapped her wrist significantly, and gave me a brief, comical shrug. I nodded, and slid my chair back from the table.

'It's been delightful, M. Debierue, the dinner by candlelight,' I lied socially, 'but I have another appointment in Palm Beach tonight, and we have to drive back.'

'Of course,' he replied, standing, 'but please keep your seat a few moments more. Already, you see, it is past the time for me to get ready. I must go to the movies tonight. I must go to the movies every night,' he added, by way of fuller explanation, 'and I must now change my clothes.'

'The movies?' I asked stupidly.

His face brightened and he rubbed his hands together briskly. 'Oh, yes, perhaps you did not see it – the Dixie Drive-in Movie Theater . . .' He pointed in the general direction of the drive-in. 'Tonight there are three long features, two films with the Bowery Boys and the film about a werewolf. And before these, the regular films, there are always two and sometimes three cartoons. The first long film tonight is *The Bowery Boys Meet Frankenstein*, a very special treat, no? And if you will kindly drive me—'

'Certainly, I said, eagerly, 'I'll be happy to take you in the car.'

'My ignorance,' Debierue chuckled reminiscently, 'it was the amusing thing. When I was first here and taking a walk one evening, I saw the automobiles driving inside the Dixie Drive-in Theater. I did not then know the American custom, and I thought that one must have the automobile to enter the movie. Never before had I seen the drive-in movies, and I said to myself, 'Why not see if the permission to go from the manager can be arranged?' So I talked then to the manager, M. Albert Price. He arranged for me to go, and gave me the Senior Citizen Golden Years' membership card.' Debierue fumbled his wallet out of his hip pocket, extracted the card, which entitled him to a 15 percent discount on movie tickets, and proudly showed it to us. It was made out to Eugene V. Debs.

'That's very nice,' Berenice said, smiling.

'M. Price is a very nice man,' Debierue said, carefully replacing the card in his thin, calfskin wallet. 'There are very good seats in front of the snack bar. The parents with the automobiles sometimes send their children to sit in these seats, and they are also for those patrons who do not have the automobile, as M. Price explained to me. Over to the right of these seats is the zinc slide and little swings, the Kiddyland for these, the children, who become tired of watching the movie screen. I *like* the children – I am a Frenchman – but the little children begin to make too much noise playing in the Kiddyland after the cartoons are finished. This arrangement is good for the parents inside the cars with speakers, but not for me. The noise becomes too loud for me. M. Price and I are now good friends, and he reserves for me each night a seat and special earphones. I hear only the movie with the earphones and no more the children.'

I smiled. 'Can you understand American English, the way the Bowery Boys speak it?'

'No, not always,' he replied seriously. 'But it is no matter. These Bowery Boys are too wonderful comedians – the Surrealist actors, no? I like M. Huntz Hall. He is very droll. Last week there were the three pictures one night with the bourgeois couple and their new house, Papa and Mama Kettle. I like them very much, and also John Wayne.' He shook his fingers as if he had burned them badly on a hot stove. 'Oh ho! *He* is the tough guy, no?'

'Yes, sir, he certainly is. But you've surprised me again, M. Debierue. I had no idea you were a movie fan.'

'It is pleasant to see the cinema in the evenings.' He shrugged. 'And I like also the grape snow cone. Do you like these, the grape snow cones, M. Figueras?'

'I haven't had one in a long time.'

'Very good. Fifteen cents at the snack bar.'

'That's quite a long walk down there and back every night, M. Debierue. And as long as you haven't seen these

557

old movies anyway, why don't you buy a television? There are at least a half-dozen films on TV every night, and—'

'No,' he said loyally, 'this is not good advice. M. Price had already explained to me that the TV was harmful to the eyes. The little screen, he said, will give one bad headaches after one or two hours of watching.'

I was going to refute this, but changed my mind and lit a cigarette instead. Debierue excused himself and left for his bedroom. I stubbed out the cigarette in the sticky remains of the imitation cranberry sauce well in the TV dinner plate. My mouth was too dry to smoke.

'Have you got any tranquilizers in your purse?'

'No, but I've got a Ritalin, I think.' Berenice untied the drawstring and searched for her pillbox.

'OK, and give me two Excedrins while you're at it.'

'I've only got Bufferin—'

I took two Bufferin and the tiny Ritalin pill and chased them with the remainder of my orange juice.

'It looks as though things are going to break for us after all,' I said softly.

'What do you mean?'

'What do you think I mean?'

She looked at me with the blank vacant stare that always infuriated me. 'I don't know.'

'Never mind. We'll talk about it later.'

Within a few minutes Debierue returned, wearing his moviegoer's 'costume'. He had exchanged the short-sleeved polo shirt for a long-sleeved dress shirt, and it was buttoned at the neck and cuffs. He wore long white duck trousers instead of shorts, and had pulled his white socks up over the cuffs and secured them with bicycle clips. With his tennis shoes and Navy blue beret he resembled some exclusive tennis club's oldest living member. In his left hand he carried a pair of cotton Iron Boy work gloves. It was a peculiar getup, but it was a practical uniform for a man who was determined to sit for six hours in a mosquito-infested drive-in movie.

Debierue locked the front door and dropped the key into a red pottery pot containing a thirsty azalea, and trailed us to the car. Berenice sat in the middle, and as I drove cautiously down the grassy road toward the highway she and the old man discussed mosquitoes and mosquito control. His beloved M. Price had a huge smoke-spraying machine on a truck that made the circuit of the theater before the films began and again at intermission, but Debierue had to take the gloves along because the mosquitoes were so fierce on his walk home. She told him about, and recommended, a spray repellent called Festrol, and I was repelled by the banality of their conversation. But with his mind on the movies, it was too late for me to ask him any final questions about his art.

I pulled over in the driveway short of the ticket window and waved a car by. I gave the old man one of my business cards with the magazine's New York address and telephone number, and wedged in a parting comment that if he changed his mind about letting me see his pictures he could call me collect at any time. He nodded impatiently and, without looking at the card, dropped it into his shirt pocket. We shook hands, the quick one-up-and-one-down handshake, Berenice gave him a peck on his beard, and he got out of the car. By the time I got the car turned around, he had disappeared into the darkness of the theater. Music and insane woodpecker laughter filled the night suddenly as I turned onto the highway. Berenice sighed.

'What's the matter?'

'Oh, I was just thinking,' she said. 'We held him up too long and now he'll have to wait until intermission to get his grape snow cone.'

'Yeah. That's tough.'

Chapter Four

I drove into Debierue's private road, stopped, and switched off the headlights. Before she could say anything I turned to Berenice and said, 'Before you say anything I'm going to tell you. Then, if you have questions, ask them. I'm going down now to take a look at Debierue's pictures. He said he had painted a few, and now that I know there are pictures in his studio I can't go back without one for Mr Cassidy.'

'Why not? He doesn't know that there are any.'

'I made a deal. And even if I decide not to take one back, which I doubt, I still have to see them for myself. If you don't understand that, you don't understand me very well.'

'I understand, but it's dangerous—'

'With Debierue in the movies, it's safer than houses. He dropped the door key into a potted plant on the porch. You saw him too, didn't you?'

'But the studio is still locked, and—'

'I don't want to get you involved any more than you are already. But I want you to stay here by the highway, just in case. Debierue might think about the key himself and come back for it. I don't believe he will, but if he does you can run down the road and warn me and we'll get the hell out. Okay?'

'I can't stand out here in the dark all by myself! I'm scared and there are all these mosquitoes and I want to go with you!'

'We're wasting time. It's one thing for me to be a house-breaker, but it's something else for you – as a schoolteacher.

There's nothing to be frightened about – I'm sorry about the mosquitoes – but if you're really afraid I'll take you down the highway to a gas station. You can lock yourself in the women's room till I come back for you.'

'I don't want to lock myself up in—'

'Get out of the car. I want to get this over with.'

'Let me have your cigarettes.'

I handed her my half-empty pack, not the full one, and she climbed resignedly out of the car. 'How long are you going to be?'

'I don't know. That depends upon how many paintings I have to look at.'

'Don't do it, James. Please don't do it!'

'Why, for God's sake?'

'Because Debierue doesn't want you to, that's why!'

'That's not a reason.'

'I – I may not be here when you get back, James.'

'Good! In that case, I can say you weren't with me at all tonight if I'm caught and you won't get into any trouble.'

Without lights I eased the car down the road, but turned them on again as soon as I was well into the pines and around the first bend. There was no good reason not to have taken Berenice with me except that I didn't want her along. That is, there was no rational reason. She had looked rather pitiful standing in the tall grass beside the road. Maybe I thought she would be in the way, or that she would talk all the time. Something . . . It might have been something in my subconscious mind warning me about what I would find. As soon as I parked in front of the house I considered, for a brief moment, going back for her. I got out of the car instead, but left the headlights on.

Because of the rain-washed air the few visible stars seemed to be light years higher in the void than they usually were. There was no moon as yet, and the night was inky. In the black swamp beyond the house a lonesome

561

bull alligator roared erotically. This was such a miserable, isolated location for an artist to live. I was grateful that the old painter had a place to go every night – and not only because the house was so easy to break into. If I had to live out here all alone, I too would have been looking forward to seeing the Bowery Boys and three color cartoons.

Debierue's 'hiding' of the key was evidently a habitual practice, a safeguard to prevent its loss as he walked to and from the theater each night. I doubted that the idea entered his head that I would return to his empty house to make an illegal use of the key. But I didn't really know. My guilt, if any, was light. I felt no more guilt that that of a professional burglar. A burglar must make a living, and to steal he must first invade the locked home where the items he wants to steal are safeguarded. I meant no harm to the old artist. Any picture I took, and I was only going to take one, Debierue, could paint again. And except for the visual impressions of his painting in my mind – and a few photos – I would take nothing else. There was no reason to feel guilty.

So I cannot account for the dryness of my mouth, the dull stasis of my blood, the tightness of the muscles surrounding my stomach, and the noticeable increase in my rate of breathing. These signs of anxiety were ridiculous. The old man was sitting in the drive-in with a pair of headphones clamped to his ears, and even if he caught me inside the house, the worst he could so would be to express dismay. He couldn't hurt me physically, and he would hardly report me to the police. But I was an amateur. I had never broken into anyone's house before, so I supposed that my anxiety stemmed from the melodramatic idea that I was engaged in a romantic adventure. But after I had unlocked the front door and let it swing inward, I had to muster a good deal of courage before I could force my hand to reach inside to flip on the living-room lights.

The light coming through the window would be bright enough to see my way back from the car. I switched off the headlights, and returned hurriedly to the house with a tire iron and a hammer I got from the trunk. But as it turned out, these tools were unnecessary.

The only barrier to the studio was the hasp and the heavy Yale lock on the door. Once broken there would be no way to prevent Debierue from guessing that I had returned. But if the artist had been afraid he might lose his house key, it also seemed unlikely that he would take the studio padlock key to the theater.

Switching on the lights as I searched, I made a hasty, fruitless examination of the kitchen before moving on to the bedroom. Two keys together on a short twist of copper wire, both of them identical, were in plain view on top of the highboy dresser. I unlocked the padlock, opened the studio door, and flipped the row of toggles on the wall. The boxlike windowless room, after hesitant blue white flickers, brightened into an icy, intense brilliance. There were a dozen overhead fluorescent tubes in parallel sets of three (two blue white to one yellow) flush with the ceiling. Under this cold light I noticed first the patching of new brickwork that filled the spaces where two windows had been before, despite the new coat of white enamel that covered the walls.

Blinking my eyes to accustom them to the intense overhead light, I closed the door behind me. My thumping heart was prepared for the impact of the unusual, the unique, for the miraculous in visual art, but instead of wine and fish I didn't even find bread and water.

There were canvases, at least two dozen of them, and all of these pristine canvases were the same size, 24" × 30". They were stacked in white plastic racks against the western wall. The racks were the commercial kind one often finds in art supply stores. I checked every one of these glittering white canvases. None of them had been touched by paint or charcoal.

There was a new, gunmetal desk in the southwest corner of the studio, with a matching chair cushioned in light gray Naugahyde. On the desk there was a fruit jar filled with sharpened pencils and ballpoint pens, a square glass paperweight (slightly magnified) holding down some correspondence, and a beautiful desk calendar (an Almanacco Artistico Italiano product in brilliant colors, made by Alfieri & Lacroix, Milano). Without shame, I read the two letters that had been held down by the paperweight. One was a letter from a Parisian clipping service, stating that Debierue's name had been mentioned twice in the foreword to a new art history pictorial collection, but inasmuch as the illustrated volume was quite expensive, the manager had written to the publisher and requested a courtesy copy for Debierue. He would send it along as soon as – or if – he received it. There was a news clipping from *Paris Soir*, an unsigned review of a Man Ray retrospective exhibit in Paris, and Debierue's name was mentioned, together with the names of a dozen other artists, in a listing of Dadaists who had known Man Ray during the 1920s.

Debierue had answered the manager of the clipping service in a crabbed, backhanded script with cursive letters so microscopic he must have written the letter with the aid of the magnified paperweight. He merely told the manager not to send the book if he got a free copy, and not to buy it if he did not. Except for Debierue's surname (the tiny lower-case letters 'e' through 'e' were all contained within a large capital 'D') there was no complimentary closing. Debierue had a unique signature. I folded the letter and put it into the breast pocket of my jumpsuit.

As I looked through the unlocked drawers of the desk, I found nothing else to hold my interest, except for a scrapbook of clippings. The scrapbook, 10" × 12", bound in gray cardboard covers, was less than half filled, and from the first clipping to the last one pasted in, covered an eighteen-month period. Most of the earlier clippings were reports of the fire that had burned down his villa, similar accounts from many different newspapers. The more recent clippings were shorter – like the mention of his name in the Man Ray art review. The items in the other drawers were what one expected to find. Stationery and supplies, stamps, glue, correspondence in manila folders – unusual perhaps because of the meticulous neatness one doesn't associate with desk drawers.

There was a two-shelf imitation walnut bookcase beside the desk that held about thirty books. Most of them were paperbacks, five *policiers* from the Série Noire, three Simenons and two by Chester Himes, Pascal's *Pensées, From Caligari to Hitler, Godard on Godard*, an autographed copy of Samuel Beckett's *Proust*, and several paperback novels by French authors I had never heard of before. The hardcover books were all well worn. A French-English dictionary and a French-German dictionary, library reference size, a tattered copy of *Heidi* (in German), a boxed two-volume edition of Schopenhauer's *The World as Will and Idea* (also in German), *Les Fleurs du Mal*, and an autographed copy of August Hauptmann's *Debierue*. I fought down my impulse to steal the autographed copy of Beckett's *Proust*, the only book in the small library I coveted, and scribbled the list of book titles into my notebook.

In addition to the books, there were several neat piles of art magazines, including *Fine Arts: The Americas*, all of them in chronological order, with the most recent issues on the top of each stack, arranged along the wall. I considered leafing through these magazines to look for drawings, but it would be absurd for Debierue, with his keen sense of order, to hide sketches in magazines.

In the center of the studio was a maple worktable (in furniture catalogues, they are called 'Early American Harvest' tables), and this table, in a rather finicky arrangement, held a terracotta jar with several new camel-hair brushes in varying lengths and brush widths, four rubber-banded, faggoty bundles of charcoal drawing sticks, four one-quart cans of linseed oil and four one-quart cans of turpentine, all unopened, and a long row of king-sized tubes of oil paint in almost every shade and tint on the spectrum.

There were at least a hundred tubes of oil paint, in colors, and three of zinc white. None of the tubes had been opened or squeezed. There was a square piece of clear glass, about 12" × 12", a fumed oak artist's palette, a pair of white gloves (size 9/12), a twelve-inch brass ruler, a palette knife, an unopened box of assorted color pencils, and a heaped flat pile of clean white rags. There were other unused art materials as well, but the crushing impression of this neatly ordered table was that of a commercial layout of art materials in an art supply showroom.

Beside the table was an unpainted wooden A-frame easel and a tall metal kitchen stool painted in white enamel. There was an untouched 24" × 30" canvas on the easel. Bewildered, and with a feeling of nausea in the pit of my stomach, I climbed onto the high stool facing the easel and lit a cigarette. A single silver filament, a spider's letdown thread, shimmering in the brilliant light washing the room from the overhead fluorescents, trailed from the right-hand corner of the canvas to the floor. The spider who had left this evidence of passage had disappeared.

Except for the pole-axed numbness of a steer, my mind was too stunned for a contiguous reaction of any kind. I neither laughed nor cried. For minutes I was unable to formulate any coherent thoughts, not until the cigarette burned my fingers, and even then I remember looking at it stupidly for a second or so before dropping it to the floor.

Debierue's aseptically forlorn studio is as clear in my mind now as if I were still sitting on that hard metal stool.

I had expected something, but not Nothing.

I had expected almost anything, but not Nothing.

Prepared for attendance and appreciation, my mind could not undo its readiness for perception and accept the unfulfilled *preparation* for painting it encountered.

Here was a qualified Nothing, a Nothing of such deep despair, I could not be absolved of my aesthetic responsibility – a nonhope Nothing, a non-Nothing – and yet, also before my eyes was the evidence of a dedication to artistic expression so unyieldingly vast in its implications that my mind – at least at first – bluntly refused to accept the evidence.

I had to work it out.

The synecdochic relationship between the place and the person was undeniable. An artist has a studio: Debierue had a studio: Debierue was an artist.

Here, in deadly readiness, Debierue sat daily in fruitless preparation for a painting that he would never paint, waiting for pictorial adventures that would never happen. *Waiting*, the incredibly patient waiting for an idea to materialize, for a single idea that could be transferred onto the ready canvas – but no ideas ever came to him. Never.

Debierue worked four hours a day, he claimed, which meant sitting on this stool staring at an empty canvas from eight until noon, every day, seven days a week, waiting for an idea to come – every single day! At that precise moment I *knew*, despite all of the published documentary evidence to the contrary, that he was not merely suffering a so-called dry period, a temporary inability to paint since moving to Florida. Without any other evidence (my own eyes were witness enough, together with my practiced critical intuition), I *knew* that Jacques Debierue had never had a plastic idea, nor had he painted a picture of any kind in his entire lifetime!

Debierue was a slave to hope. He had never accepted the fact that he couldn't paint a picture. But each day he faced the slavery of the attempt to paint, and the subsequent daily failure. After each day of failure he was destroyed, only to be reborn on the next day – each new day bringing with it a new chance, a new opportunity. How could be he so strong-willed to face this daily death, this vain slavery to hope? He had dedicated his life to Nothing.

The most primitive nescience in man cannot remain completely negative – or so I had always believed. Forms and the spectrum range of colors, the sounds a man makes with his mouth, the thousands of daily perceptions of sight and sound, invade our senses from moment to moment, consciously and subconsciously. And all of these sights and sounds – and touch, too, of course – demand an artistic interpretation. Knowing this basic natural truth, I knew that Debierue, an intelligent, sentient human being, must have had hundreds, no, literally thousands of ideas for paintings during the innumerable years he sat before an empty canvas. But these ideas were unexpressed, locked inside his head, withheld from graphic presentation because of his fear of releasing them. He was afraid to take a chance, he was unable to risk the possibility – a distinct possibility – of failure. His dread of failure was not a concern with what others might think of his work. It was a fear of what he, Debierue, the Artist, might think of his accomplished work. The moment an artist expresses himself and fails, or commits himself to an act of self-expression by action, and realizes that he did not, that he cannot, succeed, and that he will never be able to capture on canvas that which he sees so vividly in his mind's eye, he will know irrevocably that he is a failure as an artist.

So why should he paint? In fact, how can he paint?

How many times had Debierue leaned forward, reaching out timidly toward the shining canvas before him with a crumbling piece of charcoal in his trembling fingers? How many times? – and with the finished, varnished, luminous masterpiece glowing upon the museum wall of his febrile mind? – only to stay his hand at the last possible moment, the tip of the black charcoal a fraction of an inch away from the virgin canvas?

'Nonono! Not yet!'

The fear-crazed neural message would race down the full length of the motor neuron in his extended arm (vaulting synapse junctions), and in time, always in the nick of time, the quavery hand would be jerked back. The virgin canvas, safe for another day, would once again remain unviolated.

Another day, another morning of uncommitted, untested accomplishment had been hurdled, but what difference did it make? What did anything matter, at high noon, so long as he had delayed, put off until tomorrow, postponed the execution of the feeble idea he had today when there would be a much better idea tomorrow? If he did not prove to himself today that he could paint the image in his mind, or that he could *not* paint it, a tendril of comfort remained. And hope.

Faith in his untried skills provided a continuum.

Why not? Wasn't he trying? Yes. Was he not a dedicated artist? Yes. Did he ever fail to put in his scheduled work period every day? No. Was he not faithful to the sustained effort? – the devoted, painful, mental concentration? – the agony of creation? Yes, yes and yes again.

And who knew? Who knows? The day might arrive soon, perhaps tomorrow! That bright day when an idea for a painting would come to him that was so powerful, so tremendous in scope and conception, that his paint-loaded brush could no longer be withheld from the canvas! He would strike at last, and a pictorial masterpiece would be born, delivered, created, a painting that would live forever in the hearts of men!

All through life we protect ourselves from countless hurtful truths by being a little blind here – by ignoring the something trying to flag our attention on the outer edges of our peripheral vision, by being a little shortsighted there – by being a trifle too quick to accept the easiest answer, and by squinting our eyes against the bright, incoming light all of the time. Emerson wrote once that even a corpse is beautiful if you shine enough light on it.

But that is horseshit.

Too much light means unbearable truth, and too much truthful light sears a man's eyes into an unraging blindness. The blind man can only smell the crap of his life, and the sounds in his ears are cacophonous corruptions. Without vision, the terrible beauty of life is irrevocably gone. Gone!

And as I thought of all Debierue's lost visions, never to appear on canvas for the exhilaration of my eyes, scalding tears ran down my cheeks.

PART THREE

If anything was comprehensible, it would be incommunicable

Chapter One

I took my time.

What I had to do had to be done right or not at all. Once I committed, although my concern for Berenice (frightened and waiting for me in the tall grass by the highway) did not diminish, it would have been foolhardy to rush. I might have overlooked something important.

I looked in the kitchen for string and wrapping paper, but there was neither. There was newspaper, but it would have been awkward to wrap a canvas in newspaper when there was no string to tie the bundle. There were several large brown paper grocery sacks under the sink, and I took one of these back to the studio to hold the art materials I would need. I took a clean sheet from the hall linen closet and wrapped one of the new canvases from the plastic rack in it. I then filled the brown sack with several camel-hair brushes, a can of turpentine, one of linseed oil, and a half-dozen tubes of oil paint. With cadmium red, chrome yellow, Prussian blue, and zinc white I can mix almost any shade or tint of color I desire (this much I had learned in my first oil painting course because the tyrannical teacher had made us learn how to mix primary colors if he taught us nothing else). I added tubes of burnt sienna and lampblack to the others because they were useful for skin tones (there were no compositional ideas in my mind at the time, just nebulous multi-colored swirls floating loosely about in my head) if some figures became involved in the composition. The palette knife was also useful and I dropped it into the sack, but I didn't take the expensive palette. It was too expensive and could be traced, and I wouldn't want to be caught with it in my possession.

These art materials could be purchased anywhere, of course, as could the prepared 30" × 24" canvas, but I needed Debierue's materials in the event the authenticity of the painting was ever questioned. Mr Cassidy, who had purchased everything for Debierue, would have a bill from the art store listing these materials, their brands, and so would Rex Art. My mind was racing, but I was clearheaded enough to realize how close a scrutiny the painting would receive when and if it were ever painted and exhibited.

I put the wrapped canvas, the sackful of supplies, and the hammer and tire iron into the trunk of the car, and returned to the studio.

I ran into trouble with the fire. Turpentine is flammable, highly flammable, but I had difficulty in getting it lighted and in keeping it burning once it was lit. I finally had to take the remains of the *Miami Herald*, crumple each separate page into a ball, and partially soak each sheet with turpentine before I could get a roaring fire started beneath the Early American Harvest table.

Once it got started, however, the fire burned beautifully. I poured most of the last can on the studio door, and dribbled the rest to the blaze beneath the table. I then tossed the new canvases into the fire and backed out of the room. Because the fire would need a draft, I left the studio door and the front door standing open. Whether the house burned down or not was unimportant. The important thing was a charred and well-gutted studio. I wanted no evidence of any paintings left behind, and the crackling prepared canvases, sized with white lead, burned rapidly.

Satisfied, I turned out the living room and kitchen lights and got into the car. When I reached the highway and stopped, Berenice was gone. I shouted her name twice and panicked momentarily. Had she hitchhiked a ride back to Palm Beach? If she stuck out her thumb, any truck driver who saw it would stop and pick her up. But I calmed down by putting myself in her place, turned toward the drive-in theater instead of turning left for Palm Beach, and found her waiting for me in the gravel road of the driveway, standing near the well-lighted marquee.

'What took you so long?' Her voice wasn't angry. She was too relieved to see me, happy to be in the car again. 'I thought you were never coming back.'

'I'm sorry. It look longer than I expected.'

'Did you stea – take a picture?'

'Yeah.'

'What were they like? The pictures?'

'I'll turn over here US One. There're too many trucks on Seven.'

'How long do you think it'll be, before he misses the picture?'

'I've got to go back to New York, Berenice. Tonight. So as soon as we get back to the apartment I'll pack – you're still packed, practically – and then I can drop you off at the airport. Or, if you'd rather, you can stay on for a few more days. The rent's paid till the end of the month, so . . .'

'If you're going to New York so am I!'

'But what's the point? You've got your school year contract, and you have to go back to work, don't you? Besides, I'm going to be busy. I won't have any time for you at all. First, there's the Debierue article to write, and the deadline is tighter than hell now. I'll have to find a place to crash. The man in my pad has still got another month on the sub-lease, you see. I'm almost broke, and I'll have to borrow some money, and—'

'Money isn't a problem, James. I've got almost five hundred dollars in traveler's checks, and more than five thousand in savings in the credit union. I'm going to New York with you.'

'Okay,' I said bitterly, 'but you'll have to help me drive.'

'Watch out!' she shrilled. 'That car's only got one headlight!'

'I don't mean *that* way. I mean to spell me at the wheel on the way up, so we can make better time.'

'I know what you meant, but you might have thought it was a motorcycle. We can trade off every two hours.'

'No. When I get tired, we'll trade.'

'All right. How're you going to get your twenty dollars back?'

'What twenty dollars?'

'The deposit at the electric company. If we leave tonight, you won't be able to have them cut off the electricity or get your deposit back.'

'Jesus, I don't know. I can let the landlady handle it and send me the money later. They'll subtract what I owe anyway. Please, Berenice, I'm trying to think. I've got so much on my mind I don't want to hear any more domestic crap, and those damned non sequiturs of yours drive me up the goddamned tree.'

'I'm sorry.'

'So am I. We're both sorry, but just be quiet.'

'I will. I won't say anything else!'

'Nothing else! Please!'

Berenice gulped, closing her generous mouth, and puckered her lips into a prim pout. She looked straight ahead through the windshield and twisted her gloves, which she had removed, in her lap. I had shouted at her, but in my agitation, somehow, had consented to take her with me to New York. This was the last thing I wanted to do. It would take two days, perhaps three, to write the article on Debierue – and I had to do something about the painting for Mr Cassidy. It wasn't a task I could have done for me, although I knew a dozen painters in New York who could have produced anything on canvas I asked them to put there, and the product would have been a professional job.

But no one could be trusted. It was something I had to do myself, to fit Debierue's 'American Period' – at that moment I coined the title for my article: 'Debierue: The American Harvest Period.' It was a major improvement over my previous title, and 'American Harvest'— the idea must have come to me from the worktable in his studio – would provide me with a springboard for generating associative ideas.

But there was still Berenice, and the problem of what to do with her – but wasn't it better to have her with me than to simply turn her loose where she could learn about the fire by reading about it in a newspaper, or by hearing a newscast? How soon would the report go out? Would Debierue telephone Mr Cassidy and tell him about it? That depended upon the extent of the fire, probably, but Cassidy would be the only person Debierue knew to contact, and I could certainly trust Cassidy to make the correct decision. He might inform the news media, and again he might not. Before doing anything, he would want to know whether I got a picture for him before the fire started. And although Cassidy might suspect me of setting the fire, he wouldn't know for sure, and he wouldn't give a damn about the other 'paintings' destroyed in the fire so long as he got his.

I still had about three hours, or perhaps closer to four, to contact Cassidy before Debierue learned about the fire and managed to telephone him.

And Berenice? It would be best to keep her with me. At least for now. Once we reached New York, I could settle her in a hotel for a few days until I finished doing the things I had to do, and then we could work out a compromise of some kind. The best compromise, and I could work out the details later, would be for her to return to Duluth and teach until the summer vacation. In this way, we could reflect upon how we *really* felt about each other – at a sane distance, without passion interfering – and, if we both felt as if we still loved each other, in truth, and our affair was not just a *physical* thing, well, we could then work out some kind of life arrangement together when we met in New York – or somewhere – during her two-month summer vacation.

This was an idea I could sell, I decided, but until I had time for it, she could stay with me for the ride. It would take hours of argument to get rid of her now, and I simply couldn't spare the time on polemics when I had to concentrate every faculty I possessed on Debierue, his 'American Harvest' period, his painting, and what I was going to write.

I took the Lake Worth bridge to pick up A1A, to enter Palm Beach from the southern end of the island, and Berenice shifted suddenly in her seat.

'Do you know that we've driven for more than forty-five minutes, and you haven't said a single word?'

'Crack your wind-wing a little, honey,' I said, 'and we'll get some more air.'

'Oh!' She cracked the window. 'You're the most exasperating man I've ever met in my life, and if I didn't love you so much I'd tell you so!'

By leaving the food in the refrigerator, and the canned food and staples on the shelves, it didn't take us long to pack. I put my clean clothes in my small suitcase, and the dirty clothes, which made up the bulk of my belongings, all went into the big valopack with my suits, slacks, and jackets. While Berenice looked around to see if we had forgotten anything, I took my bags and typewriter to the car and tossed them into the back seat.

On my way back for Berenice's luggage I stopped at the landlady's apartment, gave her the receipt for the power company's twenty-dollar deposit, and told her to take the money that remained to pay someone to clean the apartment. When she began to protest that this small sum wouldn't be enough to pay a cleaning woman, I told her to add the balance of the rent money I had paid her in advance instead of returning it to me and she said: 'I hope you have a pleasant trip back to New York, Mr Figueras, and perhaps you'll drop me a card sometime from Spanish Harlem.'

She was a real bitch, but I shrugged off her parting remark and returned to the apartment for Berenice and her things.

I stopped at the Western Union office in Riviera Beach and sent two telegrams. The first one, to my managing editor in New York, was easy:

HOLD MY SPACE 5000 WORDS PERSONAL ARTICLE ON DEBIERUE DRIVING WITH IT NOW TO NY FIGUERAS

This telegram would put Tom Russell into a frenzy, but he would hold the space, or rip out something else already set for a piece on Debierue. But he would be so astonished about my having an article written on Debierue he wouldn't know whether to believe me or not. And yet, he would be afraid not to believe me. I gave the operator his home address on Long Island, and the New York magazine address as well, with instructions to telephone the message to him before delivering it. The girl assured me that he would have it before midnight, which assured me that Tom would have a sleepless night. Well, so would I.

The wire to Joseph Cassidy at the Royal Palm Towers, only a twenty-minute drive from Riviera Beach at this time of evening, was more difficult to compose. I threw away the first three drafts, and then sent the following as

579

a night letter, with instructions not to deliver it until at
least 8 a.m.:

EMERGENCY STOP URGENT I REPORT TO NY
MAGAZINE OFFICE STOP WILL WRITE AND
SEND PICTURE FROM THERE FIGUERAS

There was ambiguity in the wording, but I wanted it to
read that way. He would not be able to ascertain from
the way the wire was worded whether I would write and
fill him in on the 'emergency,' or whether I would be
sending Debierue's 'picture' from New York. If nothing
else, the wire would make him cautious about what he
would say to the press about Debierue and the fire,
although I knew he would have to release something.
Knowing that *he* didn't set the fire, and without knowing
for sure that *I* had set it, Debierue would most certainly
contact Cassidy. If he suspected that the fire had been
set by vandals, Debierue would probably be afraid to stay
at the isolated location even though the rest of the house
was only slightly damaged.

Berenice, happy to have her way about going to New
York, sat in the car while I sent the telegrams and, except
for humming or singing snatches of Rodgers and Hart songs,
confined her conversation to reminding me occasionally to
dim my lights or to kick them to bright again. Brooding
about what to write, and how to write it, especially after
we got onto the straight, mind-dulling Sunshine Parkway,
I needed frequent reminders about the headlights.

The rest-stop islands, with filling stations at each end,
and Dobbs House concession restaurants sandwiched
between the gas stations, are staggered at uneven distances
along the Parkway. Because they are unevenly spaced, it
wasn't possible to stop at every other one (sometimes it
was only twenty-eight miles to a rest stop, whereas the

next one would be sixty miles away), and a decision, usually to halt, had to be made every time. Berenice always went to the can twice, once upon debarking, and again after we had a cup of coffee. I said nothing about the delay (as a man I could have stopped anywhere along the highway, but I would have been insane to make such a suggestion to a middle-western schoolteacher), and besides, the rest stops soon became useful. Sitting at the counter over coffee with my notebook, I organized my vagrant thoughts about Debierue's 'American Harvest' Florida paintings, and by writing down my ideas at each stop, I retained the good ones, eliminated the poor ones, and gradually developed a complicated, but pyramiding, gestalt for the article.

I allowed Berenice to drive between the Fort Pierce and Yeehaw Junction rest stops, but, finding that I thought better at the wheel, persuaded her to put her head on my shoulder and go to sleep with the promise that she could drive all the next morning while I slept. Toward morning the air became nippy, but by 9 a.m., with Berenice driving, as we entered the long wide thoroughfare leading into downtown Valdosta, I knew that we had to stop.

If I didn't write the piece on Debierue now, while my ideas were still fresh, the article would suffer a hundred metamorphoses in my mind during the long haul to New York. I would be bone tired by then, confused, and unable to write anything. There were some references, dates, names, and so on, I would have to check in New York, but I could write the piece now and leave those spaces blank. Besides, Tom Russell would want to read the piece the moment I got into the city. I also had to paint a picture before I wrote the article. By looking at it (whatever it turned out to be), it would be a simple matter to describe the painting with it sitting in front of me, and I could tie the other paintings to it somehow.

'Berenice,' I said, 'we're going to stop here in Valdosta, not in a motel, but in the hotel downtown, if they have one. In a hotel we can get room service, and two rooms, one for you and—'

'Why two rooms? Why can't I—'

'I know you mean well, sweetheart, and you're awfully quiet when I'm working, but you also know how it bugs me to have you tiptoeing around while I'm trying to write. I won't have time to talk to you while I'm working, and I won't stop, once I start, until I've got at least a good rough draft on paper. Take a long nap, a good tub bath – motels only have showers, you know – and then go to a movie this afternoon. And tonight, if I'm fairly well along with it, we can have dinner together.'

'Shouldn't you sleep for a few hours first? I had some catnaps, but you haven't closed your eyes.'

'I'll take a couple of bennies. I'm afraid if I go to sleep I'll lose my ideas.'

Being reasonable with Berenice worked for once. Downtown, we stopped at the tattered-awninged entrance of a six-story brick hotel, The Valdosta Arms. I asked the ancient black doorman if the hotel had a parking garage.

'Yes, sir,' he said. 'If you checking in, drive right aroun' the corner there and under the buildin'. I'll have a bellman waitin' there for your bags.'

I reached across Berenice and handed the old man two quarters.

'If you want out here, I'll carry your car aroun' myself,' he offered.

'No,' I shook my head. 'I like to know where my car is parked.'

He was limping for the house phone beside the revolving glass doors before Berenice got the car into gear.

I wanted to know where the car was parked because I intended to return for the canvas and art materials after getting Berenice settled in. The bellman had a luggage truck waiting, and we followed him into the service elevator and up to the lobby.

'Two singles, please,' I said to the desk clerk. A bored middle-aged man, his eyes didn't even light up when he looked at Berenice.

'Do you have a reservation, sir?'

'No.'

'All right. I can give you connecting rooms on three, if you like.'

'Fine,' Berenice said.

'No.' I smiled and shook my head. 'You'd better separate them. I have to do some typing, and we've been driving all night and it might disturb her sleep.'

'Five-ten, and Five-oh-five.' He shifted his weary deadpan to address Berenice. 'You'll be dreckly across the hall from him, Miss.'

I signed a register card, and while Berenice was signing hers, crossed to the newsstand and looked for her favorite magazine on the rack. Unable to find it, I asked the woman behind the glass display case if she had sold out of *Cosmopolitan*. Setting her lips in a prim line, she reached beneath the counter and silently placed a copy on the glass top. I handed her a dollar and she rang it up (a man who buys 'under the counter' magazines has to pay a little more). I joined Berenice and the bellman at the elevators and we went up to our rooms.

The first thing I did after tipping the bellman and closing the door was to change out of my jumpsuit. From the guarded but indignant looks I had received in the lobby from the newsstand woman, the bellman, and two blue-suited men with narrow ties (the desk clerk's face wouldn't have registered surprise if I had worn jockey shorts), gentlemen were not expected to wear jumpsuits in downtown Valdosta. And I didn't want people to stare at me when I went down to the basement garage for my art materials. I put on a pair of gray slacks, a white silk shirt, with a white-on-white brocade tie, and a lime sports jacket, the only unrumpled clothes I had.

By taking the service elevator down and up, I was back in my room in fewer than five minutes. The room was hot and close. I stripped to my underwear, turned the air conditioner to 'Cool,' and put the canvas against the back of a straight laddered chair. There was a large, fairly flat, green ceramic ashtray on the coffee table. This ashtray served to steady the canvas upright against the back of the chair, and would perform double duty as a palette. I squeezed blobs of blue, yellow, red, and white paint onto the ashtray, opened the cans of turpentine and linseed oil, lined up the brushes on the coffee table, and stared at the canvas. After fifteen minutes, I brought the other straight-backed chair over from the desk, sat down on it, and stared at the blank canvas some more.

Twenty minutes later, still staring at the white canvas, I was shivering. I turned the reverse-cycle air conditioner to 'Heat,' and fifteen minutes later I was roasting, with perspiration bursting out of my forehead and clammy streams of sweat rolling down my sides from my damp armpits. I turned off the air conditioner and tried to raise the window. The huge air conditioner occupied the bottom half of the window, and the top half of the window was nailed shut, with rusty red paint covering the nailheads. But there was an overhead fan, and the switch still worked. The fan, with wobbly two-foot blades, turned lazily in the high ceiling. The room was still close, so I unlocked the door, and kept it ajar with an old-fashioned brass hook-and-eye attachment that held the door cracked open for approximately four inches. No one could see in from the corridor and within minutes the room was perfectly comfortable with just enough fresh air coming in from the hallway to be gently wafted about by the slow and not unpleasantly creaking overhead fan.

An hour later I was still physically comfortable. I had smoked three Kools. I was still staring at the virgin canvas, and realized, finally, that I was unable to paint an original Debierue painting. Not even if I sat there for four straight hours every day . . .

Chapter Two

My eyes, bright and alert, stared at the blank, shining canvas, and my stout heart, stepped up slightly, if inaudibly, from the depressing uppityness of two nugatory bennies, pumped willing blood to my even more willing fingers. I had forgotten, for two wasted hours, the hard-learned lesson of our times. In this, the Age of Specialization, where we can only point to Hugh Hefner or, wilder yet, to the early Marlon Brando as our contemporary 'Renaissance Men,' I had tackled my problem ass-backwards.

I was a writer confined by choice but still confined to contemporary art – writing about it, not painting it. I could wield a paintbrush, of course, passably. I had learned to paint in college studio courses before going on to my higher calling, in the same way that a man who wants to become a brigadier general and command an Air Force wing must first learn how to fly an airplane. The general does not have to be a superior pilot to command a wing, but he attains his position because, as an ex- or now part-time pilot, he understands the daily flight problems of the pilots under his command. The system doesn't work very well, of course, because the man who wants to fly an Air Force jet, and plans his career accordingly, seldom enters that active occupation with the preconceived plan of ending up some day at a desk where he rarely files. The 'hot' pilot does not make a good paper-shuffling general because the makeup of a man who wants to fly does not include a love of administration, learning letters, and enforcing discipline.

I had learned how to paint because I had to learn the problems confronting painters, and I had taught college students because that was what I had to do to survive as an art historian. But in my secret heart I had intended to become an art critic from the very beginning. And although my major passion was contemporary art, during my year in Europe I had grimly made my rounds in the Louvre, in Florence, in Rome, tramping dutifully through ancient galleries because I knew that I had to examine the art of the past to understand the art of the present.

I was a writer, not a painter, and a writer gets his ideas from a blank piece of paper, not from a blank piece of canvas. I moved my chair to the desk and my typewriter and immediately started to write.

This is the way it works. The contemporary painter approaches his canvas without an idea (in most cases), fools around with charcoal, experimenting the lines and forms, filling in here, using a shaping thumb, perhaps, to add some depth to a form that is beginning to interest him, and sooner or later he sees something. The painting develops into a composition and he completes it. His subconscious takes over, and the completed painting may turn out well or, more often than not, like most writing, turn out badly. Even when the painter begins with an idea of some kind his subconscious takes over the painting once he starts working on it. The same theory, essentially, holds true for the writer. A man paints or writes both consciously and subconsciously beginning with, at most, a few relevant mental notes.

So once I sat at my typewriter, the article began to take shape. One idea led quickly to another. It was an inspired piece of work, because it was morally right to write it. My honor and Debierue's were both at stake. And yet, although it was in some respects easy to write, it was one of the most difficult pieces I had ever written because of the fictional elements it contained.

My creative talents flagged when it came to describing the pictures Debierue had failed to paint, although, once over this block, it was a simple matter to interpret the paintings because I could visualize them perfectly in my mind's eye. I was familiar enough with Debierue's background to summarize the historical details of his earlier accomplishments. It was also simple enough to record a tightly edited version of our conversation, with a few embellishments for clarity, and a few bits of profundity for reader interest. Perhaps there is a little something of the fiction writer inside every professional journalist.

My imaginative powers were strong enough to describe the paintings that I, myself, would have liked to paint if I had had the ability to paint them, but I ran into conceptual difficulties because, at first, I thought I had to describe the paintings that *Debierue* wanted to paint. But this was a futile path. I could not possibly see the world as Debierue did. And if I was unable to live in his arcane world, I could never verbalize it into visual art.

My predetermined term, 'American Harvest,' for Debierue's so-called American period, provided me with the correlative link I needed to visualize mental pictures I was capable of describing. I began with red, white and blue – the colors of France's noble tricolor and our own American flag. Seeing these three colors on three separate panels I began to rearrange the panels in my mind. Side by side, in a row, close together, well separated, overlapping, horizontal and vertical with the floor, and scattered throughout a room on three different walls. But there are four walls to a room. A fourth panel was required – not for symmetry, because that doesn't matter – but for variety, for the sake of an ordered environment. Florida, Sun. Orange. An autumnal sun for Debierue's declining years. Burnt orange. But not a panel of burnt orange in toto – that would be heresy, because Debierue, even at his great age, was still painting, still creating, still growing. So the ragged square of burnt orange required a lustrous border of blue to surround the dying sun and to overflow the edges of the rectangle. Bluebird sky? Sky blue? No, not sky nor Dufy blue, because that meant using cobalt oil paint, and cobalt blue, with the passage of years, gradually turns to bluish gray. Prussian blue, with a haughty whisper of zinc white added to make it bitterly cold. Besides, right here in this hotel room, I had a full tube of Prussian blue.

Texture? Tactile quality? Little, if any. Pure, smooth even colors.

The four paintings, 30" × 24", were the only paintings Debierue had painted since coming to Florida. The paintings were for his personal aesthetic satisfaction, to enjoy during the harvest years of his stay in American, and yet they were in keeping with his traditionally established principles of Nihilistic Surrealism.

Every morning when Debierue arose at 6 a.m., depending upon his waking mood, he hung one of the red, white, or blue panels next to the permanently centered burnt orange, blue-bordered panel, the painting representing the painter – the painter's 'self.' For the remainder of the day, when he was not engaged in the planning of another (undisclosed to the writer) work of art, he studied and contemplated the two bilateral paintings which reminded him of America's multiple 'manifest destinies,' the complexities of American life in general, and his personal artistic commitment to the new world.

Did he ever awaken in a mood buoyant enough to hang two or perhaps three panels at once alongside the burnt orange panel?
'No,' he said.

I had typed eighteen pages for a total of 4,347 words. Now that the concept was firmly established, I could have gone on to write another dozen pages of interpretive commentary, but I forced myself to stop with the negative. Wasn't it about time? Does every contemporary work of art have to end with an affirmative? Joyce, with his coda of yesses in *Ulysses*, Beckett, with the 'I will go on' of his trilogy, and those 1,001 phallically erected obelisks and church spires pointing optimistically toward the heavens – for once, just once, let a negative prevail.

My conclusion was not a lucky accident. It was a valid, pertinent statement of Debierue's life and art. Skipping two spaces, I put a '—30—' to the piece.

I was suddenly tired. My neck and shoulders were sore and my back ached. I looked at my watch. Six o'clock. There was a plaintive rumble in my hollow stomach. Except for going into the can three times, I had been at the typewriter for almost six straight hours. I got up, stretched, rubbed the back of my neck, and walked around the coffee table shaking my hands and fingers above my head to get rid of the numb feeling in my arms.

I was tired but I wasn't sleepy. I was exhilarated by completing the article in such a short time. Every part had fallen neatly into place, and I knew that it was a good piece of writing. I had never felt better in my entire life.

I sighed, put the cover on the Hermes, moved the typewriter to the bed, and sat at the desk again to read and correct the article. I righted spelling errors, changed some diction, and penciled in a rough transitional sentence between two disparate paragraphs. It wasn't good enough, and I made a note in the margin to rewrite it. One long convoluted sentence with three semicolons and two colons made me laugh aloud. My mind had really been racing on that one. I reduced it, without any trouble, to four clear, separate sentences—

The phone rang, a loud, jangling ring designed to arouse traveling salesmen who had been drinking too much before going to bed. I almost jumped out of my chair.

Berenice's voice was husky. 'I'm hungry.'

'Who isn't?'

'I've been sleeping.'

'I've been working.'

'I've been awake for a half hour, but I'm too lazy to get out of bed. Why don't you come over and get in with me?'

'Jesus, Berenice, I've been working all day and I'm tired as hell.'

'If you eat something, you'll feel better.'

'All right. Give me an hour, and I'll be over.'

'Should I order dinner sent up?'

'No. I prefer to eat something hot, and I've never had a hot meal served in a hotel room. We'll go down to the dining room.'

'I'll do my nails.'

'In an hour.' I racked the phone.

I finished reading and proofing the typescript and put the manuscript in a manila envelope before tucking it safely away in my suitcase. There were only minimal changes to be made in New York. Only two pages would require rewriting. I put the canvas, ashtray palette, and other art materials into the closet. I could paint the picture after dinner.

The tub in the bathroom was huge, the old-fashioned kind with big claw feet clutching metal balls. The hot water came boiling out, and I shaved while the tub filled. The water was much too hot to get into, but I added a little cold water at a time until the temperature dropped to the level I could stand. Sliding down into the steaming, man-sized tub until I was fully submerged, except for my face, I soaked up the heat. The soreness gradually left my back and shoulders. I finished with a cold shower, and by the time I was dressed, I felt as if I had had eight hours' sleep. I called the bar, ordered two Gibsons to be sent to 510, Berenice's room, and studied the road maps I had picked up at the last Standard station.

After dinner, I figured I could paint the picture in an hour or at most an hour and a half. Now that the article was finished there was no point in staying overnight in a hotel. I wasn't sleepy, and with both of us driving we could make it to New York in about thirty hours. The front wheels of the old car started to shimmy if I tried to push it beyond fifty-five mph, but thirty hours from Valdosta was a fairly accurate estimate. I had forty dollars in my wallet and some loose change. My Standard credit card would get the car to New York, but I decided to save my cash. Berenice had traveler's checks, and she could use some of them to pay the hotel tab. Through the cracked door, I heard the bellman knock on 510 across the way. I waited until Berenice signed the chit and the waiter had caught the down elevator before I crossed the hallway and knocked on her door.

Berenice was willowy in a blue slack suit with lemon, quarter-inch lines forming windowpane checks, and the four tightly grouped buttons of the double-breasted jacket were genuine lapis lazuli. The bells of the slacks were fully sixteen inches in diameter, and only the toes of her white wedgies were exposed. There was a silk penny-colored scarf around her neck. She had done her nails in Chen Yu nail varnish, that peculiar decadent shade of red that resembles dried blood (the sexiest shade of red ever made, and so Germanic thirtiesish that Visconti made Ingrid Thulin wear it in *The Damned*), and she had painted her lips to match. During her six weeks in Palm Beach, Berenice had learned some peculiar things about fashion, but the schoolteacher from Duluth had not disappeared.

She giggled and pointed to the tray on the coffee table. 'These are supposed to be Gibsons!'

There were two miniatures of Gilbey's gin and another of Stock dry vermouth (two tenths of gin, an eighth of vermouth), a glass pitcher with chunks, not cubes, of ice, and a tiny glass bowl containing several cocktail onions.

I shrugged. 'I don't think they're allowed to serve mixed drinks in this Georgia county, although the waiter would've mixed them for you if you'd tipped him. Actually' – I twisted the metal caps off the two gin miniatures – 'it's better this way. Most bartenders overuse vermouth in Gibsons, and I'd rather make my own anyway.'

'It just struck me funny, that's all,' Berenice said.

While I mixed the Gibsons, I tried to work out a simple plan and a way of presenting it to Berenice to keep her away from my room until we were ready to leave.

'Did you go to a movie this afternoon?'

She shook her head, and sipped her cocktail. 'I wouldn't go to a movie alone back home, much less in a strange town. I'm not the scary type, you know that, James, but there are some things a woman shouldn't do alone, and that's one of them.'

'At any rate, you got through the day.'

'I slept like the dead. How's the article coming?'

'That's what I wanted to talk to you about. I finished it.'

'Already? That's wonderful, James!'

'It's a good rough draft,' I admitted, 'but it'll need a few things filled in up in New York—'

'Am I in it? Can I read it?'

'No. It's an article about Debierue and his art, not about you and me. When did you become interested in art criticism?' I grinned.

'When I met Mr Debierue, that's when.' She smiled. 'He's the nicest, sweetest old gentleman I ever met.'

'I'd rather you'd wait till I have the final draft, if you don't mind. I want to get back to New York as soon as possible to finish it. So after dinner, I'll take a short nap until midnight, and then we can check out of here and get rolling. If we trade off on the driving, we can reach the city in about thirty hours.'

'You won't get much sleep if we leave at midnight . . .'

'I don't need much, and you've already had enough. You wouldn't be able to sleep much tonight anyway, not after being in the sack all day.'

'I'm not arguing, James, I was just worried about you—'

'In that case, let's go downstairs to dinner, so I can come back up and get some sleep before midnight.'

During dinner, Berenice asked me if she could see Debierue's picture, but I put her off by telling her it was all wrapped up securely in the trunk of the car, and that it wouldn't be a good idea for anyone to see us looking at a painting in the basement garage. I reminded her conspiratorially that it was a 'hot' picture, and we didn't want anyone suspecting us and making enquiries. Because I half-whispered this explanation, she nodded solemnly and accepted it.

The food was excellent – medium-rare sirloins, corn on the cob, okra and tomatoes, creamed scalloped potatoes, a cucumber and onion salad, with a chocolate pudding dessert topped with real whipped cream, not sprayed from a can – and I ate every bit of it, including four hot biscuits with butter (my two, and Berenice's two). I felt somewhat lethargic following the heavy meal, but after drinking two cups of black coffee, although I was uncomfortably stuffed, I still wasn't sleepy.

I signed the check and penciled in my room number. 'After all that food, I'm sleepy.' I said.

Berenice took my arm as we left the dining room to cross the lobby to the elevators. 'Wouldn't you like a little nightcap,' she squeezed my arm, 'to make you sleep better – in my room?'

'No,' I replied, 'and when I say No to an offer like that you know I'm sleepy enough already.'

I took her room key, opened the door, and kissed her good night. 'I'll leave a call for eleven thirty, and then I'll knock on your door. Try and get some more sleep.'

'If I can,' she replied, 'and if not, I'll watch television. Let me have another one of those good-night kisses . . .'

My room was musty and close again, although I had not turned off the overhead fan. I didn't want to go through the too-hot, too-cold routine with the reverse-cycle air-conditioner – which had far too many BTUs for the size of the small room – so I cracked the door again and clamped it open with the brass hook-and-eye attachment. I stripped down to my shorts and T-shirt, took the art materials out of the closet, and got busy with the picture.

I mixed Prussian blue, adding zinc white a dollop at a time, until I had a color the shade of an Air Force uniform. I thinned it slightly with turpentine and brushed a patch on the bottom of the canvas. It was still too dark, and I added white until the blue became much bolder. I then mixed enough of the diluted blue to paint a slightly ragged border, not less than an inch in width, nor more than three inches, around the four sides of the rectangle. To fill the remaining white space with burnt orange was simple enough, once I was able to get the exact shade I wanted, but it took me much longer than I expected to mix it, because it wasn't easy to match a color that I could see in my mind, but not in front of me.

But the color was rich when I achieved it to my satis-faction. Not quite brown, not quite mustardy, but a kind of burnished burnt orange with a felt, rather than an observable, sense of yellow. I mixed more of the paint than I would need, to be sure that I would have enough, and thinned the glowing pile with enough linseed oil and turpentine to spread it smoothly on the canvas. Using the largest brush, I filled in the center of the canvas almost to the blue border, and then changed to a smaller brush to carefully fill in the narrow ring of white space that remained.

I backed to the wall for a long view of the completed painting, and decided that the blue border was not quite ragged enough. This was remedied in a few minutes, and the painting was as good as my description of it in my article. In fact, the picture was so bright and shining under the floor lamp, it looked even better than I had expected.

All it needed was Debierue's signature.

I had a sharp debate with myself whether to sign it or not, wondering whether it was in keeping with the philosophy of the 'American Harvest' period for him to put his name on one of the pictures. But inasmuch as the burnt orange, blue-bordered painting represented the 'self' of Debierue, I concluded that if he ever signed a painting, this was one he would *have* to sign. I made a mental note to add this information to my article – that this was the first real picture Debierue had ever signed (it would certainly raise the value for Mr Cassidy to possess a signed painting!).

Debierue's letter to the manager of the French clipping service was still in my jumpsuit. I took it out and studied Debierue's cramped signature, sighing gratefully over the uniqueness of the design. Forgers love a tricky signature: it makes forgery much simpler for them because it is much easier to copy a complicated signature than it is a plain, straightforward signature. There are two ways to forge a signature. One is to practice writing it over and over again until it is perfected. That is the hard way. The easy way is to turn the signature upside down and draw it, not write it, but copy it the way one would imitate any other line drawing. And this is what I did. Actually, I didn't have to turn the canvas upside down. By copying Debierue's signature onto the upper left-hand side upside down, when the picture itself was turned upside down the top would then be the bottom, and the signature would be rightside up and in the lower right-hand corner where it belonged.

Nevertheless, it took me a long time to copy it, because I was trying to paint it as small as possible in keeping with Debierue's practice of writing tiny letters. To put *ebierue* inside the 'D' wasn't simple, and I had to remember to 'write' with my brushstrokes up instead of down, because that is the way the strokes would have to be when the painting was turned upside down.

'James!'

Berenice called out my name. I was so deeply engrossed in what I was doing I wasn't certain whether this was the first or the second time she had called it out. But it was too late to do anything about it. I was sitting in the straight-backed chair facing the canvas, and I barely had time to turn and look at her, much less get to my feet, before she lifted the brass hook, opened the door, and entered the room.

'James,' she repeated flatly, halting abruptly with her hand still on the doorknob. She had removed her makeup, and her pale pink lips made a round 'O' as she stared at me, the canvas, and the makeshift palette on the low coffee table. The sheet I had used to wrap the once-blank canvas was on the floor and gathered about the chair I was using as an easel. I had spread it there to prevent paint from dropping onto the rug.

'Yes?' I said quietly.

Berenice shut the door, and leaned against it. She supported herself with her hands flat against the door panels. 'Just now . . . on TV,' she said, not looking at me, but with her rounded blue eyes staring at the canvas, '. . . on the ten thirty news, the newscaster said that Debierue's house had burned down.'

'Anything else?'

She nodded. 'Pending an investigation – something like that – Mr Debierue will be the house guest of the famous criminal lawyer Joseph Cassidy, in Palm Beach.'

I swallowed, and nodded my head. I am a highly verbal individual, but for once in my life I was at a loss for words. One lie after another struggled for expression in my mind, but each lie, in turn, was rejected before it could be voiced.

'Is that Debierue's painting?' Berenice said, as she crossed the room toward my chair.

'Yes. I needed to look at it again, you see, to check it against the description in my article. It was slightly damaged – Debierue's signature – so I thought I'd touch it up some.'

Berenice pressed her forefinger to the exact center of the painting. She examined the wet smear on her fingertip.

'Oh, James,' she said unhappily, 'you painted this awful picture . . . !'

Chapter Three

Looking back (and faced with the same set of circumstances), I don't know that I would have handled the problem any differently – except for some minor changes from the way that I did solve it. Ignorant women have destroyed the careers, the ambitions, and the secret plans of a good many honorable men throughout history.

It would have been easy enough to blame myself for allowing Berenice to discover the painting. If I had locked the door, instead of being concerned with my physical discomfort in the hotel room, I could have hidden the painting from her before allowing her into the room. This one little slip on my part destroyed everything, if one wants to look at it that way. But the problem was greater than this – not a matter of just one little slip. There was an entire string of unfortunate coincidences, going back to the unwitting moment I had allowed Berenice to move in on me, and continuing through my foolhardy decision to allow her to accompany me to Debierue's house.

And now of course, caught red handed – or burnt orange handed – Berenice was in possession of a lifelong hold over me if I carried my deception through – with the publication of the article, with the sending of the painting to Joseph Cassidy, to say nothing of the future, *my* future, and the subsequent furor that the publication of an article on Debierue would arouse in the art world.

Berenice loved me, or so she had declared again and again, and if I had married her, perhaps she would have kept her mouth shut, carrying her secret knowledge, and mine, to her grave. I don't know. I doubted it then, and I doubt it now. Love, according to my experience, is a fragile, transitory emotion. Not only does love fall a good many years short of lasting forever, a long stretch for love to last is a few months, or even a few weeks. If I think about my friends and acquaintances in New York – and don't consider casual acquaintances I have known else-where, in Palm Beach, for example – I can't think of a single friend, male or female, who hasn't been divorced at least once. And most of them, *more* than once. The milieu I live in is that way. The art world is not only egocentric, it is ecoeccentric. The environment is not conducive to lasting friendships, let alone lasting marriages. And that was my world . . .

My remaining choice, which was too stupid even to consider seriously, was a bitter one. I could have destroyed The Burnt Orange Heresy (such was the title I assigned to the painting), and torn up the article I had written, which would mean that the greatest opportunity I had ever had to make a name for myself as an art critic would be lost.

These thoughts were jumbled together in my mind as I confronted Berenice, but not in any particular order. Emotionally, I was only mildly annoyed at the time, knowing I had a major problem to solve, but bereft, at least for the moment, of any solution.

'You may believe that this is an "awful" picture,' I said coldly to Berenice, 'and it's your privilege to think so if, and the key word is *if*, if you can substantiate your opinion with valid reasons as to *why* it's an "awful" picture. Otherwise, you're not entitled to any value judgments concerning Debierue's work.'

'I – I just can't believe it!' Berenice said, shaking her head. 'You're not going to try to pass this off as a painting by Debierue, are you?'

'It *is* a painting by Debierue. Didn't I just tell you that I was touching it up a little because it was damaged slightly in transit?'

'I'm not *blind*, James.' She made a helpless, fluttering gesture with her hands, her big eyes taking in the evidence of the art materials and the painting itself. 'How do you expect to get away with something so *raw*? Don't you know that Mr Cassidy will *show* this painting to Debierue, and that—'

'Berenice!' I brought her up sharply. 'You're sticking your mid-western nose into something that is none of your damned business! Now get the hell out of here, get packed, and if you aren't ready to leave in twenty minutes, you can damned well stay here in Valdosta!'

Her face flushed, and she took two steps backward. She nodded, nibbled her nether lip, and nodded again. 'All *right*! There is obviously something going on that I don't understand, but that isn't any reason to blow off at me like that. You can at least explain it to me. You can't blame me for being bewildered, can you? I can see that, well, the way it looks is *funny*, that's all!'

I got up from the chair, put my arm around her shoulders, and gave her a friendly hug. 'I'm sorry,' I said gently, 'I shouldn't have woofed at you like that. And don't worry. I'll explain everything to you in the car. There's a good girl. Just get packed, and we can get out of here and be on our way in a few minutes. Okay?'

I held open the door. Still nodding her head, Berenice crossed the hallway to her room.

The moment her door closed, I wrapped the art materials in the sheet, washed the ashtray palette under the bathtub hot water tap and dried it with a towel. I slipped on my trousers and a shirt, and took the painting and the small bundle of art materials down to the basement garage on the elevator. I dumped the bundle in a garbage can, and placed the painting carefully, wet side up, in the trunk of my car. It took another three minutes to unfasten the canvas convertible top, fold it back, and snap the fasteners of the plastic cover. It would be chilly riding with the top back at this time of night, but I could put it up again later. The night garage attendant, a young black man wearing white overalls, stood in the doorway of the small, lighted office, watching me silently as I struggled with the top. Finished, I crossed the garage, handed him a quarter, and told him I was checking out.

'Call the desk, please,' I said, 'and tell the clerk to send a bellman with a truck to get our baggage in five-ten and five-oh-five in about fifteen minutes. Tell the bellman to pile it on the back seat when he comes down. The trunk is already filled with other things.'

'Yes, sir,' he said.

I returned to my room, packed in less than five minutes, pulled a sleeveless sweater on over my shirt, and slipped into my sports coat. Berenice wasn't ready yet, but I helped her close her suitcases, and advised her to wear her warm polo coat over her slack suit. The bellman came with his truck, and when he got off at the lobby to check out, he continued on down to the basement to put our luggage in the car. Berenice paid the bill, which was surprisingly reasonable, by cashing two traveler's checks, and the bellman had the car out in front for us before we had finished checking out. The night deskman didn't ask questions about why we were leaving in the middle of the night, and I didn't volunteer any information.

The night air was chilly when we got into the car, and there was a light, misty fog hovering fifty feet or so above the deserted city streets. I lit two cigarettes, handed Berenice one of them, and pulled away from the curb. She shivered slightly and huddled down in her seat.

'You're probably wondering why I put the top back,' I said.

'Yes, I am. But after the way you barked at me last time, I'm almost afraid to ask any questions.'

I laughed and patted her leg. 'If it gets too cold, I'll put it up again. But I thought it would be best to get as much fresh air as possible to keep myself awake. It isn't really cold, and there won't be much traffic this time of night, so we should make fairly good time.'

Berenice accepted this moronic explanation, and I increased the speed the moment we got out of the downtown area and onto the new four-lane highway that was still bordered by residential streets containing two- and three-story houses.

From my examination of the map I knew that there were several small lakes between Valdosta and Tifton, and a few pine reserves as well, first- and second-growth forests to feed the Augusta paper mills. Most of the rich, red land was cultivated, however – tobacco, for the major crop, but also with melons, corn, peas, or anything else that a farmer wanted to grow, including flax. East of Valdosta was the Great Okefonokee Swamp, which filled a large section of southeast Georgia, and there were many small lakes, streams, and brooks that filtered well-silted water into the swamp.

I was unfamiliar with the highway and the countryside, and I didn't know precisely what I was looking for, other than a grove of pines, a finger of swamp, and a rarely used access road. I slowed down considerably a few miles north of Valdosta, as soon as I was in open country with only widely scattered farmhouses, and I began to keep my eyes open for side roads leading nowhere. Berenice, who had been as silent as a martyr, and suffering from my silence as well, finally had to open her mouth.

'Well?' she said.

'Well, what?'

'I'm waiting for the explanation, that's what. You said you'd explain, what are you waiting for?'

'I've been thinking things over, Berenice, and I'm beginning to come to my senses. You really don't think it would be a good idea, do you, to send that painting to Mr Cassidy?'

'That's your business, James. It isn't up to me to tell you what to do, but if you're asking me for an opinion, I'd say no. But as you said, I don't know all there is to know about what it is you're trying to do – so until I do, I'll keep my long "mid-western nose" out of your business.'

'I apologized for that, sweetheart.'

'That's all right. I know that my nose fits my face. What does bother me though is that I've been more or less forced to think that you set fire to Debierue's house.'

'Me?' I laughed. 'What makes you think I'd do something like that?'

'Well, for one thing, you didn't show any surprise,' she said shrewdly, 'when I told you about the news of the fire on television.'

'Why should I be surprised? His villa in France burned down, too. It does surprise me, however, that you would think that I did it.'

'Then tell me that you didn't do it, and I'll believe you.'

'What would my motive be for doing such a thing?'

'Why not give me a simple yes or no?'

'There are no simple yes or no answers in this world, Big Girl – none that I've ever found. There are only qualified yes and no answers, and not many of them.'

'All right, James, I can't think of a valid motive, to use one of your favorite words, "valid," but I can think of a motive that *you* might consider valid. I think you've faked an article about some paintings that Debierue was supposed to paint, but didn't paint. You looked at the paintings he did paint and didn't like them, probably because they didn't meet your high standards of what you thought they should be, so you burned them by setting fire to the house. You then invented some nonexistent paintings of your own and wrote about them instead.'

'Jesus, do you realize how crazy that sounds?'

'Yes, I do. But you can show me how crazy it is by letting me read the article you wrote. If there's no mention of that weird orange—'

'Burnt orange—'

'All right, *burnt* orange painting in your article, then you can easily prove me wrong. I'll apologize, and that'll be that.'

'That'll be *that*, just like that? And then you'll expect me to forgive your wild accusation as if you'd never made it, right?'

'I said that I might be wrong, and I sincerely hope that I am. It's easy enough to prove me wrong, isn't it? What I *do* know, though, and there's nothing you can ever say to persuade me that I'm wrong, is that Debierue never painted that picture in your hotel room. *You* painted it. It was still wet when I touched it – including Debierue's signature. And the only reason I can possibly come up with for you to do such a thing is because you want to write about it, and pass it off as Debierue's work. I – I don't know what to think, James, the whole thing has given me a headache. And really – you may not believe this – I actually don't care! *Honestly*, I don't! But I don't want you to get into any trouble, either. Arson is a very serious offence, James.'

'No shit?'

'It isn't funny. I'll tell you that much. And if you did set fire to Debierue's house, you should tell me!'

'Why? So you can turn me in to the police for arson?'

'Oh, James,' she wailed. Berenice put her face into cupped hands and began to cry.

'All right, Berenice,' I said quietly, after I had let her cry for a minute or so. 'I'll tell you what I'm going to do.' I handed her my handkerchief.

She shook her head, took a Kleenex tissue out of her purse, and blew her nose with a refined honk.

'You're right, Berenice, on all counts,' I continued, 'and I might as well admit it. I guess I got carried away, but it isn't too late. Setting the fire was an accident. I didn't do it on purpose. The old man had spilled some turpentine, and I accidentally dropped my cigarette and it caught. I thought I'd put it out, but apparently it flared up again. Do you see?'

She nodded. 'I thought it was something like that.'

'That's the way it happened, I guess. But painting the picture was another matter. I don't know how I expected to get away with it, and the chances are I would've chickened out at the last minute anyway. What I'll do is throw the picture away, and then rewrite the article altogether, using the information I've actually got.'

'He told us lots of interesting things.'

'Sure he did.'

There was a dirt road on the right, leading into a thick stand of pines. I made the turn, shifted down to second gear, but kept up the engine speed because of the sand.

'Where are you going?'

'I'm going to drive back in here well off the highway and burn the painting.'

'You can wait until morning, can't you?'

'No. I think that the sooner I get rid of it the better. If I kept it I might change my mind again. It *would* be possible, you know, to get away with it—'

'No, it wouldn't, James,' she said crisply.

The sandy road, after more than a mile, ended in a small clearing. The clearing was filled with knee-high grass, and we were completely surrounded by second-growth slash pines. It would be another two years, at least, before these trees would be tall enough to cut. I left the lights on and cut the engine. Without another word I got out of the car, opened the trunk with the key, and picked up the tire iron. It was about ten inches long, quite hefty, and the flattened end, although it wasn't sharp, was thin enough to make a good cutting edge. Rounding the car on Berenice's side, I brought the heavy iron down on her head.

'Ooauh!' She expelled her breath, clasped both hands over her head, and turned her face toward me. Her eyes were wide and staring, but her face was expressionless. I hadn't hit her hard enough, or I had miscalculated the thickness of her hair, piled on top of her head, which had cushioned the blow. I hit her on top of the head again, much harder this time, and she slumped down in the seat.

I opened the door, grabbed the thick collar of her polo coat, and dragged her out of the car. She was inert, unbelievably heavy, and her left leg was still in the front seat. I was working one-handed, still clutching the tire iron in my right hand, and trying to free her leg from the car door, when she convulsed, rolled over, and came up off the ground, head down, butting me in the stomach like a goat.

Caught by surprise, I fell backward and my shoulder hit a splintered tree stump. At the same time my left elbow banged against the ground sharply, right on the ulna bone. My right shoulder felt as if it were on fire, and crazy prickles from my banged funny bone danced inside my forearm. I dropped the tire iron, rubbed my right shoulder with the fingers of my left hand, and the pain in my elbow and shoulder gradually subsided. Through the trees, and getting farther away every second, Berenice's voice screamed shrilly. I picked up the tire iron.

I turned off the headlights and started after her, judging direction by the sound of her screams, which were growing fainter, in the dark forest. Berenice ran awkwardly, like

607

most women, and she was hampered by the knee-length coat. I didn't think she could run far, but I was unable to catch up with her. I tried to run myself, but after tripping over a stump and sprawling full length on the damp ground, I settled for a fast walk.

The screaming stopped, and so did I. The abrupt silence startled me and, for the first time, I was frightened. I had to find her. If she got away, everything was over for me – everything.

I moved ahead, walking slower now, searching every foot of ground, now that my eyes had become adjusted to the dim light. A light mist hovered a hundred feet above the trees, but there was a moon, and I could see a little better with every passing moment. The trees thinned out and the wet ground began to get mushy. I was on the edge of a swamp, and after another fifty yards or so, I came to the edge of a lake of black, stagnant water. I knew Berenice well enough to know that she wouldn't have plunged into that inky water. The way was easier going toward the left, and I took it, figuring that she would do the same.

I found her a few minutes later, catching sight of her light-colored coat. She was in a prone position, with her legs spread awkwardly, partially hidden under a spreading dogwood tree. Afraid to touch her, I rolled her over on her back. A pale shaft of moonlight filtered through the tree branches, lighting her bloody face and wide staring eyes.

I didn't know whether she was dead or not, but I had to make certain. There was one thing I did know. I wouldn't have been able to hit her again. As I knelt down beside her and opened her coat, an aroma of Patou's 'Joy' filled my nostrils with loss. I put my head down on her chest and listened for a heartbeat. Nothing. Berenice was dead, but my blows on her head hadn't killed her. She had died from shock. No one, mortally wounded, would have been able to run so far. On the other hand, both of us for a few moments had been gifted with superhuman strength. She was a big woman, stronger than hell, and she had been fighting for her life.

But so had I.

I dragged her to the edge of the water and wedged her body under a fallen tree that was half in and half out of the swamp. By leaning dead branches and by piling brush over the unsubmerged part of the tree, she was completely hidden from view. Debierue knew that she was with me, and if she were to be found, and if he learned that she had been killed, he would tell Cassidy immediately. That is, he would tell Cassidy if her body was found before he received the tear sheets of my article on his American Harvest period. He would be so delighted by my article he wouldn't risk mentioning Berenice's name to anyone. His reputation, as well as mine, depended upon that article. But there would be time, plenty of time. Months, perhaps years, would pass before her body was found.

Suddenly I was weak and dispirited. All of my strength disappeared. I leaned against the nearest tree and vomited my dinner – the corn, the tomatoes and okra, the stringy chunks of sirloin, the biscuits, everything. Panting and sobbing until I caught my breath, I returned to the dogwood tree and picked up my tire iron. It had my fingerprints on it, and in case I had a flat tire on my way to New York, I would need it again.

I started back toward the car, and after walking for five minutes or so I discovered that I was lost. I panicked and began to run. I tripped and fell, banging my head against a tree, scratching a painful gash in my forehead. As Freud said, there are no accidents. Fighting down my panic by taking long deep breaths, I calmed down further by forcing myself to sit quietly on the damp ground, with my back against a tree, and by smoking a cigarette down to the cork tip. I was all right. Everything was going to be all right.

Calmer now, although my hands were still trembling, I managed to retrace my path back to the swamp and Berenice. I now had a sense of direction. I started back in what I thought was the general direction of the car, and hit the sandy road, missing the clearing and the car by about fifty yards. My face was flushed with heat, and I was shivering at the same time with cold. Before setting out, I put up the canvas top, and then kicked over the engine.

Two weeks later, back in New York, when I was cleaning out the car in order to sell it, I found one of Berenice's fingers, or a part of one – the first two joints and the Chen Yu-ed fingernail. She must have got it lopped off when she had put her hands over her head in the car. I wrapped the finger in a handkerchief and put it safely away. Perhaps a day would come, I thought, when I would be able to look at this finger without fear, pain, or remorse.

Chapter Four

The photograph of Debierue 'reading' the flaming copy of the *Miami Herald*, which illustrated my article in *Fine Arts: The Americas* was republished in *Look* and *Newsweek*, and in the fine arts section of the *Sunday New York Times*. UPI, after dickering with my agent, finally bought the photo and sent it out on the wire to their subscribers. The money I made from this photo provided me with my first tailor-made suit. Coat and trousers, four hundred dollars.

I had made one side trip off the superhighway to Baltimore, on my way back to New York, where I checked Berenice's luggage in two lockers inside the Greyhouse bus station (including her handbag and traveler's checks, knowing that her mother could use this money someday, if and when the bags were ever claimed). Except for this brief stopover, I drove straight through to the city.

There were five message slips in my office telling me to telephone Joseph Cassidy, collect, immediately, so I called him before I did anything else.

'Did you get the picture?' he asked.

'Yes, of course.'

'Good! Good! Hold it for a few days before sending it down. I want to get Mr Debierue settled in a good nursing home, you see – he doesn't know that you have the painting, does he?'

'No, and it'll be better if he doesn't. I've mentioned it in my article, although I won't run a photograph of it. Before sending it to Palm Beach I intend to take some good color plates of The Burnt Orange Heresy for *eventual* publication, if you get what I mean …'

'Naturally – is that the title, The Burnt Orange Heresy? That's great!'

'Yeah. It'll probably have an additional title, too. Self-portrait.'

'Jesus, James, I can hardly wait to see it!'

'Just let me know when, Mr Cassidy, and I'll send it down to you air express.'

'Don't worry, I'll call you. And listen, James, I'm not going to forget this. When the time comes to exhibit it, you've got an exclusive to cover the opening.'

'Thanks.'

'My problem right now is to persuade Debierue to enter a rest home. He's much too old to take care of himself. If he had been asleep when the fire started, he would've been killed you know. And when I think of those paintings that went up in smoke – Jesus!'

'Did he tell you anything about them?'

'Not a word. You know how he is. And nothing seems to faze him. He spends most of his time just sitting around watching old movies on TV and drinking orange juice. He can do that in a rest home. Well, you'll hear from me. This is a long distance call, you know.'

'Sure. Later.'

He didn't call me again, however. He sent me a special delivery letter after he had settled Debierue in the Regal Pines Nursing Home, near Melbourne, Florida. I sent Cassidy the painting, air express collect, although I had to pay the insurance fee, in advance, before they would agree to send it collect.

The critical reaction to my article, when it appeared in *Fine Arts: The Americas*, followed the pattern I had anticipated. Canaday, in the *Times*, had reservations. Perreault, in *The Village Voice*, was enthusiastic, and there was a short two-paragraph item in *The LA Free Press* recommending the article to would-be revolutionary painters in Southern California. This was more newspaper coverage than I expected.

My real concern was with the concentric ripples in the art journals and critical quarterlies. This reaction was slow in coming, because a lot of thought had to be put into them. The best single article, which set off a long string of letters in the correspondence department, appeared in *Spectre*, and was written by Pierre Montrand. A French chauvinist, he saw Debierue's 'American Harvest' period as a socialistic rejection of Gaullism. This was an absurd idea, but beautifully expressed, and controversial as hell.

With my photograph of Debierue, many newspapers printed sketchy accounts of Debierue's mysterious immigration to the United States, but I kept my promise to Cassidy and the old man. I never divulged Debierue's Florida address after Cassidy had him admitted under a false name to the Regal Pines Nursing Home, and Cassidy had covered his tracks so well the reporters never found him. I mailed Debierue the tearsheets of my article, a dozen 8" × 10" photographs of the burning newspaper shot, and an autographed copy of my book, *Art and the Preschool Child*. He didn't acknowledge the package, but I knew that he received it because I had mailed it Return Receipt Requested.

For the first week after my return to New York I bought a daily copy of the *Atlanta Journal-Constitution* (it 'covers Dixie like the dew'), and searched through the pages to see if there was any mention of a body being found near Valdosta. But I disliked the newspaper, and searching for such news every day was making me morbid. I quit buying the paper. If they found her, they found her, and there was nothing I could do about it. Inevitably, though, a reaction appeared in my psyche, caused, naturally enough, by the death of

Berenice. It wasn't that my conscience bothered me, although that was a part of my reaction. It was a second-thought overlap of self-doubt, a feeling of ambivalence that vitiated my value judgments of the new work I witnessed. I overcame this feeling, or overreaction, by compartmentalizing Debierue in a corner of my mind. I was able to rid myself of my ambivalence by setting Debierue apart from other artists as a 'one-of-a-kind' painter, and by not considering him in connection with the mainstream of contemporary art. It didn't take too many weeks before I adjusted to this mental suggestion. I was able to function normally again on my regular critical assignments.

My reputation as a critic didn't soar, but my workload doubled and, with it, my income. Tom Russell gave me a fifty dollar raise, which brought me up to $450 a month at the magazine. My lecture fee was raised, and I gave more lectures, including a lecture at Columbia on 'New Trends in Contemporary Art' to the art majors – and the Fine Arts Department paid me a $600 lecture fee. To lecture in my old school, where I had once been a poverty-stricken graduate student, was perhaps the high point of the entire year.

My agent unloaded some older, unsold articles I had written months before – two of them to art magazines which had earlier rejected them.

I had always done a certain amount of jury work, judging art shows for 'expenses only,' and more often without any compensation at all. I now began to receive some decent cash offers to judge and hang important exhibits at major museums. On a jury show I served on at Hartford, there was a Herb Westcott painting entered in the show. Westcott had changed his style to Romantic Realism, and his fine, almost delicate draftsmanship was well suited to the new style. The Hartford show had an anti-pollution theme, and Westcott had painted an enormous blowup of a 1925 postcard view of Niagara Falls. The painting wasn't in the First Prize category, but I was able to persuade the other jury members (the museum director and Maury Katz, a hard-edge painter) to tag Westcott's painting with an honorable mention and a thousand-dollar purchase prize. I had treated Westcott rather shabbily in Palm Beach, running out on him and his show at Gloria's gallery, and it pleased me to give him a leg up – which he well deserved in any case.

Now included in my books to review were books that the managing editor used to reserve for himself – beautiful, expensive, handsomely illustrated, coffee-table art books – that retailed for $25, $35, and even $50. After being reviewed, these expensive books can be sold at half of their wholesale price to bookdealers. This pocketed cash is found money IRS investigators cannot discover easily.

I no longer slept well. I didn't sleep well at all.

I knew that Debierue had read my article, and although I had made an educated guess that he would say nothing, I could not be positive that he would continue to say nothing. I had dared to assume that four important European art critics had also invented imaginary paintings by Debierue to write about. But *they* couldn't denounce me. Only Debierue could do that and, thanks to the fire I had set, he couldn't actually prove anything.

Nevertheless, late at night, I often awoke from a fitful sleep, covered with perspiration. Sitting in the dark on the edge of my bed, trying to keep my mind as blank as possible, I would light one cigarette after another, afraid to go back to sleep. In time, I would tell myself, all in good time, my nightmares would run their course and stop.

A year after, almost to the day that I returned to New York, Debierue died in Florida. Mr Cassidy wired me, inviting me to the funeral, but I was tied up with other work and couldn't get away on such short notice. Bodies, in Florida, must be buried within twenty-four hours, according to the state law. I wrote the obituary – a black-bordered one-page tribute – for the magazine, of course, inasmuch as I was *the* authority on Debierue, and had already written the definitive piece on him for the forthcoming *International Encyclopedia of Fine Arts*.

Ten days after Debierue's death I received a long, bulky package at the office. When I unwrapped it at my desk I discovered the dismantled baroque frame that had once been Debierue's famous *No. One*. This unexpected gift from beyond the grave made me cry, the first time I had wept in several months. There was no personal note or card with the frame. Debierue had probably left word with someone at the nursing home to mail it to me after he died. But the fact that he sent me the frame meant exoneration. Not only a complete exoneration, it proved that he had been pleased by my critique of his American Harvest period. From all of his many critics, Debierue had singled me out as his beneficiary for *No. One*.

The dismantled frame had no intrinsic value, of course. I probably could have sold it somewhere, or donated it to the Museum of Modern Art for its curiosity value, but I couldn't do that to the old man. His gesture deeply moved me.

I walked down the hall to throw the frame down the incinerator. As I opened the metal door, I noticed a small dead fly scotch-taped to one of the sides of the frame. The old man, despite his age, had a keen memory. After seeing the fly, I couldn't throw the parts down the chute. On my way home from the office I left the bundled frame under my seat in the subway instead.

I had some correspondence with Joseph Cassidy concerning The Burnt Orange Heresy. He wanted me to suggest the best place for unveiling it for the public, New York or Chicago. I advised him to wait and to exhibit the painting at Palm Beach instead, at the opening of the next season, to coincide, as nearly as possible, with the publication date of the *International Encyclopedia of Fine Arts*, which would have a full-page color plate of the painting facing my definitive article on the painter . . .

. . . I opened the heavy volume and found my piece on Jacques Debierue. The color plate of The Burnt Orange Heresy was a beautiful reproduction of the painting. Reduced in size, color photographs often look better than the original oils. And this colored photo, on expensive, white-coated stock, shone like burnished gold.

I read my article carefully. There were no errors in spelling, and no typographical errors. My name was spelled correctly at the end of the article. A short bibliography of the books and major critical articles on Debierue followed my byline, set in 5½ point agate boldface. There were no typos in the bibliography either.

Satisfied, I began to leaf through some of the other volumes of the *Encyclopedia*, here and there, to check the writing and the quality of the work. I read pieces on some of my favorites – Goya, El Greco, Piranesi, Michelangelo.

My stomach became queasy, and I had a peculiar premonition. The articles I had read were well researched and well written, particularly the piece on Piranesi, but my stomach felt as it if had been filled with raw bread dough that was beginning to rise and swell inside me. I opened my desk drawer and took out my brass ruler. Taking my time, to make certain there would be no mistakes, I measured the column inches in the *Encyclopedia* to see how many inches had been allotted to Goya, El Greco, Piranesi, Michelangelo – and Debierue.

Goya had nine and one-half inches. El Greco had twelve. Piranesi had eight. Michelangelo had fourteen. But Debierue had *sixteen column inches*! The old man, insofar as *space* was concerned, had topped the greatest artists of all time.

I closed the books, all of them, and returned them to the crate. I lit a cigarette and moved to the window. The buttery sunlight of Palm Beach scattered gold coins beneath the poinciana tree outside my window. The dark green grass in the apartment-house courtyard was still wet from the sprinklers the yardman had recently turned off. The pale blue sky, without any clouds, unpolluted by industrial smoke, was as clear as expensively bottled water. I wasn't fooled by the air-conditioning of the room. It was hotter than hell outside in the sun.

But my work was over. Debierue had triumphed over everyone, and so had I. There would never be another Jacques Debierue, not in my lifetime, and I would never want to meet another one like him if one ever did come along. There was no place else for me to go as an art critic. How could I top myself? Not in *this* world.

But what about Berenice Hollis? Could I pass the test? In a cigar box in the bottom drawer of my dresser, together with a picture of my father, taken when he was seven years old, and a dry, rough periwinkle shell (a reminder, because I had picked it up on the beach as a kid, that I was born in Puerto Rico), was Berenice's dried finger, wrapped in a linen handkerchief. I unrolled the handkerchief and looked at the shriveled finger. The blood-red Chen Yu nail varnish was dull, and some of it had flaked off. I looked at the finger for a long time without feeling fear, pain or remorse.

Debierue, and his achievement, had been worth it, and there was nothing else left for me to do. Somebody else, another critic, could cover the unveiling of Cassidy's only signed Debierue at the Everglades Club. The time had come for me to pay my dues for the death of Berenice Hollis.

I showered, shaved, and put on my tailor-made suit, together with a white shirt, a wide red-white-and-blue striped tie, black silk socks, and polished cordovan shoes.

Taking my time, strolling, I walked through the late afternoon streets to the Spanish-style Palm Beach police station. No one else would ever know the truth about Debierue, and no one, other than myself, knew the truth about my part in his apotheosis. And I would never tell, never, but I had to pay for Berenice. The man who achieves success in America must pay for it. It's the American way, and no one knows this fact of life any better than I, a de-islanded Puerto Rican.

There were a sergeant and two patrolmen inside the station. One patrolman was going on duty and the other was going off, but they both looked so clean and well groomed it would have been impossible to tell them apart. All three policemen were looking at a copy of *Palm Beach Life*, the slick, seasonal magazine that covers Palm Beach society. The policeman going off duty had his picture in it – a shot of a group of women on a garden tour, and he was smiling in the background.

'Good afternoon, sir,' the sergeant said politely, getting to his feet, 'may I help you?'

I nodded. 'Good afternoon, Sergeant,' I replied. I unfolded the handkerchief on the table, and Berenice's finger rolled out. 'I want to confess to a crime of passion.'

BOOK FOUR

The Machine in Ward Eleven

The Machine in Ward Eleven

I like Ruben. He is a nice guy. He doesn't lock my door at night. He closes it, naturally, so that none of the doctors nor any of the other nurses will notice that it isn't locked when they're just walking past, but he doesn't lock it. (An unlocked door gives me a delicately delightful sense of insecurity.) And this is the kind of thing a man appreciates in a place like this.

A little thing here is a big thing; the differences between this place and the private hospital are much greater than fifty dollars a day.

Ruben also lights my cigarettes and, what's more, he doesn't mind lighting them. The day nurse, Fred, always appears to be exasperated when I call out to him for a light. I don't blame Fred, of course. The day nurse has many things to do compared to Ruben's duties. He has to get the hallway and latrines cleaned, the privileged patients off to OT. And all of the meals are eaten during the day, too. Fred is responsible for the cart, the collection of the trays and spoons afterward, and so on. I've never had a chance to talk much to Fred, but at night, I talk to Ruben quite a little. Which means I listen, and that's what I need to do. There's a dark, liquid vacuum to fill. What Ruben tells me, I often remember. Like the cigarettes.

The American Red Cross furnishes each patient with a carton of cigarettes every week, although there isn't any limitation – at least I don't think there is – on how many cigarettes we can smoke in a week. A carton a week is plenty for me. But we aren't allowed to have matches or a lighter. The male nurse is supposed to open the cell door and light them for us when we call him. If the nurse is busy, a man has to wait, that's all. There have been times when I've had to wait so long that when Fred or one of the loose patients (there are quite a few of these loose ones who are allowed to carry matches, and they do little odd jobs around the hospital, only their work details are called 'therapy') came around to light my cigarette, I actually forgot what I called out for in the first place.

But at night it is different. The men in the other eleven (that number always makes my stomach feel queasy) cells in this locked ward are all good sleepers. Except for Old Man Reddington. Right after the supper meal, or within an hour or so, most of them are asleep. Old Man Reddington, in Number Four, has nightmares that are truly terrible. If I had nightmares like his I'd never go to sleep. But when I've mentioned his nightmares to him, he denied having any, so I guess he doesn't remember them. I wonder if I have nightmares? That's something I'll have to pump Ruben about some time. The reason I don't go to sleep early is because of my long, peaceful afternoon nap every day. I'm not allowed to go to Occupational Therapy, so when the other patients leave the ward for OT after lunch I'm locked in my cell. It's quiet then, and I sleep. I have nothing to think about; my memory is almost all gone, except for isolated, unsatisfactory, and unresolved little incidents. Trying to remember things, however, is a fascinating little game.

I like Ruben. He is a nice guy. Oh, yes, it was about the cigarettes!

'I don't really care, Ruben,' I said to him the other night (I know it wasn't tonight), 'but every week when the Gray Lady comes around with the cigarettes I get a different brand. And even though I'm satisfied with whatever brand I'm given, I don't think it's right. I realize that smoking is a privilege, but I've also concluded that any man who smoked all the time would sooner or later decide that he preferred one particular brand. And if he did, he'd buy and smoke the same brand all the time. Is it because we're crazy that we get a different brand every week, or what?'

Ruben frowned quizzically, and looked at me for a long time. He is a good-looking young guy (in a rather coarse way), twenty-five or six, with strong white teeth, and friendly enough, but when he examines me for a long time that way without replying I have a premonition that he doesn't truly like me, and that he might possibly be a doctor's spy. But then Ruben grinned fraternally, and I knew that he was all right.

'Do you know something, Blake,' he said with unfeigned sincerity, 'you're the only nut in my whole ward who's got good sense.'

This incongruous remark struck both of us as funny, and we had to laugh. 'No, seriously,' Ruben went on, 'that comment was a sign of progress, Blake. Do you possibly remember, from before maybe, smoking one particular brand of cigarettes? Think hard.'

'No,' although I didn't even try to think, 'but this talk about cigarettes makes me want one. How about a light?'

'Sure.' As he flipped his lighter he said, 'If you ever do feel a preference for any particular brand, let me know. Nobody's trying to deliberately deprive anyone of their favorite cigarettes. But I've been working here for two years now, and you're the first patient who's ever mentioned the subject.'

'Then maybe I'm not so crazy after all?' I smiled.

'Oh, you're crazy all right!' Ruben laughed. 'Would you like some coffee? I'm going to make a fresh pot.'

I remember this conversation well; the smoking of the cigarette; and yet I'm not absolutely certain whether he came back with the coffee later or whether I went to bed without it. I've had coffee with Ruben late at night on many, many occasions, but that particular night is a disconnected memory.

I cannot always orientate the sequence of daily events. It's probably because of the sameness here. The only real difference between day and night is that it's quieter at night (except for Old Man Reddington in Number Four); and there is quite a bit of activity in the mornings. Breakfast, the cleaning up, the doctor making his rounds, and I have my chess problems to puzzle over every morning. I work out two or three problems every morning, although I'd never admit it to Dr Adams.

'A man's mind is a tricky thing, Blake,' Dr Adams said, the day he brought me the board and chessmen. He made this statement as though I were unaware of this basic tenet. 'But if you exercise your brain every day – and I think you'll enjoy working out these chess problems – it'll be excellent therapy for you. In fact, your memory will probably come back to you in its entirety – all at once.' He snapped his soft, pudgy fingers. 'But I don't want you to sit around *trying* to remember things. That's too hard. Do you understand?' And he handed me an elementary paperback book of chess problems to go with the chess set.

'Yes, I understand, Dr Adams.' I nodded solemnly. 'I understand that you're a condescending son of a bitch.'

'Of course I am, Blake,' he agreed easily, humoring me, 'but solving chess problems is merely an exercise to help you. For instance, a person with weak arches can strengthen them by picking up marbles with his toes, and—'

'I haven't lost my marbles,' I broke in angrily. 'They've only rolled to one side.'

'Of course, of course,' he said wearily, looking away from me. I've learned how to discomfit these expressionless psychiatrists every time. I stare straight into their moronic, unblinking eyes. 'But you will try to work some of the problems, won't you, Blake?'

'I might.' A noncommittal answer is the only kind a headshrinker understands.

So I've never given Adams the satisfaction of knowing that I work three or four problems every morning. When he asks me how I'm getting along I tell him I'm still on the first problem in the book, although I've been through the book four times already – or is it five? Ah! Here's Ruben with my coffee.

The coffee is strong, just the way I like it, with plenty of sugar and armored cow. And Ruben is relating the story again about why he elected to become a male nurse. He's told me all this before, but each time he tells it a little differently. His fresh details don't fool me, however. He actually took the two-year junior college nursing course to be the only male student in a class of thirty-eight girls. But talking to me at night – or should I say, at me? – is probably good 'therapy' for Ruben.

'By the way, Blake, your wife's scheduled to visit you tomorrow. You asked me to remind you.'

'Already?' I made a clucking sound in my throat. 'My, my, how time flies. It seems like only yesterday, and yet thirty happy, carefree days have sped by.' I shook my head with mock dismay.

'Not for me,' he said grimly. 'Let me have your cup.' And he closed my door.

I'm beginning to get accustomed to my wife now, but it was difficult at first. The first time she visited me I didn't even know the woman. I still don't recall marrying her or living with her before assuming the bachelor residence of this cell. But I had uncommonly good taste. Maria is a real beauty, still well under thirty, and she's a movie actress (she keeps reminding me). The first time they took me to the visiting room to see here I made the undiplomatic mistake of asking her what her name was—and she cried. I felt so sorry for her I've never made the same mistake again. Now, when I occasionally forget that her name is Maria I call her Honey or Sweetie-pants. She likes these pet names.

We usually spend our whole hour together talking about the movies, about technical details mostly, and she often asks me intelligent questions about acting techniques. (The doctor probably briefed her to ask me such questions to help me regain my memory, but I enjoy giving Maria advice.) I'm an expert in the field of falsely induced emotions, and although I don't remember directing any of the plays or movies or TV shows she told me I directed, I am apparently well acquainted with all of the terms and practically every aspect of the craft – or so it seems. Maria may be lying to me, of course. It's quite possible that this vast store of film intelligence I dredge up and dispense with so freely during our monthly visits was gained by reading books on the subject before I came here. And it might be possible that a freak memory breakthrough allows me to remember film subjects as a person does who is blessed or cursed with a photographic memory. That isn't a bad *double entendre*: I think I'll mention it to Maria tomorrow – if I don't forget it by then.

But if Maria truly is an actress, she's a most convincing actress, because I always believe her when she tells me that I was a director. And there's a sharp, single scene that keeps recurring to me at odd and unexpected times, but it doesn't seem to be truly alive, despite the verisimilitude and living color. So whether it really happened, or whether it's an imagined scene I happened to create in my mind because Maria told me that I was a director – I simply do not know:

The sun is so hot!

This our fifth straight twelve-hour day on desert location, and this will be the twentieth episode of the series. Nineteen more to go after this one, and if Red Faris doesn't change his attitude soon, we'll never finish them all, which means, of course, that I will not. We may never finish this one, *The Pack Rats*, which is, in my skilled opinion, the lousiest script I've ever directed. But Red is brilliant; he knows *everything*. This is Red's third year as the star of the series, and he now owns a juicy fifty percent. A big, stupid, six-foot-two ex-football player who never had anything better than a walk-on at the Pasadena Playhouse before he lucked into this Western series, and yet he tries to tell *me* how to direct his scenes. And when I explain some basic acting rule to him he nods condescendingly, and winks broadly at the grinning crew members he plays poker with when he should be studying his lines.

Take Twelve coming up, far too many takes for the budget, but every time Red does some annoying little thing wrong. Purposely? I'm beginning to wonder. The scene is unimportant; even a poor take would be valid enough, but I seem to have some sort of uncontrollable compulsion to shoot it over and over again until it's perfect. The arid heat must be at least 110 degrees, but the enmity from everybody on the set is hotter than that, much hotter. They all hate me now, every one of them, they hate my guts. Wonderful!

'Okay, Red?' I grin pleasantly at our stupid star, who stands petulantly beside his sweaty gray horse. 'I know I'm a real bastard, Red, but let's try it one more time. Rolling a cigarette is supposed to be a piece of business just as natural as breathing to a cowboy, and yet—'

'After riding across the desert, I'm supposed to be tired, Jake! And after about fifty goddamned takes—'

'Eleven,' I emended cheerfully.

'—I'm not faking it! I *am* tired.'

'All right, get mounted.' I ignore his childish outburst, turn my back on him. 'Here we go again, kiddies,' I announce to the sullen crew.

No one moves; they avoid my eyes. They're looking past me toward Red Faris. I turn. Red is still standing stubbornly beside his horse. He glares at me, pouting with his upper lip only (which is no mean feat for a television actor). He looks toward the number one camera, raising his dimpled chin.

'That's it, everybody!' he shouts fiercely, in stentorian, but untrained pectoral tones.

A triumphant crew cheer mingles with the desert heat waves, thirty-one enthusiastic voices, including the script girl's parched, cigarette-contralto. My face freezes as Red winningly flashes his famous trademark, the sneer-snarlsmile, an endearing grimace which has been described with loving detail in seven trade mags.

'And on the way back,' he calls out again, raising a long right arm (the football signal for free catch,) 'the steaks are on me at Palm Springs!'

Another happy orgiastic rejoinder, followed immediately by the sounds of furious tearing down, leave-taking noises.

'I've been fired before, Red,' I mention quietly, 'but not this way, not crudely and publicly.'

'Hell, you aren't fired, Jake! It's been a rough week, that's all. Danny (Danny Olmstead was the unit's chief film editor) can piece together at least one decent take out of the eleven, and if he can't,' he shrugged, 'we'll simply junk the scene. Okay, Jake?' Sneersnarlsmile. A patronizing hand reaches for my shoulder, but before it touches me I back away quickly.

'No, it isn't okay. I can't direct unless I have full authority. It's one of the little rules a good director lives by.'

'Don't go hard-nosed on me; I haven't done anything to hurt your authority, J.C. I submitted damned well, I think, to every stupid idea you've had this week. And you know as well as I do, there isn't another star in television who'd go through eleven straight takes in a row without sounding off!' Sneersnarlsmile. 'Look, Jake, we'll have us a few cold ones at the Springs, rustle up some girls and a few laughs – and Monday's another week. Right? There's no use getting sore—'

I swung for his dimpled chin – and missed. It should have been a fairly decent fight, but it wasn't. Although I'm shorter than Red, five-eleven, I'm well over two hundred pounds; but Red's hard right fist slammed into my jaw as if it contained a roll of nickels. And that's all I remember. The color film snapped. Clicketyclickety-clicketyclicketyclack, as the crazy reel rolled 'round and 'round the endless track.

At first, the thing-in-itself confused me. Bam! A slam in the jaw, no matter how hard, could not, or did not, at my initial awakening, add up to two thickly bandaged wrists. I was snugly warm, in bed; I was lethargically comfortable, and my wrists, bound with white gauze, didn't hurt at all. I was fighting the will to remember, and then total recall washed over the surface of my mind in a humiliating torrent:

No, I hadn't stopped with the gang in Palm Springs. I had driven my sea-green Porsche, top down, at a forbidden speed, all of the way home to my craggy redwood retreat in the Verdugo Woodlands above the LA smogbelt. A drink, alone on the sundeck, except for my fear. Economic fear. Failure fear. I had been wrong; Red Faris had been reasonable; I was through. Aware of this, I awaited the confirming telephone call. The sundeck was cool and breezy after a week in the desert. A dozen giant potted plants with green waxed leaves, placed strategically here and there, masked successfully the dusty chapparal of the steep olive-colored hills. In some kind of wild optimism my eyes returned repeatedly to the white telephone on the big circular coffee table. Would I finish one, two, three, or four drinks before it rang? The total was six, and I had just sat down again with number seven when—

'Jake-O, baby!' It was my agent, Weldon Murray.

'Willy, boy! Now don't tell me you've found a new series for me already! You're the greatest, Willy – I shall not want—'

'I *did* manage to keep you on the payroll, Jake-O. Only you'll have to be satisfied with the standard director's contract – one-eighty per week. But it stays in effect until Red's series plays out – and that may be forever. I still haven't heard your side, baby, and everybody always has a side. If it's a fight they want, we can do that, too. Why didn't you call me first, baby? I didn't have any ammo to shoot with—'

'And I didn't have any to give you, Willy.'

'I don't suppose, for just once in your life, that you'd be willing to cry a little, kiss and make up?'

'No, and it wouldn't do any good anyway. It's been coming on for weeks. And I'm tired, Willy, tired.'

'I love you, sweetheart, but you're going to get a damned long rest this time, I'm afraid. Three is the fatal charm, it's been said in high places, and this is the third time for you in less than a year. They can't afford perfectionists in TV, baby—'

'I know.'

'It's just that TV isn't the movies, and today even the movies can't—'

'Please. No lecture, Willy,' I said wearily.

'Have you called Maria?'

'No. She's in London – I think.'

'Want me to call her for you?'

'No, I'll call her later. But thanks, Willy.'

After racking the phone I fished a squirming, many-legged arthropod out of my drink. How many men, I wondered curiously, are all washed-up at the age thirty-two meridional? Was I ahead of or behind schedule? And yet, I don't think that I was really depressed. I wasn't completely indifferent, but I had a rather sickening sense of relief. The useless struggle was finally over. The End.

I drank slowly, steadily, spacing my drinks, enjoying the silent evening and the yellow sky above Glendale far below. Hours, or many minutes later, I was giggling, lurching through the empty house in search of a razor blade. A sixty-thousand dollar home, mortgaged for seventy-five, a swimming pool, and no blades. How can a man slash his wrists with an electric razor? The phone kept ringing all the time. Needlers. Sympathizers. At last I found a blade, a used, rusty blade, in an old plaid train case that had belonged to my wife. The ancient blade had once nibbled persistent stubble from her long legs, in all probability. I giggled again as I eased the blade with concentrated caution into a fresh cake of soap. I didn't want to accidentally cut the fingers holding the blade – too painful – and yet I wanted to slice my wrists. Such paradoxical prudence was very amusing indeed.

The private hospital was a warm white womb.

There was a glass-enclosed porch parallel to the end of our ward, and the meals were served right on schedule in the dining room. I liked every one of my fellow eighteen patients – a charming, mixed-up group – and I would have been content to remain dormant in this friendly ward forever. My closest friend was Dave Tucker, an actor who had been possessed (literally) by the devil. He had played *The Devil and Daniel Webster* in summer stock a few months before, and while he was immersed in the role of Daniel, the devil had actually managed to get inside of his skin. Our unimaginative doctor, unfortunately, couldn't exorcise the devil from poor old Dave because the psychiatrist didn't believe that the devil was really under Dave's hide.

'The worst thing about Him, J.C.,' Dave told me, scratching under his pajama jacket, 'is the constant itching. He squirms around so much I itch all the time, and scratching can't get to Him.'

Poor Dave. I believed him, of course. Why would any man lie about something like that? But I still couldn't resist giving Dave the business once in awhile. 'Your case is the inevitable result of method acting,' I told him, 'but it could've been worse.'

'How's that?'

'You could've been playing *Jumbo*.'

'Move,' he said irritably, clawing his chest, 'it's your move.' And we continued our chess game on the sunny porch.

I see now that it was a mistake to become friendly with Dave Tucker, or for that matter, with anyone. It hurt me too much – it was only a few days later – when the devil finally got him. We were playing chess again, smoking, not saying much of anything, when Dave urgently stage-whispered my name: 'Jake! Get the doctor, somebody! He turned on the heat!'

I looked up from the chessboard, startled. Dave's handsome face was as fiery as a record jacket featuring exotic Hawaiian music. There was no perspiration; the devil had caught Dave in an unguarded moment, and he didn't even have enough time to perspire.

I rushed frantically into the ward, yelling my head off for the doctor. And I returned to the porch with Dr Fellerman within a minute and a half – two minutes at most – but Dave was dead. The devil had boiled Dave's blood for him and fled. I was unreasonable then, more than a little hysterical, and I cursed Fellerman for all he was worth (which wasn't much), although it hadn't been entirely his fault. It was a matter of time; the devil would have taken Dave sooner or later anyway. But the swiftness of the attack unnerved me, and I had a long, miserable crying spell.

After Dave, I dropped out of sight. No more friends for me. Not after Dave. I simply couldn't stand the emotional damage, and I was wise enough to see that much.

A truly successful, nigrescent depression has to be nourished, cherished. The strong rock wall can keep everything out and everything in, but it must be built stone by stone; each brick must be carved patiently from igneous rock; and every added layer must be layed meticulously, the stones so close together that no mortar is required.

Before retiring to my walled-in secret garden – before Dave – I'd been on the Camino Real, the road to recovery. All of the senseless oral and written psychological tests had been taken docilely; the tiny needles had been inserted into my scalp for the recording of the brain waves; and I had been a reluctant, but participating, member of Ward Fourteen's Group Therapy group. We met on Mondays, Wednesdays and Fridays at 11 a.m. in Ward Eleven, under the joint chairmanship of Doctors Fellerman and Mullinare.

There were four of us, not counting the two doctors (they merely observed and listened): Tommy Amato, a seventeen-year-old boy, the son of a well-known male movie star, and every night Tommy drowned his bed; Randolph Hicks, an ex-hotel manager who had deliberately crashed his car and now had a corrugated skull and a permanent eye-squinting headache; Marvin Morris, a pop songwriter, who, like me, had attempted suicide unsuccessfully – and there was me.

I never did understand fully what we were supposed to accomplish during these triweekly sessions. The doctors never uttered a sound; they sat impassively in their metal folding chairs looking us over like a pair of bespectacled owls caught out at high noon. We, the sick ones, were supposed to talk out our problems; I believe that was the general idea. But the atmosphere in the scaly, gray-walled ward was not conducive to talk of any kind; it was too depressing. The first five minutes of each meeting were always awkward, taut with the clearings of dry, apprehensive throats. Ward Eleven was an unused ward, pressed into service as a group therapy meeting place because of hospital space shortage, and we sat around in a rough semicircle, chain-smoking cigarettes. It was difficult to keep our eyes away from the six unoccupied mattresses – each covered with a soiled white sheet – on the floor near the doorway. The electroshock machine rested on a small gray table in one corner of the room, and there was a padded, rubber-sheeted treatment table beside it. When the shock treatments were given early in the morning, the unconscious bodies were deposited on the mattresses until they awakened, and then the dazed patients were led away to eat breakfast. No, this ward was not an inspiring meeting hall to discuss problems of the mind.

It's against federal law to photograph nuts in a Funny Factory, but these group therapy sessions were great human comedies that should have been captured on film. They were the kind of comedies that cause strong men to weep copious tears. Albert McCleery would have loved to film them on television's old *Cameo Theater*, cutting back and forth from one face to the next.

After the nervous silence became almost unbearable, young Tommy was invariably first to break into the uneasiness.

'I wet my bed again last night.' A simple statement of fact. Tommy was no longer embarrassed by his chronic enuresis, now that the doctors had convinced him that his was a psychosomatic condition, and he felt that we older men could help him. We were grateful to Tommy every time, of course, for breaking the sound barrier, and we wanted to help him.

'Ah, did you try elevating your feet?' Marvin would ask eagerly.

'Yes, I slept with three pillows under my feet last night, but they didn't do any good.'

And then the group therapy session was underway. Once started, it was easier to talk than it was to just stare at each other. We discussed the movies, BB, Russia, bridge, paperback novels, the quality of the hospital food, taxes, the LA traffic problem, the long distance dial system; everything; everything, in fact, except our individual and personal problems. Tommy, however, was always provided with fresh, thoughtful suggestions for *his* little problem— not that any of them ever worked. The two doctors never took notes, they never made any comments or suggestions, and they never attempted to steer our conversations. For their silence we were grateful, all of us, and I believe we did our best to entertain them so they wouldn't be too bored during their listening-in hour. But maybe the meetings did the doctors some good – I really don't know. After Dave, I refused flatly to attend the mental torture sessions anymore.

Ward Fourteen wasn't a locked ward, and within the hospital we had considerable freedom. There were movies at night (16 mm) in the patients' lounge. There was a library, a TV set on the porch, and there was a snack bar where the patients could sit around drinking coffee and eating sandwiches between meals. But I gave up these frivolous activities for the full-time occupation of my uncomfortable bedside chair. I ate my three full meals every day, marching to the dining room with the others when it was our ward's turn to eat, but I returned immediately to my chair. After supper each night I went to bed, and slept dreamlessly until 6:30 a.m. I could've slept all the time, I think, but we weren't allowed on our beds during the day. Unable to drowse in my hard metal chair, I meditated and read, meditated and read again – and it was always the same book: *The Silent Life*, by Thomas Merton.

I was fascinated by these accounts of monastic life; the Carthusians, particularly, with their isolated hermitages, were brilliant men who had found the right answer to the complexities of life, and I was saddened by the knowledge that I could never be one of them. These holy monks had a curious mixture of humility and vanity I could never hope to achieve. They believed that if they were humble enough they would see God when they died – surely this was a naive vanity – so innocent and touching the tears welled from my eyes. But I knew that God would never look at a wretch like me. However, there was another path, and now that I had time to think – more time than I'd ever had in my life before – the tantalizing challenge appealed to me more and more. To reach the top wasn't really difficult; I'd been up there three times already – but the pyramid at the bottom was much broader.

How many American males had consciously directed every effort to achieving the absolute bottom of the pile, burrowing their way deliberately to the exact center of the bottom of humanity? If I could only get down there, really down, all the way down, without any outside help— ah! – here was a unique and terrible aspiration! How? How? An intelligent man could meditate for years on this fascinating challenge!

My deliberations were interrupted one morning by Dr Fellerman. He had approached my bed in a surreptitious manner and tapped me on the shoulder. He asked me if I would like to talk to him alone in his office twice a week.

'I've got an hour open on Thursday, Mr Blake, and another on Monday. I'll squeeze you in.'

'Squeeze in somebody else,' I told him coldly. 'I have nothing to say to you.' Unbidden, uninvited, he had interrupted a very important train of thought, and I glared at him to express my annoyance. Fellerman was a tall, almost cadaverous man, with a concave chest. His face was lined, tired; an ostensibly overworked man. In his loose, knee-length white coat, with his humped shoulders, and with his narrow head cocked to one side, he always reminded me of an unskilled mechanic listening to an unidentifiable engine knock.

'And you won't return to our little group therapy sessions, either?'

'No. But if I come up with a valid suggestion for Tommy Amato's bed-wetting problem,' I said sarcastically, 'I'll write it down and give it to him in the dining room.'

I arose from my chair, turned my back on the doctor, and sat down again facing the wall, thereby terminating the unwelcome interview. This brief discussion took place on a Monday afternoon. On Wednesday morning, right after breakfast, the male nurse, Luchessi, told me that I had to visit Dr Fellerman's office. Any mental patient has the privilege of arguing with his doctor, but only a crazy man will argue with a male nurse. Without protest, I accompanied Luchessi to Fellerman's private office.

'Mr Blake,' Fellerman said calmly, without preamble, 'I've decided to give you a short series of nine electro-shock treatments.' The sentence was a nail on a slate.

The hand, my right, carrying the cigarette to my mouth, was arrested in midair. I was frightened, yes, but my astonishment was even greater. The hair at the nape of my neck bristled; goose bumps crawled on my arms. The six, white-sheeted mattresses on the floor in Ward Eleven appeared vividly, sickeningly, in my mind. And the small electroshock machine, which resembled a cheap portable phonograph when the lid was closed, became a leather-covered symbol of terror – sudden, terrible death!

'No!' I blurted, shaking my head. 'You aren't serious!'

He shrugged. 'I don't know what else to do with you, Mr Blake. You won't help yourself, you won't attend the group therapy sessions, you've refused private conferences. Do you still believe that it was the devil, instead of apoplexy, that killed your actor friend, Mr Tucker?'

I said nothing; he was trying to trap me.

'You aren't getting any better, and the shock treatments will help you.'

'Depression is something I can learn to live with,' I said bitterly, 'but I can't live with death.'

'Now you're being melodramatic.'

'Am I? How many people survive electric shock treatments?'

'The fatality percentage is so small it's practically unimportant.'

'It's important to me! What is the percentage?'

'I don't know offhand; less than one fatality in every three or four thousand, if that high—'

'Nine treatments in a row drops those odds down to a damned dangerous level!'

'If we thought there was any real danger, Mr Blake,' he said quietly, 'we wouldn't give you shock therapy. You're a strong healthy man, although you're a little overweight. To lessen the convulsion, we'll give you curare to relax you first.'

'Poison? If the shock doesn't kill me, the curare will! Is that the idea?'

'I assure you, you have nothing to worry about. The treatments start tomorrow. Don't go to breakfast in the morning.'

'And if I refuse?'

'Don't you want to get well?'

'Not if I have to take shock treatments I don't!'

'There's no pain, none whatsoever.'

'I don't care about pain, but I don't want to lose my memory. My memories may be bitter, but they're all I've got left and I want every single one of them.'

'There's a slight loss of memory, but it's only a temporary condition—'

'Well, I refuse to take the treatments. And that's final!' The cigarette burned my fingers, and I dropped it into his desk ashtray – a white ceramic skull. The ashtray alone, if more evidence was needed, gave the key to the psychiatrist's sadistic nature.

'The choice isn't yours to make,' he reminded me gently.

'You're frightening me now, Doctor—'

'You needn't be. Your wife has consented to the treatments, and—'

'I don't believe you!'

'It's true, nevertheless. Don't build these simple treatments up out of all proportion in your mind. If all goes well, as expected, you may not need all nine of them. Sometimes six are plenty, and you'll be going home before you know it.'

'But I don't *want* to go home,' I wailed unhappily. The tears I could no longer restrain washed my face. 'All I want, all I ever wanted, is to be let alone . . .' Blubbering childishly into my sleeve I stumbled blindly out of the office and Luchessi took me back to the ward.

Later, and considerably calmer, I realized upon reflection that most of my knowledge about electroshock therapy had been learned secondhand from a fellow patient, Nathan Wanless, during idle bull sessions on the porch. Unintentionally, Nate had implanted dread of the little machine in my head by innocently underplaying the description of his own course of treatments.

'I didn't mind too much, Mr Blake,' he told me quietly. His eyes already had a puzzled expression, and at the time he had only had three treatments. 'On the first one I asked to go first, you see, because I was a little scared and wanted to get it over with. I climbed up on the table in Ward Eleven and four male nurses – Luchessi's one of them – grabbed me by the pajamas and bathrobe. One guy held both feet. When the old electricity shoots through your brain you get one helluva big convulsion, and if these guys didn't hold you in a tight brace you'd get your back broken. It'd snap like a match. Anyway, Dr Fellerman slipped the little harness over my head, and it's got a chromium electrode that clamps tight over each temple. Then they stick a curved piece of rubber hose in your mouth to bite down on and that's it.'

'What do you mean, that's it?' I asked him tensely.

'Blooey, that's all.'

'Blooey?'

'Blooey. I didn't feel anything. Next thing I know I'm awake and looking up at the ceiling, flat on my back on one of the mattresses in Ward Eleven. You know the—'

'I know, I know. But what did you feel? Did you have any screwy dreams while you were out, anything like that?'

'No, just blooey, that's all. One minute I was wide awake, a little scared, looking up at Dr Fellerman, and then I was on the mattress looking at the ceiling instead. A funny feeling. Soon's the nurse sees you're awake, he sends you across the hall to the little kitchen in Ward Ten for scrambled eggs. Ward Ten's the locked ward, you know.'

'I know. But there must be more to the treatments than that, Nate. You make the whole business sound too simple.'

'It is simple, Mr Blake. The second time I watched some of the other guys take theirs to see how it worked, and that was it. Soon's the electrodes are in place Dr Fellerman turns on the two knobs on the machine. There can't be more'n one hundred and ten volts, because the cord's just plugged into the wall socket. All the same, I imagine Dr Fellerman watches the needle pretty close.'

'What needle?'

'There's a needle on the gauge. The machine might be preset, but I don't think there's any rheostat, so when the needle hits the right number on the gauge the doctor turns off the machine. And that's it.'

'The patient on the table. What kind of a convulsion does he have?'

'You can't really tell, not with all those guys holding him and all. All in all, I guess it's a very humane machine. I imagine the electric chair works the same way when they execute somebody. They put the guy in the chair, flip the old switch, and blooey, that's all. Of course,' Nate frowned thoughtfully, 'they have to strap the guy into the electric chair because the electricity's so much more powerful.' He giggled. 'The guy's back must get broken anyway, but he's dead by that time so it doesn't make any difference.'

'The analogy – electric chair and shock machine— doesn't seem humane to me, Nate.' I shuddered.

'Why not? It doesn't hurt you none. Blooey, that's all, except that on shock treatments you wake up later. In the electric chair you don't – not in this lousy world anyway.'

Nate Wanless was no longer with us. The course of shock treatments had helped him – perhaps they had eliminated his mental depression altogether – and he had been discharged from the hospital. But after a few treatments he'd developed a frowning, perplexed expression. He was unable to recall entering the hospital, or any of the events that had led up to his admission. I had talked to him several times before his release, and except for his memory block, which worried him very little, he was a rational, perfectly normal – nothing – that was it, nothing! He was neither excited nor depressed. He was stonily indifferent to his past and future, and he had *believed* Dr Fellerman when he was told that his memory would return, all in good time.

But I didn't believe it, not for a damned second I didn't!

My palms were wet. My throat was dry. For the first time in my life I knew true fear! Ordinary fear was a familiar emotion I'd known intimately, many times – the fear of losing an arm or a leg or an eye in battle, when I had fought (for a blissfully short three months toward the very end) in Korea; the fear of being absolutely broke; the fear of success and the fear of failure; and certainly, the fear of death. And I had also known that secret, unvoiced fear, the kind no one ever admits to anyone, and only rarely to himself; the unknown terror of afterdeath. Is there an afterlife or is there not? And if there is, how will a man fare there? Will he be able to withstand the punishment meted out to him according to his earthly record?

But what were any of these childish, mundane fears in comparison with the worst fear on earth, the worst possible misfortune that could happen to mortal man? The fear of becoming a vegetable. Could any misfortune be worse?

His memories, his ability to laugh at his follies and stupidities – when the chips were finally down, these were the only things a man had left to him. Otherwise, a man is a pine tree, a turnip, a daisy, a weed, existing through the grace of the sun and photosynthesis during the day, and ridding himself of excess carbon dioxide during the long night. I was still a fairly young man; if the choice had been the simple one of life and death I could have accepted it, I believe, at any age. Perhaps I could have even feigned some kind of insouciant bravery if I had to choose death – I didn't really know.

But I had only to go to the glass windows on the porch and look out over the verdant hospital grounds. From the windows I could always see three or four hospitalized human vegetables sitting on their benches beneath the sun. Most of them were old men, white-thatched, harmless, of course, and when the weather was nice they were allowed to remain outside all day long. They never bothered anyone, they didn't think, they couldn't remember anything, not even their names, and their ability to laugh was completely gone. Plants. Vegetables.

Mental patients live for an uncommonly long time, and I was only thirty-two. I was also gifted with that accursed trait that every director or actor must have to achieve any measure of success in the world of make-believe: the ability to put myself into someone else's place. Empathy. I could project myself now into the future, near and far; Blake the Vegetable, sitting in the sunlight year after year until he was a feeble, drooling old man of eighty – no, ninety! – the damned busy-body medicos were learning more about geriatrics every day.

No longer was I J.C. Blake the Arrogant, the one man in Hollywood who had never taken anything from anybody. I was transformed instantaneously by my cool, logical imagination into Blake the Abject, Blake the Beggar, Blake the Craven. All right, then. If Dr Fellerman wanted me to crawl I would crawl. If he wanted me humbled, if he wanted his feet washed, I would wash his feet and anoint them with scented oils. The gelid dread that twisted my entrails was panicky, and there was so little time! The clock above Luchessi's desk told me that it was 11:40. I had to see Fellerman now, before he left the hospital at noon. When tomorrow morning came it would be too late; they would inject their South American curare into my veins and then destroy my fine mind forever with their machine. Controlling my inner conflict as well as I could I approached Luchessi's desk.

'You should've reminded me,' I said, smiling, 'about the group therapy session in Ward Eleven.'

'I thought you dropped out of group therapy?' But he wasn't suspicious; he was already filling in a hall pass for me.

'I did, Luchessi, but I was supposed to start back today. That's what the doctor wanted to see me about this morning.'

'You're late, you know.' Luchessi frowned as he handed me the pass. 'But it isn't my fault.'

'I know; it's mine, but I simply forgot about it. It's probably too late to go at all now, but if I didn't make the attempt Dr Fellerman would say that I was being uncooperative. You know how he is.'

'Sure. You'd better get a move on.'

I had escaped legally from the ward, and if an official stopped me in the corridor on my way to Ward Eleven the pass would be a valid ticket. When I reached the ward the group therapy meeting was just breaking up. Tommy Amato was the first patient through the door. I nodded absently to him before he could start a conversation, brushed by the other three emerging patients and entered the ward. Dr Fellerman and Dr Mullinare were still seated in their metal chairs at the far end of the ward – holding a post-mortem on the session, I supposed. I hesitated, not allowing myself to look to the right, toward the shock machine and treatment table.

'Well, hello there, Blake!' Mullinare called out cheerily. 'Long time no see.' (This Mullinare character was a real cornball.)

'Good morning, Dr Mullinare,' I responded pleasantly. 'Sorry to intrude on you gentlemen this way, but I wanted to talk for a few moments with Dr Fellerman.' I moved toward them, holding myself erect, my back stiff.

'That's quite all right, Blake,' Fellerman said. 'We're finished here.' He winked at Mullinare. 'Call me tonight, Kevin, and we'll see.'

'Sure.' Mullinare clasped my shoulder with a meaty, sweaty hand. 'We've missed you at our little sessions, Blake,' he said lightly.

'I've missed them, too, Doctor,' I lied. 'Perhaps Dr Fellerman will let me rejoin the group.'

Mullinare didn't reply. He left the ward, closing the doors behind him. I wet my parched lips, wondering how to begin. The rehearsed, practiced silence peculiar to psychiatrists puts every patient on the defensive from the first moment on. These doctors rarely, if ever, ask questions, except perhaps with their incurious, unblinking eyes. But even their eyes are distorted unnaturally, as a rule, behind glasses. Fellerman, his skinny shoulders hunched, his narrow head cocked to the right as he looked up at me from his seated position, gave me no help. How could any man, a human being, approach such a machine?

'I've been hoping, sir,' I began humbly – and I regretted the lack of a Balkan peasant cap that could have been snatched respectfully from my head as I began to address him—'that you might reconsider your idea of putting me on shock treatments. My attitude has been poor all along, sir, and I realize that now. And I apologize, most sincerely. If I am to help myself, I must cooperate fully with you and the other doctors. And I want you to know, Dr Fellerman, I'm ready to turn over a new leaf. If you'll only allow me to do so, I'll return gladly to the group therapy sessions. And if you still have those two free hours open you mentioned I'd like to take advantage of them, too. Why,' I smiled, 'when I finally got it through this thick dumb head of mine, Doctor, that I was only hurting myself by my incorrigible attitude, I began to feel better right away. Yes, sir, and that's the truth! Why I'm not nearly so depressed as I was when I talked to you earlier this morning!'

I essayed a light laugh then, and it was indeed a pitiful, strangling sound. Is there anything more heart-rending than the forced sound of false gaiety?

'And what's more, sir,' I plodded on, 'I think my change in attitude will be beneficial to my fellow patients, too. I really do. Outside in the hall just now, when I bumped into

Tommy Amato, my heart went out to that young boy. I realized how selfish I've been all along, thinking only of myself instead of others. And as you remember, Doctor, I talked quite a bit at group therapy, just as much if not more than any of the other patients. I've got a *good* mind, Dr Fellerman, and if I truly put all of my intelligence to work, I'll bet you any amount you care to wager that I can come up with a valid solution to Tommy's bed-wetting problem. Yes, sir! If you'll just cancel those shock treatments I'll get a notebook and pencil and I'll start working on young Tommy's problem right away. I know it sounds funny, now that I'm a mental patient, but when I was in college I got straight A's in Logic. And I'll just bet you, sir,' (for a brief instant I considered injecting another forced, merry little laugh into my monologue, but I swiftly changed my mind, knowing I couldn't pull it off convincingly) 'that once I solve Tommy's problem I'll also solve my own!

'From what little knowledge I have about Freud – of course, I don't pretend to know nearly as much as you do, what with your wonderful training and the brilliant record you've established, and all – but it's a sign of progress, isn't it? I mean, when a mental patient begins to think about the feelings of others instead of just himself, isn't that a sign of recovery? Well, maybe not. But what I want to get over to you is that I'm not in any badly depressed state any longer. Shock treatments are for people who really need them, and when we get into our private consultations – just the two of us – I don't like to confess too really personal experiences in a group therapy session, but when it's just you and me, I'll tell you everything!'

I lowered my voice confidentially, to an intimate level.

'Sex, for instance. I know how interested you psychiatrists are in sex, and you are aware, of course, that I'm married to Maria Chavez, the movie star. Well, when we were first married we were very much in love, you see.

And we did all kinds of things together when we made love. I know you're anxious to go to lunch now, but when we meet alone I'll tell you every tiny detail. I'll make some notes, so I don't forget a single moment of it. With my screen experience I've learned how to tell a story well, and I'll tell you all about our love life together so you'll be able to get a real vicarious thrill out of it. I'll do anything, anything, only please, please, please—!'

I was unable to continue; my invention had flagged. Dr Fellerman's expression hadn't changed once. Nothing I had said (or possibly could say) made any impression on the man. I dropped abjectly to my knees and kissed his shoes. He wore black, rather old-fashioned, high-topped shoes, and white socks. I was furious with myself because I couldn't cry. The needed tears refused to flow, and I had a desperate need for every crutch on the emotional scale to elicit sympathy from this stone, this dehumanized machine.

'Get up, Blake, get up from the floor,' Fellerman ordered quietly.

'Yes, sir.' I scrambled hurriedly to my feet. 'You'll take me back into group therapy, sir? And you won't put me on shock treatments?'

He got up, stretching his long skinny arms as he yawned, and *yawn* he did. 'No, Blake, I'm convinced that electro-shock treatments will do you a lot of good.' Without a backward glance he started toward the exit doors.

Before he took three steps I caught up with him. My fingers dug into his neck before he could cry out. He struggled, but he didn't have a chance. I kicked his feet out from under him and followed him to the floor, still clutching his scrawny neck. I squeezed relentlessly until my fingers tingled with pain, but the moment I was positive his limpness was unfeigned I dragged his unconscious body to the treatment table in the corner. Using ripped strips of a sheet I took from one of the mattresses on the

649

floor, I quickly tied his body to the table. As I began to stuff his slack mouth with wadded paper towels from the pile on the smaller table, Fellerman gagged slightly and opened his eyes. Without his thick glasses, which had been dislodged during our unrehearsed wrestling match, Dr Fellerman's big brown eyes were very expressive indeed, particularly when my fumbling fingers adjusted the elastic harness over his head and I centered the shiny electrodes to his temples.

A simple, impersonal, uncomplicated machine. I plugged the long cord into the wall outlet, turned the two plastic knobs as far to the right as they would go and left them there. The sensitive needle on the gauge banged against the red plus-pole so hard it almost bent, jiggled slightly, and remained there without a quiver. The body convulsions were terrible to see, and I turned my head away. I couldn't bear the sight of this long, skinny body buckling and jerking beneath the steady flow of electricity. I lit a cigarette and left the ward. As I hurried down the corridor (it was time to get into the lunch line for the march to the dining room) I considered the involved technical problems of capturing this unusual scene on film. Handled exactly right, the scene would scare the hell out of any average movie audience. Good background music was mandatory. When a man takes six or seven aspirin tablets his ears ring; this amplified ringing sound would be excellent on the sound track. But if the scene weren't done perfectly – only one little slip up, and a nervous audience would burst into a giggling, embarrassed type of laughter. A point of view would have to be decided upon— Fellerman's or mine? Here was a scene that couldn't be left to the discreet, unblinking eye of the camera – no.

My transfer to the state hospital came through quickly, but I was never given electroshock treatments. They gave me insulin shock treatments instead. Every morning they awakened me at 3 a.m., dragging me down the corridor kicking and screaming to a dark little room where I was tied hands and feet to another bed and my veins were filled with insulin. And there they destroyed my mind – or so they thought. The dreams under insulin were too real to be dreams, but I finally had enough of the horrors to stop fighting them. And when I stopped fighting them, they stopped the treatments. My spirit isn't broken yet, but they don't know it, by God!

'―――――――!'

'Are you all right, Blake?' Ruben's voice is genuinely concerned. 'What's the matter?'

'I'm all right, Ruben. Every once in a long while a peal of that screwy laughter gets away from me inadvertently. I'm sorry. But after all, if I weren't crazy I wouldn't be locked up permanently in the State Asylum for the Criminally Insane – or would I?'

'Take it easy, Blake. You don't want to get Old Man Reddington started, do you?' He closed the door; this time he locked it.

I like Ruben. He is a nice guy. But I'll have to watch myself more carefully, particularly that wild dramatic laughter. So long as I keep my big mouth shut and do everything they tell me to do (within reason), I'll be able to stay here forever. I doubt if they would ever try me now for the murder of Fellerman, but if they found out that most of my memory has returned, they'd return me to the outside world again as soon as they could. After all, I still haven't reached rock bottom yet, and I must bear in mind that the competition for my hard-won private cell is getting keener all the time.

All the time . . .

Selected Incidents

*The only art and the only creation possible to humanity
is that of giving new form to an old idea.*
Anatole France

Well – you're right on time, Charlie. Come in, come in!
Sit down. Drink?

I'll pour one for you, anyway, whether you drink it or
not. It's a sort of stupid rule I have – at least here in the
office. I happen to want a drink, and I don't feel right
when I drink alone. One won't hurt you; *one* drink never
did anything to anybody.

To tell you the truth, I – that's funny, isn't it? To tell
you the truth. Christ; that's what I've been doing for an
hour every day since you started to write my autobiography. Telling you the truth. How long has it been now?

That long, eh? Well, there's no big hurry about the
book. And the first three chapters you finished were first-
rate, Charlie, absolutely first-rate. As I told you before,
my wife was after me for months to write my autobiography, but I hesitated, kept putting it off. A lot of these
'as told to' autobiographies sound so damned much alike;
the way they read, I mean. Especially our Hollywood
variety – the entire industry's less than sixty-five years
old. And if you read many of the biogs you start running
into the same stale anecdotes and stories, except that
they're attributed to different people in different books.
You keep that in mind, Carlos; I don't want my autobiography to read like any of these tired stereotypes—

No, it reads fine, at least the first three chapters. But you know what I mean. Names'll be dropped, naturally, but I still want the book to be my personal story. One of the reasons I put off starting it so long was on account of the new trend. When Groucho Marx wrote his autobiography all by himself, a lot of us out here didn't like the idea at all. It was damned presumptuous of him, if you ask me. The trend was started, however, and although most of the stars and old-time producers still have their books ghosted, they now feel that they have to say that they were written on their lonesome. Groucho didn't have his book ghosted; I know that as a fact.

But the more I thought about the idea, especially after I tried to make some preliminary notes and so on, the more disgusted I got. After all, I pay writers to write scripts, studio publicity, ads, my letters, and everything else for God's sake, so why should I try to write my own autobiography?

I'm a producer, not a writer, and if a man wants a professional writing job he hires a professional writer. Besides, with your name on the 'as told to,' the books'll sell better. You've established a reputation in this field, and your name on the cover along with mine lets the book buyers know that it's a professional job.

Have it your way, Chaz. But the book'll sell well regardless, even if Cheetah was the co-author. Remember, I've got ten different series working these days on the networks. And that fact means all the network book plugs I want, ingenious plugs, too. You can sell anything on TV, Charles, and that's a fact. It's a matter of percentages, and with enough plugs my autobiography would be a best seller if you wrote it in Sanskrit. I've never tried this, but I know it would work – if I were to advertise on TV that viewers could have their right arm cut off, absolutely free, simply by reporting to such-and-such a hospital by 10 a.m., a certain percentage of televiewers would show

653

up at the hospital the next morning with their right sleeves rolled up.

It isn't funny, Chaz, it's a matter of percentage advertising and good copy. So any man who writes his own autobiography when he isn't a professional writer is simply feeding a big fat ego . . . And that goes for all these weird generals, too, not only movie personalities.

I'm having another drink – how about you?

Suit yourself. No – don't hook up your tape recorder, and no notes today, either. As I started to tell you when you first came in – I intended to call you at home and ask you not to come at all today. I'm rather upset this morning. That mess – perhaps you read it in the *Times* this morning?

J.C. Blake, slashing his wrists. A terrible thing. Of course I knew Jake; I knew him well. According to the publicity, I was the producer who first discovered him. I didn't, of course, although I may have helped him up the ladder for a few rungs, at least in the beginning. But that doesn't mean anything. If I hadn't helped him, someone would have had to – a damned talented director. But more than talent, he had conviction of purpose and drive. Talent by itself means nothing, as you know yourself, Charlie. But as I say, this hour was already kept open for you, and if I'd canceled our appointment, I'd have been sitting in here brooding about J.C. Blake. So, well, you're here, and for the dough I'm paying you, you can afford to waste an hour.

No, not at all. I don't mind talking about J.C. I just don't feel like talking about myself, that's all; telling you how great I am and everything when a director like Blake is in the hospital – maybe the morgue by now – with two slashed wrists.

Incidentally, did you ever see the wreathes I send to funerals? I have them made up special by the Norton Floral Company – they're beautiful things. Round, in the shape of a film can, you see, with my message in two words in tiny red rosebuds: 'We Remember.' Then the name, of course. 'Elgee Productions.' If there's anything I hate, it's these cheap people who put notices in the paper—'Don't send flowers.' To send flowers is a beautiful gesture; it shows that we have respect for our dead out here, that's all. And if you've ever attended one of these funerals where they didn't have any flowers, you'd know what I mean.

Blake? You never met him? It's just as well. Nobody ever really knew him anyway – not really. Perhaps it's the difference between a biographer like you and a novelist. I can talk to you easily, but I can't talk to a novelist for five minutes. They don't listen, you see – they're thinking of something else all the time. Blake was that way; he was a filmmaker, but he was an artist, you see.

The first time I met J.C. I thought somebody was pulling a practical joke on me – it was really funny – but it worked. He had a gimmick; even a man as talented as J.C. Blake had to have a trick to put himself over. It's almost a rule out here – the way a man has to keep topping himself and others to get ahead.

Yes. He had an appointment all right. Certainly. But it was only for ten minutes. And yet he stretched it out for more than an hour, and went to lunch with me besides.

What? You're damned right I haven't taken you to lunch yet. And I don't intend to! I don't eat lunch anymore; I eat cottage cheese, and sometimes a cup of hot bouillon. And I eat alone. I simply can't stand to see some healthy irresponsible writer like you eating steak and french fries when I'm forced to eat cottage cheese. Anyway – yes – to get back to Blake.

He had an agent, and his agent made the appointment for him. That's another rule. If a man doesn't have an agent he's a non-professional and I don't talk to him. I can't even see all the professionals I should see, let alone amateurs.

I was also vaguely aware of Blake's name. In this business, you have to keep up with those people who've got something on the ball. And the reports, in synopsis form, come in all the time.

Blake had already directed a play in New York, and it had received above average critical acclaim. It was one of those weird, sadistic off-Broadway things. Most of these crazy New York plays are awful things nowadays – incest, cannibalism, homosexuality, insanity, every taboo forbidden to us on TV – and they pass back there as entertainment. It's the current trend. A good many of these plays are written by screenwriters, because – as they put it, 'television censorship stifles their creativity.' Which is all a lot of crap, because we buy the same sick plays that hit it on Broadway, clean them up, add entertainment values, and make them into fairly decent movies.

And nine times out of ten, Chazz, the same guy who wrote the play also gets a nice fat fee to write the movie adaptation and to make the mandatory revisions. So where is his so-called artistic integrity then? It's just another gimmick, that's all. The same tourists who visit New York on a vacation, and sit drooling through some of these sadistic plays – paying scalpers ten bucks a ducat – would flood us with indignant letters if we gave them the same plays for absolutely nothing on televsion.

In any event, Blake had directed this one play, and it had considerable notoriety value, despite a short run, but it wasn't made into a movie. It was one of those anti-dramas, as I recall – no story, just mean and meaningless dialogue by several mean characters. The studio that bought the play got stuck with it. They could've fixed up a story all right, but the title was too long for a theater marquee. Without being able to use the original title, getting the benefit of the publicity value, there was no use fooling with the play. Exhibitors don't like long titles for their marquees.

But Blake was more than just a sometime legitimate stage director. He'd made a couple of avant garde sixteen millimeter films, and although I hadn't seen either one of them at the time, I had heard about them. The motion picture is an art form, Charles, all of us know that, and most of us keep private film libraries at home the way book publishers keep home libraries full of books. A man doesn't reach my position in the industry without a knowledge of art. That's something you might remember for my autobiography. Later on, I'll show you my film library, run off a few unusual films for you. It may open your eyes as to what we could really do with movies if the public would let us make a little money out of them in the bargain.

The point is: we keep abreast of the avant garde trend in the sixteen millimeter film club circles and rentals. The improved sixteen millimeter equipment, and the cheaper sound processing techniques, have brought a lot of gifted amateurs into filmmaking for the various film societies. Sometimes we pick up one of these devoted cinematographers who has a knack for special effects and give him a job in the technical department.

When Blake was ushered into my office, however, his personal appearance was definitely against him. He had a short red beard and a thick moustache. His hair was coal black, and too damned long. A lot of dark-haired men sprout red beards, but a beard of any color is held against a man out here. Every fall semester I conduct a seminar at UCLA for graduate students who are working for their master's degrees in Cinema, and I always stress to these young men that they should observe conservatism in their dress and personal appearances. Cinema, whether it's

657

television or movies, is a business. We must present a concerted public image, and there's no place in any business for nonconformists and eccentrics.

But I was distracted from Blake's appearance by all of the equipment he had with him. He had a sixteen millimeter projector, a portable screen, and a can of film. The moment he came in he started to set all this stuff up, right here in the office, without saying a word.

'Look, Blake,' I said to him, 'your appointment's only for ten minutes.'

'Make it twelve,' he replied, 'I've got a film to show you.'

I had to smile. We've got a dozen comfortable projection rooms here at the studio, and here's a man setting up a projector and screen in my office for a home movie arrangement. I mentioned this to Blake, and he said that he was aware of my various studio projection rooms.

'My films are designed for small groups,' he said, 'from three to ten people at most, and they should be shown in small intimate rooms – not in theaters. So I want you to see the film under normal conditions.'

This wasn't an original idea, of course. We always try to keep in mind that our television plays are to be seen by small groups and families, but it was a different idea for a movie to be planned this way. Interested by the idea, I allowed him to go ahead with the preparations, and I even lowered the Venetian blinds myself.

And now, Charles, I'm going to speak pontifically – a bad habit I've picked up from these lecture and seminar sessions at UCLA – but ours is a private conversation; so I can let myself go a little bit with you. With colleagues, this is a side of myself that's best to keep submerged.

But Blake flattered me, and I responded to this type of flattery. He didn't insult my intelligence by going into an involved explanation, the way I'm doing with you because I don't have the film to show you. He merely showed the film. Within a few dozen frames I recognized where he got his inspiration, and what he was trying to do. When it comes to art, there's nothing really new, you know, not if you've thoroughly explored the subject.

Back in the tenth century, in China, most of the artists were subsidized by the court, or they managed to get commissions from the wealthy. These were the professionals. But there were quite a few gifted amateurs with private means who also painted, and these people began to break with traditional forms. A parallel today is the new interest by private individuals who are making their noncommercial sixteen millimeter films.

The Chinese amateur painters weren't faced with deadlines; they had plenty of time at their disposal and they used it, you see. You may not be aware of it, Chaz, but the entire movie industry is based upon a biological accident – the fact that the retina can retain an image for a momentary period. When the next frame appears, the remembered frame is retained long enough to merge with the next one, and we then have the appearance of movement. Movies don't slither through the projector; each frame stops for a moment – held in place by the maltese cross before the next frame appears.

I'm sorry, Charles. I know this is basic knowledge today, but not too many people realize that many of the finest painters in China during the late tenth century were also aware of the same phenomenon.

But Blake knew it, and somehow, he must've known that I did, too. The Chinese painters – this was during the latter period of the Five Dynasties – painted landscapes on scrolls, some of them more than fifty in length. One person, two or three at most, would sit down and unroll the scroll from right to left, and only a small section of the painting could be seen at a time. The sequence of the scroll required a good memory – moods, motifs and details were often repeated, and they had to be remembered for a full appreciation. The perspectives also were shifted – but to return to Blake's film, which was what we call pure cinema, he'd accomplished the same thing. Only by using moving images, it sure as hell taxed your memory and your skill as a moviegoer. The title was *Selected Incidents;* storyless, plotless, of course, but it was a beautiful showcase for Blake's talents and to show his mastery of the medium. There were a series of tight shots; the overall impression of the montage gave an impressionistic viewpoint of a drunk's outlook on the world – a drunk or a schizophrenic's – but that isn't important in pure cinema. The viewer has to work when he sees a film of this kind and, depending upon his own knowledge, experience, and personal contributions to his seeing, well, every viewer can very easily have a different interpretation.

There was no sound, no subtitles; merely images merging skillfully, evenly, and flowing like a fast mountain stream. A closeup, for example, of a thickly coated dark tongue— and almost before you recognized it for what it was, the image was followed by a black, wet asphalt street, which led, in turn, to a black velvet coat collar, and so on.

A short, but very impressive film. And I recognized something else. A layman, Carlos, probably wouldn't recognize it, and it isn't easy to describe precisely what I mean. How Blake managed the thing so early in his career, I don't know, but he had developed a personal cinematic style.

Take a look, for a moment, at that unhappy clown on the wall above the couch. It's a Roualt, as you know, twenty-five thousand bucks worth of oil paint. Incidentally, I didn't buy the painting as a hedge against inflation; I bought it because I like it.

Everyone knows that Roualt had a distinctive style; you can recognize an original Roualt as far as you can see one. His style is inimitable. Most painters – you might say all of them – have a distinctive, personal style. The paintbrush is an extension of their mind, emotion, and body when they paint. But a camera isn't a paintbrush, Chaz. Less than a dozen filmmakers have ever achieved a truly personal style. Nowadays, it's almost impossible – the production of a film is a group effort. To really pull it off, a director must write and film his own script, do his own editing, do damned near everything by himself. But even then, another indefinable quality must be added if he wants a personal statement on film, because everything—almost everything – has been done already. So if he isn't original, truly original, the ideas he thinks of as new will probably be derivative. Blake, at least, was intelligent enough to go back to early Chinese art for his inspiration. By combining movement to the earlier static forms, he did contribute something cinematically fresh and original.

You still don't follow me?

Well, you aren't an expert, Charlie, that's why. And to be frank, there are plenty of producers out here who would've tossed Blake out without a hearing. Not everybody can recognize a personal film style. The distinction is more subtle than it is in a painting. Here's a better example; we'll take a checkwriting machine. The man writing the check holds one pen, and as he signs his name four more pens also sign his name on four more checks. A handwriting expert can examine all five signatures and pick out the original signature with no trouble at all. I mean the one where the checkwriter held the pen. You and I could look at the five signatures all day long without seeing any difference in them.

But when it comes to cinema, *I* am an expert. And on Blake's short twelve-minute film, his personal stamp on the picture was as obvious to me as the unusual style of some writer, we'll say, is to you.

Blake knew damned well I'd recognize this quality; that's why he brought the film along and ran it off for me.

Yes, I hired him, but that was some time later on.

What he really wanted to discuss during that first meeting was a film script he'd written. It was a beautiful screenplay; absolutely the finest I've ever read. A wonderful script.

Back in the thirties, Chazz, well before your time, F. Scott Fitzgerald wrote a series of short stories which were published in *Esquire* magazine. They were all of the short-short variety, most of them biter-bit, running from twelve to fifteen hundred words in length. The fictional hero of the series was a broken-down screenwriter named Pat Hobby. This unlikely hero was middle-aged, a drunk, a lousy screenwriter – barely literate, in fact – but the old boy had been around Hollywood for a long time. Once in awhile, out of sentiment, I suppose, for the presound days, some producer would hire Pat Hobby for a week or two at two- or two-fifty a week. Just as a handout, you see. But during the week Hobby held the special writing job, doing additional dialogue or something, the old has-been would dream up some ingenious method to remain on the studio payroll for an extra week or so. That was the gist of most of the tales, anyway; they were clever, but built around this general idea.

Well, J.C. Blake had rediscovered these old Fitzgerald stories. For two full years Jake worked on a feature-length screenplay about Pat Hobby. And by incorporating only the very best of the stories into one ninety-minute script, he'd written one of the cleverest, funniest, and most touching movies I've ever read. The script was a master-piece. For one thing, there were more than six hundred numbered shots in the script. Ordinarily, feature-lengths rarely run more than three hundred numbered shots – and that's a lot. So you have an idea of how tightly the script was written. But each shot was so well-considered, tying in so well with the next, if two or three shots had been cut out of the script the gaps would've been noticeable.

I must admit that the script had special interest for me. I had met Fitzgerald once or twice in the old days, although I'd forgotten about the old Pat Hobby stories in *Esquire*. But as Blake related some of these stories to me, at lunch, it started me off – reminiscing about the depression days when everything was a hell of a lot more fun out here than it is today.

He left the scenario with me, naturally, and I read it that afternoon and reread it again that night, sitting up at home until after 2 a.m. I simply couldn't get over the labor and the actual man hours Blake had put into the writing. The idea of any screenwriter putting in two full years on the writing of a single screenplay is ridiculous, don't you know. Ben Hecht and Selznick wrote the first half of *Gone With The Wind* in a single weekend – and look what that picture's grossed!

Nevertheless, Charles, new vistas were opened to me. For the first time; no, not really for the first time – I've always had my personal ideas and intimations of what could really be done with cinema. After all, I've been in the business for thirty-six years. But despite the fact that this script of Blake's was a masterpiece of its kind, it was all so damned futile.

You see, if the script had been filmed to the letter, as it was written, the time and the costs would've been fantastic. The editing alone would've taken months. In many of the scenes he not only had the time limit down in seconds, the number of frames was counted! In a way, it was a little frightening; the devotion to detail, I mean. No writer who ever lived – and certainly not Fitzgerald— deserved such dedicated treatment. Not for a movie script—

All I have to do, Chazz, is pick up the phone. Within three minutes I can have three writers in here – or a dozen

– all pros, all paid-up guild members. In another five minutes I can block out an ad-libbed movie story of some kind, just a sentence even: 'Department store; write a feature-length about employees in an expensive, high-class department store.'

The three writers will have a passable shooting script about a department store on my desk within a couple of weeks – the whole bit – theme, main plot, sub-plot, a dual-love story, the works. And it would make a movie, and money would be made. These details are easily worked out by the writers. The script wouldn't be great, but it would be a competent, professional job. In turn, the assigned director studies the script, adds his know-how and skill during the shooting. A couple of stars, with their familiar personalities, and the movie's ready to be scheduled for distribution.

You've written several books, Charles, but let's say now that you're going to write a movie script.

In your description of the hero you'd probably go into considerable detail, wouldn't you? 'John Hansen is a personable young man in his late twenties; blond, wavy hair; an infectious smile; tall and broad-shouldered; and yet, he has a boyish quality, an appealing shyness – and so on.' That description's off the top of my head, of course, but I could make it as detailed as an inventory of a woman's handbag, and so could you.

But for a screenplay, it would all be wasted effort. Unnecessary writing. A professional screenwriter would only put down three words: 'Tab Hunter type.'

If the budget were high enough, and if we deemed the story good enough to warrant the dough, we'd even get Tab Hunter to play the role. Why not? On a low-budget, we'd merely cast someone like him. It's easier that way for everybody concerned. When the audience saw Tab Hunter's name on the theater marquee, or in the newspapers, they'd be clued in as to the kind of picture they'd see because he'd be the lead, you see. We've got our audiences trained for typage thinking, and that makes it easier all around for both fans and moviemakers. To use another analogy, magazines are the same. A person subscribes to the *Saturday Evening Post* because he knows damned well he's going to reread the same short story every week. If they ran a different kind of a story from the one he was used to every week the poor guy would get nervous, apprehensive – then he'd cancel his subscription. You know this as well as I do. It's basic.

But J.C. Blake . . . He found a simple job that didn't tax his energy too much, night man for a filling station on the Ridge Route, somewhere between here and Bakersfield up in the mountains. He rented an abandoned trapper's cabin, he told me, not too far away from the gas station, and that's where he worked for two years on the screenplay.

Why or how the man got the patience and fortitude is still beyond my comprehension, at least for the writing of a screenplay. They say that James Joyce spent seven years on *Ulysses*, and maybe he did. Well, I'd say that two years' work on one screenplay would be comparable to ten years of work on a novel. Any day.

But when Blake's script was analyzed, as fine as it was, it still boiled down to just another comedy. A fabulous comedy, true enough, but so finely drawn that the average American audience would know whether to laugh or weep. It's the same with Joyce's *Ulysses*, in a way. I've read the book, naturally, and I considered it as an earthy, well-written humorous novel. But D.H. Lawrence, of all people, called it a *dirty* book. And then, we have the scholarly types. Did you know that there's a quarterly magazine that's been published for many years now called *The James Joyce Review*? That may not be the exact title, but it's similar to that. And in every quarterly issue scholars are still finding new things to write about *Ulysses* and other Joycean writings. After all these years.

Who, for God's sake, could ever take movies that seriously? Or any one movie?

Now you follow me. Jake Blake did. Right.

Well, when you read the run-of-the-mill scripts I get in here day after day, it was a curious pleasure for me to read a script like his. Honest to Jesus, Charlie, some of the scripts sent in were written for other shows and other studios, and then rejected. And when I get them, the agents and writers are too damned lazy to rewrite another title page to fit any of my shows. This happens all the time.

Disregarding technical work, Blake's major mistake was this, although he must've made the mistake deliberately. In a comedy, let's say, especially in a comedy, the hero must be likeable. The audience can laugh at him or with him, but they must like him well enough to want him to come out on top in the end. This is a tricky bit, particularly if the guy is one of those stupid, ineffectual comics. In this case, we don't often let the comic get the girl— unless she's the same stupid type – because even though the audience likes the hero, they have a tendency to feel sorry for the girl who gets stuck in a marriage with some sap, you see.

This may sound like hair-splitting, but it isn't. No matter how well the audience *likes* the hero, they can never be allowed to really *care* about the things that happen to him. This was Charlie Chaplin's secret. People liked him all right, but he saw to it by his makeup and ridiculous costume that people would never believe that the on-screen personage was a real person. He was always a character, and the fact that he could jerk tears and laughter both out of an audience as a character was only due to the period of suspended belief during the running time of the movie.

Please, don't let me get off on the genius of Chaplin—

In Fitzgerald's Pat Hobby stories, no one could really identify themselves with the character. The readers, I suppose, enjoyed the stories because they liked to see an ignorant person outmaneuver a big shot.

Blake's Pat Hobby had an extra dimension, although he was basically the same character Fitzgerald created. Can you read a script and see it on the screen as you read it? I can. An audience would've *cared* about Pat Hobby on the screen. When you really love someone, you can't laugh when he gets hurt. Pat Hobby was a drunk and a failure—funny, yes, but pathetically so. If you have an enemy, and he becomes an alcoholic, it's human nature to rejoice to a certain extent at his downfall. But you can't laugh at any alcoholic, no matter how funny the things are that he does, if he's a member of your immediate family.

This was a special type of movie, a beautiful screenplay, and it's a shame it was never filmed. Blake overdid it; the characterization was too good.

And the way it was written, it was mandatory that an unknown actor had to play the part of Hobby. Any well-known actor, with his image impressed indelibly on the mass-audience mind through dozens of movie exposures, would've completely spoiled the script. Blake had planned it that way.

No, it makes no difference how great the actor is; in movies the audience has the actor and the character fused. So you see the problem. Chaplin and his screen character were one, and no matter how emotionally involved the audience became during one of his movies, when they left the theater they knew that Chaplin was actually a millionaire living in Hollywood. It's the system, Charlie.

667

Hell, yes, I bought the script! I'd have been a fool not to – somebody else would've grabbed it. I called Blake's agent the next morning and paid five thousand dollars for it – although I probably could've got it for less.

At the time there was considerable public interest in Fitzgerald. They had done a ninety-minute TV play about then, an adaptation of his unfinished novel, *The Last Tycoon*. And Fitzgerald's former mistress had written an 'as told to' book about their shacking up days out here. She must've really hated his guts to publish that sordid book; it was in poor taste, to say the least. But even the staid old publishing firm of Scribner's had begun to reissue Fitzgerald's old novels in quality-type paperbacks, so Blake's screenplay was a good property. I bought it, and had it registered.

A few months later, as I said, I hired Blake as a director. I needed a replacement director for the series we were filming then called *City Block*. We shot three fifteen-minute scripts every week for sale to independent stations. They could be used as morning or afternoon filler; it was strictly daytime stuff. For variety we had about fifty actors on a roster for this series, but the three directors – one for each show – were semipermanent. Every Friday we mailed out sides, not complete scripts, to the actors we'd need for the three plays the next week. They learned their lines at home, and when they reported to the studio the director gave them a couple of runthroughs and then put the play on film. It was only a fifteen-minute daytime show, and most directors were off the set by noon.

But Blake took all day, and sometimes went into overtime. Here's the deal – most of the actors had never seen each other before; they didn't even know the plot of the story, because they only had their own parts and cue lines. But Blake still wanted to lecture them about motivation and all that stuff, and some of these people had other shows to do in the afternoon and in the evening. There were conflicts, you see, and in addition to overtime, the spontaneity of the barely rehearsed actors was the only thing that gave any life to the substandard scripts. Blake got the actors to thinking, emoting, and the scripts couldn't stand it. There's a time to shoot the works and a time to be practical. I had to let him go.

It wasn't long after he left us when he did a color Western for one of the independents. One reliable rumor has it that he ran them eight hundred thousand bucks over the budget. If you cut that in half, which is closer to the truth, it's still a goodly sum. It was a good Western, but after all, Chazz, what can anybody do with a Western? It was cleverly done for an oater, but a Western in color is merely a Western that isn't in black-and-white.

After that Jake drifted back East for a year or so, and picked up financial backing for a version of *Everyman* he'd written. He did the play in Middle English, too, so it was a critical success. Those college professor critics who do New York reviews eat that stuff up, but it flopped at the box office. New York audiences don't even understand good English, let alone Middle English.

But Mammoth bought the script anyway, and brought J.C. out here to direct. The movie didn't break even in the US, but an odd thing happened. He filmed the movie the way the old morality plays were originally staged in England during the seventeenth century. Each scene was performed on a different wagon, and these plays were put on at fairs. When a scene was done the wagon moved on to another waiting group of spectators and the next wagon and the next scene pulled in. The technique was so old it almost seemed fresh, and because his budget was low, J.C. shot the movie with unknown actors.

But here's what's funny. It flopped in the US, but for some reason the movie really appealed to Latin Americans.

Everyman, with Spanish subtitles, has been running for several years now to a packed house in Mexico City. It's the same story in Spain and other South American countries, and Mammoth actually made some fair money on the film.

Why? Well, I don't know if it's true or not, but according to one theory the Mexicans and other Spanish-speaking people think the movie is in Basic English instead of Middle English. The same people go again and again to see it, so it's believed that they're trying to learn how to speak English from the film. Odd, isn't it?

Yes, of course. Blake made more movies. He did a mystery and at least two more oaters, plus some others. And I hired him to direct an hour-long special, *Roller-Skating, USA* He also directed a television series called *Camp Cook*. This was supposed to be a nonviolent type of Western for children; a stupid idea that was doomed before it even started. But J.C.'s been working right along, and he finally got a reputation as a good, competent director – as a man who knows his job. It simply doesn't make any sense for a man as talented as J.C. Blake to slice his wrists—

The old Pat Hobby scenario?

Yeah, I finally used it; that is, I managed to salvage a lot of good bits and pieces out of the script. I put two contract writers on it and they turned the script into a thirteen-week series.

We junked the middle-aged screenwriter character. We named the show *The Man and The Method*. We changed the drunken screenwriter to struggling young actor here in Hollywood. Instead of a writer trying to get studio writing jobs, the young actor tried to get various TV parts every week. And he always got the part he wanted each week by pulling some clever ruse or working out a gimmick of some kind. Audience response was excellent, especially from teenagers. We had a little sponsor trouble, but otherwise we could've had at least two seasons out of the series. It goes into reruns in 1964.

But I'm tired of talking, Charlie. About the business, even about myself – at least for today. I'll be all right again tomorrow. It's just that – well, when a brilliant man like J.C. Blake cuts his wrists, you sometimes wonder what in the hell the whole damned business is all about. That's all.

Thank *you*, for coming in . . .

A Letter to A.A. (Almost Anybody)

Dear sir,

Or maybe you're a lady, or a disparate group – I don't know. I am an alcoholic, or should that be capitalized? All right. I make you a gift of the Capital. I am an Alcoholic, and I need your help. At least I think I do; I'm not sure. I'm not sure of anything anymore except that I am an Alcoholic, and a sober one at that; and if there is anything more disgusting than a sober alc – pardon – *Alcoholic*, I don't know what it is. Being sober all the time has me befuddled and confused, although up to now I was under the impression that being sober was supposed to be an ideal – or at least idealistic – state for an Alcoholic. I know I feel better even though I feel worse, and if you can make good sense out of that then you are a better man, or a woman, or an Alcoholic than I am.

'Talk it out, George, that's the only way to get at the roots of the thing.' That's what Fred; he's the chairman at our local AA chapter, and that's what Fred – I never asked him what his last name was, although I know what it is, and he never asked for mine although he knew it— but you know the rules about last names as well as I do, and all I'm trying to do now is follow Fred's advice as he said I ought to do: Talk it out, George!

Down to it, get down to it – I keep trying to delay, to put it off, to sneak around it and avoid the over, under, or through; I even went back and read my last paragraph. Like Faulkner, man, *sir*, I mean, and now I know how he wrote all of those compounded and involved syntaxes – he was sober, he had to be. But I'll start, and if the beginning doesn't make me reach for that brown unopened bottle in front of me nothing else will, or so I think but really don't know. I do know, or think I know, that by the time I finish this letter, or scream, if I can finish it, and if you get it, which you will, I suppose, if I mail it, and I'll mail it if I can find a stamp around the house some place, and if you *do* get it, which you will if it is delivered, my problem will be solved long before then. Mr Anthony, I have a problem – what ever became of Mr Anthony, anyway?

All right. The beginning. If I don't weep, and maybe this time I won't; isn't it possible that the time will come when the beginning will no longer make a man cry? Don't the tears ever dry up and go away somewhere? Like how many times does a man have to pay for it? I mean the beginning, and I was drunk even then, although I wasn't then a drunk – an Alcoholic. I became a drunk – an Alcoholic – because I was drunk at the time. And because I was drunk at the time, that's how it happened, although I wasn't an *Alcoholic* at the time; I was only drunk, which isn't the same, as you know.

My wife's arm.

Some, several minutes have gone by, fifteen of them maybe. I smoked a cigarette, taking my time; I didn't open the bottle, and I didn't weep. A milestone. This is the first time for this test, the written test, and I was able to think about *it* without trying to drown it, or *pickle* it is a better term, although drinking never really worked anyway.

My wife's arm. There; it was much easier to write the second time. Arm. Arm, arm, arm, arm, arm. Nothing, none.

Maybe I'm finished inside, all gone, empty, voided, like my wife's arm. It is gone and I did it and I'm an Alcoholic, a sober Alcoholic right now, but I was one of the drunkest Alcoholics anybody ever saw around this town for the last four years. And even though this is a small city, there have been some mighty fine drunks residing here, including my friend Fred before *he* sobered up and then did the same for me. I drank with the best of them, boy, I mean, sir (madame?), although later on I preferred to drink alone; that is, around the house where I could see her, because she never touched a drop after – My wife, and her arm—or where the arm used to be. It sort of kept the evil spirits up – no *double entendre* intended – I'm not trying to be funny, for God's sake, I'm trying to get down to it.

The accident, and my wife's arm. (And how can I tell about it without sounding like a lugubrious, fatuous ass?) Although, if I hadn't been drunk at the time – I said this – there wouldn't have been any accident and my wife would still have her arm. Her left arm; that's the arm that was 'sheared off at the shoulder,' as the newspaper reported it. Sheared off; the car door did it, but I really did it because I was drunk at the time and driving home from the country club dance, recklessly – the same old monotonous Saturday night dance that is held every Saturday night during the summer – outside on the patio when the weather's nice (with Japanese lanterns), and inside when it rains, and maybe the dances are still being held. I never went back to the club again, not after the accident. I was too afraid that somebody would commiserate with me, or worse, pretend to talk about something else while they were really thinking about my wife's lost arm and me drunk and smashing up the car. And I didn't even get a scratch, not a scratch.

I was *lucky*, my mother told me, even as she was bawling, and dead now (she died, Mother, eight months after the accident, the old liver trouble she had had for years, poor sweet soul), but in that dismal, horrible, gray Sunday dawn at the hospital – and I was sober *then*, all right, hanging around first in the hall and then in the waiting room and back to the hall, unable to sit down, not even for a second, the beard stubble on my face making me feel dirty, and the damned cigarette machine in the corridor only took a quarter and a nickel, not three dimes, and nobody had any change, of course, and my mother picked this time to say, crying, 'You were lucky, George.'

'Lucky!' The strangled scream hurt my throat, and then the doctor came and I was crying wildly and carrying on, hitting the innocent white walls with my fists; and he gave me a shot that didn't work and told me to go home.

Not me. I went to the White Springs Hotel instead and bought two fifths of Old Grandpappy from the night bellhop. Even *before* I became an Alcoholic I had the professional Alcoholic's cunning instinct for knowing when, where, and how to get a needed bottle or so when the bars and package stores were closed. Those two bottles and a good many more saw me through during the days before my wife came home from the hospital – minus her arm.

And I visited her every single day, trying to get the precise, exact balance into my system so I'd have enough of the magic fluid inside me to get me there – to the hospital – and into Louise's private room, and not too much so she would notice any effects on me, but I *never* did get the perfect balance, or enough inside me not to notice that her arm wasn't there anymore. And each time, before I left home to go to the hospital, I'd say to myself, 'Now this time, don't look! Look into her bright, bright eyes, or simply read to her from a book, or look at the floor and count the cracks and wet-mop marks, or look at the table, the bedspread, or even the new red scar on her temple, but don't look at her arm!'

But the moment I entered Louise's room, trying to smile, trying to say something cheerful, and most of the time struggling to say just something, anything, my eyes couldn't keep away from that – I could never stay put for the full two-hour visiting period without excusing myself and going to the men's room down the hall for a drink. I always stashed a bottle in there before going to my wife's room; just plain old common horse sense (the kind that convinces us that the world is flat), because I never would have made it otherwise, unless – I think I could have taken it a little better, perhaps, if Louise had only berated me, cursed me. This idea is only supposition, but Louise took it too well, too bravely, like a saint. And she lost so much weight so fast she even looked like a saint, too. There was always the touch of pink on her lips, the lipstick a little crooked; awkwardly applied, of course, the pitiful *effort* to fix-herself-up for my daily visit. And the too-too sweet martyr's smile, and the round wet eyes, wet, but without tears. No bitterness, ever, never a whimper out of her, not a word about its being all my fault. There's a Christian for you, every damned time.

But that's enough about the beginning, and all that, but it led to later, much later, some four years later when everything was gone, my business, at least my half of it; I sold out at less than a tenth of what my half was worth because I had to have the cash. (I was a public accountant, not a CPA, but we were doing all right, Herb and I, counting the increased income tax business and all; and Herb got up the price I asked for my half because I had set it so deliberately and ridiculously low. All was fair, and I have no complaints on that score. I certainly wasn't pulling my share of the load; after the accident I didn't go to the office more than once or twice a week. And then I didn't go at all because I couldn't do any work if I did go; for more than a year before I sold out to Herb I didn't set foot in the place. I just phoned and asked Herb to call the bank and okay a ten or a twenty-dollar check for me when I needed dough. And when Herb came to his senses and refused to okay any more checks for me, I sold out to him – and that money went, too.)

The money all went so fast. The hospital bills. The doctors. I couldn't afford the private room for Louise in the first place, but I couldn't afford *not* to have it; or the exorbitant, accompanying medical consultations, which were nothing but money thrown down the drain. The savings, the bonds all went (there were the expensive private 'rehabilitation' lessons for my wife), and then our home went, too. The car, of course, was a total loss; I used the insurance money as one of the hospital payments. And Mother died, and I had to pay for her funeral. Although Mother didn't have any money of her own, I inherited her tiny house, naturally, which was fortuitous, if it was anything. Louise and I moved into it, and here we were:

Louise, with only one arm, was making like a housewife, and I was making like a drunk with both of my arms, and there was no money coming in – suddenly, just like that, we were on Relief! The bounty of the County. But I didn't really care, not at first – at least Mother never lived to see the Day – she *would* have cared. All at once we were on the 'poor and needy' rolls of all the weird churches and women's clubs in the city. The Methodists, the Baptists, the Church of God's Flock, the Presbyterians, and naturally, the Unitarians took this *avid* interest in our affairs. The Unitarians were in on it because of *Mother*, and all of the ministers from these various churches kept coming around to commiserate with my wife. A new one every day, it seemed, and my wife and the visiting minister would be kneeling and praying and talking in undertones by the hour in the living room while I sat in the kitchen trying to drown their funereal voices with a bottle. *Très gai*, it was, but I couldn't say anything about it, one way or the other, because this sort of thing was all the pleasure my wife had left to her – evidently; she couldn't talk to me, and I couldn't talk to her—

The social worker's name was Miss Whiteside. Mary Ellen Whiteside. She was about thirty-two, give a few years, and her weekly visits to the house with the weekly check were like clockwork. Miss Whiteside didn't resemble the social worker stereotype, except perhaps for her absurd hats and white gloves, and she drove a Buick, not last year's Ford or Chevvy like most of them drive. But she was right there with the fifty-five dollar check every week, on time, and in person. With Alcoholics, the social worker is required to bring the weekly check in person instead of mailing them (only idiots, imbeciles and morons are entitled to get their relief checks via the mails). Alcoholics can't be trusted, it seems. Miss Whiteside would hand me the check, and after I signed it she pointedly handed it to my wife – another rule – and then departed in her baby-blue Buick. My good wife, who now walked a little lopsided, despite the expensive rehabilitation lessons, would then trot down to the corner, cash the check, and bring the money – all of it – back to me. I would give Louise ten or fifteen magnanimous dollars, and drink through the rest of it. Oh, my wife never said a word about my drinking – not to me, anyway – the martyr bit, don't you know. I think it was Shaw who said something about martyrs, that martyrdom is the way to recognition for the person of no talent or ability – something like that – the exact quotation doesn't make any difference.

If we had only fought, or talked things over 'sensibly,' or if she had only screamed her head off at me, piling enough curses on my head to enable me to desert the woman in all good conscience, but no; it was always pretend, pretend, pretend. Everything is lovely. Of course, her arm was gone, and she had an unsightly four-inch scar on her forehead, as well as the jagged scar on her temple, and she had dropped from a well-shaped 120 pounds down to a scrawny eighty-six pounds (the arm hadn't weighed

678

that much!), and me, her blottery husband – I was a drunk, my business was gone, my money was gone, our beautiful home was gone, and we were on Relief.

Relief. Daily, the churches delivered food baskets to our door. We had no children, but that didn't make any difference – we got toys delivered to the house just the same. Ladies' clubs and auxiliaries were driving up in groups and depositing clothes, dresses, suits, shirts, shoes, and all kinds of stuff on our front porch. Last Christmas, for example, we got six basketfuls of assorted groceries, three turkeys – one of them already cooked and stuffed— and two Christmas trees, complete with ornaments, delivered right to the door by these good, God-fearing people.

Oh, no, nothing was wrong. Nothing had happened, the way Louise and I acted toward each other, so very polite and all – we accepted all of this stuff with mumbled thanks to the donors as though it were the way people were supposed to live. We didn't sleep together anymore— that sort of thing would have been impossible for me – and Louise never mentioned it.

So I would drink up the money at Nelson's, the bar nearest to the house, setting them up for the boys when I had the cash (after rat-holing some of my weekly stipend first for package stuff later in the week); and after the money was gone I pawned some of the clothing the women's clubs and auxiliaries brought around for the purpose. And so it all went until Fred managed to get through to me and straightened me out.

Fred was an Alcoholic, he said, and it was time that I, too, recognized the fact that I was an Alcoholic.

'Okay,' I said, 'so I'm an Alcoholic.'

'So we talk it out,' Fred said.

And talk it out I did, as well as I could, although I had reached the point where I didn't care whether I was an Alcoholic or not – or so I thought. I couldn't talk to my disabled wife, and Fred didn't judge me; he was easy to talk to, after I got started. We attended AA meetings together, although I went to these meetings as a favor to Fred, at first. Sitting there that way, in the rented hall, listening to those people – Alcoholics like myself – and hearing some of the terrible stories they told which were worse than mine – well, perhaps not. No man ever has troubles that are greater than another man's, but these stories were sort of inspiring to me: comebacks had been made, after all; and almost overnight, it seemed, I quit drinking. I didn't taper off, I merely quit, just like that, and just for a day at a time, as Fred had suggested. And it was easy because I knew it was only for the day, and I could start drinking the next morning if I wanted to – but I didn't. I began to get a few friendly, encouraging visits from other AA members, and they were all decent guys . . .

It took about a month. I was fairly well straightened out, but I was restless. A man has to do something, and I wasn't doing anything because I had lost my full-time job of drinking. I started thinking about a job. Naturally, I didn't go back and see old Herb, or try for anything in the accounting line. I wasn't ready yet; too many people around town knew that I was a drunk; and I wasn't about to put any of my former friends on the spot by forcing them to turn me down for a job. But there was a brand new supermarket that had opened recently only six blocks away from the house, and I applied there for a position, talking frankly to the manager.

'I'm an Alcoholic,' I told him bluntly, 'but I've joined AA, and I haven't had a drink now for more than a month. I need a job, and I have to get my self-respect back. I know figures, I'm a competent accountant, and if you'll give me a chance I can mark prices on cans, total inventories for you, and—'

'Grab a broom,' he said.

The manager gave me a chance, and thirty-five dollars a week. I was issued a black leather bow tie, a clean apron, and a new broom. There were tears of gratitude in my eyes; I could have kissed his feet, then and there . . .

And all week long I've been working – sweeping, dusting, mopping, carrying – and shivering happily in the frigid air-conditioning of the new store.

Miss Whiteside came around this afternoon, on my first day off, with the weekly relief check. I laughed; with the excitement and all, I had forgotten to telephone her about my new job.

'I've got a job, Miss Whiteside,' I said proudly. I tore the relief check in half, and handed her the pieces.

She flushed slightly, started to say something, but my wife caught her eye. The two women went outside and sat, talking, in Miss Whiteside's car for about twenty minutes; and then the social worker drove away, for what I thought was the last time. But it was just a few minutes ago, before I started to write this letter, when Miss Whiteside returned. After my wife let her in and retired behind the closed door of her bedroom, Miss Whiteside placed a fifth of whiskey on the kitchen table before me.

'Let's talk for awhile, George,' Miss Whiteside began, favoring me with a friendly smile. 'For once in your life, I think you should think about somebody else instead of yourself.'

'What—?'

'Please, let me talk.' She placed a white-gloved hand on my arm. 'You, George, are an Alcoholic. You know it and I know it, so why pretend that you aren't?'

'Who's pretending?' I protested.

'You are, George. You won't keep that sweeper's job for two weeks, and in your heart you know it. You can't possibly keep away from liquor, George, because you're an Alcoholic. Besides, what are they paying you? Thirty-five dollars a week. We're already paying you fifty-five dollars a week, so what do you think you're gaining by pretending to be something you're not? And if you don't have any feelings left for your poor crippled wife, who'll be cut off from every organized charity in town the moment it gets around that you're working again, what about me?'

'You?'

'Haven't I been decent to you ever since I took your case? Did I ever lecture you, bawl you out for drinking?'

'No.' I shook my head.

'Have I ever been late with your check? Have I ever asked for a kickback?'

'No,' I replied defensively. 'But I'm entitled to some credit myself. I've always been here to sign it when you came, whether I've been drunk or sober!'

'Granted. And don't think I haven't appreciated it either, George. But for a moment, just for a moment, I want you to hear my side of the story. Do you know that there are only thirty-two cases left on the county relief rolls? The truth of the matter is, George, I'm already in trouble. If I don't come up with at least two or three more active cases by the beginning of the fiscal year I'm liable to lose my job – or at best, be transferred into the city. And I've got my roots here, George. I support my mother, and it isn't easy to find new social worker positions nowadays – not in these prosperous times,' she added bitterly. To my astonishment her lips trembled, but before I could say anything she went ahead with it. 'The truth of the matter is this, George: I need you on my rolls, and you and your wife need me. So for once in your life, show a little selflessness. You want a drink right now, don't you?' She pushed the bottle toward me.

'No,' I said honestly, 'I really don't want a drink, Miss Whiteside. One drink would probably get me started all over again. But I honestly didn't know that the times were so good – I mean, so *bad*, from your point of view.'

'It so happens that they are, George.' She sighed. The corners of her worried mouth turned up slightly, but it wasn't even a good imitation of a brave smile; and her eyes behind her glasses were much too bright.

'I know you won't let me down, George.' She touched me lightly, timidly, on the shoulder. 'Or your poor wife, either.' She turned away, and smoothed the skirt wrinkles down over her hips. 'I'll leave the bottle,' she added, without looking back.

For a long time after Miss Whiteside left the house I just sat here at the table, staring bewilderedly at the bottle of whiskey without really seeing it, and then I began to write this long, desperate – yes, what else? – meaningless letter. And now that I've finished it I'm going to open the bottle and have a small drink, and then, perhaps another. Why not? When next Christmas rolls around, maybe we'll get *eight* lousy turkeys—

Nobody's,

I Am an Alcoholic

Jake's Journal

First Entry (Undated)

This ledger and more than two dozen ballpoint pens have all been here in the tower for a long time. I do not know why I did not start a journal, or diary, long before now. If I had started in the beginning I might have been able to at least put down the date. Not that I have a great deal to relate since this assignment, but I have had lately a suspicion (a slight one to be sure), that all is not right here. And a certain evilness is beginning to make itself felt in the atmosphere. As my mind comes close to perceiving what I believe, in time, will be a complete revelation of everything, the thought slips away from me, like a dark cloud merging with another cloud, and I am further away from the truth than before. But then, I am not really surprised. Very few men know the answers to anything, much less everything.

I will begin with a description of my surroundings. I know this dark field better now than I know the streets of Los Angeles, my home town. But writing this way, putting the image of this place into words, is as good a way to start as any I can think of, and if writing helps to pass the time, that in itself is a fair reward.

There are no maps in the tower, so I cannot place the geographical location with any exactness. I believe this auxiliary landing field lies somewhere in Tibet, although I am not even certain of that. As yet I have not seen a native of the place, and before a native could get to this field he would have to fly in by airplane like I did. I do not believe it would be possible to climb, on foot, the terrible mountains we flew over to reach this field, although I have hoped innumerable times that someone, anyone, would come stumbling down the snowy mountainside to this lonely tower.

The field is not a large one. The strip is not much larger than a football field. The surface of the landing strip is made of crushed black stones. These glistening stones are peculiar in that they are warm to the touch. Not hot, but warm, warm enough to melt the everfalling snow as it touches the field. As I look out from the tower now, in the black night, the field shines like an onyx lake. The lake is surrounded on all sides by high, clean banks of snow, terraced back naturally by the wind to the four jagged mountain peaks pointing at the field. Due west is a kind of a pass and the only decent approach to the field by airplane. When the pilot dropped me off here he must have landed from that direction. And if another airplane ever lands here, it will also have to come in from the west. I am not a pilot, and perhaps it might be possible to glide down one of these sheer mountains by barely skimming along the surface if the wind was not blowing. But the wind is always blowing. Since I have been stationed here the wind has always blown with great force straight from the pass, causing a sharp, steep updraft which would surely cause any airplane to crash if it attempted to fly down and into the field.

Perhaps a helicopter could make it.

Along the edges of the field there are little red and green lights spaced four thirty-inch steps apart.

Squaring the field, the lights are alternated, red-green, red-green, all of the way around. There is also a small searchlight atop the tower that circles once around every sixty seconds. That is my job: I replace the bulbs as they burn out. When it gets dark I turn on the field lights and the searchlight. In the morning I turn them off. Not much of a job, but I make the square of the field once a day looking for bulbs that have burned out. The temperature is considerably below zero and I am always glad to get back to the tower. In addition to these simple maintenance duties I am also supposed to service any airplane forced to land here. There are several hundred drums of fuel lining the field and I do not know how many more buried under the snow behind the tower for this purpose. So far, no airplane has landed. Whoever it was who planned this emergency field greatly overestimated the air traffic. Although I am only a Basic Airman, I am certain the government is wasting their money by keeping me here. Not that I have been paid in all of the months I have been here, and even if I were paid, I do not know how I could spend my money.

The tower itself is not large. The downstairs part has two storerooms in addition to my sleeping-living room. Right above my bedroom, where I am writing this, is this glassed-in tower room. In the tower is this broad metal desk which takes in the entire front window overlooking the field. The other three sides are filled with radio equipment. None of it works. During the first few months I was here I fiddled and worked with the radio equipment for hours with no results. I do not know anything about electronics, but I do know that none of the stuff up here works. In the center of the floor there is a hole and a wooden ladder to the downstairs room. The downstairs room contains my wooden bunk, a gasoline stove, a chair, and a wardrobe made out of a packing-case where I keep my uniforms. That is another thing that irritates me. Coming here from the Philippine Islands like I did, all I had were cotton khaki uniforms. They should have issued me woolen uniforms for Tibet. If it were not for the dirty sheepskin jacket left here by the previous custodian I do not know how I would make my daily rounds of the field without freezing to death.

The two storerooms each have a door into my sleeping room. The door to the outside is made of heavy oak. One of the storerooms contains my provisions and the other has nothing in it except electric light bulbs. The provisions allow for no variety in meal planning. One side of the storeroom is piled high with canned Argentine corned beef, and the other side is stacked to the ceiling with one hundred pound sacks of small, white dried beans. This is a rotten diet for a man, and whoever provisioned this tower should have thought to lay in a supply of coffee. I drink hot water instead, and although it warms my stomach, it is a poor substitute for coffee.

About thirty yards away from the tower is the shed with the generator and the two-cylinder gasoline engine for the field and tower lights. That is about it. No books, no radio, no magazines, and no company. How the Air Force ever expected a man to be contented in a place like this is beyond me.

This is enough for the first entry. My fingers are a bit cramped, not being used to writing, although I did enjoy writing this down. I wish, now, that I had thought of it sooner.

Second Entry (Undated)

Just before starting this entry I reread the first one and found it pleasant to have something to read. It isn't strange to read something you wrote yourself and I wouldn't be surprised if writers themselves didn't go back and read their own books over and over. Inasmuch as I have nothing to read except what I write myself it will be better and better the more I put down. In time when I get a lot written I can go back and by merely reading what I've put down I can kill several hours at a time. Considering that, it will pay me to write as well as I can.

Being alone as I have for so long now that I hesitate to guess, and with little to do, my mind takes a lot of strange journeys. This morning I was thinking of books, and I thought I should have brought at least one book along with me. This in turn led me to think, 'What book?' Such speculation can kill a lot of time. I tried my best to remember all the books I've read, going back to when I first started with *The Little Red Hen;* and although I left out a lot of them, surely, I ended up thinking about the last one I read, or one of the last, *Look Homeward, Angel,* by Thomas Wolfe. The latter was read at the insistence of Red Galvin, my onetime bunkmate at Pampanga, because he said it was good. I didn't think so because there wasn't much plot to it and was mostly about a common Southern family. But as Galvin said, it was funny, and for a place like this, with just one good book, if I had it, it would be good because it was thick. Thickness in books made me think of the Bible. I remembered a magazine piece where several people were asked what book they considered the most valuable to have in their library, and about eight out of ten of them said, the Bible. I've never read the Bible, although I've skimmed through it a few times, and I won one once at Sunday School for memorizing a few pet phrases of our teacher's. I wouldn't, if I had a choice, bring a Bible here, but I'd settle for almost any thick book.

Then I thought about music. In Pampanga, when I was living with Elena Espeneida, I had a small wind-up phonograph and two records. One was a Bing Crosby and the other was *Afternoon of a Faun,* parts one and two. I enjoyed both of those records very much. After I taught Elena how to work the phonograph she played them over and over for me. She was partial to the second part of *Afternoon of a Faun* but she also liked the Bing Crosby record. I guess she still has the phonograph and the two records. I like to think that as she plays them now she thinks of me. In fact I *know* she must think of me every time she plays them. And as much as I would like to have that phonograph and the two records here, I wouldn't deprive Elena of them. I was the only decent thing that ever happened to that girl and I would never destroy her wonderful memories of me.

The whole affair with Elena was a strange one. My memories of her are sweet and sad, leaving a taste like burned bacon in my mouth as I recall the termination of that affair.

I was driving the fire truck those days. This left me free time every other morning when the rest of the squadron was working and I took advantage of it.

Two miles away from the field was the little *barrio* of Sapang Bato which we used to call Sloppy Bottom. I don't know why it was called that. Maybe Sapang Bato means Sloppy Bottom in English. On the edge of this little *barrio*, the fringe, was the Air Force Settlement. This was a group of eight or ten shacks rented by wealthier airmen like sergeants and enlisted crew members on flying pay. In the shacks they installed their Filipino women, their house furnishings, and their demijohns of gin and rum. To a Basic Airman like myself, these women were fair prey. Knowing they were available but difficult to be had, I spent several weeks in thought before finding a solution that worked; a plan that would get me into the houses when none of their men were around. Although most of these women were passed on to another NCO when a man left for the States, there was a lot of talk (by the men who paid the rent and girl) about how faithful their girls were and how well they could be trusted. Of course, the more money, clothes, candy and PX items they gave their girls, the more faithful they were. But there were some of the stingier sergeants who thought their girls would be faithful on the most minimum kind of allowance; thinking in their stupid way that the girls 'loved' them. The more stupid the man is the happier he is, it seems.

'Honeymoon Lotion' proved to be the solution to my problem. This was a milky-white fluid in a green bottle sold exclusively in the Hindu's Gift Shop. Contents were one litre, which is about a fifth of a gallon. This lotion smelled malodorous to an American nose. It was an unpleasant mixture of coconut oil, wintergreen, burnt sugar and I don't know what all. Filipino girls, however, loved the smell of it. They used 'Honeymoon Lotion' on their hair; they rubbed it on their bodies; and when it was used in large enough amounts it covered the fact they hadn't bathed recently. It made their brown skins shine with the oily shine of a fish stinking in the moonlight. They loved it. It only cost one peso, and I had credit with the Hindu.

It was on a morning off that I met Elena. I had a bottle of 'Honeymoon Lotion' in my hand, and had walked the two miles from the barracks to the *barrio*, taking the shortcut through the Baluga village. My plan was simple and foolproof. I usually went directly to the Air Force Settlement swinging the green bottle in my hand. The girls would watch me from the porches of their stilted shacks. Sooner or later one of the girls would engage me in conversation. We would then go inside for a drink of her man's gin or rum. I would engage the girl in promiscuous intercourse and then depart. I always left behind the bottle of 'Honeymoon Lotion.' I didn't mind the smell, but I know that several sergeants were bitter about it when they got home from the base, wondering where the women got the lotion.

But this particular morning, I had paused at the well which was centrally located in the *barrio*. A slender girl was filling her five-gallon Standard Oil can with water. I thought she was beautiful and wondered how I had missed seeing her before. She was young and appeared to be shy. Her upper lip was beaded slightly with perspiration and her skin was the color of buttered toast that has been made just right. In the early sunshine she glistened and her thick black hair was a plaited rope hanging down her back. She was barefooted and she wore a faded blue dress.

I caught the sun with my bottle and the reflection put a greenish light on her face. She paid no attention, and I moved in closer.

I cleared my throat almost in her ear. She was startled and stepped back, her chin on her chest. She said nothing and kept her eyes looking down at the ground. I raised her chin with my hand and looked into her eyes. She was blind. It was like looking into two almond-sized pools of cream.

'I didn't mean to frighten you,' I said. 'I admired your beauty so much I was trying to start a conversation.'

'I didn't know anyone was watching me. But I wasn't frightened.'

'I wasn't watching you. I was staring, but I didn't know you were blind.'

'I must go home.' She smiled. Her voice was tiny; it was the voice of a princess in an animated cartoon. She would have lifted her can of water but I took it away from her.

'Go on home. I'll carry it for you.' She hesitated a moment, then surefooted and confidently she led the way through rubbish-laden back alleys, in and out of yard-ways, and up a deadend dirt street to the house at the end of it. The little house was on stilts like the rest of the *barrio* houses, and she stopped beneath the ladder.

'I live here.' She pointed directly above her head to the hole in the floor that was used as a door. I marveled at her ability to walk unerringly to her house as I put the can of water on the ground.

'Are you sure this is your house?' I asked.

'Oh, yes!' She laughed girlishly and I had to join in. It was that kind of a laugh.

At this moment an old man stuck his head through the hole and started spouting in Tagalog. The girl climbed swiftly up the ladder and inside. The old man clambered down; his face was dark red with rage.

'Go away! You keep away from here! Elena is blind girl. No good for you!' He shook his little fist in my face.

'Take it easy, Papasan,' I said. 'Nobody's going to hurt your little girl.' I twisted his arm behind his back and flung him into a nearby bush. He was up in an instant; his eyes were like shiny, black marbles. Then, probably realizing the futility of it all, he began to cry.

'You just take it easy, Pop,' I told him. I lighted two cigarettes and gave him one. He started to smoke it, and calmed down. 'You can't hide a girl like that forever, Pop. They grow up on you. I'll be back tonight.'

I whistled and the girl stuck her head through the hole. I climbed the ladder and put the bottle of 'Honeymoon Lotion' in her hand.

'I'll be back tonight,' I said and dropped to the ground. I patted the old man on the shoulder and left.

That night I went back. I gave the old man several sacks of tobacco and some cigarette papers. I took the girl before I left. I was happy with her and spent several weeks at the little house. I often stayed all night and on most of my free weekends. I bought her the phonograph, on credit from the Hindu, and the two records. It was refreshing to have a girl like Elena after the hard-bitten professional girls who lived with the sergeants.

The breakup came as a surprise, even though I should have seen it coming. The airmen at Pampanga were so stupid I could hardly speak to them. I had one friend, Red Galvin, at the time, and when I wanted to talk to someone I talked to him. It was my own fault for not realizing that my little deal with Elena would cause vicious jealousy.

I'd been drinking gin in the shack and talking to Elena until almost midnight. She had fanned me, as I talked, with a palm leaf and it had been an enjoyable evening. Instead of staying the night I decided to go back to the barracks.

I cut through the Baluga village and was on the trail that led across the plain when I was jumped by three men. Ducky Halpert, Vernon Watson and Melvin Powell were the three. Between them they worked me over pretty well. I got in a few good licks, of course, but the viciousness of their attack caught me by surprise and I took quite a beating. After I was down, and after I was kicked a few times I said I'd had enough. They let me up and the night was quiet except for the heavy breathing all of us were doing. Watson was the spokesman for the ambushers.

'Blake,' he said, 'you've had this coming for a long time. I've seen some rotten bastards in my time but you top them all. Anybody that would take advantage of a poor little blind girl ought to be killed instead of just being beaten up. But I'm telling you now, if I ever hear of you going over there again I'll personally kill you. Do you understand?'

'Yes, I understand. I understand your jealousy.'

'No,' he said. 'I guess you wouldn't understand. That's why I'm telling you.'

Ducky picked up a piece of wood and started for me. 'Let me kill him now,' he said.

'No,' Watson said. 'He isn't worth it.' They went on toward the *barrio* and I limped back to the barracks.

For several days after that I was black and blue, and I had lost a tooth during the fracas. My one small satisfaction

693

was the black eye I'd given to Ducky Halpert. It is best to avoid vicious people. I never went back to see Elena. I still believe Airman First Class Watson would have killed me if I had gone back, but now I shall never know.

Poor Elena Espeneida, my little lost brown flower. May this stupid world treat you kindly and may your days be short and sweet.

Third Entry (Undated)

I believe I should write something about the miserable quality of the food at this dark field. It is certainly most unreasonable to station a man in the midst of nowhere and then go off and leave him with a storeroom containing nothing except canned corned beef and small, white dried beans. The first week or two the rations were all right. I managed to eat the stuff three times a day, but now I can eat only one meal a day and I have to force myself to do that.

There is no variety. To be sure, there is the choice of one or the other, and for a short time I could spend a few moments in thought as to which it would be, or both. But now, the thought that I have to eat either one makes my stomach turn over with disgust. So what I do is just put a pot of beans on the stove and dump a can of corned beef into it. This horrible mess simmers along, and when it begins to dry out I throw more snow into it. This concoction I eat once a day. And that is one too many times.

Often at night I dream of meat, of the huge hamburgers I used to buy in the summertime at Ocean Park, with the thick slice of tomato, the slab of Bermuda onion, the relish, the mustard, the thinly sliced tart dill pickle, and the great quarter pound patty of meat; hot, greasy and dripping. The dream wakes me, and I find that I've been drooling in my sleep; and in the dead silent air of my sleeping room

I can almost smell the lingering traces of cooking hamburger and onions. At such times I'm so hungry it is impossible to go back to sleep. In desperation I go to the bean pot and take one huge bite of beans. I have to spit it out, finding that I cannot swallow such food with my recent visions so fresh in my mind.

The only virtue corned beef has is that it is greasy. By being careful I can scrape enough white fat from a newly opened can to wash my face and hands. It's as good, if not better, than regular soap. It is nice that the canned corned beef is good for something.

About my second or third week here I thought there might be game of some sort about. A country as wild as this should have some kind of animal living in it. It is wild enough for any animal. In addition to my daily round of the field I took a few short trips away from the field looking for tracks. I never found any. I haven't seen a bird, or even an insect for that matter. Of course, I can't go too far away from the tower. It's too cold, and a man could freeze quickly too long away from warmth. But there is nothing here anyway. Any animal who would pick this section of Tibet for a residence would be stupid.

In a way it is funny. There is food enough here to last one man for fifty years, and yet I am hungry. Really hungry.

I am hungry all the time.

Fourth Entry (Undated)

Today I have been thinking about The Man in the Black Robe.

I know positively that there is such a Man and I wonder, sometimes, if He will find me here in Tibet, or wherever it is that I am now. So far, I haven't even seen His shadow. I doubt if He will ever come here for me, but I know that He exists. But at the time I didn't believe it. Only old Sinkiewicz believed it and he was right and I, for once, was wrong. Of course, the ten-day drunk Sinkiewicz was on had something to do with it. I have often noticed that alcohol sharpens a man's perception and he sees things he would not otherwise see. I suppose that is the way it was with old Sinkiewicz.

It was after midnight when the Pollack woke me. I was sleeping soundly and I shrugged his shaking hand away several times before I actually awoke. There he was, Airman Sinkiewicz, a four-day stubble of beard on his face, tears in his marbled eyes; thin arms jerking up and down in the moonlight like a man with Dengue fever.

'What'd you say, Sinkiewicz?' I asked him.

'The Man in the Black Robe . . .' he mumbled through his clattering false teeth. 'He's after me again!'

'Look, Pop,' I said, irritated, 'go on back to bed and get some sleep.'

'I haven't been to bed in three days, Blake! If I go to sleep now, He'll get me for sure!' Juicy tears rolled down his wrinkled cheeks. There is something horrible about an old man crying, and old Sinkiewicz must have been forty-five years old if he was a day. I swung my feet to the floor, pulled on my khaki shorts and lit a cigarette.

'What do you want me to do about it?' I asked wearily. I couldn't go back to sleep and let the old man cry.

'I need me some sleep, Blake; I ain't slept in three days. If you'll only stand guard for me, just an hour, that's all I ask, so I can get me some sleep, I can fight Him off when I wake up.'

'Fight who off?'

'The Man in the Black Robe!' he whispered impatiently. 'Who'd you think I was talking about?' He rubbed his eyes with the back of his right hand, trying to look at me and over his shoulder at the same time.

'Where is He?' I was interested. 'I'd like to get a look at Him.'

'You don't believe me, do you?'

'Sure. But I'd like to see Him, that's all.'

Compressing his lips over his loose plate, Sinkiewicz nodded and weaved toward the stairwell. I followed, barefooted, exhilarated by the novelty of having something unexpected to do. Downstairs, on the long front gallery, Sinkiewicz retrieved his grande of gin from its hiding place behind the squadron bulletin board. He had a rough time taking out the cork, took a long pull, wiped the neck on his shirt and handed the bottle to me. I took a short one, and returned the bottle.

'Thanks. Now where is The Man in the Black Robe?'

'Follow me.' Sinkiewicz held his shoulders back; the drink had steadied him. Doing his best to stay on tiptoes, he staggered down the porch. I padded along behind and when we reached the end of the barracks I came to an abrupt halt when he flattened his back to the wall and pointed a trembling finger around the corner of the building.

'The Man in the Black Robe!' he whispered dramatically.

Cautiously, I peeked around the corner and took in the scene. There was a pile of wood, ready for the kitchen stove in the morning; three windblown bamboo trees; the woodshed; and the well-known row of tightly covered garbage cans. Nothing else that I could see.

'Do you see Him?' Sinkiewicz hissed anxiously.

'No.'

'Let me look!' Gripping my arms at the biceps, he peered over my shoulder. Quickly pulling his head back, he flattened his back to the wall again and trembled all over like a twanged rubber band. 'He's there all right! Waiting for me behind the bamboo tree!'

I looked again. All I could see by the bamboo cluster were the wavering shadows caused by the slight breeze wafting up from the south. The moon was three-quarter and if there had been anything else back there I would have been able to see it with ease. My vision is fifteen-fifteen.

'You're nuts,' I said. 'There's nobody back there.'

'You don't believe me,' Sinkiewicz said childishly. A moment later, tears rolled down his cheeks again.

'Quit crying, for Christ's sake. Go on up to your bunk and I'll stay down here on guard for you.' I was trying to humor him, but he shook his head craftily.

'Best not to go inside. Too dark. I'll just lay the body down right here and you watch me for one hour. Okay? One hour. That's all I ask.'

'All right.'

I don't suppose the old rummy had slept for three days at that. As soon as he stretched his skinny body out on the porch he began to snore. Taking another shot of gin from his bottle I returned to my bunk. I took the gin along with me and stowed it away in my footlocker before climbing back into bed. Sinkiewicz had been drunk too long; it was time for him to taper off. Without further thought about the matter, I fell asleep and didn't wake until first call.

The Charge-of-Quarters found Sinkiewicz at 9:30 a.m. the next morning. His head was bashed in at the back and he was curled up fetuslike on the concrete floor of the shower boiler room. I happened to be in the barracks when the CQ found him because I had just returned from sick call. The CQ, Staff Sergeant Haxby, was all excited by his find and I followed the crowd into the boiler room. Haxby, the mess sergeant, the first sergeant, two Filipino KPs, Sinkiewicz and myself, made quite a crowd in the little room. A few other men, off-duty, hovered about outside the door. A good ten feet above the floor, on the concrete wall, there was a bloody spot as big as a man's hand. A few brown hairs, the same color as Sinkiewicz's hair, were mixed with the blood. A mystery. But a mystery easily solved by the brainy first sergeant.

'Here's the way I construct it,' the Top said, pursing his lips. 'Old Sinkiewicz was hanging by his knees from that pipe up there, and by swinging himself back and forth he kept banging his head against the wall until he killed himself.'

'That must've been the way it happened, Top,' Sergeant Haxby agreed.

'I don't think so,' I said.

'Who asked you, Blake?' The first sergeant turned on me angrily. 'And how come you ain't down on the line anyway?'

'I just got back from sick call.'

'Then get your ass down to the line! You think I don't know a suicide when I see one?'

'Clear-cut,' I said, and I left the boiler room, thereby making room for another observer.

The ambulance pulled up quietly as I started down the dirt road toward the hangar. The correct thing to have done, I suppose, would have been for me to tell the doctor about The Man in the Black Robe, but if I had, all I would have received for my pains would have been a reputation for being nuts. I ended up by not telling anybody anything about The Man in the Black Robe, and I suppose it is just as well. But now that it is written down; even on paper it doesn't make a hell of a lot of difference.

Not to me, anyway.

And I'll never see The Man in the Black Robe in this lousy place.

Fifth Entry (Undated)

Tonight I am really excited and it is with great pride that I make this entry in my journal. Many days have passed by and I have entered nothing. I have entered nothing because nothing happens here. And to describe things of no consequence doesn't seem to be quite right. But all day today I've been writing a poem. In fact, I was so engrossed in it I almost forgot to make the rounds of the field to check the little red and green lights. But I did remember, and now; as the night hangs over the dark field like the evil witch she is; and as my searchlight shows her up every sixty seconds, I can inscribe the poem I have labored on all day. It is beautiful and true and sad and it almost has the answer . . . I wonder why I didn't know before this that the fashioning of a poem could bring such bittersweet tragedy to a young man's heart?

MY HOUSE

My house has windows and doors that open both ways.
My house catches the night's southern rays.
The silence of death sleeps in my house.
And I am alone, all alone in my house.
My calling calls for the light of blackness
With a single searching ray of infrared—
Turning inward to see inside my shaking head.
This is my house, a vessel for my clumsy soul,
Set aside to repeat a senseless role,
Again and again throughout the matchless blackness.
Come Witch! And come Ghoul!
Let us examine the stool.
Let us see the beginning of that which is not
Outside the center of this house's inner rot!
For I am the Kingdom and the Glory for all Time;
The unheard lyrics of a speechless mime.

And

My house has windows and doors that open both ways.

And

My house catches the night's southern rays.

This is a very sad poem. And what makes it sadder still is that I cannot share it with anybody. I've never been one to talk much. I have been, if anything, a man of action. It is boring to talk to strangers and fools and most people are one or the other. But I have always liked to listen to people talking, and now, even that is denied me. I listen instead to the two-cylinder engine and the generator. I listen to the wind as it whips out of the western pass. I listen to the softly falling snow, and it is like listening to nothing. There is an air of futile unreality about this dark field that bothers me. I feel, sometimes, that I have been forgotten here, that I have been left here on purpose and that they don't intend to replace me . . . that I have been left here forever. Yet I know that such a thing is impossible. Every Air Force man must be accounted for, someplace. Although I am only a Basic Airman, I have my own little square in a column headed AMN on a morning report somewhere, and I cannot mean nothing. There has been some oversight. They are having difficulty in finding a replacement. That may be the answer. Perhaps the weather for flying is too bad? Many things can go wrong. But forgotten? It makes me laugh. No. I am not forgotten. Not me. Not Jacob C. Blake. I am a poet.

A poet cannot be forgotten.

Sixth Entry (Undated)

Last night I couldn't sleep. I am never tired, but usually I can get to sleep all right; last night I couldn't. Without

701

cigarettes, without coffee, without anything to read I was restless. It was too cold to go outside, so I decided to tire myself by doing calisthenics.

I ran through all of the exercises I could remember from basic training at Lackland Air Force Base, and then finished by doing push-ups. Push-ups are hard, and I had never been able to do more than twenty-five in my entire life. But last night I started, and I counted as I did each one, counting aloud, and I passed twenty-five, kept going, hit fifty, and when I got to one hundred I stopped of my own accord and sat down on the edge of my bunk.

One hundred! And I wasn't a bit tired; I could have kept on doing push-ups all night long, two hundred, a thousand of them if I wanted. Just before making this entry I did a hundred push-ups and I wasn't even breathing hard.

So one thing I can say for the dark field. It is healthy. Despite the lousy chow and all I am in better physical shape now than I have ever been in my entire life. I'm going to do some more.

I did five hundred. Nothing to it.

Seventh Entry (Undated)

It was Sunday morning. I was in bed and Red Galvin was shaking me by the shoulder. It was Flagellante Day and I had forgotten.

'Get up,' he said. 'It's after seven.' Galvin was dressed and when he saw that I was awake he left me and went downstairs. I put on a pair of khaki shorts and a polo shirt and joined Galvin in the dayroom.

'We can eat breakfast at the Iron Star in Angeles,' he said. 'Did you ever eat coconut pancakes dripping with rancid goat butter?'

'No.' I shook my head sleepily.

'A fine way to start the day.'

The taxi arrived and we rode to Angeles in silence. I was far from enthusiastic about seeing the Flagellantes but Red had been insistent that I go with him.

'These guys are true religious fanatics,' he said. 'A man should always observe fanaticism when he gets the chance. It is rare when people can be anything about anything, and maybe we can learn something.'

'What can you learn from a bunch of Filipinos beating themselves with bamboo whips?' I asked.

'Love,' Galvin said, and he would have spat out the window but it wasn't rolled down.

The taxicab pulled up and stopped in front of the Iron Star and I signed the chit.

We ate breakfast at the Iron Star and the pancakes were all right. The goat butter wasn't. I'm not much for goat butter. Several whores from the Bull-Pen, hearing that two airmen were in town already, began to drift sleepily into the Iron Star. The Moro, two Elena's, The Igorote and Blondie were among the first arrivals. I didn't like to look at Blondie. She had peroxided her hair with terrible success, and it was an ugly reddish-orange color with the jet roots growing out again for almost an inch close to her dirty scalp. Despite the weird color of her hair she got a surprising play on payday.

Red sent the Moro to the Chinaman's for a bottle of gin. We sat drinking gin highballs until ten thirty. It was hot by that time and I was feeling the effects of the gin. It was pleasant, sitting there, looking across the dusty plaza at the dancing heatwaves.

'It should be about time,' Red said. We left the semi-coolness of the Iron Star and started out for the white-washed church and the beginning of the climb. Before we reached the church we got another grande of gin at the Chinaman's. A Filipino and his young girl friend were in the Chinaman's and Galvin patted the girl on her rear end. Her boy friend didn't like it and shoved Galvin. Galvin hit the man in the stomach and he doubled over, fell on the floor, and was sick. The girl ran into the back darkened section of the store and, trembling, flattened herself against the wall.

'Never push a redhead,' Galvin told the man on the floor. I signed a chit for the grande and we went to the church.

There was a large crowd gathered. Several officers and their dependents were in the crowd, all of them with cameras, taking pictures of the Flagellantes. A couple of dependents gave Galvin and me dirty looks, but the officers pretended not to notice us. The Flagellantes were getting into the mood; about twenty-five of them altogether. Fiber ropes were tied tightly around their arms and legs and more than half of them wore heavy crosses tied across their backs. They held limp bamboo switches in each hand which they swished gingerly across their backs as the priest chanted to them. There was a huge crowd of Filipinos, all of them dressed in their best clothes. The women prayed and counted the number of beads on their rosaries. It was a colorful sight and I was glad I was there to see it.

The procession started, the black-robed priest leading the way. The Flagellantes were going to end up at a hilltop almost three miles away for the finish of the ceremony. They seemed to get more fervor as the climb started and were soon switching themselves very hard. Their backs began to bleed and from time to time they would shout in ecstasy; bitter, incomprehensible cries.

Galvin and I followed along, stopping now and then to have a drink from the bottle. The crowd thinned quickly, officers and dependents being the first to leave. It was really too hot to be out in the blazing sun. Perspiration ran down my bare legs and squished in my shoes as I walked.

We had started with the head of the column, but after stopping a few times we were all alone on the trail.

'The hell with this,' I said. 'Let's sit down.'

'I guess we've seen enough for one day at that,' Galvin said.

We sat on a cluster of rocks by the side of the trail under the shade of a banana tree. I took a long swig of gin. The searing fluid burned my throat and filled me with elation.

'Yaow!' I yelled.

Galvin had another drink but he didn't yell. He was more dignified with every drink. The last of the Flagellantes was coming up the hill. I nudged Galvin and we watched the man struggle up the steep incline. He was small, even for a Filipino, and his cross appeared to be much larger and heavier than those of the other Flagellantes. His dark, sienna body was drenched with sweat and his arms were streaked with blood from cross-handed switching with the sharp twisted strips of bamboo.

As he came abreast of us he dropped, exhausted, to the ground. He struggled to rise, couldn't and then lay there in the dust, shuddering with great rasping sobs. It made me more tired than I was already just to listen to him.

Galvin got up from his rock and kicked the Flagellante in the ribs. I heard the ribs crack, and I could see the scuffed skin on the man's side where the point of Galvin's heavy shoe had landed.

'Get up,' Galvin said, and he kicked him again. The man made no effort to rise. Galvin kicked him in the face and blood ran from the man's mouth, bubbling. I watched his eyes. They were the eyes of a dog with a full belly; full to bursting, and yet begging at the table for more food. He didn't cry out. There wasn't a shred of hate in his eyes. Just love.

'You wanted to suffer. Now suffer!' Galvin said, and he kicked him in the head again. The man continued

705

his rasping breathing. Galvin sat down and we had another drink.

'Galvin,' I said, 'this man loves us.' It was hard to believe but I knew it was so. I could see it in the man's eyes. The realization was like an electric shock to me.

'Sure he does,' Galvin said. 'Today he is Jesus. But watch out for the son of a bitch tomorrow. He'll cut your head off with a *bolo*.'

'No. Not this man. He loves us.' I began to cry. I couldn't help it. 'No one has ever loved me before,' I said.

'You're drunk, you bastard,' Galvin said.

This was true. I was very drunk. Yet I knew this little Flagellante loved me and it made me cry. Sobbing, I got to my feet. I wanted to help the Flagellante up, but I tripped over the cross and fell down. This made Galvin laugh and in a moment I was laughing too. We killed the remainder of the gin, and leaving the man in the middle of the trail, we lurched down the hill.

We were singing when we reached Angeles again. We had a drink at the Chinaman's and I signed a chit for another grande of gin. The young girl came into the store, the same girl Glavin had patted before we left. She saw Galvin and tried to run out, but he caught her by the arm and held her.

'I'm going to the Iron Star,' I said.

'Go ahead.' Galvin didn't look at me. He was holding the girl with one hand and tickling her with the other. She squirmed and kicked him. The Chinaman was giggling like he was the one being tickled.

Sergeant Ratilinsky was sitting at a table in the Iron Star eating a big bowlful of *pansit*. He waved me over and I ordered a bowl for myself. After we ate, we drank gin highballs made with *lemonada*. A Filipino Army recruit came into the cafe wearing a .45 pistol on his hip.

'Do you know how to take that gun apart, boy?' Sergeant Ratilinsky asked him.

'No, sir.' He handed his weapon obediently to Ratilinsky, when the sergeant held out his hand.

Ratilinsky detail-stripped the pistol down as far as it would go. The parts were spread all over the top of the greasy, *pansit*-smeared table. I was laughing. Ratilinsky had a false look of intense concentration on his face. He eyed the scattered pistol stupidly. He scratched his head.

'Do you know how to put this gun together again, boy?' he asked the young soldier.

'No, sir.'

'Neither do I,' Sergeant Ratilinsky said, with a straight face.

I was laughing so hard by that time I fell off my chair. No sounds were coming from my throat. It was a terrible breath-choking laugh. The old *mamasan* came from behind the counter and stood over me.

'Whassa matter, you? Whassa matter, you?' she asked.

I passed out.

Later I remember riding back to the field in a taxi with Abe Harris and Sergeant Ratilinsky. Abe spotted Galvin lying by the side of the road and we had the driver stop. He was dead weight and we had to drag him into the taxi.

At the barracks I was sobered quite a bit from the ride, and I helped Abe carry Galvin upstairs. We threw him on his bunk.

The next morning Red Galvin was dead. Somebody had stabbed him with a knife. It must have been a thin blade. He bled internally. Just to look at the tiny wound, it was nothing. The Air Police never found out who killed him.

The Sunday following his death, I picked some flowers in the jungle, walked to the base cemetery, and put them on his grave.

They were the only flowers he got.

Eighth Entry (Undated)

A strange thing happened today and it adds to the evil that hangs over this dark field like a foul mildewed blanket.

I wanted to see what my beard looked like. Before coming here I shaved every day except Sunday. But in my haste to get here I only had four blades in my shaving kit. These were used up long ago and, consequently, my beard has grown thick and long since I stopped shaving. I don't have a mirror and I wondered what I looked like with a beard. I came up here to the tower and tried to catch my reflection in the window. I could not. I thought then that it was because I was on the inside lookout and the light wasn't right. I went outside and shifted a few empty fuel drums to make a sort of a ladder, and stood at the apex to look in the window from the outside. I still couldn't see any reflection. All I could see was the inside of the tower room. It was disconcerting. I boiled a cup of water and drank it to settle my tense nerves. I still can't understand it.

I talked to myself about it. These conversations I hold with myself are more frequent of late, but they are harmless, and at times, interesting. I've divided myself into two persons to tell myself apart. The man with the beard is Mr Blake and the man I was before without the beard is Jake. It's easier that way.

'Well, Jake,' I said, 'how do I look with a beard?'

'It does nothing for you.'

'You'd say that, not having a beard yourself.'

'Look for yourself then.'

'I tried to and couldn't.'

'Mr Blake, I'm going to tell you something for your own good—'

'Don't tell me anything for my own good!' I broke in.

'All right. For my own good then. Having known you for a long time I feel I can speak frankly and sincerely to you. I've always had your welfare at heart even though I haven't always shown it by my actions.'

'I know that, Jake. You're my best friend.'

'I'm more than that. I'm your only friend.'

'And that goes for me too.'

'I'm filled with mutual admiration for you.'

'With and without the beard?'

'With and without the beard.'

'What were you going to tell me for my own good, Jake?'

'You can't see your reflection because you only see the things there are for you and not the things there are.'

'Do you mind running over that again?'

'Not at all. Have you ever cast reflections on yourself?'

'Well, I . . .'

'Of course you haven't. It takes a person like myself, a man who is close to you, a friend, a confidant, to see and tell you of your imperfections.'

'What makes you such an authority?' I scratched my throat through my beard.

'I can only reply with another question. Who knows you better than I know you?'

'That isn't an answer, Jake. When a man is standing too close, things become magnified in his eyes. He should stand back, way back, and get an overall picture.'

'True. But if he gets too far away the imperfections have a tendency to diminish in his eyes.'

'What's wrong with that?' I said innocently.

'Mr Blake, Mr Blake.' I shook my head sadly. 'You're hedging.'

I shifted uncomfortably in my chair. The beardless youth was getting on my nerves.

'Now look here, Jake. You've got a bunch of generalizations stored up in that young mind of yours and none of them make any sense! If you're going to tell me something, tell it!'

'If you'll stop that scratching and listen for a minute I will tell you.'

'The beard makes my neck itch. All right. I'll stop.'

'Mr Blake,' I continued. 'I've been doing a lot of thinking in the months I've been stationed here. In a way, this lonely assignment has been the best thing that ever happened to me. It's an opportunity few men get in a dreary lifetime. So involved are men with their foolish, but necessary, grubby, day to day existence, scratching around in the filth for wherewithal and sustenance; they never get the chance that you and I have: The chance to actually sit, to get completely rested, and to ask themselves, 'What is it all about?' and to then provide themselves with the answer. Do you follow me?'

'I'm listening. Go ahead.'

'I've already said it. Ask yourself.'

'You mean I should ask myself what it's all about?'

'Of course. Weren't you listening?'

'All right! What is it all about?' I asked it bitterly, and I didn't expect an answer.

'Open the door and look outside.'

I opened the door. The sun was gone. It had gone down behind the western peak. It was dark; time to make my square of the field and check the lights.

I flicked the switches on, shrugged into the dirty sheepskin jacket, and by the light of the searchlight as it circled every sixty seconds, I made my rounds.

I still don't know what I look like with my beard, but I imagine I look as well as anyone else with one.

Ninth Entry (Undated)

I have noticed, by keeping this journal, that I usually feel a lot better after writing something down. And it always gives me a lot of pleasure to go back over what I've written and read it. I only wish I was able to write something down every day. But I cannot. It is difficult to get started. It is hard to think of a subject, or a plan, and things are always more interesting when they are put down in a certain groove and lead up to something. My life so far has been so uneventful I must wrack my brain to think of anything worth writing and then I discard the ideas I do get as too mundane.

Tonight, though, I thought I would write about the Baluga. It could get me into trouble to write about it, should anybody get their hands on this journal, but I have never been sure I did the right thing in killing that Baluga anyway, and perhaps, by putting it down on paper, I might come to some sort of conclusion.

The Balugas of Pinatuba in the Philippines are a Negrito race; a race of little men and women rarely growing more than three and a half feet tall. They are mighty primitive, not even speaking Tagalog, the main Filipino dialect, and no English at all. Most of them live on and around Mount Pinatuba, eking out a bare existence by planting sweet potatoes, and by eating small animals they manage to bag with bows and arrows. They never wash and their little black bodies are scaly most of the time, unless they happen to be surprised by a quick tropical rain. Nearby our Pampanga field there was a small villageful of them, perhaps twenty families in all, and they were a bit more civilized than the rest of the tribe that lived on Mount Pinatuba. We airmen always passed through the little village on our way to the *barrio* and the Air Force Settlement. It was interesting to watch their activities in community living. There was one huge black pot in the middle of the sandy street, and the older Balugas, men and women, kept a hot fire going under it all of the time. The younger men, after foraging in the jungle, would throw what they caught or bagged into the pot. The young women would throw in sweet potatoes from time to time, or else wrap the potatoes in banana leaves and shove them under the coals. When hungry, they would pick up a pointed stick and stab it into the pot and eat what they speared; a lizard, a section of a snake, a field mouse, a portion of rabbit or a sweet potato. It was an honest, communistic way of living.

On paydays, five or six of the young Baluga men would come to the field and stand around hoping some airman would buy a bow and arrow set. In this manner the Balugas obtained cash. The arrows, as I recall, were three pesos apiece and the bows sold for ten. You couldn't haggle about price because they couldn't understand you. The price never varied and they wouldn't take five pesos for an arrow or two and a half; it had to be three. Several airmen bought sets consisting of a bow and three arrows and mailed them back to the States. I guess they wanted them for souvenirs. I never bought any because they were too crudely made to suit me, and besides, I wouldn't have had any use for them.

One of the Balugas worked for the squadron. He was very old, but his job wasn't difficult. He pulled a weighted burlap sack over the sand greens of our nine-hole golf course every day. It was a strange sight, when I first arrived at the field, to sit on the porch railing and look across the road to hole number five and see this tiny black man in a dirty loin cloth, clutching a bow and arrow in one hand and dragging a burlap sack around and around the sand green. He was serious about this work and I often wondered how the job had been explained to him in the first place. He didn't speak a word of English. On payday the Charge of Quarters would get a ten-peso check from the first sergeant and take the Baluga into the PX to cash it. The Baluga would make an X on the back, and after the CQ countersigned the check he would give the Baluga ten one-peso bills.

Many of the men tried to kid the old Baluga. They would question him and he always listened attentively. After listening for a decent interval he would say: *'Junque cigarillo mo!'* meaning, 'Give me your cigarette!' or actually, to give him a cigarette. He would take the cigarette that was offered, light it, and put it between his teeth with the fire part inside his mouth and smoke it. The interview was over, so far as he was concerned, after he got the cigarette. He would leave then, and wouldn't be seen until the next day. There he would be again, out on the golf course dragging the burlap sack around the greens. After a few weeks I was used to the sight and it no longer seemed strange to me. I still can't work up any excitement about his death and it means nothing to me. Perhaps it should. That's why I'm writing this down; to see if I should be affected in any way with what happened. I would like to know.

Guard duty was a fairly simple matter at Pampanga. There were two posts, watchman type, the detail calling for two NCOs and four airmen. One post was at the hangar area and the other was around the barracks area and the officer's row. The shifts were from six to midnight and from midnight to six. The next day, following a guard shift, was an off day unless there happened to be a prisoner in our little guardhouse, and if there were, (sometimes Leech Hudson was in for a few days) the four Airmen of the guard split the day four ways and worked the prisoner. Guard duty wasn't too bad and it only came around about twice a month.

The night this happened I was on the midnight to six shift on Post Number Two; the barracks area and officer's row. There was a telephone in the dayroom by the barracks and another one in the garage at the end of the officers'

713

row of houses behind a captain's residence. It took fifteen minutes to patrol from the dayroom to the garage and one of the orders was to call the sergeant of the guard every twenty minutes to tell him everything was all right. Once from the dayroom phone and twenty minutes later from the garage phone. I learned early in the game that it was just as easy to sit on a box in the garage and make several calls from there instead of doing the tedious patrolling and the sergeant wouldn't know the difference anyway. Another order on Post Number Two was to shoot all loose dogs. The reason for this order was that in the tropical heat the dogs that abounded in the *barrios* caught rabies quite easily, and the diet they lived on, consisting mostly of fish heads and the leftover rice the Filipinos gave them, caused them to lose their hair and raised large red sores on their bodies. Such an animal could spread disease. It was best to shoot them. I mention this order to prove I was entirely within my rights on this night I am writing about. The sentinel carried a riot gun, commonly called a sawed-off shotgun, and four shells. I was always on the lookout for dogs in the hope I could shoot one to break the monotony of the long night.

It was about 2 a.m. and I had just made a call from the garage telling the sergeant everything was okay. I saw a light coining down the alley and got to my feet, cocked my gun and took the safety off. I stepped out of the shadow and challenged.

'Halt! Who's there?'

The light kept coming. It was the old Baluga who worked on the golf course and he was carrying a candle stuck on a board. He stopped and grimaced at me, holding the candle up so I could see his face. He had no business being there at that time of night, but was using the alley as a shortcut to get to the trail leading to the Baluga village.

'Looks to me like you're lost, old man,' I said.

'*Junque cigarillo mo!*' he said.

The feeling I got when he said those three words filled me with compassion for the old man. He was on the bottom rung of the ladder. It was a feeling of great pity I felt, and at the same time one of great love. It swelled inside me. I couldn't hold all of it. My heart was filled with the strong emotions. I wanted to do something for him. This primitive little man. He had nothing. He would never have anything.

I knew there was only one thing I could do for him and I had to do it. My eyes began to blur and just before the tears rolled down my cheeks I pulled the trigger. The shot caught him full in the chest and he fell backward, slammed to the ground. His candle went out as it fell in the thick dust of the alley. I put the safety on and stood silently for a full minute, listening to the night. It was a still night and I knew the sergeant of the guard heard the shot at the other end of the field. I called the guardhouse from the garage.

'This is Post Number Two, Sergeant Irby. I just shot at a dog, but I missed him.'

'All right. I heard the shot. Be sure you get him next time. These shells cost the government twenty cents apiece.'

'I know what they cost. I'm going to stay on the officers' row for a few more minutes in case he comes back.'

'Okay,' he said and he hung up.

That gave me twenty minutes before I had to call again.

The tears that had been rolling down my cheeks were gone. My hands began to shake and I was afraid. I was afraid of being caught. Although my motives had been good and I had meant well, I knew that I would be court-martialed if they found me with a dead Baluga. I put the shotgun inside the garage by the telephone. I carried the dead Baluga into the open field behind the row of houses. It was a rocky field, scattered here and

715

there with grey fieldstones and thick patches of lush grass. The Baluga was very light in my arms. I found a shallow sandy depression in the uneven field, scooped it deeper with my foot, and put the little man into it. I covered him with a layer of sand and small rocks and brushed the grave clear of footprints and markings with a piece of brush. I returned to the road for his bow and arrows and piece of board with candle. I buried these in the field. Looking at my watch I noticed the twenty minutes were up. I called the guardhouse.

'Post Number Two. Everything okay,' I said.

'Did you see the dog again?'

'No. But I'm keeping an eye out.'

'Okay.' He hung up.

I knew I had to kill a dog; I had to kill one to discourage suspicion. Our squadron commander had a dog. Prince. A boxer. I took my shotgun and walked up the alley to the major's house. Prince was tied to his latticed doghouse in the back yard. He was awake and licked my hand when I patted him on the head. I untied him, and holding him by the collar, I led him down the alley for a hundred yards or so. Foolishly, I turned him loose and the frisky animal galloped away. He was playful and ran around in circles. He would jump up on me and then dart away. I called him softly. He paid no attention. I chased the beast and after five miserable minutes he allowed me to catch him. Holding him by the collar I held the muzzle of the shotgun against his side with my free hand and pulled the trigger. He dropped to the dust. I called the guardhouse.

'This is Post Number Two. I shot the dog.'

'Good.'

'I don't think it's a *barrio* dog though.'

'You don't?'

'No. It looks a lot like Prince.'

'The major's dog?'

'Yes. I think it is,' I said.

'Jesus!'

'How was I to know? He was running loose.'

'I'm coming up there. Wait for me by the garage phone.'

Sergeant Irby examined Prince and we covered the dog with a burlap sack I found in the garage. He wrote a report for his guard book the way I described it. At 6 a.m. I was relieved. I ate breakfast in the mess hall and went to bed. I was dead tired.

At 10 a.m. the Charge of Quarters woke me.

'The major wants to see you in the orderly room. Get dressed.'

'What does he want to see me about?' I asked.

'I can't imagine,' the CQ said.

I reported to the first sergeant in the orderly room. I didn't like the first sergeant very well. He always had something unpleasant to say to everybody. He was in his late forties, bald, and his large teeth looked as if they were slipcovered with Muscat grape skins. His mouth was smiling at me.

'The old man wants to see you, Blake. Do you know how to report?'

'Of course I do.'

'I suppose you've got a good story ready?'

'What do you mean, Sergeant?'

'All right, Blake. Report to the major.'

I knocked on the inner door and the major told me to come in. I halted one pace away from his desk, saluted, and reported.

'Sir. Basic Airman Blake reports to the squadron commander as directed by the first sergeant.'

He returned my salute and stared at me. His face was old; his skin was furrowed and creased with deep wrinkles. His eyes, however, were bright and alert. They looked me over like two tropical fish exploring a new aquarium.

'Blake. Why did you shoot my dog?'

'He was running loose. I didn't recognize him.'

'You're a liar, Blake.'

'No, sir.'

'Then why did you shoot my dog?'

'He was running loose like I said, sir. I missed him with my first shot and then when he came around again I bagged him. I didn't know it was Prince, sir.'

'Blake, there were powder burns on his side. The muzzle of that gun was so close the shot didn't even have a chance to scatter.'

'He was running by me pretty fast, sir.'

He didn't say anything for a long time. He just looked at me. I was still standing at attention. Perspiration was flowing down my back under my starched khaki shirt. I saw the tears start in his eyes, and I watched them roll down his cheeks. I was ashamed for him and then I was sorry for him. He felt about me just like I had felt about the Baluga. I was glad he didn't have a shotgun in his hand.

'That's all, Blake.'

'Yes, sir.' I saluted, did an about face, and closed the door behind me.

'You ought to feel real proud of yourself,' the first sergeant said.

'I didn't write the guard orders. You people did,' I said.

'Get the hell out of here!' he yelled at me. I went back to bed.

As far as I know they have never found the buried Baluga. I imagine the ants have got him by now.

Now that I've written all of this down I find that I still feel sorry for the Baluga. But unlike the major, at least I tried to do the right thing.

Tenth Entry (Undated)

718

I've stopped eating altogether now. Just the last two days. I don't feel any ill effects at all. I feel much better in fact. I don't suppose I can continue to ignore food, but I've decided to try it for a while. I'm as strong as I ever was and can make my round of the field all right. After a few days I'll go back to eating one meal a day, but it's restful to know that I don't have to eat the horrible beans and corned beef for a few days.

If somebody were to come up to me now and say, 'Blake, what do you want more than anything else in the world?' I would say, 'Popcorn! And don't spare the butter!'

Eleventh Entry (Undated)

I still can't understand why I was assigned to this field. I'm a truck driver not a maintenance man. It was probably the major's idea, because I'm certain he didn't like me after I shot his dog. But all the same, personal prejudice is not supposed to enter into the assignments of airmen, and perhaps it is wrong for me to blame the major for this assignment. He was just doing his duty, I imagine, and when my name came up for this job he gave it to me and let it go at that.

It was on a Saturday morning, right after the inspection. I was changing into khaki shorts and a polo shirt when the Charge of Quarters came running up the stairs screaming my name. Pollack NCOs always scream.

'I'm over here,' I said. 'I'm not deaf either.'

'You've got to get hot, Blake,' he said. 'There's a plane waiting for you down on the line!' He was excited.

'A plane for what?'

'An 0-19. You're leaving.'

'Leaving for where?'

719

'I don't know.' He shrugged his shoulders. 'The first sergeant called from the line and said for you to throw some stuff in a barracks bag. You're being transferred.'

'What about my footlocker and my stuff in the laundry?'

'I don't know anything about that. I suppose it'll be sent to you. Here. I'll give you a hand.' He threw my uniforms and stuff into a barracks bag while I changed back into my inspection uniform. I shouldered my barracks bag and went downstairs. The squadron jeep was out front and the driver drove me down to the flight line.

The major and the first sergeant were waiting for me by an all-fabric 0-19 that had its prop turning over. There was a pilot in the plane but I didn't know who he was. He had his helmet and goggles on and the lower part of his face was muffled by a white silk scarf. The major took me by the arm and led me away from the plane where it wasn't so noisy. The first sergeant threw my barracks bag into the rear cockpit.

'Blake,' the major said, 'you've been assigned to Tibet.'

'Tibet?'

'Yes. You're assigned there temporarily as a field maintenance man. Your job is to keep the lights on at night, and act as alert man for any planes forced down in that area. You know how to service planes, don't you?'

'I drove the gas truck for two months.'

'Fine.'

'What about the rest of my stuff?'

'We'll send it to you. The pilot's waiting now, so you'd better hurry.'

The first sergeant was holding a heavy flying suit for me and I struggled into it, putting it on over my uniform. I put on the helmet and the goggles he handed me and climbed into the plane. The pilot taxied to the end of the field. On the takeoff we passed in front of the hangar, and it looked like the entire squadron was in formation

720

on the concrete apron, all of them at hand salute. It was nice of so many to see me off that way.

There wasn't any radio contact with the pilot from the rear cockpit. I looked around and couldn't find a headset. The pilot never turned around, but kept his eyes straight ahead, his mind on the business of flying the obsolete aircraft. After three hours we landed at a small grassy field and a Filipino boy gassed the ship. I started to dismount to help him but the pilot shook his head, no. We took off again.

We flew over water after that and were soon out of sight of land. The next stop was an island field. It was a little island and I didn't see it at first. There was a slight haze on the water and for a moment I thought the pilot was off his rocker, but then the bare, low-flying island appeared and he put the 0-19 down on a crushed coral strip. The man who gassed the plane this time had a turban wrapped around his head. I took him for a Hindu. We flew away from the island.

It began to get dark and it was cold. Despite the heavy flying suit the cold settled in my arms and back and I felt miserable. I didn't have flying boots on and my feet were like a couple of rocks. The night was black before the pilot set the plane down again. We landed on a small diamond-shaped field without landing lights; just the probing wing lights of the plane picking the way. We rolled to a stop and an ancient Chinaman hobbled out to the plane. Taxiing, the pilot followed the Chinaman to a stone shed and cut the engine. After we were refueled I yelled to the Chinaman.

'What have you got to eat?'

He didn't understand me. By sign language I got across the idea that I was hungry. He grinned, nodded his head, and brought me a can of corned beef from the stone shed. Before I got it open the pilot was taking off. I ate the corned beef in the plane. It was the last time I remember tasting corned beef and liking it.

There were two more similar stops for fuel before we started over the mountains. The pilot was a good one. I knew the ceiling was much too low for an old crate like the O-19, yet he managed to nurse it up and up, the engine protesting every foot of ascent. He stayed in the passes as much as possible and at times I could see the snowy heights of mountains rising up and almost out of sight. Huge mountains they were, shaped like daggers, like bears, like dragons. I fell asleep after a time despite my growing numbness and when I awoke we were on the ground. The pilot was shaking me by the shoulder with his gloved hand. When he saw I was awake he pointed to the tower of this dark field and signaled for me to get out. I got out with my barracks bag, took off the flying suit and helmet and handed them up to him. The prop was still whirring and without a word he twisted the ship about, catching me with a blast of icy propwash. I dodged back as he taxied to the end of the field. I watched him take off and fly into the opening of the pass; then I lost sight of the plane as it disappeared into the gently falling snow. He could have waved goodbye to me. I expected it. But he didn't.

Shivering in my khakis I ran to the tower, threw my barracks bag on the floor and started the gas stove. I ate a can of corned beef. I found the gasoline engine, started it; found the light switches and turned them on. I've been here ever since. I have been ready to leave ever since that first night.

I am overdue for a change of assignment.

I must be.

Twelfth Entry (Undated)

It has now been ten days since I've eaten anything. I still make hot water out of snow and drink it but I haven't tasted either beans or corned beef. I should feel weak but

I feel stronger than I've ever felt in my life. I'm in a better humor too. I spent all morning singing all of the old songs I could remember. 'Flirtation Walk', 'Isn't It Romantic?', 'You're the Top', lots of them. It's funny how the words to these songs come back to a man. I don't even remember learning most of them. 'Deep Purple' brings back a lot of wonderful memories. All puppy love stuff of course, and of a girl who wouldn't interest me now, but the singing of the song brought many memories back to me. They were great days, those LA days. Los Angeles is a wonderful city to grow up in. There are so many fine things to do in LA. Childhood, after everything is said and done, is perhaps the best time of all.

I didn't like school when I was growing up, but none of the guys did. It was so dull. I passed every time but so did everyone else. They have to pass you on to the next class. Other kids are pushing their way up and if they didn't pass you there wouldn't be any room. 'Deep Purple' is a good song. Probably the best song ever written. I thought of a little prayer.

> *If I should die before I eat,*
> *I pray the Lord my soul to meet.*

It's a funny little poem, sardonic too, a twist on the regular bedtime prayer they teach to kids. *If I should die before I wake, I pray the Lord my soul to take.* Mine is better. I'm not going to die anyway. I'll be right here when the time comes to leave. There is a lot of back pay coming to me and I intend to draw and spend every cent of it. This afternoon, even if I have to force myself I'm going to start eating again. I feel good today. Real good.

This dark field isn't so bad once you get used to it. At first I couldn't see it. It was too lonely. But it's good to be by yourself. It gives a man a chance to realize some of the mistakes he has made. If I had it to do all over again I wouldn't have enlisted in the service. I'd have gotten married, gone to college, or maybe to a good trade school. But it isn't too late to do any of these things. When my enlistment is up I can still go to school. I can start all over again. I'll be all the wiser for this experience. Certainly I will. I know one thing. They can't keep me at this field after my enlistment is up. That's one thing they can't do. It's the law. So why shouldn't I feel happy?

What I'm going to do right now is go downstairs and cook up a big pot of beans and eat every bite. Then I'm going to sing some more old songs. My baritone sounds pretty good. If I practice singing every day and get so I'm really good at it I can sing in night clubs when I get out. Make records. Might get in the big money. I don't smoke anymore. I don't even miss the cigarettes anymore. That's why my voice sounds so good.

After looking this entry over I see it doesn't mean much. But in case I don't feel so happy after a couple of days I can come back and reread it.

At least I feel happy today!

Last Entry (Undated)

I might as well tie this up.

Two hours ago I was making my daily round of the field. I was replacing a burned-out bulb in one of the field lights almost directly across the field from the tower. Then I heard my name.

'AIRMAN JAKE BLAKE! REPORT THE TOWER!'

I ran, running as fast as I've ever run in my life. All the way across the field my name kept booming out of the tower: 'BLAKE! COME IN, BLAKE! BLAKE! COME IN, BLAKE!' I cursed myself as I ran for my attention to duty.

I reached the big oak door and pulled it open. The voice was booming from upstairs. I climbed the ladder. The voice was coming out of the speaker. The radio equipment on all three sides of the tower room was brilliantly lighted; humming like a million bees; the radio equipment that had never worked in all the time I'd been there! I searched frantically for the microphone, found it, plugged it into the female socket.

'Blake!' I yelled. 'This is Blake! Come in!' I was out of breath.

'AIRMAN BLAKE?' the voice asked.

'Who else!' I shouted bitterly. I couldn't help it.

'GET READY TO LEAVE.'

'When?'

'GET READY TO LEAVE. OVER AND OUT.'

The transmitter and receiver lights went off. Click! The angry humming stopped. The room was silent again. More silent than ever. I stared dumbly at the speaker. Had I heard it speak? Did a voice tell me to get ready to leave or was everything a dream? I was still panting, puffing, out of breath. I knew that I'd heard the voice and yet I couldn't believe it. I felt the top of the transmitter. It was warm!

'Yaow!' I shouted.

Downstairs, I stuffed my uniforms and underwear into my barracks bag. I brought this ledger and the ballpoint pen I'm writing with from upstairs, threw them into the bag. I stripped off my dirty sheepskin jacket and tossed it on the bunk. There would be another man to take my place and he would need it. For a moment I almost felt sorry for my unknown replacement. But I was too elated to feel sorry for anyone very long. I climbed to the tower and watched the opening in the pass for the airplane that was to take me away.

I could hear the plane before I could see it. It was a two-engine job. The engines weren't synchronized and I could hear them counter-coughing at each other. The transport loomed in the pass like a silver angel, leveled, and roared down to a perfect landing. I dropped down the ladder, grabbed my barracks bag, opened the door, and rushed onto the field. The door opened as I reached the plane. There wasn't a ladder and there wasn't anybody to give me a hand up, but I didn't mind that. I threw my bag in, and pulled myself up and over the edge of the doorway. As I got to my feet inside the door slammed shut. The plane taxied to the end of the runway. With an accelerated roar it picked up flying speed down the field and in a moment was airborne and heading for the pass. I didn't look out the window at the dark field. I never wanted to see it again, and I still don't.

Except for myself, my barracks bag, and a parachute with my name stenciled on it, the interior of the massive ship was empty. The door leading to the pilot's compartment was closed and I wanted to talk to him. I wanted to talk to anybody. But I waited. The pilot would have to clear the pass and I didn't want to interfere with his flying.

After waiting for approximately five minutes I opened the door to the cockpit.

There wasn't any pilot.

There was no one in the pilot's compartment.

The controls were steady as I watched them. The instruments on the panel reflected the things that were happening. The altimeter, air speed, all of the instruments were working nicely, but there was no one in the airplane except myself.

There still isn't.

I sat down on the floor next to my barracks bag. I don't know how long I sat without moving, but I know it was quite a while. I was in a state of semi-shock or something as the realization of my predicament overwhelmed me. The plane roared through the night. It sank in after a while as I stared at the parachute. I didn't have to stay in the airplane. I could slip into the parachute, so kindly provided, open the door, and jump. So easy. Well, I don't want the easy way.

I opened the door and kicked the parachute out. No, Jacob C. Blake is not so easily tricked. After being stationed at the dark field for as long as I have been, I'll just go ahead and take my chances on my next assignment.

Either place – so long as there are people – will suit me right down to the ground—

(The journal breaks off here.)

'Just Like on Television—'

Arresting Off.:
Det. Sgt. G.E. Rouse, LAPD
Interviewing Off.:
Det. Lt. E.M. Harbold, LAPD

STATEMENT

IO: State your name and address.
Suspect: Billy T. Berkowitz. 3428½ South Normandy.
   The half's because I live around to the back. It's a
   garage apartment, but I don't have a car or anything—
IO: Simply answer the questions. Where do you live?
Suspect: I just said: 3428½ South—
IO: No, no. The city.
Suspect: Jesus. Los Angeles. Where else?
IO: And your full name?
Suspect: Billy T. Berko—
IO: The 'T'; what's the 'T' stand for?
Suspect: That's okay, I never use my middle name.
IO: We don't give a damn whether you use it or not.
   What's your middle name?
Suspect: Terence. After my grandfather; he was Irish.
IO: Is that your real middle name? You don't look Irish
   to me.
Suspect: I never said I was Irish; I said my grandfather
   was Irish.
IO: — — —. Never mind that, Steno, strike it out.
   Now, Billy, tell us in your own words about your move-
   ments on October 23. Start in the morning, and finish

up with the morning of the twenty-fourth. Do you understand? And remember that although this statement is voluntary, it may be used against you.

Suspect: I got to go back further than that. I can't explain everything right if I have to start on the morning of the twenty-third, because I just went to work like always.

IO: All right. How far back?

Suspect: Not far. Just enough to explain my original idea, because it's a little involved. But it didn't come to me all at once, so it stands to reason I can't explain it all at once, don't it?

IO: Go ahead.

Suspect: Television. That's where I got the idea. I watch TV every night, but I don't have no set of my own so I look at the sets in the four different bars I hang around in regular. That's what I am; I'm what you might call a habitué, a cocktail bar habitué – although I'm a beer drinker, not a hard liquor man. Not that I wouldn't drink whiskey all the time if I could afford it, but with my lousy job at only forty-five bucks a week and all—

IO: Get on with it, Billy.

Suspect: I am getting on with it, but this is the background part, and if you don't have the fill-in part, the rest don't make sense. It was funny the way the idea came to me – not laughing funny, but funny funny, the way this idea came to me. Just like that. And from television, too.

Now my favorite kind of TV show is the private eye type – *Sunset Strip*, *Boston Blackie* reruns, *Mike Hammer*, *Hawaiian Eye*—

IO: Skip the commercials.

Suspect: I'm only trying to explain the kind of shows I like. Anyway, I guess there are two or three good private eye shows every night, and knowing the schedule so well, I don't miss many. Even when I was going from one bar to the next on my regular rounds I'd plan my time so I wouldn't miss a private eye show. It was research to watch them, to improve my business. In fact, if you will take a look in my little notebook you took away from me you'll see the way I've got them all rated. I give four stars for 'superior,' three stars for 'excellent,' two—

IO: We aren't interested in your TV ratings.

Suspect: Well, no, I guess not. My ratings don't mean much, except to me, but a man has got to set up some sort of a standard to go by. And watching all these private eye shows, especially the series kind, nursing a beer – making only forty-five bucks a week at the su-permarket, I have to nurse one beer a long time, except when somebody buys me a free one, but I don't like to accept a free one because they expect you to buy one back, and—

IO: Get to the point, if there is a point.

Suspect: Sure there's a point. The point is this: By concentrating on this one kind of show, just because I liked them at first, after a while I began to see the pat-tern – the formula, you might call it. I don't mean all private eye shows are alike, I mean exactly the same, the way Westerns are; I mean that all these detectives, the private eyes, have a regular routine they more or less have to follow to solve the case. And it stands to reason that when most of these shows are a half-hour long, and the hero has to find the guy he's looking for to solve the case in a hurry, he has got a tough problem. So what does he do?

Just like in real life, the way any detective works – when he has to find out where somebody lives he has to ask some guy who knows. Like here in LA, where most of the private eye shows take place. If you're hunting for some guy, what do you do—? Start down the street in any old direction knocking on every single door asking for the guy? Of course not. You'd never find him that way, and especially you wouldn't in a half-hour TV show. So in every show, they all got this one thing in common, there's always one guy who knows the answer. It had to be that way, I figured, and they just don't make up people like that for TV, either. The way I saw it there had to be a few guys in every town a cop or a private eye could go to and find out where the guy he was looking for lived. Or where he happened to be at that particular time.

IO: You're a thinker, Billy, a real thinker.

Suspect: Thanks. And that was my original idea, you see, that's the idea that came to me. After all, I thought, what did I do after work anyway? I work six days— Saturday's our biggest day at the supermarket – but when I get through, there are only two choices of something to do. I can go home to my cruddy garage apartment where there isn't anything to do, or I can go to a bar somewhere, nurse a beer, and watch TV. I could go to the movies, I suppose, but TV doesn't cost anything, and it is about the same anyway except for the smaller screen.

So when I got this idea I really got excited.

IO: What idea?

Suspect: The pattern. Becoming a part of the pattern. I realized that I could become a part of the detective work, the private eye pattern myself. After work. I even had the right kind of qualifications, just like the actors who played this kind of part on TV. For one thing, the guy the private eye asks for information is always a character. That was me; I'm something of a character myself.

IO: You are a character all right.

Suspect: Thanks. And another thing. The guy who hangs around in the bar knowing where everybody is – well,

it's not easy to come right out and admit it this way –
he always has what you might call an 'obnoxious personality.' And for some reason – I don't know why – I
seem to be a little obnoxious to other people. I try to
be friendly and all, but most people just don't like me
very much. But in this case, when I thought it over,
having this somewhat obnoxious personality, and being
something of a character besides, well, it made me a
natural for the barroom habitué and answerman. Here
was a way for me to make a little dough on the side.
Once I got myself established in the pattern I knew I
could make some extra money this way.

IO: How?

Suspect: How? I'm coming to that. Let me give you an
    example. Take any regular private eye half-hour story.
    Here's one that is used every week or so.

Some criminal, usually an escaped criminal from prison,
hates the private eye hero and wants to kill him. So
what he does first, he kidnaps the private eye's girl
friend. The hero goes out with his gun looking for the
kidnapper. He knows his name because somebody
telephones him, or else there's a note slipped under his
door. But he don't know where the kidnapper's hide-
out is, and he has to find out quick. What the criminal-
kidnapper usually does, you see, to add a little suspense
to the story, is to have the girl friend call the eye. Then
he pinches her or something to make her scream over
the phone, and then he hangs up quick. This drives the
eye crazy. So the angry hero drives his convertible to
some particular bar where there's a habitué who always
knows where everybody is all the time.

The detective orders a drink, and looks sideways at the
    habitué, who is usually a little drunk.

'You know Blackjack Mussurgorsky?' the hero asks the
    habitué—

IO: Spell that out.

Suspect: I don't know how to spell it; I just made it up. I think he was a football player or something, I don't know.

IO: Okay. Go on.

Suspect: Anyway, the habitué just sits there; he don't even look at the private eye. 'The name is not unfamiliar,' he says, real cool-like. 'Blackjack Matthews—'

IO: You said Mussurgorsky before.

Suspect: But now I'm giving you the guy's real name, which could have been Matthews, the other name being an alias, or something. I'm trying to make this up as I go along, and when you break in this way I forget where I was—

IO: Go on. Get on with it.

Suspect: All right. So the habitué says, real cool, you know: 'Blackjack Mussurgorsky—'

IO: Make up your mind. Mussurgorsky or Matthews? You're confusing the steno.

Steno: No, he isn't.

Suspect: Mussurgorsky. And then the habitué says, 'Whittier Reformatory for Boys, 1933–36; Preston Industrial Reformatory for Youthful Offenders, 1939–41; San Quentin, 1947–51; and Folsom Prison, 1953–57. Occupation: Strongarm boy, armed robbery, and handy with a rod.'

The private eye nods his head—

IO: Just a minute. Sergeant Rouse. Run a make on Blackjack Mussurgorsky.

Sgt. Rouse: Yes, sir. Matthews, too?

IO: Yes, Matthews, too.

Suspect: But I made those names up, I told you—

IO: Never mind. Get on with it.

Suspect: Where was I?

Steno: 'The private eye nods his head—'

Suspect: Right. And he says, the private eye says, 'That's Blackjack Mussurgorsky, all right. Know where he is now?'

But this time the habitué doesn't say anything. Instead, he smiles *knowingly* into his drink. The eye gets the message, and lays a twenty-dollar bill on the bar. But the habitué ignores this bill; he waits for the eye to put another one down before he picks up the dough. 'Try,' he says then, '3428½ South Normandy. It's a salmon-colored duplex, upstairs.'

IO: Not a garage apartment?

Suspect: I just used my own address for convenience. Anyway, that's the end of the habitué's part in the show. Of course, to finish the story, when the hero gets to 3428½ Normandy, or whatever the address is, he shoots it out with Blackjack Mussurgorsky, saves his girl friend, and that's the end of the show.

IO: Somehow, the point of all this escapes me.

Suspect: But that was me; that's what I wanted to be – a professional habitué, in real life. Only I must admit that I didn't know how to go about getting established at first. Before I could sell any information I had to get hold of some first, which only stands to reason. And that was the hardest part of the plan. First, I bought myself a notebook. Then I picked out the four nicest bars in my neighborhood and worked out a regular route and time schedule so I could hit each bar at the same time each night. Before the week was out I knew every bartender by name, and they all knew me as Billy. When I left one bar to go to the next, for instance, I'd tell the bartender, 'Anybody asks for me, I'm at the Dew Drop Inn.' Then when I got to the Dew Drop, I'd phone back to the bar I just left and ask the bartender if he'd seen Billy around tonight. And then he'd tell me over the phone that Billy had just left to go to the Dew

Drop Inn. It was a good system, you see. When I got a chance to work it into a conversation, I'd say to these different bartenders, 'I don't know how I do it, but I probably know more people in this neighborhood than anybody else.' All this was groundwork, I figured, for later on.

Starting out with my new notebook, I wasn't selective about the names I put in it, because I really didn't know anybody at first. I picked up various names from listening in on bar conversations, and I always introduced myself to the strangers in various bars so they'd give me their names in return. Every time I picked up a new name I'd go into the men's room and write it down in my notebook.

IO: You just picked up names indiscriminately?

Suspect: I had to start somewhere, but getting the addresses was harder, the hardest part of all. A guy who's drinking will tell you his name all right, most of the time, anyway, but if you ask for his address he gets a little suspicious. So to tell you the truth, I got most of the addresses out of the phone book. If you know the name, that's the easiest way, if the guy's got a phone. If he hasn't, the next best bet is the City Register.

IO: This is a weird way to kill time in a bar.

Suspect: I guess it does sound a little weird, but like I said, I didn't have nothing else to do, and I figured that my information would pay off sooner or later. Just like on television. If I could pick up a few dollars, simply by giving out some guy's address to a private eye or a cop, well – do you have any idea what an extra ten bucks or so means to a guy who's only making forty-five a week?

IO: Get on with your statement.

Suspect: I'm coming to it now. It was about ten-fifteen, and I was in the Dew Drop Inn, 1425 Vermont Avenue, my regular bar for that time slot, and I was

watching TV. There was only one other guy in the bar,
not counting the bartender, Eddie McSwain, Figueroa
Hotel, Room 419.

IO: Who was the other man?

Suspect: Mr Bert Plouden, sells hand-painted neckties
to exclusive shops; lives with his mother at 2715 41st
Place.

IO: Don't you have to check your notebook for these
addresses?

Suspect: No, it would be unprofessional. During the day
at the supermarket, when I was stacking cans or something, I'd open the notebook and read one page over
and over till I memorized all the names I had in the
book.

And then it happened, just like a dream, or a private eye
show coming to life. This man comes into the bar, goes
straight to the bartender and shows him a photograph.
It was a regular eight-by-ten photo, and I recognized
the old *Dragnet* pattern right away. On *Dragnet* it's almost a *rule* for Sergeant Friday to carry a photo around
to show bartenders.

'You know this woman?' the man asks Eddie. 'She ever
come in here?'

Eddie takes a look and shakes his head. Meantime, I'm
watching the man close. Sure enough, I spot the bulge
under his armpit, so I know he's got a pistol in a shoulder holster.

'I'm sorry,' Eddie tells him, 'but I've never seen her in
here.'

The man starts to leave, and then Eddie stopped him—
just the way I knew he would when the right time
came. 'Hey!' Eddie says, 'why don't you ask Billy?' He
jerks his thumb at me. 'Billy doesn't know how he does
it, but he knows more people around here than anybody.' Eddie was a little sarcastic, the way he said this,

but I didn't mind. I wanted a look at the photograph. So the man comes down to my end of the bar and flashes the photo at me.

'D'you know this woman?'

Well, it just so happened that I did. Her name was Gloria, Gloria Latham. In fact, her name and address is the last entry listed in my little notebook. The whole thing was just a lucky accident, you might say. Only you can't really call it an accident, because I was in the *business* of getting names and addresses.

I'd met Miss Latham only the night before, just casually, in Skinny's Bar and Grill. Skinny's bar is always my last stop on the way home. Anyway, this Gloria Latham was pretty loaded. It was about fifteen minutes before closing, and she staggered when she went out the front door. She was too drunk to drive her car, and she knew it. I heard her tell the bartender, when he cautioned her about driving, that she was going to get a cab at the corner.

IO: Did you follow her outside?

Suspect: Sure, I followed her out. At this time, I only knew that her first name was Gloria. And I needed her last name to get her address out of the phone book. I was going to follow her to the cabstand and listen in if I could when she gave the hack driver her address. Then I could write it down, and check her last name later, you see. But there weren't any cabs at the stand. So I said to her, 'Gloria, I'm Billy. I met you earlier at Skinny's tonight, if you remember—'

'Sure,' she said, 'I know you, Billy old Billy, old Billy goat you.' Being intoxicated, she said my name that way three times – I don't know why, though.

'I don't have a car myself, Gloria,' I told her, 'but if you want me to take you home, I'll drive yours.'

So even though she was really lit, she was smart enough

to give me her car keys. And I drove her home – the Drexel Arms, 2746 Santa Barbara Avenue, Apartment 307. She gave me her address as soon as we got in the car, which was all I wanted. It was the only reason I offered to drive her home, but she didn't know that. I parked in front of the apartment house, helped her through the front door, and gave her back her keys.

IO: You didn't go into her apartment?

Suspect: No. By checking the row of mailboxes in the outside foyer I matched up Gloria to the last name— Latham – and wrote it down in my book, along with the address. The procedure was very simple; it was one of the easiest names and addresses I ever picked up.

IO: Then what did you do?

Suspect: I'm telling you now. I'm back in the bar now, as I said, looking at this photograph. And I see that it's Gloria Latham right away. But I play it cool. 'Maybe I know her and maybe I don't,' I say, and I shrug my shoulders.

He gives me the long look, the once-over, just like on TV, and then he frowns. 'Take a better look,' he says, real tough.

And I talked back just as tough. 'I don't need another look.' But I had a feeling that I wasn't getting through to the man, so I rubbed my thumb back and forth across my fingers. Everybody knows what that means; it's the signal to grease the old palm with cash. He gets the idea immediately, and puts a ten-dollar bill on the bar. I didn't try for a second tenner, the way they do on TV, I picked it up quick before he could change his mind.

'Her name is Gloria Latham.'

'Do you know where she lives?'

I smile then, one of the knowing kinds, and then I figured that I might as well try for the second ten. So I make the old thumb and fingers rub again, and he puts down another ten-dollar bill. 'The Drexel Arms,' I told him, picking up the bill, '2746 Santa Barbara Avenue, Apartment 307.'

'And your name is Billy?'

'That's right. Billy. Billy T. Berkowitz. And any time you need a little information, I'm right here in the Dew Drop every night from ten to eleven.'

But when I reached back to get my wallet, in order to put the money away, he slapped the lousy handcuffs on me and brought me down here to the station. And I'm telling you again that I don't know anything else about the woman, just her name and address like I said. I certainly didn't kill her, for God's sake! I didn't even know she was dead till you guys told me she was. All I am is just a poor workingman with a lousy job in a supermarket. I was only trying to beat inflation by picking up a little extra dough as a professional barroom habitué. That's the whole truth, and I'll swear to it!

IO: Why did Miss Latham write 'Billy' in lipstick on her bathroom mirror before she died?

Suspect: I don't know, but that don't mean I killed her! Being so drunk and all, she might've been afraid she'd forget my name. Sure, that's it! She must have wrote my name down that way so she'd remember it the next morning, figuring she'd thank me for driving her home the next time she saw me. That must be it. It's the only logical explanation, and it stands to reason. I'm an innocent man. I didn't kill her, and that's all I got to say.

IO: You don't expect us to believe all this crap, do you?

Suspect: That's my statement, Lieutenant. Type it up and I'll sign it.

IO: — — — —Strike that out, Steno!

Signed & Typed

Billy T. Berkowitz, October 25, 1962

739

The Alectryomancer*

Where did the old alectryomancer come from in the first place? I didn't see or hear him approach on the soft sand. I looked up from the sea and there he was, waiting patiently for me to recognize him. The blue denim rags covering his thin shanks were clean, and so was his faded blue work shirt. His dusky skin was the shade of wet number two emery paper, and he respectfully held a shredded brimmed straw hat in his right hand. Once he had my attention he nodded his head amiably and smiled, exposing toothless gums the color of a rotten mango.

'What do you want?' I said rudely. One of my chief reasons for renting a cottage on the tiny island of Bequia was the private beach.

'Please excuse my intrusion on your privacy, Mr Waxman,' the native said politely, 'but when I heard that the author of *Cockfighting in the Zone of Interior* had rented a cottage on Princess Margaret Beach I wanted to congratulate him in person.'

I was mollified, and at the same time, taken aback. Of course, I had written *Cockfighting in the Zone of Interior*, but it was a thin pamphlet, privately printed, issued in a limited edition of five hundred copies. The pamphlet had been written at the request of two well-heeled Florida cock-fighters who had hoped to gain support for the sport from an eastern syndicate, and I had been paid more than the job was worth. But it certainly wasn't the type of booklet to wind up in the hands of a Bequian native in the West Indies.

* Originally appeared in *Alfred Hitchcock's Mystery Magazine* as 'A Genuine Alectryomancer,' © 1959 by H.S.D. Publications, Inc.

'Where did you get a copy of that?' I said, getting to my feet and brushing the damp sand off my swimming trunks.

'Gamecocks, Mr Waxman, are my source of livelihood,' he replied simply. 'And I read everything I can find concerning game fowl. Your pamphlet, sir, was highly informative.'

'Thank you, but my information was excellent. I didn't know you fought gamecocks on Bequia, however. According to the British Mandate passed in 1857, cockfighting was forbidden throughout the Empire.'

'I don't fight gamecocks, Mr Waxman.' He smiled again and held up a protesting hand. 'My interest in game fowl lies in a parallel art: alectryomancy.'

I laughed, but I was interested all the same. I had gone to Bequia because it was a peaceful little island in the Grenadines, and I had hoped to begin and finish a novel. But in three months' time I hadn't written a line. Bored, and with little to do but stare sullenly at the sea, I found myself enjoying this curious encounter.

'That's a parallel art,' I agreed good naturedly, 'but I didn't know there were any practitioners of alectryomancy left in the Atomic Age.'

'My rooster has made some fascinating predictions concerning the atom, Mr Waxman,' the alectryomancer confided. 'If you would care to visit me sometime – at your convenience, of course – we could discuss his findings. Or possibly, you might be more interested in obtaining a personal reading—'

'I don't need any gamecock to make predictions for me,' I said truthfully. 'If I don't get some work done on my book soon I'll run out of money and be forced to return to the States and look for work.'

'Isn't your writing going well?'

'It isn't going at all.'

'Then there must be a reason. And only through alectryomancy can—'

I cut the interview short and returned to my cottage. After boiling some water for a cup of instant coffee and thinking about the odd meeting for a few minutes I concluded that there might be an article in the old man and his black art. Why not? Three or four thousand fast words on the old fellow's unusual occupation might conceivably find a market in the US, and I sure as hell wasn't getting anywhere with my novel project.

Alectryomancy, of course, is usually considered as a false science, on a par with astrology, if not as popular with the superstitious. A circle is described on the bare ground; the letters of the alphabet are then written around the outer edge of the circle and a grain or so of corn is placed on each letter. A rooster, preferably a cock from a gamestrain, is tethered to a stake in the center by his left leg, and then as he pecks a grain of corn from the various letters, the letters are written down by the alectryomancer, in order, and a message of – the 'science' is crazy – really! For one thing, before there could be any validity to the message the rooster would have to be able to understand a language. And a chicken's brain is about the size of a BB. Still, an article about a practicing alectryomancer would be of interest to a great many readers, and I needed the money.

I didn't look the old alectryomancer up immediately; things are not done so speedily in the West Indies. I prepared myself for the impending interview by thinking about it for a couple of days, and then made my way to the seer's shack on Mount Pleasant. Bequia is a tiny island, and it was simple enough to find out where the old man lived.

'Where,' I asked my simple-minded maid, 'does the old man with the rooster live?'

It is to the woman's credit, I suppose, that she knew to whom I referred, because every indigenous resident owns a few chickens and at least one rooster. She gave me directions I could understand, and even went so far as to draw a crude map with her finger on the sandy beach in front of the cottage.

Mount Pleasant is not a high mountain, as mountains go, but the path was crooked and steep and the forty-minute climb had winded me by the time I reached the old man's shack at the peak. He greeted me warmly and without surprise, and invited me to enjoy the lovely pano-rama of his view. Nine sea miles away the verdant, volcanic mass of St. Vincent loomed above the dark sea and, behind us toward the southwest, the smaller islands of the Grenadines glittered like emeralds in the sunlight.

'Your prospect is beautiful,' I said, when I was breathing normally again.

'We like it, Mr Waxman.' The old native nodded his head.

'We?'

'My rooster and me.'

'Oh, yes,' I said casually, snapping my fingers. 'I'd like to take a look at him.'

At a low whistle from the alectryomancer the rooster marched sedately out of the shack and joined us in the clearing. He was a large whitish bird of about six or seven pounds, with brown and red feathers splashing his wings and chest. His limp comb was undipped, and his dark red wattles dangled almost to his breast. He eyed me suspi-ciously for a moment, cocking his head alertly, and crowed deep in his throat as he stretched his long neck. He then turned away from us to scratch listlessly in the dirt.

'He looks like a Whitehackle cross,' I observed.

'Correct, Mr Waxman,' the alectryomancer said respect-fully. 'His mother was a purebred *Gallus bankiva.*'

'I suspected as much. Only purebred gamecocks should be utilized in alectryomancy, as you must know,' I added pedantically.

743

'Of course.'

For a few moments we sat quietly on the ground watching the stupid rooster, who was amusing himself by twisting his head sharply to the right, and then to the left, like a jay-walker looking for a lurking policeman. I cleared my throat. 'As long as I'm here, I may as well have a reading.'

'I'll change my clothes.' The old man smiled, exposing his raw gums for my inspection, and then hobbled painfully into his shack.

The shack itself was reminiscent of the old Hooverville residences of the 1930s; it was built of five-gallon oil tins, smashed flat, and the roof was topped by a mauve fifty-gallon oil drum, which held, I presumed, rain water. Forming an even square around the clearing before the shack were several dozen five-gallon tins, each containing a young arrowroot plant. An alectryomancer, I supposed, wouldn't have too much business on a small island, and the arrowroot plants probably supplemented the old man's income.

I was unprepared for the change in attire and I started in spite of myself when the alectryomancer reappeared. A dirty white cotton turban had been wrapped around his bald head, and he wore a long-sleeved blue work shirt buttoned to the neck. Tiny red felt hearts, clubs, spades and diamonds had been sewn in thick profusion on the shirt, and larger card symbols had been sewn on the pair of faded khaki trousers he now wore instead of the ragged blue denim shorts. His splayed feet were still bare, however, which rather spoiled the effect.

'That's a unique costume, Mr—?'

'Wainscoting. Two Moons Wainscoting. Thank you, sir.'

'Is Two Moons your actual given name, Mr Wainscoting?'

'You might say that. It was given to me when I was a small boy. My father took me across the channel in his fishing boat to St. Vincent when I was eleven years old.

When I returned my friends asked me what I had seen over there. 'St. Vincent has a moon, too,' I told them. And I've been called Two Moons ever since.'

'It's a romantic name, but quite appropriate for an alectryomancer.'

'I have always regarded it highly. And now . . .' Two Moons tethered the Whitehackle cross to a stake in the clearing with a piece of brown twine, and proceeded to draw a circle around him with a pointed stick.

'The ancient Greeks,' I said, to reveal to the man that I knew a few things about alectryomancy, 'always described the circle on the ground *prior* to tethering the gamecock in the center.'

'Yes,' he agreed, and his face assumed for a moment a resentful expression, 'but that isn't the way we do it in the West Indies. Every island race has its own traditions and rituals. I have nothing against the Greeks, and I can see some merit in describing the circle first, but on the other hand, it is possible that a portion of the circle will be rubbed out inadvertently when re-entering the ring to tether the cock. I have tried both methods, and in all probability I shall use the Greek method again sometime in the future. But the system employed doesn't affect the reading, or so I have learned through many years of experience.'

'You could get into a technical argument on that statement.'

'Undoubtedly. You can have an argument on any point pertaining to alectryomancy,' Two Moons added cheerfully; and he began to draw the letters of the alphabet in a clockwise direction about the outer perimeter of the circle. He apparently took considerable pride in his work, drawing large block capital letters with his pointed stick, rubbing them out and doing them over gain when they didn't come up to his high standards. He measured the distances between each letter, using his stick as a ruler, and found it necessary to redraw the S and T because they were too close together.

'Now,' he said when he was finished, surveying his handiwork, 'the hard part is over. First, a personal question: what is your birth date, Mr Waxman?'

'2 January, 1919.'

'You'll have to speak a little louder, Mr Waxman,' Two Moons said apologetically. 'My old rooster's beginning to get somewhat deaf, and I don't believe he heard you.'

I repeated my birthday loudly, enunciating carefully for the rooster's benefit, although I felt rather foolish.

Two Moons paced counterclockwise about the circle, dropping a grain of corn in the center of each letter, and then sat beside me before signaling the bird with an abrupt motion of his pointed stick. The bird crowed, wheeled about twice, and pecked up the grain of corn on the letter M. Two Moons wrote M on the ground, and followed it with the O, R, and T as the chicken made his choices. After eating the fourth grain of corn, the rooster returned to the center of the circle, leaned wearily, almost dispiritedly, against the stake, and hung his head down to the ground. We waited, but it was quite evident from the apathy of the chicken that he was finished.

'Maybe he isn't hungry?' I suggested.

'We'll soon find out.' Two Moons untied the cord from the rooster's left leg and carried him out of the circle. He scattered a few grains of corn, released the cock, and the bird scratched up and gobbled down cracked corn as if it were famished.

'He was hungry enough, Mr Waxman; your reading is full and complete. M - O - R - T.' Two Moons muttered the letters, savoring the sounds with his eyes half-closed. 'Mort. Tell me: is your middle name Mort, by any chance?'

'No. Harry Waxman, only. I dropped my middle name when I became a writer, but it wasn't Mort.'

'Any relatives named Mort?'

I thought carefully. 'No, none at all, not that I know of, anyway.'

'That's too bad.' Two Moons shook his head. 'I had hoped . . .' His voice trailed away.

'Hoped what?'

'That Mort didn't mean what I knew in my heart that it did mean.' He thumped his breast with a closed fist. '*Mort* is a French word meaning death, Mr Waxman.'

'So? How does it apply to me? I'm not a Frenchman; I'm an American. If the rooster's predicting anything about me he should do so in English. Right?'

'He doesn't know any English,' Two Moons explained patiently. 'I bought this rooster in Martinique, after my last gamecock died. All he knows is French. On difficult readings I often have to consult a French-English dictionary—'

'Maybe he was going to write 'MORTGAGE'?' I broke in.

'I sympathize with you, Mr Waxman.' Two Moons shook his head, almost dislodging his dirty turban. 'But in alectryomancy we must go only by what the gamecock does write, not by what he does not. Otherwise—' He spread his hands wide, and shrugged hopelessly.

'Let's try another reading.'

'Another time, perhaps. It's a nervous strain on my rooster, making predictions, and I only allow him to make one a day.'

'Tomorrow, then,' I said, getting to my feet.

'Perhaps tomorrow,' he agreed reluctantly.

I took my wallet out of my hip pocket. 'What do I owe you?'

'Nothing.' The alectryomancer spread his arms, palms up, and shrugged. 'I would appreciate it, however, if you would be kind enough to autograph my copy of your pamphlet, *Cockfighting in the Zone of Interior.*'

I felt my shirt pocket. 'When I come up tomorrow. I didn't bring my fountain pen with me today—'

'If you don't mind, Mr Waxman,' Two Moons said reasonably. 'In view of the prediction, I would prefer to have the autograph today. If you'll wait a moment, I have the pamphlet and a ballpoint pen inside the house . . .'

I slept fitfully that night, which meant little, if anything, to me. I had slept fitfully every night of the three months I had been on Bequia. No one had informed me of the fierceness of the sand flies on Princess Margaret Beach, and I had neglected to purchase a mosquito bar before departing from Trinidad. But between waking and sleeping, the prediction of the Whitehackle cross at least gave me something to think about. I was far from satisfied with Two Moons' interpretation of the word 'mort.'

The suggestion was too pat. And yet, as I lay there scratching in my bed, no better meaning suggested itself to me. Toward 2 a.m. I was reduced to considering MORT as initials standing for a secret sentence of some kind. During the war I received several letters from a girl in California with SWAK written across the back of the envelope: this cryptic message meant 'Sealed With A Kiss.' But when this piece of romantic tripe crossed my mind I cursed myself as a fool, downed three searing tumblers of Mount Gay rum, and slept soundly until dawn.

By 8:30 a.m. I was on the mountain trail to Two Moons' metal residence. Halfway up the mountain I stopped for breath and a slow cigarette, regretting my decision to settle for coffee but no breakfast, and almost changed my mind about asking the old man for another reading. Curiosity and a few moments rest got the better of my judgment and I climbed on. When I topped the last crest to the clearing, Two Moons was seated cross-legged in the sunlight, humming happily, and plaiting a fish trap out of green palm leaf strips. He dropped his lower jaw the moment he saw me, and his yellow eyeballs popped in their sockets.

'Why, Mr Waxman,' he said, with well-feigned astonishment, 'I didn't expect you this morning!'

'You needn't act so damned surprised,' I scowled at him. 'I told you I'd be back this morning.'

'Please forgive my outburst; I apologize. But your case was remarkably similar to a reading I gave a student at Oxford, and I—'

'You attended Oxford?' It was my turn to be surprised.

'Baliol College, but for a year and a half only,' Two Moons admitted modestly. 'I was putting myself through college by practicing alectryomancy in London's West End. I had a poor but steady clientele; actors, actresses, producers, and two or three dozen playwrights.'

'I fail to see how an Oxford man could end up back on Bequia,' I said, looking at the Alectryomancer with new respect.

'An English Dom did it,' Two Moons said ruefully.

'Got mixed up with a woman, eh?'

'No, sir. Not a woman, a Dom. A truly beautiful gamestrain, the English Dom. Pure white, with a lemon bill and feet to match. I bought the rooster in Sussex, and before utilizing his services for my clients, I had him make a practice prediction for me. Without hesitating the Dom pecked out 'Bequia.' I ate the fowl as a farewell supper, packed my belongings, and departed on the next ship leaving England for Barbados. I've been here on Bequia ever since, thirty-two years this coming October.'

'At any rate,' I said, moved by the unhappy story, 'one of your predictions came true.'

'They all come true, when they are correctly interpreted by a skilled alectryomancer.'

'We'll see. How about my second reading?'

'Yes, sir.' Two Moons held out his right hand. 'That will be ten dollars, please – in advance.'

'Very well.' I parted with a brown BWI ten-dollar bill. 'Bring on your French-pecking rooster.'

The rigmarole was unchanged from the previous day. Two Moons changed from his blue denim shorts into his homemade costume and turban, tethered the gamecock, and drew the circle and block-letter alphabet as carefully as he had done for my first reading. He signaled with the pointed stick and the idiotic rooster pecked M, O, R, T and stopped. After crowing half-heartedly, the bird leaned against the stake with his head down, his bill touching the ground. I was unable to understand how the mere pecking up of four measly grains of corn could make the rooster so weary.

'Let's wait a bit, Two Moons.' I cleared my dry throat. 'Maybe he'll continue.'

'As you wish, Mr Waxman.'

The minutes ticked away. The mid-morning sun was hot. The back of my neck stung with prickly heat. Mango flies and tiny eye gnats buzzed and feinted about my dripping face, but I waited. Five minutes, ten, fifteen minutes, and the rooster still remained immobilized in the center of the circle.

Two Moons clucked his tongue. '*Mort*,' he said pityingly, 'comes to us all, in time.'

'An undeniable truth,' I agreed indifferently, getting to my feet and stretching. 'Well, thanks for the prediction, Two Moons. But it's a hot day and I'm going for a swim.'

I started down the trail without a backward glance, my hands balled into tight fists inside the pockets of my khaki shorts.

'Watch out for barracuda,' Two Moons shouted after me, 'and the tricky crosscurrents!'

'Thanks!' I said drily, over my shoulder.

I didn't go swimming.

I didn't do anything.

I brooded. Sitting in the tiny living room of my screenless cottage, staring out the window at the bright blue, cheerful waters of the bay, I pondered dark thoughts. The first *mort* wasn't so bad, but when it came to two *morts* in a row I was forced to do a little quiet thinking. Like all Americans who consider themselves intelligent, I laugh at superstition. Ha ha! The pinch of salt, tossed carelessly over the shoulder – a meaningless precaution, but I did it all the time, without thinking about it. Did I ever place a hat upon a bed? Never! Why not? Well, just because, that's why. Did I ever walk under a ladder? No, of course not – a can of paint might spill over a man from above. That was prudence, not superstition. I wasn't really superstitious. Not really. It was just that that gamecock had been so positive, so cocksure . . . !

Three days later I fired my maid. The stubborn woman refused to taste my food, claiming falsely that she didn't like canned pork and beans. I issued an angry ultimatum, and when she still flatly but politely refused to eat a bite, and therefore prevent me from the possibility of being poisoned, I gave her the sack, and tossed the uneaten beans into the bay.

Without anyone else around the house, my life became more complicated, but I preferred to be alone. I had to meet the MV *Madinina* when she steamed into the harbor each Friday to get my provisions, and I had to have a list of foodstuffs ready to hand the captain. But I didn't mind the activity. I wasn't hungry, either, and the little I did eat was best prepared by myself. I woried, however. A bad tin of corned beef, a can of sour condensed milk, or even some undetected botulized canned string beans, and pouf! *Mort!* I drank a lot of Mount Gay rum, and very little water.

Three weeks after my second reading I paid a third visit to Two Moons Wainscoting. I was unable to stand the fear and suspense any longer; I needed additional, and concrete, information. I hadn't shaved for several days. Suppose I had cut myself with a rusty razor blade? Where could I get a tetanus shot on isolated Bequia? My sleep was no longer fitful; I couldn't sleep at all. Three full inches had disappeared from my waistline.

'Two Moons,' I said anxiously, as soon as I stepped into his clearing, 'I've got to have another reading.'

'I've been expecting you, Mr Waxman,' Two Moons said sympathetically. 'That is, I've been expecting word concerning you; but I must turn down your request for a third reading. This is not an arbitrary decision. The life of an alectryomancer on Bequia isn't an easy one, and I would welcome the prospect of another ten-dollar bill. But I am not a man totally lacking in compassion, so I must refuse—'

'I'll give you twenty dollars—'

Two Moons held up a hand to silence me. 'Please, Mr Waxman. My decision is not a matter of mere money! Let me summarize: you have had two flat predictions, both of them identical. *Mort!* An ugly word, whether in English or French, but *mort* all the same. Suppose, on a third prediction, that my gamecock were to peck out a W.E.D.S., or even a simple F.R.I.? Do you see the implications? You're a writer, Mr Waxman; you are not without imagination. A gamecock is incapable of deceit, of deliberately telling a falsehood; and if my rooster pecked F.R.I. – which he could do in all innocence – this is the abbreviation for 'Friday.' Today is Tuesday. How would you feel tomorrow, on Wednesday? And then Thursday? The next day would be Friday, and Friday would be the day for what? *Mort!*' He pointed a long brown forefinger at my chest, and shook his head unhappily.

A shudder danced icily down my spine. 'But—'

'Please, Mr Waxman. I simply cannot risk another reading. An alectryomancer has a conscience, just like everyone else, and I would suffer along with you, so I must refuse your request for a third reading. I cannot; I will not do it!'

'I'm a young man,' I croaked hoarsely, 'and I'm not ready to die. I'm barely into my forties – the prime of life.'

'Well,' Two Moons pursed his lips, 'there's an alternative.' He peered at me intently. 'But I hesitate to mention it to a man with so little faith.'

'Mention it,' I said sharply. 'By all means, mention it.'

'Are you cognizant of the West Indian *obeah*?'

'I think so. It's a spell or charm of some kind, isn't it?'

'In a way, yes. There are all kinds of *obeah*; they can be made for good or evil, just as African *jujus* are made for good or evil. Unfortunately,' he sighed, 'many West Indians have a vindictive character, and they often cast about for a means of vengeance for a very small grievance. This deplorable trait of character, I am happy to state, is not a universal West Indian—'

'Right now,' I broke in, 'I'm not interested in the character traits of the average West Indian. I have problems of my own.'

'To be sure. To shorten the rather interesting story I was preparing to tell you, I possess an *obeah* that will ward off *mort* for an indefinite period.'

'Let me take a look at it.'

'Not so fast. Like all spells, charms, and *jujus*, an *obeah* also has a condition attached.'

'What are the conditions?'

'Condition.' He raised a long forefinger. 'Singular, Mr Waxman. A simple condition, but a condition nevertheless. Belief. Blind, unquestioning belief. So long as you believe in the *obeah* you shall have life. Not everlasting life, as is promised by your optimistic Christian *obeahs*, but life for a reasonable period of time. The Grenadian who fashioned this *obeah*, for example, lived to be one hundred and ten.'

'That's a long time.'

'A very long time.'

'I believe,' I said quickly. 'Give me the *obeah*!'

'You are an impulsive young man, Mr Waxman. This is a valuable *obeah*, and before I can consider giving it to you I must test your belief. The *obeah* has a price of seventy-five dollars.'

I passed the test.

Happier than I had been in days I ran down the mountain trail, a small leather sack tied around my neck. The sack was securely fastened with a square knot in the rawhide thong at the back of my neck, and from time to time I fingered the knot to make certain it wouldn't slip.

Night fell. I sat in my tiny living room, trying to relax with a cigar and a light grog. The pale light of my kerosene lamp – there is no electricity on Bequia – made my shadow dance on the wall like a boxer. The wind, as well as my quick, inadvertent movements, was responsible for my flickering shadow, but I felt like a boxer, fighting the deadly logic of the gamecock's prediction. I clutched the thick leather sack at my neck, feeling vaguely the strange objects inside, wondering what in the devil they were. Two Moons had warned me not to look inside—'Never look a gift horse in the mouth'—were his exact words, but I was curious all the same. If I stopped believing in the *obeah*, death – *mort* – could strike me suddenly, at any moment. The great wisdom of Two Moons Wainscoting, in denying me a third, and final, prediction, was the only bright spot in my thinking. Even with the *obeah* in my possession, I couldn't live forever . . .

Not that I had any particular reason to go on living, to extend my life for an indefinite period. I wasn't happy now, and I never had been happy. I was single, no dependents, no real purpose in life – really, except for the writing of novels, and an occasional short story. But I wanted to hang on, if for no other reason than to see what would happen next. I had lost all desire to write an article on alectryomancy.

I fingered the strange objects inside the *obeah* sack. What were they? Why did they have this mysterious power? I jerked my hand away quickly. What if my fingers recognized one or more of the objects inside the leather sack? How could I go on believing in the efficacy of the *obeah*, if I discovered what the sack contained? A nasty situation, all the way around.

In the daytime, life wasn't so bad. The bright sunlight and blue skies chased away the problems of the night. But everything I did, which wasn't much, was done judiciously, carefully. I still swam every day, but never ventured more than a few yards from shore, fearing the treacherous cross-currents. I continued to take daily hikes, but I walked slowly, like an old man with brittle bones. And I carried a cane. Most of the time I sat quietly on the narrow front porch of my cottage drinking rum and water, staring moodily at the sea. The *obeah* was doing a good job of protecting me from accidental death, but sometimes I wished that *mort* would come to me in the night, in my sleep, so that it would be all over and done with.

After a few lonely, disconsolate evenings I began to go to the hotel in the evenings, picking my way along the beach path, playing my flashlight on every shadow before taking another cautious step. There wasn't any electricity at the hotel either, but the verandah and small outside bar were lighted by Coleman lanterns, and they didn't cast shadows.

Just a few short hours ago I was sitting at a wicker table on the hotel verandah staring glumly into my glass, when Bob Corbett sat down across from me. One quick glance at his red, serious face and orange moustache, and I shook my head.

755

'No. No nattering tonight, Bob,' I said firmly. 'I'm not up to it.'

Bob Corbett had one of those vague British civil service jobs that seemed to provide him with more free time than work. He made periodic trips to various islands looking for fungus or something, but the government provided a house for him on Bequia – although he did not have an office. Like many of the bored civil servants posted to the Windward Islands for three years, Bob had become addicted to the game of 'nattering.' Nattering is a kind of game where two persons trade insults until one of them gets angry enough to fight. The person who has the best self-control wins, even though he ends up more often than not with a bloody nose. During the apprentice years of my writing career I had served time as a desk clerk at a Los Angeles hotel for almost two years and, as a consequence, I had bested Bob Corbett in every nattering session he started. In the last set-to we played, Bob had taken a swing at me with an empty Black & White bottle.

'No nattering,' Bob agreed readily, signaling the barmaid to refill our glasses. 'I came over to make amends, to tell you the truth. I've been standing at the bar for almost an hour without a sign of recognition from you, and if it's an apology you want you can have it. But I really didn't hit you with that bottle, old man—'

'I'm sorry, Bob. I didn't cut you on purpose; I didn't see you,' I apologized. All at once, I felt an overwhelming desire to confide in Bob Corbett, to take advantage of his unimaginative common sense, and I yielded impulsively to the desire. The dark thoughts had been bottled up inside me too long; I had to get them out into the open.

'Listen, Bob,' I began, 'did you ever hear of alectryomancy?' And I unfolded the whole story, from my first meeting with Two Moons on the beach.

'Ho-ho-ho!' Bob laughed wetly, when I had finished. 'You've been had, old man!'

'What're you talking about?'

'Had. Taken. Bilked! And you're a Californian, too! That's what makes it so funny!' Another string of bubbling ho-ho-hos followed, and I drummed my fingers impatiently on the table.

'Old Two Moons is a notorious character in the islands, Harry,' Bob said at last, wiping the corners of his eyes with the back of his freckled left hand. 'This old faker and his trained rooster have caused I don't know how many complaints to the Administrator on St. Vincent from irate tourists. His rooster, you see, is trained to peck out the word '*mort*'! And the convincing mumbo jumbo Two Moons puts with it has sucked you in. That's all.'

'I don't believe you, Bob. I'd like to, but I can't.'

'I'll prove it to you,' Bob said, leaning across the table. 'After the rooster pecked the four grains of corn, ostensibly spelling '*mort*,' he hung his head down. Right?'

'Right.'

'Following this, then, didn't Two Moons remove the chicken from the circle and feed him some more corn? And didn't the rooster scratch it up and eat it?'

'Of course. That's what made the reading so effective.'

'No, Harry. It proves only that the rooster is trained. Think a bit, man. To train animals of any kind, you must always reward them with food after they do their trick. And food is the only reward an animal recognizes! A trained rooster is no different from a trained bear that's been given a bottle of beer for doing a dance. A bloke I knew in Newfoundland had a bloody wolf chained in his garage, and one—'

I left the table, not waiting to hear about the bloody wolf in Newfoundland, and, flashing my torch before me, ran all the way home along the beach path. As soon as my kerosene lamp was lighted, and the wick trimmed, I untied the thong at the back of my neck, and dumped the contents of the leather sack on the dining table. Inventory: one plastic toothpick (red); one round, highly polished obsidian pebble; two withered jackfish eyes (lacquered); one dried chameleon tail, approximately three inches long; one red chess pawn (plastic); three battered and curiously bent Coca-Cola bottle caps; one chicken feather (yellow); six assorted and unidentifiable (to me) small dried bones; and one brass disc entitling the bearer to a ten-cent beer at Freddy Ming's Cafe, Port-of-Spain, Trinidad.

A scorching red film seared my eyes. I stared stupidly at the contents of the *obeah* and cursed Two Moons Wainscoting aloud for at least five minutes. Then I scooped the objects into the leather sack, tightened the thong drawstring, went outside, and tossed the thing into the sea. The buoyant sack floated on the surface, bobbing gently, drifting away from the shore on the outgoing tide. Still sullen with anger, a great idea occurred to me. I would recover the *obeah* from the sea, pay a return visit to Two Moons' establishment – and feed him each object in the bag, one at a time.

This idea delighted me so much I kicked off my sandals, on impulse, waded into the water, and then dived after the *obeah*, which was now sailing away from me as though it were fitted out with a spinnaker. I soon found, with mounting apprehension, that in spite of all the strokes I was taking, I wasn't making much headway. The *obeah* floated, bobbing, just beyond my grasp, while the riptide tore at my chest and shorts. I panicked, and as my strokes grew weaker I knew that the *obeah* was my only hope of salvation; and yet it always floated, tantalizing me, just beyond my grasp. The night was so black I didn't even know where the land was anymore, and I began to think about the night-feeding barracuda—

'Obeah!' I screamed. '*I believe in you! I believe, I believe, I believe! I—*' An angry wave crashed against my open mouth.

When I regained consciousness, dawn was showing itself whitely in the sea pools along the shore, although the sky was still as dark as polaroid glass. I was waterlogged and, for longer than I care to remember, I was sick to my stomach. Despite my weakness and nausea, however, I was filled with a wild, almost overwhelming sense of elation: the *obeah* was clutched tightly in my right hand!

At last I staggered to my feet, and, bent almost double by my cramping stomach, I made my way weakly down the beach toward my cottage. I had the title – *This Is My God* – and most of the first chapter of my novel outlined in my mind, and I was anxious to get these words on paper while the details were fresh and pure.

THE END

Acknowledgments

Chapter 1, 'The Machine in Ward Eleven' was published by *Playboy* (1961) in slightly different form; Chapter 2, 'Selected Incidents', appeared in *Gent* as 'The Sin of Integrity'; Chapter 4, 'The Alectryomancer', appeared in *Alfred Hitchcock's Mystery Magazine*.